The Best Short Stories and Novellas of Henry James

A Digireads.com Book
Digireads.com Publishing
16212 Riggs Rd
Stilwell, KS, 66085

The Best Short Stories and Novellas of Henry James
By Henry James
ISBN: 1-4209-3141-5

Please visit *www.digireads.com*

CONTENTS

DAISY MILLER

PART I

At the little town of Vevey, in Switzerland, there is a particularly comfortable hotel. There are, indeed, many hotels, for the entertainment of tourists is the business of the place, which, as many travelers will remember, is seated upon the edge of a remarkably blue lake—a lake that it behooves every tourist to visit. The shore of the lake presents an unbroken array of establishments of this order, of every category, from the "grand hotel" of the newest fashion, with a chalk-white front, a hundred balconies, and a dozen flags flying from its roof, to the little Swiss pension of an elder day, with its name inscribed in German-looking lettering upon a pink or yellow wall and an awkward summerhouse in the angle of the garden. One of the hotels at Vevey, however, is famous, even classical, being distinguished from many of its upstart neighbors by an air both of luxury and of maturity. In this region, in the month of June, American travelers are extremely numerous; it may be said, indeed, that Vevey assumes at this period some of the characteristics of an American watering place. There are sights and sounds which evoke a vision, an echo, of Newport and Saratoga. There is a flitting hither and thither of "stylish" young girls, a rustling of muslin flounces, a rattle of dance music in the morning hours, a sound of high-pitched voices at all times. You receive an impression of these things at the excellent inn of the "Trois Couronnes" and are transported in fancy to the Ocean House or to Congress Hall. But at the "Trois Couronnes," it must be added, there are other features that are much at variance with these suggestions: neat German waiters, who look like secretaries of legation; Russian princesses sitting in the garden; little Polish boys walking about held by the hand, with their governors; a view of the sunny crest of the Dent du Midi and the picturesque towers of the Castle of Chillon.

I hardly know whether it was the analogies or the differences that were uppermost in the mind of a young American, who, two or three years ago, sat in the garden of the "Trois Couronnes," looking about him, rather idly, at some of the graceful objects I have mentioned. It was a beautiful summer morning, and in whatever fashion the young American looked at things, they must have seemed to him charming. He had come from Geneva the day before by the little steamer, to see his aunt, who was staying at the hotel—Geneva having been for a long time his place of residence. But his aunt had a headache—his aunt had almost always a headache—and now she was shut up in her room, smelling camphor, so that he was at liberty to wander about. He was some seven-and-twenty years of age; when his friends spoke of him, they usually said that he was at Geneva "studying." When his enemies spoke of him, they said—but, after all, he had no enemies; he was an extremely amiable fellow, and universally liked. What I should say is, simply, that when certain persons spoke of him they affirmed that the reason of his spending so much time at Geneva was that he was extremely devoted to a lady who lived there—a foreign lady—a person older than himself. Very few Americans—indeed, I think none—had ever seen this lady, about whom there were some singular stories. But Winterbourne had an old attachment for the little metropolis of Calvinism; he had been put to school there as a boy, and he had afterward gone to college there—circumstances which had led to his forming a great many youthful friendships. Many of these he had kept, and they were a source of great satisfaction to him.

After knocking at his aunt's door and learning that she was indisposed, he had taken a walk about the town, and then he had come in to his breakfast. He had now finished his breakfast; but he was drinking a small cup of coffee, which had been served to him on a little table in the garden by one of the waiters who looked like an *attaché*. At last he finished his coffee and lit a cigarette. Presently a small boy came walking along the path—an urchin of nine or ten. The child, who was diminutive for his years, had an aged expression of countenance, a pale complexion, and sharp little features. He was dressed in knickerbockers, with red stockings, which displayed his poor little spindle-shanks; he also wore a brilliant red cravat. He carried in his hand a long alpenstock, the sharp point of which he thrust into everything that he approached—the flowerbeds, the garden benches, the trains of the ladies' dresses. In front of Winterbourne he paused, looking at him with a pair of bright, penetrating little eyes.

"Will you give me a lump of sugar?" he asked in a sharp, hard little voice—a voice immature and yet, somehow, not young.

Winterbourne glanced at the small table near him, on which his coffee service rested, and saw that several morsels of sugar remained. "Yes, you may take one," he answered; "but I don't think sugar is good for little boys."

This little boy stepped forward and carefully selected three of the coveted fragments, two of which he buried in the pocket of his knickerbockers, depositing the other as promptly in another place. He poked his alpenstock, lance-fashion, into Winterbourne's bench and tried to crack the lump of sugar with his teeth.

"Oh, blazes; it's har-r-d!" he exclaimed, pronouncing the adjective in a peculiar manner.

Winterbourne had immediately perceived that he might have the honor of claiming him as a fellow countryman. "Take care you don't hurt your teeth," he said, paternally.

"I haven't got any teeth to hurt. They have all come out. I have only got seven teeth. My mother counted them last night, and one came out right afterward. She said she'd slap me if any more came out. I can't help it. It's this old Europe. It's the climate that makes them come out. In America they didn't come out. It's these hotels."

Winterbourne was much amused. "If you eat three lumps of sugar, your mother will certainly slap you," he said.

"She's got to give me some candy, then," rejoined his young interlocutor. "I can't get any candy here—any American candy. American candy's the best candy."

"And are American little boys the best little boys?" asked Winterbourne.

"I don't know. I'm an American boy," said the child.

"I see you are one of the best!" laughed Winterbourne.

"Are you an American man?" pursued this vivacious infant. And then, on Winterbourne's affirmative reply—"American men are the best," he declared.

His companion thanked him for the compliment, and the child, who had now got astride of his alpenstock, stood looking about him, while he attacked a second lump of sugar. Winterbourne wondered if he himself had been like this in his infancy, for he had been brought to Europe at about this age.

"Here comes my sister!" cried the child in a moment. "She's an American girl."

Winterbourne looked along the path and saw a beautiful young lady advancing. "American girls are the best girls," he said cheerfully to his young companion.

"My sister ain't the best!" the child declared. "She's always blowing at me."

"I imagine that is your fault, not hers," said Winterbourne. The young lady meanwhile had drawn near. She was dressed in white muslin, with a hundred frills and flounces, and knots of pale-colored ribbon. She was bareheaded, but she balanced in her hand a large parasol, with a deep border of embroidery; and she was strikingly, admirably pretty. "How pretty they are!" thought Winterbourne, straightening himself in his seat, as if he were prepared to rise.

The young lady paused in front of his bench, near the parapet of the garden, which overlooked the lake. The little boy had now converted his alpenstock into a vaulting pole, by the aid of which he was springing about in the gravel and kicking it up not a little.

"Randolph," said the young lady, "what *are* you doing?"

"I'm going up the Alps," replied Randolph. "This is the way!" And he gave another little jump, scattering the pebbles about Winterbourne's ears.

"That's the way they come down," said Winterbourne.

"He's an American man!" cried Randolph, in his little hard voice.

The young lady gave no heed to this announcement, but looked straight at her brother. "Well, I guess you had better be quiet," she simply observed.

It seemed to Winterbourne that he had been in a manner presented. He got up and stepped slowly toward the young girl, throwing away his cigarette. "This little boy and I have made acquaintance," he said, with great civility. In Geneva, as he had been perfectly aware, a young man was not at liberty to speak to a young unmarried lady except under certain rarely occurring conditions; but here at Vevey, what conditions could be better than these?—a pretty American girl coming and standing in front of you in a garden. This pretty American girl, however, on hearing Winterbourne's observation, simply glanced at him; she then turned her head and looked over the parapet, at the lake and the opposite mountains. He wondered whether he had gone too far, but he decided that he must advance farther, rather than retreat. While he was thinking of something else to say, the young lady turned to the little boy again.

"I should like to know where you got that pole," she said.

"I bought it," responded Randolph.

"You don't mean to say you're going to take it to Italy?"

"Yes, I am going to take it to Italy," the child declared.

The young girl glanced over the front of her dress and smoothed out a knot or two of ribbon. Then she rested her eyes upon the prospect again. "Well, I guess you had better leave it somewhere," she said after a moment.

"Are you going to Italy?" Winterbourne inquired in a tone of great respect.

The young lady glanced at him again. "Yes, sir," she replied. And she said nothing more.

"Are you—a—going over the Simplon?" Winterbourne pursued, a little embarrassed.

"I don't know," she said. "I suppose it's some mountain. Randolph, what mountain are we going over?"

"Going where?" the child demanded.

"To Italy," Winterbourne explained.

"I don't know," said Randolph. "I don't want to go to Italy. I want to go to America."

"Oh, Italy is a beautiful place!" rejoined the young man.

"Can you get candy there?" Randolph loudly inquired.

"I hope not," said his sister. "I guess you have had enough candy, and mother thinks so too."

"I haven't had any for ever so long—for a hundred weeks!" cried the boy, still jumping about.

The young lady inspected her flounces and smoothed her ribbons again; and Winterbourne presently risked an observation upon the beauty of the view. He was ceasing to be embarrassed, for he had begun to perceive that she was not in the least embarrassed herself. There had not been the slightest alteration in her charming complexion; she was evidently neither offended nor flattered. If she looked another way when he spoke to her, and seemed not particularly to hear him, this was simply her habit, her manner. Yet, as he talked a little more and pointed out some of the objects of interest in the view, with which she appeared quite unacquainted, she gradually gave him more of the benefit of her glance; and then he saw that this glance was perfectly direct and unshrinking. It was not, however, what would have been called an immodest glance, for the young girl's eyes were singularly honest and fresh. They were wonderfully pretty eyes; and, indeed, Winterbourne had not seen for a long time anything prettier than his fair countrywoman's various features—her complexion, her nose, her ears, her teeth. He had a great relish for feminine beauty; he was addicted to observing and analyzing it; and as regards this young lady's face he made several observations. It was not at all insipid, but it was not exactly expressive; and though it was eminently delicate, Winterbourne mentally accused it—very forgivingly—of a want of finish. He thought it very possible that Master Randolph's sister was a coquette; he was sure she had a spirit of her own; but in her bright, sweet, superficial little visage there was no mockery, no irony. Before long it became obvious that she was much disposed toward conversation. She told him that they were going to Rome for the winter—she and her mother and Randolph. She asked him if he was a "real American"; she shouldn't have taken him for one; he seemed more like a German—this was said after a little hesitation—especially when he spoke. Winterbourne, laughing, answered that he had met Germans who spoke like Americans, but that he had not, so far as he remembered, met an American who spoke like a German. Then he asked her if she should not be more comfortable in sitting upon the bench which he had just quitted. She answered that she liked standing up and walking about; but she presently sat down. She told him she was from New York State—"if you know where that is." Winterbourne learned more about her by catching hold of her small, slippery brother and making him stand a few minutes by his side.

"Tell me your name, my boy," he said.

"Randolph C. Miller," said the boy sharply. "And I'll tell you her name"; and he leveled his alpenstock at his sister.

"You had better wait till you are asked!" said this young lady calmly.

"I should like very much to know your name," said Winterbourne.

"Her name is Daisy Miller!" cried the child. "But that isn't her real name; that isn't her name on her cards."

"It's a pity you haven't got one of my cards!" said Miss Miller.

"Her real name is Annie P. Miller," the boy went on.

"Ask him *his* name," said his sister, indicating Winterbourne.

But on this point Randolph seemed perfectly indifferent; he continued to supply information with regard to his own family. "My father's name is Ezra B. Miller," he announced. "My father ain't in Europe; my father's in a better place than Europe."

Winterbourne imagined for a moment that this was the manner in which the child had been taught to intimate that Mr. Miller had been removed to the sphere of celestial reward. But Randolph immediately added, "My father's in Schenectady. He's got a big business. My father's rich, you bet!"

"Well!" ejaculated Miss Miller, lowering her parasol and looking at the embroidered border. Winterbourne presently released the child, who departed, dragging his alpenstock along the path. "He doesn't like Europe," said the young girl. "He wants to go back."

"To Schenectady, you mean?"

"Yes; he wants to go right home. He hasn't got any boys here. There is one boy here, but he always goes round with a teacher; they won't let him play."

"And your brother hasn't any teacher?" Winterbourne inquired.

"Mother thought of getting him one, to travel round with us. There was a lady told her of a very good teacher; an American lady—perhaps you know her—Mrs. Sanders. I think she came from Boston. She told her of this teacher, and we thought of getting him to travel round with us. But Randolph said he didn't want a teacher traveling round with us. He said he wouldn't have lessons when he was in the cars. And we ARE in the cars about half the time. There was an English lady we met in the cars—I think her name was Miss Featherstone; perhaps you know her. She wanted to know why I didn't give Randolph lessons—give him 'instruction,' she called it. I guess he could give me more instruction than I could give him. He's very smart."

"Yes," said Winterbourne; "he seems very smart."

"Mother's going to get a teacher for him as soon as we get to Italy. Can you get good teachers in Italy?"

"Very good, I should think," said Winterbourne.

"Or else she's going to find some school. He ought to learn some more. He's only nine. He's going to college." And in this way Miss Miller continued to converse upon the affairs of her family and upon other topics. She sat there with her extremely pretty hands, ornamented with very brilliant rings, folded in her lap, and with her pretty eyes now resting upon those of Winterbourne, now wandering over the garden, the people who passed by, and the beautiful view. She talked to Winterbourne as if she had known him a long time. He found it very pleasant. It was many years since he had heard a young girl talk so much. It might have been said of this unknown young lady, who had come and sat down beside him upon a bench, that she chattered. She was very quiet; she sat in a charming, tranquil attitude; but her lips and her eyes were constantly moving. She had a soft, slender, agreeable voice, and her tone was decidedly sociable. She gave Winterbourne a history of her movements and intentions and those of her mother and brother, in Europe, and enumerated, in particular, the various hotels at which they had stopped. "That English lady in the cars," she said—"Miss Featherstone—asked me if we didn't all live in hotels in America. I told her I had never been in so many hotels in my life as since I came to Europe. I have never seen so many—it's nothing but hotels." But Miss Miller did not make this remark with a querulous accent; she appeared to be in the best humor with everything. She declared that the hotels were very good, when once you got used to their ways, and that Europe was perfectly sweet. She was not disappointed—not a bit. Perhaps it was because she had heard so much about it before. She had ever so many intimate friends that had been there ever so many times. And then she had had ever so many dresses and things from Paris. Whenever she put on a Paris dress she felt as if she were in Europe.

"It was a kind of a wishing cap," said Winterbourne.

"Yes," said Miss Miller without examining this analogy; "it always made me wish I was here. But I needn't have done that for dresses. I am sure they send all the pretty ones to America; you see the most frightful things here. The only thing I don't like," she proceeded, "is the society. There isn't any society; or, if there is, I don't know where it keeps itself. Do you? I suppose there is some society somewhere, but I haven't seen anything of it. I'm very fond of society, and I have always had a great deal of it. I don't mean only in Schenectady, but in New York. I used to go to New York every winter. In New York I had lots of society. Last winter I had seventeen dinners given me; and three of them were by gentlemen," added Daisy Miller. "I have more friends in New York than in Schenectady—more gentleman friends; and more young lady friends too," she resumed in a moment. She paused again for an instant; she was looking at Winterbourne with all her prettiness in her lively eyes and in her light, slightly monotonous smile. "I have always had," she said, "a great deal of gentlemen's society."

Poor Winterbourne was amused, perplexed, and decidedly charmed. He had never yet heard a young girl express herself in just this fashion; never, at least, save in cases where to say such things seemed a kind of demonstrative evidence of a certain laxity of deportment. And yet was he to accuse Miss Daisy Miller of actual or potential *inconduite*, as they said at Geneva? He felt that he had lived at Geneva so long that he had lost a good deal; he had become dishabituated to the American tone. Never, indeed, since he had grown old enough to appreciate things, had he encountered a young American girl of so pronounced a type as this. Certainly she was very charming, but how deucedly sociable! Was she simply a pretty girl from New York State? Were they all like that, the pretty girls who had a good deal of gentlemen's society? Or was she also a designing, an audacious, an unscrupulous young person? Winterbourne had lost his instinct in this matter, and his reason could not help him. Miss Daisy Miller looked extremely innocent. Some people had told him that, after all, American girls were exceedingly innocent; and others had told him that, after all, they were not. He was inclined to think Miss Daisy Miller was a flirt—a pretty American flirt. He had never, as yet, had any relations with young ladies of this category. He had known, here in Europe, two or three women—persons older than Miss Daisy Miller, and provided, for respectability's sake, with husbands—who were great coquettes—dangerous, terrible women, with whom one's relations were liable to take a serious turn. But this young girl was not a coquette in that sense; she was very unsophisticated; she was only a pretty American flirt. Winterbourne was almost grateful for having found the formula that applied to Miss Daisy Miller. He leaned back in his seat; he remarked to himself that she had the most charming nose he had ever seen; he wondered what were the regular conditions and limitations of one's intercourse with a pretty American flirt. It presently became apparent that he was on the way to learn.

"Have you been to that old castle?" asked the young girl, pointing with her parasol to the far-gleaming walls of the Chateau de Chillon.

"Yes, formerly, more than once," said Winterbourne. "You too, I suppose, have seen it?"

"No; we haven't been there. I want to go there dreadfully. Of course I mean to go there. I wouldn't go away from here without having seen that old castle."

"It's a very pretty excursion," said Winterbourne, "and very easy to make. You can drive, you know, or you can go by the little steamer."

"You can go in the cars," said Miss Miller.

"Yes; you can go in the cars," Winterbourne assented.

"Our courier says they take you right up to the castle," the young girl continued. "We were going last week, but my mother gave out. She suffers dreadfully from dyspepsia. She said she couldn't go. Randolph wouldn't go either; he says he doesn't think much of old castles. But I guess we'll go this week, if we can get Randolph."

"Your brother is not interested in ancient monuments?" Winterbourne inquired, smiling.

"He says he don't care much about old castles. He's only nine. He wants to stay at the hotel. Mother's afraid to leave him alone, and the courier won't stay with him; so we haven't been to many places. But it will be too bad if we don't go up there." And Miss Miller pointed again at the Chateau de Chillon.

"I should think it might be arranged," said Winterbourne. "Couldn't you get some one to stay for the afternoon with Randolph?"

Miss Miller looked at him a moment, and then, very placidly, "I wish *you* would stay with him!" she said.

Winterbourne hesitated a moment. "I should much rather go to Chillon with you."

"With me?" asked the young girl with the same placidity.

She didn't rise, blushing, as a young girl at Geneva would have done; and yet Winterbourne, conscious that he had been very bold, thought it possible she was offended. "With your mother," he answered very respectfully.

But it seemed that both his audacity and his respect were lost upon Miss Daisy Miller. "I guess my mother won't go, after all," she said. "She don't like to ride round in the afternoon. But did you really mean what you said just now—that you would like to go up there?"

"Most earnestly," Winterbourne declared.

"Then we may arrange it. If mother will stay with Randolph, I guess Eugenio will."

"Eugenio?" the young man inquired.

"Eugenio's our courier. He doesn't like to stay with Randolph; he's the most fastidious man I ever saw. But he's a splendid courier. I guess he'll stay at home with Randolph if mother does, and then we can go to the castle."

Winterbourne reflected for an instant as lucidly as possible—"we" could only mean Miss Daisy Miller and himself. This program seemed almost too agreeable for credence; he felt as if he ought to kiss the young lady's hand. Possibly he would have done so and quite spoiled the project, but at this moment another person, presumably Eugenio, appeared. A tall, handsome man, with superb whiskers, wearing a velvet morning coat and a brilliant watch chain, approached Miss Miller, looking sharply at her companion. "Oh, Eugenio!" said Miss Miller with the friendliest accent.

Eugenio had looked at Winterbourne from head to foot; he now bowed gravely to the young lady. "I have the honor to inform mademoiselle that luncheon is upon the table."

Miss Miller slowly rose. "See here, Eugenio!" she said; "I'm going to that old castle, anyway."

"To the Chateau de Chillon, mademoiselle?" the courier inquired. "Mademoiselle has made arrangements?" he added in a tone which struck Winterbourne as very impertinent.

Eugenio's tone apparently threw, even to Miss Miller's own apprehension, a slightly ironical light upon the young girl's situation. She turned to Winterbourne, blushing a little—a very little. "You won't back out?" she said.

"I shall not be happy till we go!" he protested.

"And you are staying in this hotel?" she went on. "And you are really an American?"

The courier stood looking at Winterbourne offensively. The young man, at least, thought his manner of looking an offense to Miss Miller; it conveyed an imputation that she "picked up" acquaintances. "I shall have the honor of presenting to you a person who will tell you all about me," he said, smiling and referring to his aunt.

"Oh, well, we'll go some day," said Miss Miller. And she gave him a smile and turned away. She put up her parasol and walked back to the inn beside Eugenio. Winterbourne stood looking after her; and as she moved away, drawing her muslin furbelows over the gravel, said to himself that she had the *tournure* of a princess.

He had, however, engaged to do more than proved feasible, in promising to present his aunt, Mrs. Costello, to Miss Daisy Miller. As soon as the former lady had got better of her headache, he waited upon her in her apartment; and, after the proper inquiries in regard to her health, he asked her if she had observed in the hotel an American family—a mamma, a daughter, and a little boy.

"And a courier?" said Mrs. Costello. "Oh yes, I have observed them. Seen them—heard them—and kept out of their way." Mrs. Costello was a widow with a fortune; a person of much distinction, who frequently intimated that, if she were not so dreadfully liable to sick headaches, she would probably have left a deeper impress upon her time. She had a long, pale face, a high nose, and a great deal of very striking white hair, which she wore in large puffs and *rouleaux* over the top of her head. She had two sons married in New York and another who was now in Europe. This young man was amusing himself at Hamburg, and, though he was on his travels, was rarely perceived to visit any particular city at the moment selected by his mother for her own appearance there. Her nephew, who had come up to Vevey expressly to see her, was therefore more attentive than those who, as she said, were nearer to her. He had imbibed at Geneva the idea that one must always be attentive to one's aunt. Mrs. Costello had not seen him for many years, and she was greatly pleased with him, manifesting her approbation by initiating him into many of the secrets of that social sway which, as she gave him to understand, she exerted in the American capital. She admitted that she was very exclusive; but, if he were acquainted with New York, he would see that one had to be. And her picture of the minutely hierarchical constitution of the society of that city, which she presented to him in many different lights, was, to Winterbourne's imagination, almost oppressively striking.

He immediately perceived, from her tone, that Miss Daisy Miller's place in the social scale was low. "I am afraid you don't approve of them," he said.

"They are very common," Mrs. Costello declared. "They are the sort of Americans that one does one's duty by not—not accepting."

"Ah, you don't accept them?" said the young man.

"I can't, my dear Frederick. I would if I could, but I can't."

"The young girl is very pretty," said Winterbourne in a moment.

"Of course she's pretty. But she is very common."

"I see what you mean, of course," said Winterbourne after another pause.

"She has that charming look that they all have," his aunt resumed. "I can't think where they pick it up; and she dresses in perfection—no, you don't know how well she dresses. I can't think where they get their taste."

"But, my dear aunt, she is not, after all, a Comanche savage."

"She is a young lady," said Mrs. Costello, "who has an intimacy with her mamma's courier."

"An intimacy with the courier?" the young man demanded.

"Oh, the mother is just as bad! They treat the courier like a familiar friend—like a gentleman. I shouldn't wonder if he dines with them. Very likely they have never seen a man with such good manners, such fine clothes, so like a gentleman. He probably corresponds to the young lady's idea of a count. He sits with them in the garden in the evening. I think he smokes."

Winterbourne listened with interest to these disclosures; they helped him to make up his mind about Miss Daisy. Evidently she was rather wild. "Well," he said, "I am not a courier, and yet she was very charming to me."

"You had better have said at first," said Mrs. Costello with dignity, "that you had made her acquaintance."

"We simply met in the garden, and we talked a bit."

"*Tout bonnement!* And pray what did you say?"

"I said I should take the liberty of introducing her to my admirable aunt."

"I am much obliged to you."

"It was to guarantee my respectability," said Winterbourne.

"And pray who is to guarantee hers?"

"Ah, you are cruel!" said the young man. "She's a very nice young girl."

"You don't say that as if you believed it," Mrs. Costello observed.

"She is completely uncultivated," Winterbourne went on. "But she is wonderfully pretty, and, in short, she is very nice. To prove that I believe it, I am going to take her to the Chateau de Chillon."

"You two are going off there together? I should say it proved just the contrary. How long had you known her, may I ask, when this interesting project was formed? You haven't been twenty-four hours in the house."

"I have known her half an hour!" said Winterbourne, smiling.

"Dear me!" cried Mrs. Costello. "What a dreadful girl!"

Her nephew was silent for some moments. "You really think, then," he began earnestly, and with a desire for trustworthy information—"you really think that—" But he paused again.

"Think what, sir?" said his aunt.

"That she is the sort of young lady who expects a man, sooner or later, to carry her off?"

"I haven't the least idea what such young ladies expect a man to do. But I really think that you had better not meddle with little American girls that are uncultivated, as you call them. You have lived too long out of the country. You will be sure to make some great mistake. You are too innocent."

"My dear aunt, I am not so innocent," said Winterbourne, smiling and curling his mustache.

"You are guilty too, then!"

Winterbourne continued to curl his mustache meditatively. "You won't let the poor girl know you then?" he asked at last.

"Is it literally true that she is going to the Chateau de Chillon with you?"

"I think that she fully intends it."

"Then, my dear Frederick," said Mrs. Costello, "I must decline the honor of her acquaintance. I am an old woman, but I am not too old, thank Heaven, to be shocked!"

"But don't they all do these things—the young girls in America?" Winterbourne inquired.

Mrs. Costello stared a moment. "I should like to see my granddaughters do them!" she declared grimly.

This seemed to throw some light upon the matter, for Winterbourne remembered to have heard that his pretty cousins in New York were "tremendous flirts." If, therefore,

Miss Daisy Miller exceeded the liberal margin allowed to these young ladies, it was probable that anything might be expected of her. Winterbourne was impatient to see her again, and he was vexed with himself that, by instinct, he should not appreciate her justly.

Though he was impatient to see her, he hardly knew what he should say to her about his aunt's refusal to become acquainted with her; but he discovered, promptly enough, that with Miss Daisy Miller there was no great need of walking on tiptoe. He found her that evening in the garden, wandering about in the warm starlight like an indolent sylph, and swinging to and fro the largest fan he had ever beheld. It was ten o'clock. He had dined with his aunt, had been sitting with her since dinner, and had just taken leave of her till the morrow. Miss Daisy Miller seemed very glad to see him; she declared it was the longest evening she had ever passed.

"Have you been all alone?" he asked.

"I have been walking round with mother. But mother gets tired walking round," she answered.

"Has she gone to bed?"

"No; she doesn't like to go to bed," said the young girl. "She doesn't sleep—not three hours. She says she doesn't know how she lives. She's dreadfully nervous. I guess she sleeps more than she thinks. She's gone somewhere after Randolph; she wants to try to get him to go to bed. He doesn't like to go to bed."

"Let us hope she will persuade him," observed Winterbourne.

"She will talk to him all she can; but he doesn't like her to talk to him," said Miss Daisy, opening her fan. "She's going to try to get Eugenio to talk to him. But he isn't afraid of Eugenio. Eugenio's a splendid courier, but he can't make much impression on Randolph! I don't believe he'll go to bed before eleven." It appeared that Randolph's vigil was in fact triumphantly prolonged, for Winterbourne strolled about with the young girl for some time without meeting her mother. "I have been looking round for that lady you want to introduce me to," his companion resumed. "She's your aunt." Then, on Winterbourne's admitting the fact and expressing some curiosity as to how she had learned it, she said she had heard all about Mrs. Costello from the chambermaid. She was very quiet and very *comme il faut*; she wore white puffs; she spoke to no one, and she never dined at the *table d'hote*. Every two days she had a headache. "I think that's a lovely description, headache and all!" said Miss Daisy, chattering along in her thin, gay voice. "I want to know her ever so much. I know just what *your* aunt would be; I know I should like her. She would be very exclusive. I like a lady to be exclusive; I'm dying to be exclusive myself. Well, we *are* exclusive, mother and I. We don't speak to everyone—or they don't speak to us. I suppose it's about the same thing. Anyway, I shall be ever so glad to know your aunt."

Winterbourne was embarrassed. "She would be most happy," he said; "but I am afraid those headaches will interfere."

The young girl looked at him through the dusk. "But I suppose she doesn't have a headache every day," she said sympathetically.

Winterbourne was silent a moment. "She tells me she does," he answered at last, not knowing what to say.

Miss Daisy Miller stopped and stood looking at him. Her prettiness was still visible in the darkness; she was opening and closing her enormous fan. "She doesn't want to know me!" she said suddenly. "Why don't you say so? You needn't be afraid. I'm not afraid!" And she gave a little laugh.

Winterbourne fancied there was a tremor in her voice; he was touched, shocked, mortified by it. "My dear young lady," he protested, "she knows no one. It's her wretched health."

The young girl walked on a few steps, laughing still. "You needn't be afraid," she repeated. "Why should she want to know me?" Then she paused again; she was close to the parapet of the garden, and in front of her was the starlit lake. There was a vague sheen upon its surface, and in the distance were dimly seen mountain forms. Daisy Miller looked out upon the mysterious prospect and then she gave another little laugh. "Gracious! she *is* exclusive!" she said. Winterbourne wondered whether she was seriously wounded, and for a moment almost wished that her sense of injury might be such as to make it becoming in him to attempt to reassure and comfort her. He had a pleasant sense that she would be very approachable for consolatory purposes. He felt then, for the instant, quite ready to sacrifice his aunt, conversationally; to admit that she was a proud, rude woman, and to declare that they needn't mind her. But before he had time to commit himself to this perilous mixture of gallantry and impiety, the young lady, resuming her walk, gave an exclamation in quite another tone. "Well, here's Mother! I guess she hasn't got Randolph to go to bed." The figure of a lady appeared at a distance, very indistinct in the darkness, and advancing with a slow and wavering movement. Suddenly it seemed to pause.

"Are you sure it is your mother? Can you distinguish her in this thick dusk?" Winterbourne asked.

"Well!" cried Miss Daisy Miller with a laugh; "I guess I know my own mother. And when she has got on my shawl, too! She is always wearing my things."

The lady in question, ceasing to advance, hovered vaguely about the spot at which she had checked her steps.

"I am afraid your mother doesn't see you," said Winterbourne. "Or perhaps," he added, thinking, with Miss Miller, the joke permissible—"perhaps she feels guilty about your shawl."

"Oh, it's a fearful old thing!" the young girl replied serenely. "I told her she could wear it. She won't come here because she sees you."

"Ah, then," said Winterbourne, "I had better leave you."

"Oh, no; come on!" urged Miss Daisy Miller.

"I'm afraid your mother doesn't approve of my walking with you."

Miss Miller gave him a serious glance. "It isn't for me; it's for you—that is, it's for *her*. Well, I don't know who it's for! But mother doesn't like any of my gentlemen friends. She's right down timid. She always makes a fuss if I introduce a gentleman. But I *do* introduce them—almost always. If I didn't introduce my gentlemen friends to Mother," the young girl added in her little soft, flat monotone, "I shouldn't think I was natural."

"To introduce me," said Winterbourne, "you must know my name." And he proceeded to pronounce it.

"Oh, dear, I can't say all that!" said his companion with a laugh. But by this time they had come up to Mrs. Miller, who, as they drew near, walked to the parapet of the garden and leaned upon it, looking intently at the lake and turning her back to them. "Mother!" said the young girl in a tone of decision. Upon this the elder lady turned round. "Mr. Winterbourne," said Miss Daisy Miller, introducing the young man very frankly and prettily. "Common," she was, as Mrs. Costello had pronounced her; yet it was a wonder to Winterbourne that, with her commonness, she had a singularly delicate grace.

Her mother was a small, spare, light person, with a wandering eye, a very exiguous nose, and a large forehead, decorated with a certain amount of thin, much frizzled hair. Like her daughter, Mrs. Miller was dressed with extreme elegance; she had enormous diamonds in her ears. So far as Winterbourne could observe, she gave him no greeting—she certainly was not looking at him. Daisy was near her, pulling her shawl straight. "What are you doing, poking round here?" this young lady inquired, but by no means with that harshness of accent which her choice of words may imply.

"I don't know," said her mother, turning toward the lake again.

"I shouldn't think you'd want that shawl!" Daisy exclaimed.

"Well I do!" her mother answered with a little laugh.

"Did you get Randolph to go to bed?" asked the young girl.

"No; I couldn't induce him," said Mrs. Miller very gently. "He wants to talk to the waiter. He likes to talk to that waiter."

I was telling Mr. Winterbourne," the young girl went on; and to the young man's ear her tone might have indicated that she had been uttering his name all her life.

"Oh, yes!" said Winterbourne; "I have the pleasure of knowing your son."

Randolph's mamma was silent; she turned her attention to the lake. But at last she spoke. "Well, I don't see how he lives!"

"Anyhow, it isn't so bad as it was at Dover," said Daisy Miller.

"And what occurred at Dover?" Winterbourne asked.

"He wouldn't go to bed at all. I guess he sat up all night in the public parlor. He wasn't in bed at twelve o'clock: I know that."

"It was half-past twelve," declared Mrs. Miller with mild emphasis.

"Does he sleep much during the day?" Winterbourne demanded.

"I guess he doesn't sleep much," Daisy rejoined.

"I wish he would!" said her mother. "It seems as if he couldn't."

"I think he's real tiresome," Daisy pursued.

Then, for some moments, there was silence. "Well, Daisy Miller," said the elder lady, presently, "I shouldn't think you'd want to talk against your own brother!"

"Well, he *is* tiresome, Mother," said Daisy, quite without the asperity of a retort.

"He's only nine," urged Mrs. Miller.

"Well, he wouldn't go to that castle," said the young girl. "I'm going there with Mr. Winterbourne."

To this announcement, very placidly made, Daisy's mamma offered no response. Winterbourne took for granted that she deeply disapproved of the projected excursion; but he said to himself that she was a simple, easily managed person, and that a few deferential protestations would take the edge from her displeasure. "Yes," he began; "your daughter has kindly allowed me the honor of being her guide."

Mrs. Miller's wandering eyes attached themselves, with a sort of appealing air, to Daisy, who, however, strolled a few steps farther, gently humming to herself. "I presume you will go in the cars," said her mother.

"Yes, or in the boat," said Winterbourne.

"Well, of course, I don't know," Mrs. Miller rejoined. "I have never been to that castle."

"It is a pity you shouldn't go," said Winterbourne, beginning to feel reassured as to her opposition. And yet he was quite prepared to find that, as a matter of course, she meant to accompany her daughter.

"We've been thinking ever so much about going," she pursued; "but it seems as if we couldn't. Of course Daisy—she wants to go round. But there's a lady here—I don't know her name—she says she shouldn't think we'd want to go to see castles *here*; she should think we'd want to wait till we got to Italy. It seems as if there would be so many there," continued Mrs. Miller with an air of increasing confidence. "Of course we only want to see the principal ones. We visited several in England," she presently added.

"Ah yes! in England there are beautiful castles," said Winterbourne. "But Chillon here, is very well worth seeing."

"Well, if Daisy feels up to it—" said Mrs. Miller, in a tone impregnated with a sense of the magnitude of the enterprise. "It seems as if there was nothing she wouldn't undertake."

"Oh, I think she'll enjoy it!" Winterbourne declared. And he desired more and more to make it a certainty that he was to have the privilege of a *tête-à-tête* with the young lady, who was still strolling along in front of them, softly vocalizing. "You are not disposed, madam," he inquired, "to undertake it yourself?"

Daisy's mother looked at him an instant askance, and then walked forward in silence. Then—"I guess she had better go alone," she said simply. Winterbourne observed to himself that this was a very different type of maternity from that of the vigilant matrons who massed themselves in the forefront of social intercourse in the dark old city at the other end of the lake. But his meditations were interrupted by hearing his name very distinctly pronounced by Mrs. Miller's unprotected daughter.

"Mr. Winterbourne!" murmured Daisy.

"Mademoiselle!" said the young man.

"Don't you want to take me out in a boat?"

"At present?" he asked.

"Of course!" said Daisy.

"Well, Annie Miller!" exclaimed her mother.

"I beg you, madam, to let her go," said Winterbourne ardently; for he had never yet enjoyed the sensation of guiding through the summer starlight a skiff freighted with a fresh and beautiful young girl.

"I shouldn't think she'd want to," said her mother. "I should think she'd rather go indoors."

"I'm sure Mr. Winterbourne wants to take me," Daisy declared. "He's so awfully devoted!"

"I will row you over to Chillon in the starlight."

"I don't believe it!" said Daisy.

"Well!" ejaculated the elder lady again.

"You haven't spoken to me for half an hour," her daughter went on.

"I have been having some very pleasant conversation with your mother," said Winterbourne.

"Well, I want you to take me out in a boat!" Daisy repeated. They had all stopped, and she had turned round and was looking at Winterbourne. Her face wore a charming smile, her pretty eyes were gleaming, she was swinging her great fan about. No; it's impossible to be prettier than that, thought Winterbourne.

"There are half a dozen boats moored at that landing place," he said, pointing to certain steps which descended from the garden to the lake. "If you will do me the honor to accept my arm, we will go and select one of them."

Daisy stood there smiling; she threw back her head and gave a little, light laugh. "I like a gentleman to be formal!" she declared.

"I assure you it's a formal offer."

"I was bound I would make you say something," Daisy went on.

"You see, it's not very difficult," said Winterbourne. "But I am afraid you are chaffing me."

"I think not, sir," remarked Mrs. Miller very gently.

"Do, then, let me give you a row," he said to the young girl.

"It's quite lovely, the way you say that!" cried Daisy.

"It will be still more lovely to do it."

"Yes, it would be lovely!" said Daisy. But she made no movement to accompany him; she only stood there laughing.

"I should think you had better find out what time it is," interposed her mother.

"It is eleven o'clock, madam," said a voice, with a foreign accent, out of the neighboring darkness; and Winterbourne, turning, perceived the florid personage who was in attendance upon the two ladies. He had apparently just approached.

"Oh, Eugenio," said Daisy, "I am going out in a boat!"

Eugenio bowed. "At eleven o'clock, mademoiselle?"

"I am going with Mr. Winterbourne—this very minute."

"Do tell her she can't," said Mrs. Miller to the courier.

"I think you had better not go out in a boat, mademoiselle," Eugenio declared.

Winterbourne wished to Heaven this pretty girl were not so familiar with her courier; but he said nothing.

"I suppose you don't think it's proper!" Daisy exclaimed. "Eugenio doesn't think anything's proper."

"I am at your service," said Winterbourne.

"Does mademoiselle propose to go alone?" asked Eugenio of Mrs. Miller.

"Oh, no; with this gentleman!" answered Daisy's mamma.

The courier looked for a moment at Winterbourne—the latter thought he was smiling—and then, solemnly, with a bow, "As mademoiselle pleases!" he said.

"Oh, I hoped you would make a fuss!" said Daisy. "I don't care to go now."

"I myself shall make a fuss if you don't go," said Winterbourne.

"That's all I want—a little fuss!" And the young girl began to laugh again.

"Mr. Randolph has gone to bed!" the courier announced frigidly.

"Oh, Daisy; now we can go!" said Mrs. Miller.

Daisy turned away from Winterbourne, looking at him, smiling and fanning herself. "Good night," she said; "I hope you are disappointed, or disgusted, or something!"

He looked at her, taking the hand she offered him. "I am puzzled," he answered.

"Well, I hope it won't keep you awake!" she said very smartly; and, under the escort of the privileged Eugenio, the two ladies passed toward the house.

Winterbourne stood looking after them; he was indeed puzzled. He lingered beside the lake for a quarter of an hour, turning over the mystery of the young girl's sudden familiarities and caprices. But the only very definite conclusion he came to was that he should enjoy deucedly "going off" with her somewhere.

Two days afterward he went off with her to the Castle of Chillon. He waited for her in the large hall of the hotel, where the couriers, the servants, the foreign tourists, were lounging about and staring. It was not the place he should have chosen, but she had appointed it. She came tripping downstairs, buttoning her long gloves, squeezing her folded parasol against her pretty figure, dressed in the perfection of a soberly elegant traveling costume. Winterbourne was a man of imagination and, as our ancestors used to say, sensibility; as he looked at her dress and, on the great staircase, her little rapid, confiding step, he felt as if there were something romantic going forward. He could have believed he was going to elope with her. He passed out with her among all the idle people that were assembled there; they were all looking at her very hard; she had begun to chatter as soon as she joined him. Winterbourne's preference had been that they should be conveyed to Chillon in a carriage; but she expressed a lively wish to go in the little steamer; she declared that she had a passion for steamboats. There was always such a lovely breeze upon the water, and you saw such lots of people. The sail was not long, but Winterbourne's companion found time to say a great many things. To the young man himself their little excursion was so much of an escapade—an adventure—that, even allowing for her habitual sense of freedom, he had some expectation of seeing her regard it in the same way. But it must be confessed that, in this particular, he was disappointed. Daisy Miller was extremely animated, she was in charming spirits; but she was apparently not at all excited; she was not fluttered; she avoided neither his eyes nor those of anyone else; she blushed neither when she looked at him nor when she felt that people were looking at her. People continued to look at her a great deal, and Winterbourne took much satisfaction in his pretty companion's distinguished air. He had been a little afraid that she would talk loud, laugh overmuch, and even, perhaps, desire to move about the boat a good deal. But he quite forgot his fears; he sat smiling, with his eyes upon her face, while, without moving from her place, she delivered herself of a great number of original reflections. It was the most charming garrulity he had ever heard. he had assented to the idea that she was "common"; but was she so, after all, or was he simply getting used to her commonness? Her conversation was chiefly of what metaphysicians term the objective cast, but every now and then it took a subjective turn.

"What on *earth* are you so grave about?" she suddenly demanded, fixing her agreeable eyes upon Winterbourne's.

"Am I grave?" he asked. "I had an idea I was grinning from ear to ear."

"You look as if you were taking me to a funeral. If that's a grin, your ears are very near together."

"Should you like me to dance a hornpipe on the deck?"

"Pray do, and I'll carry round your hat. It will pay the expenses of our journey."

"I never was better pleased in my life," murmured Winterbourne.

She looked at him a moment and then burst into a little laugh. "I like to make you say those things! You're a queer mixture!"

In the castle, after they had landed, the subjective element decidedly prevailed. Daisy tripped about the vaulted chambers, rustled her skirts in the corkscrew staircases, flirted back with a pretty little cry and a shudder from the edge of the oubliettes, and turned a singularly well-shaped ear to everything that Winterbourne told her about the place. But he saw that she cared very little for feudal antiquities and that the dusky traditions of Chillon made but a slight impression upon her. They had the good fortune to have been able to walk about without other companionship than that of the custodian; and Winterbourne arranged with this functionary that they should not be hurried—that they should linger and pause wherever they chose. The custodian interpreted the bargain generously—Winterbourne, on his side, had been generous—and ended by leaving them quite to themselves. Miss Miller's observations were not remarkable for logical consistency; for anything she wanted to say she was sure to find a pretext. She found a great many pretexts in the rugged embrasures of Chillon for asking Winterbourne sudden questions about himself—his family, his previous history, his tastes, his habits, his intentions—and for supplying information upon corresponding points in her own personality. Of her own tastes, habits, and intentions Miss Miller was prepared to give the most definite, and indeed the most favorable account.

"Well, I hope you know enough!" she said to her companion, after he had told her the history of the unhappy Bonivard. "I never saw a man that knew so much!" The history of Bonivard had evidently, as they say, gone into one ear and out of the other. But Daisy went on to say that she wished Winterbourne would travel with them and "go round" with them; they might know something, in that case. "Don't you want to come and teach Randolph?" she asked. Winterbourne said that nothing could possibly please him so much, but that he unfortunately other occupations. "Other occupations? I don't believe it!" said Miss Daisy. "What do you mean? You are not in business." The young man admitted that he was not in business; but he had engagements which, even within a day or two, would force him to go back to Geneva. "Oh, bother!" she said; "I don't believe it!" and she began to talk about something else. But a few moments later, when he was pointing out to her the pretty design of an antique fireplace, she broke out irrelevantly, "You don't mean to say you are going back to Geneva?"

"It is a melancholy fact that I shall have to return to Geneva tomorrow."

"Well, Mr. Winterbourne," said Daisy, "I think you're horrid!"

"Oh, don't say such dreadful things!" said Winterbourne—"just at the last!"

"The last!" cried the young girl; "I call it the first. I have half a mind to leave you here and go straight back to the hotel alone." And for the next ten minutes she did nothing but call him horrid. Poor Winterbourne was fairly bewildered; no young lady had as yet done him the honor to be so agitated by the announcement of his movements. His companion, after this, ceased to pay any attention to the curiosities of Chillon or the beauties of the lake; she opened fire upon the mysterious charmer in Geneva whom she appeared to have instantly taken it for granted that he was hurrying back to see. How did Miss Daisy Miller know that there was a charmer in Geneva? Winterbourne, who denied the existence of such a person, was quite unable to discover, and he was divided between amazement at the rapidity of her induction and amusement at the frankness of her *persiflage*. She seemed to him, in all this, an extraordinary mixture of innocence and crudity. "Does she never allow you more than three days at a time?" asked Daisy ironically. "Doesn't she give you a vacation in summer? There's no one so hard worked but they can get leave to go off somewhere at this season. I suppose, if you stay another day, she'll come after you in the boat. Do wait over till Friday, and I will go down to the landing to see her arrive!" Winterbourne began to think he had been wrong to feel disappointed in the temper in which the young lady had embarked. If he had missed the personal accent, the personal accent was now making its appearance. It sounded very distinctly, at last, in her telling him she would stop "teasing" him if he would promise her solemnly to come down to Rome in the winter.

"That's not a difficult promise to make," said Winterbourne. "My aunt has taken an apartment in Rome for the winter and has already asked me to come and see her."

"I don't want you to come for your aunt," said Daisy; "I want you to come for me." And this was the only allusion that the young man was ever to hear her make to his invidious kinswoman. He declared that, at any rate, he would certainly come. After this Daisy stopped teasing. Winterbourne took a carriage, and they drove back to Vevey in the dusk; the young girl was very quiet.

In the evening Winterbourne mentioned to Mrs. Costello that he had spent the afternoon at Chillon with Miss Daisy Miller.

"The Americans—of the courier?" asked this lady.

"Ah, happily," said Winterbourne, "the courier stayed at home."

"She went with you all alone?"

"All alone."

Mrs. Costello sniffed a little at her smelling bottle. "And that," she exclaimed, "is the young person whom you wanted me to know!"

PART II

Winterbourne, who had returned to Geneva the day after his excursion to Chillon, went to Rome toward the end of January. His aunt had been established there for several weeks, and he had received a couple of letters from her. "Those people you were so devoted to last summer at Vevey have turned up here, courier and all," she wrote. "They seem to have made several acquaintances, but the courier continues to be the most *intime*. The young lady, however, is also very intimate with some third-rate Italians, with whom she rackets about in a way that makes much talk. Bring me that pretty novel of Cherbuliez's—Paule Mere—and don't come later than the 23rd."

In the natural course of events, Winterbourne, on arriving in Rome, would presently have ascertained Mrs. Miller's address at the American banker's and have gone to pay his compliments to Miss Daisy. "After what happened at Vevey, I think I may certainly call upon them," he said to Mrs. Costello.

"If, after what happens—at Vevey and everywhere—you desire to keep up the acquaintance, you are very welcome. Of course a man may know everyone. Men are welcome to the privilege!"

"Pray what is it that happens—here, for instance?" Winterbourne demanded.

"The girl goes about alone with her foreigners. As to what happens further, you must apply elsewhere for information. She has picked up half a dozen of the regular Roman fortune hunters, and she takes them about to people's houses. When she comes to a party she brings with her a gentleman with a good deal of manner and a wonderful mustache."

"And where is the mother?"

"I haven't the least idea. They are very dreadful people."

Winterbourne meditated a moment. "They are very ignorant—very innocent only. Depend upon it they are not bad."

"They are hopelessly vulgar," said Mrs. Costello. "Whether or no being hopelessly vulgar is being 'bad' is a question for the metaphysicians. They are bad enough to dislike, at any rate; and for this short life that is quite enough."

The news that Daisy Miller was surrounded by half a dozen wonderful mustaches checked Winterbourne's impulse to go straightway to see her. He had, perhaps, not definitely flattered himself that he had made an ineffaceable impression upon her heart, but he was annoyed at hearing of a state of affairs so little in harmony with an image that had lately flitted in and out of his own meditations; the image of a very pretty girl looking out of an old Roman window and asking herself urgently when Mr. Winterbourne would arrive. If, however, he determined to wait a little before reminding Miss Miller of his claims to her consideration, he went very soon to call upon two or three other friends. One of these friends was an American lady who had spent several winters at Geneva, where she had placed her children at school. She was a very accomplished woman, and she lived in the Via Gregoriana. Winterbourne found her in a little crimson drawing room on a third floor; the room was filled with southern sunshine. He had not been there ten minutes when the servant came in, announcing "Madame Mila!" This announcement was presently followed by the entrance of little Randolph Miller, who stopped in the middle of the room and stood staring at Winterbourne. An instant later his pretty sister crossed the threshold; and then, after a considerable interval, Mrs. Miller slowly advanced.

"I know you!" said Randolph.

"I'm sure you know a great many things," exclaimed Winterbourne, taking him by the hand. "How is your education coming on?"

Daisy was exchanging greetings very prettily with her hostess, but when she heard Winterbourne's voice she quickly turned her head. "Well, I declare!" she said.

"I told you I should come, you know," Winterbourne rejoined, smiling.

"Well, I didn't believe it," said Miss Daisy.

"I am much obliged to you," laughed the young man.

"You might have come to see me!" said Daisy.

"I arrived only yesterday."

"I don't believe that!" the young girl declared.

Winterbourne turned with a protesting smile to her mother, but this lady evaded his glance, and, seating herself, fixed her eyes upon her son. "We've got a bigger place than this," said Randolph. "It's all gold on the walls."

Mrs. Miller turned uneasily in her chair. "I told you if I were to bring you, you would say something!" she murmured.

"I told *you!*" Randolph exclaimed. "I tell *you*, sir!" he added jocosely, giving Winterbourne a thump on the knee. "It *is* bigger, too!"

Daisy had entered upon a lively conversation with her hostess; Winterbourne judged it becoming to address a few words to her mother. "I hope you have been well since we parted at Vevey," he said.

Mrs. Miller now certainly looked at him—at his chin. "Not very well, sir," she answered.

"She's got the dyspepsia," said Randolph. "I've got it too. Father's got it. I've got it most!"

This announcement, instead of embarrassing Mrs. Miller, seemed to relieve her. "I suffer from the liver," she said. "I think it's this climate; it's less bracing than Schenectady, especially in the winter season. I don't know whether you know we reside at Schenectady. I was saying to Daisy that I certainly hadn't found any one like Dr. Davis, and I didn't believe I should. Oh, at Schenectady he stands first; they think everything of him. He has so much to do, and yet there was nothing he wouldn't do for me. He said he never saw anything like my dyspepsia, but he was bound to cure it. I'm sure there was nothing he wouldn't try. He was just going to try something new when we came off. Mr. Miller wanted Daisy to see Europe for herself. But I wrote to Mr. Miller that it seems as if I couldn't get on without Dr. Davis. At Schenectady he stands at the very top; and there's a great deal of sickness there, too. It affects my sleep."

Winterbourne had a good deal of pathological gossip with Dr. Davis's patient, during which Daisy chattered unremittingly to her own companion. The young man asked Mrs. Miller how she was pleased with Rome. "Well, I must say I am disappointed," she answered. "We had heard so much about it; I suppose we had heard too much. But we couldn't help that. We had been led to expect something different."

"Ah, wait a little, and you will become very fond of it," said Winterbourne.

"I hate it worse and worse every day!" cried Randolph.

"You are like the infant Hannibal," said Winterbourne.

"No, I ain't!" Randolph declared at a venture.

"You are not much like an infant," said his mother. "But we have seen places," she resumed, "that I should put a long way before Rome." And in reply to Winterbourne's interrogation, "There's Zurich," she concluded, "I think Zurich is lovely; and we hadn't heard half so much about it."

"The best place we've seen is the City of Richmond!" said Randolph.

"He means the ship," his mother explained. "We crossed in that ship. Randolph had a good time on the City of Richmond."

"It's the best place I've seen," the child repeated. "Only it was turned the wrong way."

"Well, we've got to turn the right way some time," said Mrs. Miller with a little laugh. Winterbourne expressed the hope that her daughter at least found some gratification in Rome, and she declared that Daisy was quite carried away. "It's on account of the society—the society's splendid. She goes round everywhere; she has made a great number of acquaintances. Of course she goes round more than I do. I must say they have been very sociable; they have taken her right in. And then she knows a great many gentlemen. Oh, she thinks there's nothing like Rome. Of course, it's a great deal pleasanter for a young lady if she knows plenty of gentlemen."

By this time Daisy had turned her attention again to Winterbourne. "I've been telling Mrs. Walker how mean you were!" the young girl announced.

"And what is the evidence you have offered?" asked Winterbourne, rather annoyed at Miss Miller's want of appreciation of the zeal of an admirer who on his way down to Rome had stopped neither at Bologna nor at Florence, simply because of a certain sentimental impatience. He remembered that a cynical compatriot had once told him that American women—the pretty ones, and this gave a largeness to the axiom—were at once the most exacting in the world and the least endowed with a sense of indebtedness.

"Why, you were awfully mean at Vevey," said Daisy. "You wouldn't do anything. You wouldn't stay there when I asked you."

"My dearest young lady," cried Winterbourne, with eloquence, "have I come all the way to Rome to encounter your reproaches?"

"Just hear him say that!" said Daisy to her hostess, giving a twist to a bow on this lady's dress. "Did you ever hear anything so quaint?"

"So quaint, my dear?" murmured Mrs. Walker in the tone of a partisan of Winterbourne.

"Well, I don't know," said Daisy, fingering Mrs. Walker's ribbons. "Mrs. Walker, I want to tell you something."

"Mother-r," interposed Randolph, with his rough ends to his words, "I tell you you've got to go. Eugenio'll raise—something!"

"I'm not afraid of Eugenio," said Daisy with a toss of her head. "Look here, Mrs. Walker," she went on, "you know I'm coming to your party."

"I am delighted to hear it."

"I've got a lovely dress!"

"I am very sure of that."

"But I want to ask a favor—permission to bring a friend."

"I shall be happy to see any of your friends," said Mrs. Walker, turning with a smile to Mrs. Miller.

"Oh, they are not my friends," answered Daisy's mamma, smiling shyly in her own fashion. "I never spoke to them."

"It's an intimate friend of mine—Mr. Giovanelli," said Daisy without a tremor in her clear little voice or a shadow on her brilliant little face.

Mrs. Walker was silent a moment; she gave a rapid glance at Winterbourne. "I shall be glad to see Mr. Giovanelli," she then said.

"He's an Italian," Daisy pursued with the prettiest serenity. "He's a great friend of mine; he's the handsomest man in the world—except Mr. Winterbourne! He knows plenty of Italians, but he wants to know some Americans. He thinks ever so much of Americans. He's tremendously clever. He's perfectly lovely!"

It was settled that this brilliant personage should be brought to Mrs. Walker's party, and then Mrs. Miller prepared to take her leave. "I guess we'll go back to the hotel," she said.

"You may go back to the hotel, Mother, but I'm going to take a walk," said Daisy.

"She's going to walk with Mr. Giovanelli," Randolph proclaimed.

"I am going to the Pincio," said Daisy, smiling.

"Alone, my dear—at this hour?" Mrs. Walker asked. The afternoon was drawing to a close—it was the hour for the throng of carriages and of contemplative pedestrians. "I don't think it's safe, my dear," said Mrs. Walker.

"Neither do I," subjoined Mrs. Miller. "You'll get the fever, as sure as you live. Remember what Dr. Davis told you!"

"Give her some medicine before she goes," said Randolph.

The company had risen to its feet; Daisy, still showing her pretty teeth, bent over and kissed her hostess. "Mrs. Walker, you are too perfect," she said. "I'm not going alone; I am going to meet a friend."

"Your friend won't keep you from getting the fever," Mrs. Miller observed.

"Is it Mr. Giovanelli?" asked the hostess.

Winterbourne was watching the young girl; at this question his attention quickened. She stood there, smiling and smoothing her bonnet ribbons; she glanced at Winterbourne. Then, while she glanced and smiled, she answered, without a shade of hesitation, "Mr. Giovanelli—the beautiful Giovanelli."

"My dear young friend," said Mrs. Walker, taking her hand pleadingly, "don't walk off to the Pincio at this hour to meet a beautiful Italian."

"Well, he speaks English," said Mrs. Miller.

"Gracious me!" Daisy exclaimed, "I don't to do anything improper. There's an easy way to settle it." She continued to glance at Winterbourne. "The Pincio is only a hundred yards distant; and if Mr. Winterbourne were as polite as he pretends, he would offer to walk with me!"

Winterbourne's politeness hastened to affirm itself, and the young girl gave him gracious leave to accompany her. They passed downstairs before her mother, and at the door Winterbourne perceived Mrs. Miller's carriage drawn up, with the ornamental courier whose acquaintance he had made at Vevey seated within. "Goodbye, Eugenio!" cried Daisy; "I'm going to take a walk." The distance from the Via Gregoriana to the beautiful garden at the other end of the Pincian Hill is, in fact, rapidly traversed. As the day was splendid, however, and the concourse of vehicles, walkers, and loungers numerous, the young Americans found their progress much delayed. This fact was highly agreeable to Winterbourne, in spite of his consciousness of his singular situation. The slow-moving, idly gazing Roman crowd bestowed much attention upon the extremely pretty young foreign lady who was passing through it upon his arm; and he wondered what on earth had been in Daisy's mind when she proposed to expose herself, unattended, to its appreciation. His own mission, to her sense, apparently, was to consign her to the hands of Mr. Giovanelli; but Winterbourne, at once annoyed and gratified, resolved that he would do no such thing.

"Why haven't you been to see me?" asked Daisy. "You can't get out of that."

"I have had the honor of telling you that I have only just stepped out of the train."

"You must have stayed in the train a good while after it stopped!" cried the young girl with her little laugh. "I suppose you were asleep. You have had time to go to see Mrs. Walker."

"I knew Mrs. Walker—" Winterbourne began to explain.

"I know where you knew her. You knew her at Geneva. She told me so. Well, you knew me at Vevey. That's just as good. So you ought to have come." She asked him no other question than this; she began to prattle about her own affairs. "We've got splendid rooms at the hotel; Eugenio says they're the best rooms in Rome. We are going to stay all winter, if we don't die of the fever; and I guess we'll stay then. It's a great deal nicer than I thought; I thought it would be fearfully quiet; I was sure it would be awfully poky. I was sure we should be going round all the time with one of those dreadful old men that explain about the pictures and things. But we only had about a week of that, and now I'm enjoying myself. I know ever so many people, and they are all so charming. The society's extremely select. There are all kinds—English, and Germans, and Italians. I think I like the English best. I like their style of conversation. But there are some lovely Americans. I never saw anything so hospitable. There's something or other every day. There's not much dancing; but I must say I never thought dancing was everything. I was always fond of conversation. I guess I shall have plenty at Mrs. Walker's, her rooms are so small." When they had passed the gate of the Pincian Gardens, Miss Miller began to wonder where Mr. Giovanelli might be. "We had better go straight to that place in front," she said, "where you look at the view."

"I certainly shall not help you to find him," Winterbourne declared.

"Then I shall find him without you," cried Miss Daisy.

"You certainly won't leave me!" cried Winterbourne.

She burst into her little laugh. "Are you afraid you'll get lost—or run over? But there's Giovanelli, leaning against that tree. He's staring at the women in the carriages: did you ever see anything so cool?"

Winterbourne perceived at some distance a little man standing with folded arms nursing his cane. He had a handsome face, an artfully poised hat, a glass in one eye, and a nosegay in his buttonhole. Winterbourne looked at him a moment and then said, "Do you mean to speak to that man?"

"Do I mean to speak to him? Why, you don't suppose I mean to communicate by signs?"

"Pray understand, then," said Winterbourne, "that I intend to remain with you."

Daisy stopped and looked at him, without a sign of troubled consciousness in her face, with nothing but the presence of her charming eyes and her happy dimples. "Well, she's a cool one!" thought the young man.

"I don't like the way you say that," said Daisy. "It's too imperious."

"I beg your pardon if I say it wrong. The main point is to give you an idea of my meaning."

The young girl looked at him more gravely, but with eyes that were prettier than ever. "I have never allowed a gentleman to dictate to me, or to interfere with anything I do."

"I think you have made a mistake," said Winterbourne. "You should sometimes listen to a gentleman—the right one."

Daisy began to laugh again. "I do nothing but listen to gentlemen!" she exclaimed. "Tell me if Mr. Giovanelli is the right one?"

The gentleman with the nosegay in his bosom had now perceived our two friends, and was approaching the young girl with obsequious rapidity. He bowed to Winterbourne as well as to the latter's companion; he had a brilliant smile, an intelligent eye; Winterbourne thought him not a bad-looking fellow. But he nevertheless said to Daisy, "No, he's not the right one."

Daisy evidently had a natural talent for performing introductions; she mentioned the name of each of her companions to the other. She strolled alone with one of them on each side of her; Mr. Giovanelli, who spoke English very cleverly—Winterbourne afterward learned that he had practiced the idiom upon a great many American heiresses—addressed her a great deal of very polite nonsense; he was extremely urbane, and the young American, who said nothing, reflected upon that profundity of Italian cleverness which enables people to appear more gracious in proportion as they are more acutely disappointed. Giovanelli, of course, had counted upon something more intimate; he had not bargained for a party of three. But he kept his temper in a manner which suggested far-stretching intentions. Winterbourne flattered himself that he had taken his measure. "He is not a gentleman," said the young American; "he is only a clever imitation of one. He is a music master, or a penny-a-liner, or a third-rate artist. Damn his good looks!" Mr. Giovanelli had certainly a very pretty face; but Winterbourne felt a superior indignation at his own lovely fellow countrywoman's not knowing the difference between a spurious gentleman and a real one. Giovanelli chattered and jested and made himself wonderfully agreeable. It was true that, if he was an imitation, the imitation was brilliant. "Nevertheless," Winterbourne said to himself, "a nice girl ought to know!" And then he came back to the question whether this was, in fact, a nice girl. Would a nice girl, even allowing for her being a little American flirt, make a rendezvous with a presumably low-lived foreigner? The rendezvous in this case, indeed, had been in broad daylight and in the most crowded corner of Rome, but was it not impossible to regard the choice of these circumstances as a proof of extreme cynicism? Singular though it may seem, Winterbourne was vexed that the young girl, in joining her amoroso, should not appear more impatient of his own company, and he was vexed because of his inclination. It was impossible to regard her as a perfectly well-conducted young lady; she was wanting in a certain indispensable delicacy. It would therefore simplify matters greatly to be able to treat her as the object of one of those sentiments which are called by romancers "lawless passions." That she should seem to wish to get rid of him would help him to think more lightly of her, and to be able to think more lightly of her would make her much less perplexing. But Daisy, on this occasion, continued to present herself as an inscrutable combination of audacity and innocence.

She had been walking some quarter of an hour, attended by her two cavaliers, and responding in a tone of very childish gaiety, as it seemed to Winterbourne, to the pretty speeches of Mr. Giovanelli, when a carriage that had detached itself from the revolving train drew up beside the path. At the same moment Winterbourne perceived that his friend Mrs. Walker—the lady whose house he had lately left—was seated in the vehicle and was beckoning to him. Leaving Miss Miller's side, he hastened to obey her summons. Mrs. Walker was flushed; she wore an excited air. "It is really too dreadful," she said. "That girl must not do this sort of thing. She must not walk here with you two men. Fifty people have noticed her."

Winterbourne raised his eyebrows. "I think it's a pity to make too much fuss about it."

"It's a pity to let the girl ruin herself!"

"She is very innocent," said Winterbourne.

"She's very crazy!" cried Mrs. Walker. "Did you ever see anything so imbecile as her mother? After you had all left me just now, I could not sit still for thinking of it. It seemed too pitiful, not even to attempt to save her. I ordered the carriage and put on my bonnet, and came here as quickly as possible. Thank Heaven I have found you!"

"What do you propose to do with us?" asked Winterbourne, smiling.

"To ask her to get in, to drive her about here for half an hour, so that the world may see she is not running absolutely wild, and then to take her safely home."

"I don't think it's a very happy thought," said Winterbourne; "but you can try."

Mrs. Walker tried. The young man went in pursuit of Miss Miller, who had simply nodded and smiled at his interlocutor in the carriage and had gone her way with her companion. Daisy, on learning that Mrs. Walker wished to speak to her, retraced her steps with a perfect good grace and with Mr. Giovanelli at her side. She declared that she was delighted to have a chance to present this gentleman to Mrs. Walker. She immediately achieved the introduction, and declared that she had never in her life seen anything so lovely as Mrs. Walker's carriage rug.

"I am glad you admire it," said this lady, smiling sweetly. "Will you get in and let me put it over you?"

"Oh, no, thank you," said Daisy. "I shall admire it much more as I see you driving round with it."

"Do get in and drive with me!" said Mrs. Walker.

"That would be charming, but it's so enchanting just as I am!" and Daisy gave a brilliant glance at the gentlemen on either side of her.

"It may be enchanting, dear child, but it is not the custom here," urged Mrs. Walker, leaning forward in her victoria, with her hands devoutly clasped.

"Well, it ought to be, then!" said Daisy. "If I didn't walk I should expire."

"You should walk with your mother, dear," cried the lady from Geneva, losing patience.

"With my mother dear!" exclaimed the young girl. Winterbourne saw that she scented interference. "My mother never walked ten steps in her life. And then, you know," she added with a laugh, "I am more than five years old."

"You are old enough to be more reasonable. You are old enough, dear Miss Miller, to be talked about."

Daisy looked at Mrs. Walker, smiling intensely. "Talked about? What do you mean?"

"Come into my carriage, and I will tell you."

Daisy turned her quickened glance again from one of the gentlemen beside her to the other. Mr. Giovanelli was bowing to and fro, rubbing down his gloves and laughing very agreeably; Winterbourne thought it a most unpleasant scene. "I don't think I want to know what you mean," said Daisy presently. "I don't think I should like it."

Winterbourne wished that Mrs. Walker would tuck in her carriage rug and drive away, but this lady did not enjoy being defied, as she afterward told him. "Should you prefer being thought a very reckless girl?" she demanded.

"Gracious!" exclaimed Daisy. She looked again at Mr. Giovanelli, then she turned to Winterbourne. There was a little pink flush in her cheek; she was tremendously pretty. "Does Mr. Winterbourne think," she asked slowly, smiling, throwing back her head, and glancing at him from head to foot, "that, to save my reputation, I ought to get into the carriage?"

Winterbourne colored; for an instant he hesitated greatly. It seemed so strange to hear her speak that way of her "reputation." But he himself, in fact, must speak in accordance with gallantry. The finest gallantry, here, was simply to tell her the truth; and the truth, for Winterbourne, as the few indications I have been able to give have made him known to the reader, was that Daisy Miller should take Mrs. Walker's advice. He looked at her exquisite prettiness, and then he said, very gently, "I think you should get into the carriage."

Daisy gave a violent laugh. "I never heard anything so stiff! If this is improper, Mrs. Walker," she pursued, "then I am all improper, and you must give me up. Goodbye; I hope you'll have a lovely ride!" and, with Mr. Giovanelli, who made a triumphantly obsequious salute, she turned away.

Mrs. Walker sat looking after her, and there were tears in Mrs. Walker's eyes. "Get in here, sir," she said to Winterbourne, indicating the place beside her. The young man answered that he felt bound to accompany Miss Miller, whereupon Mrs. Walker declared that if he refused her this favor she would never speak to him again. She was evidently in earnest. Winterbourne overtook Daisy and her companion, and, offering the young girl his hand, told her that Mrs. Walker had made an imperious claim upon his society. He expected that in answer she would say something rather free, something to commit herself still further to that "recklessness" from which Mrs. Walker had so charitably endeavored to dissuade her. But she only shook his hand, hardly looking at him, while Mr. Giovanelli bade him farewell with a too emphatic flourish of the hat.

Winterbourne was not in the best possible humor as he took his seat in Mrs. Walker's victoria. "That was not clever of you," he said candidly, while the vehicle mingled again with the throng of carriages.

"In such a case," his companion answered, "I don't wish to be clever; I wish to be *earnest!*"

"Well, your earnestness has only offended her and put her off."

"It has happened very well," said Mrs. Walker. "If she is so perfectly determined to compromise herself, the sooner one knows it the better; one can act accordingly."

"I suspect she meant no harm," Winterbourne rejoined.

"So I thought a month ago. But she has been going too far."

"What has she been doing?"

"Everything that is not done here. Flirting with any man she could pick up; sitting in corners with mysterious Italians; dancing all the evening with the same partners; receiving visits at eleven o'clock at night. Her mother goes away when visitors come."

"But her brother," said Winterbourne, laughing, "sits up till midnight."

"He must be edified by what he sees. I'm told that at their hotel everyone is talking about her, and that a smile goes round among all the servants when a gentleman comes and asks for Miss Miller."

"The servants be hanged!" said Winterbourne angrily. "The poor girl's only fault," he presently added, "is that she is very uncultivated."

"She is naturally indelicate," Mrs. Walker declared. Take that example this morning. How long had you known her at Vevey?"

"A couple of days."

"Fancy, then, her making it a personal matter that you should have left the place!"

Winterbourne was silent for some moments; then he said, "I suspect, Mrs. Walker, that you and I have lived too long at Geneva!" And he added a request that she should inform him with what particular design she had made him enter her carriage.

"I wished to beg you to cease your relations with Miss Miller—not to flirt with her—to give her no further opportunity to expose herself—to let her alone, in short."

"I'm afraid I can't do that," said Winterbourne. "I like her extremely."

"All the more reason that you shouldn't help her to make a scandal."

"There shall be nothing scandalous in my attentions to her."

"There certainly will be in the way she takes them. But I have said what I had on my conscience," Mrs. Walker pursued. "If you wish to rejoin the young lady I will put you down. Here, by the way, you have a chance."

The carriage was traversing that part of the Pincian Garden that overhangs the wall of Rome and overlooks the beautiful Villa Borghese. It is bordered by a large parapet, near which there are several seats. One of the seats at a distance was occupied by a gentleman and a lady, toward whom Mrs. Walker gave a toss of her head. At the same moment these persons rose and walked toward the parapet. Winterbourne had asked the coachman to stop; he now descended from the carriage. His companion looked at him a moment in silence; then, while he raised his hat, she drove majestically away. Winterbourne stood there; he had turned his eyes toward Daisy and her cavalier. They evidently saw no one; they were too deeply occupied with each other. When they reached the low garden wall, they stood a moment looking off at the great flat-topped pine clusters of the Villa Borghese; then Giovanelli seated himself, familiarly, upon the broad ledge of the wall. The western sun in the opposite sky sent out a brilliant shaft through a couple of cloud bars, whereupon Daisy's companion took her parasol out of her hands and opened it. She came a little nearer, and he held the parasol over her; then, still holding it, he let it rest upon her shoulder, so that both of their heads were hidden from Winterbourne. This young man lingered a moment, then he began to walk. But he walked—not toward the couple with the parasol; toward the residence of his aunt, Mrs. Costello.

He flattered himself on the following day that there was no smiling among the servants when he, at least, asked for Mrs. Miller at her hotel. This lady and her daughter, however, were not at home; and on the next day after, repeating his visit, Winterbourne again had the misfortune not to find them. Mrs. Walker's party took place on the evening of the third day, and, in spite of the frigidity of his last interview with the hostess, Winterbourne was among the guests. Mrs. Walker was one of those American ladies who, while residing abroad, make a point, in their own phrase, of studying European society, and she had on this occasion collected several specimens of her diversely born fellow mortals to serve, as it were, as textbooks. When Winterbourne arrived, Daisy Miller was not there, but in a few moments he saw her mother come in alone, very shyly and ruefully. Mrs. Miller's hair above her exposed-looking temples was more frizzled than ever. As she approached Mrs. Walker, Winterbourne also drew near.

"You see, I've come all alone," said poor Mrs. Miller. "I'm so frightened; I don't know what to do. It's the first time I've ever been to a party alone, especially in this country. I wanted to bring Randolph or Eugenio, or someone, but Daisy just pushed me off by myself. I ain't used to going round alone."

"And does not your daughter intend to favor us with her society?" demanded Mrs. Walker impressively.

"Well, Daisy's all dressed," said Mrs. Miller with that accent of the dispassionate, if not of the philosophic, historian with which she always recorded the current incidents of her daughter's career. "She got dressed on purpose before dinner. But she's got a friend of hers there; that gentleman—the Italian—that she wanted to bring. They've got going at the piano; it seems as if they couldn't leave off. Mr. Giovanelli sings splendidly. But I guess they'll come before very long," concluded Mrs. Miller hopefully.

"I'm sorry she should come in that way," said Mrs. Walker.

"Well, I told her that there was no use in her getting dressed before dinner if she was going to wait three hours," responded Daisy's mamma. "I didn't see the use of her putting on such a dress as that to sit round with Mr. Giovanelli."

"This is most horrible!" said Mrs. Walker, turning away and addressing herself to Winterbourne. "*Elle s'affiche*. It's her revenge for my having ventured to remonstrate with her. When she comes, I shall not speak to her."

Daisy came after eleven o'clock; but she was not, on such an occasion, a young lady to wait to be spoken to. She rustled forward in radiant loveliness, smiling and chattering, carrying a large bouquet, and attended by Mr. Giovanelli. Everyone stopped talking and turned and looked at her. She came straight to Mrs. Walker. "I'm afraid you thought I never was coming, so I sent mother off to tell you. I wanted to make Mr. Giovanelli practice some things before he came; you know he sings beautifully, and I want you to ask him to sing. This is Mr. Giovanelli; you know I introduced him to you; he's got the most lovely voice, and he knows the most charming set of songs. I made him go over them this evening on purpose; we had the greatest time at the hotel." Of all this Daisy delivered herself with the sweetest, brightest audibleness, looking now at her hostess and now round the room, while she gave a series of little pats, round her shoulders, to the edges of her dress. "Is there anyone I know?" she asked.

"I think every one knows you!" said Mrs. Walker pregnantly, and she gave a very cursory greeting to Mr. Giovanelli. This gentleman bore himself gallantly. He smiled and bowed and showed his white teeth; he curled his mustaches and rolled his eyes and performed all the proper functions of a handsome Italian at an evening party. He sang very prettily half a dozen songs, though Mrs. Walker afterward declared that she had been quite unable to find out who asked him. It was apparently not Daisy who had given him his orders. Daisy sat at a distance from the piano, and though she had publicly, as it were, professed a high admiration for his singing, talked, not inaudibly, while it was going on.

"It's a pity these rooms are so small; we can't dance," she said to Winterbourne, as if she had seen him five minutes before.

"I am not sorry we can't dance," Winterbourne answered; "I don't dance."

"Of course you don't dance; you're too stiff," said Miss Daisy. "I hope you enjoyed your drive with Mrs. Walker!"

"No. I didn't enjoy it; I preferred walking with you."

"We paired off: that was much better," said Daisy. "But did you ever hear anything so cool as Mrs. Walker's wanting me to get into her carriage and drop poor Mr.

Giovanelli, and under the pretext that it was proper? People have different ideas! It would have been most unkind; he had been talking about that walk for ten days."

"He should not have talked about it at all," said Winterbourne; "he would never have proposed to a young lady of this country to walk about the streets with him."

"About the streets?" cried Daisy with her pretty stare. "Where, then, would he have proposed to her to walk? The Pincio is not the streets, either; and I, thank goodness, am not a young lady of this country. The young ladies of this country have a dreadfully poky time of it, so far as I can learn; I don't see why I should change my habits for *them*."

"I am afraid your habits are those of a flirt," said Winterbourne gravely.

"Of course they are," she cried, giving him her little smiling stare again. "I'm a fearful, frightful flirt! Did you ever hear of a nice girl that was not? But I suppose you will tell me now that I am not a nice girl."

"You're a very nice girl; but I wish you would flirt with me, and me only," said Winterbourne.

"Ah! thank you—thank you very much; you are the last man I should think of flirting with. As I have had the pleasure of informing you, you are too stiff."

"You say that too often," said Winterbourne.

Daisy gave a delighted laugh. "If I could have the sweet hope of making you angry, I should say it again."

"Don't do that; when I am angry I'm stiffer than ever. But if you won't flirt with me, do cease, at least, to flirt with your friend at the piano; they don't understand that sort of thing here."

"I thought they understood nothing else!" exclaimed Daisy.

"Not in young unmarried women."

"It seems to me much more proper in young unmarried women than in old married ones," Daisy declared.

"Well," said Winterbourne, "when you deal with natives you must go by the custom of the place. Flirting is a purely American custom; it doesn't exist here. So when you show yourself in public with Mr. Giovanelli, and without your mother—"

"Gracious! poor Mother!" interposed Daisy.

"Though you may be flirting, Mr. Giovanelli is not; he means something else."

"He isn't preaching, at any rate," said Daisy with vivacity. "And if you want very much to know, we are neither of us flirting; we are too good friends for that: we are very intimate friends."

"Ah!" rejoined Winterbourne, "if you are in love with each other, it is another affair."

She had allowed him up to this point to talk so frankly that he had no expectation of shocking her by this ejaculation; but she immediately got up, blushing visibly, and leaving him to exclaim mentally that little American flirts were the queerest creatures in the world. "Mr. Giovanelli, at least," she said, giving her interlocutor a single glance, "never says such very disagreeable things to me."

Winterbourne was bewildered; he stood, staring. Mr. Giovanelli had finished singing. He left the piano and came over to Daisy. "Won't you come into the other room and have some tea?" he asked, bending before her with his ornamental smile.

Daisy turned to Winterbourne, beginning to smile again. He was still more perplexed, for this inconsequent smile made nothing clear, though it seemed to prove, indeed, that she had a sweetness and softness that reverted instinctively to the pardon of offenses. "It has never occurred to Mr. Winterbourne to offer me any tea," she said with her little tormenting manner.

"I have offered you advice," Winterbourne rejoined.

"I prefer weak tea!" cried Daisy, and she went off with the brilliant Giovanelli. She sat with him in the adjoining room, in the embrasure of the window, for the rest of the evening. There was an interesting performance at the piano, but neither of these young people gave heed to it. When Daisy came to take leave of Mrs. Walker, this lady conscientiously repaired the weakness of which she had been guilty at the moment of the young girl's arrival. She turned her back straight upon Miss Miller and left her to depart with what grace she might. Winterbourne was standing near the door; he saw it all. Daisy turned very pale and looked at her mother, but Mrs. Miller was humbly unconscious of any violation of the usual social forms. She appeared, indeed, to have felt an incongruous impulse to draw attention to her own striking observance of them. "Good night, Mrs. Walker," she said; "we've had a beautiful evening. You see, if I let Daisy come to parties without me, I don't want her to go away without me." Daisy turned away, looking with a pale, grave face at the circle near the door; Winterbourne saw that, for the first moment, she was too much shocked and puzzled even for indignation. He on his side was greatly touched.

"That was very cruel," he said to Mrs. Walker.

"She never enters my drawing room again!" replied his hostess.

Since Winterbourne was not to meet her in Mrs. Walker's drawing room, he went as often as possible to Mrs. Miller's hotel. The ladies were rarely at home, but when he found them, the devoted Giovanelli was always present. Very often the brilliant little Roman was in the drawing room with Daisy alone, Mrs. Miller being apparently constantly of the opinion that discretion is the better part of surveillance. Winterbourne noted, at first with surprise, that Daisy on these occasions was never embarrassed or annoyed by his own entrance; but he very presently began to feel that she had no more surprises for him; the unexpected in her behavior was the only thing to expect. She showed no displeasure at her *tête-à-tête* with Giovanelli being interrupted; she could chatter as freshly and freely with two gentlemen as with one; there was always, in her conversation, the same odd mixture of audacity and puerility. Winterbourne remarked to himself that if she was seriously interested in Giovanelli, it was very singular that she should not take more trouble to preserve the sanctity of their interviews; and he liked her the more for her innocent-looking indifference and her apparently inexhaustible good humor. He could hardly have said why, but she seemed to him a girl who would never be jealous. At the risk of exciting a somewhat derisive smile on the reader's part, I may affirm that with regard to the women who had hitherto interested him, it very often seemed to Winterbourne among the possibilities that, given certain contingencies, he should be afraid—literally afraid—of these ladies; he had a pleasant sense that he should never be afraid of Daisy Miller. It must be added that this sentiment was not altogether flattering to Daisy; it was part of his conviction, or rather of his apprehension, that she would prove a very light young person.

But she was evidently very much interested in Giovanelli. She looked at him whenever he spoke; she was perpetually telling him to do this and to do that; she was constantly "chaffing" and abusing him. She appeared completely to have forgotten that Winterbourne had said anything to displease her at Mrs. Walker's little party. One Sunday afternoon, having gone to St. Peter's with his aunt, Winterbourne perceived Daisy strolling about the great church in company with the inevitable Giovanelli. Presently he pointed out the young girl and her cavalier to Mrs. Costello. This lady looked at them a moment through her eyeglass, and then she said:

"That's what makes you so pensive in these days, eh?"

"I had not the least idea I was pensive," said the young man.

"You are very much preoccupied; you are thinking of something."

"And what is it," he asked, "that you accuse me of thinking of?"

"Of that young lady's—Miss Baker's, Miss Chandler's—what's her name?—Miss Miller's intrigue with that little barber's block."

"Do you call it an intrigue," Winterbourne asked—"an affair that goes on with such peculiar publicity?"

"That's their folly," said Mrs. Costello; "it's not their merit."

"No," rejoined Winterbourne, with something of that pensiveness to which his aunt had alluded. "I don't believe that there is anything to be called an intrigue."

"I have heard a dozen people speak of it; they say she is quite carried away by him."

"They are certainly very intimate," said Winterbourne.

Mrs. Costello inspected the young couple again with her optical instrument. "He is very handsome. One easily sees how it is. She thinks him the most elegant man in the world, the finest gentleman. She has never seen anything like him; he is better, even, than the courier. It was the courier probably who introduced him; and if he succeeds in marrying the young lady, the courier will come in for a magnificent commission."

"I don't believe she thinks of marrying him," said Winterbourne, "and I don't believe he hopes to marry her."

"You may be very sure she thinks of nothing. She goes on from day to day, from hour to hour, as they did in the Golden Age. I can imagine nothing more vulgar. And at the same time," added Mrs. Costello, "depend upon it that she may tell you any moment that she is 'engaged.'"

"I think that is more than Giovanelli expects," said Winterbourne.

"Who is Giovanelli?"

"The little Italian. I have asked questions about him and learned something. He is apparently a perfectly respectable little man. I believe he is, in a small way, a *cavaliere avvocato*. But he doesn't move in what are called the first circles. I think it is really not absolutely impossible that the courier introduced him. He is evidently immensely charmed with Miss Miller. If she thinks him the finest gentleman in the world, he, on his side, has never found himself in personal contact with such splendor, such opulence, such expensiveness as this young lady's. And then she must seem to him wonderfully pretty and interesting. I rather doubt that he dreams of marrying her. That must appear to him too impossible a piece of luck. He has nothing but his handsome face to offer, and there is a substantial Mr. Miller in that mysterious land of dollars. Giovanelli knows that he hasn't a title to offer. If he were only a count or a *marchese!* He must wonder at his luck, at the way they have taken him up."

"He accounts for it by his handsome face and thinks Miss Miller a young lady *qui se passe ses fantaisies!*" said Mrs. Costello.

"It is very true," Winterbourne pursued, "that Daisy and her mamma have not yet risen to that stage of—what shall I call it?—of culture at which the idea of catching a count or a *marchese* begins. I believe that they are intellectually incapable of that conception."

"Ah! but the *cavaliere* can't believe it," said Mrs. Costello.

Of the observation excited by Daisy's "intrigue," Winterbourne gathered that day at St. Peter's sufficient evidence. A dozen of the American colonists in Rome came to talk with Mrs. Costello, who sat on a little portable stool at the base of one of the great pilasters. The vesper service was going forward in splendid chants and organ tones in the adjacent choir, and meanwhile, between Mrs. Costello and her friends, there was a great deal said about poor little Miss Miller's going really "too far." Winterbourne was not pleased with what he heard, but when, coming out upon the great steps of the church, he saw Daisy, who had emerged before him, get into an open cab with her accomplice and roll away through the cynical streets of Rome, he could not deny to himself that she was going very far indeed. He felt very sorry for her—not exactly that he believed that she had completely lost her head, but because it was painful to hear so much that was pretty, and undefended, and natural assigned to a vulgar place among the categories of disorder. He made an attempt after this to give a hint to Mrs. Miller. He met one day in the Corso a friend, a tourist like himself, who had just come out of the Doria Palace, where he had been walking through the beautiful gallery. His friend talked for a moment about the superb portrait of Innocent X by Velasquez which hangs in one of the cabinets of the palace, and then said, "And in the same cabinet, by the way, I had the pleasure of contemplating a picture of a different kind—that pretty American girl whom you pointed out to me last week." In answer to Winterbourne's inquiries, his friend narrated that the pretty American girl—prettier than ever—was seated with a companion in the secluded nook in which the great papal portrait was enshrined.

"Who was her companion?" asked Winterbourne.

"A little Italian with a bouquet in his buttonhole. The girl is delightfully pretty, but I thought I understood from you the other day that she was a young lady *du meilleur monde*."

"So she is!" answered Winterbourne; and having assured himself that his informant had seen Daisy and her companion but five minutes before, he jumped into a cab and went to call on Mrs. Miller. She was at home; but she apologized to him for receiving him in Daisy's absence.

"She's gone out somewhere with Mr. Giovanelli," said Mrs. Miller. "She's always going round with Mr. Giovanelli."

"I have noticed that they are very intimate," Winterbourne observed.

"Oh, it seems as if they couldn't live without each other!" said Mrs. Miller. "Well, he's a real gentleman, anyhow. I keep telling Daisy she's engaged!"

"And what does Daisy say?"

"Oh, she says she isn't engaged. But she might as well be!" this impartial parent resumed; "she goes on as if she was. But I've made Mr. Giovanelli promise to tell me, if *she* doesn't. I should want to write to Mr. Miller about it—shouldn't you?"

Winterbourne replied that he certainly should; and the state of mind of Daisy's mamma struck him as so unprecedented in the annals of parental vigilance that he gave up as utterly irrelevant the attempt to place her upon her guard.

After this Daisy was never at home, and Winterbourne ceased to meet her at the houses of their common acquaintances, because, as he perceived, these shrewd people had quite made up their minds that she was going too far. They ceased to invite her; and they intimated that they desired to express to observant Europeans the great truth that, though Miss Daisy Miller was a young American lady, her behavior was not representative—was regarded by her compatriots as abnormal. Winterbourne wondered how she felt about all the cold shoulders that were turned toward her, and sometimes it annoyed him to suspect that she did not feel at all. He said to himself that she was too light and childish, too uncultivated and unreasoning, too provincial, to have reflected upon her ostracism, or even to have perceived it. Then at other moments he believed that she carried about in her elegant and irresponsible little organism a defiant, passionate, perfectly observant consciousness of the impression she produced. He asked himself whether Daisy's defiance came from the consciousness of innocence, or from her being, essentially, a young person of the reckless class. It must be admitted that holding one's self to a belief in Daisy's "innocence" came to seem to Winterbourne more and more a matter of fine-spun gallantry. As I have already had occasion to relate, he was angry at finding himself reduced to chopping logic about this young lady; he was vexed at his want of instinctive certitude as to how far her eccentricities were generic, national, and how far they were personal. From either view of them he had somehow missed her, and now it was too late. She was "carried away" by Mr. Giovanelli.

A few days after his brief interview with her mother, he encountered her in that beautiful abode of flowering desolation known as the Palace of the Caesars. The early Roman spring had filled the air with bloom and perfume, and the rugged surface of the Palatine was muffled with tender verdure. Daisy was strolling along the top of one of those great mounds of ruin that are embanked with mossy marble and paved with monumental inscriptions. It seemed to him that Rome had never been so lovely as just then. He stood, looking off at the enchanting harmony of line and color that remotely encircles the city, inhaling the softly humid odors, and feeling the freshness of the year and the antiquity of the place reaffirm themselves in mysterious interfusion. It seemed to him also that Daisy had never looked so pretty, but this had been an observation of his whenever he met her. Giovanelli was at her side, and Giovanelli, too, wore an aspect of even unwonted brilliancy.

"Well," said Daisy, "I should think you would be lonesome!"

"Lonesome?" asked Winterbourne.

"You are always going round by yourself. Can't you get anyone to walk with you?"

"I am not so fortunate," said Winterbourne, "as your companion."

Giovanelli, from the first, had treated Winterbourne with distinguished politeness. He listened with a deferential air to his remarks; he laughed punctiliously at his pleasantries; he seemed disposed to testify to his belief that Winterbourne was a superior young man. He carried himself in no degree like a jealous wooer; he had obviously a great deal of tact; he had no objection to your expecting a little humility of him. It even seemed to Winterbourne at times that Giovanelli would find a certain mental relief in being able to have a private understanding with him—to say to him, as an intelligent man, that, bless you, *he* knew how extraordinary was this young lady, and didn't flatter himself with delusive—or at least *too* delusive—hopes of matrimony and dollars. On this occasion he strolled away from his companion to pluck a sprig of almond blossom, which he carefully arranged in his buttonhole.

"I know why you say that," said Daisy, watching Giovanelli. "Because you think I go round too much with *him*." And she nodded at her attendant.

"Every one thinks so—if you care to know," said Winterbourne.

"Of course I care to know!" Daisy exclaimed seriously. "But I don't believe it. They are only pretending to be shocked. They don't really care a straw what I do. Besides, I don't go round so much."

"I think you will find they do care. They will show it disagreeably."

Daisy looked at him a moment. "How disagreeably?"

"Haven't you noticed anything?" Winterbourne asked.

"I have noticed you. But I noticed you were as stiff as an umbrella the first time I saw you."

"You will find I am not so stiff as several others," said Winterbourne, smiling.

"How shall I find it?"

"By going to see the others."

"What will they do to me?"

"They will give you the cold shoulder. Do you know what that means?"

Daisy was looking at him intently; she began to color. "Do you mean as Mrs. Walker did the other night?"

"Exactly!" said Winterbourne.

She looked away at Giovanelli, who was decorating himself with his almond blossom. Then looking back at Winterbourne, "I shouldn't think you would let people be so unkind!" she said.

"How can I help it?" he asked.

"I should think you would say something."

"I do say something"; and he paused a moment. "I say that your mother tells me that she believes you are engaged."

"Well, she does," said Daisy very simply.

Winterbourne began to laugh. "And does Randolph believe it?" he asked.

"I guess Randolph doesn't believe anything," said Daisy. Randolph's skepticism excited Winterbourne to further hilarity, and he observed that Giovanelli was coming back to them. Daisy, observing it too, addressed herself again to her countryman. "Since you have mentioned it," she said, "I *am* engaged." . . . Winterbourne looked at her; he had stopped laughing. "You don't believe!" she added.

He was silent a moment; and then, "Yes, I believe it," he said.

"Oh, no, you don't!" she answered. "Well, then—I am not!"

The young girl and her cicerone were on their way to the gate of the enclosure, so that Winterbourne, who had but lately entered, presently took leave of them. A week afterward he went to dine at a beautiful villa on the Caelian Hill, and, on arriving, dismissed his hired vehicle. The evening was charming, and he promised himself the satisfaction of walking home beneath the Arch of Constantine and past the vaguely lighted monuments of the Forum. There was a waning moon in the sky, and her radiance was not brilliant, but she was veiled in a thin cloud curtain which seemed to diffuse and equalize it. When, on his return from the villa (it was eleven o'clock), Winterbourne approached the dusky circle of the Colosseum, it recurred to him, as a lover of the picturesque, that the interior, in the pale moonshine, would be well worth a glance. He turned aside and walked to one of the empty arches, near which, as he observed, an open carriage—one of the little Roman street-cabs—was stationed. Then he passed in, among the cavernous shadows of the great structure, and emerged upon the clear and silent arena. The place had never seemed to him more impressive. One-half of the gigantic circus was in deep shade, the other was sleeping in the luminous dusk. As he stood there he began to murmur Byron's famous lines, out of "Manfred," but before he had finished his quotation he remembered that if nocturnal meditations in the Colosseum are recommended by the poets, they are deprecated by the doctors. The historic atmosphere was there, certainly; but the historic atmosphere, scientifically considered, was no better than a villainous miasma. Winterbourne walked to the middle of the arena, to take a more general glance, intending thereafter to make a hasty retreat. The great cross in the center was covered with shadow; it was only as he drew near it that he made it out distinctly. Then he saw that two persons were stationed upon the low steps which formed its base. One of these was a woman, seated; her companion was standing in front of her.

Presently the sound of the woman's voice came to him distinctly in the warm night air. "Well, he looks at us as one of the old lions or tigers may have looked at the Christian martyrs!" These were the words he heard, in the familiar accent of Miss Daisy Miller.

"Let us hope he is not very hungry," responded the ingenious Giovanelli. "He will have to take me first; you will serve for dessert!"

Winterbourne stopped, with a sort of horror, and, it must be added, with a sort of relief. It was as if a sudden illumination had been flashed upon the ambiguity of Daisy's behavior, and the riddle had become easy to read. She was a young lady whom a gentleman need no longer be at pains to respect. He stood there, looking at her—looking at her companion and not reflecting that though he saw them vaguely, he himself must have been more brightly visible. He felt angry with himself that he had bothered so much about the right way of regarding Miss Daisy Miller. Then, as he was going to advance again, he checked himself, not from the fear that he was doing her injustice, but from a sense of the danger of appearing unbecomingly exhilarated by this sudden revulsion from cautious criticism. He turned away toward the entrance of the place, but, as he did so, he heard Daisy speak again.

"Why, it was Mr. Winterbourne! He saw me, and he cuts me!"

What a clever little reprobate she was, and how smartly she played at injured innocence! But he wouldn't cut her. Winterbourne came forward again and went toward the great cross. Daisy had got up; Giovanelli lifted his hat. Winterbourne had now begun to think simply of the craziness, from a sanitary point of view, of a delicate young girl lounging away the evening in this nest of malaria. What if she *were* a clever little reprobate? that was no reason for her dying of the *perniciosa*. "How long have you been here?" he asked almost brutally.

Daisy, lovely in the flattering moonlight, looked at him a moment. Then—"All the evening," she answered, gently. . . . "I never saw anything so pretty."

"I am afraid," said Winterbourne, "that you will not think Roman fever very pretty. This is the way people catch it. I wonder," he added, turning to Giovanelli, "that you, a native Roman, should countenance such a terrible indiscretion."

"Ah," said the handsome native, "for myself I am not afraid."

"Neither am I—for you! I am speaking for this young lady."

Giovanelli lifted his well-shaped eyebrows and showed his brilliant teeth. But he took Winterbourne's rebuke with docility. "I told the Signorina it was a grave indiscretion, but when was the Signorina ever prudent?"

"I never was sick, and I don't mean to be!" the Signorina declared. "I don't look like much, but I'm healthy! I was bound to see the Colosseum by moonlight; I shouldn't have wanted to go home without that; and we have had the most beautiful time, haven't we, Mr. Giovanelli? If there has been any danger, Eugenio can give me some pills. He has got some splendid pills."

"I should advise you," said Winterbourne, "to drive home as fast as possible and take one!"

"What you say is very wise," Giovanelli rejoined. "I will go and make sure the carriage is at hand." And he went forward rapidly.

Daisy followed with Winterbourne. He kept looking at her; she seemed not in the least embarrassed. Winterbourne said nothing; Daisy chattered about the beauty of the place. "Well, I *have* seen the Colosseum by moonlight!" she exclaimed. "That's one good thing." Then, noticing Winterbourne's silence, she asked him why he didn't speak. He made no answer; he only began to laugh. They passed under one of the dark archways;

Giovanelli was in front with the carriage. Here Daisy stopped a moment, looking at the young American. "*did* you believe I was engaged, the other day?" she asked.

"It doesn't matter what I believed the other day," said Winterbourne, still laughing.

"Well, what do you believe now?"

"I believe that it makes very little difference whether you are engaged or not!"

He felt the young girl's pretty eyes fixed upon him through the thick gloom of the archway; she was apparently going to answer. But Giovanelli hurried her forward. "Quick! quick!" he said; "if we get in by midnight we are quite safe."

Daisy took her seat in the carriage, and the fortunate Italian placed himself beside her. "Don't forget Eugenio's pills!" said Winterbourne as he lifted his hat.

"I don't care," said Daisy in a little strange tone, "whether I have Roman fever or not!" Upon this the cab driver cracked his whip, and they rolled away over the desultory patches of the antique pavement.

Winterbourne, to do him justice, as it were, mentioned to no one that he had encountered Miss Miller, at midnight, in the Colosseum with a gentleman; but nevertheless, a couple of days later, the fact of her having been there under these circumstances was known to every member of the little American circle, and commented accordingly. Winterbourne reflected that they had of course known it at the hotel, and that, after Daisy's return, there had been an exchange of remarks between the porter and the cab driver. But the young man was conscious, at the same moment, that it had ceased to be a matter of serious regret to him that the little American flirt should be "talked about" by low-minded menials. These people, a day or two later, had serious information to give: the little American flirt was alarmingly ill. Winterbourne, when the rumor came to him, immediately went to the hotel for more news. He found that two or three charitable friends had preceded him, and that they were being entertained in Mrs. Miller's salon by Randolph.

"It's going round at night," said Randolph—"that's what made her sick. She's always going round at night. I shouldn't think she'd want to, it's so plaguey dark. You can't see anything here at night, except when there's a moon. In America there's always a moon!" Mrs. Miller was invisible; she was now, at least, giving her daughter the advantage of her society. It was evident that Daisy was dangerously ill.

Winterbourne went often to ask for news of her, and once he saw Mrs. Miller, who, though deeply alarmed, was, rather to his surprise, perfectly composed, and, as it appeared, a most efficient and judicious nurse. She talked a good deal about Dr. Davis, but Winterbourne paid her the compliment of saying to himself that she was not, after all, such a monstrous goose. "Daisy spoke of you the other day," she said to him. "Half the time she doesn't know what she's saying, but that time I think she did. She gave me a message she told me to tell you. She told me to tell you that she never was engaged to that handsome Italian. I am sure I am very glad; Mr. Giovanelli hasn't been near us since she was taken ill. I thought he was so much of a gentleman; but I don't call that very polite! A lady told me that he was afraid I was angry with him for taking Daisy round at night. Well, so I am, but I suppose he knows I'm a lady. I would scorn to scold him. Anyway, she says she's not engaged. I don't know why she wanted you to know, but she said to me three times, 'Mind you tell Mr. Winterbourne.' And then she told me to ask if you remembered the time you went to that castle in Switzerland. But I said I wouldn't give any such messages as that. Only, if she is not engaged, I'm sure I'm glad to know it."

But, as Winterbourne had said, it mattered very little. A week after this, the poor girl died; it had been a terrible case of the fever. Daisy's grave was in the little Protestant cemetery, in an angle of the wall of imperial Rome, beneath the cypresses and the thick spring flowers. Winterbourne stood there beside it, with a number of other mourners, a number larger than the scandal excited by the young lady's career would have led you to expect. Near him stood Giovanelli, who came nearer still before Winterbourne turned away. Giovanelli was very pale: on this occasion he had no flower in his buttonhole; he seemed to wish to say something. At last he said, "She was the most beautiful young lady I ever saw, and the most amiable"; and then he added in a moment, "and she was the most innocent."

Winterbourne looked at him and presently repeated his words, "And the most innocent?"

"The most innocent!"

Winterbourne felt sore and angry. "Why the devil," he asked, "did you take her to that fatal place?"

Mr. Giovanelli's urbanity was apparently imperturbable. He looked on the ground a moment, and then he said, "For myself I had no fear; and she wanted to go."

"That was no reason!" Winterbourne declared.

The subtle Roman again dropped his eyes. "If she had lived, I should have got nothing. She would never have married me, I am sure."

"She would never have married you?"

"For a moment I hoped so. But no. I am sure."

Winterbourne listened to him: he stood staring at the raw protuberance among the April daisies. When he turned away again, Mr. Giovanelli, with his light, slow step, had retired.

Winterbourne almost immediately left Rome; but the following summer he again met his aunt, Mrs. Costello at Vevey. Mrs. Costello was fond of Vevey. In the interval Winterbourne had often thought of Daisy Miller and her mystifying manners. One day he spoke of her to his aunt—said it was on his conscience that he had done her injustice.

"I am sure I don't know," said Mrs. Costello. "How did your injustice affect her?"

"She sent me a message before her death which I didn't understand at the time; but I have understood it since. She would have appreciated one's esteem."

"Is that a modest way," asked Mrs. Costello, "of saying that she would have reciprocated one's affection?"

Winterbourne offered no answer to this question; but he presently said, "You were right in that remark that you made last summer. I was booked to make a mistake. I have lived too long in foreign parts."

Nevertheless, he went back to live at Geneva, whence there continue to come the most contradictory accounts of his motives of sojourn: a report that he is "studying" hard—an intimation that he is much interested in a very clever foreign lady.

FOUR MEETINGS

I saw her but four times, though I remember them vividly; she made her impression on me. I thought her very pretty and very interesting—a touching specimen of a type with which I had had other and perhaps less charming associations. I'm sorry to hear of her death, and yet when I think of it why *should* I be? The last time I saw her she was certainly not—! But it will be of interest to take our meetings in order.

I

The first was in the country, at a small tea-party, one snowy night of some seventeen years ago. My friend Latouche, going to spend Christmas with his mother, had insisted on my company, and the good lady had given in our honour the entertainment of which I speak. To me it was really full of savour—it had all the right marks: I had never been in the depths of New England at that season. It had been snowing all day and the drifts were knee-high. I wondered how the ladies had made their way to the house; but I inferred that just those general rigours rendered any assembly offering the attraction of two gentlemen from New York worth a desperate effort.

Mrs. Latouche in the course of the evening asked me if I "didn't want to" show the photographs to some of the young ladies. The photographs were in a couple of great portfolios, and had been brought home by her son, who, like myself, was lately returned from Europe. I looked round and was struck with the fact that most of the young ladies were provided with an object of interest more absorbing than the most vivid sun-picture. But there was a person alone near the mantel-shelf who looked round the room with a small vague smile, a discreet, a disguised yearning, which seemed somehow at odds with her isolation. I looked at her a moment and then chose. "I should like to show them to that young lady."

"Oh yes," said Mrs. Latouche, "she's just the person. She doesn't care for flirting—I'll speak to her." I replied that if she didn't care for flirting she wasn't perhaps just the person; but Mrs. Latouche had already, with a few steps, appealed to her participation. "She's delighted," my hostess came back to report; "and she's just the person—so quiet and so bright." And she told me the young lady was by name Miss Caroline Spencer—with which she introduced me.

Miss Caroline Spencer was not quite a beauty, but was none the less, in her small odd way, formed to please. Close upon thirty, by every presumption, she was made almost like a little girl and had the complexion of a child. She had also the prettiest head, on which her hair was arranged as nearly as possible like the hair of a Greek bust, though indeed it was to be doubted if she had ever seen a Greek bust. She was "artistic," I suspected, so far as the polar influences of North Verona could allow for such yearnings or could minister to them. Her eyes were perhaps just too round and too inveterately surprised, but her lips had a certain mild decision and her teeth, when she showed them, were charming. About her neck she wore what ladies call, I believe, a "ruche" fastened with a very small pin of pink coral, and in her hand she carried a fan made of plaited straw and adorned with pink ribbon. She wore a scanty black silk dress. She spoke with slow soft neatness, even without smiles showing the prettiness of her teeth, and she seemed extremely pleased, in fact quite fluttered, at the prospect of my demonstrations. These went forward very smoothly after I had moved the portfolios out of their corner and placed a couple of chairs near a lamp. The photographs were usually things I knew—large views of Switzerland, Italy and Spain, landscapes, reproductions of famous buildings, pictures and statues. I said what I could for them, and my companion, looking at them as I held them up, sat perfectly still, her straw fan raised to her under-lip and gently, yet, as I could feel, almost excitedly, rubbing it. Occasionally, as I laid one of the pictures down, she said without confidence, which would have been too much: "Have you seen that place?" I usually answered that I had seen it several times—I had been a great traveller, though I was somehow particularly admonished not to swagger—and then I felt her look at me askance for a moment with her pretty eyes. I had asked her at the outset whether she had been to Europe; to this she had answered "No, no, no"—almost as much below her breath as if the image of such an event scarce, for solemnity, brooked phrasing. But after that, though she never took her eyes off the pictures, she said so little that I feared she was at last bored. Accordingly when we had finished one portfolio I offered, if she desired it, to desist. I rather guessed the exhibition really held her, but her reticence puzzled me and I wanted to make her speak. I turned round to judge better and then saw a faint flush in each of her cheeks. She kept waving her little fan to and fro. Instead of looking at me she fixed her eyes on the remainder of the collection, which leaned, in its receptacle, against the table.

"Won't you show me that?" she quavered, drawing the long breath of a person launched and afloat but conscious of rocking a little.

"With pleasure," I answered, "if you're really not tired."

"Oh I'm not tired a bit. I'm just fascinated." With which as I took up the other portfolio she laid her hand on it, rubbing it softly. "And have you been here too?"

On my opening the portfolio it appeared I had indeed been there. One of the first photographs was a large view of the Castle of Chillon by the Lake of Geneva. "Here," I said, "I've been many a time. Isn't it beautiful?" And I pointed to the perfect reflexion of the rugged rocks and pointed towers in the clear still water. She didn't say "Oh enchanting!" and push it away to see the next picture. She looked a while and then asked if it weren't where Bonnivard, about whom Byron wrote, had been confined. I assented, trying to quote Byron's verses, but not quite bringing it off.

She fanned herself a moment and then repeated the lines correctly, in a soft flat voice but with charming conviction. By the time she had finished, she was nevertheless blushing. I complimented her and assured her she was perfectly equipped for visiting Switzerland and Italy. She looked at me askance again, to see if I might be serious, and I added that if she wished to recognise Byron's descriptions she must go abroad speedily—Europe was getting sadly dis-Byronised. "How soon must I go?" she thereupon enquired.

"Oh I'll give you ten years."

"Well, I guess I can go in *that* time," she answered as if measuring her words.

"Then you'll enjoy it immensely," I said; "you'll find it of the highest interest." Just then I came upon a photograph of some nook in a foreign city which I had been very fond of and which recalled tender memories. I discoursed (as I suppose) with considerable spirit; my companion sat listening breathless.

"Have you been *very* long over there?" she asked some time after I had ceased.

"Well, it mounts up, put all the times together."

"And have you travelled everywhere?"

"I've travelled a good deal. I'm very fond of it and happily have been able."

Again she turned on me her slow shy scrutiny. "Do you know the foreign languages?"

"After a fashion."

"Is it hard to speak them?"

"I don't imagine you'd find it so," I gallantly answered.

"Oh I shouldn't want to speak—I should only want to listen." Then on a pause she added: "They say the French theatre's so beautiful."

"Ah the best in the world."

"Did you go there very often?"

"When I was first in Paris I went every night."

"Every night!" And she opened her clear eyes very wide. "That to me is"—and her expression hovered—"as if you tell me a fairy-tale." A few minutes later she put to me: "And which country do you prefer?"

"There's one I love beyond any. I think you'd do the same."

Her gaze rested as on a dim revelation and then she breathed "Italy?"

"Italy," I answered softly too; and for a moment we communed over it. She looked as pretty as if instead of showing her photographs I had been making love to her. To increase the resemblance she turned off blushing. It made a pause which she broke at last by saying: "That's the place which—in particular—I thought of going to."

"Oh that's the place—that's the place!" I laughed.

She looked at two or three more views in silence. "They say it's not very dear."

"As some other countries? Well, one gets back there one's money. That's not the least of the charms."

"But it's *all* very expensive, isn't it?"

"Europe, you mean?"

"Going there and travelling. That has been the trouble. I've very little money. I teach, you know," said Miss Caroline Spencer.

"Oh of course one must have money," I allowed; "but one can manage with a moderate amount judiciously spent."

"I think I should manage. I've saved and saved up, and I'm always adding a little to it. It's all for that." She paused a moment, and then went on with suppressed eagerness, as if telling me the story were a rare, but possibly an impure satisfaction. "You see it hasn't been only the money—it has been everything. Everything has acted against it. I've waited and waited. It has been my castle in the air. I'm almost afraid to talk about it. Two or three times it has come a little nearer, and then I've talked about it and it has melted away. I've talked about it too much," she said hypocritically—for I saw such talk was now a small tremulous ecstasy. "There's a lady who's a great friend of mine—she doesn't want to go, but I'm always at her about it. I think I must tire her dreadfully. She told me just the other day she didn't know what would become of me. She guessed I'd go crazy if I didn't sail, and yet certainly I'd go crazy if I did."

"Well," I laughed, "you haven't sailed up to now—so I suppose you *are* crazy."

She took everything with the same seriousness. "Well, I guess I must be. It seems as if I couldn't think of anything else—and I don't require photographs to work me up! I'm always right *on* it. It kills any interest in things nearer home—things I ought to attend to. That's a kind of craziness."

"Well then the cure for it's just to go," I smiled—"I mean the cure for this kind. Of course you may have the other kind worse," I added—"the kind you get over there."

"Well, I've a faith that I'll go *some* time all right!" she quite elatedly cried. "I've a relative right there on the spot," she went on, "and I guess he'll know how to control me." I expressed the hope that he would, and I forget whether we turned over more photographs; but when I asked her if she had always lived just where I found her, "Oh no sir," she quite eagerly replied; "I've spent twenty-two months and a half in Boston." I met it with the inevitable joke that in this case foreign lands might prove a disappointment to her, but I quite failed to alarm her. "I know more about them than you might think"—her earnestness resisted even that. "I mean by reading—for I've really read considerable. In fact I guess I've prepared my mind about as much as you *can*—in advance. I've not only read Byron—I've read histories and guide-books and articles and lots of things. I know I shall rave about everything."

"'Everything' is saying much, but I understand your case," I returned. "You've the great American disease, and you've got it 'bad'—the appetite, morbid and monstrous, for colour and form, for the picturesque and the romantic at any price. I don't know whether we come into the world with it—with the germs implanted and antecedent to experience; rather perhaps we catch it early, almost before developed consciousness—we *feel*, as we look about, that we're going (to save our souls, or at least our senses) to be thrown back on it hard. We're like travellers in the desert—deprived of water and subject to the terrible mirage, the torment of illusion, of the thirst-fever. They hear the plash of fountains, they see green gardens and orchards that are hundreds of miles away. So we with *our* thirst—except that with us it's *more* wonderful: we have before us the beautiful old things we've never seen at all, and when we do at last see them—if we're lucky!—we simply recognise them. What experience does is merely to confirm and consecrate our confident dream."

She listened with her rounded eyes. "The way you express it's too lovely, and I'm sure it will be just like that. I've dreamt of everything—I'll know it all!"

"I'm afraid," I pretended for harmless comedy, "that you've wasted a great deal of time."

"Oh yes, that has been my great wickedness!" The people about us had begun to scatter; they were taking their leave. She got up and put out her hand to me, timidly, but as if quite shining and throbbing.

"I'm going back there—one *has* to," I said as I shook hands with her. "I shall look out for you."

Yes, she fairly glittered with her fever of excited faith. "Well, I'll tell you if I'm disappointed." And she left me, fluttering all expressively her little straw fan.

II

A few months after this I crossed the sea eastward again and some three years elapsed. I had been living in Paris and, toward the end of October, went from that city to the Havre, to meet a pair of relatives who had written me they were about to arrive there. On reaching the Havre I found the steamer already docked—I was two or three hours late. I repaired directly to the hotel, where my travellers were duly established. My sister had gone to bed, exhausted and disabled by her voyage; she was the unsteadiest of sailors and her sufferings on this occasion had been extreme. She desired for the moment undisturbed rest and was able to see me but five minutes—long enough for us to agree to stop over, restoratively, till the morrow. My brother-in-law, anxious about his wife, was unwilling to leave her room; but she insisted on my taking him a walk for aid to recovery of his spirits and his land-legs.

The early autumn day was warm and charming, and our stroll through the bright-coloured busy streets of the old French seaport beguiling enough. We walked along the sunny noisy quays and then turned into a wide pleasant street which lay half in sun and half in shade—a French provincial street that resembled an old water-colour drawing: tall grey steep-roofed red-gabled many-storied houses; green shutters on windows and old scroll-work above them; flower-pots in balconies and white-capped women in doorways. We walked in the shade; all this stretched away on the sunny side of the vista and made a picture. We looked at it as we passed along; then suddenly my companion stopped—pressing my arm and staring. I followed his gaze and saw that we had paused just before reaching a cafe where, under an awning, several tables and chairs were disposed upon the pavement. The windows were open behind; half a dozen plants in tubs were ranged beside the door; the pavement was besprinkled with clean bran. It was a dear little quiet old-world cafe; inside, in the comparative dusk, I saw a stout handsome woman, who had pink ribbons in her cap, perched up with a mirror behind her back and smiling at some one placed out of sight. This, to be exact, I noted afterwards; what I first observed was a lady seated alone, outside, at one of the little marble-topped tables. My brother-in-law had stopped to look at her. Something had been put before her, but she only leaned back, motionless and with her hands folded, looking down the street and away from us. I saw her but in diminished profile; nevertheless I was sure I knew on the spot that we must already have met.

"The little lady of the steamer!" my companion cried.

"Was she on your steamer?" I asked with interest.

"From morning till night. She was never sick. She used to sit perpetually at the side of the vessel with her hands crossed that way, looking at the eastward horizon."

"And are you going to speak to her?"

"I don't know her. I never made acquaintance with her. I wasn't in form to make up to ladies. But I used to watch her and—I don't know why—to be interested in her. She's a dear little Yankee woman. I've an idea she's a school-mistress taking a holiday—for which her scholars have made up a purse."

She had now turned her face a little more into profile, looking at the steep grey house-fronts opposite. On this I decided. "I shall speak to her myself."

"I wouldn't—she's very shy," said my brother-in-law.

"My dear fellow, I know her. I once showed her photographs at a tea-party." With which I went up to her, making her, as she turned to look at me, leave me in no doubt of her identity. Miss Caroline Spencer had achieved her dream. But she was less quick to recognise me and showed a slight bewilderment. I pushed a chair to the table and sat down. "Well," I said, "I hope you're not disappointed!"

She stared, blushing a little—then gave a small jump and placed me. "It was you who showed me the photographs—at North Verona."

"Yes, it was I. This happens very charmingly, for isn't it quite for me to give you a formal reception here—the official welcome? I talked to you so much about Europe."

"You didn't say too much. I'm so intensely happy!" she declared.

Very happy indeed she looked. There was no sign of her being older; she was as gravely, decently, demurely pretty as before. If she had struck me then as a thin-stemmed mild-hued flower of Puritanism it may be imagined whether in her present situation this clear bloom was less appealing. Beside her an old gentleman was drinking absinthe; behind her the *dame de comptoir* in the pink ribbons called "Alcibiade, Alcibiade!" to the long-aproned waiter. I explained to Miss Spencer that the gentleman with me had lately been her shipmate, and my brother-in-law came up and was introduced to her. But she looked at him as if she had never so much as seen him, and I remembered he had told me her eyes were always fixed on the eastward horizon. She had evidently not noticed him, and, still timidly smiling, made no attempt whatever to pretend the contrary. I staid with her on the little terrace of the cafe while he went back to the hotel and to his wife. I remarked to my friend that this meeting of ours at the first hour of her landing partook, among all chances, of the miraculous, but that I was delighted to be there and receive her first impressions.

"Oh I can't tell you," she said—"I feel so much in a dream. I've been sitting here an hour and I don't want to move. Everything's so delicious and romantic. I don't know whether the coffee has gone to my head—it's *so* unlike the coffee of my dead past."

"Really," I made answer, "if you're so pleased with this poor prosaic Havre you'll have no admiration left for better things. Don't spend your appreciation all the first day—remember it's your intellectual letter of credit. Remember all the beautiful places and things that are waiting for you. Remember that lovely Italy we talked about."

"I'm not afraid of running short," she said gaily, still looking at the opposite houses. "I could sit here all day—just saying to myself that here I am at last. It's so dark and strange—so old and different."

"By the way then," I asked, "how come you to be encamped in this odd place? Haven't you gone to one of the inns?" For I was half-amused, half-alarmed at the good conscience with which this delicately pretty woman had stationed herself in conspicuous isolation on the edge of the sidewalk.

"My cousin brought me here and—a little while ago—left me," she returned. "You know I told you I had a relation over here. He's still here—a real cousin. Well," she pursued with unclouded candour, "he met me at the steamer this morning."

It was absurd—and the case moreover none of my business; but I felt somehow disconcerted. "It was hardly worth his while to meet you if he was to desert you so soon."

"Oh he has only left me for half an hour," said Caroline Spencer. "He has gone to get my money."

I continued to wonder. "Where *is* your money?"

She appeared seldom to laugh, but she laughed for the joy of this. "It makes me feel very fine to tell you! It's in circular notes."

"And where are your circular notes?"

"In my cousin's pocket."

This statement was uttered with such clearness of candour that—I can hardly say why—it gave me a sensible chill. I couldn't at all at the moment have justified my lapse from ease, for I knew nothing of Miss Spencer's cousin. Since he stood in that relation to her—dear respectable little person—the presumption was in his favour. But I found myself wincing at the thought that half an hour after her landing her scanty funds should have passed into his hands. "Is he to travel with you?" I asked.

"Only as far as Paris. He's an art-student in Paris—I've always thought that so splendid. I wrote to him that I was coming, but I never expected him to come off to the ship. I supposed he'd only just meet me at the train in Paris. It's very kind of him. But he *is*," said Caroline Spencer, "very kind—and very bright."

I felt at once a strange eagerness to see this bright kind cousin who was an art-student. "He's gone to the banker's?" I enquired.

"Yes, to the banker's. He took me to an hotel—such a queer quaint cunning little place, with a court in the middle and a gallery all round, and a lovely landlady in such a beautifully fluted cap and such a perfectly fitting dress! After a while we came out to walk to the banker's, for I hadn't any French money. But I was very dizzy from the motion of the vessel and I thought I had better sit down. He found this place for me here—then he went off to the banker's himself. I'm to wait here till he comes back."

Her story was wholly lucid and my impression perfectly wanton, but it passed through my mind that the gentleman would never come back. I settled myself in a chair beside my friend and determined to await the event. She was lost in the vision and the imagination of everything near us and about us—she observed, she recognised and admired, with a touching intensity. She noticed everything that was brought before us by the movement of the street—the peculiarities of costume, the shapes of vehicles, the big Norman horses, the fat priests, the shaven poodles. We talked of these things, and there was something charming in her freshness of perception and the way her book-nourished fancy sallied forth for the revel.

"And when your cousin comes back what are you going to do?" I went on.

For this she had, a little oddly, to think. "We don't quite know."

"When do you go to Paris? If you go by the four o'clock train I may have the pleasure of making the journey with you."

"I don't think we shall do that." So far she was prepared. "My cousin thinks I had better stay here a few days."

"Oh!" said I—and for five minutes had nothing to add. I was wondering what our absentee was, in vulgar parlance, "up to." I looked up and down the street, but saw nothing that looked like a bright and kind American art-student. At last I took the liberty of observing that the Havre was hardly a place to choose as one of the aesthetic stations of a European tour. It was a place of convenience, nothing more; a place of transit, through which transit should be rapid. I recommended her to go to Paris by the afternoon train and meanwhile to amuse herself by driving to the ancient fortress at the mouth of the harbour—that remarkable circular structure which bore the name of Francis the First and figured a sort of small Castle of Saint Angelo. (I might really have foreknown that it was to be demolished.)

She listened with much interest—then for a moment looked grave. "My cousin told me that when he returned he should have something particular to say to me, and that we could do nothing or decide nothing till I should have heard it. But I'll make him tell me right off, and then we'll go to the ancient fortress. Francis the First, did you say? Why, that's lovely. There's no hurry to get to Paris; there's plenty of time."

She smiled with her softly severe little lips as she spoke those last words, yet, looking at her with a purpose, I made out in her eyes, I thought, a tiny gleam of apprehension. "Don't tell me," I said, "that this wretched man's going to give you bad news!"

She coloured as if convicted of a hidden perversity, but she was soaring too high to drop. "Well, I guess it's a *little* bad, but I don't believe it's *very* bad. At any rate I must listen to it."

I usurped an unscrupulous authority. "Look here; you didn't come to Europe to listen—you came to *see*!" But now I was sure her cousin would come back; since he had something disagreeable to say to her he'd infallibly turn up. We sat a while longer and I asked her about her plans of travel. She had them on her fingers' ends and told over the names as solemnly as a daughter of another faith might have told over the beads of a rosary: from Paris to Dijon and to Avignon, from Avignon to Marseilles and the Cornice road; thence to Genoa, to Spezia, to Pisa, to Florence, to Rome. It apparently had never occurred to her that there could be the least incommodity in her travelling alone; and since she was unprovided with a companion I of course civilly abstained from disturbing her sense of security.

At last her cousin came back. I saw him turn toward us out of a side-street, and from the moment my eyes rested on him I knew he could but be the bright, if not the kind, American art-student. He wore a slouch hat and a rusty black velvet jacket, such as I had often encountered in the Rue Bonaparte. His shirt-collar displayed a stretch of throat that at a distance wasn't strikingly statuesque. He was tall and lean, he had red hair and freckles. These items I had time to take in while he approached the cafe, staring at me with natural surprise from under his romantic brim. When he came up to us I immediately introduced myself as an old acquaintance of Miss Spencer's, a character she serenely permitted me to claim. He looked at me hard with a pair of small sharp eyes, then he gave me a solemn wave, in the "European" fashion, of his rather rusty sombrero.

"You weren't on the ship?" he asked.

"No, I wasn't on the ship. I've been in Europe these several years."

He bowed once more, portentously, and motioned me to be seated again. I sat down, but only for the purpose of observing him an instant—I saw it was time I should return to my sister. Miss Spencer's European protector was, by my measure, a very queer quantity. Nature hadn't shaped him for a Raphaelesque or Byronic attire, and his velvet doublet and exhibited though not columnar throat weren't in harmony with his facial attributes. His hair was cropped close to his head; his ears were large and ill-adjusted to the same. He had a lackadaisical carriage and a sentimental droop which were peculiarly at variance with his keen conscious strange-coloured eyes—of a brown that was almost red. Perhaps I was prejudiced, but I thought his eyes too shifty. He said nothing for some time; he leaned his hands on his stick and looked up and down the street. Then at last, slowly lifting the stick and pointing with it, "That's a very nice bit," he dropped with a certain flatness. He had his head to one side—he narrowed his ugly lids. I followed the direction of his stick; the object it indicated was a red cloth hung out of an old window. "Nice bit of colour," he continued; and without moving his head transferred his half-closed gaze to me. "Composes well. Fine old tone. Make a nice thing." He spoke in a charmless vulgar voice.

"I see you've a great deal of eye," I replied. "Your cousin tells me you're studying art." He looked at me in the same way, without answering, and I went on with deliberate urbanity: "I suppose you're at the studio of one of those great men." Still on this he continued to fix me, and then he named one of the greatest of that day; which led me to ask him if he liked his master.

"Do you understand French?" he returned.

"Some kinds."

He kept his little eyes on me; with which he remarked: "Je suis fou de la peinture!"

"Oh I understand that kind!" I replied. Our companion laid her hand on his arm with a small pleased and fluttered movement; it was delightful to be among people who were on such easy terms with foreign tongues. I got up to take leave and asked her where, in Paris, I might have the honour of waiting on her. To what hotel would she go?

She turned to her cousin enquiringly and he favoured me again with his little languid leer. "Do you know the Hotel des Princes?"

"I know where it is."

"Well, that's the shop."

"I congratulate you," I said to Miss Spencer. "I believe it's the best inn in the world; but, in case I should still have a moment to call on you here, where are you lodged?"

"Oh it's such a pretty name," she returned gleefully. "A la Belle Normande."

"I guess I know my way round!" her kinsman threw in; and as I left them he gave me with his swaggering head-cover a great flourish that was like the wave of a banner over a conquered field.

III

My relative, as it proved, was not sufficiently restored to leave the place by the afternoon train; so that as the autumn dusk began to fall I found myself at liberty to call at the establishment named to me by my friends. I must confess that I had spent much of the interval in wondering what the disagreeable thing was that the less attractive of these had been telling the other. The *auberge* of the Belle Normande proved an hostelry in a shady by-street, where it gave me satisfaction to think Miss Spencer must have encountered local colour in abundance. There was a crooked little court, where much of the hospitality of the house was carried on; there was a staircase climbing to bedrooms on the outer side of the wall; there was a small trickling fountain with a stucco statuette set in the midst of it; there was a little boy in a white cap and apron cleaning copper vessels at a conspicuous kitchen door; there was a chattering landlady, neatly laced, arranging apricots and grapes into an artistic pyramid upon a pink plate. I looked about, and on a green bench outside of an open door labelled Salle-à-Manger, I distinguished Caroline Spencer. No sooner had I looked at her than I was sure something had happened since the morning. Supported by the back of her bench, with her hands clasped in her lap, she kept her eyes on the other side of the court where the landlady manipulated the apricots.

But I saw that, poor dear, she wasn't thinking of apricots or even of landladies. She was staring absently, thoughtfully; on a nearer view I could have certified she had been crying. I had seated myself beside her before she was aware; then, when she had done so, she simply turned round without surprise and showed me her sad face. Something very bad indeed had happened; she was completely changed, and I immediately charged her with it. "Your cousin has been giving you bad news. You've had a horrid time."

For a moment she said nothing, and I supposed her afraid to speak lest her tears should again rise. Then it came to me that even in the few hours since my leaving her she had shed them all—which made her now intensely, stoically composed. "My poor cousin has been having one," she replied at last. "He has had great worries. His news was bad." Then after a dismally conscious wait: "He was in dreadful want of money."

"In want of yours, you mean?"

"Of any he could get—honourably of course. Mine IS all—well, that's available."

Ah it was as if I had been sure from the first! "And he has taken it from you?"

Again she hung fire, but her face meanwhile was pleading. "I gave him what I had."

I recall the accent of those words as the most angelic human sound I had ever listened to—which is exactly why I jumped up almost with a sense of personal outrage. "Gracious goodness, madam, do you call that his getting it 'honourably'?"

I had gone too far—she coloured to her eyes. "We won't speak of it."

"We *must* speak of it," I declared as I dropped beside her again. "I'm your friend—upon my word I'm your protector; it seems to me you need one. What's the matter with this extraordinary person?"

She was perfectly able to say. "He's just badly in debt."

"No doubt he is! But what's the special propriety of your—in such tearing haste!—paying for that?"

"Well, he has told me all his story. I *feel* for him so much."

"So do I, if you come to that! But I hope," I roundly added, "he'll give you straight back your money."

As to this she was prompt. "Certainly he will—as soon as ever he can."

"And when the deuce will that be?"

Her lucidity maintained itself. "When he has finished his great picture."

It took me full in the face. "My dear young lady, damn his great picture! Where is this voracious man?"

It was as if she must let me feel a moment that I did push her!—though indeed, as appeared, he was just where he'd naturally be. "He's having his dinner."

I turned about and looked through the open door into the salle-à-manger. There, sure enough, alone at the end of a long table, was the object of my friend's compassion—the bright, the kind young art-student. He was dining too attentively to notice me at first, but in the act of setting down a well-emptied wine-glass he caught sight of my air of observation. He paused in his repast and, with his head on one side and his meagre jaws slowly moving, fixedly returned my gaze. Then the landlady came brushing lightly by with her pyramid of apricots.

"And that nice little plate of fruit is for him?" I wailed.

Miss Spencer glanced at it tenderly. "They seem to arrange everything so nicely!" she simply sighed.

I felt helpless and irritated. "Come now, really," I said; "do you think it right, do you think it decent, that that long strong fellow should collar your funds?" She looked away from me—I was evidently giving her pain. The case was hopeless; the long strong fellow had "interested" her.

"Pardon me if I speak of him so unceremoniously," I said. "But you're really too generous, and he hasn't, clearly, the rudiments of delicacy. He made his debts himself—he ought to pay them himself."

"He has been foolish," she obstinately said—"of course I know that. He has told me everything. We had a long talk this morning—the poor fellow threw himself on my charity. He has signed notes to a large amount."

"The more fool he!"

"He's in real distress—and it's not only himself. It's his poor young wife."

"Ah he has a poor young wife?"

"I didn't know—but he made a clean breast of it. He married two years since—secretly."

"Why secretly?"

My informant took precautions as if she feared listeners. Then with low impressiveness: "She was a Countess!"

"Are you very sure of that?"

"She has written me the most beautiful letter."

"Asking you—whom she has never seen—for money?"

"Asking me for confidence and sympathy"—Miss Spencer spoke now with spirit. "She has been cruelly treated by her family—in consequence of what she has done for him. My cousin has told me every particular, and she appeals to me in her own lovely way in the letter, which I've here in my pocket. It's such a wonderful old-world romance," said my prodigious friend. "She was a beautiful young widow—her first husband was a Count, tremendously high-born, but really most wicked, with whom she hadn't been happy and whose death had left her ruined after he had deceived her in all sorts of ways.

My poor cousin, meeting her in that situation and perhaps a little too recklessly pitying her and charmed with her, found her, don't you see?"—Caroline's appeal on this head was amazing!—"but too ready to trust a better man after all she had been through. Only when her 'people,' as he says—and I do like the word!—understood she *would* have him, poor gifted young American art-student though he simply was, because she just adored him, her great-aunt, the old Marquise, from whom she had expectations of wealth which she could yet sacrifice for her love, utterly cast her off and wouldn't so much as speak to her, much less to *him*, in their dreadful haughtiness and pride. They *can* be haughty over here, it seems," she ineffably developed—"there's no mistake about that! It's like something in some famous old book. The family, my cousin's wife's," she by this time almost complacently wound up, "are of the oldest Provencal noblesse."

I listened half-bewildered. The poor woman positively found it so interesting to be swindled by a flower of that stock—if stock or flower or solitary grain of truth was really concerned in the matter—as practically to have lost the sense of what the forfeiture of her hoard meant for her. "My dear young lady," I groaned, "you don't want to be stripped of every dollar for such a rigmarole!"

She asserted, at this, her dignity—much as a small pink shorn lamb might have done. "It isn't a rigmarole, and I shan't be stripped. I shan't live any worse than I *have* lived, don't you see? And I'll come back before long to stay with them. The Countess—he still gives her, he says, her title, as they do to noble widows, that is to 'dowagers,' don't you know? in England—insists on a visit from me *some* time. So I guess for *that* I can start afresh—and meanwhile I'll have recovered my money."

It was all too heart-breaking. "You're going home then at once?"

I felt the faint tremor of voice she heroically tried to stifle. "I've nothing left for a tour."

"You gave it *all* up?"

"I've kept enough to take me back."

I uttered, I think, a positive howl, and at this juncture the hero of the situation, the happy proprietor of my little friend's sacred savings and of the infatuated *grande dame* just sketched for me, reappeared with the clear consciousness of a repast bravely earned and consistently enjoyed. He stood on the threshold an instant, extracting the stone from a plump apricot he had fondly retained; then he put the apricot into his mouth and, while he let it gratefully dissolve there, stood looking at us with his long legs apart and his hands thrust into the pockets of his velvet coat. My companion got up, giving him a thin glance that I caught in its passage and which expressed at once resignation and fascination—the last dregs of her sacrifice and with it an anguish of upliftedness. Ugly vulgar pretentious dishonest as I thought him, and destitute of every grace of plausibility, he had yet appealed successfully to her eager and tender imagination. I was deeply disgusted, but I had no warrant to interfere, and at any rate felt that it would be vain. He waved his hand meanwhile with a breadth of appreciation. "Nice old court. Nice mellow old place. Nice crooked old staircase. Several pretty things."

Decidedly I couldn't stand it, and without responding I gave my hand to my friend. She looked at me an instant with her little white face and rounded eyes, and as she showed her pretty teeth I suppose she meant to smile. "Don't be sorry for me," she sublimely pleaded; "I'm very sure I shall see something of this dear old Europe yet."

I refused however to take literal leave of her—I should find a moment to come back next morning. Her awful kinsman, who had put on his sombrero again, flourished it off at me by way of a bow—on which I hurried away.

On the morrow early I did return, and in the court of the inn met the landlady, more loosely laced than in the evening. On my asking for Miss Spencer, "*Partie*, monsieur," the good woman said. "She went away last night at ten o'clock, with her—her—not her husband, eh?—in fine her Monsieur. They went down to the American ship." I turned off—I felt the tears in my eyes. The poor girl had been some thirteen hours in Europe.

IV

I myself, more fortunate, continued to sacrifice to opportunity as I myself met it. During this period—of some five years—I lost my friend Latouche, who died of a malarious fever during a tour in the Levant. One of the first things I did on my return to America was to go up to North Verona on a consolatory visit to his poor mother. I found her in deep affliction and sat with her the whole of the morning that followed my arrival—I had come in late at night—listening to her tearful descant and singing the praises of my friend. We talked of nothing else, and our conversation ended only with the arrival of a quick little woman who drove herself up to the door in a "carry-all" and whom I saw toss the reins to the horse's back with the briskness of a startled sleeper throwing off the bedclothes. She jumped out of the carry-all and she jumped into the room. She proved to be the minister's wife and the great town-gossip, and she had evidently, in the latter capacity, a choice morsel to communicate. I was as sure of this as I was that poor Mrs. Latouche was not absolutely too bereaved to listen to her. It seemed to me discreet to retire, and I described myself as anxious for a walk before dinner.

"And by the way," I added, "if you'll tell me where my old friend Miss Spencer lives I think I'll call on her."

The minister's wife immediately responded. Miss Spencer lived in the fourth house beyond the Baptist church; the Baptist church was the one on the right, with that queer green thing over the door; they called it a portico, but it looked more like an old-fashioned bedstead swung in the air. "Yes, do look up poor Caroline," Mrs. Latouche further enjoined. "It will refresh her to see a strange face."

"I should think she had had enough of strange faces!" cried the minister's wife.

"To see, I mean, a charming visitor"—Mrs. Latouche amended her phrase.

"I should think she had had enough of charming visitors!" her companion returned. "But *you* don't mean to stay ten years," she added with significant eyes on me.

"Has she a visitor of that sort?" I asked in my ignorance.

"You'll make out the sort!" said the minister's wife. "She's easily seen; she generally sits in the front yard. Only take care what you say to her, and be very sure you're polite."

"Ah she's so sensitive?"

The minister's wife jumped up and dropped me a curtsey—a most sarcastic curtsey. "That's what she is, if you please. 'Madame la Comtesse!'"

And pronouncing these titular words with the most scathing accent, the little woman seemed fairly to laugh in the face of the lady they designated. I stood staring, wondering, remembering.

"Oh I shall be very polite!" I cried; and, grasping my hat and stick, I went on my way.

I found Miss Spencer's residence without difficulty. The Baptist church was easily identified, and the small dwelling near it, of a rusty white, with a large central chimney-stack and a Virginia creeper, seemed naturally and properly the abode of a withdrawn old maid with a taste for striking effects inexpensively obtained. As I approached I slackened my pace, for I had heard that some one was always sitting in the front yard, and I wished to reconnoitre. I looked cautiously over the low white fence that separated the small garden-space from the unpaved street, but I descried nothing in the shape of a Comtesse. A small straight path led up to the crooked door-step, on either side of which was a little grass-plot fringed with currant-bushes. In the middle of the grass, right and left, was a large quince-tree, full of antiquity and contortions, and beneath one of the quince-trees were placed a small table and a couple of light chairs. On the table lay a piece of unfinished embroidery and two or three books in bright-coloured paper covers. I went in at the gate and paused halfway along the path, scanning the place for some further token of its occupant, before whom—I could hardly have said why—I hesitated abruptly to present myself. Then I saw the poor little house to be of the shabbiest and felt a sudden doubt of my right to penetrate, since curiosity had been my motive and curiosity here failed of confidence. While I demurred a figure appeared in the open doorway and stood there looking at me. I immediately recognised Miss Spencer, but she faced me as if we had never met. Gently, but gravely and timidly, I advanced to the door-step, where I spoke with an attempt at friendly banter.

"I waited for you over there to come back, but you never came."

"Waited where, sir?" she quavered, her innocent eyes rounding themselves as of old. She was much older; she looked tired and wasted.

"Well," I said, "I waited at the old French port."

She stared harder, then recognised me, smiling, flushing, clasping her two hands together. "I remember you now—I remember that day." But she stood there, neither coming out nor asking me to come in. She was embarrassed.

I too felt a little awkward while I poked at the path with my stick. "I kept looking out for you year after year."

"You mean in Europe?" she ruefully breathed.

"In Europe of course! Here apparently you're easy enough to find."

She leaned her hand against the unpainted door-post and her head fell a little to one side. She looked at me thus without speaking, and I caught the expression visible in women's eyes when tears are rising. Suddenly she stepped out on the cracked slab of stone before her threshold and closed the door. Then her strained smile prevailed and I saw her teeth were as pretty as ever. But there had been tears too. "Have you been there ever since?" she lowered her voice to ask.

"Until three weeks ago. And you—you never came back?"

Still shining at me as she could, she put her hand behind her and reopened the door. "I'm not very polite," she said. "Won't you come in?"

"I'm afraid I incommode you."

"Oh no!"—she wouldn't hear of it now. And she pushed back the door with a sign that I should enter.

I followed her in. She led the way to a small room on the left of the narrow hall, which I supposed to be her parlour, though it was at the back of the house, and we passed the closed door of another apartment which apparently enjoyed a view of the quince-trees. This one looked out upon a small wood-shed and two clucking hens. But I thought it pretty until I saw its elegance to be of the most frugal kind; after which, presently, I thought it prettier still, for I had never seen faded chintz and old mezzotint engravings, framed in varnished autumn leaves, disposed with so touching a grace. Miss Spencer sat down on a very small section of the sofa, her hands tightly clasped in her lap. She looked ten years older, and I needn't now have felt called to insist on the facts of her person. But

I still thought them interesting, and at any rate I was moved by them. She was peculiarly agitated. I tried to appear not to notice it; but suddenly, in the most inconsequent fashion—it was an irresistible echo of our concentrated passage in the old French port—I said to her: "I do incommode you. Again you're in distress."

She raised her two hands to her face and for a moment kept it buried in them. Then taking them away, "It's because you remind me," she said.

"I remind you, you mean, of that miserable day at the Havre?"

She wonderfully shook her head. "It wasn't miserable. It was delightful."

Ah was it? my manner of receiving this must have commented. "I never was so shocked as when, on going back to your inn the next morning, I found you had wretchedly retreated."

She waited an instant, after which she said: "Please let us not speak of that."

"Did you come straight back here?" I nevertheless went on.

"I was back here just thirty days after my first start."

"And here you've remained ever since?"

"Every minute of the time."

I took it in; I didn't know what to say, and what I presently said had almost the sound of mockery. "When then are you going to make that tour?" It might be practically aggressive; but there was something that irritated me in her depths of resignation, and I wished to extort from her some expression of impatience.

She attached her eyes a moment to a small sunspot on the carpet; then she got up and lowered the window-blind a little to obliterate it. I waited, watching her with interest—as if she had still something more to give me. Well, presently, in answer to my last question, she gave it. "Never!"

"I hope at least your cousin repaid you that money," I said.

At this again she looked away from me. "I don't care for it now."

"You don't care for your money?"

"For ever going to Europe."

"Do you mean you wouldn't go if you could?"

"I can't—I can't," said Caroline Spencer. "It's all over. Everything's different. I never think of it."

"The scoundrel never repaid you then!" I cried.

"Please, please—!" she began.

But she had stopped—she was looking toward the door. There had been a rustle and a sound of steps in the hall.

I also looked toward the door, which was open and now admitted another person—a lady who paused just within the threshold. Behind her came a young man. The lady looked at me with a good deal of fixedness—long enough for me to rise to a vivid impression of herself. Then she turned to Caroline Spencer and, with a smile and a strong foreign accent, "*Pardon, ma chère*! I didn't know you had company," she said. "The gentleman came in so quietly." With which she again gave me the benefit of her attention. She was very strange, yet I was at once sure I had seen her before. Afterwards I rather put it that I had only seen ladies remarkably like her. But I had seen them very far away from North Verona, and it was the oddest of all things to meet one of them in that frame. To what quite other scene did the sight of her transport me? To some dusky landing before a shabby Parisian *quatrième*—to an open door revealing a greasy ante-chamber and to Madame leaning over the banisters while she holds a faded wrapper together and bawls down to the portress to bring up her coffee. My friend's guest was a very large lady, of middle age, with a plump dead-white face and hair drawn back *à la chinoise*. She had a small penetrating eye and what is called in French *le sourire agréable*. She wore an old pink cashmere dressing-gown covered with white embroideries, and, like the figure in my momentary vision, she confined it in front with a bare and rounded arm and a plump and deeply-dimpled hand.

"It's only to spick about my cafe," she said to her hostess with her *sourire agréable*. "I should like it served in the garden under the leetle tree."

The young man behind her had now stepped into the room, where he also stood revealed, though with rather less of a challenge. He was a gentleman of few inches but a vague importance, perhaps the leading man of the world of North Verona. He had a small pointed nose and a small pointed chin; also, as I observed, the most diminutive feet and a manner of no point at all. He looked at me foolishly and with his mouth open.

"You shall have your coffee," said Miss Spencer as if an army of cooks had been engaged in the preparation of it.

"C'est bien!" said her massive inmate. "Find your bouk"—and this personage turned to the gaping youth.

He gaped now at each quarter of the room. "My grammar, d' ye mean?"

The large lady however could but face her friend's visitor while persistently engaged with a certain laxity in the flow of her wrapper. "Find your bouk," she more absently repeated.

"My poetry, d' ye mean?" said the young man who also couldn't take his eyes off me.

"Never mind your bouk"—his companion reconsidered. "To-day we'll just talk. We'll make some conversation. But we mustn't interrupt Mademoiselle's. Come, come"—and she moved off a step. "Under the leetle tree," she added for the benefit of Mademoiselle. After which she gave me a thin salutation, jerked a measured "Monsieur!" and swept away again with her swain following.

I looked at Miss Spencer, whose eyes never moved from the carpet, and I spoke, I fear, without grace. "Who in the world's that?"

"The Comtesse—that *was*: my *cousine* as they call it in French."

"And who's the young man?"

"The Countess's pupil, Mr. Mixter." This description of the tie uniting the two persons who had just quitted us must certainly have upset my gravity; for I recall the marked increase of my friend's own as she continued to explain. "She gives lessons in French and music, the simpler sorts—"

"The simpler sorts of French?" I fear I broke in.

But she was still impenetrable, and in fact had now an intonation that put me vulgarly in the wrong. "She has had the worst reverses—with no one to look to. She's prepared for any exertion—and she takes her misfortunes with gaiety."

"Ah well," I returned—no doubt a little ruefully, "that's all I myself am pretending to do. If she's determined to be a burden to nobody, nothing could be more right and proper."

My hostess looked vaguely, though I thought quite wearily enough, about: she met this proposition in no other way. "I must go and get the coffee," she simply said.

"Has the lady many pupils?" I none the less persisted.

"She has only Mr. Mixter. She gives him all her time." It might have set me off again, but something in my whole impression of my friend's sensibility urged me to keep strictly decent. "He pays very well," she at all events inscrutably went on. "He's not very bright—as a pupil; but he's very rich and he's very kind. He has a buggy—with a back, and he takes the Countess to drive."

"For good long spells I hope," I couldn't help interjecting—even at the cost of her so taking it that she had still to avoid my eyes. "Well, the country's beautiful for miles," I went on. And then as she was turning away: "You're going for the Countess's coffee?"

"If you'll excuse me a few moments."

"Is there no one else to do it?"

She seemed to wonder who there should be. "I keep no servants."

"Then can't I help?" After which, as she but looked at me, I bettered it. "Can't she wait on herself?"

Miss Spencer had a slow headshake—as if that too had been a strange idea. "She isn't used to *manual* labour."

The discrimination was a treat, but I cultivated decorum. "I see—and you *are*." But at the same time I couldn't abjure curiosity. "Before you go, at any rate, please tell me this: who *is* this wonderful lady?"

"I told you just who in France—that extraordinary day. She's the wife of my cousin, whom you saw there."

"The lady disowned by her family in consequence of her marriage?"

"Yes; they've never seen her again. They've completely broken with her."

"And where's her husband?"

"My poor cousin's dead."

I pulled up, but only a moment. "And where's your money?"

The poor thing flinched—I kept her on the rack. "I don't know," she woefully said.

I scarce know what it didn't prompt me to—but I went step by step. "On her husband's death this lady at once came to you?"

It was as if she had had too often to describe it. "Yes, she arrived one day."

"How long ago?"

"Two years and four months."

"And has been here ever since?"

"Ever since."

I took it all in. "And how does she like it?"

"Well, not *very* much," said Miss Spencer divinely.

That too I took in. "And how do *you*—?"

She laid her face in her two hands an instant as she had done ten minutes before. Then, quickly, she went to get the Countess's coffee.

Left alone in the little parlour I found myself divided between the perfection of my disgust and a contrary wish to see, to learn more. At the end of a few minutes the young man in attendance on the lady in question reappeared as for a fresh gape at me. He was inordinately grave—to be dressed in such parti-coloured flannels; and he produced with no great confidence on his own side the message with which he had been charged. "She wants to know if you won't come right out."

"Who wants to know?"

"The Countess. That French lady."

"She has asked you to bring me?"

"Yes sir," said the young man feebly—for I may claim to have surpassed him in stature and weight.

I went out with him, and we found his instructress seated under one of the small quince-trees in front of the house; where she was engaged in drawing a fine needle with a very fat hand through a piece of embroidery not remarkable for freshness. She pointed graciously to the chair beside her and I sat down. Mr. Mixter glanced about him and then accommodated himself on the grass at her feet; whence he gazed upward more gapingly than ever and as if convinced that between us something wonderful would now occur.

"I'm sure you spick French," said the Countess, whose eyes were singularly protuberant as she played over me her agreeable smile.

"I do, madam—*tant bien que mal*," I replied, I fear, more dryly.

"*Ah voilà*!" she cried as with delight. "I knew it as soon as I looked at you. You've been in my poor dear country."

"A considerable time."

"You love it then, *mon pays de France*?"

"Oh it's an old affection." But I wasn't exuberant.

"And you know Paris well?"

"Yes, *sans me vanter*, madam, I think I really do." And with a certain conscious purpose I let my eyes meet her own.

She presently, hereupon, moved her own and glanced down at Mr. Mixter. "What are we talking about?" she demanded of her attentive pupil.

He pulled his knees up, plucked at the grass, stared, blushed a little. "You're talking French," said Mr. Mixter.

"*La belle découverte*!" mocked the Countess. "It's going on ten months," she explained to me, "since I took him in hand. Don't put yourself out not to say he's *la bêtise même*," she added in fine style. "He won't in the least understand you."

A moment's consideration of Mr. Mixter, awkwardly sporting at our feet, quite assured me that he wouldn't. "I hope your other pupils do you more honour," I then remarked to my entertainer.

"I have no others. They don't know what French—or what anything else—is in this place; they don't want to know. You may therefore imagine the pleasure it is to me to meet a person who speaks it like yourself." I could but reply that my own pleasure wasn't less, and she continued to draw the stitches through her embroidery with an elegant curl of her little finger. Every few moments she put her eyes, near-sightedly, closer to her work—this as if for elegance too. She inspired me with no more confidence than her late husband, if husband he was, had done, years before, on the occasion with which this one so detestably matched: she was coarse, common, affected, dishonest—no more a Countess than I was a Caliph. She had an assurance—based clearly on experience; but this couldn't have been the experience of "race." Whatever it was indeed it did now, in a yearning fashion, flare out of her. "Talk to me of Paris, *mon beau Paris* that I'd give my eyes to see. The very name of it *me fait languir*. How long since you were there?"

"A couple of months ago."

"*Vous avez de la chance*! Tell me something about it. What were they doing? Oh for an hour of the Boulevard!"

"They were doing about what they're always doing—amusing themselves a good deal."

"At the theatres, *hein*?" sighed the Countess. "At the cafes-concerts? *sous ce beau ciel*—at the little tables before the doors? *Quelle existence*! You know I'm a Parisienne, monsieur," she added, "to my finger-tips."

"Miss Spencer was mistaken then," I ventured to return, "in telling me you're a Provençale."

She stared a moment, then put her nose to her embroidery, which struck me as having acquired even while we sat a dingier and more desultory air. "Ah I'm a Provençale by birth, but a Parisienne by—inclination." After which she pursued: "And by the saddest events of my life—as well as by some of the happiest, helas!"

"In other words by a varied experience!" I now at last smiled.

She questioned me over it with her hard little salient eyes. "Oh experience!—I could talk of that, no doubt, if I wished. *On en a de toutes les sortes*—and I never dreamed that mine, for example, would ever have *this* in store for me." And she indicated with her large bare elbow and with a jerk of her head all surrounding objects; the little white house, the pair of quince-trees, the rickety paling, even the rapt Mr. Mixter.

I took them all bravely in. "Ah if you mean you're decidedly in exile—!"

"You may imagine what it is. These two years of my *épreuve—elles m'en ont données, des heures, des heures*! One gets used to things"—and she raised her shoulders to the highest shrug ever accomplished at North Verona; "so that I sometimes think I've got used to this. But there are some things that are always beginning again. For example my coffee."

I so far again lent myself. "Do you always have coffee at this hour?"

Her eyebrows went up as high as her shoulders had done. "At what hour would you propose to me to have it? I must have my little cup after breakfast."

"Ah you breakfast at this hour?"

"At mid-day—*comme cela se fait*. Here they breakfast at a quarter past seven. That 'quarter past' is charming!"

"But you were telling me about your coffee," I observed sympathetically.

"My *cousine* can't believe in it; she can't understand it. *C'est une fille charmante*, but that little cup of black coffee with a drop of '*fine*,' served at this hour—they exceed her comprehension. So I have to break the ice each day, and it takes the coffee the time you see to arrive. And when it does arrive, monsieur—! If I don't press it on *you*—though monsieur here sometimes joins me!—it's because you've drunk it on the Boulevard."

I resented extremely so critical a view of my poor friend's exertions, but I said nothing at all—the only way to be sure of my civility. I dropped my eyes on Mr. Mixter, who, sitting cross-legged and nursing his knees, watched my companion's foreign graces with an interest that familiarity had apparently done little to restrict. She became aware, naturally, of my mystified view of him and faced the question with all her boldness. "He adores me, you know," she murmured with her nose again in her tapestry—"he dreams of becoming *mon amoureux*. Yes, *il me fait une cour acharnée*—such as you see him. That's what we've come to. He has read some French novel—it took him six months. But ever since that he has thought himself a hero and me—such as I am, monsieur—*je ne sais quelle dévergondée*!"

Mr. Mixter may have inferred that he was to that extent the object of our reference; but of the manner in which he was handled he must have had small suspicion—preoccupied as he was, as to my companion, with the ecstasy of contemplation. Our hostess moreover at this moment came out of the house, bearing a coffee-pot and three cups on a neat little tray. I took from her eyes, as she approached us, a brief but intense appeal—the mute expression, as I felt, conveyed in the hardest little look she had yet addressed me, of her longing to know what, as a man of the world in general and of the French world in particular, I thought of these allied forces now so encamped on the stricken field of her life. I could only "act" however, as they said at North Verona, quite impenetrably—only make no answering sign. I couldn't intimate, much less could I frankly utter, my inward sense of the Countess's probable past, with its measure of her virtue, value and accomplishments, and of the limits of the consideration to which she could properly pretend. I couldn't give my friend a hint of how I myself personally "saw" her interesting pensioner—whether as the runaway wife of a too-jealous hair-dresser or of a too-morose pastry-cook, say; whether as a very small bourgeoise, in fine, who had vitiated her case beyond patching up, or even as some character, of the nomadic sort, less edifying still. I couldn't let in, by the jog of a shutter, as it were, a hard informing ray and then, washing my hands of the business, turn my back for ever. I could on the contrary but save the situation, my own at least, for the moment, by pulling myself together with a master hand and appearing to ignore everything but that the dreadful person between us *was* a "grande dame." This effort was possible indeed but as a retreat in good order and with all the forms of courtesy. If I couldn't speak, still less could I stay, and I think I must, in spite of everything, have turned black with disgust to see Caroline Spencer stand there like a waiting-maid. I therefore won't answer for the shade of success that may have attended my saying to the Countess, on my feet and as to leave her: "You expect to remain some time in these *parages*?"

What passed between us, as from face to face, while she looked up at me, *that* at least our companion may have caught, that at least may have sown, for the after-time, some seed of revelation. The Countess repeated her terrible shrug. "Who knows? I don't see my way—! It isn't an existence, but when one's in misery—! *Chère belle*," she added as an appeal to Miss Spencer, "you've gone and forgotten the '*fine*'!"

I detained that lady as, after considering a moment in silence the small array, she was about to turn off in quest of this article. I held out my hand in silence—I had to go. Her wan set little face, severely mild and with the question of a moment before now quite cold in it, spoke of extreme fatigue, but also of something else strange and conceived—whether a desperate patience still, or at last some other desperation, being more than I can say. What was clearest on the whole was that she was glad I was going. Mr. Mixter had risen to his feet and was pouring out the Countess's coffee. As I went back past the Baptist church I could feel how right my poor friend had been in her conviction at the other, the still intenser, the now historic crisis, that she should still see something of that dear old Europe.

IN THE CAGE

CHAPTER I

It had occurred to her early that in her position—that of a young person spending, in framed and wired confinement, the life of a guinea-pig or a magpie—she should know a great many persons without their recognising the acquaintance. That made it an emotion the more lively—though singularly rare and always, even then, with opportunity still very much smothered—to see any one come in whom she knew outside, as she called it, any one who could add anything to the meanness of her function. Her function was to sit there with two young men—the other telegraphist and the counter-clerk; to mind the "sounder," which was always going, to dole out stamps and postal-orders, weigh letters, answer stupid questions, give difficult change and, more than anything else, count words as numberless as the sands of the sea, the words of the telegrams thrust, from morning to night, through the gap left in the high lattice, across the encumbered shelf that her forearm ached with rubbing. This transparent screen fenced out or fenced in, according to the side of the narrow counter on which the human lot was cast, the duskiest corner of a shop pervaded not a little, in winter, by the poison of perpetual gas, and at all times by the presence of hams, cheese, dried fish, soap, varnish, paraffin and other solids and fluids that she came to know perfectly by their smells without consenting to know them by their names.

The barrier that divided the little post-and-telegraph-office from the grocery was a frail structure of wood and wire; but the social, the professional separation was a gulf that fortune, by a stroke quite remarkable, had spared her the necessity of contributing at all publicly to bridge. When Mr. Cocker's young men stepped over from behind the other counter to change a five-pound note—and Mr. Cocker's situation, with the cream of the "Court Guide" and the dearest furnished apartments, Simpkin's, Ladle's, Thrupp's, just round the corner, was so select that his place was quite pervaded by the crisp rustle of these emblems—she pushed out the sovereigns as if the applicant were no more to her than one of the momentary, the practically featureless, appearances in the great procession; and this perhaps all the more from the very fact of the connexion (only recognised outside indeed) to which she had lent herself with ridiculous inconsequence. She recognised the others the less because she had at last so unreservedly, so irredeemably, recognised Mr. Mudge. However that might be, she was a little ashamed of having to admit to herself that Mr. Mudge's removal to a higher sphere—to a more commanding position, that is, though to a much lower neighbourhood—would have been described still better as a luxury than as the mere simplification, the corrected awkwardness, that she contented herself with calling it. He had at any rate ceased to be all day long in her eyes, and this left something a little fresh for them to rest on of a Sunday. During the three months of his happy survival at Cocker's after her consent to their engagement she had often asked herself what it was marriage would be able to add to a familiarity that seemed already to have scraped the platter so clean. Opposite there, behind the counter of which his superior stature, his whiter apron, his more clustering curls and more present, too present, *h*'s had been for a couple of years the principal ornament, he had moved to and fro before her as on the small sanded floor of their contracted future. She was conscious now of the improvement of not having to take her present and her future at once. They were about as much as she could manage when taken separate.

She had, none the less, to give her mind steadily to what Mr. Mudge had again written her about, the idea of her applying for a transfer to an office quite similar—she couldn't yet hope for a place in a bigger—under the very roof where he was foreman, so that, dangled before her every minute of the day, he should see her, as he called it, "hourly," and in a part, the far N.W. district, where, with her mother, she would save on their two rooms alone nearly three shillings. It would be far from dazzling to exchange Mayfair for Chalk Farm, and it wore upon her much that he could never drop a subject; still, it didn't wear as things had worn, the worries of the early times of their great misery, her own, her mother's and her elder sister's—the last of whom had succumbed to all but absolute want when, as conscious and incredulous ladies, suddenly bereft, betrayed, overwhelmed, they had slipped faster and faster down the steep slope at the bottom of which she alone had rebounded. Her mother had never rebounded any more at the bottom than on the way; had only rumbled and grumbled down and down, making, in respect of caps, topics and "habits," no effort whatever—which simply meant smelling much of the time of whiskey.

CHAPTER II

It was always rather quiet at Cocker's while the contingent from Ladle's and Thrupp's and all the other great places were at luncheon, or, as the young men used vulgarly to say, while the animals were feeding. She had forty minutes in advance of this to go home for her own dinner; and when she came back and one of the young men took his turn there was often half an hour during which she could pull out a bit of work or a book—a book from the place where she borrowed novels, very greasy, in fine print and all about fine folks, at a ha'penny a day. This sacred pause was one of the numerous ways in which the establishment kept its finger on the pulse of fashion and fell into the rhythm of the larger life. It had something to do, one day, with the particular flare of importance of an arriving customer, a lady whose meals were apparently irregular, yet whom she was destined, she afterwards found, not to forget. The girl was blasée; nothing could belong more, as she perfectly knew, to the intense publicity of her profession; but she had a whimsical mind and wonderful nerves; she was subject, in short, to sudden flickers of antipathy and sympathy, red gleams in the grey, fitful needs to notice and to "care," odd caprices of curiosity. She had a friend who had invented a new career for women—that of being in and out of people's houses to look after the flowers. Mrs. Jordan had a manner of her own of sounding this allusion; "the flowers," on her lips, were, in fantastic places, in happy homes, as usual as the coals or the daily papers. She took charge of them, at any rate, in all the rooms, at so much a month, and people were quickly finding out what it was to make over this strange burden of the pampered to the widow of a clergyman. The widow, on her side, dilating on the initiations thus opened up to her, had been splendid to her young friend, over the way she was made free of the greatest houses—the way, especially when she did the dinner-tables, set out so often for twenty, she felt that a single step more would transform her whole social position. On its being asked of her then if she circulated only in a sort of tropical solitude, with the upper servants for picturesque natives, and on her having to assent to this glance at her limitations, she had found a reply to the girl's invidious question. "You've no imagination, my dear!"—that was because a door more than half open to the higher life couldn't be called anything but a thin partition. Mrs. Jordan's imagination quite did away with the thickness.

Our young lady had not taken up the charge, had dealt with it good-humouredly, just because she knew so well what to think of it. It was at once one of her most cherished complaints and most secret supports that people didn't understand her, and it was accordingly a matter of indifference to her that Mrs. Jordan shouldn't; even though Mrs. Jordan, handed down from their early twilight of gentility and also the victim of reverses, was the only member of her circle in whom she recognised an equal. She was perfectly aware that her imaginative life was the life in which she spent most of her time; and she would have been ready, had it been at all worth while, to contend that, since her outward occupation didn't kill it, it must be strong indeed. Combinations of flowers and green-stuff, forsooth! What she could handle freely, she said to herself, was combinations of men and women. The only weakness in her faculty came from the positive abundance of her contact with the human herd; this was so constant, it had so the effect of cheapening her privilege, that there were long stretches in which inspiration, divination and interest quite dropped. The great thing was the flashes, the quick revivals, absolute accidents all, and neither to be counted on nor to be resisted. Some one had only sometimes to put in a penny for a stamp and the whole thing was upon her. She was so absurdly constructed that these were literally the moments that made up—made up for the long stiffness of sitting there in the stocks, made up for the cunning hostility of Mr. Buckton and the importunate sympathy of the counter-clerk, made up for the daily deadly flourishy letter from Mr. Mudge, made up even for the most haunting of her worries, the rage at moments of not knowing how her mother did "get it."

She had surrendered herself moreover of late to a certain expansion of her consciousness; something that seemed perhaps vulgarly accounted for by the fact that, as the blast of the season roared louder and the waves of fashion tossed their spray further over the counter, there were more impressions to be gathered and really—for it came to that—more life to be led. Definite at any rate it was that by the time May was well started the kind of company she kept at Cocker's had begun to strike her as a reason—a reason she might almost put forward for a policy of procrastination. It sounded silly, of course, as yet, to plead such a motive, especially as the fascination of the place was after all a sort of torment. But she liked her torment; it was a torment she should miss at Chalk Farm. She was ingenious and uncandid, therefore, about leaving the breadth of London a little longer between herself and that austerity. If she hadn't quite the courage in short to say to Mr. Mudge that her actual chance for a play of mind was worth any week the three shillings he desired to help her to save, she yet saw something happen in the course of the month that in her heart of hearts at least answered the subtle question. This was connected precisely with the appearance of the memorable lady.

CHAPTER III

She pushed in three bescribbled forms which the girl's hand was quick to appropriate, Mr. Buckton having so frequent a perverse instinct for catching first any eye that promised the sort of entertainment with which she had her peculiar affinity. The amusements of captives are full of a desperate contrivance, and one of our young friend's ha'pennyworths had been the charming tale of "Picciola." It was of course the law of the place that they were never to take no notice, as Mr. Buckton said, whom they served; but this also never prevented, certainly on the same gentleman's own part, what he was fond of describing as the underhand game. Both her companions, for that matter, made no secret of the number of favourites they had among the ladies; sweet familiarities in spite of which she had repeatedly caught each of them in stupidities and mistakes, confusions of identity and lapses of observation that never failed to remind her how the cleverness of men ends where the cleverness of women begins. "Marguerite, Regent Street. Try on at six. All Spanish lace. Pearls. The full length." That was the first; it had no signature. "Lady Agnes Orme, Hyde Park Place. Impossible to-night, dining Haddon. Opera to-morrow, promised Fritz, but could do play Wednesday. Will try Haddon for Savoy, and anything in the world you like, if you can get Gussy. Sunday Montenero. Sit Mason Monday, Tuesday. Marguerite awful. Cissy." That was the second. The third, the girl noted when she took it, was on a foreign form: "Everard, Hôtel Brighton, Paris. Only understand and believe. 22nd to 26th, and certainly 8th and 9th. Perhaps others. Come. Mary."

Mary was very handsome, the handsomest woman, she felt in a moment, she had ever seen—or perhaps it was only Cissy. Perhaps it was both, for she had seen stranger things than that—ladies wiring to different persons under different names. She had seen all sorts of things and pieced together all sorts of mysteries. There had once been one—not long before—who, without winking, sent off five over five different signatures.

Perhaps these represented five different friends who had asked her—all women, just as perhaps now Mary and Cissy, or one or other of them, were wiring by deputy. Sometimes she put in too much—too much of her own sense; sometimes she put in too little; and in either case this often came round to her afterwards, for she had an extraordinary way of keeping clues. When she noticed she noticed; that was what it came to. There were days and days, there were weeks sometimes, of vacancy. This arose often from Mr. Buckton's devilish and successful subterfuges for keeping her at the sounder whenever it looked as if anything might arouse; the sounder, which it was equally his business to mind, being the innermost cell of captivity, a cage within the cage, fenced oft from the rest by a frame of ground glass. The counter-clerk would have played into her hands; but the counter-clerk was really reduced to idiocy by the effect of his passion for her. She flattered herself moreover, nobly, that with the unpleasant conspicuity of this passion she would never have consented to be obliged to him. The most she would ever do would be always to shove off on him whenever she could the registration of letters, a job she happened particularly to loathe. After the long stupors, at all events, there almost always suddenly would come a sharp taste of something; it was in her mouth before she knew it; it was in her mouth now.

To Cissy, to Mary, whichever it was, she found her curiosity going out with a rush, a mute effusion that floated back to her, like a returning tide, the living colour and splendour of the beautiful head, the light of eyes that seemed to reflect such utterly other things than the mean things actually before them; and, above all, the high curt consideration of a manner that even at bad moments was a magnificent habit and of the very essence of the innumerable things—her beauty, her birth, her father and mother, her cousins and all her ancestors—that its possessor couldn't have got rid of even had she wished. How did our obscure little public servant know that for the lady of the telegrams this was a bad moment? How did she guess all sorts of impossible things, such as, almost on the very spot, the presence of drama at a critical stage and the nature of the tie with the gentleman at the Hôtel Brighton? More than ever before it floated to her through the bars of the cage that this at last was the high reality, the bristling truth that she had hitherto only patched up and eked out—one of the creatures, in fine, in whom all the conditions for happiness actually met, and who, in the air they made, bloomed with an unwitting insolence. What came home to the girl was the way the insolence was tempered by something that was equally a part of the distinguished life, the custom of a flowerlike bend to the less fortunate—a dropped fragrance, a mere quick breath, but which in fact pervaded and lingered. The apparition was very young, but certainly married, and our fatigued friend had a sufficient store of mythological comparison to recognise the port of Juno. Marguerite might be "awful," but she knew how to dress a goddess.

Pearls and Spanish lace—she herself, with assurance, could see them, and the "full length" too, and also red velvet bows, which, disposed on the lace in a particular manner (she could have placed them with the turn of a hand) were of course to adorn the front of a black brocade that would be like a dress in a picture. However, neither Marguerite nor Lady Agnes nor Haddon nor Fritz nor Gussy was what the wearer of this garment had really come in for. She had come in for Everard—and that was doubtless not his true name either. If our young lady had never taken such jumps before it was simply that she had never before been so affected. She went all the way. Mary and Cissy had been round together, in their single superb person, to see him—he must live round the corner; they had found that, in consequence of something they had come, precisely, to make up for or to have another scene about, he had gone off—gone off just on purpose to make them feel it; on which they had come together to Cocker's as to the nearest place; where they had put in the three forms partly in order not to put in the one alone. The two others in a manner, covered it, muffled it, passed it off. Oh yes, she went all the way, and this was a specimen of how she often went. She would know the hand again any time. It was as handsome and as everything else as the woman herself. The woman herself had, on learning his flight, pushed past Everard's servant and into his room; she had written her missive at his table and with his pen. All this, every inch of it, came in the waft that she blew through and left behind her, the influence that, as I have said, lingered. And among the things the girl was sure of, happily, was that she should see her again.

CHAPTER IV

She saw her in fact, and only ten days later; but this time not alone, and that was exactly a part of the luck of it. Not unaware—as how could her observation have left her so?—of the possibilities through which it could range, our young lady had ever since had in her mind a dozen conflicting theories about Everard's type; as to which, the instant they came into the place, she felt the point settled with a thump that seemed somehow addressed straight to her heart. That organ literally beat faster at the approach of the gentleman who was this time with Cissy, and who, as seen from within the cage, became on the spot the happiest of the happy circumstances with which her mind had invested the friend of Fritz and Gussy. He was a very happy circumstance indeed as, with his cigarette in his lips and his broken familiar talk caught by his companion, he put down the half-dozen telegrams it would take them together several minutes to dispatch. And here it occurred, oddly enough, that if, shortly before the girl's interest in his companion had sharpened her sense for the messages then transmitted, her immediate vision of himself had the effect, while she counted his seventy words, of preventing intelligibility. His words were mere numbers, they told her nothing whatever; and after he had gone she was in possession of no name, of no address, of no meaning, of nothing but a vague sweet sound and an immense impression. He had been there but five minutes, he had smoked in her face, and, busy with his telegrams, with the tapping pencil and the conscious danger, the odious betrayal that would come from a mistake, she had had no wandering glances nor roundabout arts to spare. Yet she had taken him in; she knew everything; she had made up her mind.

He had come back from Paris; everything was re-arranged; the pair were again shoulder to shoulder in their high encounter with life, their large and complicated game. The fine soundless pulse of this game was in the air for our young woman while they remained in the shop. While they remained? They remained all day; their presence continued and abode with her, was in everything she did till nightfall, in the thousands of other words she counted, she transmitted, in all the stamps she detached and the letters she weighed and the change she gave, equally unconscious and unerring in each of these particulars, and not, as the run on the little office thickened with the afternoon hours, looking up at a single ugly face in the long sequence, nor really hearing the stupid questions that she patiently and perfectly answered. All patience was possible now, all questions were stupid after his, all faces were ugly. She had been sure she should see the lady again; and even now she should perhaps, she should probably, see her often. But for him it was totally different; she should never never see him. She wanted it too much. There was a kind of wanting that helped—she had arrived, with her rich experience, at that generalisation; and there was another kind that was fatal. It was this time the fatal kind; it would prevent.

Well, she saw him the very next day, and on this second occasion it was quite different; the sense of every syllable he paid for was fiercely distinct; she indeed felt her progressive pencil, dabbing as if with a quick caress the marks of his own, put life into every stroke. He was there a long time—had not brought his forms filled out but worked them off in a nook on the counter; and there were other people as well—a changing pushing cluster, with every one to mind at once and endless right change to make and information to produce. But she kept hold of him throughout; she continued, for herself, in a relation with him as close as that in which, behind the hated ground glass, Mr. Buckton luckily continued with the sounder. This morning everything changed, but rather to dreariness; she had to swallow the rebuff to her theory about fatal desires, which she did without confusion and indeed with absolute levity; yet if it was now flagrant that he did live close at hand—at Park Chambers—and belonged supremely to the class that wired everything, even their expensive feelings (so that, as he never wrote, his correspondence cost him weekly pounds and pounds, and he might be in and out five times a day) there was, all the same, involved in the prospect, and by reason of its positive excess of light, a perverse melancholy, a gratuitous misery. This was at once to give it a place in an order of feelings on which I shall presently touch.

Meanwhile, for a month, he was very constant. Cissy, Mary, never re-appeared with him; he was always either alone or accompanied only by some gentleman who was lost in the blaze of his glory. There was another sense, however—and indeed there was more than one—in which she mostly found herself counting in the splendid creature with whom she had originally connected him. He addressed this correspondent neither as Mary nor as Cissy; but the girl was sure of whom it was, in Eaten Square, that he was perpetually wiring to—and all so irreproachably!—as Lady Bradeen. Lady Bradeen was Cissy, Lady Bradeen was Mary, Lady Bradeen was the friend of Fritz and of Gussy, the customer of Marguerite, and the close ally in short (as was ideally right, only the girl had not yet found a descriptive term that was) of the most magnificent of men. Nothing could equal the frequency and variety of his communications to her ladyship but their extraordinary, their abysmal propriety. It was just the talk—so profuse sometimes that she wondered what was left for their real meetings—of the very happiest people. Their real meetings must have been constant, for half of it was appointments and allusions, all swimming in a sea of other allusions still, tangled in a complexity of questions that gave a wondrous image of their life. If Lady Bradeen was Juno it was all certainly Olympian. If the girl, missing the answers, her ladyship's own outpourings, vainly reflected that Cocker's should have been one of the bigger offices where telegrams arrived as well as departed, there were yet ways in which, on the whole, she pressed the romance closer by reason of the very quantity of imagination it demanded and consumed. The days and hours of this new friend, as she came to account him, were at all events unrolled, and however much more she might have known she would still have wished to go beyond. In fact she did go beyond; she went quite far enough.

But she could none the less, even after a month, scarce have told if the gentlemen who came in with him recurred or changed; and this in spite of the fact that they too were always posting and wiring, smoking in her face and signing or not signing. The gentlemen who came in with him were nothing when he was there. They turned up alone at other times—then only perhaps with a dim richness of reference. He himself, absent as well as present, was all. He was very tall, very fair, and had, in spite of his thick preoccupations, a good-humour that was exquisite, particularly as it so often had the effect of keeping him on. He could have reached over anybody, and anybody—no matter who—would have let him; but he was so extraordinarily kind that he quite pathetically waited, never waggling things at her out of his turn nor saying "Here!" with horrid sharpness. He waited for pottering old ladies, for gaping slaveys, for the perpetual Buttonses from Thrupp's; and the thing in all this that she would have liked most unspeakably to put to the test was the possibility of her having for him a personal identity that might in a particular way appeal. There were moments when he actually struck her as on her side, as arranging to help, to support, to spare her.

But such was the singular spirit of our young friend that she could remind herself with a pang that when people had awfully good manners—people of that class,—you couldn't tell. These manners were for everybody, and it might be drearily unavailing for any poor particular body to be overworked and unusual. What he did take for granted was all sorts of facility; and his high pleasantness, his relighting of cigarettes while he waited, his unconscious bestowal of opportunities, of boons, of blessings, were all a part of his splendid security, the instinct that told him there was nothing such an existence as his could ever lose by. He was somehow all at once very bright and very grave, very young and immensely complete; and whatever he was at any moment it was always as much as all the rest the mere bloom of his beatitude. He was sometimes Everard, as he had been at the Hôtel Brighton, and he was sometimes Captain Everard. He was sometimes Philip with his surname and sometimes Philip without it. In some directions he was merely Phil, in others he was merely Captain. There were relations in which he was none of these things, but a quite different person—"the Count." There were several friends for whom he was William. There were several for whom, in allusion perhaps to his complexion, he was "the Pink 'Un." Once, once only by good luck, he had, coinciding comically, quite miraculously, with another person also near to her, been "Mudge." Yes, whatever he was, it was a part of his happiness—whatever he was and probably whatever he wasn't. And his happiness was a part—it became so little by little—of something that, almost from the first of her being at Cocker's, had been deeply with the girl.

CHAPTER V

This was neither more nor less than the queer extension of her experience, the double life that, in the cage, she grew at last to lead. As the weeks went on there she lived more and more into the world of whiffs and glimpses, she found her divinations work faster and stretch further. It was a prodigious view as the pressure heightened, a panorama fed with facts and figures, flushed with a torrent of colour and accompanied with wondrous world-music. What it mainly came to at this period was a picture of how London could amuse itself; and that, with the running commentary of a witness so exclusively a witness, turned for the most part to a hardening of the heart. The nose of this observer was brushed by the bouquet, yet she could never really pluck even a daisy. What could still remain fresh in her daily grind was the immense disparity, the difference and contrast, from class to class, of every instant and every motion. There were times when all the wires in the country seemed to start from the little hole-and-corner where she plied for a livelihood, and where, in the shuffle of feet, the flutter of "forms," the straying of stamps and the ring of change over the counter, the people she had fallen into the habit of remembering and fitting together with others, and of having her theories and interpretations of, kept up before her their long procession and rotation. What twisted the knife in her vitals was the way the profligate rich scattered about them, in extravagant chatter over their extravagant pleasures and sins, an amount of money that would have held the stricken household of her frightened childhood, her poor pinched mother and tormented father and lost brother and starved sister, together for a lifetime. During her first weeks she had often gasped at the sums people were willing to pay for the stuff they transmitted—the "much love"s, the "awful" regrets, the compliments and wonderments and vain vague gestures that cost the price of a new pair of boots. She had had a way then of glancing at the people's faces, but she had early learnt that if you became a telegraphist you soon ceased to be astonished. Her eye for types amounted nevertheless to genius, and there were those she liked and those she hated, her feeling for the latter of which grew to a positive possession, an instinct of observation and detection. There were the brazen women, as she called them, of the higher and the lower fashion, whose squanderings and graspings, whose struggles and secrets and love-affairs and lies, she tracked and stored up against them till she had at moments, in private, a triumphant vicious feeling of mastery and ease, a sense of carrying their silly guilty secrets in her pocket, her small retentive brain, and thereby knowing so much more about them than they suspected or would care to think. There were those she would have liked to betray, to trip up, to bring down with words altered and fatal; and all through a personal hostility provoked by the lightest signs, by their accidents of tone and manner, by the particular kind of relation she always happened instantly to feel.

There were impulses of various kinds, alternately soft and severe, to which she was constitutionally accessible and which were determined by the smallest accidents. She was rigid in general on the article of making the public itself affix its stamps, and found a special enjoyment in dealing to that end with some of the ladies who were too grand to touch them. She had thus a play of refinement and subtlety greater, she flattered herself, than any of which she could be made the subject; and though most people were too stupid to be conscious of this it brought her endless small consolations and revenges. She recognised quite as much those of her sex whom she would have liked to help, to warn, to rescue, to see more of; and that alternative as well operated exactly through the hazard of personal sympathy, her vision for silver threads and moonbeams and her gift for keeping the clues and finding her way in the tangle. The moonbeams and silver threads presented at moments all the vision of what poor she might have made of happiness. Blurred and blank as the whole thing often inevitably, or mercifully, became, she could still, through crevices and crannies, be stupefied, especially by what, in spite of all seasoning, touched the sorest place in her consciousness, the revelation of the golden shower flying about without a gleam of gold for herself. It remained prodigious to the end, the money her fine friends were able to spend to get still more, or even to complain to fine friends of their own that they were in want. The pleasures they proposed were equalled only by those they declined, and they made their appointments often so expensively that she was left wondering at the nature of the delights to which the mere approaches were so paved with shillings. She quivered on occasion into the perception of this and that one whom she would on the chance have just simply liked to be. Her conceit, her baffled vanity, was possibly monstrous; she certainly often threw herself into a defiant conviction that she would have done the whole thing much better. But her greatest comfort, mostly, was her comparative vision of the men; by whom I mean the unmistakeable gentlemen, for she had no interest in the spurious or the shabby and no mercy at all for the poor. She could have found a sixpence, outside, for an appearance of want; but her fancy, in some directions so alert, had never a throb of response for any sign of the sordid. The men she did track, moreover, she tracked mainly in one relation, the relation as to which the cage convinced her, she believed, more than anything else could have done, that it was quite the most diffused.

She found her ladies, in short, almost always in communication with her gentlemen, and her gentlemen with her ladies, and she read into the immensity of their intercourse stories and meanings without end. Incontestably she grew to think that the men cut the best figure; and in this particular, as in many others, she arrived at a philosophy of her own, all made up of her private notations and cynicisms. It was a striking part of the business, for example, that it was much more the women, on the whole, who were after the men than the men who were after the women: it was literally visible that the general attitude of the one sex was that of the object pursued and defensive, apologetic and attenuating, while the light of her own nature helped her more or less to conclude as to the attitude of the other. Perhaps she herself a little even fell into the custom of pursuit in occasionally deviating only for gentlemen from her high rigour about the stamps. She had early in the day made up her mind, in fine, that they had the best manners; and if there were none of them she noticed when Captain Everard was there, there were plenty she could place and trace and name at other times, plenty who, with their way of being "nice" to her, and of handling, as if their pockets were private tills loose mixed masses of silver and gold, were such pleasant appearances that she could envy them without dislike. They never had to give change—they only had to get it. They ranged through every suggestion, every shade of fortune, which evidently included indeed lots of bad luck as well as of good, declining even toward Mr. Mudge and his bland firm thrift, and ascending, in wild signals and rocket-flights, almost to within hail of her highest standard. So from month to month she went on with them all, through a thousand ups and downs and a thousand pangs and indifferences. What virtually happened was that in the shuffling herd that passed before her by far the greater part only passed—a proportion but just appreciable stayed. Most of the elements swam straight away, lost themselves in the bottomless common, and by so doing really kept the page clear. On the clearness therefore what she did retain stood sharply out; she nipped and caught it, turned it over and interwove it.

CHAPTER VI

She met Mrs. Jordan when she could, and learned from her more and more how the great people, under her gentle shake and after going through everything with the mere shops, were waking up to the gain of putting into the hands of a person of real refinement the question that the shop-people spoke of so vulgarly as that of the floral decorations. The regular dealers in these decorations were all very well; but there was a peculiar magic in the play of taste of a lady who had only to remember, through whatever intervening dusk, all her own little tables, little bowls and little jars and little other arrangements, and the wonderful thing she had made of the garden of the vicarage. This small domain, which her young friend had never seen, bloomed in Mrs. Jordan's discourse like a new Eden, and she converted the past into a bank of violets by the tone in which she said "Of course you always knew my one passion!" She obviously met now, at any rate, a big contemporary need, measured what it was rapidly becoming for people to feel they could trust her without a tremor. It brought them a peace that—during the quarter of an hour before dinner in especial—was worth more to them than mere payment could express. Mere payment, none the less, was tolerably prompt; she engaged by the month, taking over the whole thing; and there was an evening on which, in respect to our heroine, she at last returned to the charge. "It's growing and growing, and I see that I must really divide the work. One wants an associate—of one's own kind, don't you know? You know the look they want it all to have?—of having come, not from a florist, but from one of themselves. Well, I'm sure you could give it—because you are one. Then we should win. Therefore just come in with me."

"And leave the P.O.?"

"Let the P.O. simply bring you your letters. It would bring you lots, you'd see: orders, after a bit, by the score." It was on this, in due course, that the great advantage again came up: "One seems to live again with one's own people." It had taken some little time (after their having parted company in the tempest of their troubles and then, in the glimmering dawn, finally sighted each other again) for each to admit that the other was, in her private circle, her only equal, but the admission came, when it did come, with an honest groan; and since equality was named, each found much personal profit in exaggerating the other's original grandeur. Mrs. Jordan was ten years the older, but her young friend was struck with the smaller difference this now made: it had counted otherwise at the time when, much more as a friend of her mother's, the bereaved lady, without a penny of provision and with stopgaps, like their own, all gone, had, across the sordid landing on which the opposite doors of the pair of scared miseries opened and to which they were bewilderedly bolted, borrowed coals and umbrellas that were repaid in potatoes and postage-stamps. It had been a questionable help, at that time, to ladies submerged, floundering, panting, swimming for their lives, that they were ladies; but such an advantage could come up again in proportion as others vanished, and it had grown very great by the time it was the only ghost of one they possessed. They had literally watched it take to itself a portion of the substance of each that had departed; and it became prodigious now, when they could talk of it together, when they could look back at it across a desert of accepted derogation, and when, above all, they could together work up a credulity about it that neither could otherwise work up. Nothing was really so marked as that they felt the need to cultivate this legend much more after having found their feet and stayed their stomachs in the ultimate obscure than they had done in the upper air of mere frequent shocks. The thing they could now oftenest say to each other was that they knew what they meant; and the sentiment with which, all round, they knew it was known had well-nigh amounted to a promise not again to fall apart.

Mrs. Jordan was at present fairly dazzling on the subject of the way that, in the practice of her fairy art, as she called it, she more than peeped in—she penetrated. There was not a house of the great kind—and it was of course only a question of those, real homes of luxury—in which she was not, at the rate such people now had things, all over the place. The girl felt before the picture the cold breath of disinheritance as much as she had ever felt it in the cage; she knew moreover how much she betrayed this, for the experience of poverty had begun, in her life, too early, and her ignorance of the requirements of homes of luxury had grown, with other active knowledge, a depth of simplification. She had accordingly at first often found that in these colloquies she could only pretend she understood. Educated as she had rapidly been by her chances at Cocker's, there were still strange gaps in her learning—she could never, like Mrs. Jordan, have found her way about one of the "homes." Little by little, however, she had caught on, above all in the light of what Mrs. Jordan's redemption had materially made of that lady, giving her, though the years and the struggles had naturally not straightened a feature, an almost super-eminent air. There were women in and out of Cocker's who were quite nice and who yet didn't look well; whereas Mrs. Jordan looked well and yet, with her extraordinarily protrusive teeth, was by no means quite nice. It would seem, mystifyingly, that it might really come from all the greatness she could live with. It was fine to hear her talk so often of dinners of twenty and of her doing, as she said, exactly as she liked with them. She spoke as if, for that matter, she invited the company. "They simply give me the table—all the rest, all the other effects, come afterwards."

CHAPTER VII

"Then you do see them?" the girl again asked.

Mrs. Jordan hesitated, and indeed the point had been ambiguous before. "Do you mean the guests?"

Her young friend, cautious about an undue exposure of innocence, was not quite sure. "Well—the people who live there."

"Lady Ventnor? Mrs. Bubb? Lord Rye? Dear, yes. Why they like one."

"But does one personally know them?" our young lady went on, since that was the way to speak. "I mean socially, don't you know?—as you know me."

"They're not so nice as you!" Mrs. Jordan charmingly cried. "But I shall see more and more of them."

Ah this was the old story. "But how soon?"

"Why almost any day. Of course," Mrs. Jordan honestly added, "they're nearly always out."

"Then why do they want flowers all over?"

"Oh that doesn't make any difference." Mrs. Jordan was not philosophic; she was just evidently determined it shouldn't make any. "They're awfully interested in my ideas, and it's inevitable they should meet me over them."

Her interlocutress was sturdy enough. "What do you call your ideas?"

Mrs. Jordan's reply was fine. "If you were to see me some day with a thousand tulips you'd discover."

"A thousand?"—the girl gaped at such a revelation of the scale of it; she felt for the instant fairly planted out. "Well, but if in fact they never do meet you?" she none the less pessimistically insisted.

"Never? They often do—and evidently quite on purpose. We have grand long talks."

There was something in our young lady that could still stay her from asking for a personal description of these apparitions; that showed too starved a state. But while she considered she took in afresh the whole of the clergyman's widow. Mrs. Jordan couldn't help her teeth, and her sleeves were a distinct rise in the world. A thousand tulips at a shilling clearly took one further than a thousand words at a penny; and the betrothed of Mr. Mudge, in whom the sense of the race for life was always acute, found herself wondering, with a twinge of her easy jealousy, if it mightn't after all then, for her also, be better—better than where she was—to follow some such scent. Where she was was where Mr. Buckton's elbow could freely enter her right side and the counter-clerk's breathing—he had something the matter with his nose—pervade her left ear. It was something to fill an office under Government, and she knew but too well there were places commoner still than Cocker's; but it needed no great range of taste to bring home to her the picture of servitude and promiscuity she couldn't but offer to the eye of comparative freedom. She was so boxed up with her young men, and anything like a margin so absent, that it needed more art than she should ever possess to pretend in the least to compass, with any one in the nature of an acquaintance—say with Mrs. Jordan herself, flying in, as it might happen, to wire sympathetically to Mrs. Bubb—an approach to a relation of elegant privacy. She remembered the day when Mrs. Jordan had, in fact, by the greatest chance, come in with fifty-three words for Lord Rye and a five-pound note to change. This had been the dramatic manner of their reunion—their mutual recognition was so great an event. The girl could at first only see her from the waist up, besides making but little of her long telegram to his lordship. It was a strange whirligig that had converted the clergyman's widow into such a specimen of the class that went beyond the sixpence.

Nothing of the occasion, all the more, had ever become dim; least of all the way that, as her recovered friend looked up from counting, Mrs. Jordan had just blown, in explanation, through her teeth and through the bars of the cage: "I do flowers, you know." Our young woman had always, with her little finger crooked out, a pretty movement for counting; and she had not forgotten the small secret advantage, a sharpness of triumph it might even have been called, that fell upon her at this moment and avenged her for the incoherence of the message, an unintelligible enumeration of numbers, colours, days, hours. The correspondence of people she didn't know was one thing; but the correspondence of people she did had an aspect of its own for her even when she couldn't understand it. The speech in which Mrs. Jordan had defined a position and announced a profession was like a tinkle of bluebells; but for herself her one idea about flowers was that people had them at funerals, and her present sole gleam of light was that lords probably had them most. When she watched, a minute later, through the cage, the swing of her visitor's departing petticoats, she saw the sight from the waist down; and when the counter-clerk, after a mere male glance, remarked, with an intention unmistakeably low, "Handsome woman!" she had for him the finest of her chills: "She's the widow of a bishop." She always felt, with the counter-clerk, that it was impossible sufficiently to put it on; for what she wished to express to him was the maximum of her contempt, and that element in her nature was confusedly stored. "A bishop" was putting it on, but the counter-clerk's approaches were vile. The night, after this, when, in the fulness of time, Mrs. Jordan mentioned the grand long talks, the girl at last brought out: "Should I see them?—I mean if I were to give up everything for you."

Mrs. Jordan at this became most arch. "I'd send you to all the bachelors!"

Our young lady could be reminded by such a remark that she usually struck her friend as pretty. "Do they have their flowers?"

"Oceans. And they're the most particular." Oh it was a wonderful world. "You should see Lord Rye's."

"His flowers?"

"Yes, and his letters. He writes me pages on pages—with the most adorable little drawings and plans. You should see his diagrams!"

CHAPTER VIII

The girl had in course of time every opportunity to inspect these documents, and they a little disappointed her; but in the mean while there had been more talk, and it had led to her saying, as if her friend's guarantee of a life of elegance were not quite definite: "Well, I see every one at my place."

"Every one?"

"Lots of swells. They flock. They live, you know, all round, and the place is filled with all the smart people, all the fast people, those whose names are in the papers—mamma has still the *Morning Post*—and who come up for the season."

Mrs. Jordan took this in with complete intelligence. "Yes, and I dare say it's some of your people that I do."

Her companion assented, but discriminated. "I doubt if you 'do' them as much as I! Their affairs, their appointments and arrangements, their little games and secrets and vices—those things all pass before me."

This was a picture that could make a clergyman's widow not imperceptibly gasp; it was in intention moreover something of a retort to the thousand tulips. "Their vices? Have they got vices?"

Our young critic even more overtly stared then with a touch of contempt in her amusement: "Haven't you found that out?" The homes of luxury then hadn't so much to give. "I find out everything."

Mrs. Jordan, at bottom a very meek person, was visibly struck. "I see. You do 'have' them."

"Oh I don't care! Much good it does me!"

Mrs. Jordan after an instant recovered her superiority. "No—it doesn't lead to much." Her own initiations so clearly did. Still—after all; and she was not jealous: "There must be a charm."

"In seeing them?" At this the girl suddenly let herself go. "I hate them. There's that charm!"

Mrs. Jordan gaped again. "The real 'smarts'?"

"Is that what you call Mrs. Bubb? Yes—it comes to me; I've had Mrs. Bubb. I don't think she has been in herself, but there are things her maid has brought. Well, my dear!"—and the young person from Cocker's, recalling these things and summing them up, seemed suddenly to have much to say. She didn't say it, however; she checked it; she only brought out: "Her maid, who's horrid—she must have her!" Then she went on with indifference: "They're too real! They're selfish brutes."

Mrs. Jordan, turning it over, adopted at last the plan of treating it with a smile. She wished to be liberal. "Well, of course, they do lay it out."

"They bore me to death," her companion pursued with slightly more temperance.

But this was going too far. "Ah that's because you've no sympathy!"

The girl gave an ironic laugh, only retorting that nobody could have any who had to count all day all the words in the dictionary; a contention Mrs. Jordan quite granted, the more that she shuddered at the notion of ever failing of the very gift to which she owed the vogue—the rage she might call it—that had caught her up. Without sympathy—or without imagination, for it came back again to that—how should she get, for big dinners, down the middle and toward the far corners at all? It wasn't the combinations, which were easily managed: the strain was over the ineffable simplicities, those that the bachelors above all, and Lord Rye perhaps most of any, threw off—just blew off like cigarette-puffs—such sketches of. The betrothed of Mr. Mudge at all events accepted the explanation, which had the effect, as almost any turn of their talk was now apt to have, of bringing her round to the terrific question of that gentleman. She was tormented with the desire to get out of Mrs. Jordan, on this subject, what she was sure was at the back of Mrs. Jordan's head; and to get it out of her, queerly enough, if only to vent a certain irritation at it. She knew that what her friend would already have risked if she hadn't been timid and tortuous was: "Give him up—yes, give him up: you'll see that with your sure chances you'll be able to do much better."

Our young woman had a sense that if that view could only be put before her with a particular sniff for poor Mr. Mudge she should hate it as much as she morally ought. She was conscious of not, as yet, hating it quite so much as that. But she saw that Mrs. Jordan was conscious of something too, and that there was a degree of confidence she was waiting little by little to arrive at. The day came when the girl caught a glimpse of what was still wanting to make her friend feel strong; which was nothing less than the prospect of being able to announce the climax of sundry private dreams. The associate of the aristocracy had personal calculations—matter for brooding and dreaming, even for peeping out not quite hopelessly from behind the window-curtains of lonely lodgings. If she did the flowers for the bachelors, in short, didn't she expect that to have consequences very different from such an outlook at Cocker's as she had pronounced wholly desperate? There seemed in very truth something auspicious in the mixture of bachelors and flowers, though, when looked hard in the eye, Mrs. Jordan was not quite prepared to say she had expected a positive proposal from Lord Rye to pop out of it. Our young woman arrived at last, none the less, at a definite vision of what was in her mind. This was a vivid foreknowledge that the betrothed of Mr. Mudge would, unless conciliated in advance by a successful rescue, almost hate her on the day she should break a particular piece of news. How could that unfortunate otherwise endure to hear of what, under the protection of Lady Ventnor, was after all so possible.

CHAPTER IX

Meanwhile, since irritation sometimes relieved her, the betrothed of Mr. Mudge found herself indebted to that admirer for amounts of it perfectly proportioned to her fidelity. She always walked with him on Sundays, usually in the Regent's Park, and quite often, once or twice a month he took her, in the Strand or thereabouts, to see a piece that was having a run. The productions he always preferred were the really good ones—Shakespeare, Thompson or some funny American thing; which, as it also happened that she hated vulgar plays, gave him ground for what was almost the fondest of his approaches, the theory that their tastes were, blissfully, just the same. He was for ever reminding her of that, rejoicing over it and being affectionate and wise about it. There were times when she wondered how in the world she could "put up with" him, how she could put up with any man so smugly unconscious of the immensity of her difference. It was just for this difference that, if she was to be liked at all, she wanted to be liked, and if that was not the source of Mr. Mudge's admiration, she asked herself what on earth could be? She was not different only at one point, she was different all round; unless perhaps indeed in being practically human, which her mind just barely recognised that he also was. She would have made tremendous concessions in other quarters: there was no limit for instance to those she would have made to Captain Everard; but what I have named was the most she was prepared to do for Mr. Mudge. It was because he was different that, in the oddest way, she liked as well as deplored him; which was after all a proof that the disparity, should they frankly recognise it, wouldn't necessarily be fatal. She felt that, oleaginous—too oleaginous—as he was, he was somehow comparatively primitive: she had once, during the portion of his time at Cocker's that had overlapped her own, seen him collar a drunken soldier, a big violent man who, having come in with a mate to get a postal-order cashed, had made a grab at the money before his friend could reach it and had so determined, among the hams and cheeses and the lodgers from Thrupp's, immediate and alarming reprisals, a scene of scandal and consternation. Mr. Buckton and the counter-clerk had crouched within the cage, but Mr. Mudge had, with a very quiet but very quick step round the counter, an air of masterful authority she shouldn't soon forget, triumphantly interposed in the scrimmage, parted the combatants and shaken the delinquent in his skin. She had been proud of him at that moment, and had felt that if their affair had not already been settled the neatness of his execution would have left her without resistance.

Their affair had been settled by other things: by the evident sincerity of his passion and by the sense that his high white apron resembled a front of many floors. It had gone a great way with her that he would build up a business to his chin, which he carried quite in the air. This could only be a question of time; he would have all Piccadilly in the pen behind his ear. That was a merit in itself for a girl who had known what she had known. There were hours at which she even found him good-looking, though, frankly there could be no crown for her effort to imagine on the part of the tailor or the barber some such treatment of his appearance as would make him resemble even remotely a man of the world. His very beauty was the beauty of a grocer, and the finest future would offer it none too much room consistently to develop. She had engaged herself in short to the perfection of a type, and almost anything square and smooth and whole had its weight for a person still conscious herself of being a mere bruised fragment of wreckage. But it contributed hugely at present to carry on the two parallel lines of her experience in the cage and her experience out of it. After keeping quiet for some time about this opposition she suddenly—one Sunday afternoon on a penny chair in the Regent's Park—broke, for him, capriciously, bewilderingly, into an intimation of what it came to. He had naturally pressed more and more on the point of her again placing herself where he could see her hourly, and for her to recognise that she had as yet given him no sane reason for delay he had small need to describe himself as unable to make out what she was up to. As if, with her absurd bad reasons, she could have begun to tell him! Sometimes she thought it would be amusing to let him have them full in the face, for she felt she should die of him unless she once in a while stupefied him; and sometimes she thought it would be disgusting and perhaps even fatal. She liked him, however, to think her silly, for that gave her the margin which at the best she would always require; and the only difficulty about this was that he hadn't enough imagination to oblige her. It produced none the less something of the desired effect—to leave him simply wondering why, over the matter of their reunion, she didn't yield to his arguments. Then at last, simply as if by accident and out of mere boredom on a day that was rather flat, she preposterously produced her own. "Well, wait a bit. Where I am I still see things." And she talked to him even worse, if possible, than she had talked to Jordan.

Little by little, to her own stupefaction, she caught that he was trying to take it as she meant it and that he was neither astonished nor angry. Oh the British tradesman—this gave her an idea of his resources! Mr. Mudge would be angry only with a person who, like the drunken soldier in the shop, should have an unfavourable effect on business. He seemed positively to enter, for the time and without the faintest flash of irony or ripple of laughter, into the whimsical grounds of her enjoyment of Cocker's custom, and instantly to be casting up whatever it might, as Mrs. Jordan had said, lead to. What he had in mind was not of course what Mrs. Jordan had had: it was obviously not a source of speculation with him that his sweetheart might pick up a husband. She could see perfectly that this was not for a moment even what he supposed she herself dreamed of. What she had done was simply to give his sensibility another push into the dim vast of trade. In that direction it was all alert, and she had whisked before it the mild fragrance of a "connexion." That was the most he could see in any account of her keeping in, on whatever roundabout lines, with the gentry; and when, getting to the bottom of this, she quickly proceeded to show him the kind of eye she turned on such people and to give him a sketch of what that eye discovered, she reduced him to the particular prostration in which he could still be amusing to her.

CHAPTER X

"They're the most awful wretches, I assure you—the lot all about there."

"Then why do you want to stay among them?"

"My dear man, just because they are. It makes me hate them so."

"Hate them? I thought you liked them."

"Don't be stupid. What I 'like' is just to loathe them. You wouldn't believe what passes before my eyes."

"Then why have you never told me? You didn't mention anything before I left."

"Oh I hadn't got round to it then. It's the sort of thing you don't believe at first; you have to look round you a bit and then you understand. You work into it more and more. Besides," the girl went on, "this is the time of the year when the worst lot come up. They're simply packed together in those smart streets. Talk of the numbers of the poor! What I can vouch for is the numbers of the rich! There are new ones every day, and they seem to get richer and richer. Oh, they do come up!" she cried, imitating for her private recreation—she was sure it wouldn't reach Mr. Mudge—the low intonation of the counter-clerk.

"And where do they come from?" her companion candidly enquired.

She had to think a moment; then she found something. "From the 'spring meetings.' They bet tremendously."

"Well, they bet enough at Chalk Farm, if that's all."

"It isn't all. It isn't a millionth part!" she replied with some sharpness. "It's immense fun"—she had to tantalise him. Then as she had heard Mrs. Jordan say, and as the ladies at Cocker's even sometimes wired, "It's quite too dreadful!" She could fully feel how it was Mr. Mudge's propriety, which was extreme—he had a horror of coarseness and attended a Wesleyan chapel—that prevented his asking for details. But she gave him some of the more innocuous in spite of himself, especially putting before him how, at Simpkin's and Ladle's, they all made the money fly. That was indeed what he liked to hear: the connexion was not direct, but one was somehow more in the right place where the money was flying than where it was simply and meagrely nesting. The air felt that stir, he had to acknowledge, much less at Chalk Farm than in the district in which his beloved so oddly enjoyed her footing. She gave him, she could see, a restless sense that these might be familiarities not to be sacrificed; germs, possibilities, faint foreshowings—heaven knew what—of the initiation it would prove profitable to have arrived at when in the fulness of time he should have his own shop in some such paradise. What really touched him—that was discernible—was that she could feed him with so much mere vividness of reminder, keep before him, as by the play of a fan, the very wind of the swift bank-notes and the charm of the existence of a class that Providence had raised up to be the blessing of grocers. He liked to think that the class was there, that it was always there, and that she contributed in her slight but appreciable degree to keep it up to the mark. He couldn't have formulated his theory of the matter, but the exuberance of the aristocracy was the advantage of trade, and everything was knit together in a richness of pattern that it was good to follow with one's finger-tips. It was a comfort to him to be thus assured that there were no symptoms of a drop. What did the sounder, as she called it, nimbly worked, do but keep the ball going?

What it came to therefore for Mr. Mudge was that all enjoyments were, as might be said, inter-related, and that the more people had the more they wanted to have. The more flirtations, as he might roughly express it, the more cheese and pickles. He had even in his own small way been dimly struck with the linkèd sweetness connecting the tender passion with cheap champagne, or perhaps the other way round. What he would have liked to say had he been able to work out his thought to the end was: "I see, I see. Lash them up then, lead them on, keep them going: some of it can't help, some time, coming our way." Yet he was troubled by the suspicion of subtleties on his companion's part that spoiled the straight view. He couldn't understand people's hating what they liked or liking what they hated; above all it hurt him somewhere—for he had his private delicacies—to see anything but money made out of his betters. To be too enquiring, or in any other way too free, at the expense of the gentry was vaguely wrong; the only thing that was distinctly right was to be prosperous at any price. Wasn't it just because they were up there aloft that they were lucrative? He concluded at any rate by saying to his young friend: "If it's improper for you to remain at Cocker's, then that falls in exactly with the other reasons I've put before you for your removal."

"Improper?"—her smile became a prolonged boldness. "My dear boy, there's no one like you!"

"I dare say," he laughed; "but that doesn't help the question."

"Well," she returned, "I can't give up my friends. I'm making even more than Mrs. Jordan."

Mr. Mudge considered. "How much is she making?"

"Oh you dear donkey!"—and, regardless of all the Regent's Park, she patted his cheek. This was the sort of moment at which she was absolutely tempted to tell him that she liked to be near Park Chambers. There was a fascination in the idea of seeing if, on a mention of Captain Everard, he wouldn't do what she thought he might; wouldn't weigh against the obvious objection the still more obvious advantage. The advantage of course could only strike him at the best as rather fantastic; but it was always to the good to keep hold when you had hold, and such an attitude would also after all involve a high tribute to her fidelity. Of one thing she absolutely never doubted: Mr. Mudge believed in her with a belief—! She believed in herself too, for that matter: if there was a thing in the world no one could charge her with it was being the kind of low barmaid person who rinsed tumblers and bandied slang. But she forbore as yet to speak; she had not spoken even to Mrs. Jordan; and the hush that on her lips surrounded the Captain's name maintained itself as a kind of symbol of the success that, up to this time, had attended something or other—she couldn't have said what—that she humoured herself with calling, without words, her relation with him.

CHAPTER XI

She would have admitted indeed that it consisted of little more than the fact that his absences, however frequent and however long, always ended with his turning up again. It was nobody's business in the world but her own if that fact continued to be enough for her. It was of course not enough just in itself; what it had taken on to make it so was the extraordinary possession of the elements of his life that memory and attention had at last given her. There came a day when this possession on the girl's part actually seemed to enjoy between them, while their eyes met, a tacit recognition that was half a joke and half a deep solemnity. He bade her good morning always now; he often quite raised his hat to her. He passed a remark when there was time or room, and once she went so far as to say to him that she hadn't seen him for "ages." "Ages" was the word she consciously and carefully, though a trifle tremulously used; "ages" was exactly what she meant. To this he replied in terms doubtless less anxiously selected, but perhaps on that account not the less remarkable, "Oh yes, hasn't it been awfully wet?" That was a specimen of their give and take; it fed her fancy that no form of intercourse so transcendent and distilled had ever been established on earth. Everything, so far as they chose to consider it so, might mean almost anything. The want of margin in the cage, when he peeped through the bars, wholly ceased to be appreciable. It was a drawback only in superficial commerce. With Captain Everard she had simply the margin of the universe. It may be imagined therefore how their unuttered reference to all she knew about him could in this immensity play at its ease. Every time he handed in a telegram it was an addition to her knowledge: what did his constant smile mean to mark if it didn't mean to mark that? He never came into the place without saying to her in this manner: "Oh yes, you have me by this time so completely at your mercy that it doesn't in the least matter what I give you now. You've become a comfort, I assure you!"

She had only two torments; the greatest of which was that she couldn't, not even once or twice, touch with him on some individual fact. She would have given anything to have been able to allude to one of his friends by name, to one of his engagements by date, to one of his difficulties by the solution. She would have given almost as much for just the right chance—it would have to be tremendously right—to show him in some sharp sweet way that she had perfectly penetrated the greatest of these last and now lived with it in a kind of heroism of sympathy. He was in love with a woman to whom, and to any view of whom, a lady-telegraphist, and especially one who passed a life among hams and cheeses, was as the sand on the floor; and what her dreams desired was the possibility of its somehow coming to him that her own interest in him could take a pure and noble account of such an infatuation and even of such an impropriety. As yet, however, she could only rub along with the hope that an accident, sooner or later, might give her a lift toward popping out with something that would surprise and perhaps even, some fine day, assist him. What could people mean moreover—cheaply sarcastic people—by not feeling all that could be got out of the weather? *She* felt it all, and seemed literally to feel it most when she went quite wrong, speaking of the stuffy days as cold, of the cold ones as stuffy, and betraying how little she knew, in her cage, of whether it was foul or fair. It was for that matter always stuffy at Cocker's, and she finally settled down to the safe proposition that the outside element was "changeable." Anything seemed true that made him so radiantly assent.

This indeed is a small specimen of her cultivation of insidious ways of making things easy for him—ways to which of course she couldn't be at all sure he did real justice. Real justice was not of this world: she had had too often to come back to that; yet, strangely, happiness was, and her traps had to be set for it in a manner to keep them unperceived by Mr. Buckton and the counter-clerk. The most she could hope for apart from the question, which constantly flickered up and died down, of the divine chance of his consciously liking her, would be that, without analysing it, he should arrive at a vague sense that

Cocker's was—well, attractive; easier, smoother, sociably brighter, slightly more picturesque, in short more propitious in general to his little affairs, than any other establishment just thereabouts. She was quite aware that they couldn't be, in so huddled a hole, particularly quick; but she found her account in the slowness—she certainly could bear it if he could. The great pang was that just thereabouts post-offices were so awfully thick. She was always seeing him in imagination in other places and with other girls. But she would defy any other girl to follow him as she followed. And though they weren't, for so many reasons, quick at Cocker's, she could hurry for him when, through an intimation light as air, she gathered that he was pressed.

When hurry was, better still, impossible, it was because of the pleasantest thing of all, the particular element of their contact—she would have called it their friendship—that consisted of an almost humorous treatment of the look of some of his words. They would never perhaps have grown half so intimate if he had not, by the blessing of heaven, formed some of his letters with a queerness—! It was positive that the queerness could scarce have been greater if he had practised it for the very purpose of bringing their heads together over it as far as was possible to heads on different sides of a wire fence. It had taken her truly but once or twice to master these tricks, but, at the cost of striking him perhaps as stupid, she could still challenge them when circumstances favoured. The great circumstance that favoured was that she sometimes actually believed he knew she only feigned perplexity. If he knew it therefore he tolerated it; if he tolerated it he came back; and if he came back he liked her. This was her seventh heaven; and she didn't ask much of his liking—she only asked of it to reach the point of his not going away because of her own. He had at times to be away for weeks; he had to lead lets life; he had to travel—there were places to which he was constantly wiring for "rooms": all this she granted him, forgave him; in fact, in the long run, literally blessed and thanked him for. If he had to lead his life, that precisely fostered his leading it so much by telegraph: therefore the benediction was to come in when he could. That was all she asked—that he shouldn't wholly deprive her.

Sometimes she almost felt that he couldn't have deprived her even had he been minded, by reason of the web of revelation that was woven between them. She quite thrilled herself with thinking what, with such a lot of material, a bad girl would do. It would be a scene better than many in her ha'penny novels, this going to him in the dusk of evening at Park Chambers and letting him at last have it. "I know too much about a certain person now not to put it to you—excuse my being so lurid—that it's quite worth your while to buy me off. Come, therefore; buy me!" There was a point indeed at which such flights had to drop again—the point of an unreadiness to name, when it came to that, the purchasing medium. It wouldn't certainly be anything so gross as money, and the matter accordingly remained rather vague, all the more that *she* was not a bad girl. It wasn't for any such reason as might have aggravated a mere minx that she often hoped he would again bring Cissy. The difficulty of this, however, was constantly present to her, for the kind of communion to which Cocker's so richly ministered rested on the fact that Cissy and he were so often in different places. She knew by this time all the places—Suchbury, Monkhouse, Whiteroy, Finches—and even how the parties on these occasions were composed; but her subtlety found ways to make her knowledge fairly protect and promote their keeping, as she had heard Mrs. Jordan say, in touch. So, when he actually sometimes smiled as if he really felt the awkwardness of giving her again one of the same old addresses, all her being went out in the desire—which her face must have expressed—that he should recognise her forbearance to criticise as one of the finest tenderest sacrifices a woman had ever made for love.

CHAPTER XII

She was occasionally worried, however this might be, by the impression that these sacrifices, great as they were, were nothing to those that his own passion had imposed; if indeed it was not rather the passion of his confederate, which had caught him up and was whirling him round like a great steam-wheel. He was at any rate in the strong grip of a dizzy splendid fate; the wild wind of his life blew him straight before it. Didn't she catch in his face at times, even through his smile and his happy habit, the gleam of that pale glare with which a bewildered victim appeals, as he passes, to some pair of pitying eyes? He perhaps didn't even himself know how scared he was; but *she* knew. They were in danger, they were in danger, Captain Everard and Lady Bradeen: it beat every novel in the shop. She thought of Mr. Mudge and his safe sentiment; she thought of herself and blushed even more for her tepid response to it. It was a comfort to her at such moments to feel that in another relation—a relation supplying that affinity with her nature that Mr. Mudge, deluded creature, would never supply—she should have been no more tepid than her ladyship. Her deepest soundings were on two or three occasions of finding herself almost sure that, if she dared, her ladyship's lover would have gathered relief from "speaking" to her. She literally fancied once or twice that, projected as he was toward his doom, her own eyes struck him, while the air roared in his ears, as the one pitying pair in the crowd. But how could he speak to her while she sat sandwiched there between the counter-clerk and the sounder?

She had long ago, in her comings and goings made acquaintance with Park Chambers and reflected as she looked up at their luxurious front that *they* of course would supply the ideal setting for the ideal speech. There was not an object in London that, before the season was over, was more stamped upon her brain. She went roundabout to pass it, for it was not on the short way; she passed on the opposite side of the street and always looked up, though it had taken her a long time to be sure of the particular set of windows. She had made that out finally by an act of audacity that at the time had almost stopped her heart-beats and that in retrospect greatly quickened her blushes. One evening she had lingered late and watched—watched for some moment when the porter, who was in uniform and often on the steps, had gone in with a visitor. Then she followed boldly, on the calculation that he would have taken the visitor up and that the hall would be free. The hall *was* free, and the electric light played over the gilded and lettered board that showed the names and numbers of the occupants of the different floors. What she wanted looked straight at her—Captain Everard was on the third. It was as if, in the immense intimacy of this, they were, for the instant and the first time, face to face outside the cage. Alas! they were face to face but a second or two: she was whirled out on the wings of a panic fear that he might just then be entering or issuing. This fear was indeed, in her shameless deflexions, never very far from her, and was mixed in the oddest way with depressions and disappointments. It was dreadful, as she trembled by, to run the risk of looking to him as if she basely hung about; and yet it was dreadful to be obliged to pass only at such moments as put an encounter out of the question.

At the horrible hour of her first coming to Cocker's he was always—it was to be hoped—snug in bed; and at the hour of her final departure he was of course—she had such things all on her fingers'-ends—dressing for dinner. We may let it pass that if she couldn't bring herself to hover till he was dressed, this was simply because such a process for such a person could only be terribly prolonged. When she went in the middle of the day to her own dinner she had too little time to do anything but go straight, though it must be added that for a real certainty she would joyously have omitted the repast. She had made up her mind as to there being on the whole no decent pretext to justify her flitting casually past at three o'clock in the morning. That was the hour at which, if the ha'penny novels were not all wrong, he probably came home for the night. She was therefore reduced to the vainest figuration of the miraculous meeting toward which a hundred impossibilities would have to conspire. But if nothing was more impossible than the fact, nothing was more intense than the vision. What may not, we can only moralise, take place in the quickened muffled perception of a young person with an ardent soul? All our humble friend's native distinction, her refinement of personal grain, of heredity, of pride, took refuge in this small throbbing spot; for when she was most conscious of the objection of her vanity and the pitifulness of her little flutters and manoeuvres, then the consolation and the redemption were most sure to glow before her in some just discernible sign. He did like her!

CHAPTER XIII

He never brought Cissy back, but Cissy came one day without him, as fresh as before from the hands of Marguerite, or only, at the season's end, a trifle less fresh. She was, however, distinctly less serene. She had brought nothing with her and looked about with impatience for the forms and the place to write. The latter convenience, at Cocker's, was obscure and barely adequate, and her clear voice had the light note of disgust which her lover's never showed as she responded with a "There?" of surprise to the gesture made by the counter-clerk in answer to her sharp question. Our young friend was busy with half a dozen people, but she had dispatched them in her most businesslike manner by the time her ladyship flung through the bars this light of re-appearance. Then the directness with which the girl managed to receive the accompanying missive was the result of the concentration that had caused her to make the stamps fly during the few minutes occupied by the production of it. This concentration, in turn, may be described as the effect of the apprehension of imminent relief. It was nineteen days, counted and checked off, since she had seen the object of her homage; and as, had he been in London, she should, with his habits, have been sure to see him often, she was now about to learn what other spot his presence might just then happen to sanctify. For she thought of them, the other spots, as ecstatically conscious of it, expressively happy in it.

But, gracious, how handsome *was* her ladyship, and what an added price it gave him that the air of intimacy he threw out should have flowed originally from such a source! The girl looked straight through the cage at the eyes and lips that must so often have been so near as own—looked at them with a strange passion that for an instant had the result of filling out some of the gaps, supplying the missing answers, in his correspondence. Then as she made out that the features she thus scanned and associated were totally unaware of it, that they glowed only with the colour of quite other and not at all guessable thoughts, this directly added to their splendour, gave the girl the sharpest impression she had yet received of the uplifted, the unattainable plains of heaven, and yet at the same time caused her to thrill with a sense of the high company she did somehow keep. She was with the absent through her ladyship and with her ladyship through the absent. The only pang—but it didn't matter—was the proof in the admirable face, in the sightless preoccupation of its possessor, that the latter hadn't a notion of her. Her folly had gone to the point of half believing that the other party to the affair must sometimes mention in Eaton Square the extraordinary little person at the place from which he so often wired. Yet the perception of her visitor's blankness actually helped this extraordinary little person, the next instant, to take refuge in a reflexion that could be as proud as it liked. "How little she knows, how little she knows!" the girl cried to herself; for what did that show after all but that Captain Everard's telegraphic confidant was Captain Everard's charming secret? Our young friend's perusal of her ladyship's telegram was literally prolonged by a momentary daze: what swam between her and the words, making her see them as through rippled shallow sun-shot water, was the great, the perpetual flood of "How much *I* know—how much *I* know!" This produced a delay in her catching that, on the face, these words didn't give her what she wanted, though she was prompt enough with her remembrance that her grasp was, half the time, just of what *was* not on the face. "Miss Dolman, Parade Lodge, Parade Terrace, Dover. Let him instantly know right one, Hôtel de France, Ostend. Make it seven nine four nine six one. Wire me alternative Burfield's."

The girl slowly counted. Then he was at Ostend. This hooked on with so sharp a click that, not to feel she was as quickly letting it all slip from her, she had absolutely to hold it a minute longer and to do something to that end. Thus it was that she did on this occasion what she never did—threw off a "Reply paid?" that sounded officious, but that she partly made up for by deliberately affixing the stamps and by waiting till she had done so to give change. She had, for so much coolness, the strength that she considered she knew all about Miss Dolman.

"Yes—paid." She saw all sorts of things in this reply, even to a small suppressed start of surprise at so correct an assumption; even to an attempt the next minute at a fresh air of detachment. "How much, with the answer?" The calculation was not abstruse, but our intense observer required a moment more to make it, and this gave her ladyship time for a second thought. "Oh just wait!" The white begemmed hand bared to write rose in sudden nervousness to the side of the wonderful face which, with eyes of anxiety for the paper on the counter, she brought closer to the bars of the cage. "I think I must alter a word!" On this she recovered her telegram and looked over it again; but she had a new, an obvious trouble, and studied it without deciding and with much of the effect of making our young woman watch her.

This personage, meanwhile, at the sight of her expression, had decided on the spot. If she had always been sure they were in danger her ladyship's expression was the best possible sign of it. There was a word wrong, but she had lost the right one, and much clearly depended on her finding it again. The girl, therefore, sufficiently estimating the affluence of customers and the distraction of Mr. Buckton and the counter-clerk, took the jump and gave it. "Isn't it Cooper's?"

It was as if she had bodily leaped—cleared the top of the cage and alighted on her interlocutress. "Cooper's?"—the stare was heightened by a blush. Yes, she had made Juno blush.

This was all the greater reason for going on. "I mean instead of Burfield's."

Our young friend fairly pitied her; she had made her in an instant so helpless, and yet not a bit haughty nor outraged. She was only mystified and scared. "Oh, you know—?"

"Yes, I know!" Our young friend smiled, meeting the other's eyes, and, having made Juno blush, proceeded to patronise her. "*I'll* do it"—she put out a competent hand. Her ladyship only submitted, confused and bewildered, all presence of mind quite gone; and the next moment the telegram was in the cage again and its author out of the shop. Then quickly, boldly, under all the eyes that might have witnessed her tampering, the extraordinary little person at Cocker's made the proper change. People were really too giddy, and if they *were*, in a certain case, to be caught, it shouldn't be the fault of her own grand memory. Hadn't it been settled weeks before?—for Miss Dolman it was always to be "Cooper's."

CHAPTER XIV

But the summer "holidays" brought a marked difference; they were holidays for almost every one but the animals in the cage. The August days were flat and dry, and, with so little to feed it, she was conscious of the ebb of her interest in the secrets of the refined. She was in a position to follow the refined to the extent of knowing—they had made so many of their arrangements with her aid—exactly where they were; yet she felt quite as if the panorama had ceased unrolling and the band stopped playing. A stray member of the latter occasionally turned up, but the communications that passed before her bore now largely on rooms at hotels, prices of furnished houses, hours of trains, dates of sailings and arrangements for being "met"; she found them for the most part prosaic and coarse. The only thing was that they brought into her stuffy corner as straight a whiff of Alpine meadows and Scotch moors as she might hope ever to inhale; there were moreover in especial fat hot dull ladies who had out with her, to exasperation, the terms for seaside lodgings, which struck her as huge, and the matter of the number of beds required, which was not less portentous: this in reference to places of which the names—Eastbourne, Folkestone, Cromer, Scarborough, Whitby—tormented her with something of the sound of the plash of water that haunts the traveller in the desert. She had not been out of London for a dozen years, and the only thing to give a taste to the present dead weeks was the spice of a chronic resentment. The sparse customers, the people she did see, were the people who were "just off"—off on the decks of fluttered yachts, off to the uttermost point of rocky headlands where the very breeze was then playing for the want of which she said to herself that she sickened.

There was accordingly a sense in which, at such a period, the great differences of the human condition could press upon her more than ever; a circumstance drawing fresh force in truth from the very fact of the chance that at last, for a change, did squarely meet her—the chance to be "off," for a bit, almost as far as anybody. They took their turns in the cage as they took them both in the shop and at Chalk Farm; she had known these two months that time was to be allowed in September—no less than eleven days—for her personal private holiday. Much of her recent intercourse with Mr. Mudge had consisted of the hopes and fears, expressed mainly by himself, involved in the question of their getting the same dates—a question that, in proportion as the delight seemed assured, spread into a sea of speculation over the choice of where and how. All through July, on the Sunday evenings and at such other odd times as he could seize, he had flooded their talk with wild waves of calculation. It was practically settled that, with her mother, somewhere "on the south coast" (a phrase of which she liked the sound) they should put in their allowance together; but she already felt the prospect quite weary and worn with the way he went round and round on it. It had become his sole topic, the theme alike of his most solemn prudences and most placid jests, to which every opening led for return and revision and in which every little flower of a foretaste was pulled up as soon as planted. He had announced at the earliest day—characterising the whole business, from that moment, as their "plans," under which name he handled it as a Syndicate handles a Chinese or other Loan—he had promptly declared that the question must be thoroughly studied, and he produced, on the whole subject, from day to day, an amount of information that excited her wonder and even, not a little, as she frankly let him know, her disdain. When she thought of the danger in which another pair of lovers rapturously lived she enquired of him anew why he could leave nothing to chance. Then she got for answer that this profundity was just his pride, and he pitted Ramsgate against Bournemouth and even Boulogne against Jersey—for he had great ideas—with all the mastery of detail that was some day, professionally, to carry him afar.

The longer the time since she had seen Captain Everard the more she was booked, as she called it, to pass Park Chambers; and this was the sole amusement that in the lingering August days and the twilights sadly drawn out it was left her to cultivate. She had long since learned to know it for a feeble one, though its feebleness was perhaps scarce the reason for her saying to herself each evening as her time for departure approached: "No, no—not to-night." She never failed of that silent remark, any more than she failed of feeling, in some deeper place than she had even yet fully sounded, that one's remarks were as weak as straws and that, however one might indulge in them at eight o'clock, one's fate infallibly declared itself in absolute indifference to them at about eight-fifteen. Remarks were remarks, and very well for that; but fate was fate, and this young lady's was to pass Park Chambers every night in the working week. Out of the immensity of her knowledge of the life of the world there bloomed on these occasions as specific remembrance that it was regarded in that region, in August and September, as rather pleasant just to be caught for something or other in passing through town. Somebody was always passing and somebody might catch somebody else. It was in full cognisance of this subtle law that she adhered to the most ridiculous circuit she could have made to get home. One warm dull featureless Friday, when an accident had made her start from Cocker's a little later than usual, she became aware that something of which the infinite possibilities had for so long peopled her dreams was at last prodigiously upon her, though the perfection in which the conditions happened to present it was almost rich enough to be but the positive creation of a dream. She saw, straight before her, like a vista painted in a picture, the empty street and the lamps that burned pale in the dusk not yet established. It was into the convenience of this quiet twilight that a gentleman on the doorstep of the Chambers gazed with a vagueness that our young lady's little figure violently trembled, in the approach, with the measure of its power to dissipate. Everything indeed grew in a flash terrific and distinct; her old uncertainties fell away from her, and, since she was so familiar with fate, she felt as if the very nail that fixed it were driven in by the hard look with which, for a moment, Captain Everard awaited her.

The vestibule was open behind him and the porter as absent as on the day she had peeped in; he had just come out—was in town, in a tweed suit and a pot hat, but between two journeys—duly bored over his evening and at a loss what to do with it. Then it was that she was glad she had never met him in that way before: she reaped with such ecstasy the benefit of his not being able to think she passed often. She jumped in two seconds to the determination that he should even suppose it to be the very first time and the very oddest chance: this was while she still wondered if he would identify or notice her. His original attention had not, she instinctively knew, been for the young woman at Cocker's; it had only been for any young woman who might advance to the tune of her not troubling the quiet air, and in fact the poetic hour, with ugliness. Ah but then, and just as she had reached the door, came his second observation, a long light reach with which, visibly and quite amusedly, he recalled and placed her. They were on different sides, but the street, narrow and still, had only made more of a stage for the small momentary drama. It was not over, besides, it was far from over, even on his sending across the way, with the pleasantest laugh she had ever heard, a little lift of his hat and an "Oh good evening!" It was still less over on their meeting, the next minute, though rather indirectly and awkwardly, in the middle, of the road—a situation to which three or four steps of her own had unmistakeably contributed—and then passing not again to the side on which she had arrived, but back toward the portal of Park Chambers.

"I didn't know you at first. Are you taking a walk?"

"Ah I don't take walks at night! I'm going home after my work."

"Oh!"

That was practically what they had meanwhile smiled out, and his exclamation to which for a minute he appeared to have nothing to add, left them face to face and in just such an attitude as, for his part, he might have worn had he been wondering if he could properly ask her to come in. During this interval in fact she really felt his question to be just "*How* properly—?" It was simply a question of the degree of properness.

CHAPTER XV

She never knew afterwards quite what she had done to settle it, and at the time she only knew that they presently moved, with vagueness, yet with continuity, away from the picture of the lighted vestibule and the quiet stairs and well up the street together. This also must have been in the absence of a definite permission, of anything vulgarly articulate, for that matter, on the part of either; and it was to be, later on, a thing of remembrance and reflexion for her that the limit of what just here for a longish minute passed between them was his taking in her thoroughly successful deprecation, though conveyed without pride or sound or touch, of the idea that she might be, out of the cage, the very shop-girl at large that she hugged the theory she wasn't. Yes, it was strange, she afterwards thought, that so much could have come and gone and yet not disfigured the dear little intense crisis either with impertinence or with resentment, with any of the horrid notes of that kind of acquaintance. He had taken no liberty, as she would have so called it; and, through not having to betray the sense of one, she herself had, still more charmingly, taken none. On the spot, nevertheless, she could speculate as to what it meant that, if his relation with Lady Bradeen continued to be what her mind had built it up to, he should feel free to proceed with marked independence. This was one of the questions he was to leave her to deal with—the question whether people of his sort still asked girls up to their rooms when they were so awfully in love with other women. Could people of his sort do that without what people of *her* sort would call being "false to their love"? She had already a vision of how the true answer was that people of her sort didn't, in such cases, matter—didn't count as infidelity, counted only as something else: she might have been curious, since it came to that, to see exactly what.

Strolling together slowly in their summer twilight and their empty corner of Mayfair, they found themselves emerge at last opposite to one of the smaller gates of the Park; upon which, without any particular word about it—they were talking so of other things—they crossed the street and went in and sat down on a bench. She had gathered by this time one magnificent hope about him—the hope he would say nothing vulgar. She knew thoroughly what she meant by that; she meant something quite apart from any matter of his being "false." Their bench was not far within; it was near the Park Lane paling and the patchy lamplight and the rumbling cabs and 'buses. A strange emotion had come to her, and she felt indeed excitement within excitement; above all a conscious joy in testing him with chances he didn't take. She had an intense desire he should know the type she really conformed to without her doing anything so low as tell him, and he had surely begun to know it from the moment he didn't seize the opportunities into which a common man would promptly have blundered. These were on the mere awkward surface, and their relation was beautiful behind and below them. She had questioned so little on the way what they might be doing that as soon as they were seated she took straight hold of it. Her hours, her confinement, the many conditions of service in the post-office, had—with a glance at his own postal resources and alternatives—formed, up to this stage, the subject of their talk. "Well, here we are, and it may be right enough; but this isn't the least, you know, where I was going."

"You were going home?"

"Yes, and I was already rather late. I was going to my supper."

"You haven't had it?"

"No indeed!"

"Then you haven't eaten—?"

He looked of a sudden so extravagantly concerned that she laughed out. "All day? Yes, we do feed once. But that was long ago. So I must presently say good-bye."

"Oh deary *me*!" he exclaimed with an intonation so droll and yet a touch so light and a distress so marked—a confession of helplessness for such a case, in short, so unrelieved—that she at once felt sure she had made the great difference plain. He looked at her with the kindest eyes and still without saying what she had known he wouldn't. She had known he wouldn't say "Then sup with *me*!" but the proof of it made her feel as if she had feasted.

"I'm not a bit hungry," she went on.

"Ah you *must* be, awfully!" he made answer, but settling himself on the bench as if, after all, that needn't interfere with his spending his evening. "I've always quite wanted the chance to thank you for the trouble you so often take for me."

"Yes, I know," she replied; uttering the words with a sense of the situation far deeper than any pretence of not fitting his allusion. She immediately felt him surprised and even a little puzzled at her frank assent; but for herself the trouble she had taken could only, in these fleeting minutes—they would probably never come back—be all there like a little hoard of gold in her lap. Certainly he might look at it, handle it, take up the pieces. Yet if he understood anything he must understand all. "I consider you've already immensely thanked me." The horror was back upon her of having seemed to hang about for some reward. "It's awfully odd you should have been there just the one time—!"

"The one time you've passed my place?"

"Yes; you can fancy I haven't many minutes to waste. There was a place to-night I had to stop at."

"I see, I see—" he knew already so much about her work. "It must be an awful grind—for a lady."

"It is, but I don't think I groan over it any more than my companions—and you've seen *they're* not ladies!" She mildly jested, but with an intention. "One gets used to things, and there are employments I should have hated much more." She had the finest conception of the beauty of not at least boring him. To whine, to count up her wrongs, was what a barmaid or a shop-girl would do, and it was quite enough to sit there like one of these.

"If you had had another employment," he remarked after a moment, "we might never have become acquainted."

"It's highly probable—and certainly not in the same way." Then, still with her heap of gold in her lap and something of the pride of it in her manner of holding her head, she continued not to move—she only smiled at him. The evening had thickened now; the scattered lamps were red; the Park, all before them, was full of obscure and ambiguous life; there were other couples on other benches whom it was impossible not to see, yet at whom it was impossible to look. "But I've walked so much out of my way with you only just to show you that—that"—with this she paused; it was not after all so easy to express—"that anything you may have thought is perfectly true."

"Oh I've thought a tremendous lot!" her companion laughed. "Do you mind my smoking?"

"Why should I? You always smoke *there*."

"At your place? Oh yes, but here it's different."

"No," she said as he lighted a cigarette, "that's just what it isn't. It's quite the same."

"Well, then, that's because 'there' it's so wonderful!"

"Then you're conscious of how wonderful it is?" she returned.

He jerked his handsome head in literal protest at a doubt. "Why that's exactly what I mean by my gratitude for all your trouble. It has been just as if you took a particular interest." She only looked at him by way of answer in such sudden headlong embarrassment, as she was quite aware, that while she remained silent he showed himself checked by her expression. "You *have*—haven't you?—taken a particular interest?"

"Oh a particular interest!" she quavered out, feeling the whole thing—her headlong embarrassment—get terribly the better of her, and wishing, with a sudden scare, all the more to keep her emotion down. She maintained her fixed smile a moment and turned her eyes over the peopled darkness, unconfused now, because there was something much more confusing. This, with a fatal great rush, was simply the fact that they were thus together. They were near, near, and all she had imagined of that had only become more true, more dreadful and overwhelming. She stared straight away in silence till she felt she looked an idiot; then, to say something, to say nothing, she attempted a sound which ended in a flood of tears.

CHAPTER XVI

Her tears helped her really to dissimulate, for she had instantly, in so public a situation, to recover herself. They had come and gone in half a minute, and she immediately explained them. "It's only because I'm tired. It's that—it's that!" Then she added a trifle incoherently: "I shall never see you again."

"Ah but why not?" The mere tone in which her companion asked this satisfied her once for all as to the amount of imagination for which she could count on him. It was naturally not large: it had exhausted itself in having arrived at what he had already touched upon—the sense of an intention in her poor zeal at Cocker's. But any deficiency of this kind was no fault in him: *he* wasn't obliged to have an inferior cleverness—to have second-rate resources and virtues. It had been as if he almost really believed she had simply cried for fatigue, and he accordingly put in some kind confused plea—"You ought really to take something: won't you have something or other *somewhere*?" to which she had made no response but a headshake of a sharpness that settled it. "Why shan't we all the more keep meeting?"

"I mean meeting this way—only this way. At my place there—*that* I've nothing to do with, and I hope of course you'll turn up, with your correspondence, when it suits you. Whether I stay or not, I mean; for I shall probably not stay."

"You're going somewhere else?" he put it with positive anxiety.

"Yes, ever so far away—to the other end of London. There are all sorts of reasons I can't tell you; and it's practically settled. It's better for me, much; and I've only kept on at Cocker's for *you*."

"For me?"

Making out in the dusk that he fairly blushed, she now measured how far he had been from knowing too much. Too much, she called it at present; and that was easy, since it proved so abundantly enough for her that he should simply be where he was. "As we shall never talk this way but to-night—never, never again!—here it all is. I'll say it; I don't care what you think; it doesn't matter; I only want to help you. Besides, you're kind—you're kind. I've been thinking then of leaving for ever so long. But you've come so often—at times—and you've had so much to do, and it has been so pleasant and interesting, that I've remained, I've kept putting off any change. More than once, when I had nearly decided, you've turned up again and I've thought 'Oh no!' That's the simple fact!" She had by this time got her confusion down so completely that she could laugh. "This is what I meant when I said to you just now that I 'knew.' I've known perfectly that you knew I took trouble for you; and that knowledge has been for me, and I seemed to see it was for you, as if there were something—I don't know what to call it!—between us. I mean something unusual and good and awfully nice—something not a bit horrid or vulgar."

She had by this time, she could see, produced a great effect on him; but she would have spoken the truth to herself had she at the same moment declared that she didn't in the least care: all the more that the effect must be one of extreme perplexity. What, in it all, was visibly clear for him, none the less, was that he was tremendously glad he had met her. She held him, and he was astonished at the force of it; he was intent, immensely considerate. His elbow was on the back of the seat, and his head, with the pot-hat pushed quite back, in a boyish way, so that she really saw almost for the first time his forehead and hair, rested on the hand into which he had crumpled his gloves. "Yes," he assented, "it's not a bit horrid or vulgar."

She just hung fire a moment, then she brought out the whole truth. "I'd do anything for you. I'd do anything for you." Never in her life had she known anything so high and fine as this, just letting him have it and bravely and magnificently leaving it. Didn't the place, the associations and circumstances, perfectly make it sound what it wasn't? and wasn't that exactly the beauty?

So she bravely and magnificently left it, and little by little she felt him take it up, take it down, as if they had been on a satin sofa in a boudoir. She had never seen a boudoir, but there had been lots of boudoirs in the telegrams. What she had said at all events sank into him, so that after a minute he simply made a movement that had the result of placing his hand on her own—presently indeed that of her feeling herself firmly enough grasped. There was no pressure she need return, there was none she need decline; she just sat admirably still, satisfied for the time with the surprise and bewilderment of the impression she made on him. His agitation was even greater on the whole than she had at first allowed for. "I say, you know, you mustn't think of leaving!" he at last broke out.

"Of leaving Cocker's, you mean?"

"Yes, you must stay on there, whatever happens, and help a fellow."

She was silent a little, partly because it was so strange and exquisite to feel him watch her as if it really mattered to him and he were almost in suspense. "Then you *have* quite recognised what I've tried to do?" she asked.

"Why, wasn't that exactly what I dashed over from my door just now to thank you for?"

"Yes; so you said."

"And don't you believe it?"

She looked down a moment at his hand, which continued to cover her own; whereupon he presently drew it back, rather restlessly folding his arms. Without answering his question she went on: "Have you ever spoken of me?"

"Spoken of you?"

"Of my being there—of my knowing, and that sort of thing."

"Oh never to a human creature!" he eagerly declared.

She had a small drop at this, which was expressed in another pause, and she then returned to what he had just asked her. "Oh yes, I quite believe you like it—my always being there and our taking things up so familiarly and successfully: if not exactly where we left them," she laughed, "almost always at least at an interesting point!" He was about to say something in reply to this, but her friendly gaiety was quicker. "You want a great many things in life, a great many comforts and helps and luxuries—you want everything as pleasant as possible. Therefore, so far as it's in the power of any particular person to contribute to all that—" She had turned her face to him smiling, just thinking.

"Oh see here!" But he was highly amused. "Well, what then?" he enquired as if to humour her.

"Why the particular person must never fail. We must manage it for you somehow."

He threw back his head, laughing out; he was really exhilarated. "Oh yes, somehow!"

"Well, I think we each do—don't we?—in one little way and another and according to our limited lights. I'm pleased at any rate, for myself, that you are; for I assure you I've done my best."

"You do better than any one!" He had struck a match for another cigarette, and the flame lighted an instant his responsive finished face, magnifying into a pleasant grimace the kindness with which he paid her this tribute. "You're awfully clever, you know; cleverer, cleverer, cleverer—!" He had appeared on the point of making some tremendous statement; then suddenly, puffing his cigarette and shifting almost with violence on his seat, he let it altogether fall.

CHAPTER XVII

In spite of this drop, if not just by reason of it, she felt as if Lady Bradeen, all but named out, had popped straight up; and she practically betrayed her consciousness by waiting a little before she rejoined: "Cleverer than who?"

"Well, if I wasn't afraid you'd think I swagger, I should say—than anybody! If you leave your place there, where shall you go?" he more gravely asked.

"Oh too far for you ever to find me!"

"I'd find you anywhere."

The tone of this was so still more serious that she had but her one acknowledgement. "I'd do anything for you—I'd do anything for you," she repeated. She had already, she felt, said it all; so what did anything more, anything less, matter? That was the very reason indeed why she could, with a lighter note, ease him generously of any awkwardness produced by solemnity, either his own or hers. "Of course it must be nice for you to be able to think there are people all about who feel in such a way."

In immediate appreciation of this, however, he only smoked without looking at her. "But you don't want to give up your present work?" he at last threw out. "I mean you *will* stay in the post-office?"

"Oh yes; I think I've a genius for that."

"Rather! No one can touch you." With this he turned more to her again. "But you can get, with a move, greater advantages?"

"I can get in the suburbs cheaper lodgings. I live with my mother. We need some space. There's a particular place that has other inducements."

He just hesitated. "Where is it?"

"Oh quite out of *your* way. You'd never have time."

"But I tell you I'd go anywhere. Don't you believe it?"

"Yes, for once or twice. But you'd soon see it wouldn't do for you."

He smoked and considered; seemed to stretch himself a little and, with his legs out, surrender himself comfortably. "Well, well, well—I believe everything you say. I take it from you—anything you like—in the most extraordinary way." It struck her certainly—and almost without bitterness—that the way in which she was already, as if she had been an old friend, arranging for him and preparing the only magnificence she could muster, was quite the most extraordinary. "Don't, *don't* go!" he presently went on. "I shall miss you too horribly!"

"So that you just put it to me as a definite request?"—oh how she tried to divest this of all sound of the hardness of bargaining! That ought to have been easy enough, for what was she arranging to get? Before he could answer she had continued: "To be perfectly fair I should tell you I recognise at Cocker's certain strong attractions. All you people come. I like all the horrors."

"The horrors?"

"Those you all—you know the set I mean, *your* set—show me with as good a conscience as if I had no more feeling than a letter-box."

He looked quite excited at the way she put it. "Oh they don't know!"

"Don't know I'm not stupid? No, how should they?"

"Yes, how should they?" said the Captain sympathetically. "But isn't 'horrors' rather strong?"

"What you *do* is rather strong!" the girl promptly returned.

"What I do?"

"Your extravagance, your selfishness, your immorality, your crimes," she pursued, without heeding his expression.

"I *say*!"—her companion showed the queerest stare.

"I like them, as I tell you—I revel in them. But we needn't go into that," she quietly went on; "for all I get out of it is the harmless pleasure of knowing. I know, I know, I know!"—she breathed it ever so gently.

"Yes; that's what has been between us," he answered much more simply.

She could enjoy his simplicity in silence, and for a moment she did so. "If I do stay because you want it—and I'm rather capable of that—there are two or three things I think you ought to remember. One is, you know, that I'm there sometimes for days and weeks together without your ever coming."

"Oh I'll come every day!" he honestly cried.

She was on the point, at this, of imitating with her hand his movement of shortly before; but she checked herself, and there was no want of effect in her soothing substitute. "How can you? How can you?" He had, too manifestly, only to look at it there, in the vulgarly animated gloom, to see that he couldn't; and at this point, by the mere action of his silence, everything they had so definitely not named, the whole presence round which they had been circling, became part of their reference, settled in solidly between them. It was as if then for a minute they sat and saw it all in each other's eyes, saw so much that there was no need of a pretext for sounding it at last. "Your danger, your danger—!" Her voice indeed trembled with it, and she could only for the moment again leave it so.

During this moment he leaned back on the bench, meeting her in silence and with a face that grew more strange. It grew so strange that after a further instant she got straight up. She stood there as if their talk were now over, and he just sat and watched her. It was as if now—owing to the third person they had brought in—they must be more careful; so that the most he could finally say was: "That's where it is!"

"That's where it is!" the girl as guardedly replied. He sat still, and she added: "I won't give you up. Good-bye."

"Good-bye?"—he appealed, but without moving.

"I don't quite see my way, but I won't give you up," she repeated. "There. Good-bye."

It brought him with a jerk to his feet, tossing away his cigarette. His poor face was flushed. "See here—see here!"

"No, I won't; but I must leave you now," she went on as if not hearing him.

"See here—see here!" He tried, from the bench, to take her hand again.

But that definitely settled it for her: this would, after all, be as bad as his asking her to supper. "You mustn't come with me—no, no!"

He sank back, quite blank, as if she had pushed him. "I mayn't see you home?"

"No, no; let me go." He looked almost as if she had struck him, but she didn't care; and the manner in which she spoke—it was literally as if she were angry—had the force of a command. "Stay where you are!"

"See here—see here!" he nevertheless pleaded.

"I won't give you up!" she cried once more—this time quite with passion; on which she got away from him as fast as she could and left him staring after her.

CHAPTER XVIII

Mr. Mudge had lately been so occupied with their famous "plans" that he had neglected for a while the question of her transfer; but down at Bournemouth, which had found itself selected as the field of their recreation by a process consisting, it seemed, exclusively of innumerable pages of the neatest arithmetic in a very greasy but most orderly little pocket-book, the distracting possible melted away—the fleeting absolute ruled the scene. The plans, hour by hour, were simply superseded, and it was much of a rest to the girl, as she sat on the pier and overlooked the sea and the company, to see them evaporate in rosy fumes and to feel that from moment to moment there was less left to cipher about. The week proves blissfully fine, and her mother, at their lodgings—partly to her embarrassment and partly to her relief—struck up with the landlady an alliance that left the younger couple a great deal of freedom. This relative took her pleasure of a week at Bournemouth in a stuffy back-kitchen and endless talks; to that degree even that Mr.

Mudge himself—habitually inclined indeed to a scrutiny of all mysteries and to seeing, as he sometimes admitted, too much in things—made remarks on it as he sat on the cliff with his betrothed, or on the decks of steamers that conveyed them, close-packed items in terrific totals of enjoyment, to the Isle of Wight and the Dorset coast.

He had a lodging in another house, where he had speedily learned the importance of keeping his eyes open, and he made no secret of his suspecting that sinister mutual connivances might spring, under the roof of his companions, from unnatural sociabilities. At the same time he fully recognised that as a source of anxiety, not to say of expense, his future mother-in law would have weighted them more by accompanying their steps than by giving her hostess, in the interest of the tendency they considered that they never mentioned, equivalent pledges as to the tea-caddy and the jam-pot. These were the questions—these indeed the familiar commodities—that he had now to put into the scales; and his betrothed had in consequence, during her holiday, the odd and yet pleasant and almost languid sense of an anticlimax. She had become conscious of an extraordinary collapse, a surrender to stillness and to retrospect. She cared neither to walk nor to sail; it was enough for her to sit on benches and wonder at the sea and taste the air and not be at Cocker's and not see the counter-clerk. She still seemed to wait for something—something in the key of the immense discussions that had mapped out their little week of idleness on the scale of a world-atlas. Something came at last, but without perhaps appearing quite adequately to crown the monument.

Preparation and precaution were, however, the natural flowers of Mr. Mudge's mind, and in proportion as these things declined in one quarter they inevitably bloomed elsewhere. He could always, at the worst, have on Tuesday the project of their taking the Swanage boat on Thursday, and on Thursday that of their ordering minced kidneys on Saturday. He had moreover a constant gift of inexorable enquiry as to where and what they should have gone and have done if they hadn't been exactly as they were. He had in short his resources, and his mistress had never been so conscious of them; on the other hand they never interfered so little with her own. She liked to be as she was—if it could only have lasted. She could accept even without bitterness a rigour of economy so great that the little fee they paid for admission to the pier had to be balanced against other delights. The people at Ladle's and at Thrupp's had *their* ways of amusing themselves, whereas she had to sit and hear Mr. Mudge talk of what he might do if he didn't take a bath, or of the bath he might take if he only hadn't taken something else. He was always with her now, of course, always beside her; she saw him more than "hourly," more than ever yet, more even than he had planned she should do at Chalk Farm. She preferred to sit at the far end, away from the band and the crowd; as to which she had frequent differences with her friend, who reminded her often that they could have only in the thick of it the sense of the money they were getting back. That had little effect on her, for she got back her money by seeing many things, the things of the past year, fall together and connect themselves, undergo the happy relegation that transforms melancholy and misery, passion and effort, into experience and knowledge.

She liked having done with them, as she assured herself she had practically done, and the strange thing was that she neither missed the procession now nor wished to keep her place for it. It had become there, in the sun and the breeze and the sea-smell, a far-away story, a picture of another life. If Mr. Mudge himself liked processions, liked them at Bournemouth and on the pier quite as much as at Chalk Farm or anywhere, she learned after a little not to be worried by his perpetual counting of the figures that made them up. There were dreadful women in particular, usually fat and in men's caps and write shoes, whom he could never let alone—not that *she* cared; it was not the great world, the world of Cocker's and Ladle's and Thrupp's, but it offered an endless field to his faculties of memory, philosophy, and frolic. She had never accepted him so much, never arranged so successfully for making him chatter while she carried on secret conversations. This separate commerce was with herself; and if they both practised a great thrift she had quite mastered that of merely spending words enough to keep him imperturbably and continuously going.

He was charmed with the panorama, not knowing—or at any rate not at all showing that he knew—what far other images peopled her mind than the women in the navy caps and the shop-boys in the blazers. His observations on these types, his general interpretation of the show, brought home to her the prospect of Chalk Farm. She wondered sometimes that he should have derived so little illumination, during his period, from the society at Cocker's. But one evening while their holiday cloudlessly waned he gave her such a proof of his quality as might have made her ashamed of her many suppressions. He brought out something that, in all his overflow, he had been able to keep back till other matters were disposed of. It was the announcement that he was at last ready to marry—that he saw his way. A rise at Chalk Farm had been offered him; he was to be taken into the business, bringing with him a capital the estimation of which by other parties constituted the handsomest recognition yet made of the head on his shoulders. Therefore their waiting was over—it could be a question of a near date. They would settle this date before going back, and he meanwhile had his eye on a sweet little home. He would take her to see it on their first Sunday.

CHAPTER XIX

His having kept this great news for the last, having had such a card up his sleeve and not floated it out in the current of his chatter and the luxury of their leisure, was one of those incalculable strokes by which he could still affect her; the kind of thing that reminded her of the latent force that had ejected the drunken soldier—an example of the profundity of which his promotion was the proof. She listened a while in silence, on this occasion, to the wafted strains of the music; she took it in as she had not quite done before that her future was now constituted. Mr. Mudge was distinctly her fate; yet at this moment she turned her face quite away from him, showing him so long a mere quarter of her cheek that she at last again heard his voice. He couldn't see a pair of tears that were partly the reason of her delay to give him the assurance he required; but he expressed at a venture the hope that she had had her fill of Cocker's.

She was finally able to turn back. "Oh quite. There's nothing going on. No one comes but the Americans at Thrupp's, and *they* don't do much. They don't seem to have a secret in the world."

"Then the extraordinary reason you've been giving me for holding on there has ceased to work?"

She thought a moment. "Yes, that one. I've seen the thing through—I've got them all in my pocket."

"So you're ready to come?"

For a little again she made no answer. "No, not yet, all the same. I've still got a reason—a different one."

He looked her all over as if it might have been something she kept in her mouth or her glove or under her jacket—something she was even sitting upon. "Well, I'll have it, please."

"I went out the other night and sat in the Park with a gentleman," she said at last.

Nothing was ever seen like his confidence in her and she wondered a little now why it didn't irritate her. It only gave her ease and space, as she felt, for telling him the whole truth that no one knew. It had arrived at present at her really wanting to do that, and yet to do it not in the least for Mr. Mudge, but altogether and only for herself. This truth filled out for her there the whole experience about to relinquish, suffused and coloured it as a picture that she should keep and that, describe it as she might, no one but herself would ever really see. Moreover she had no desire whatever to make Mr. Mudge jealous; there would be no amusement in it, for the amusement she had lately known had spoiled her for lower pleasures. There were even no materials for it. The odd thing was how she never doubted that, properly handled, his passion was poisonable; what had happened was that he had cannily selected a partner with no poison to distil. She read then and there that she should never interest herself in anybody as to whom some other sentiment, some superior view, wouldn't be sure to interfere for him with jealousy. "And what did you get out of that?" he asked with a concern that was not in the least for his honour.

"Nothing but a good chance to promise him I wouldn't forsake him. He's one of my customers."

"Then it's for him not to forsake you."

"Well, he won't. It's all right. But I must just keep on as long as he may want me."

"Want you to sit with him in the Park?"

"He may want me for that—but I shan't. I rather liked it, but once, under the circumstances, is enough. I can do better for him in another manner."

"And what manner, pray?"

"Well, elsewhere."

"Elsewhere?—I *say*!"

This was an ejaculation used also by Captain Everard, but oh with what a different sound! "You needn't 'say'—there's nothing to be said. And yet you ought perhaps to know."

"Certainly I ought. But what—up to now?"

"Why exactly what I told him. That I'd do anything for him."

"What do you mean by 'anything'?"

"Everything."

Mr. Mudge's immediate comment on this statement was to draw from his pocket a crumpled paper containing the remains of half a pound of "sundries." These sundries had figured conspicuously in his prospective sketch of their tour, but it was only at the end of three days that they had defined themselves unmistakeably as chocolate-creams. "Have another?—*that* one," he said. She had another, but not the one he indicated, and then he continued: "What took place afterwards?"

"Afterwards?"

"What did you do when you had told him you'd do everything?"

"I simply came away."

"Out of the Park?"

"Yes, leaving him there. I didn't let him follow me."

"Then what did you let him do?"

"I didn't let him do anything."

Mr. Mudge considered an instant. "Then what did you go there for?" His tone was even slightly critical.

"I didn't quite know at the time. It was simply to be with him, I suppose—just once. He's in danger, and I wanted him to know I know it. It makes meeting him—at Cocker's, since it's that I want to stay on for—more interesting."

"It makes it mighty interesting for *me*!" Mr. Mudge freely declared. "Yet he didn't follow you?" he asked. "*I* would!"

"Yes, of course. That was the way you began, you know. You're awfully inferior to him."

"Well, my dear, you're not inferior to anybody. You've got a cheek! What's he in danger of?"

"Of being found out. He's in love with a lady—and it isn't right—and *I've* found him out."

"That'll be a look-out for *me*!" Mr. Mudge joked. "You mean she has a husband?"

"Never mind what she has! They're in awful danger, but his is the worst, because he's in danger from her too."

"Like me from you—the woman *I* love? If he's in the same funk as me—"

"He's in a worse one. He's not only afraid of the lady—he's afraid of other things."

Mr. Mudge selected another chocolate-cream. "Well, I'm only afraid of one! But how in the world can you help this party?"

"I don't know—perhaps not at all. But so long as there's a chance—"

"You won't come away?"

"No, you've got to wait for me."

Mr. Mudge enjoyed what was in his mouth. "And what will he give you?"

"Give me?"

"If you do help him."

"Nothing. Nothing in all the wide world."

"Then what will he give *me*?" Mr. Mudge enquired. "I mean for waiting."

The girl thought a moment; then she got up to walk. "He never heard of you," she replied.

"You haven't mentioned me?"

"We never mention anything. What I've told you is just what I've found out."

Mr. Mudge, who had remained on the bench, looked up at her; she often preferred to be quiet when he proposed to walk, but now that he seemed to wish to sit she had a desire to move. "But you haven't told me what *he* has found out."

She considered her lover. "He'd never find *you*, my dear!"

Her lover, still on his seat, appealed to her in something of the attitude in which she had last left Captain Everard, but the impression was not the same. "Then where do I come in?"

"You don't come in at all. That's just the beauty of it!"—and with this she turned to mingle with the multitude collected round the band. Mr. Mudge presently overtook her and drew her arm into his own with a quiet force that expressed the serenity of possession; in consonance with which it was only when they parted for the night at her door that he referred again to what she had told him.

"Have you seen him since?"

"Since the night in the Park? No, not once."

"Oh, what a cad!" said Mr. Mudge.

CHAPTER XX

It was not till the end of October that she saw Captain Everard again, and on that occasion—the only one of all the series on which hindrance had been so utter—no communication with him proved possible. She had made out even from the cage that it was a charming golden day: a patch of hazy autumn sunlight lay across the sanded floor and also, higher up, quickened into brightness a row of ruddy bottled syrups. Work was slack and the place in general empty; the town, as they said in the cage, had not waked up, and the feeling of the day likened itself to something than in happier conditions she would have thought of romantically as Saint Martin's summer. The counter-clerk had gone to his dinner; she herself was busy with arrears of postal jobs, in the midst of which she became aware that Captain Everard had apparently been in the shop a minute and that Mr. Buckton had already seized him.

He had as usual half a dozen telegrams; and when he saw that she saw him and their eyes met he gave, on bowing to her, an exaggerated laugh in which she read a new consciousness. It was a confession of awkwardness; it seemed to tell her that of course he knew he ought better to have kept his head, ought to have been clever enough to wait, on some pretext, till he should have found her free. Mr. Buckton was a long time with him, and her attention was soon demanded by other visitors; so that nothing passed between them but the fulness of their silence. The look she took from him was his greeting, and the other one a simple sign of the eyes sent her before going out. The only token they exchanged therefore was his tacit assent to her wish that since they couldn't attempt a certain frankness they should attempt nothing at all. This was her intense preference; she could be as still and cold as any one when that was the sole solution.

Yet more than any contact hitherto achieved these counted instants struck her as marking a step: they were built so—just in the mere flash—on the recognition of his now definitely knowing what it was she would do for him. The "anything, anything" she had uttered in the Park went to and fro between them and under the poked-out china that interposed. It had all at last even put on the air of their not needing now clumsily to manoeuvre to converse: their former little postal make-believes, the intense implications of questions and answers and change, had become in the light of the personal fact, of their having had their moment, a possibility comparatively poor. It was as if they had met for all time—it exerted on their being in presence again an influence so prodigious. When she watched herself, in the memory of that night, walk away from him as if she were making an end, she found something too pitiful in the primness of such a gait. Hadn't she precisely established on the part of each a consciousness that could end only with death?

It must be admitted that in spite of this brave margin an irritation, after he had gone, remained with her; a sense that presently became one with a still sharper hatred of Mr. Buckton, who, on her friend's withdrawal, had retired with the telegrams to the sounder and left her the other work. She knew indeed she should have a chance to see them, when she would, on file; and she was divided, as the day went on, between the two impressions of all that was lost and all that was re-asserted. What beset her above all, and as she had almost never known it before, was the desire to bound straight out, to overtake the autumn afternoon before it passed away for ever and hurry off to the Park and perhaps be with him there again on a bench. It became for an hour a fantastic vision with her that he might just have gone to sit and wait for her. She could almost hear him, through the tick of the sounder, scatter with his stick, in his impatience, the fallen leaves of October. Why should such a vision seize her at this particular moment with such a shake? There was a time—from four to five—when she could have cried with happiness and rage.

Business quickened, it seemed, toward five, as if the town did wake up; she had therefore more to do, and she went through it with little sharp stampings and jerkings: she made the crisp postal-orders fairly snap while she breathed to herself "It's the last day—the last day!" The last day of what? She couldn't have told. All she knew now was that if she were out of the cage she wouldn't in the least have minded, this time, its not yet being dark. She would have gone straight toward Park Chambers and have hung about there till no matter when. She would have waited, stayed, rung, asked, have gone in, sat on the stairs. What the day was the last of was probably, to her strained inner sense, the group of golden ones, of any occasion for seeing the hazy sunshine slant at that angle into the smelly shop, of any range of chances for his wishing still to repeat to her the two words she had in the Park scarcely let him bring out. "See here—see here!"—the sound of these two words had been with her perpetually; but it was in her ears to-day without mercy, with a loudness that grew and grew. What was it they then expressed? what was it he had wanted her to see? She seemed, whatever it was, perfectly to see it now—to see that if she should just chuck the whole thing, should have a great and beautiful courage, he would somehow make everything up to her. When the clock struck five she was on the very point of saying to Mr. Buckton that she was deadly ill and rapidly getting worse. This announcement was on her lips, and she had quite composed the pale hard face she would offer him: "I can't stop—I must go home. If I feel better, later on, I'll come back. I'm very sorry, but I *must* go." At that instant Captain Everard once more stood there, producing in her agitated spirit, by his real presence, the strangest, quickest revolution. He stopped her off without knowing it, and by the time he had been a minute in the shop she felt herself saved.

That was from the first minute how she thought of it. There were again other persons with whom she was occupied, and again the situation could only be expressed by their silence. It was expressed, of a truth, in a larger phrase than ever yet, for her eyes now spoke to him with a kind of supplication. "Be quiet, be quiet!" they pleaded; and they saw his own reply: "I'll do whatever you say; I won't even look at you—see, see!" They kept conveying thus, with the friendliest liberality, that they wouldn't look, quite positively wouldn't. What she was to see was that he hovered at the other end of the counter, Mr. Buckton's end, and surrendered himself again to that frustration. It quickly proved so great indeed that what she was to see further was how he turned away before he was attended to, and hung off, waiting, smoking, looking about the shop; how he went over to Mr. Cocker's own counter and appeared to price things, gave in fact presently two or three orders and put down money, stood there a long time with his back to her, considerately abstaining from any glance round to see if she were free. It at last came to pass in this way that he had remained in the shop longer than she had ever yet known to do, and that, nevertheless, when he did turn about she could see him time himself—she was freshly taken up—and cross straight to her postal subordinate, whom some one else had released. He had in his hand all this while neither letters nor telegrams, and now that he was close to her—for she was close to the counter-clerk—it brought her heart into her mouth merely to see him look at her neighbour and open his lips. She was too nervous to bear it. He asked for a Post-Office Guide, and the young man whipped out a new one; whereupon he said he wished not to purchase, but only to consult one a moment; with which, the copy kept on loan being produced, he once more wandered off.

What was he doing to her? What did he want of her? Well, it was just the aggravation of his "See here!" She felt at this moment strangely and portentously afraid of him—had in her ears the hum of a sense that, should it come to that kind of tension, she must fly on the spot to Chalk Farm. Mixed with her dread and with her reflexion was the idea that, if he wanted her so much as he seemed to show, it might be after all simply to do for him the "anything" she had promised, the "everything" she had thought it so fine to bring out to Mr. Mudge. He might want her to help him, might have some particular appeal; though indeed his manner didn't denote that—denoted on the contrary an embarrassment, an indecision, something of a desire not so much to be helped as to be treated rather more nicely than she had treated him the other time. Yes, he considered quite probably that he had help rather to offer than to ask for. Still, none the less, when he again saw her free he continued to keep away from her; when he came back with his thumbed Guide it was Mr. Buckton he caught—it was from Mr. Buckton he obtained half-a-crown's-worth of stamps.

After asking for the stamps he asked, quite as a second thought, for a postal-order for ten shillings. What did he want with so many stamps when he wrote so few letters? How could he enclose a postal-order in a telegram? She expected him, the next thing, to go into the corner and make up one of his telegrams—half a dozen of them—on purpose to prolong his presence. She had so completely stopped looking at him that she could only guess his movements—guess even where his eyes rested. Finally she saw him make a dash that might have been toward the nook where the forms were hung; and at this she suddenly felt that she couldn't keep it up. The counter-clerk had just taken a telegram from a slavey, and, to give herself something to cover her, she snatched it out of his hand. The gesture was so violent that he gave her in return an odd look, and she also perceived that Mr. Buckton noticed it. The latter personage, with a quick stare at her, appeared for an instant to wonder whether his snatching it in *his* turn mightn't be the thing she would least like, and she anticipated this practical criticism by the frankest glare she had ever given him. It sufficed: this time it paralysed him; and she sought with her trophy the refuge of the sounder.

CHAPTER XXI

It was repeated the next day; it went on for three days; and at the end of that time she knew what to think. When, at the beginning, she had emerged from her temporary shelter Captain Everard had quitted the shop; and he had not come again that evening, as it had struck her he possibly might—might all the more easily that there were numberless persons who came, morning and afternoon, numberless times, so that he wouldn't necessarily have attracted attention. The second day it was different and yet on the whole worse. His access to her had become possible—she felt herself even reaping the fruit of her yesterday's glare at Mr. Buckton; but transacting his business with him didn't simplify—it could, in spite of the rigour of circumstance, feed so her new conviction. The rigour was tremendous, and his telegrams—not now mere pretexts for getting at her—were apparently genuine; yet the conviction had taken but a night to develop. It could be simply enough expressed; she had had the glimmer of it the day before in her idea that he needed no more help than she had already given; that it was help he himself was prepared to render. He had come up to town but for three or four days; he had been absolutely obliged to be absent after the other time; yet he would, now that he was face to face with her, stay on as much longer as she liked. Little by little it was thus clarified, though from the first flash of his re-appearance she had read into it the real essence.

That was what the night before, at eight o'clock, her hour to go, had made her hang back and dawdle. She did last things or pretended to do them; to be in the cage had suddenly become her safety, and she was literally afraid of the alternate self who might be waiting outside. *He* might be waiting; it was he who was her alternate self, and of him she was afraid. The most extraordinary change had taken place in her from the moment of her catching the impression he seemed to have returned on purpose to give her. Just before she had done so, on that bewitched afternoon, she had seen herself approach without a scruple the porter at Park Chambers; then as the effect of the rush of a consciousness quite altered she had on at last quitting Cocker's, gone straight home for the first time since her return from Bournemouth. She had passed his door every night for weeks, but nothing would have induced her to pass it now. This change was the tribute of her fear—the result of a change in himself as to which she needed no more explanation than his mere face vividly gave her; strange though it was to find an element of deterrence in the object that she regarded as the most beautiful in the world. He had taken it from her in the Park that night that she wanted him not to propose to her to sup; but he had put away the lesson by this time—he practically proposed supper every time he looked at her. This was what, for that matter, mainly filled the three days. He came in twice on each of these, and it was as if he came in to give her a chance to relent. That was after all, she said to herself in the intervals, the most that he did. There were ways, she fully recognised, in which he spared her, and other particular ways as to which she meant that her silence should be full to him of exquisite pleading. The most particular of all was his not being outside, at the corner, when she quitted the place for the night. This he might so easily have been—so easily if he hadn't been so nice. She continued to recognise in his forbearance the fruit of her dumb supplication, and the only compensation he found for it was the harmless freedom of being able to appear to say: "Yes, I'm in town only for three or four days, but, you know, I *would* stay on." He struck her as calling attention each day, each hour, to the rapid ebb of time; he exaggerated to the point of putting it that there were only two days more, that there was at last, dreadfully, only one.

There were other things still that he struck her as doing with a special intention; as to the most marked of which—unless indeed it were the most obscure—she might well have marvelled that it didn't seem to her more horrid. It was either the frenzy of her imagination or the disorder of his baffled passion that gave her once or twice the vision of his putting down redundant money—sovereigns not concerned with the little payments he was perpetually making—so that she might give him some sign of helping him to slip them over to her. What was most extraordinary in this impression was the amount of excuse that, with some incoherence, she found for him. He wanted to pay her because there was nothing to pay her for. He wanted to offer her things he knew she wouldn't take. He wanted to show her how much he respected her by giving her the supreme chance to show him she was respectable. Over the dryest transactions, at any rate, their eyes had out these questions. On the third day he put in a telegram that had evidently something of the same point as the stray sovereigns—a message that was in the first place concocted and that on a second thought he took back from her before she had stamped it. He had given her time to read it and had only then bethought himself that he had better not send it. If it was not to Lady Bradeen at Twindle—where she knew her ladyship then to be—this was because an address to Doctor Buzzard at Brickwood was just as good, with the added merit of its not giving away quite so much a person whom he had still, after all, in a manner to consider. It was of course most complicated, only half lighted; but there was, discernibly enough, a scheme of communication in which Lady Bradeen at Twindle and Dr. Buzzard at Brickwood were, within limits, one and the same person. The words he had shown her and then taken back consisted, at all events, of the brief but vivid phrase "Absolutely impossible." The point was not that she should transmit it; the point was just that she should see it. What was absolutely impossible was that before he had settled something at Cocker's he should go either to Twindle or to Brickwood.

The logic of this, in turn, for herself, was that she could lend herself to no settlement so long as she so intensely knew. What she knew was that he was, almost under peril of life, clenched in a situation: therefore how could she also know where a poor girl in the P.O. might really stand? It was more and more between them that if he might convey to her he was free, with all the impossible locked away into a closed chapter, her own case might become different for her, she might understand and meet him and listen. But he could convey nothing of the sort, and he only fidgeted and floundered in his want of power. The chapter wasn't in the least closed, not for the other party; and the other party had a pull, somehow and somewhere: this his whole attitude and expression confessed, at the same time that they entreated her not to remember and not to mind. So long as she did remember and did mind he could only circle about and go and come, doing futile things of which he was ashamed. He was ashamed of his two words to Dr. Buzzard; he went out of the shop as soon as he had crumpled up the paper again and thrust it into his pocket. It had been an abject little exposure of dreadful impossible passion. He appeared in fact to be too ashamed to come back. He had once more left town, and a first week elapsed, and a second. He had had naturally to return to the real mistress of his fate; she had insisted—she knew how to insist, and he couldn't put in another hour. There was always a day when she called time. It was known to our young friend moreover that he had now been dispatching telegrams from other offices. She knew at last so much that she had quite lost her earlier sense of merely guessing. There were no different shades of distinctness—it all bounced out.

CHAPTER XXII

Eighteen days elapsed, and she had begun to think it probable she should never see him again. He too then understood now: he had made out that she had secrets and reasons and impediments, that even a poor girl at the P.O. might have her complications. With the charm she had cast on him lightened by distance he had suffered a final delicacy to speak to him, had made up his mind that it would be only decent to let her alone. Never so much as during these latter days had she felt the precariousness of their relation—the happy beautiful untroubled original one, if it could only have been restored—in which the public servant and the casual public only were concerned. It hung at the best by the merest silken thread, which was at the mercy of any accident and might snap at any minute. She arrived by the end of the fortnight at the highest sense of actual fitness, never doubting that her decision was now complete. She would just give him a few days more to come back to her on a proper impersonal basis—for even to an embarrassing representative of the casual public a public servant with a conscience did owe something—and then would signify to Mr. Mudge that she was ready for the little home. It had been visited, in the further talk she had had with him at Bournemouth, from garret to cellar, and they had especially lingered, with their respectively darkened brows, before the niche into which it was to be broached to her mother that she must find means to fit.

He had put it to her more definitely than before that his calculations had allowed for that dingy presence, and he had thereby marked the greatest impression he had ever made on her. It was a stroke superior even again to his handling of the drunken soldier. What she considered that in the face of it she hung on at Cocker's for was something she could only have described as the common fairness of a last word. Her actual last word had been, till it should be superseded, that she wouldn't forsake her other friend, and it stuck to her through thick and thin that she was still at her post and on her honour. This other friend had shown so much beauty of conduct already that he would surely after all just re-appear long enough to relieve her, to give her something she could take away. She saw it, caught it, at times, his parting present; and there were moments when she felt herself sitting like a beggar with a hand held out to almsgiver who only fumbled. She hadn't taken the sovereigns, but she *would* take the penny. She heard, in imagination, on the counter, the ring of the copper. "Don't put yourself out any longer," he would say, "for so bad a case. You've done all there is to be done. I thank and acquit and release you. Our lives take us. I don't know much—though I've really been interested—about yours, but I suppose you've got one. Mine at any rate will take *me*—and where it will. Heigh-ho! Good-bye." And then once more, for the sweetest faintest flower of all: "Only, I say—see here!" She had framed the whole picture with a squareness that included also the image of how again she would decline to "see there," decline, as she might say, to see anywhere, see anything. Yet it befell that just in the fury of this escape she saw more than ever.

He came back one night with a rush, near the moment of their closing, and showed her a face so different and new, so upset and anxious, that almost anything seemed to look out of it but clear recognition. He poked in a telegram very much as if the simple sense of pressure, the distress of extreme haste, had blurred the remembrance of where in particular he was. But as she met his eyes a light came; it broke indeed on the spot into a positive conscious glare. That made up for everything, since it was an instant proclamation of the celebrated "danger"; it seemed to pour things out in a flood. "Oh yes, here it is—it's upon me at last! Forget, for God's sake, my having worried or bored you, and just help me, just *save* me, by getting this off without the loss of a second!" Something grave had clearly occurred, a crisis declared itself. She recognised immediately the person to whom the telegram was addressed—the Miss Dolman of Parade Lodge to whom Lady Bradeen had wired, at Dover, on the last occasion, and whom she had then, with her recollection of previous arrangements, fitted into a particular setting. Miss Dolman had figured before and not figured since, but she was now the subject of an imperative appeal. "Absolutely necessary to see you. Take last train Victoria if you can catch it. If not, earliest morning, and answer me direct either way."

"Reply paid?" said the girl. Mr. Buckton had just departed and the counter-clerk was at the sounder. There was no other representative of the public, and she had never yet, as it seemed to her, not even in the street or in the Park, been so alone with him.

"Oh yes, reply paid, and as sharp as possible, please."

She affixed the stamps in a flash. "She'll catch the train!" she then declared to him breathlessly, as if she could absolutely guarantee it.

"I don't know—I hope so. It's awfully important. So kind of you. Awfully sharp, please." It was wonderfully innocent now, his oblivion of all but his danger. Anything else that had ever passed between them was utterly out of it. Well, she had wanted him to be impersonal!

There was less of the same need therefore, happily, for herself; yet she only took time, before she flew to the sounder, to gasp at him: "You're in trouble?"

"Horrid, horrid—there's a row!" But they parted, on it, in the next breath; and as she dashed at the sounder, almost pushing, in her violence, the counter-clerk off the stool, she caught the bang with which, at Cocker's door, in his further precipitation, he closed the apron of the cab into which he had leaped. As he rebounded to some other precaution suggested by his alarm, his appeal to Miss Dolman flashed straight away.

But she had not, on the morrow, been in the place five minutes before he was with her again, still more discomposed and quite, now, as she said to herself, like a frightened child coming to its mother. Her companions were there, and she felt it to be remarkable how, in the presence of his agitation, his mere scared exposed nature, she suddenly ceased to mind. It came to her as it had never come to her before that with absolute directness and assurance they might carry almost anything off. He had nothing to send—she was sure he had been wiring all over—and yet his business was evidently huge. There was nothing but that in his eyes—not a glimmer of reference or memory. He was almost haggard with anxiety and had clearly not slept a wink. Her pity for him would have given her any courage, and she seemed to know at last why she had been such a fool. "She didn't come?" she panted.

"Oh yes, she came; but there has been some mistake. We want a telegram."

"A telegram?"

"One that was sent from here ever so long ago. There was something in it that has to be recovered. Something very, *very* important, please—we want it immediately."

He really spoke to her as if she had been some strange young woman at Knightsbridge or Paddington; but it had no other effect on her than to give her the measure of his tremendous flurry. Then it was that, above all, she felt how much she had missed in the gaps and blanks and absent answers—how much she had had to dispense with: it was now black darkness save for this little wild red flare. So much as that she saw, so much her mind dealt with. One of the lovers was quaking somewhere out of town, and the other was quaking just where he stood. This was vivid enough, and after an instant she knew it was all she wanted. She wanted no detail, no fact—she wanted no nearer vision of discovery or shame. "When was your telegram? Do you mean you sent it from here?" She tried to do the young woman at Knightsbridge.

"Oh yes, from here—several weeks ago. Five, six, seven"—he was confused and impatient—"don't you remember?"

"Remember?" she could scarcely keep out of her face, at the word, the strangest of smiles.

But the way he didn't catch what it meant was perhaps even stranger still. "I mean, don't you keep the old ones?"

"For a certain time."

"But how long?"

She thought; she *must* do the young woman, and she knew exactly what the young woman would say and, still more, wouldn't. "Can you give me the date?"

"Oh God, no! It was some time or other in August—toward the end. It was to the same address as the one I gave you last night."

"Oh!" said the girl, knowing at this the deepest thrill she had ever felt. It came to her there, with her eyes on his face, that she held the whole thing in her hand, held it as she held her pencil, which might have broken at that instant in her tightened grip. This made her feel like the very fountain of fate, but the emotion was such a flood that she had to press it back with all her force. That was positively the reason, again, of her flute-like Paddington tone. "You can't give us anything a little nearer?" Her "little" and her "us" came straight from Paddington. These things were no false note for him—his difficulty absorbed them all. The eyes with which he pressed her, and in the depths of which she read terror and rage and literal tears, were just the same he would have shown any other prim person.

"I don't know the date. I only know the thing went from here, and just about the time I speak of. It wasn't delivered, you see. We've got to recover it."

CHAPTER XXIII

She was as struck with the beauty of his plural pronoun as she had judged he might be with that of her own; but she knew now so well what she was about that she could almost play with him and with her new-born joy. "You say 'about the time you speak of.' But I don't think you speak of an exact time—*do* you?"

He looked splendidly helpless. "That's just what I want to find out. Don't you keep the old ones?—can't you look it up?"

Our young lady—still at Paddington—turned the question over. "It wasn't delivered?"

"Yes, it *was*; yet, at the same time, don't you know? it wasn't." He just hung back, but he brought it out. "I mean it was intercepted, don't you know? and there was something in it." He paused again and, as if to further his quest and woo and supplicate success and recovery, even smiled with an effort at the agreeable that was almost ghastly and that turned the knife in her tenderness. What must be the pain of it all, of the open gulf and the throbbing fever, when this was the mere hot breath? "We want to get what was in it—to know what it was."

"I see—I see." She managed just the accent they had at Paddington when they stared like dead fish. "And you have no clue?"

"Not at all—I've the clue I've just given you."

"Oh the last of August?" If she kept it up long enough she would make him really angry.

"Yes, and the address, as I've said."

"Oh the same as last night?"

He visibly quivered, as with a gleam of hope; but it only poured oil on her quietude, and she was still deliberate. She ranged some papers. "Won't you look?" he went on.

"I remember your coming," she replied.

He blinked with a new uneasiness; it might have begun to come to him, through her difference, that he was somehow different himself. "You were much quicker then, you know!"

"So were you—you must do me that justice," she answered with a smile. "But let me see. Wasn't it Dover?"

"Yes, Miss Dolman—"

"Parade Lodge, Parade Terrace?"

"Exactly—thank you so awfully much!" He began to hope again. "Then you *have* it—the other one?"

She hesitated afresh; she quite dangled him. "It was brought by a lady?"

"Yes; and she put in by mistake something wrong. That's what we've got to get hold of!"

Heavens, what was he going to say?—flooding poor Paddington with wild betrayals! She couldn't too much, for her joy, dangle him, yet she couldn't either, for his dignity, warn or control or check him. What she found herself doing was just to treat herself to the middle way. "It was intercepted?"

"It fell into the wrong hands. But there's something in it," he continued to blurt out, "that may be all right. That is, if it's wrong, don't you know? It's all right if it's wrong," he remarkably explained.

What *was* he, on earth, going to say? Mr. Buckton and the counter-clerk were already interested; no one *would* have the decency to come in; and she was divided between her particular terror for him and her general curiosity. Yet she already saw with what brilliancy she could add, to carry the thing off, a little false knowledge to all her real. "I quite understand," she said with benevolent, with almost patronising quickness. "The lady has forgotten what she did put."

"Forgotten most wretchedly, and it's an immense inconvenience. It has only just been found that it didn't get there; so that if we could immediately have it—"

"Immediately?"

"Every minute counts. You *have*," he pleaded, "surely got them on file?"

"So that you can see it on the spot?"

"Yes, please—this very minute." The counter rang with his knuckles, with the knob of his stick, with his panic of alarm. "Do, *do* hunt it up!" he repeated.

"I dare say we could get it for you," the girl sweetly returned.

"Get it?"—he looked aghast. "When?"

"Probably by to-morrow."

"Then it isn't here?"—his face was pitiful.

She caught only the uncovered gleams that peeped out of the blackness, and she wondered what complication, even among the most supposable, the very worst, could be bad enough to account for the degree of his terror. There were twists and turns, there were places where the screw drew blood, that she couldn't guess. She was more and more glad she didn't want to. "It has been sent on."

"But how do you know if you don't look?"

She gave him a smile that was meant to be, in the absolute irony of its propriety, quite divine. "It was August 23rd, and we've nothing later here than August 27th."

Something leaped into his face. "27th—23rd? Then you're sure? You know?"

She felt she scarce knew what—as if she might soon be pounced upon for some lurid connexion with a scandal. It was the queerest of all sensations, for she had heard, she had read, of these things, and the wealth of her intimacy with them at Cocker's might be supposed to have schooled and seasoned her. This particular one that she had really quite lived with was, after all, an old story; yet what it had been before was dim and distant beside the touch under which she now winced. Scandal?—it had never been but a silly word. Now it was a great tense surface, and the surface was somehow Captain Everard's wonderful face. Deep down in his eyes a picture, a scene—a great place like a chamber of justice, where, before a watching crowd, a poor girl, exposed but heroic, swore with a quavering voice to a document, proved an *alibi*, supplied a link. In this picture she bravely took her place. "It was the 23rd."

"Then can't you get it this morning—or some time to-day?"

She considered, still holding him with her look, which she then turned on her two companions, who were by this time unreservedly enlisted. She didn't care—not a scrap, and she glanced about for a piece of paper. With this she had to recognise the rigour of official thrift—a morsel of blackened blotter was the only loose paper to be seen. "Have you got a card?" she said to her visitor. He was quite away from Paddington now, and the next instant, pocket-book in hand, he had whipped a card out. She gave no glance at the name on it—only turned it to the other side. She continued to hold him, she felt at present, as she had never held him; and her command of her colleagues was for the moment not less marked. She wrote something on the back of the card and pushed it across to him.

He fairly glared at it. "Seven, nine, four—"

"Nine, six, one"—she obligingly completed the number. "Is it right?" she smiled.

He took the whole thing in with a flushed intensity; then there broke out in him a visibility of relief that was simply a tremendous exposure. He shone at them all like a tall lighthouse, embracing even, for sympathy, the blinking young men. "By all the powers—it's wrong!" And without another look, without a word of thanks, without time for anything or anybody, he turned on them the broad back of his great stature, straightened his triumphant shoulders, and strode out of the place.

She was left confronted with her habitual critics. "'If it's wrong it's all right!'" she extravagantly quoted to them.

The counter-clerk was really awe-stricken. "But how did you know, dear?"

"I remembered, love!"

Mr. Buckton, on the contrary, was rude. "And what game is that, miss?"

No happiness she had ever known came within miles of it, and some minutes elapsed before she could recall herself sufficiently to reply that it was none of his business.

CHAPTER XXIV

If life at Cocker's, with the dreadful drop of August, had lost something of its savour, she had not been slow to infer that a heavier blight had fallen on the graceful industry of Mrs. Jordan.

With Lord Rye and Lady Ventnor and Mrs. Bubb all out of town, with the blinds down on all the homes of luxury, this ingenious woman might well have found her wonderful taste left quite on her hands. She bore up, however, in a way that began by exciting much of her young friend's esteem; they perhaps even more frequently met as the wine of life flowed less free from other sources, and each, in the lack of better diversion, carried on with more mystification for the other an intercourse that consisted not a little in peeping out and drawing back. Each waited for the other to commit herself, each profusely curtained for the other the limits of low horizons. Mrs. Jordan was indeed probably the more reckless skirmisher; nothing could exceed her frequent incoherence unless it was indeed her occasional bursts of confidence. Her account of her private affairs rose and fell like a flame in the wind—sometimes the bravest bonfire and sometimes a handful of ashes. This our young woman took to be an effect of the position, at one moment and another, of the famous door of the great world. She had been struck in one of her ha'penny volumes with the translation of a French proverb according to which such a door, any door, had to be either open or shut; and it seemed part of the precariousness of Mrs. Jordan's life that hers mostly managed to be neither. There had been occasions when it appeared to gape wide—fairly to woo her across its threshold; there had been others, of an order distinctly disconcerting, when it was all but banged in her face. On the whole, however, she had evidently not lost heart; these still belonged to the class of things in spite of which she looked well. She intimated that the profits of her trade had swollen so as to float her through any state of the tide, and she had, besides this, a hundred profundities and explanations.

She rose superior, above all, on the happy fact that there were always gentlemen in town and that gentlemen were her greatest admirers; gentlemen from the City in especial—as to whom she was full of information about the passion and pride excited in such breasts by the elements of her charming commerce. The City men *did* in short go in for flowers. There was a certain type of awfully smart stockbroker—Lord Rye called them Jews and bounders, but she didn't care—whose extravagance, she more than once threw out, had really, if one had any conscience, to be forcibly restrained. It was not perhaps a pure love of beauty: it was a matter of vanity and a sign of business; they wished to crush their rivals, and that was one of their weapons. Mrs. Jordan's shrewdness was extreme; she knew in any case her customer—she dealt, as she said, with all sorts; and it was at the worst a race for her—a race even in the dull months—from one set of chambers to another. And then, after all, there were also still the ladies; the ladies of stockbroking circles were perpetually up and down. They were not quite perhaps Mrs. Bubb or Lady Ventnor; but you couldn't tell the difference unless you quarrelled with them, and then you knew it only by their making-up sooner. These ladies formed the branch of her subject on which she most swayed in the breeze; to that degree that her confidant had ended with an inference or two tending to banish regret for opportunities not embraced. There were indeed tea-gowns that Mrs. Jordan described—but tea-gowns were not the whole of respectability, and it was odd that a clergyman's widow should sometimes speak as if she almost thought so. She came back, it was true, unfailingly to Lord Rye, never, evidently, quite losing sight of him even on the longest excursions. That he was kindness itself had become in fact the very moral it all pointed—pointed in strange flashes of the poor woman's nearsighted eyes. She launched at her young friend portentous looks, solemn heralds of some extraordinary communication. The communication itself, from week to week, hung fire; but it was to the facts over which it hovered that she owed her power of going on. "They *are*, in one way *and* another," she often emphasised, "a tower of strength"; and as the allusion was to the aristocracy the girl could quite wonder why, if they were so in "one way," they should require to be so in two. She thoroughly knew, however, how many ways Mrs. Jordan counted in. It all meant simply that her fate was pressing her close. If that fate was to be sealed at the matrimonial altar it was perhaps not remarkable that she shouldn't come all at once to the scratch of overwhelming a mere telegraphist. It would necessarily present to such a person a prospect of regretful sacrifice. Lord Rye—if it *was* Lord Rye—wouldn't be "kind" to a nonentity of that sort, even though people quite as good had been.

One Sunday afternoon in November they went, by arrangement, to church together; after which—on the inspiration of the moment the arrangement had not included it—they proceeded to Mrs. Jordan's lodging in the region of Maida Vale. She had raved to her friend about her service of predilection; she was excessively "high," and had more than once wished to introduce the girl to the same comfort and privilege. There was a thick brown fog and Maida Vale tasted of acrid smoke; but they had been sitting among chants and incense and wonderful music, during which, though the effect of such things on her mind was great, our young lady had indulged in a series of reflexions but indirectly related to them. One of these was the result of Mrs. Jordan's having said to her on the way, and with a certain fine significance, that Lord Rye had been for some time in town. She had spoken as if it were a circumstance to which little required to be added—as if the bearing of such an item on her life might easily be grasped. Perhaps it was the wonder of whether Lord Rye wished to marry her that made her guest, with thoughts straying to that quarter, quite determine that some other nuptials also should take place at Saint Julian's. Mr. Mudge was still an attendant at his Wesleyan chapel, but this was the least of her worries—it had never even vexed her enough for her to so much as name it to Mrs. Jordan. Mr. Mudge's form of worship was one of several things—they made up in superiority and beauty for what they wanted in number—that she had long ago settled he should take from her, and she had now moreover for the first time definitely established her own. Its principal feature was that it was to be the same as that of Mrs. Jordan and Lord Rye; which was indeed very much what she said to her hostess as they sat together later on. The brown fog was in this hostess's little parlour, where it acted as a postponement of the question of there being, besides, anything else than the teacups and a pewter pot and a very black little fire and a paraffin lamp without a shade. There was at any rate no sign of a flower; it was not for herself Mrs. Jordan gathered sweets. The girl waited till they had had a cup of tea—waited for the announcement that she fairly believed her friend had, this time, possessed herself of her formally at last to make; but nothing came, after the interval, save a little poke at the fire, which was like the clearing of a throat for a speech.

CHAPTER XXV

"I think you must have heard me speak of Mr. Drake?" Mrs. Jordan had never looked so queer, nor her smile so suggestive of a large benevolent bite.

"Mr. Drake? Oh yes; isn't he a friend of Lord Rye?"

"A great and trusted friend. Almost—I may say—a loved friend."

Mrs. Jordan's "almost" had such an oddity that her companion was moved, rather flippantly perhaps, to take it up. "Don't people as good as love their friends when they I trust them?"

It pulled up a little the eulogist of Mr. Drake. "Well, my dear, I love *you*—"

"But you don't trust me?" the girl unmercifully asked.

Again Mrs. Jordan paused—still she looked queer. "Yes," she replied with a certain austerity; "that's exactly what I'm about to give you rather a remarkable proof of." The sense of its being remarkable was already so strong that, while she bridled a little, this held her auditor in a momentary muteness of submission. "Mr. Drake has rendered his lordship for several years services that his lordship has highly appreciated and that make it all the more—a—unexpected that they should, perhaps a little suddenly, separate."

"Separate?" Our young lady was mystified, but she tried to be interested; and she already saw that she had put the saddle on the wrong horse. She had heard something of Mr. Drake, who was a member of his lordship's circle—the member with whom, apparently, Mrs. Jordan's avocations had most happened to throw her. She was only a little puzzled at the "separation." "Well, at any rate," she smiled, "if they separate as friends—!"

"Oh his lordship takes the greatest interest in Mr. Drake's future. He'll do anything for him; he has in fact just done a great deal. There *must*, you know, be changes—!"

"No one knows it better than I," the girl said. She wished to draw her interlocutress out. "There will be changes enough for me."

"You're leaving Cocker's?"

The ornament of that establishment waited a moment to answer, and then it was indirect. "Tell me what *you're* doing."

"Well, what will you think of it?"

"Why that you've found the opening you were always so sure of."

Mrs. Jordan, on this, appeared to muse with embarrassed intensity. "I was always sure, yes—and yet I often wasn't!"

"Well, I hope you're sure now. Sure, I mean, of Mr. Drake."

"Yes, my dear, I think I may say I *am*. I kept him going till I was."

"Then he's yours?"

"My very own."

"How nice! And awfully rich?" our young woman went on.

Mrs. Jordan showed promptly enough that she loved for higher things. "Awfully handsome—six foot two. And he *has* put by."

"Quite like Mr. Mudge, then!" that gentleman's friend rather desperately exclaimed.

"Oh not *quite*!" Mr. Drake's was ambiguous about it, but the name of Mr. Mudge had evidently given her some sort of stimulus. "He'll have more opportunity now, at any rate. He's going to Lady Bradeen."

"To Lady Bradeen?" This was bewilderment. "'Going—'?"

The girl had seen, from the way Mrs. Jordan looked at her, that the effect of the name had been to make her let something out. "Do you know her?"

She floundered, but she found her feet. "Well, you'll remember I've often told you that if you've grand clients I have them too."

"Yes," said Mrs. Jordan; "but the great difference is that you hate yours, whereas I really love mine. *Do* you know Lady Bradeen?" she pursued.

"Down to the ground! She's always in and out."

Mrs. Jordan's foolish eyes confessed, in fixing themselves on this sketch, to a degree of wonder and even of envy. But she bore up and, with a certain gaiety, "Do you hate *her*?" she demanded.

Her visitor's reply was prompt. "Dear no!—not nearly so much as some of them. She's too outrageously beautiful."

Mrs. Jordan continued to gaze. "Outrageously?"

"Well, yes; deliciously." What was really delicious was Mrs. Jordan's vagueness. "You don't know her—you've not seen her?" her guest lightly continued.

"No, but I've heard a great deal about her."

"So have I!" our young lady exclaimed.

Jordan looked an instant as if she suspected her good faith, or at least her seriousness. "You know some friend—?"

"Of Lady Bradeen's? Oh yes—I know one."

"Only one?"

The girl laughed out. "Only one—but he's so intimate."

Mrs. Jordan just hesitated. "He's a gentleman?"

"Yes, he's not a lady."

Her interlocutress appeared to muse. "She's immensely surrounded."

"She *will* be—with Mr. Drake!"

Mrs. Jordan's gaze became strangely fixed. "Is she *very* good-looking?"

"The handsomest person I know."

Mrs. Jordan continued to brood. "Well, I know some beauties." Then with her odd jerkiness: "Do you think she looks *good*?"

"Because that's not always the case with the good-looking?"—the other took it up. "No, indeed, it isn't: that's one thing Cocker's has taught me. Still, there are some people who have everything. Lady Bradeen, at any rate, has enough: eyes and a nose and a mouth, a complexion, a figure—"

"A figure?" Mrs. Jordan almost broke in.

"A figure, a head of hair!" The girl made a little conscious motion that seemed to let the hair all down, and her companion watched the wonderful show. "But Mr. Drake *is* another—?"

"Another?"—Mrs. Jordan's thoughts had to come back from a distance.

"Of her ladyship's admirers. He's 'going,' you say, to her?"

At this Mrs. Jordan really faltered. "She has engaged him."

"Engaged him?"—our young woman was quite at sea.

"In the same capacity as Lord Rye."

"And was Lord Rye engaged?"

CHAPTER XXVI

Mrs. Jordan looked away from her now—looked, she thought, rather injured and, as if trifled with, even a little angry. The mention of Lady Bradeen had frustrated for a while the convergence of our heroine's thoughts; but with this impression of her old friend's combined impatience and diffidence they began again to whirl round her, and continued it till one of them appeared to dart at her, out of the dance, as if with a sharp peck. It came to her with a lively shock, with a positive sting, that Mr. Drake was—could it be possible? With the idea she found herself afresh on the edge of laughter, of a sudden and strange perversity of mirth. Mr. Drake loomed, in a swift image, before her; such a figure as she had seen in open doorways of houses in Cocker's quarter—majestic, middle-aged, erect, flanked on either side by a footman and taking the name of a visitor. Mr. Drake then verily *was* a person who opened the door! Before she had time, however, to recover from the effect of her evocation, she was offered a vision which quite engulfed it. It was communicated to her somehow that the face with which she had seen it rise prompted Mrs. Jordan to dash, a bit wildly, at something, at anything, that might attenuate criticism. "Lady Bradeen's re-arranging—she's going to be married."

"Married?" The girl echoed it ever so softly, but there it was at last.

"Didn't you know it?"

She summoned all her sturdiness. "No, she hasn't told me."

"And her friends—haven't they?"

"I haven't seen any of them lately. I'm not so fortunate as *you*."

Mrs. Jordan gathered herself. "Then you haven't even heard of Lord Bradeen's death?"

Her comrade, unable for a moment to speak, gave a slow headshake. "You know it from Mr. Drake?" It was better surely not to learn things at all than to learn them by the butler.

"She tells him everything."

"And he tells *you*—I see." Our young lady got up; recovering her muff and her gloves she smiled. "Well, I haven't unfortunately any Mr. Drake. I congratulate you with all my heart. Even without your sort of assistance, however, there's a trifle here and there that I do pick up. I gather that if she's to marry any one it must quite necessarily be my friend."

Mrs. Jordan was now also on her feet. "Is Captain Everard your friend?"

The girl considered, drawing on a glove. "I saw, at one time, an immense deal of him."

Mrs. Jordan looked hard at the glove, but she hadn't after all waited for that to be sorry it wasn't cleaner. "What time was that?"

"It must have been the time you were seeing so much of Mr. Drake." She had now fairly taken it in: the distinguished person Mrs. Jordan was to marry would answer bells and put on coals and superintend, at least, the cleaning of boots for the other distinguished person whom *she* might—well, whom she might have had, if she had wished, so much more to say to. "Good-bye," she added; "good-bye."

Mrs. Jordan, however, again taking her muff from her, turned it over, brushed it off and thoughtfully peeped into it. "Tell me this before you go. You spoke just now of your own changes. Do you mean that Mr. Mudge—?"

"Mr. Mudge has had great patience with me—he has brought me at last to the point. We're to be married next month and have a nice little home. But he's only a grocer, you know"—the girl met her friend's intent eyes—"so that I'm afraid that, with the set you've got into, you won't see your way to keep up our friendship."

Mrs. Jordan for a moment made no answer to this; she only held the muff up to her face, after which she gave it back. "You don't like it. I see, I see."

To her guest's astonishment there were tears now in her eyes. "I don't like what?" the girl asked.

"Why my engagement. Only, with your great cleverness," the poor lady quavered out, "you put it in your own way. I mean that you'll cool off. You already *have*—!" And on this, the next instant, her tears began to flow. She succumbed to them and collapsed; she sank down again, burying her face and trying to smother her sobs.

Her young friend stood there, still in some rigour, but taken much by surprise even if not yet fully moved to pity. "I don't put anything in any 'way,' and I'm very glad you're suited. Only, you know, you did put to me so splendidly what, even for me, if I had listened to you, it might lead to."

Mrs. Jordan kept up a mild thin weak wail; then, drying her eyes, as feebly considered this reminder. "It has led to my not starving!" she faintly gasped.

Our young lady, at this, dropped into the place beside her, and now, in a rush, the small silly misery was clear. She took her hand as a sign of pitying it, then, after another instant, confirmed this expression with a consoling kiss. They sat there together; they looked out, hand in hand, into the damp dusky shabby little room and into the future, of no such very different suggestion, at last accepted by each. There was no definite utterance, on either side, of Mr. Drake's position in the great world, but the temporary collapse of his prospective bride threw all further necessary light; and what our heroine saw and felt for in the whole business was the vivid reflexion of her own dreams and delusions and her own return to reality. Reality, for the poor things they both were, could only be ugliness and obscurity, could never be the escape, the rise. She pressed her friend—she had tact enough for that—with no other personal question, brought on no need of further revelations, only just continued to hold and comfort her and to acknowledge by stiff little forbearances the common element in their fate. She felt indeed magnanimous in such matters; since if it was very well, for condolence or reassurance, to suppress just then invidious shrinkings, she yet by no means saw herself sitting down, as she might say, to the same table with Mr. Drake. There would luckily, to all appearance, be little question of tables; and the circumstance that, on their peculiar lines, her friend's interests would still attach themselves to Mayfair flung over Chalk Farm the first radiance it had shown. Where was one's pride and one's passion when the real way to judge of one's luck was by making not the wrong but the right comparison? Before she had again gathered herself to go she felt very small and cautious and thankful. "We shall have our own house," she said, "and you must come very soon and let me show it you."

"*We* shall have our own too," Mrs. Jordan replied; "for, don't you know? he makes it a condition that he sleeps out?"

"A condition?"—the girl felt out of it.

"For any new position. It was on that he parted with Lord Rye. His lordship can't meet it. So Mr. Drake has given him up."

"And all for you?"—our young woman put it as cheerfully as possible.

"For me and Lady Bradeen. Her ladyship's too glad to get him at any price. Lord Rye, out of interest in us, has in fact quite *made* her take him. So, as I tell you, he will have his own establishment."

Mrs. Jordan, in the elation of it, had begun to revive; but there was nevertheless between them rather a conscious pause—a pause in which neither visitor nor hostess brought out a hope or an invitation. It expressed in the last resort that, in spite of submission and sympathy, they could now after all only look at each other across the social gulf. They remained together as if it would be indeed their last chance, still sitting, though awkwardly, quite close, and feeling also—and this most unmistakeably—that there was one thing more to go into. By the time it came to the surface, moreover, our young friend had recognised the whole of the main truth, from which she even drew again a slight irritation. It was not the main truth perhaps that most signified; but after her momentary effort, her embarrassment and her tears Mrs. Jordan had begun to sound afresh—and even without speaking—the note of a social connexion. She hadn't really let go of it that she was marrying into society. Well, it was a harmless compensation, and it was all the prospective bride of Mr. Mudge had to leave with her.

CHAPTER XXVII

This young lady at last rose again, but she lingered before going. "And has Captain Everard nothing to say to it?"

"To what, dear?"

"Why, to such questions—the domestic arrangements, things in the house."

"How *can* he, with any authority, when nothing in the house is his?"

"Not his?" The girl wondered, perfectly conscious of the appearance she thus conferred on Mrs. Jordan of knowing, in comparison with herself, so tremendously much about it. Well, there were things she wanted so to get at that she was willing at last, though it hurt her, to pay for them with humiliation. "Why are they not his?"

"Don't you know, dear, that he has nothing?"

"Nothing?" It was hard to see him in such a light, but Mrs. Jordan's power to answer for it had a superiority that began, on the spot, to grow. "Isn't he rich?"

Mrs. Jordan looked immensely, looked both generally and particularly, informed. "It depends upon what you call—! Not at any rate in the least as *she* is. What does he bring? Think what she has. And then, love, his debts."

"His debts?" His young friend was fairly betrayed into helpless innocence. She could struggle a little, but she had to let herself go; and if she had spoken frankly she would have said: "Do tell me, for I don't know so much about him as *that*!" As she didn't speak frankly she only said: "His debts are nothing—when she so adores him."

Mrs. Jordan began to fix her again, and now she saw that she must only take it all. That was what it had come to: his having sat with her there on the bench and under the trees in the summer darkness and put his hand on her, making her know what he would have said if permitted; his having returned to her afterwards, repeatedly, with supplicating eyes and a fever in his blood; and her having, on her side, hard and pedantic, helped by some miracle and with her impossible condition, only answered him, yet supplicating back, through the bars of the cage,—all simply that she might hear of him, now for ever lost, only through Mrs. Jordan, who touched him through Mr. Drake, who reached him through Lady Bradeen. "She adores him—but of course that wasn't all there was about it."

The girl met her eyes a minute, then quite surrendered. "What was there else about it?"

"Why, don't you know?"—Mrs. Jordan was almost compassionate.

Her interlocutress had, in the cage, sounded depths, but there was a suggestion here somehow of an abyss quite measureless. "Of course I know she would never let him alone."

"How *could* she—fancy!—when he had so compromised her?"

The most artless cry they had ever uttered broke, at this, from the younger pair of lips. "*Had* he so—?"

"Why, don't you know the scandal?"

Our heroine thought, recollected there was something, whatever it was, that she knew after all much more of than Mrs. Jordan. She saw him again as she had seen him come that morning to recover the telegram—she saw him as she had seen him leave the shop. She perched herself a moment on this. "Oh there was nothing public."

"Not exactly public—no. But there was an awful scare and an awful row. It was all on the very point of coming out. Something was lost—something was found."

"Ah yes," the girl replied, smiling as if with the revival of a blurred memory; "something was found."

"It all got about—and there was a point at which Lord Bradeen had to act."

"Had to—yes. But he didn't."

Mrs. Jordan was obliged to admit it. "No, he didn't. And then, luckily for them, he died."

"I didn't know about his death," her companion said.

"It was nine weeks ago, and most sudden. It has given them a prompt chance."

"To get married?"—this was a wonder—"within nine weeks?"

"Oh not immediately, but—in all the circumstances—very quietly and, I assure you, very soon. Every preparation's made. Above all she holds him."

"Oh yes, she holds him!" our young friend threw off. She had this before her again a minute; then she continued: "You mean through his having made her talked about?"

"Yes, but not only that. She has still another pull."

"Another?"

Mrs. Jordan hesitated. "Why, he was in something."

Her comrade wondered. "In what?"

"I don't know. Something bad. As I tell you, something was found."

The girl stared. "Well?"

"It would have been very bad for him. But, she helped him some way—she recovered it, got hold of it. It's even said she stole it!"

Our young woman considered afresh. "Why it was what was found that precisely saved him."

Mrs. Jordan, however, was positive. "I beg your pardon. I happen to know."

Her disciple faltered but an instant. "Do you mean through Mr. Drake? Do they tell *him* these things?"

"A good servant," said Mrs. Jordan, now thoroughly superior and proportionately sententious, "doesn't need to be told! Her ladyship saved—as a woman so often saves!—the man she loves."

This time our heroine took longer to recover herself, but she found a voice at last. "Ah well—of course I don't know! The great thing was that he got off. They seem then, in a manner," she added, "to have done a great deal for each other."

"Well, it's she that has done most. She has him tight."

"I see, I see. Good-bye." The women had already embraced, and this was not repeated; but Mrs. Jordan went down with her guest to the door of the house. Here again the younger lingered, reverting, though three or four other remarks had on the way passed between them, to Captain Everard and Lady Bradeen. "Did you mean just now that if she hadn't saved him, as you call it, she wouldn't hold him so tight?"

"Well, I dare say." Mrs. Jordan, on the doorstep, smiled with a reflexion that had come to her; she took one of her big bites of the brown gloom. "Men always dislike one when they've done one an injury."

"But what injury had he done her?"

"The one I've mentioned. He *must* marry her, you know."

"And didn't he want to?"

"Not before."

"Not before she recovered the telegram?"

Mrs. Jordan was pulled up a little. "Was it a telegram?"

The girl hesitated. "I thought you said so. I mean whatever it was."

"Yes, whatever it was, I don't think she saw *that*."

"So she just nailed him?"

"She just nailed him." The departing friend was now at the bottom of the little flight of steps; the other was at the top, with a certain thickness of fog. "And when am I to think of you in your little home?—next month?" asked the voice from the top.

"At the very latest. And when am I to think of you in yours?"

"Oh even sooner. I feel, after so much talk with you about it, as if I were already there!" Then "*Good*-bye!" came out of the fog.

"Good-*bye*!" went into it. Our young lady went into it also, in the opposed quarter, and presently, after a few sightless turns, came out on the Paddington canal. Distinguishing vaguely what the low parapet enclosed she stopped close to it and stood a while very intently, but perhaps still sightlessly, looking down on it. A policeman; while she remained, strolled past her; then, going his way a little further and half lost in the atmosphere, paused and watched her. But she was quite unaware—she was full of her thoughts. They were too numerous to find a place just here, but two of the number may at least be mentioned. One of these was that, decidedly, her little home must be not for next month, but for next week; the other, which came indeed as she resumed her walk and went her way, was that it was strange such a matter should be at last settled for her by Mr. Drake.

OWEN WINGRAVE

I

"Upon my honour you must be off your head!" cried Spencer Coyle, as the young man, with a white face, stood there panting a little and repeating "Really, I've quite decided," and "I assure you I've thought it all out." They were both pale, but Owen Wingrave smiled in a manner exasperating to his interlocutor, who however still discriminated sufficiently to see that his grimace (it was like an irrelevant leer) was the result of extreme and conceivable nervousness.

"It was certainly a mistake to have gone so far; but that is exactly why I feel I mustn't go further," poor Owen said, waiting mechanically, almost humbly (he wished not to swagger, and indeed he had nothing to swagger about) and carrying through the window to the stupid opposite houses the dry glitter of his eyes.

"I'm unspeakably disgusted. You've made me dreadfully ill," Mr. Coyle went on, looking thoroughly upset.

"I'm very sorry. It was the fear of the effect on you that kept me from speaking sooner."

"You should have spoken three months ago. Don't you know your mind from one day to the other?"

The young man for a moment said nothing. Then he replied with a little tremor: "You're very angry with me, and I expected it. I'm awfully obliged to you for all you've done for me. I'll do anything else for you in return, but I can't do that. Everyone else will let me have it, of course. I'm prepared for it—I'm prepared for everything. That's what has taken the time: to be sure I was prepared. I think it's your displeasure I feel most and regret most. But little by little you'll get over it."

"You'll get over it rather faster, I suppose!" Spencer Coyle satirically exclaimed. He was quite as agitated as his young friend, and they were evidently in no condition to prolong an encounter in which they each drew blood. Mr. Coyle was a professional 'coach'; he prepared young men for the army, taking only three or four at a time, to whom he applied the irresistible stimulus of which the possession was both his secret and his fortune. He had not a great establishment; he would have said himself that it was not a wholesale business. Neither his system, his health nor his temper could have accommodated itself to numbers; so he weighed and measured his pupils and turned away more applicants than he passed. He was an artist in his line, caring only for picked subjects and capable of sacrifices almost passionate for the individual. He liked ardent young men (there were kinds of capacity to which he was indifferent) and he had taken a particular fancy to Owen Wingrave. This young man's facility really fascinated him. His candidates usually did wonders, and he might have sent up a multitude. He was a person of exactly the stature of the great Napoleon, with a certain flicker of genius in his light blue eye: it had been said of him that he looked like a pianist. The tone of his favourite pupil now expressed, without intention indeed, a superior wisdom which irritated him. He had not especially suffered before from Wingrave's high opinion of himself, which had seemed justified by remarkable parts; but to-day it struck him as intolerable. He cut short the discussion, declining absolutely to regard their relations as terminated, and remarked to his pupil that he had better go off somewhere (down to Eastbourne, say; the sea would bring him round) and take a few days to find his feet and come to his senses. He could afford the time, he was so well up: when Spencer Coyle remembered how well up he was he could have boxed his ears. The tall, athletic young man was not physically a subject for simplified reasoning; but there was a troubled gentleness in his handsome face, the index of compunction mixed with pertinacity, which signified that if it could have done any good he would have turned both cheeks. He evidently didn't pretend that his wisdom was superior; he only presented it as his own. It was his own career after all that was in question. He couldn't refuse to go through the form of trying Eastbourne or at least of holding his tongue, though there was that in his manner which implied that if he should do so it would be really to give Mr. Coyle a chance to recuperate. He didn't feel a bit overworked, but there was nothing more natural than that with their tremendous pressure Mr. Coyle should be. Mr. Coyle's own intellect would derive an advantage from his pupil's holiday. Mr. Coyle saw what he meant, but he controlled himself; he only demanded, as his right, a truce of three days. Owen Wingrave granted it, though as fostering sad illusions this went visibly against his conscience; but before they separated the famous crammer remarked: "All the same I feel as if I ought to see someone. I think you mentioned to me that your aunt had come to town?"

"Oh yes; she's in Baker Street. Do go and see her," the boy said comfortingly.

Mr. Coyle looked at him an instant. "Have you broached this folly to her?"

"Not yet—to no one. I thought it right to speak to you first."

"Oh, what you 'think right'!" cried Spencer Coyle, outraged by his young friend's standards. He added that he would probably call on Miss Wingrave; after which the recreant youth got out of the house.

The latter didn't, none the less, start at once for Eastbourne; he only directed his steps to Kensington Gardens, from which Mr. Coyle's desirable residence (he was terribly expensive and had a big house) was not far removed. The famous coach 'put up' his pupils, and Owen had mentioned to the butler that he would be back to dinner. The spring day was warm to his young blood, and he had a book in his pocket which, when he had passed into the gardens and, after a short stroll, dropped into a chair, he took out with the slow, soft sigh that finally ushers in a pleasure postponed. He stretched his long legs and began to read it; it was a volume of Goethe's poems. He had been for days in a state of the highest tension, and now that the cord had snapped the relief was proportionate; only it was characteristic of him that this deliverance should take the form of an intellectual pleasure. If he had thrown up the probability of a magnificent career it was not to dawdle along Bond Street nor parade his indifference in the window of a club. At any rate he had in a few moments forgotten everything—the tremendous pressure, Mr. Coyle's disappointment, and even his formidable aunt in Baker Street. If these watchers had overtaken him there would surely have been some excuse for their exasperation. There was no doubt he was perverse, for his very choice of a pastime only showed how he had got up his German.

"What the devil's the matter with him, do you know?" Spencer Coyle asked that afternoon of young Lechmere, who had never before observed the head of the establishment to set a fellow such an example of bad language. Young Lechmere was not only Wingrave's fellow-pupil, he was supposed to be his intimate, indeed quite his best friend, and had unconsciously performed for Mr. Coyle the office of making the promise of his great gifts more vivid by contrast. He was short and sturdy and as a general thing uninspired, and Mr. Coyle, who found no amusement in believing in him, had never thought him less exciting than as he stared now out of a face from which you could never guess whether he had caught an idea. Young Lechmere concealed such achievements as if they had been youthful indiscretions. At any rate he could evidently conceive no reason why it should be thought there was anything more than usual the matter with the companion of his studies; so Mr. Coyle had to continue: "He declines to go up. He chucks the whole thing!"

The first thing that struck young Lechmere in the case was the freshness it had imparted to the governor's vocabulary.

"He doesn't want to go to Sandhurst?"

"He doesn't want to go anywhere. He gives up the army altogether. He objects," said Mr. Coyle, in a tone that made young Lechmere almost hold his breath, "to the military profession."

"Why, it has been the profession of all his family!"

"Their profession? It has been their religion! Do you know Miss Wingrave?"

"Oh, yes. Isn't she awful?" young Lechmere candidly ejaculated.

His instructor demurred.

"She's formidable, if you mean that, and it's right she should be; because somehow in her very person, good maiden lady as she is, she represents the might, she represents the traditions and the exploits of the British army. She represents the expansive property of the English name. I think his family can be trusted to come down on him, but every influence should be set in motion. I want to know what yours is. Can you do anything in the matter?"

"I can try a couple of rounds with him," said young Lechmere reflectively. "But he knows a fearful lot. He has the most extraordinary ideas."

"Then he has told you some of them—he has taken you into his confidence?"

"I've heard him jaw by the yard," smiled the honest youth. "He has told me he despises it."

"What is it he despises? I can't make out."

The most consecutive of Mr. Coyle's nurslings considered a moment, as if he were conscious of a responsibility.

"Why, I think, military glory. He says we take the wrong view of it."

"He oughtn't to talk to you that way. It's corrupting the youth of Athens. It's sowing sedition."

"Oh, I'm all right!" said young Lechmere. "And he never told me he meant to chuck it. I always thought he meant to see it through, simply because he had to. He'll argue on any side you like. It's a tremendous pity—I'm sure he'd have a big career."

"Tell him so, then; plead with him; struggle with him—for God's sake."

"I'll do what I can—I'll tell him it's a regular shame."

"Yes, strike that note—insist on the disgrace of it."

The young man gave Mr. Coyle a more perceptive glance. "I'm sure he wouldn't do anything dishonourable."

"Well—it won't look right. He must be made to feel that—work it up. Give him a comrade's point of view—that of a brother-in-arms."

"That's what I thought we were going to be!" young Lechmere mused romantically, much uplifted by the nature of the mission imposed on him. "He's an awfully good sort."

"No one will think so if he backs out!" said Spencer Coyle.

"They mustn't say it to me!" his pupil rejoined with a flush.

Mr. Coyle hesitated a moment, noting his tone and aware that in the perversity of things, though this young man was a born soldier, no excitement would ever attach to his alternatives save perhaps on the part of the nice girl to whom at an early day he was sure to be placidly united. "Do you like him very much—do you believe in him?"

Young Lechmere's life in these days was spent in answering terrible questions; but he had never been subjected to so queer an interrogation as this. "Believe in him? Rather!"

"Then save him!"

The poor boy was puzzled, as if it were forced upon him by this intensity that there was more in such an appeal than could appear on the surface; and he doubtless felt that he was only entering into a complex situation when after another moment, with his hands in his pockets, he replied hopefully but not pompously: "I daresay I can bring him round!"

II

Before seeing young Lechmere Mr. Coyle had determined to telegraph an inquiry to Miss Wingrave. He had prepaid the answer, which, being promptly put into his hand, brought the interview we have just related to a close. He immediately drove off to Baker Street, where the lady had said she awaited him, and five minutes after he got there, as he sat with Owen Wingrave's remarkable aunt, he repeated over several times, in his angry sadness and with the infallibility of his experience: "He's so intelligent—he's so intelligent!" He had declared it had been a luxury to put such a fellow through.

"Of course he's intelligent, what else could he be? We've never, that I know of, had but one idiot in the family!" said Jane Wingrave. This was an allusion that Mr. Coyle could understand, and it brought home to him another of the reasons for the disappointment, the humiliation as it were, of the good people at Paramore, at the same time that it gave an example of the conscientious coarseness he had on former occasions observed in his interlocutress. Poor Philip Wingrave, her late brother's eldest son, was literally imbecile and banished from view; deformed, unsocial, irretrievable, he had been relegated to a private asylum and had become among the friends of the family only a little hushed lugubrious legend. All the hopes of the house, picturesque Paramore, now unintermittently old Sir Philip's rather melancholy home (his infirmities would keep him there to the last) were therefore collected on the second boy's head, which nature, as if in compunction for her previous botch, had, in addition to making it strikingly handsome, filled with marked originalities and talents. These two had been the only children of the old man's only son, who, like so many of his ancestors, had given up a gallant young life to the service of his country. Owen Wingrave the elder had received his death-cut, in close-quarters, from an Afghan sabre; the blow had come crashing across his skull. His wife, at that time in India, was about to give birth to her third child; and when the event took place, in darkness and anguish, the baby came lifeless into the world and the mother sank under the multiplication of her woes. The second of the little boys in England, who was at Paramore with his grandfather, became the peculiar charge of his aunt, the only unmarried one, and during the interesting Sunday that, by urgent invitation, Spencer Coyle, busy as he was, had, after consenting to put Owen through, spent under that roof, the celebrated crammer received a vivid impression of the influence exerted at least in intention by Miss Wingrave. Indeed the picture of this short visit remained with the observant little man a curious one—the vision of an impoverished Jacobean house, shabby and remarkably 'creepy', but full of character still and full of felicity as a setting for the distinguished figure of the peaceful old soldier. Sir Philip Wingrave, a relic rather than a celebrity, was a small brown, erect octogenarian, with smouldering eyes and a studied courtesy. He liked to do the diminished honours of his house, but even when with a shaky hand he lighted a bedroom candle for a deprecating guest it was impossible not to feel that beneath the surface he was a merciless old warrior. The eye of the imagination could glance back into his crowded Eastern past—back at episodes in which his scrupulous forms would only have made him more terrible.

Mr. Coyle remembered also two other figures—a faded inoffensive Mrs. Julian, domesticated there by a system of frequent visits as the widow of an officer and a particular friend of Miss Wingrave, and a remarkably clever little girl of eighteen, who was this lady's daughter and who struck the speculative visitor as already formed for other relations. She was very impertinent to Owen, and in the course of a long walk that he had taken with the young man and the effect of which, in much talk, had been to clinch his high opinion of him, he had learned (for Owen chattered confidentially) that Mrs. Julian was the sister of a very gallant gentleman, Captain Hume-Walker, of the Artillery, who had fallen in the Indian Mutiny and between whom and Miss Wingrave (it had been that lady's one known concession) a passage of some delicacy, taking a tragic turn, was believed to have been enacted. They had been engaged to be married, but she had given way to the jealousy of her nature—had broken with him and sent him off to his fate, which had been horrible. A passionate sense of having wronged him, a hard eternal remorse had thereupon taken possession of her, and when his poor sister, linked also to a soldier, had by a still heavier blow been left almost without resources, she had devoted herself charitably to a long expiation. She had sought comfort in taking Mrs. Julian to live much of the time at Paramore, where she became an unremunerated though not uncriticised housekeeper, and Spencer Coyle suspected that it was a part of this comfort that she could at her leisure trample on her. The impression of Jane Wingrave was not the faintest he had gathered on that intensifying Sunday—an occasion singularly tinged for him with the sense of bereavement and mourning and memory, of names never mentioned of the far-away plaint of widows and the echoes of battles and bad news. It was all military indeed, and Mr. Coyle was made to shudder a little at the profession of which he helped to open the door to harmless young men. Miss Wingrave moreover might have made such a bad conscience worse—so cold and clear a good one looked at him out of her hard, fine eyes and trumpeted in her sonorous voice.

She was a high, distinguished person; angular but not awkward, with a large forehead and abundant black hair, arranged like that of a woman conceiving perhaps excusably of her head as 'noble', and irregularly streaked to-day with white. If however she represented for Spencer Coyle the genius of a military race it was not that she had the step of a grenadier or the vocabulary of a camp-follower; it was only that such sympathies were vividly implied in the general fact to which her very presence and each of her actions and glances and tones were a constant and direct allusion—the paramount valour of her family. If she was military it was because she sprang from a military house and because she wouldn't for the world have been anything but what the Wingraves had been. She was almost vulgar about her ancestors, and if one had been tempted to quarrel with her one would have found a fair pretext in her defective sense of proportion. This temptation however said nothing to Spencer Coyle, for whom as a strong character revealing itself in colour and sound she was a spectacle and who was glad to regard her as a force exerted on his own side. He wished her nephew had more of her narrowness instead of being almost cursed with the tendency to look at things in their relations. He wondered why when she came up to town she always resorted to Baker Street for lodgings. He had never known nor heard of Baker Street as a residence—he associated it only with bazaars and photographers. He divined in her a rigid indifference to everything that was not the passion of her life. Nothing really mattered to her but that, and she would have occupied apartments in Whitechapel if they had been a feature in her tactics. She had received her visitor in a large, cold, faded room, furnished with slippery seats and decorated with alabaster vases and wax-flowers. The only little personal comfort for which she appeared to have looked out was a fat catalogue of the Army and Navy Stores, which reposed on a vast, desolate table-cover of false blue. Her clear forehead—it was like a porcelain slate, a receptacle for addresses and sums—had flushed when her nephew's crammer told her the extraordinary news; but he saw she was fortunately more angry than frightened. She had essentially, she would always have, too little imagination for fear, and the healthy habit moreover of facing everything had taught her that the occasion usually found her a quantity to reckon with. Mr. Coyle saw that her only fear at present could have been that of not being able to prevent her nephew from being absurd and that to such an apprehension as this she was in fact inaccessible. Practically too she was not troubled by surprise; she recognised none of the futile, none of the subtle sentiments. If Philip had for an hour made a fool of himself she was angry; disconcerted as she would have been on learning that he had confessed to debts or fallen in love with a low girl. But there remained in any annoyance the saving fact that no one could make a fool of her.

"I don't know when I've taken such an interest in a young man—I think I never have, since I began to handle them," Mr. Coyle said. "I like him, I believe in him—it's been a delight to see how he was going."

"Oh, I know how they go!" Miss Wingrave threw back her head with a familiar briskness, as if a rapid procession of the generations had flashed before her, rattling their scabbards and spurs. Spencer Coyle recognised the intimation that she had nothing to learn from anybody about the natural carriage of a Wingrave, and he even felt convicted by her next words of being, in her eyes, with the troubled story of his check, his weak complaint of his pupil, rather a poor creature. "If you like him," she exclaimed, "for mercy's sake keep him quiet!"

Mr. Coyle began to explain to her that this was less easy than she appeared to imagine; but he perceived that she understood very little of what he said. The more he insisted that the boy had a kind of intellectual independence, the more this struck her as a conclusive proof that her nephew was a Wingrave and a soldier. It was not till he mentioned to her that Owen had spoken of the profession of arms as of something that would be 'beneath' him, it was not till her attention was arrested by this intenser light on the complexity of the problem that Miss Wingrave broke out after a moment's stupefied reflection: "Send him to see me immediately!"

"That's exactly what I wanted to ask your leave to do. But I've wanted also to prepare you for the worst, to make you understand that he strikes me as really obstinate and to suggest to you that the most powerful arguments at your command—especially if you should be able to put your hand on some intensely practical one—will be none too effective."

"I think I've got a powerful argument." Miss Wingrave looked very hard at her visitor. He didn't know in the least what it was, but he begged her to put it forward without delay. He promised that their young man should come to Baker Street that evening, mentioning however that he had already urged him to spend without delay a couple of days at Eastbourne. This led Jane Wingrave to inquire with surprise what virtue there might be in that expensive remedy, and to reply with decision when Mr. Coyle had said "The virtue of a little rest, a little change, a little relief to overwrought nerves," "Ah, don't coddle him—he's costing us a great deal of money! I'll talk to him and I'll take him down to Paramore; then I'll send him back to you straightened out."

Spencer Coyle hailed this pledge superficially with satisfaction, but before he quitted Miss Wingrave he became conscious that he had really taken on a new anxiety—a restlessness that made him say to himself, groaning inwardly: 'Oh, she is a grenadier at bottom, and she'll have no tact. I don't know what her powerful argument is; I'm only afraid she'll be stupid and make him worse. The old man's better—he's capable of tact, though he's not quite an extinct volcano. Owen will probably put him in a rage. In short the difficulty is that the boy's the best of them.'

Spencer Coyle felt afresh that evening at dinner that the boy was the best of them. Young Wingrave (who, he was pleased to observe, had not yet proceeded to the seaside) appeared at the repast as usual, looking inevitably a little self-conscious, but not too original for Bayswater. He talked very naturally to Mrs. Coyle, who had thought him from the first the most beautiful young man they had ever received; so that the person most ill at ease was poor Lechmere, who took great trouble, as if from the deepest delicacy, not to meet the eye of his misguided mate. Spencer Coyle however paid the penalty of his own profundity in feeling more and more worried; he could so easily see that there were all sorts of things in his young friend that the people of Paramore wouldn't understand. He began even already to react against the notion of his being harassed—to reflect that after all he had a right to his ideas—to remember that he was of a substance too fine to be in fairness roughly used. It was in this way that the ardent little crammer, with his whimsical perceptions and complicated sympathies, was generally condemned not to settle down comfortably either into his displeasures or into his enthusiasms. His love of the real truth never gave him a chance to enjoy them. He mentioned to Wingrave after dinner the propriety of an immediate visit to Baker Street, and the young man, looking 'queer', as he thought—that is smiling again with the exaggerated glory he had shown in their recent interview—went off to face the ordeal. Spencer Coyle noted that he was scared—he was afraid of his aunt; but somehow this didn't strike him as a sign of pusillanimity. He should have been scared, he was well aware, in the poor boy's place, and the sight of his pupil marching up to the battery in spite of his terrors was a positive suggestion of the temperament of the soldier. Many a plucky youth would have shirked this particular peril.

"He has got ideas!" young Lechmere broke out to his instructor after his comrade had quitted the house. He was evidently bewildered and agitated—he had an emotion to work off. He had before dinner gone straight at his friend, as Mr. Coyle had requested, and had elicited from him that his scruples were founded on an overwhelming conviction of the stupidity—the 'crass barbarism' he called it—of war. His great complaint was that people hadn't invented anything cleverer, and he was determined to show, the only way he could, that he wasn't such an ass.

"And he thinks all the great generals ought to have been shot, and that Napoleon Bonaparte in particular, the greatest, was a criminal, a monster for whom language has no adequate name!" Mr. Coyle rejoined, completing young Lechmere's picture. "He favoured you, I see, with exactly the same pearls of wisdom that he produced for me. But I want to know what you said."

"I said they were awful rot!" Young Lechmere spoke with emphasis, and he was slightly surprised to hear Mr. Coyle laugh incongruously at this just declaration and then after a moment continue:

"It's all very curious—I daresay there's something in it. But it's a pity!"

"He told me when it was that the question began to strike him in that light. Four or five years ago, when he did a lot of reading about all the great swells and their campaigns—Hannibal and Julius Cæsar, Marlborough and Frederick and Bonaparte. He has done a lot of reading, and he says it opened his eyes. He says that a wave of disgust rolled over him. He talked about the 'immeasurable misery' of wars, and asked me why nations don't tear to pieces the governments, the rulers that go in for them. He hates poor old Bonaparte worst of all."

"Well, poor old Bonaparte was a brute. He was a frightful ruffian," Mr. Coyle unexpectedly declared. "But I suppose you didn't admit that."

"Oh, I daresay he was objectionable, and I'm very glad we laid him on his back. But the point I made to Wingrave was that his own behaviour would excite no end of remark." Young Lechmere hesitated an instant, then he added: "I told him he must be prepared for the worst."

"Of course he asked you what you meant by the 'worst'," said Spencer Coyle.

"Yes, he asked me that, and do you know what I said? I said people would say that his conscientious scruples and his wave of disgust are only a pretext. Then he asked 'A pretext for what?'"

"Ah, he rather had you there!" Mr. Coyle exclaimed with a little laugh that was mystifying to his pupil.

"Not a bit—for I told him."

"What did you tell him?"

Once more, for a few seconds, with his conscious eyes in his instructor's, the young man hung fire.

"Why, what we spoke of a few hours ago. The appearance he'd present of not having—" The honest youth faltered a moment, then brought it out: "The military temperament, don't you know? But do you know what he said to that?" young Lechmere went on.

"Damn the military temperament!" the crammer promptly replied.

Young Lechmere stared. Mr. Coyle's tone left him uncertain if he were attributing the phrase to Wingrave or uttering his own opinion, but he exclaimed:

"Those were exactly his words!"

"He doesn't care," said Mr. Coyle.

"Perhaps not. But it isn't fair for him to abuse us fellows. I told him it's the finest temperament in the world, and that there's nothing so splendid as pluck and heroism."

"Ah! there you had him."

"I told him it was unworthy of him to abuse a gallant, a magnificent profession. I told him there's no type so fine as that of the soldier doing his duty."

"That's essentially your type, my dear boy." Young Lechmere blushed; he couldn't make out (and the danger was naturally unexpected to him) whether at that moment he didn't exist mainly for the recreation of his friend. But he was partly reassured by the genial way this friend continued, laying a hand on his shoulder: "Keep at him that way! we may do something. I'm extremely obliged to you."

Another doubt however remained unassuaged—a doubt which led him to exclaim to Mr. Coyle before they dropped the painful subject:

"He doesn't care! But it's awfully odd he shouldn't!"

"So it is, but remember what you said this afternoon—I mean about your not advising people to make insinuations to you."

"I believe I should knock a fellow down!" said young Lechmere. Mr. Coyle had got up; the conversation had taken place while they sat together after Mrs. Coyle's withdrawal from the dinner-table and the head of the establishment administered to his disciple, on principles that were a part of his thoroughness, a glass of excellent claret. The disciple, also on his feet, lingered an instant, not for another 'go', as he would have called it, at the decanter, but to wipe his microscopic moustache with prolonged and unusual care. His companion saw he had something to bring out which required a final effort, and waited for him an instant with a hand on the knob of the door. Then as young Lechmere approached him Spencer Coyle grew conscious of an unwonted intensity in the round and ingenuous face. The boy was nervous, but he tried to behave like a man of the world. "Of course, it's between ourselves," he stammered, "and I wouldn't breathe such a word to any one who wasn't interested in poor Wingrave as you are. But do you think he funks it?"

Mr. Coyle looked at him so hard for an instant that he was visibly frightened at what he had said.

"Funks it! Funks what?"

"Why, what we're talking about—the service." Young Lechmere gave a little gulp and added with a naïveté almost pathetic to Spencer Coyle: "The dangers, you know!"

"Do you mean he's thinking of his skin?"

Young Lechmere's eyes expanded appealingly, and what his instructor saw in his pink face—he even thought he saw a tear—was the dread of a disappointment shocking in the degree in which the loyalty of admiration had been great.

"Is he—is he afraid?" repeated the honest lad, with a quaver of suspense.

"Dear no!" said Spencer Coyle, turning his back.

On which young Lechmere felt a little snubbed and even a little ashamed; but he felt still more relieved.

III

Less than a week after this Spencer Coyle received a note from Miss Wingrave, who had immediately quitted London with her nephew. She proposed that he should come down to Paramore for the following Sunday—Owen was really so tiresome. On the spot, in that house of examples and memories and in combination with her poor dear father, who was 'dreadfully annoyed', it might be worth their while to make a last stand. Mr. Coyle read between the lines of this letter that the party at Paramore had got over a good deal of ground since Miss Wingrave, in Baker Street, had treated his despair as superficial. She was not an insinuating woman, but she went so far as to put the question on the ground of his conferring a particular favour on an afflicted family; and she expressed the pleasure it would give them if he should be accompanied by Mrs. Coyle, for whom she enclosed a separate invitation. She mentioned that she was also writing, subject to Mr. Coyle's approval, to young Lechmere. She thought such a nice manly boy might do her wretched nephew some good. The celebrated crammer determined to embrace this opportunity; and now it was the case not so much that he was angry as that he was anxious. As he directed his answer to Miss Wingrave's letter he caught himself smiling at the thought that at bottom he was going to defend his young friend rather than to attack him. He said to his wife, who was a fair, fresh, slow woman—a person of much more presence than himself—that she had better take Miss Wingrave at her word: it was such an extraordinary, such a fascinating specimen of an old English home. This last allusion was amicably sarcastic—he had already accused the good lady more than once of being in love with Owen Wingrave. She admitted that she was, she even gloried in her passion; which shows that the subject, between them, was treated in a liberal spirit. She carried out the joke by accepting the invitation with eagerness. Young Lechmere was delighted to do the same; his instructor had good-naturedly taken the view that the little break would freshen him up for his last spurt.

It was the fact that the occupants of Paramore did indeed take their trouble hard that struck Spencer Coyle after he had been an hour or two in that fine old house. This very short second visit, beginning on the Saturday evening, was to constitute the strangest episode of his life. As soon as he found himself in private with his wife—they had retired to dress for dinner—they called each other's attention with effusion and almost with alarm to the sinister gloom that was stamped on the place. The house was admirable with its old grey front which came forward in wings so as to form three sides of a square, but Mrs. Coyle made no scruple to declare that if she had known in advance the sort of impression she was going to receive she would never have put her foot in it. She characterized it as 'uncanny', she accused her husband of not having warned her properly. He had mentioned to her in advance certain facts, but while she almost feverishly dressed she had innumerable questions to ask. He hadn't told her about the girl, the extraordinary girl, Miss Julian—that is, he hadn't told her that this young lady, who in plain terms was a mere dependent, would be in effect, and as a consequence of the way she carried herself, the most important person in the house. Mrs. Coyle was already prepared to announce that she hated Miss Julian's affectations. Her husband above all hadn't told her that they should find their young charge looking five years older.

"I couldn't imagine that," said Mr. Coyle, "nor that the character of the crisis here would be quite so perceptible. But I suggested to Miss Wingrave the other day that they should press her nephew in real earnest, and she has taken me at my word. They've cut off his supplies—they're trying to starve him out. That's not what I meant—but indeed I don't quite know to-day what I meant. Owen feels the pressure, but he won't yield." The strange thing was that, now that he was there, the versatile little coach felt still more that his own spirit had been caught up by a wave of reaction. If he was there it was because he was on poor Owen's side. His whole impression, his whole apprehension, had on the spot become much deeper. There was something in the dear boy's very resistance that began to charm him. When his wife, in the intimacy of the conference I have mentioned, threw off the mask and commended even with extravagance the stand his pupil had taken (he was too good to be a horrid soldier and it was noble of him to suffer for his convictions—wasn't he as upright as a young hero, even though as pale as a Christian martyr?) the good lady only expressed the sympathy which, under cover of regarding his young friend as a rare exception, he had already recognised in his own soul.

For, half an hour ago, after they had had superficial tea in the brown old hall of the house, his young friend had proposed to him, before going to dress, to take a turn outside, and had even, on the terrace, as they walked together to one of the far ends of it, passed his hand entreatingly into his companion's arm, permitting himself thus a familiarity unusual between pupil and master and calculated to show that he had guessed whom he could most depend on to be kind to him. Spencer Coyle on his own side had guessed something, so that he was not surprised at the boy's having a particular confidence to make. He had felt on arriving that each member of the party had wished to get hold of him first, and he knew that at that moment Jane Wingrave was peering through the ancient blur of one of the windows (the house had been modernised so little that the thick dim panes were three centuries old) to see if her nephew looked as if he were poisoning the visitor's mind. Mr. Coyle lost no time therefore in reminding the youth (and he took care to laugh as he did so) that he had not come down to Paramore to be corrupted. He had come down to make, face to face, a last appeal to him—he hoped it wouldn't be utterly vain. Owen smiled sadly as they went, asking him if he thought he had the general air of a fellow who was going to knock under.

"I think you look strange—I think you look ill," Spencer Coyle said very honestly. They had paused at the end of the terrace.

"I've had to exercise a great power of resistance, and it rather takes it out of one."

"Ah, my dear boy, I wish your great power—for you evidently possess it—were exerted in a better cause!"

Owen Wingrave smiled down at his small instructor. "I don't believe that!" Then he added, to explain why: "Isn't what you want, if you're so good as to think well of my character, to see me exert most power, in whatever direction? Well, this is the way I exert most." Owen Wingrave went on to relate that he had had some terrible hours with his grandfather, who had denounced him in a way to make one's hair stand up on one's head. He had expected them not to like it, not a bit, but he had had no idea they would make such a row. His aunt was different, but she was equally insulting. Oh, they had made him feel they were ashamed of him; they accused him of putting a public dishonour on their name. He was the only one who had ever backed out—he was the first for three hundred years. Every one had known he was to go up, and now every one would know he was a young hypocrite who suddenly pretended to have scruples. They talked of his scruples as you wouldn't talk of a cannibal's god. His grandfather had called him outrageous names. "He called me—he called me—" Here the young man faltered, his voice failed him. He looked as haggard as was possible to a young man in such magnificent health.

"I probably know!" said Spencer Coyle, with a nervous laugh.

Owen Wingrave's clouded eyes, as if they were following the far-off consequences of things, rested for an instant on a distant object. Then they met his companion's and for another moment sounded them deeply. "It isn't true. No, it isn't. It's not that!"

"I don't suppose it is! But what do you propose instead of it?"

"Instead of what?"

"Instead of the stupid solution of war. If you take that away you should suggest at least a substitute."

"That's for the people in charge, for governments and cabinets," said Owen Wingrave. "They'll arrive soon enough at a substitute, in the particular case, if they're made to understand that they'll be hung if they don't find one. Make it a capital crime—that'll quicken the wits of ministers!" His eyes brightened as he spoke, and he looked assured and exalted. Mr. Coyle gave a sigh of perplexed resignation—it was a monomania. He fancied after this for a moment that Owen was going to ask him if he too thought he was a coward; but he was relieved to observe that he either didn't suspect him of it or shrank uncomfortably from putting the question to the test. Spencer Coyle wished to show confidence, but somehow a direct assurance that he didn't doubt of his courage appeared too gross a compliment—it would be like saying he didn't doubt of his honesty. The difficulty was presently averted by Owen's continuing: "My grandfather can't break the entail, but I shall have nothing but this place, which, as you know, is small and, with the way rents are going, has quite ceased to yield an income. He has some money—not much, but such as it is he cuts me off. My aunt does the same—she has let me know her intentions. She was to have left me her six hundred a year. It was all settled; but now what's settled is that I don't get a penny of it if I give up the army. I must add in fairness that I have from my mother three hundred a year of my own. And I tell you the simple truth when I say that I don't care a rap for the loss of the money." The young man drew a long, slow breath, like a creature in pain; then he subjoined: "That's not what worries me!"

"What are you going to do?" asked Spencer Coyle.

"I don't know; perhaps nothing. Nothing great, at all events. Only something peaceful!"

Owen gave a weary smile, as if, worried as he was, he could yet appreciate the humorous effect of such a declaration from a Wingrave; but what it suggested to his companion, who looked up at him with a sense that he was after all not a Wingrave for nothing and had a military steadiness under fire, was the exasperation that such a programme, uttered in such a way and striking them as the last word of the inglorious, might well have engendered on the part of his grandfather and his aunt. 'Perhaps nothing'—when he might carry on the great tradition! Yes, he wasn't weak, and he was interesting; but there was a point of view from which he was provoking. "What is it then that worries you?" Mr. Coyle demanded.

"Oh, the house—the very air and feeling of it. There are strange voices in it that seem to mutter at me—to say dreadful things as I pass. I mean the general consciousness and responsibility of what I'm doing. Of course it hasn't been easy for me—not a bit. I assure you I don't enjoy it." With a light in them that was like a longing for justice Owen again bent his eyes on those of the little coach; then he pursued: "I've started up all the old ghosts. The very portraits glower at me on the walls. There's one of my great-great-grandfather (the one the extraordinary story you know is about—the old fellow who hangs on the second landing of the big staircase) that fairly stirs on the canvas—just heaves a little—when I come near it. I have to go up and down stairs—it's rather awkward! It's what my aunt calls the family circle. It's all constituted here, it's a kind of indestructible presence, it stretches away into the past, and when I came back with her the other day Miss Wingrave told me I wouldn't have the impudence to stand in the midst of it and say such things. I had to say them to my grandfather; but now that I've said them it seems to me that the question's ended. I want to go away—I don't care if I never come back again."

"Oh, you are a soldier; you must fight it out!" Mr. Coyle laughed.

The young man seemed discouraged at his levity, but as they turned round, strolling back in the direction from which they had come, he himself smiled faintly after an instant and replied: "Ah, we're tainted all!"

They walked in silence part of the way to the old portico; then Spencer Coyle, stopping short after having assured himself that he was at a sufficient distance from the house not to be heard, suddenly put the question: "What does Miss Julian say?"

"Miss Julian?" Owen had perceptibly coloured.

"I'm sure she hasn't concealed her opinion."

"Oh, it's the opinion of the family circle, for she's a member of it of course. And then she has her own as well."

"Her own opinion?"

"Her own family-circle."

"Do you mean her mother—that patient lady?"

"I mean more particularly her father, who fell in battle. And her grandfather, and his father, and her uncles and great-uncles—they all fell in battle."

"Hasn't the sacrifice of so many lives been sufficient? Why should she sacrifice you?"

"Oh, she hates me!" Owen declared, as they resumed their walk.

"Ah, the hatred of pretty girls for fine young men!" exclaimed Spencer Coyle.

He didn't believe in it, but his wife did, it appeared perfectly, when he mentioned this conversation while, in the fashion that has been described, the visitors dressed for dinner. Mrs. Coyle had already discovered that nothing could have been nastier than Miss Julian's manner to the disgraced youth during the half-hour the party had spent in the hall; and it was this lady's judgment that one must have had no eyes in one's head not to see that she was already trying outrageously to flirt with young Lechmere. It was a pity they had brought that silly boy: he was down in the hall with her at that moment. Spencer Coyle's version was different; he thought there were finer elements involved. The girl's footing in the house was inexplicable on any ground save that of her being predestined to Miss Wingrave's nephew. As the niece of Miss Wingrave's own unhappy intended she had been dedicated early by this lady to the office of healing by a union with Owen the tragic breach that had separated their elders; and if in reply to this it was to be said that a girl of spirit couldn't enjoy in such a matter having her duty cut out for her, Owen's enlightened friend was ready with the argument that a young person in Miss Julian's position would never be such a fool as really to quarrel with a capital chance. She was familiar at Paramore and she felt safe; therefore she might trust herself to the amusement of pretending that she had her option. But it was all innocent coquetry. She had a curious charm, and it was vain to pretend that the heir of that house wouldn't seem good enough to a girl, clever as she might be, of eighteen. Mrs. Coyle reminded her husband that the poor young man was precisely now not of that house: this problem was among the questions that exercised their wits after the two men had taken the turn on the terrace. Spencer Coyle told his wife that Owen was afraid of the portrait of his great-great-grandfather. He would show it to her, since she hadn't noticed it, on their way downstairs.

"Why of his great-great-grandfather more than of any of the others?"

"Oh, because he's the most formidable. He's the one who's sometimes seen."

"Seen where?" Mrs. Coyle had turned round with a jerk.

"In the room he was found dead in—the White Room they've always called it."

"Do you mean to say the house has a ghost?" Mrs. Coyle almost shrieked. "You brought me here without telling me?"

"Didn't I mention it after my other visit?"

"Not a word. You only talked about Miss Wingrave."

"Oh, I was full of the story—you have simply forgotten."

"Then you should have reminded me!"

"If I had thought of it I would have held my peace, for you wouldn't have come."

"I wish, indeed, I hadn't!" cried Mrs. Coyle. "What is the story?"

"Oh, a deed of violence that took place here ages ago. I think it was in George the First's time. Colonel Wingrave, one of their ancestors, struck in a fit of passion one of his children, a lad just growing up, a blow on the head of which the unhappy child died. The matter was hushed up for the hour—some other explanation was put about. The poor boy was laid out in one of those rooms on the other side of the house, and amid strange smothered rumours the funeral was hurried on. The next morning, when the household assembled, Colonel Wingrave was missing; he was looked for vainly, and at last it occurred to some one that he might perhaps be in the room from which his child had been carried to burial. The seeker knocked without an answer—then opened the door. Colonel

Wingrave lay dead on the floor, in his clothes, as if he had reeled and fallen back, without a wound, without a mark, without anything in his appearance to indicate that he had either struggled or suffered. He was a strong, sound man—there was nothing to account for such a catastrophe. He is supposed to have gone to the room during the night, just before going to bed, in some fit of compunction or some fascination of dread. It was only after this that the truth about the boy came out. But no one ever sleeps in the room."

Mrs. Coyle had fairly turned pale. "I hope not! Thank heaven they haven't put us there!"

"We're at a comfortable distance; but I've seen the gruesome chamber."

"Do you mean you've been in it?"

"For a few moments. They're rather proud of it and my young friend showed it to me when I was here before."

Mrs. Coyle stared. "And what is it like?"

"Simply like an empty, dull, old-fashioned bedroom, rather big, with the things of the 'period' in it. It's panelled from floor to ceiling, and the panels evidently, years and years ago, were painted white. But the paint has darkened with time and there are three or four quaint little ancient 'samplers', framed and glazed, hung on the walls."

Mrs. Coyle looked round with a shudder. "I'm glad there are no samplers here! I never heard anything so jumpy! Come down to dinner."

On the staircase as they went down her husband showed her the portrait of Colonel Wingrave—rather a vigorous representation, for the place and period, of a gentleman with a hard, handsome face, in a red coat and a peruke. Mrs. Coyle declared that his descendant Sir Philip was wonderfully like him; and her husband could fancy, though he kept it to himself, that if one should have the courage to walk about the old corridors of Paramore at night one might meet a figure that resembled him roaming, with the restlessness of a ghost, hand in hand with the figure of a tall boy. As he proceeded to the drawing-room with his wife he found himself suddenly wishing that he had made more of a point of his pupil's going to Eastbourne. The evening however seemed to have taken upon itself to dissipate any such whimsical forebodings, for the grimness of the family-circle, as Spencer Coyle had preconceived its composition, was mitigated by an infusion of the 'neighbourhood'. The company at dinner was recruited by two cheerful couples—one of them the vicar and his wife, and by a silent young man who had come down to fish. This was a relief to Mr. Coyle, who had begun to wonder what was after all expected of him and why he had been such a fool as to come, and who now felt that for the first hours at least the situation would not have directly to be dealt with. Indeed he found, as he had found before, sufficient occupation for his ingenuity in reading the various symptoms of which the picture before him was an expression. He should probably have an irritating day on the morrow: he foresaw the difficulty of the long decorous Sunday and how dry Jane Wingrave's ideas, elicited in a strenuous conference, would taste. She and her father would make him feel that they depended upon him for the impossible, and if they should try to associate him with a merely stupid policy he might end by telling them what he thought of it—an accident not required to make his visit a sensible mistake. The old man's actual design was evidently to let their friends see in it a positive mark of their being all right. The presence of the great London coach was tantamount to a profession of faith in the results of the impending examination. It had clearly been obtained from Owen, rather to Spencer Coyle's surprise, that he would do nothing to interfere with the apparent harmony. He let the allusions to his hard work pass and, holding his tongue about his affairs, talked to the ladies as amicably as if he had not been 'cut off'. When Spencer Coyle looked at him once or twice across the table, catching his eye, which showed an indefinable passion, he saw a puzzling pathos in his laughing face: one couldn't resist a pang for a young lamb so visibly marked for sacrifice. 'Hang him—what a pity he's such a fighter!' he privately sighed, with a want of logic that was only superficial.

This idea however would have absorbed him more if so much of his attention had not been given to Kate Julian, who now that he had her well before him struck him as a remarkable and even as a possibly fascinating young woman. The fascination resided not in any extraordinary prettiness, for if she was handsome, with her long Eastern eyes, her magnificent hair and her general unabashed originality, he had seen complexions rosier and features that pleased him more: it resided in a strange impression that she gave of being exactly the sort of person whom, in her position, common considerations, those of prudence and perhaps even a little those of decorum, would have enjoined on her not to be. She was what was vulgarly termed a dependant—penniless, patronized, tolerated; but something in her aspect and manner signified that if her situation was inferior, her spirit, to make up for it, was above precautions or submissions. It was not in the least that she was aggressive, she was too indifferent for that; it was only as if, having nothing either to gain or to lose, she could afford to do as she liked. It occurred to Spencer Coyle that she might really have had more at stake than her imagination appeared to take account of; whatever it was at any rate he had never seen a young woman at less pains to be on the safe side. He wondered inevitably how the peace was kept between Jane Wingrave and such an inmate as this; but those questions of course were unfathomable deeps. Perhaps Kate Julian lorded it even over her protectress. The other time he was at Paramore he had received an impression that, with Sir Philip beside her, the girl could fight with her back to the wall. She amused Sir Philip, she charmed him, and he liked people who weren't afraid; between him and his daughter moreover there was no doubt which was the higher in command. Miss Wingrave took many things for granted, and most of all the rigour of discipline and the fate of the vanquished and the captive.

But between their clever boy and so original a companion of his childhood what odd relation would have grown up? It couldn't be indifference, and yet on the part of happy, handsome, youthful creatures it was still less likely to be aversion. They weren't Paul and Virginia, but they must have had their common summer and their idyll: no nice girl could have disliked such a nice fellow for anything but not liking her, and no nice fellow could have resisted such propinquity. Mr. Coyle remembered indeed that Mrs. Julian had spoken to him as if the propinquity had been by no means constant, owing to her daughter's absences at school, to say nothing of Owen's; her visits to a few friends who were so kind as to 'take her' from time to time; her sojourns in London—so difficult to manage, but still managed by God's help—for 'advantages', for drawing and singing, especially drawing or rather painting, in oils, in which she had had immense success. But the good lady had also mentioned that the young people were quite brother and sister, which was a little, after all, like Paul and Virginia. Mrs. Coyle had been right, and it was apparent that Virginia was doing her best to make the time pass agreeably for young Lechmere. There was no such whirl of conversation as to render it an effort for Mr. Coyle to reflect on these things, for the tone of the occasion, thanks principally to the other guests, was not disposed to stray—it tended to the repetition of anecdote and the discussion of rents, topics that huddled together like uneasy animals. He could judge how intensely his hosts wished the evening to pass off as if nothing had happened; and this gave him the measure of their private resentment. Before dinner was over he found himself fidgety about his second pupil. Young Lechmere, since he began to cram, had done all that might have been expected of him; but this couldn't blind his instructor to a present perception of his being in moments of relaxation as innocent as a babe. Mr. Coyle had considered that the amusements of Paramore would probably give him a fillip, and the poor fellow's manner testified to the soundness of the forecast. The fillip had been unmistakably administered; it had come in the form of a revelation. The light on young Lechmere's brow announced with a candour that was almost an appeal for compassion, or at least a deprecation of ridicule, that he had never seen anything like Miss Julian.

IV

In the drawing-room after dinner the girl found an occasion to approach Spencer Coyle. She stood before him a moment, smiling while she opened and shut her fan, and then she said abruptly, raising her strange eyes: "I know what you've come for, but it isn't any use."

"I've come to look after you a little. Isn't that any use?"

"It's very kind. But I'm not the question of the hour. You won't do anything with Owen."

Spencer Coyle hesitated a moment. "What will you do with his young friend?"

She stared, looked round her.

"Mr. Lechmere? Oh, poor little lad! We've been talking about Owen. He admires him so."

"So do I. I should tell you that."

"So do we all. That's why we're in such despair."

"Personally then you'd like him to be a soldier?" Spencer Coyle inquired.

"I've quite set my heart on it. I adore the army and I'm awfully fond of my old playmate," said Miss Julian.

Her interlocutor remembered the young man's own different version of her attitude; but he judged it loyal not to challenge the girl.

"It's not conceivable that your old playmate shouldn't be fond of you. He must therefore wish to please you; and I don't see why—between you—you don't set the matter right."

"Wish to please me!" Miss Julian exclaimed. "I'm sorry to say he shows no such desire. He thinks me an impudent wretch. I've told him what I think of him, and he simply hates me."

"But you think so highly! You just told me you admire him."

"His talents, his possibilities, yes; even his appearance, if I may allude to such a matter. But I don't admire his present behaviour."

"Have you had the question out with him?" Spencer Coyle asked.

"Oh, yes, I've ventured to be frank—the occasion seemed to excuse it. He couldn't like what I said."

"What did you say?"

Miss Julian, thinking a moment, opened and shut her fan again.

"Why, that such conduct isn't that of a gentleman!"

After she had spoken her eyes met Spencer Coyle's, who looked into their charming depths.

"Do you want then so much to send him off to be killed?"

"How odd for you to ask that—in such a way!" she replied with a laugh. "I don't understand your position: I thought your line was to make soldiers!"

"You should take my little joke. But, as regards Owen Wingrave, there's no 'making' needed," Mr. Coyle added. "To my sense"—the little crammer paused a moment, as if with a consciousness of responsibility for his paradox—"to my sense he is, in a high sense of the term, a fighting man."

"Ah, let him prove it!" the girl exclaimed, turning away.

Spencer Coyle let her go; there was something in her tone that annoyed and even a little shocked him. There had evidently been a violent passage between these young people, and the reflection that such a matter was after all none of his business only made him more sore. It was indeed a military house, and she was at any rate a person who placed her ideal of manhood (young persons doubtless always had their ideals of manhood) in the type of the belted warrior. It was a taste like another; but, even a quarter of an hour later, finding himself near young Lechmere, in whom this type was embodied, Spencer Coyle was still so ruffled that he addressed the innocent lad with a certain magisterial dryness. "You're not to sit up late, you know. That's not what I brought you down for." The dinner-guests were taking leave and the bedroom candles twinkled in a monitory row. Young Lechmere however was too agreeably agitated to be accessible to a snub: he had a happy pre-occupation which almost engendered a grin.

"I'm only too eager for bedtime. Do you know there's an awfully jolly room?"

"Surely they haven't put you there?"

"No indeed: no one has passed a night in it for ages. But that's exactly what I want to do—it would be tremendous fun."

"And have you been trying to get Miss Julian's permission?"

"Oh, she can't give leave, she says. But she believes in it, and she maintains that no man dare."

"No man shall! A man in your critical position in particular must have a quiet night," said Spencer Coyle.

Young Lechmere gave a disappointed but reasonable sigh.

"Oh, all right. But mayn't I sit up for a little go at Wingrave? I haven't had any yet."

Mr. Coyle looked at his watch.

"You may smoke one cigarette."

He felt a hand on his shoulder, and he turned round to see his wife tilting candle-grease upon his coat. The ladies were going to bed and it was Sir Philip's inveterate hour; but Mrs. Coyle confided to her husband that after the dreadful things he had told her she positively declined to be left alone, for no matter how short an interval, in any part of the house. He promised to follow her within three minutes, and after the orthodox handshakes the ladies rustled away. The forms were kept up at Paramore as bravely as if the old house had no present heartache. The only one of which Spencer Coyle noticed the omission was some salutation to himself from Kate Julian. She gave him neither a word nor a glance, but he saw her look hard at Owen Wingrave. Her mother, timid and pitying, was apparently the only person from whom this young man caught an inclination of the head. Miss Wingrave marshalled the three ladies—her little procession of twinkling tapers—up the wide oaken stairs and past the watching portrait of her ill-fated ancestor. Sir Philip's servant appeared and offered his arm to the old man, who turned a perpendicular back on poor Owen when the boy made a vague movement to anticipate this office. Spencer Coyle learned afterwards that before Owen had forfeited favour it had always, when he was at home, been his privilege at bedtime to conduct his grandfather ceremoniously to rest. Sir Philip's habits were contemptuously different now. His apartments were on the lower floor and he shuffled stiffly off to them with his valet's help, after fixing for a moment significantly on the most responsible of his visitors the thick red ray, like the glow of stirred embers, that always made his eyes conflict oddly with his mild manners. They seemed to say to Spencer Coyle 'We'll let the young scoundrel have it to-morrow!' One might have gathered from them that the young scoundrel, who had now strolled to the other end of the hall, had at least forged a cheque. Mr. Coyle watched him an instant, saw him drop nervously into a chair and then with a restless movement get up. The same movement brought him back to where his late instructor stood addressing a last injunction to young Lechmere.

"I'm going to bed and I should like you particularly to conform to what I said to you a short time ago. Smoke a single cigarette with your friend here and then go to your room. You'll have me down on you if I hear of your having, during the night, tried any preposterous games." Young Lechmere, looking down with his hands in his pockets, said nothing—he only poked at the corner of a rug with his toe; so that Spencer Coyle, dissatisfied with so tacit a pledge, presently went on, to Owen: "I must request you, Wingrave, not to keep this sensitive subject sitting up—and indeed to put him to bed and turn his key in the door." As Owen stared an instant, apparently not understanding the motive of so much solicitude, he added: "Lechmere has a morbid curiosity about one of your legends—of your historic rooms. Nip it in the bud."

"Oh, the legend's rather good, but I'm afraid the room's an awful sell!" Owen laughed.

"You know you don't believe that, my boy!" young Lechmere exclaimed.

"I don't think he does," said Mr. Coyle, noticing Owen's mottled flush.

"He wouldn't try a night there himself!" young Lechmere pursued.

"I know who told you that," rejoined Owen, lighting a cigarette in an embarrassed way at the candle, without offering one to either of his companions.

"Well, what if she did?" asked the younger of these gentlemen, rather red. "Do you want them all yourself?" he continued facetiously, fumbling in the cigarette-box.

Owen Wingrave only smoked quietly; then he exclaimed:

"Yes—what if she did? But she doesn't know," he added.

"She doesn't know what?"

"She doesn't know anything!—I'll tuck him in!" Owen went on gaily to Mr. Coyle, who saw that his presence, now that a certain note had been struck, made the young men uncomfortable. He was curious, but there was a kind of discretion, with his pupils, that he had always pretended to practise; a discretion that however didn't prevent him as he took his way upstairs from recommending them not to be donkeys.

At the top of the staircase, to his surprise, he met Miss Julian, who was apparently going down again. She had not begun to undress, nor was she perceptibly disconcerted at seeing him. She nevertheless, in a manner slightly at variance with the rigour with which she had overlooked him ten minutes before, dropped the words: "I'm going down to look for something. I've lost a jewel."

"A jewel?"

"A rather good turquoise, out of my locket. As it's the only ornament I have the honour to possess—!" And she passed down.

"Shall I go with you and help you?" asked Spencer Coyle.

The girl paused a few steps below him, looking back with her Oriental eyes.

"Don't I hear voices in the hall?"

"Those remarkable young men are there."

"They'll help me." And Kate Julian descended.

Spencer Coyle was tempted to follow her, but remembering his standard of tact he rejoined his wife in their apartment. He delayed however to go to bed, and though he went into his dressing-room he couldn't bring himself even to take off his coat. He pretended for half an hour to read a novel; after which, quietly, or perhaps I should say agitatedly, he passed from the dressing-room into the corridor. He followed this passage to the door of the room which he knew to have been assigned to young Lechmere and was comforted to see that it was closed. Half an hour earlier he had seen it standing open; therefore he could take for granted that the bewildered boy had come to bed. It was of this he had wished to assure himself, and having done so he was on the point of retreating. But at the same instant he heard a sound in the room—the occupant was doing, at the window, something which showed him that he might knock without the reproach of waking his pupil up. Young Lechmere came in fact to the door in his shirt and trousers. He admitted his visitor in some surprise, and when the door was closed again Spencer Coyle said:

"I don't want to make your life a burden to you, but I had it on my conscience to see for myself that you're not exposed to undue excitement."

"Oh, there's plenty of that!" said the ingenuous youth. "Miss Julian came down again."

"To look for a turquoise?"

"So she said."

"Did she find it?"

"I don't know. I came up. I left her with poor Wingrave."

"Quite the right thing," said Spencer Coyle.

"I don't know," young Lechmere repeated uneasily. "I left them quarrelling."

"What about?"

"I don't understand. They're a quaint pair!"

Spencer Coyle hesitated. He had, fundamentally, principles and scruples, but what he had in particular just now was a curiosity, or rather, to recognise it for what it was, a sympathy, which brushed them away.

"Does it strike you that she's down on him?" he permitted himself to inquire.

"Rather!—when she tells him he lies!"

"What do you mean?"

"Why, before me. It made me leave them; it was getting too hot. I stupidly brought up the question of the haunted room again, and said how sorry I was that I had had to promise you not to try my luck with it."

"You can't pry about in that gross way in other people's houses—you can't take such liberties, you know!" Mr. Coyle interjected.

"I'm all right—see how good I am. I don't want to go near the place!" said young Lechmere, confidingly. "Miss Julian said to me 'Oh, I daresay you'd risk it, but'—and she turned and laughed at poor Owen—'that's more than we can expect of a gentleman who has taken his extraordinary line.' I could see that something had already passed between them on the subject—some teasing or challenging of hers. It may have been only chaff, but his chucking the profession had evidently brought up the question of his pluck."

"And what did Owen say?"

"Nothing at first; but presently he brought out very quietly: 'I spent all last night in the confounded place.' We both stared and cried out at this and I asked him what he had seen there. He said he had seen nothing, and Miss Julian replied that he ought to tell his story better than that—he ought to make something good of it. 'It's not a story—it's a simple fact,' said he; on which she jeered at him and wanted to know why, if he had done it, he hadn't told her in the morning, since he knew what she thought of him. 'I know, but I don't care,' said Wingrave. This made her angry, and she asked him quite seriously whether he would care if he should know she believed him to be trying to deceive us."

"Ah, what a brute!" cried Spencer Coyle.

"She's a most extraordinary girl—I don't know what she's up to."

"Extraordinary indeed—to be romping and bandying words at that hour of the night with fast young men!"

Young Lechmere reflected a moment. "I mean because I think she likes him."

Spencer Coyle was so struck with this unwonted symptom of subtlety that he flashed out: "And do you think he likes her?"

But his interlocutor only replied with a puzzled sigh and a plaintive "I don't know—I give it up!—I'm sure he did see something or hear something," young Lechmere added.

"In that ridiculous place? What makes you sure?"

"I don't know—he looks as if he had. He behaves as if he had."

"Why then shouldn't he mention it?"

Young Lechmere thought a moment. "Perhaps it's too gruesome!"

Spencer Coyle gave a laugh. "Aren't you glad then you're not in it?"

"Uncommonly!"

"Go to bed, you goose," said Spencer Coyle, with another laugh. "But before you go tell me what he said when she told him he was trying to deceive you."

"'Take me there yourself, then, and lock me in!'"

"And did she take him?"

"I don't know—I came up."

Spencer Coyle exchanged a long look with his pupil.

"I don't think they're in the hall now. Where's Owen's own room?"

"I haven't the least idea."

Mr. Coyle was perplexed; he was in equal ignorance, and he couldn't go about trying doors. He bade young Lechmere sink to slumber, and came out into the passage. He asked himself if he should be able to find his way to the room Owen had formerly shown him, remembering that in common with many of the others it had its ancient name painted upon it. But the corridors of Paramore were intricate; moreover some of the servants would still be up, and he didn't wish to have the appearance of roaming over the house. He went back to his own quarters, where Mrs. Coyle soon perceived that his inability to rest had not subsided. As she confessed for her own part, in the dreadful place, to an increased sense of 'creepiness', they spent the early part of the night in conversation, so that a portion of their vigil was inevitably beguiled by her husband's account of his colloquy with little Lechmere and by their exchange of opinions upon it. Toward two o'clock Mrs. Coyle became so nervous about their persecuted young friend, and so possessed by the fear that that wicked girl had availed herself of his invitation to put him to an abominable test, that she begged her husband to go and look into the matter at whatever cost to his own equilibrium. But Spencer Coyle, perversely, had ended, as the perfect stillness of the night settled upon them, by charming himself into a tremulous acquiescence in Owen's readiness to face a formidable ordeal—an ordeal the more formidable to an excited imagination as the poor boy now knew from the experience of the previous night how resolute an effort he should have to make. "I hope he is there," he said to his wife: "it puts them all so in the wrong!" At any rate he couldn't take upon himself to explore a house he knew so little. He was inconsequent—he didn't prepare for bed. He sat in the dressing-room with his light and his novel, waiting to find himself nodding. At last however Mrs. Coyle turned over and ceased to talk, and at last too he fell asleep in his chair. How long he slept he only knew afterwards by computation; what he knew to begin with was that he had started up, in confusion, with the sense of a sudden appalling sound. His sense cleared itself quickly, helped doubtless by a confirmatory cry of horror from his wife's room. But he gave no heed to his wife; he had already bounded into the passage. There the sound was repeated—it was the "Help! help!" of a woman in agonised terror. It came from a distant quarter of the house, but the quarter was sufficiently indicated. Spencer Coyle rushed straight before him, with the sound of opening doors and alarmed voices in his ears and the faintness of the early dawn in his eyes. At a turn of one of the passages he came upon the white figure of a girl in a swoon on a bench, and in the vividness of the revelation he read as he went that Kate Julian, stricken in her pride too late with a chill of compunction for what she had mockingly done, had, after coming to release the victim of her derision, reeled away, overwhelmed, from the catastrophe that was her work—the catastrophe that the next moment he found himself aghast at on the threshold of an open door. Owen Wingrave, dressed as he had last seen him, lay dead on the spot on which his ancestor had been found. He looked like a young soldier on a battle-field.

PANDORA

CHAPTER I

It has long been the custom of the North German Lloyd steamers, which convey passengers from Bremen to New York, to anchor for several hours in the pleasant port of Southampton, where their human cargo receives many additions. An intelligent young German, Count Otto Vogelstein, hardly knew a few years ago whether to condemn this custom or approve it. He leaned over the bulwarks of the *Donau* as the American passengers crossed the plank—the travellers who embark at Southampton are mainly of that nationality—and curiously, indifferently, vaguely, through the smoke of his cigar, saw them absorbed in the huge capacity of the ship, where he had the agreeable consciousness that his own nest was comfortably made. To watch from such a point of vantage the struggles of those less fortunate than ourselves—of the uninformed, the unprovided, the belated, the bewildered—is an occupation not devoid of sweetness, and there was nothing to mitigate the complacency with which our young friend gave himself up to it; nothing, that is, save a natural benevolence which had not yet been extinguished by the consciousness of official greatness. For Count Vogelstein was official, as I think you would have seen from the straightness of his back, the lustre of his light elegant spectacles, and something discreet and diplomatic in the curve of his moustache, which looked as if it might well contribute to the principal function, as cynics say, of the lips—the active concealment of thought. He had been appointed to the secretaryship of the German legation at Washington and in these first days of the autumn was about to take possession of his post. He was a model character for such a purpose—serious civil ceremonious curious stiff, stuffed with knowledge and convinced that, as lately rearranged, the German Empire places in the most striking light the highest of all the possibilities of the greatest of all the peoples. He was quite aware, however, of the claims to economic and other consideration of the United States, and that this quarter of the globe offered a vast field for study.

The process of inquiry had already begun for him, in spite of his having as yet spoken to none of his fellow-passengers; the case being that Vogelstein inquired not only with his tongue, but with his eyes—that is with his spectacles—with his ears, with his nose, with his palate, with all his senses and organs. He was a highly upright young man, whose only fault was that his sense of comedy, or of the humour of things, had never been specifically disengaged from his several other senses. He vaguely felt that something should be done about this, and in a general manner proposed to do it, for he was on his way to explore a society abounding in comic aspects. This consciousness of a missing measure gave him a certain mistrust of what might be said of him; and if circumspection is the essence of diplomacy our young aspirant promised well. His mind contained several millions of facts, packed too closely together for the light breeze of the imagination to draw through the mass. He was impatient to report himself to his superior in Washington, and the loss of time in an English port could only incommode him, inasmuch as the study of English institutions was no part of his mission. On the other hand the day was charming; the blue sea, in Southampton Water, pricked all over with light, had no movement but that of its infinite shimmer. Moreover he was by no means sure that he should be happy in the United States, where doubtless he should find himself soon enough disembarked. He knew that this was not an important question and that happiness was an unscientific term, such as a man of his education should be ashamed to use even in the silence of his thoughts. Lost none the less in the inconsiderate crowd and feeling himself neither in his own country nor in that to which he was in a manner accredited, he was reduced to his mere personality; so that during the hour, to save his importance, he cultivated such ground as lay in sight for a judgement of this delay to which the German steamer was subjected in English waters. Mightn't it be proved, facts, figures and documents—or at least watch—in hand, considerably greater than the occasion demanded?

Count Vogelstein was still young enough in diplomacy to think it necessary to have opinions. He had a good many indeed which had been formed without difficulty; they had been received ready-made from a line of ancestors who knew what they liked. This was of course—and under pressure, being candid, he would have admitted it—an unscientific way of furnishing one's mind. Our young man was a stiff conservative, a Junker of Junkers; he thought modern democracy a temporary phase and expected to find many arguments against it in the great Republic. In regard to these things it was a pleasure to him to feel that, with his complete training, he had been taught thoroughly to appreciate the nature of evidence. The ship was heavily laden with German emigrants, whose mission in the United States differed considerably from Count Otto's. They hung over the bulwarks, densely grouped; they leaned forward on their elbows for hours, their shoulders kept on a level with their ears; the men in furred caps, smoking long-bowled pipes, the women with babies hidden in remarkably ugly shawls. Some were yellow Germans and some were black, and all looked greasy and matted with the sea-damp. They were destined to swell still further the huge current of the Western democracy; and Count Vogelstein doubtless said to himself that they wouldn't improve its quality. Their numbers, however, were striking, and I know not what he thought of the nature of this particular evidence.

The passengers who came on board at Southampton were not of the greasy class; they were for the most part American families who had been spending the summer, or a longer period, in Europe. They had a great deal of luggage, innumerable bags and rugs and hampers and sea-chairs, and were composed largely of ladies of various ages, a little pale with anticipation, wrapped also in striped shawls, though in prettier ones than the nursing mothers of the steerage, and crowned with very high hats and feathers. They darted to and fro across the gangway, looking for each other and for their scattered parcels; they separated and reunited, they exclaimed and declared, they eyed with dismay the occupants of the forward quarter, who seemed numerous enough to sink the vessel, and their voices sounded faint and far as they rose to Vogelstein's ear over the latter's great tarred sides. He noticed that in the new contingent there were many young girls, and he remembered what a lady in Dresden had once said to him—that America was the country of the Mädchen. He wondered whether he should like that, and reflected that it would be an aspect to study, like everything else. He had known in Dresden an American family in which there were three daughters who used to skate with the officers, and some of the ladies now coming on board struck him as of that same habit, except that in the Dresden days feathers weren't worn quite so high.

At last the ship began to creak and slowly bridge, and the delay at Southampton came to an end. The gangway was removed and the vessel indulged in the awkward evolutions that were to detach her from the land. Count Vogelstein had finished his cigar, and he spent a long time in walking up and down the upper deck. The charming English coast passed before him, and he felt this to be the last of the old world. The American coast also might be pretty—he hardly knew what one would expect of an American coast; but he was sure it would be different. Differences, however, were notoriously half the charm of travel, and perhaps even most when they couldn't be expressed in figures, numbers, diagrams or the other merely useful symbols. As yet indeed there were very few among the objects presented to sight on the steamer. Most of his fellow-passengers appeared of one and the same persuasion, and that persuasion the least to be mistaken. They were Jews and commercial to a man. And by this time they had lighted their cigars and put on all manner of seafaring caps, some of them with big ear-lappets which somehow had the effect of bringing out their peculiar facial type. At last the new voyagers began to emerge from below and to look about them, vaguely, with that suspicious expression of face always to be noted in the newly embarked and which, as directed to the receding land, resembles that of a person who begins to perceive himself the victim of a trick. Earth and ocean, in such glances, are made the subject of a sweeping objection, and many travellers, in the general plight, have an air at once duped and superior, which seems to say that they could easily go ashore if they would.

It still wanted two hours of dinner, and by the time Vogelstein's long legs had measured three or four miles on the deck he was ready to settle himself in his sea-chair and draw from his pocket a Tauchnitz novel by an American author whose pages, he had been assured, would help to prepare him for some of the oddities. On the back of his chair his name was painted in rather large letters, this being a precaution taken at the recommendation of a friend who had told him that on the American steamers the passengers—especially the ladies—thought nothing of pilfering one's little comforts. His friend had even hinted at the correct reproduction of his coronet. This marked man of the world had added that the Americans are greatly impressed by a coronet. I know not whether it was scepticism or modesty, but Count Vogelstein had omitted every pictured plea for his rank; there were others of which he might have made use. The precious piece of furniture which on the Atlantic voyage is trusted never to flinch among universal concussions was emblazoned simply with his title and name. It happened, however, that the blazonry was huge; the back of the chair was covered with enormous German characters. This time there can be no doubt: it was modesty that caused the secretary of legation, in placing himself, to turn this portion of his seat outward, away from the eyes of his companions—to present it to the balustrade of the deck. The ship was passing the Needles—the beautiful uttermost point of the Isle of Wight. Certain tall white cones of rock rose out of the purple sea; they flushed in the afternoon light and their vague rosiness gave them a human expression in face of the cold expanse toward which the prow was turned; they seemed to say farewell, to be the last note of a peopled world. Vogelstein saw them very comfortably from his place and after a while turned his eyes to the other quarter, where the elements of air and water managed to make between them so comparatively poor an opposition. Even his American novelist was more amusing than that, and he prepared to return to this author. In the great curve which it described, however, his glance was arrested by the figure of a young lady who had just ascended to the deck and who paused at the mouth of the companionway.

This was not in itself an extraordinary phenomenon; but what attracted Vogelstein's attention was the fact that the young person appeared to have fixed her eyes on him. She was slim, brightly dressed, rather pretty; Vogelstein remembered in a moment that he had noticed her among the people on the wharf at Southampton. She was soon aware he had observed her; whereupon she began to move along the deck with a step that seemed to indicate a purpose of approaching him. Vogelstein had time to wonder whether she could be one of the girls he had known at Dresden; but he presently reflected that they would now be much older than that. It was true they were apt to advance, like this one, straight upon their victim. Yet the present specimen was no longer looking at him, and though she passed near him it was now tolerably clear she had come above but to take a general survey. She was a quick handsome competent girl, and she simply wanted to see what one could think of the ship, of the weather, of the appearance of England, from such a position as that; possibly even of one's fellow-passengers. She satisfied herself promptly on these points, and then she looked about, while she walked, as if in keen search of a missing object; so that Vogelstein finally arrived at a conviction of her real motive. She passed near him again and this time almost stopped, her eyes bent upon him attentively. He thought her conduct remarkable even after he had gathered that it was not at his face, with its yellow moustache, she was looking, but at the chair on which he was seated. Then those words of his friend came back to him—the speech about the tendency of the people, especially of the ladies, on the American steamers to take to themselves one's little belongings. Especially the ladies, he might well say; for here was one who apparently wished to pull from under him the very chair he was sitting on. He was afraid she would ask him for it, so he pretended to read, systematically avoiding her eye. He was conscious she hovered near him, and was moreover curious to see what she would do. It seemed to him strange that such a nice-looking girl—for her appearance was really charming—should endeavour by arts so flagrant to work upon the quiet dignity of a secretary of legation. At last it stood out that she was trying to look round a corner, as it were—trying to see what was written on the back of his chair. "She wants to find out my name; she wants to see who I am!" This reflexion passed through his mind and caused him to raise his eyes. They rested on her own—which for an appreciable moment she didn't withdraw. The latter were brilliant and expressive, and surmounted a delicate aquiline nose, which, though pretty, was perhaps just a trifle too hawk-like. It was the oddest coincidence in the world; the story Vogelstein had taken up treated of a flighty forward little American girl who plants herself in front of a young man in the garden of an hotel. Wasn't the conduct of this young lady a testimony to the truthfulness of the tale, and wasn't Vogelstein himself in the position of the young man in the garden? That young man—though with more, in such connexions in general, to go upon—ended by addressing himself to his aggressor, as she might be called, and after a very short hesitation Vogelstein followed his example. "If she wants to know who I am she's welcome," he said to himself; and he got out of the chair, seized it by the back and, turning it round, exhibited the superscription to the girl. She coloured slightly, but smiled and read his name, while Vogelstein raised his hat.

"I'm much obliged to you. That's all right," she remarked as if the discovery had made her very happy.

It affected him indeed as all right that he should be Count Otto Vogelstein; this appeared even rather a flippant mode of disposing of the fact. By way of rejoinder he asked her if she desired of him the surrender of his seat.

"I'm much obliged to you; of course not. I thought you had one of our chairs, and I didn't like to ask you. It looks exactly like one of ours; not so much now as when you sit in it. Please sit down again. I don't want to trouble you. We've lost one of ours, and I've been looking for it everywhere. They look so much alike; you can't tell till you see the back. Of course I see there will be no mistake about yours," the young lady went on with a smile of which the serenity matched her other abundance. "But we've got such a small name—you can scarcely see it," she added with the same friendly intention. "Our name's just Day—you mightn't think it *was* a name, might you? if we didn't make the most of it. If you see that on anything, I'd be so obliged if you'd tell me. It isn't for myself, it's for my mother; she's so dependent on her chair, and that one I'm looking for pulls out so beautifully. Now that you sit down again and hide the lower part it does look just like ours. Well, it must be somewhere. You must excuse me; I wouldn't disturb you."

This was a long and even confidential speech for a young woman, presumably unmarried, to make to a perfect stranger; but Miss Day acquitted herself of it with perfect simplicity and self-possession. She held up her head and stepped away, and Vogelstein could see that the foot she pressed upon the clean smooth deck was slender and shapely. He watched her disappear through the trap by which she had ascended, and he felt more than ever like the young man in his American tale. The girl in the present case was older and not so pretty, as he could easily judge, for the image of her smiling eyes and speaking lips still hovered before him. He went back to his book with the feeling that it would give him some information about her. This was rather illogical, but it indicated a certain amount of curiosity on the part of Count Vogelstein. The girl in the book had a mother, it appeared, and so had this young lady; the former had also a brother, and he now remembered that he had noticed a young man on the wharf—a young man in a high hat and a white overcoat—who seemed united to Miss Day by this natural tie. And there was some one else too, as he gradually recollected, an older man, also in a high hat, but in a black overcoat—in black altogether—who completed the group and who was presumably the head of the family. These reflexions would indicate that Count Vogelstein read his volume of Tauchnitz rather interruptedly. Moreover they represented but the loosest economy of consciousness; for wasn't he to be afloat in an oblong box for ten days with such people, and could it be doubted he should see at least enough of them?

It may as well be written without delay that he saw a great deal of them. I have sketched in some detail the conditions in which he made the acquaintance of Miss Day, because the event had a certain importance for this fair square Teuton; but I must pass briefly over the incidents that immediately followed it. He wondered what it was open to him, after such an introduction, to do in relation to her, and he determined he would push through his American tale and discover what the hero did. But he satisfied himself in a very short time that Miss Day had nothing in common with the heroine of that work save certain signs of habitat and climate—and save, further, the fact that the male sex wasn't terrible to her. The local stamp sharply, as he gathered, impressed upon her he estimated indeed rather in a borrowed than in a natural light, for if she was native to a small town in the interior of the American continent one of their fellow-passengers, a lady from New York with whom he had a good deal of conversation, pronounced her "atrociously" provincial. How the lady arrived at this certitude didn't appear, for Vogelstein observed that she held no communication with the girl. It was true she gave it the support of her laying down that certain Americans could tell immediately who other Americans were, leaving him to judge whether or no she herself belonged to the critical or only to the criticised half of the nation. Mrs. Dangerfield was a handsome confidential insinuating woman, with whom Vogelstein felt his talk take a very wide range indeed. She convinced him rather effectually that even in a great democracy there are human differences, and that American life was full of social distinctions, of delicate shades, which foreigners often lack the intelligence to perceive. Did he suppose every one knew every one else in the biggest country in the world, and that one wasn't as free to choose one's company there as in the most monarchical and most exclusive societies? She laughed such delusions to scorn as Vogelstein tucked her beautiful furred coverlet—they reclined together a great deal in their elongated chairs—well over her feet. How free an American lady was to choose her company she abundantly proved by not knowing any one on the steamer but Count Otto.

He could see for himself that Mr. and Mrs. Day had not at all her grand air. They were fat plain serious people who sat side by side on the deck for hours and looked straight before them. Mrs. Day had a white face, large cheeks and small eyes: her forehead was surrounded with a multitude of little tight black curls; her lips moved as if she had always a lozenge in her mouth. She wore entwined about her head an article which Mrs. Dangerfield spoke of as a "nuby," a knitted pink scarf concealing her hair, encircling her neck and having among its convolutions a hole for her perfectly expressionless face. Her hands were folded on her stomach, and in her still, swathed figure her little bead-like eyes, which occasionally changed their direction, alone represented life. Her husband had a stiff grey beard on his chin and a bare spacious upper lip, to which constant shaving had imparted a hard glaze. His eyebrows were thick and his nostrils wide, and when he was uncovered, in the saloon, it was visible that his grizzled hair was dense and perpendicular. He might have looked rather grim and truculent hadn't it been for the mild familiar accommodating gaze with which his large light-coloured pupils—the leisurely eyes of a silent man—appeared to consider surrounding objects. He was evidently more friendly than fierce, but he was more diffident than friendly. He liked to have you in sight, but wouldn't have pretended to understand you much or to classify you, and would have been sorry it should put you under an obligation. He and his wife spoke sometimes, but seldom talked, and there was something vague and patient in them, as if they had become victims of a wrought spell. The spell however was of no sinister cast; it was the fascination of prosperity, the confidence of security, which sometimes makes people arrogant, but which had had such a different effect on this simple satisfied pair, in whom further development of every kind appeared to have been happily arrested.

Mrs. Dangerfield made it known to Count Otto that every morning after breakfast, the hour at which he wrote his journal in his cabin, the old couple were guided upstairs and installed in their customary corner by Pandora. This she had learned to be the name of their elder daughter, and she was immensely amused by her discovery. "Pandora"—that was in the highest degree typical; it placed them in the social scale if other evidence had been wanting; you could tell that a girl was from the interior, the mysterious interior about which Vogelstein's imagination was now quite excited, when she had such a name as that. This young lady managed the whole family, even a little the small beflounced sister, who, with bold pretty innocent eyes, a torrent of fair silky hair, a crimson fez, such as is worn by male Turks, very much askew on top of it, and a way of galloping and straddling about the ship in any company she could pick up—she had long thin legs, very short skirts and stockings of every tint—was going home, in elegant French clothes, to resume an interrupted education. Pandora overlooked and directed her relatives; Vogelstein could see this for himself, could see she was very active and decided, that she had in a high degree the sentiment of responsibility, settling on the spot most of the questions that could come up for a family from the interior.

The voyage was remarkably fine, and day after day it was possible to sit there under the salt sky and feel one's self rounding the great curves of the globe. The long deck made a white spot in the sharp black circle of the ocean and in the intense sea-light, while the shadow of the smoke-streamers trembled on the familiar floor, the shoes of fellow-passengers, distinctive now, and in some cases irritating, passed and repassed, accompanied, in the air so tremendously "open," that rendered all voices weak and most remarks rather flat, by fragments of opinion on the run of the ship. Vogelstein by this time had finished his little American story and now definitely judged that Pandora Day was not at all like the heroine. She was of quite another type; much more serious and strenuous, and not at all keen, as he had supposed, about making the acquaintance of gentlemen. Her speaking to him that first afternoon had been, he was bound to believe, an incident without importance for herself; in spite of her having followed it up the next day by the remark, thrown at him as she passed, with a smile that was almost fraternal: "It's all right, sir! I've found that old chair." After this she hadn't spoken to him again and had scarcely looked at him. She read a great deal, and almost always French books, in fresh yellow paper; not the lighter forms of that literature, but a volume of Sainte-Beuve, of Renan or at the most, in the way of dissipation, of Alfred de Musset. She took frequent exercise and almost always walked alone, apparently not having made many friends on the ship and being without the resource of her parents, who, as has been related, never budged out of the cosy corner in which she planted them for the day.

Her brother was always in the smoking-room, where Vogelstein observed him, in very tight clothes, his neck encircled with a collar like a palisade. He had a sharp little face, which was not disagreeable; he smoked enormous cigars and began his drinking early in the day: but his appearance gave no sign of these excesses. As regards euchre and poker and the other distractions of the place he was guilty of none. He evidently understood such games in perfection, for he used to watch the players, and even at moments impartially advise them; but Vogelstein never saw the cards in his hand. He was referred to as regards disputed points, and his opinion carried the day. He took little part in the conversation, usually much relaxed, that prevailed in the smoking-room, but from time to time he made, in his soft flat youthful voice, a remark which every one paused to listen to and which was greeted with roars of laughter. Vogelstein, well as he knew English, could rarely catch the joke; but he could see at least that these must be choice specimens of that American humour admired and practised by a whole continent and yet to be rendered accessible to a trained diplomatist, clearly, but by some special and incalculable revelation. The young man, in his way, was very remarkable, for, as Vogelstein heard some one say once after the laughter had subsided, he was only nineteen. If his sister didn't resemble the dreadful little girl in the tale already mentioned, there was for Vogelstein at least an analogy between young Mr. Day and a certain small brother—a candy-loving Madison, Hamilton or Jefferson—who was, in the Tauchnitz volume, attributed to that unfortunate maid. This was what the little Madison would have grown up to at nineteen, and the improvement was greater than might have been expected.

The days were long, but the voyage was short, and it had almost come to an end before Count Otto yielded to an attraction peculiar in its nature and finally irresistible, and, in spite of Mrs. Dangerfield's emphatic warning, sought occasion for a little continuous talk with Miss Pandora. To mention that this impulse took effect without mentioning sundry other of his current impressions with which it had nothing to do is perhaps to violate proportion and give a false idea; but to pass it by would be still more unjust. The Germans, as we know, are a transcendental people, and there was at last an irresistible appeal for Vogelstein in this quick bright silent girl who could smile and turn vocal in an instant, who imparted a rare originality to the filial character, and whose profile was delicate as she bent it over a volume which she cut as she read, or presented it in musing attitudes, at the side of the ship, to the horizon they had left behind. But he felt it to be a pity, as regards a possible acquaintance with her, that her parents should be heavy little burghers, that her brother should not correspond to his conception of a young man of the upper class, and that her sister should be a Daisy Miller *en herbe*. Repeatedly admonished by Mrs. Dangerfield, the young diplomatist was doubly careful as to the relations he might form at the beginning of his sojourn in the United States. That lady reminded him, and he had himself made the observation in other capitals, that the first year, and even the second, is the time for prudence. One was ignorant of proportions and values; one was exposed to mistakes and thankful for attention, and one might give one's self away to people who would afterwards be as a millstone round one's neck: Mrs. Dangerfield struck and sustained that note, which resounded in the young man's imagination. She assured him that if he didn't "look out" he would be committing himself to some American girl with an impossible family. In America, when one committed one's self, there was nothing to do but march to the altar, and what should he say for instance to finding himself a near relation of Mr. and Mrs. P. W. Day?—since such were the initials inscribed on the back of the two chairs of that couple. Count Otto felt the peril, for he could immediately think of a dozen men he knew who had married American girls. There appeared now to be a constant danger of marrying the American girl; it was something one had to reckon with, like the railway, the telegraph, the discovery of dynamite, the Chassepot rifle, the Socialistic spirit: it was one of the complications of modern life.

It would doubtless be too much to say that he feared being carried away by a passion for a young woman who was not strikingly beautiful and with whom he had talked, in all, but ten minutes. But, as we recognise, he went so far as to wish that the human belongings of a person whose high spirit appeared to have no taint either of fastness, as they said in England, or of subversive opinion, and whose mouth had charming lines, should not be a little more distinguished. There was an effect of drollery in her behaviour to these subjects of her zeal, whom she seemed to regard as a care, but not as an interest; it was as if they had been entrusted to her honour and she had engaged to convey them safe to a certain point; she was detached and inadvertent, and then suddenly remembered, repented and came back to tuck them into their blankets, to alter the position of her mother's umbrella, to tell them something about the run of the ship. These little offices were usually performed deftly, rapidly, with the minimum of words, and when their daughter drew near them Mr. and Mrs. Day closed their eyes after the fashion of a pair of household dogs who expect to be scratched.

One morning she brought up the Captain of the ship to present to them; she appeared to have a private and independent acquaintance with this officer, and the introduction to her parents had the air of a sudden happy thought. It wasn't so much an introduction as an exhibition, as if she were saying to him: "This is what they look like; see how comfortable I make them. Aren't they rather queer and rather dear little people? But they leave me perfectly free. Oh I can assure you of that. Besides, you must see it for yourself." Mr. and Mrs. Day looked up at the high functionary who thus unbent to them with very little change of countenance; then looked at each other in the same way. He saluted, he inclined himself a moment; but Pandora shook her head, she seemed to be answering for them; she made little gestures as if in explanation to the good Captain of some of their peculiarities, as for instance that he needn't expect them to speak. They closed their eyes at last; she appeared to have a kind of mesmeric influence on them, and Miss Day walked away with the important friend, who treated her with evident consideration, bowing very low, for all his importance, when the two presently after separated. Vogelstein could see she was capable of making an impression; and the moral of our little matter is that in spite of Mrs. Dangerfield, in spite of the resolutions of his prudence, in spite of the limits of such acquaintance as he had momentarily made with her, in spite of Mr. and Mrs. Day and the young man in the smoking-room, she had fixed his attention.

It was in the course of the evening after the scene with the Captain that he joined her, awkwardly, abruptly, irresistibly, on the deck, where she was pacing to and fro alone, the hour being auspiciously mild and the stars remarkably fine. There were scattered talkers and smokers and couples, unrecognisable, that moved quickly through the gloom. The vessel dipped with long regular pulsations; vague and spectral under the low stars, its swaying pinnacles spotted here and there with lights, it seemed to rush through the darkness faster than by day. Count Otto had come up to walk, and as the girl brushed past him he distinguished Pandora's face—with Mrs. Dangerfield he always spoke of her as Pandora—under the veil worn to protect it from the sea-damp. He stopped, turned, hurried after her, threw away his cigar—then asked her if she would do him the honour to accept his arm. She declined his arm but accepted his company, and he allowed her to enjoy it for an hour. They had a great deal of talk, and he was to remember afterwards some of the things she had said. There was now a certainty of the ship's getting into dock the next morning but one, and this prospect afforded an obvious topic. Some of Miss Day's expressions struck him as singular, but of course, as he was aware, his knowledge of English was not nice enough to give him a perfect measure.

"I'm not in a hurry to arrive; I'm very happy here," she said. "I'm afraid I shall have such a time putting my people through."

"Putting them through?"

"Through the Custom-House. We've made so many purchases. Well, I've written to a friend to come down, and perhaps he can help us. He's very well acquainted with the head. Once I'm chalked I don't care. I feel like a kind of blackboard by this time anyway. We found them awful in Germany."

Count Otto wondered if the friend she had written to were her lover and if they had plighted their troth, especially when she alluded to him again as "that gentleman who's coming down." He asked her about her travels, her impressions, whether she had been long in Europe and what she liked best, and she put it to him that they had gone abroad, she and her family, for a little fresh experience. Though he found her very intelligent he suspected she gave this as a reason because he was a German and she had heard the Germans were rich in culture. He wondered what form of culture Mr. and Mrs. Day had brought back from Italy, Greece and Palestine—they had travelled for two years and been everywhere—especially when their daughter said: "I wanted father and mother to see the best things. I kept them three hours on the Acropolis. I guess they won't forget that!" Perhaps it was of Phidias and Pericles they were thinking, Vogelstein reflected, as they sat ruminating in their rugs. Pandora remarked also that she wanted to show her little sister everything while she was comparatively unformed ("comparatively!" he mutely gasped); remarkable sights made so much more impression when the mind was fresh: she had read something of that sort somewhere in Goethe. She had wanted to come herself when she was her sister's age; but her father was in business then and they couldn't leave Utica. The young man thought of the little sister frisking over the Parthenon and the Mount of Olives and sharing for two years, the years of the school-room, this extraordinary pilgrimage of her parents; he wondered whether Goethe's dictum had been justified in this case. He asked Pandora if Utica were the seat of her family, if it were an important or typical place, if it would be an interesting city for him, as a stranger, to see. His companion replied frankly that this was a big question, but added that all the same she would ask him to "come and visit us at our home" if it weren't that they should probably soon leave it.

"Ah, you're going to live elsewhere?" Vogelstein asked, as if that fact too would be typical.

"Well, I'm working for New York. I flatter myself I've loosened them while we've been away," the girl went on. "They won't find in Utica the same charm; that was my idea. I want a big place, and of course Utica—!" She broke off as before a complex statement.

"I suppose Utica is inferior—?" Vogelstein seemed to see his way to suggest.

"Well no, I guess I can't have you call Utica inferior. It isn't supreme—that's what's the matter with it, and I hate anything middling," said Pandora Day. She gave a light dry laugh, tossing back her head a little as she made this declaration. And looking at her askance in the dusk, as she trod the deck that vaguely swayed, he recognised something in her air and port that matched such a pronouncement.

"What's her social position?" he inquired of Mrs. Dangerfield the next day. "I can't make it out at all—it's so contradictory. She strikes me as having much cultivation and much spirit. Her appearance, too, is very neat. Yet her parents are complete little burghers. That's easily seen."

"Oh, social position," and Mrs. Dangerfield nodded two or three times portentously. "What big expressions you use! Do you think everybody in the world has a social position? That's reserved for an infinitely small majority of mankind. You can't have a social position at Utica any more than you can have an opera-box. Pandora hasn't got one; where, if you please, should she have got it? Poor girl, it isn't fair of you to make her the subject of such questions as that."

"Well," said Vogelstein, "if she's of the lower class it seems to me very—very—" And he paused a moment, as he often paused in speaking English, looking for his word.

"Very what, dear Count?"

"Very significant, very representative."

"Oh dear, she isn't of the lower class," Mrs. Dangerfield returned with an irritated sense of wasted wisdom. She liked to explain her country, but that somehow always required two persons.

"What is she then?"

"Well, I'm bound to admit that since I was at home last she's a novelty. A girl like that with such people—it *is* a new type."

"I like novelties"—and Count Otto smiled with an air of considerable resolution. He couldn't however be satisfied with a demonstration that only begged the question; and when they disembarked in New York he felt, even amid the confusion of the wharf and the heaps of disembowelled baggage, a certain acuteness of regret at the idea that Pandora and her family were about to vanish into the unknown. He had a consolation however: it was apparent that for some reason or other—illness or absence from town—the gentleman to whom she had written had not, as she said, come down. Vogelstein was glad—he couldn't have told you why—that this sympathetic person had failed her; even though without him Pandora had to engage single-handed with the United States Custom-House. Our young man's first impression of the Western world was received on the landing-place of the German steamers at Jersey City—a huge wooden shed covering a wooden wharf which resounded under the feet, an expanse palisaded with rough-hewn piles that leaned this way and that, and bestrewn with masses of heterogeneous luggage. At one end; toward the town, was a row of tall painted palings, behind which he could distinguish a press of hackney-coachmen, who brandished their whips and awaited their victims, while their voices rose, incessant, with a sharp strange sound, a challenge at once fierce and familiar. The whole place, behind the fence, appeared to bristle and resound. Out there was America, Count Otto said to himself, and he looked toward it with a sense that he should have to muster resolution. On the wharf people were rushing about amid their trunks, pulling their things together, trying to unite their scattered parcels. They were heated and angry, or else quite bewildered and discouraged. The few that had succeeded in collecting their battered boxes had an air of flushed indifference to the efforts of their neighbours, not even looking at people with whom they had been fondly intimate on the steamer. A detachment of the officers of the Customs was in attendance, and energetic passengers were engaged in attempts to drag them toward their luggage or to drag heavy pieces toward them. These functionaries were good-natured and taciturn, except when occasionally they remarked to a passenger whose open trunk stared up at them, eloquent, imploring, that they were afraid the voyage had been "rather glassy." They had a friendly leisurely speculative way of discharging their duty, and if they perceived a victim's name written on the portmanteau they addressed him by it in a tone of old acquaintance. Vogelstein found however that if they were familiar they weren't indiscreet. He had heard that in America all public functionaries were the same, that there wasn't a different *tenue*, as they said in France, for different positions, and he wondered whether at Washington the President and ministers, whom he expected to see—to *have* to see—a good deal of, would be like that.

He was diverted from these speculations by the sight of Mr. and Mrs. Day seated side by side upon a trunk and encompassed apparently by the accumulations of their tour. Their faces expressed more consciousness of surrounding objects than he had hitherto recognised, and there was an air of placid expansion in the mysterious couple which suggested that this consciousness was agreeable. Mr. and Mrs. Day were, as they would have said, real glad to get back. At a little distance, on the edge of the dock, our observer remarked their son, who had found a place where, between the sides of two big ships, he could see the ferry-boats pass; the large pyramidal low-laden ferry-boats of American waters. He stood there, patient and considering, with his small neat foot on a coil of rope, his back to everything that had been disembarked, his neck elongated in its polished cylinder, while the fragrance of his big cigar mingled with the odour of the rotting piles, and his little sister, beside him, hugged a huge post and tried to see how far she could crane over the water without falling in. Vogelstein's servant was off in search of an examiner; Count Otto himself had got his things together and was waiting to be released, fully expecting that for a person of his importance the ceremony would be brief.

Before it began he said a word to young Mr. Day, raising his hat at the same time to the little girl, whom he had not yet greeted and who dodged his salute by swinging herself boldly outward to the dangerous side of the pier. She was indeed still unformed, but was evidently as light as a feather.

"I see you're kept waiting like me. It's very tiresome," Count Otto said.

The young American answered without looking behind him. "As soon as we're started we'll go all right. My sister has written to a gentleman to come down."

"I've looked for Miss Day to bid her good-bye," Vogelstein went on; "but I don't see her."

"I guess she has gone to meet that gentleman; he's a great friend of hers."

"I guess he's her lover!" the little girl broke out. "She was always writing to him in Europe."

Her brother puffed his cigar in silence a moment. "That was only for this. I'll tell on you, sis," he presently added.

But the younger Miss Day gave no heed to his menace; she addressed herself only, though with all freedom, to Vogelstein. "This is New York; I like it better than Utica."

He had no time to reply, for his servant had arrived with one of the dispensers of fortune; but as he turned away he wondered, in the light of the child's preference, about the towns of the interior. He was naturally exempt from the common doom. The officer who took him in hand, and who had a large straw hat and a diamond breastpin, was quite a man of the world, and in reply to the Count's formal declarations only said, "Well, I guess it's all right; I guess I'll just pass you," distributing chalk-marks as if they had been so many love-pats. The servant had done some superfluous unlocking and unbuckling, and while he closed the pieces the officer stood there wiping his forehead and conversing with Vogelstein. "First visit to our country, sir?—quite alone—no ladies? Of course the ladies are what we're most after." It was in this manner he expressed himself, while the young diplomatist wondered what he was waiting for and whether he ought to slip something into his palm. But this representative of order left our friend only a moment in suspense; he presently turned away with the remark quite paternally uttered, that he hoped the Count would make quite a stay; upon which the young man saw how wrong he should have been to offer a tip. It was simply the American manner, which had a finish of its own after all. Vogelstein's servant had secured a porter with a truck, and he was about to leave the place when he saw Pandora Day dart out of the crowd and address herself with much eagerness to the functionary who had just liberated him. She had an open letter in her hand which she gave him to read and over which he cast his eyes, thoughtfully stroking his beard. Then she led him away to where her parents sat on their luggage. Count Otto sent off his servant with the porter and followed Pandora, to whom he really wished to address a word of farewell. The last thing they had said to each other on the ship was that they should meet again on shore. It seemed improbable however that the meeting would occur anywhere but just here on the dock; inasmuch as Pandora was decidedly not in society, where Vogelstein would be of course, and as, if Utica—he had her sharp little sister's word for it—was worse than what was about him there, he'd be hanged if he'd go to Utica. He overtook Pandora quickly; she was in the act of introducing the representative of order to her parents, quite in the same manner in which she had introduced the Captain of the ship. Mr. and Mrs. Day got up and shook hands with him and they evidently all prepared to have a little talk. "I should like to introduce you to my brother and sister," he heard the girl say, and he saw her look about for these appendages. He caught her eye as she did so, and advanced with his hand outstretched, reflecting the while that evidently the Americans, whom he had always heard described as silent and practical, rejoiced to extravagance in the social graces. They dawdled and chattered like so many Neapolitans.

"Good-bye, Count Vogelstein," said Pandora, who was a little flushed with her various exertions but didn't look the worse for it. "I hope you'll have a splendid time and appreciate our country."

"I hope you'll get through all right," Vogelstein answered, smiling and feeling himself already more idiomatic.

"That gentleman's sick that I wrote to," she rejoined; "isn't it too bad? But he sent me down a letter to a friend of his—one of the examiners—and I guess we won't have any trouble. Mr. Lansing, let me make you acquainted with Count Vogelstein," she went on, presenting to her fellow-passenger the wearer of the straw hat and the breastpin, who shook hands with the young German as if he had never seen him before. Vogelstein's heart rose for an instant to his throat; he thanked his stars he hadn't offered a tip to the friend of a gentleman who had often been mentioned to him and who had also been described by a member of Pandora's family as Pandora's lover.

"It's a case of ladies this time," Mr. Lansing remarked to him with a smile which seemed to confess surreptitiously, and as if neither party could be eager, to recognition.

"Well, Mr. Bellamy says you'll do anything for *him*," Pandora said, smiling very sweetly at Mr. Lansing. "We haven't got much; we've been gone only two years."

Mr. Lansing scratched his head a little behind, with a movement that sent his straw hat forward in the direction of his nose. "I don't know as I'd do anything for him that I wouldn't do for you," he responded with an equal geniality. "I guess you'd better open that one"—and he gave a little affectionate kick to one of the trunks.

"Oh mother, isn't he lovely? It's only your sea-things," Pandora cried, stooping over the coffer with the key in her hand.

"I don't know as I like showing them," Mrs. Day modestly murmured.

Vogelstein made his German salutation to the company in general, and to Pandora he offered an audible good-bye, which she returned in a bright friendly voice, but without looking round as she fumbled at the lock of her trunk.

"We'll try another, if you like," said Mr. Lansing good-humouredly.

"Oh no it has got to be this one! Good-bye, Count Vogelstein. I hope you'll judge us correctly!"

The young man went his way and passed the barrier of the dock. Here he was met by his English valet with a face of consternation which led him to ask if a cab weren't forthcoming.

"They call 'em 'acks 'ere, sir," said the man, "and they're beyond everything. He wants thirty shillings to take you to the inn."

Vogelstein hesitated a moment. "Couldn't you find a German?"

"By the way he talks he IS a German said the man; and in a moment Count Otto began his career in America by discussing the tariff of hackney-coaches in the language of the fatherland.

CHAPTER II

He went wherever he was asked, on principle, partly to study American society and partly because in Washington pastimes seemed to him not so numerous that one could afford to neglect occasions. At the end of two winters he had naturally had a good many of various kinds—his study of American society had yielded considerable fruit. When, however, in April, during the second year of his residence, he presented himself at a large party given by Mrs. Bonnycastle and of which it was believed that it would be the last serious affair of the season, his being there (and still more his looking very fresh and talkative) was not the consequence of a rule of conduct. He went to Mrs. Bonnycastle's simply because he liked the lady, whose receptions were the pleasantest in Washington, and because if he didn't go there he didn't know what he should do; that absence of alternatives having become familiar to him by the waters of the Potomac. There were a great many things he did because if he didn't do them he didn't know what he should do. It must be added that in this case even if there had been an alternative he would still have decided to go to Mrs. Bonnycastle's. If her house wasn't the pleasantest there it was at least difficult to say which was pleasanter; and the complaint sometimes made of it that it was too limited, that it left out, on the whole, more people than it took in, applied with much less force when it was thrown open for a general party. Toward the end of the social year, in those soft scented days of the Washington spring when the air began to show a southern glow and the Squares and Circles (to which the wide empty avenues converged according to a plan so ingenious, yet so bewildering) to flush with pink blossom and to make one wish to sit on benches—under this magic of expansion and condonation Mrs. Bonnycastle, who during the winter had been a good deal on the defensive, relaxed her vigilance a little, became whimsically wilful, vernally reckless, as it were, and ceased to calculate the consequences of an hospitality which a reference to the back files or even to the morning's issue of the newspapers might easily prove a mistake. But Washington life, to Count Otto's apprehension, was paved with mistakes; he felt himself in a society founded on fundamental fallacies and triumphant blunders. Little addicted as he was to the sportive view of existence, he had said to himself at an early stage of his sojourn that the only way to enjoy the great Republic would be to burn one's standards and warm one's self at the blaze. Such were the reflexions of a theoretic Teuton who now walked for the most part amid the ashes of his prejudices.

Mrs. Bonnycastle had endeavoured more than once to explain to him the principles on which she received certain people and ignored certain others; but it was with difficulty that he entered into her discriminations. American promiscuity, goodness knew, had been strange to him, but it was nothing to the queerness of American criticism. This lady would discourse to him *à perte de vue* on differences where he only saw resemblances, and both the merits and the defects of a good many members of Washington society, as this society was interpreted to him by Mrs. Bonnycastle, he was often at a loss to understand. Fortunately she had a fund of good humour which, as I have intimated, was apt to come uppermost with the April blossoms and which made the people she didn't invite to her house almost as amusing to her as those she did. Her husband was not in politics, though politics were much in him; but the couple had taken upon themselves the responsibilities of an active patriotism; they thought it right to live in America, differing therein from many of their acquaintances who only, with some grimness, thought it inevitable. They had that burdensome heritage of foreign reminiscence with which so many Americans were saddled; but they carried it more easily than most of their country-people, and one knew they had lived in Europe only by their present exultation, never in the least by their regrets. Their regrets, that is, were only for their ever having lived there, as Mrs. Bonnycastle once told the wife of a foreign minister. They solved all their problems successfully, including those of knowing none of the people they didn't wish to, and of finding plenty of occupation in a society supposed to be meagrely provided with resources for that body which Vogelstein was to hear invoked, again and again, with the mixture of desire and of deprecation that might have attended the mention of a secret vice, under the name of a leisure-class. When as the warm weather approached they opened both the wings of their house-door, it was because they thought it would entertain them and not because they were conscious of a pressure. Alfred Bonnycastle all winter indeed chafed a little at the definiteness of some of his wife's reserves; it struck him that for Washington their society was really a little too good. Vogelstein still remembered the puzzled feeling--it had cleared up somewhat now—with which, more than a year before, he had heard Mr. Bonnycastle exclaim one evening, after a dinner in his own house, when every guest but the German secretary (who often sat late with the pair) had departed Hang it, there's only a month left; let us be vulgar and have some fun—let us invite the President."

This was Mrs. Bonnycastle's carnival, and on the occasion to which I began my chapter by referring the President had not only been invited but had signified his intention of being present. I hasten to add that this was not the same august ruler to whom Alfred Bonnycastle's irreverent allusion had been made. The White House had received a new tenant—the old one was then just leaving it—and Count Otto had had the advantage, during the first eighteen months of his stay in America, of seeing an electoral campaign, a presidential inauguration and a distribution of spoils. He had been bewildered during those first weeks by finding that at the national capital in the houses he supposed to be the best, the head of the State was not a coveted guest; for this could be the only explanation of Mr. Bonnycastle's whimsical suggestion of their inviting him, as it were, in carnival. His successor went out a good deal for a President.

The legislative session was over, but this made little difference in the aspect of Mrs. Bonnycastle's rooms, which even at the height of the congressional season could scarce be said to overflow with the representatives of the people. They were garnished with an occasional Senator, whose movements and utterances often appeared to be regarded with a mixture of alarm and indulgence, as if they would be disappointing if they weren't rather odd and yet might be dangerous if not carefully watched. Our young man had come to entertain a kindness for these conscript fathers of invisible families, who had something of the toga in the voluminous folds of their conversation, but were otherwise rather bare and bald, with stony wrinkles in their faces, like busts and statues of ancient law-givers. There seemed to him something chill and exposed in their being at once so exalted and so naked; there were frequent lonesome glances in their eyes, as if in the social world their legislative consciousness longed for the warmth of a few comfortable laws ready-made. Members of the House were very rare, and when Washington was new to the inquiring secretary he used sometimes to mistake them, in the halls and on the staircases where he met them, for the functionaries engaged, under stress, to usher in guests and wait at supper. It was only a little later that he perceived these latter public characters almost always to be impressive and of that rich racial hue which of itself served as a livery. At present, however, such confounding figures were much less to be met than during the months of winter, and indeed they were never frequent at Mrs. Bonnycastle's. At present the social vistas of Washington, like the vast fresh flatness of the lettered and numbered streets, which at this season seemed to Vogelstein more spacious and vague than ever, suggested but a paucity of political phenomena. Count Otto that evening knew every one or almost every one. There were often inquiring strangers, expecting great things, from New York and Boston, and to them, in the friendly Washington way, the young German was promptly introduced. It was a society in which familiarity reigned and in which people were liable to meet three times a day, so that their ultimate essence really became a matter of importance.

"I've got three new girls," Mrs. Bonnycastle said. "You must talk to them all."

"All at once?" Vogelstein asked, reversing in fancy a position not at all unknown to him. He had so repeatedly heard himself addressed in even more than triple simultaneity.

"Oh no; you must have something different for each; you can't get off that way. Haven't you discovered that the American girl expects something especially adapted to herself? It's very well for Europe to have a few phrases that will do for any girl. The American girl isn't *any* girl; she's a remarkable specimen in a remarkable species. But you must keep the best this evening for Miss Day."

"For Miss Day!"—and Vogelstein had a stare of intelligence. "Do you mean for Pandora?"

Mrs. Bonnycastle broke on her side into free amusement. "One would think you had been looking for her over the globe! So you know her already—and you call her by her pet name?"

"Oh no, I don't know her; that is I haven't seen her or thought of her from that day to this. We came to America in the same ship."

"Isn't she an American then?"

"Oh yes; she lives at Utica—in the interior."

"In the interior of Utica? You can't mean my young woman then, who lives in New York, where she's a great beauty and a great belle and has been immensely admired this winter."

"After all," said Count Otto, considering and a little disappointed, "the name's not so uncommon; it's perhaps another. But has she rather strange eyes, a little yellow, but very pretty, and a nose a little arched?"

"I can't tell you all that; I haven't seen her. She's staying with Mrs. Steuben. She only came a day or two ago, and Mrs. Steuben's to bring her. When she wrote to me to ask leave she told me what I tell you. They haven't come yet."

Vogelstein felt a quick hope that the subject of this correspondence might indeed be the young lady he had parted from on the dock at New York, but the indications seemed to point another way, and he had no wish to cherish an illusion. It didn't seem to him probable that the energetic girl who had introduced him to Mr. Lansing would have the entree of the best house in Washington; besides, Mrs. Bonnycastle's guest was described as a beauty and belonging to the brilliant city.

"What's the social position of Mrs. Steuben?" it occurred to him to ask while he meditated. He had an earnest artless literal way of putting such a question as that; you could see from it that he was very thorough.

Mrs. Bonnycastle met it, however, but, with mocking laughter. "I'm sure I don't know! What's your own?"—and she left him to turn to her other guests, to several of whom she repeated his question. Could they tell her what was the social position of Mrs. Steuben? There was Count Vogelstein who wanted to know. He instantly became aware of course that he oughtn't so to have expressed himself. Wasn't the lady's place in the scale sufficiently indicated by Mrs. Bonnycastle's acquaintance with her? Still there were fine degrees, and he felt a little unduly snubbed. It was perfectly true, as he told his hostess, that with the quick wave of new impressions that had rolled over him after his arrival in America the image of Pandora was almost completely effaced; he had seen innumerable things that were quite as remarkable in their way as the heroine of the *Donau*, but at the touch of the idea that he might see her and hear her again at any moment she became as vivid in his mind as if they had parted the day before: he remembered the exact shade of the eyes he had described to Mrs. Bonnycastle as yellow, the tone of her voice when at the last she expressed the hope he might judge America correctly. *Had* he judged America correctly? If he were to meet her again she doubtless would try to ascertain. It would be going much too far to say that the idea of such an ordeal was terrible to Count Otto; but it may at least be said that the thought of meeting Pandora Day made him nervous. The fact is certainly singular, but I shall not take on myself to explain it; there are some things that even the most philosophic historian isn't bound to account for.

He wandered into another room, and there, at the end of five minutes, he was introduced by Mrs. Bonnycastle to one of the young ladies of whom she had spoken. This was a very intelligent girl who came from Boston and showed much acquaintance with Spielhagen's novels. "Do you like them?" Vogelstein asked rather vaguely, not taking much interest in the matter, as he read works of fiction only in case of a sea-voyage. The young lady from Boston looked pensive and concentrated; then she answered that she liked *some* of them *very* much, but that there were others she didn't like—and she enumerated the works that came under each of these heads. Spielhagen is a voluminous writer, and such a catalogue took some time; at the end of it moreover Vogelstein's question was not answered, for he couldn't have told us whether she liked Spielhagen or not.

On the next topic, however, there was no doubt about her feelings. They talked about Washington as people talk only in the place itself, revolving about the subject in widening and narrowing circles, perching successively on its many branches, considering it from every point of view. Our young man had been long enough in America to discover that after half a century of social neglect Washington had become the fashion and enjoyed the great advantage of being a new resource in conversation. This was especially the case in the months of spring, when the inhabitants of the commercial cities came so far southward to escape, after the long winter, that final affront. They were all agreed that Washington was fascinating, and none of them were better prepared to talk it over than the Bostonians. Vogelstein originally had been rather out of step with them; he hadn't seized their point of view, hadn't known with what they compared this object of their infatuation. But now he knew everything; he had settled down to the pace; there wasn't a possible phase of the discussion that could find him at a loss. There was a kind of Hegelian element in it; in the light of these considerations the American capital took on the semblance of a monstrous mystical infinite *Werden*. But they fatigued Vogelstein a little, and it was his preference, as a general thing, not to engage the same evening with more than one newcomer, one visitor in the freshness of initiation. This was why Mrs.

Bonnycastle's expression of a wish to introduce him to three young ladies had startled him a little; he saw a certain process, in which he flattered himself that he had become proficient, but which was after all tolerably exhausting, repeated for each of the damsels. After separating from his judicious Bostonian he rather evaded Mrs. Bonnycastle, contenting himself with the conversation of old friends, pitched for the most part in a lower and easier key.

At last he heard it mentioned that the President had arrived, had been some half-hour in the house, and he went in search of the illustrious guest, whose whereabouts at Washington parties was never indicated by a cluster of courtiers. He made it a point, whenever he found himself in company with the President, to pay him his respects, and he had not been discouraged by the fact that there was no association of ideas in the eye of the great man as he put out his hand presidentially and said, "Happy to meet you, sir." Count Otto felt himself taken for a mere loyal subject, possibly for an office-seeker; and he used to reflect at such moments that the monarchical form had its merits it provided a line of heredity for the faculty of quick recognition. He had now some difficulty in finding the chief magistrate, and ended by learning that he was in the tea-room, a small apartment devoted to light refection near the entrance of the house. Here our young man presently perceived him seated on a sofa and in conversation with a lady. There were a number of people about the table, eating, drinking, talking; and the couple on the sofa, which was not near it but against the wall, in a shallow recess, looked a little withdrawn, as if they had sought seclusion and were disposed to profit by the diverted attention of the others. The President leaned back; his gloved hands, resting on either knee, made large white spots. He looked eminent, but he looked relaxed, and the lady beside him ministered freely and without scruple, it was clear, to this effect of his comfortably unbending. Vogelstein caught her voice as he approached. He heard her say "Well now, remember; I consider it a promise." She was beautifully dressed, in rose-colour; her hands were clasped in her lap and her eyes attached to the presidential profile.

"Well, madam, in that case it's about the fiftieth promise I've given to-day."

It was just as he heard these words, uttered by her companion in reply, that Count Otto checked himself, turned away and pretended to be looking for a cup of tea. It wasn't usual to disturb the President, even simply to shake hands, when he was sitting on a sofa with a lady, and the young secretary felt it in this case less possible than ever to break the rule, for the lady on the sofa was none other than Pandora Day. He had recognised her without her appearing to see him, and even with half an eye, as they said, had taken in that she was now a person to be reckoned with. She had an air of elation, of success; she shone, to intensity, in her rose-coloured dress; she was extracting promises from the ruler of fifty millions of people. What an odd place to meet her, her old shipmate thought, and how little one could tell, after all, in America, who people were! He didn't want to speak to her yet; he wanted to wait a little and learn more; but meanwhile there was something attractive in the fact that she was just behind him, a few yards off, that if he should turn he might see her again. It was she Mrs. Bonnycastle had meant, it was she who was so much admired in New York. Her face was the same, yet he had made out in a moment that she was vaguely prettier; he had recognised the arch of her nose, which suggested a fine ambition. He took some tea, which he hadn't desired, in order not to go away. He remembered her *entourage* on the steamer; her father and mother, the silent senseless burghers, so little "of the world," her infant sister, so much of it, her humorous brother with his tall hat and his influence in the smoking-room. He remembered Mrs. Dangerfield's warnings—yet her perplexities too—and the letter from Mr. Bellamy, and the introduction to Mr. Lansing, and the way Pandora had stooped down on the dirty dock, laughing and talking, mistress of the situation, to open her trunk for the Customs. He was pretty sure she had paid no duties that day; this would naturally have been the purpose of Mr. Bellamy's letter. Was she still in correspondence with that gentleman, and had he got over the sickness interfering with their reunion? These images and these questions coursed through Count Otto's mind, and he saw it must be quite in Pandora's line to be mistress of the situation, for there was evidently nothing on the present occasion that could call itself her master. He drank his tea and as; he put down his cup heard the President, behind him, say: "Well, I guess my wife will wonder why I don't come home."

"Why didn't you bring her with you?" Pandora benevolently asked.

"Well, she doesn't go out much. Then she has got her sister staying with her—Mrs. Runkle, from Natchez. She's a good deal of an invalid, and my wife doesn't like to leave her."

"She must be a very kind woman"—and there was a high mature competence in the way the girl sounded the note of approval.

"Well, I guess she isn't spoiled—yet."

"I should like very much to come and see her," said Pandora.

"Do come round. Couldn't you come some night?" the great man responded.

"Well, I'll come some time. And I shall remind you of your promise."

"All right. There's nothing like keeping it up. Well," said the President, "I must bid good-bye to these bright folks."

Vogelstein heard him rise from the sofa with his companion; after which he gave the pair time to pass out of the room before him. They did it with a certain impressive deliberation, people making way for the ruler of fifty millions and looking with a certain curiosity at the striking pink person at his side. When a little later he followed them across the hall, into one of the other rooms, he saw the host and hostess accompany the President to the door and two foreign ministers and a judge of the Supreme Court address themselves to Pandora Day. He resisted the impulse to join this circle: if he should speak to her at all he would somehow wish it to be in more privacy. She continued nevertheless to occupy him, and when Mrs. Bonnycastle came back from the hall he immediately approached her with an appeal. "I wish you'd tell me something more about that girl—that one opposite and in pink."

"The lovely Day—that's what they call her, I believe? I wanted you to talk with her."

"I find she *is* the one I've met. But she seems to be so different here. I can't make it out," said Count Otto.

There was something in his expression that again moved Mrs. Bonnycastle to mirth. "How we do puzzle you Europeans! You look quite bewildered."

"I'm sorry I look so—I try to hide it. But of course we're very simple. Let me ask then a simple earnest childlike question. Are her parents also in society?"

"Parents in society? D'où tombez-vous? Did you ever hear of the parents of a triumphant girl in rose-colour, with a nose all her own, in society?"

"Is she then all alone?" he went on with a strain of melancholy in his voice.

Mrs. Bonnycastle launched at him all her laughter.

"You're too pathetic. Don't you know what she is? I supposed of course you knew."

"It's exactly what I'm asking you."

"Why she's the new type. It has only come up lately. They have had articles about it in the papers. That's the reason I told Mrs. Steuben to bring her."

"The new type? *What* new type, Mrs. Bonnycastle?" he returned pleadingly—so conscious was he that all types in America were new.

Her laughter checked her reply a moment, and by the time she had recovered herself the young lady from Boston, with whom Vogelstein had been talking, stood there to take leave. This, for an American type, was an old one, he was sure; and the process of parting between the guest and her hostess had an ancient elaboration. Count Otto waited a little; then he turned away and walked up to Pandora Day, whose group of interlocutors had now been re-enforced by a gentleman who had held an important place in the cabinet of the late occupant of the presidential chair. He had asked Mrs. Bonnycastle if she were "all alone"; but there was nothing in her present situation to show her for solitary. She wasn't sufficiently alone for our friend's taste; but he was impatient and he hoped she'd give him a few words to himself. She recognised him without a moment's hesitation and with the sweetest smile, a smile matching to a shade the tone in which she said: "I was watching you. I wondered if you weren't going to speak to me."

"Miss Day was watching him!" one of the foreign ministers exclaimed; "and we flattered ourselves that her attention was all with us."

"I mean before," said the girl, "while I was talking with the President."

At which the gentlemen began to laugh, one of them remarking that this was the way the absent were sacrificed, even the great; while another put on record that he hoped Vogelstein was duly flattered.

"Oh I was watching the President too," said Pandora. "I've got to watch *him*. He has promised me something."

"It must be the mission to England," the judge of the Supreme Court suggested. "A good position for a lady; they've got a lady at the head over there."

"I wish they would send you to my country," one of the foreign ministers suggested. "I'd immediately get recalled."

"Why perhaps in your country I wouldn't speak to you! It's only because you're here," the ex-heroine of the *Donau* returned with a gay familiarity which evidently ranked with her but as one of the arts of defence. "You'll see what mission it is when it comes out. But I'll speak to Count Vogelstein anywhere," she went on. "He's an older friend than any right here. I've known him in difficult days."

"Oh yes, on the great ocean," the young man smiled. "On the watery waste, in the tempest!"

"Oh I don't mean that so much; we had a beautiful voyage and there wasn't any tempest. I mean when I was living in Utica. That's a watery waste if you like, and a tempest there would have been a pleasant variety."

"Your parents seemed to me so peaceful!" her associate in the other memories sighed with a vague wish to say something sympathetic.

"Oh you haven't seen them ashore! At Utica they were very lively. But that's no longer our natural home. Don't you remember I told you I was working for New York? Well, I worked—I had to work hard. But we've moved."

Count Otto clung to his interest. "And I hope they're happy."

"My father and mother? Oh they will be, in time. I must give them time. They're very young yet, they've years before them. And you've been always in Washington?" Pandora continued. "I suppose you've found out everything about everything."

"Oh no—there are some things I *can't* find out."

"Come and see me and perhaps I can help you. I'm very different from what I was in that phase. I've advanced a great deal since then."

"Oh how was Miss Day in that phase?" asked a cabinet minister of the last administration.

"She was delightful of course," Count Otto said.

"He's very flattering; I didn't open my mouth!" Pandora cried. "Here comes Mrs. Steuben to take me to some other place. I believe it's a literary party near the Capitol. Everything seems so separate in Washington. Mrs. Steuben's going to read a poem. I wish she'd read it here; wouldn't it do as well?"

This lady, arriving, signified to her young friend the necessity of their moving on. But Miss Day's companions had various things to say to her before giving her up. She had a vivid answer for each, and it was brought home to Vogelstein while he listened that this would be indeed, in her development, as she said, another phase. Daughter of small burghers as she might be she was really brilliant. He turned away a little and while Mrs. Steuben waited put her a question. He had made her half an hour before the subject of that inquiry to which Mrs. Bonnycastle returned so ambiguous an answer; but this wasn't because he failed of all direct acquaintance with the amiable woman or of any general idea of the esteem in which she was held. He had met her in various places and had been at her house. She was the widow of a commodore, was a handsome mild soft swaying person, whom every one liked, with glossy bands of black hair and a little ringlet depending behind each ear. Some one had said that she looked like the *vieux jeu*, idea of the queen in *Hamlet*. She had written verses which were admired in the South, wore a full-length portrait of the commodore on her bosom and spoke with the accent of Savannah. She had about her a positive strong odour of Washington. It had certainly been very superfluous in our young man to question Mrs. Bonnycastle about her social position.

"Do kindly tell me," he said, lowering his voice, "what's the type to which that young lady belongs? Mrs. Bonnycastle tells me it's a new one."

Mrs. Steuben for a moment fixed her liquid eyes on the secretary of legation. She always seemed to be translating the prose of your speech into the finer rhythms with which her own mind was familiar. "Do you think anything's really new?" she then began to flute. "I'm very fond of the old; you know that's a weakness of we Southerners." The poor lady, it will be observed, had another weakness as well. "What we often take to be the new is simply the old under some novel form. Were there not remarkable natures in the past? If you doubt it you should visit the South, where the past still lingers."

Vogelstein had been struck before this with Mrs. Steuben's pronunciation of the word by which her native latitudes were designated; transcribing it from her lips you would have written it (as the nearest approach) the Sooth. But at present he scarce heeded this peculiarity; he was wondering rather how a woman could be at once so copious and so uninforming. What did he care about the past or even about the Sooth? He was afraid of starting her again. He looked at her, discouraged and helpless, as bewildered almost as Mrs. Bonnycastle had found him half an hour before; looked also at the commodore, who, on her bosom, seemed to breathe again with his widow's respirations. "Call it an old type then if you like," he said in a moment. "All I want to know is what type it *is*! It seems impossible," he gasped, "to find out."

"You can find out in the newspapers. They've had articles about it. They write about everything now. But it isn't true about Miss Day. It's one of the first families. Her great-grandfather was in the Revolution." Pandora by this time had given her attention again to Mrs. Steuben. She seemed to signify that she was ready to move on. "Wasn't your great-grandfather in the Revolution?" the elder lady asked. "I'm telling Count Vogelstein about him."

"Why are you asking about my ancestors?" the girl demanded of the young German with untempered brightness. "Is that the thing you said just now that you can't find out? Well, if Mrs. Steuben will only be quiet you never will."

Mrs. Steuben shook her head rather dreamily. "Well, it's no trouble for we of the Sooth to be quiet. There's a kind of languor in our blood. Besides, we have to be to-day. But I've got to show some energy to-night. I've got to get you to the end of Pennsylvania Avenue."

Pandora gave her hand to Count Otto and asked him if he thought they should meet again. He answered that in Washington people were always meeting again and that at any rate he shouldn't fail to wait upon her. Hereupon, just as the two ladies were detaching themselves, Mrs. Steuben remarked that if the Count and Miss Day wished to meet again the picnic would be a good chance—the picnic she was getting up for the following Thursday. It was to consist of about twenty bright people, and they'd go down the Potomac to Mount Vernon. The Count answered that if Mrs. Steuben thought him bright enough he should be delighted to join the party; and he was told the hour for which the tryst was taken.

He remained at Mrs. Bonnycastle's after every one had gone, and then he informed this lady of his reason for waiting. Would she have mercy on him and let him know, in a single word, before he went to rest—for without it rest would be impossible—what was this famous type to which Pandora Day belonged?

"Gracious, you don't mean to say you've not found out that type yet!" Mrs. Bonnycastle exclaimed with a return of her hilarity. "What have you been doing all the evening? You Germans may be thorough, but you certainly are not quick!"

It was Alfred Bonnycastle who at last took pity on him. "My dear Vogelstein, she's the latest freshest fruit of our great American evolution. She's the self-made girl!"

Count Otto gazed a moment. "The fruit of the great American Revolution? Yes, Mrs. Steuben told me her great-grandfather—" but the rest of his sentence was lost in a renewed explosion of Mrs. Bonnycastle's sense of the ridiculous. He bravely pushed his advantage, such as it was, however, and, desiring his host's definition to be defined, inquired what the self-made girl might be.

"Sit down and we'll tell you all about it," Mrs. Bonnycastle said. "I like talking this way, after a party's over. You can smoke if you like, and Alfred will open another window. Well, to begin with, the self-made girl's a new feature. That, however, you know. In the second place she isn't self-made at all. We all help to make her—we take such an interest in her."

"That's only after she's made!" Alfred Bonnycastle broke in. "But it's Vogelstein that takes an interest. What on earth has started you up so on the subject of Miss Day?"

The visitor explained as well as he could that it was merely the accident of his having crossed the ocean in the steamer with her; but he felt the inadequacy of this account of the matter, felt it more than his hosts, who could know neither how little actual contact he had had with her on the ship, how much he had been affected by Mrs. Dangerfield's warnings, nor how much observation at the same time he had lavished on her. He sat there half an hour, and the warm dead stillness of the Washington night—nowhere are the nights so silent—came in at the open window, mingled with a soft sweet earthy smell, the smell of growing things and in particular, as he thought, of Mrs. Steuben's Sooth. Before he went away he had heard all about the self-made girl, and there was something in the picture that strongly impressed him. She was possible doubtless only in America; American life had smoothed the way for her. She was not fast, nor emancipated, nor crude, nor loud, and there wasn't in her, of necessity at least, a grain of the stuff of which the adventuress is made. She was simply very successful, and her success was entirely personal. She hadn't been born with the silver spoon of social opportunity; she had grasped it by honest exertion. You knew her by many different signs, but chiefly, infallibly, by the appearance of her parents. It was her parents who told her story; you always saw how little her parents could have made her. Her attitude with regard to them might vary in different ways. As the great fact on her own side was that she had lifted herself from a lower social plane, done it all herself, and done it by the simple lever of her personality, it was naturally to be expected that she would leave the authors of her mere material being in the shade. Sometimes she had them in her wake, lost in the bubbles and the foam that showed where she had passed; sometimes, as Alfred Bonnycastle said, she let them slide altogether; sometimes she kept them in close confinement, resorting to them under cover of night and with every precaution; sometimes she exhibited them to the public in discreet glimpses, in prearranged attitudes. But the general characteristic of the self-made girl was that, though it was frequently understood that she was privately devoted to her kindred, she never attempted to impose them on society, and it was striking that, though in some of her manifestations a bore, she was at her worst less of a bore than they. They were almost always solemn and portentous, and they were for the most part of a deathly respectability. She wasn't necessarily snobbish, unless it was snobbish to want the best. She didn't cringe, she didn't make herself smaller than she was; she took on the contrary a stand of her own and attracted things to herself. Naturally she was possible only in America—only in a country where whole ranges of competition and comparison were absent. The natural history of this interesting creature was at last completely laid bare to the earnest stranger, who, as he sat there in the animated stillness, with the fragrant breath of the Western world in his nostrils, was convinced of what he had already suspected, that conversation in the great Republic was more yearningly, not to say gropingly, psychological than elsewhere. Another thing, as he learned, that you knew the self-made girl by was her culture, which was perhaps a little too restless and obvious. She had usually got into society more or less by reading, and her conversation was apt to be garnished with literary allusions, even with familiar quotations. Vogelstein hadn't had time to observe this element as a developed form in Pandora Day; but Alfred Bonnycastle hinted that he wouldn't trust her to keep it under in a *tête-à-tête*. It was needless to say that these young persons had always been to Europe; that was usually the first place they got to. By such arts they sometimes entered society on the other side before they did so at home; it was to be added at the same time that this resource was less and less valuable, for Europe, in the American world, had less and less prestige and people in the Western hemisphere now kept a watch on that roundabout road. All of which quite applied to Pandora Day—the journey to Europe, the culture (as exemplified in the books she read on the ship), the relegation, the effacement, of the family. The only thing that was exceptional was the rapidity of her march; for the jump she had taken since he left her in the hands of Mr. Lansing struck Vogelstein, even after he had made all allowance for the abnormal homogeneity of the American mass, as really considerable. It took all her cleverness to account for such things. When she "moved" from Utica—mobilised her commissariat—the battle appeared virtually to have been gained.

Count Otto called the next day, and Mrs. Steuben's blackamoor informed him, in the communicative manner of his race, that the ladies had gone out to pay some visits and look at the Capitol. Pandora apparently had not hitherto examined this monument, and our young man wished he had known, the evening before, of her omission, so that he might have offered to be her initiator. There is too obvious a connexion for us to fail of catching it between his regret and the fact that in leaving Mrs. Steuben's door he reminded himself that he wanted a good walk, and that he thereupon took his way along Pennsylvania Avenue. His walk had become fairly good by the time he reached the great white edifice that unfolds its repeated colonnades and uplifts its isolated dome at the end of a long vista of saloons and tobacco-shops. He slowly climbed the great steps, hesitating a little, even wondering why he had come. The superficial reason was obvious enough, but there was a real one behind it that struck him as rather wanting in the solidity which should characterise the motives of an emissary of Prince Bismarck. The superficial reason was a belief that Mrs. Steuben would pay her visit first—it was probably only a question of leaving cards—and bring her young friend to the Capitol at the hour when the yellow afternoon light would give a tone to the blankness of its marble walls. The Capitol was a splendid building, but it was rather wanting in tone. Vogelstein's curiosity about Pandora Day had been much more quickened than checked by the revelations made to him in Mrs. Bonnycastle's drawing-room. It was a relief to have the creature classified; but he had a desire, of which he had not been conscious before, to see really to the end how well, in other words how completely and artistically, a girl could make herself. His calculations had been just, and he had wandered about the rotunda for only ten minutes, looking again at the paintings, commemorative of the national annals, which occupy its lower spaces, and at the simulated sculptures, so touchingly characteristic of early American taste, which adorn its upper reaches, when the charming women he had been counting on presented themselves in charge of a licensed guide. He went to meet them and didn't conceal from them that he had marked them for his very own. The encounter was happy on both sides, and he accompanied them through the queer and endless interior, through labyrinths of bleak bare development, into legislative and judicial halls. He thought it a hideous place; he had seen it all before and asked himself what senseless game he was playing. In the lower House were certain bedaubed walls, in the basest style of imitation, which made him feel faintly sick, not to speak of a lobby adorned with artless prints and photographs of eminent defunct Congressmen that was all too serious for a joke and too comic for a Valhalla. But Pandora was greatly interested; she thought the Capitol very fine; it was easy to criticise the details, but as a whole it was the most impressive building she had ever seen. She proved a charming fellow tourist; she had constantly something to say, but never said it too much; it was impossible to drag in the wake of a *cicerone* less of a lengthening or an irritating chain. Vogelstein could see too that she wished to improve her mind; she looked at the historical pictures, at the uncanny statues of local worthies, presented by the different States—they were of different sizes, as if they had been "numbered," in a shop—she asked questions of the guide and in the chamber of the Senate requested him to show her the chairs of the gentlemen from New York. She sat down in one of them, though Mrs. Steuben told her *that* Senator (she mistook the chair, dropping into another State) was a horrid old thing.

Throughout the hour he spent with her Vogelstein seemed to see how it was she had made herself. They walked about, afterwards on the splendid terrace that surrounds the Capitol, the great marble floor on which it stands, and made vague remarks—Pandora's were the most definite—about the yellow sheen of the Potomac, the hazy hills of

Virginia, the far-gleaming pediment of Arlington, the raw confused-looking country. Washington was beneath them, bristling and geometrical; the long lines of its avenues seemed to stretch into national futures. Pandora asked Count Otto if he had ever been to Athens and, on his admitting so much, sought to know whether the eminence on which they stood didn't give him an idea of the Acropolis in its prime. Vogelstein deferred the satisfaction of this appeal to their next meeting; he was glad—in spite of the appeal—to make pretexts for seeing her again. He did so on the morrow; Mrs. Steuben's picnic was still three days distant. He called on Pandora a second time, also met her each evening in the Washington world. It took very little of this to remind him that he was forgetting both Mrs. Dangerfield's warnings and the admonitions--long familiar to him—of his own conscience. Was he in peril of love? Was he to be sacrificed on the altar of the American girl, an altar at which those other poor fellows had poured out some of the bluest blood in Germany and he had himself taken oath he would never seriously worship? He decided that he wasn't in real danger, that he had rather clinched his precautions. It was true that a young person who had succeeded so well for herself might be a great help to her husband; but this diplomatic aspirant preferred on the whole that his success should be his own: it wouldn't please him to have the air of being pushed by his wife. Such a wife as that would wish to push him, and he could hardly admit to himself that this was what fate had in reserve for him—to be propelled in his career by a young lady who would perhaps attempt to talk to the Kaiser as he had heard her the other night talk to the President. Would she consent to discontinue relations with her family, or would she wish still to borrow plastic relief from that domestic background? That her family was so impossible was to a certain extent an advantage; for if they had been a little better the question of a rupture would be less easy. He turned over these questions in spite of his security, or perhaps indeed because of it. The security made them speculative and disinterested.

They haunted him during the excursion to Mount Vernon, which took place according to traditions long established. Mrs. Steuben's confederates assembled on the steamer and were set afloat on the big brown stream which had already seemed to our special traveller to have too much bosom and too little bank. Here and there, however, he became conscious of a shore where there was something to look at, even though conscious at the same time that he had of old lost great opportunities of an idyllic cast in not having managed to be more "thrown with" a certain young lady on the deck of the North German Lloyd. The two turned round together to hang over Alexandria, which for Pandora, as she declared, was a picture of Old Virginia. She told Vogelstein that she was always hearing about it during the Civil War, ages before. Little girl as she had been at the time she remembered all the names that were on people's lips during those years of reiteration. This historic spot had a touch of the romance of rich decay, a reference to older things, to a dramatic past. The past of Alexandria appeared in the vista of three or four short streets sloping up a hill and lined with poor brick warehouses erected for merchandise that had ceased to come or go. It looked hot and blank and sleepy, down to the shabby waterside where tattered darkies dangled their bare feet from the edge of rotting wharves. Pandora was even more interested in Mount Vernon—when at last its wooded bluff began to command the river—than she had been in the Capitol, and after they had disembarked and ascended to the celebrated mansion she insisted on going into every room it contained. She "claimed for it," as she said—some of her turns were so characteristic both of her nationality and her own style—the finest situation in the world, and was distinct as to the shame of their not giving it to the President for his country-seat.

Most of her companions had seen the house often, and were now coupling themselves in the grounds according to their sympathies, so that it was easy for Vogelstein to offer the benefit of his own experience to the most inquisitive member of the party. They were not to lunch for another hour, and in the interval the young man roamed with his first and fairest acquaintance. The breath of the Potomac, on the boat, had been a little harsh, but on the softly-curving lawn, beneath the clustered trees, with the river relegated to a mere shining presence far below and in the distance, the day gave out nothing but its mildness, the whole scene became noble and genial.

Count Otto could joke a little on great occasions, and the present one was worthy of his humour. He maintained to his companion that the shallow painted mansion resembled a false house, a "wing" or structure of daubed canvas, on the stage; but she answered him so well with certain economical palaces she had seen in Germany, where, as she said, there was nothing but china stoves and stuffed birds, that he was obliged to allow the home of Washington to be after all really *gemüthlich.* What he found so in fact was the soft texture of the day, his personal situation, the sweetness of his suspense. For suspense had decidedly become his portion; he was under a charm that made him feel he was watching his own life and that his susceptibilities were beyond his control. It hung over him that things might take a turn, from one hour to the other, which would make them very different from what they had been yet; and his heart certainly beat a little faster as he wondered what that turn might be. Why did he come to picnics on fragrant April days with American girls who might lead him too far? Wouldn't such girls be glad to marry a Pomeranian count? And *would* they, after all, talk that way to the Kaiser? If he were to marry one of them he should have to give her several thorough lessons.

In their little tour of the house our young friend and his companion had had a great many fellow visitors, who had also arrived by the steamer and who had hitherto not left them an ideal privacy. But the others gradually dispersed; they circled about a kind of showman who was the authorised guide, a big slow genial vulgar heavily-bearded man, with a whimsical edifying patronising tone, a tone that had immense success when he stopped here and there to make his points—to pass his eyes over his listening flock, then fix them quite above it with a meditative look and bring out some ancient pleasantry as if it were a sudden inspiration. He made a cheerful thing, an echo of the platform before the booth of a country fair, even of a visit to the tomb of the *pater patriæ*. It is enshrined in a kind of grotto in the grounds, and Vogelstein remarked to Pandora that he was a good man for the place, but was too familiar. "Oh he'd have been familiar with Washington," said the girl with the bright dryness with which she often uttered amusing things. Vogelstein looked at her a moment, and it came over him, as he smiled, that she herself probably wouldn't have been abashed even by the hero with whom history has taken fewest liberties. "You look as if you could hardly believe that," Pandora went on. "You Germans are always in such awe of great people." And it occurred to her critic that perhaps after all Washington would have liked her manner, which was wonderfully fresh and natural. The man with the beard was an ideal minister to American shrines; he played on the curiosity of his little band with the touch of a master, drawing them at the right moment away to see the classic ice-house where the old lady had been found weeping in the belief it was Washington's grave. While this monument was under inspection our interesting couple had the house to themselves, and they spent some time on a pretty terrace where certain windows of the second floor opened—a little rootless verandah which overhung, in a manner, obliquely, all the magnificence of the view; the immense sweep of the river, the artistic plantations, the last-century garden with its big box hedges and remains of old espaliers. They lingered here for nearly half an hour, and it was in this retirement that Vogelstein enjoyed the only approach to intimate conversation appointed for him, as was to appear, with a young woman in whom he had been unable to persuade himself that he was not absorbed. It's not necessary, and it's not possible, that I should reproduce this colloquy; but I may mention that it began—as they leaned against the parapet of the terrace and heard the cheerful voice of the showman wafted up to them from a distance—with his saying to her rather abruptly that he couldn't make out why they hadn't had more talk together when they crossed the Atlantic.

"Well, I can if you can't," said Pandora. "I'd have talked quick enough if you had spoken to me. I spoke to you first."

"Yes, I remember that"—and it affected him awkwardly.

"You listened too much to Mrs. Dangerfield."

He feigned a vagueness. "To Mrs. Dangerfield?"

"That woman you were always sitting with; she told you not to speak to me. I've seen her in New York; she speaks to me now herself. She recommended you to have nothing to do with me."

"Oh how can you say such dreadful things?" Count Otto cried with a very becoming blush.

"You know you can't deny it. You weren't attracted by my family. They're charming people when you know them. I don't have a better time anywhere than I have at home," the girl went on loyally. "But what does it matter? My family are very happy. They're getting quite used to New York. Mrs. Dangerfield's a vulgar wretch—next winter she'll call on me."

"You are unlike any Mädchen I've ever seen—I don't understand you," said poor Vogelstein with the colour still in his face.

"Well, you never *will* understand me—probably; but what difference does it make?"

He attempted to tell her what difference, but I've no space to follow him here. It's known that when the German mind attempts to explain things it doesn't always reduce them to simplicity, and Pandora was first mystified, then amused, by some of the Count's revelations. At last I think she was a little frightened, for she remarked irrelevantly, with some decision, that luncheon would be ready and that they ought to join Mrs. Steuben. Her companion walked slowly, on purpose, as they left the house together, for he knew the pang of a vague sense that he was losing her.

"And shall you be in Washington many days yet?" he appealed as they went.

"It will all depend. I'm expecting important news. What I shall do will be influenced by that."

The way she talked about expecting news—and important!—made him feel somehow that she had a career, that she was active and independent, so that he could scarcely hope to stop her as she passed. It was certainly true that he had never seen any girl like her. It would have occurred to him that the news she was expecting might have reference to the favour she had begged of the President, if he hadn't already made up his mind—in the calm of meditation after that talk with the Bonnycastles—that this favour must be a pleasantry. What she had said to him had a discouraging, a somewhat chilling effect; nevertheless it was not without a certain ardour that he inquired of her whether, so long as she stayed in Washington, he mightn't pay her certain respectful attentions.

"As many as you like—and as respectful ones; but you won't keep them up for ever!"

"You try to torment me," said Count Otto.

She waited to explain. "I mean that I may have some of my family."

"I shall be delighted to see them again."

Again she just hung fire. "There are some you've never seen."

In the afternoon, returning to Washington on the steamer, Vogelstein received a warning. It came from Mrs. Bonnycastle and constituted, oddly enough, the second juncture at which an officious female friend had, while sociably afloat with him, advised him on the subject of Pandora Day.

"There's one thing we forgot to tell you the other night about the self-made girl," said the lady of infinite mirth. "It's never safe to fix your affections on her, because she has almost always an impediment somewhere in the background."

He looked at her askance, but smiled and said: "I should understand your information—for which I'm so much obliged—a little better if I knew what you mean by an impediment."

"Oh I mean she's always engaged to some young man who belongs to her earlier phase."

"Her earlier phase?"

"The time before she had made herself—when she lived unconscious of her powers. A young man from Utica, say. They usually have to wait; he's probably in a store. It's a long engagement."

Count Otto somehow preferred to understand as little as possible. "Do you mean a betrothal—to take effect?"

"I don't mean anything German and moonstruck. I mean that piece of peculiarly American enterprise a premature engagement—to take effect, but too complacently, at the end of time."

Vogelstein very properly reflected that it was no use his having entered the diplomatic career if he weren't able to bear himself as if this interesting generalisation had no particular message for him. He did Mrs. Bonnycastle moreover the justice to believe that she wouldn't have approached the question with such levity if she had supposed she should make him wince. The whole thing was, like everything else, but for her to laugh at, and the betrayal moreover of a good intention. "I see, I see—the self-made girl has of course always had a past. Yes, and the young man in the store—from Utica—is part of her past."

"You express it perfectly," said Mrs. Bonnycastle. "I couldn't say it better myself."

"But with her present, with her future, when they change like this young lady's, I suppose everything else changes. How do you say it in America? She lets him slide."

"We don't say it at all!" Mrs. Bonnycastle cried. "She does nothing of the sort; for what do you take her? She sticks to him; that at least is what we *expect* her to do," she added with less assurance. "As I tell you, the type's new and the case under consideration. We haven't yet had time for complete study."

"Oh of course I hope she sticks to him," Vogelstein declared simply and with his German accent more audible, as it always was when he was slightly agitated.

For the rest of the trip he was rather restless. He wandered about the boat, talking little with the returning picnickers. Toward the last, as they drew near Washington and the white dome of the Capitol hung aloft before them, looking as simple as a suspended snowball, he found himself, on the deck, in proximity to Mrs. Steuben. He reproached himself with having rather neglected her during an entertainment for which he was indebted to her bounty, and he sought to repair his omission by a proper deference. But the only act of homage that occurred to him was to ask her as by chance whether Miss Day were, to her knowledge, engaged.

Mrs. Steuben turned her Southern eyes upon him with a look of almost romantic compassion. "To my knowledge? Why of course I'd know! I should think you'd know too. Didn't you know she was engaged? Why she has been engaged since she was sixteen."

Count Otto gazed at the dome of the Capitol. "To a gentleman from Utica?

"Yes, a native of her place. She's expecting him soon."

"I'm so very glad to hear it," said Vogelstein, who decidedly, for his career, had promise. "And is she going to marry him?"

"Why what do people fall in love with each other *for*? I presume they'll marry when she gets round to it. Ah if she had only been from the Sooth—!"

At this he broke quickly in: "But why have they never brought it off, as you say, in so many years?"

"Well, at first she was too young, and then she thought her family ought to see Europe—of course they could see it better *with* her—and they spent some time there. And then Mr. Bellamy had some business difficulties that made him feel as if he didn't want to marry just then. But he has given up business and I presume feels more free. Of course it's rather long, but all the while they've been engaged. It's a true, true love," said Mrs. Steuben, whose sound of the adjective was that of a feeble flute.

"Is his name Mr. Bellamy?" the Count asked with his haunting reminiscence. "D. F. Bellamy, so? And has he been in a store?"

"I don't know what kind of business it was: it was some kind of business in Utica. I think he had a branch in New York. He's one of the leading gentlemen of Utica and very highly educated. He's a good deal older than Miss Day. He's a very fine man—I presume a college man. He stands very high in Utica. I don't know why you look as if you doubted it."

Vogelstein assured Mrs. Steuben that he doubted nothing, and indeed what she told him was probably the more credible for seeming to him eminently strange. Bellamy had been the name of the gentleman who, a year and a half before, was to have met Pandora on the arrival of the German steamer; it was in Bellamy's name that she had addressed herself with such effusion to Bellamy's friend, the man in the straw hat who was about to fumble in her mother's old clothes. This was a fact that seemed to Count Otto to finish the picture of her contradictions; it wanted at present no touch to be complete. Yet even as it hung there before him it continued to fascinate him, and he stared at it, detached from surrounding things and feeling a little as if he had been pitched out of an overturned vehicle, till the boat bumped against one of the outstanding piles of the wharf at which Mrs. Steuben's party was to disembark. There was some delay in getting the steamer adjusted to the dock, during which the passengers watched the process over its side and extracted what entertainment they might from the appearance of the various persons collected to receive it. There were darkies and loafers and hackmen, and also vague individuals, the loosest and blankest he had ever seen anywhere, with tufts on their chins, toothpicks in their mouths, hands in their pockets, rumination in their jaws and diamond pins in their shirt-fronts, who looked as if they had sauntered over from Pennsylvania Avenue to while away half an hour, forsaking for that interval their various slanting postures in the porticoes of the hotels and the doorways of the saloons.

"Oh I'm so glad! How sweet of you to come down!" It was a voice close to Count Otto's shoulder that spoke these words, and he had no need to turn to see from whom it proceeded. It had been in his ears the greater part of the day, though, as he now perceived, without the fullest richness of expression of which it was capable. Still less was he obliged to turn to discover to whom it was addressed, for the few simple words I have quoted had been flung across the narrowing interval of water, and a gentleman who had stepped to the edge of the dock without our young man's observing him tossed back an immediate reply.

"I got here by the three o'clock train. They told me in K Street where you were, and I thought I'd come down and meet you."

"Charming attention!" said Pandora Day with the laugh that seemed always to invite the whole of any company to partake in it; though for some moments after this she and her interlocutor appeared to continue the conversation only with their eyes. Meanwhile Vogelstein's also were not idle. He looked at her visitor from head to foot, and he was aware that she was quite unconscious of his own proximity. The gentleman before him was tall, good-looking, well-dressed; evidently he would stand well not only at Utica, but, judging from the way he had planted himself on the dock, in any position that circumstances might compel him to take up. He was about forty years old; he had a black moustache and he seemed to look at the world over some counter-like expanse on which he invited it all warily and pleasantly to put down first its idea of the terms of a transaction. He waved a gloved hand at Pandora as if, when she exclaimed "Gracious, ain't they long!" to urge her to be patient. She was patient several seconds and then asked him if he had any news. He looked at her briefly, in silence, smiling, after which he drew from his pocket a large letter with an official-looking seal and shook it jocosely above his head. This was discreetly, covertly done. No one but our young man appeared aware of how much was taking place—and poor Count Otto mainly felt it in the air. The boat was touching the wharf and the space between the pair inconsiderable.

"Department of State?" Pandora very prettily and soundlessly mouthed across at him.

"That's what they call it."

"Well, what country?"

"What's your opinion of the Dutch?" the gentleman asked for answer.

"Oh gracious!" cried Pandora.

"Well, are you going to wait for the return trip?" said the gentleman.

Our silent sufferer turned away, and presently Mrs. Steuben and her companion disembarked together. When this lady entered a carriage with Miss Day the gentleman who had spoken to the girl followed them; the others scattered, and Vogelstein, declining with thanks a "lift" from Mrs. Bonnycastle, walked home alone and in some intensity of meditation. Two days later he saw in a newspaper an announcement that the President had offered the post of Minister to Holland to Mr. D. F. Bellamy of Utica; and in the course of a month he heard from Mrs. Steuben that Pandora, a thousand other duties performed, had finally "got round" to the altar of her own nuptials. He communicated this news to Mrs. Bonnycastle, who had not heard it but who, shrieking at the queer face he showed her, met it with the remark that there was now ground for a new induction as to the self-made girl.

SIR EDMUND ORME

The statement appears to have been written, though the fragment is undated, long after the death of his wife, whom I take to have been one of the persons referred to. There is, however, nothing in the strange story to establish this point, which is, perhaps, not of importance. When I took possession of his effects I found these pages, in a locked drawer, among papers relating to the unfortunate lady's too brief career (she died in childbirth a year after her marriage), letters, memoranda, accounts, faded photographs, cards of invitation. That is the only connection I can point to, and you may easily and will probably say that the tale is too extravagant to have had a demonstrable origin. I cannot, I admit, vouch for his having intended it as a report of real occurrence—I can only vouch for his general veracity. In any case it was written for himself, not for others. I offer it to others—having full option—precisely because it is so singular. Let them, in respect to the form of the thing, bear in mind that it was written quite for himself. I have altered nothing but the names.

If there's a story in the matter I recognise the exact moment at which it began. This was on a soft, still Sunday noon in November, just after church, on the sunny Parade. Brighton was full of people; it was the height of the season, and the day was even more respectable than lovely—which helped to account for the multitude of walkers. The blue sea itself was decorous; it seemed to doze, with a gentle snore (if that be decorum), as if nature were preaching a sermon. After writing letters all the morning I had come out to take a look at it before luncheon. I was leaning over the rail which separates the King's Road from the beach, and I think I was smoking a cigarette, when I became conscious of an intended joke in the shape of a light walking-stick laid across my shoulders. The idea, I found, had been thrown off by Teddy Bostwick, of the Rifles, and was intended as a contribution to talk. Our talk came off as we strolled together—he always took your arm to show you he forgave your obtuseness about his humour—and looked at the people, and bowed to some of them, and wondered who others were, and differed in opinion as to the prettiness of the girls. About Charlotte Marden we agreed, however, as we saw her coming toward us with her mother; and there surely could have been no one who wouldn't have agreed with us. The Brighton air, of old, used to make plain girls pretty and pretty girls prettier still—I don't know whether it works the spell now. The place, at any rate, was rare for complexions, and Miss Marden's was one that made people turn round. It made *us* stop, heaven knows—at least, it was one of the things, for we already knew the ladies.

We turned with them, we joined them, we went where they were going. They were only going to the end and back—they had just come out of church. It was another manifestation of Teddy's humour that he got immediate possession of Charlotte, leaving me to walk with her mother. However, I was not unhappy; the girl was before me and I had her to talk about. We prolonged our walk, Mrs. Marden kept me, and presently she said she was tired and must sit down. We found a place on a sheltered bench—we gossiped as the people passed. It had already struck me, in this pair, that the resemblance between the mother and the daughter was wonderful even among such resemblances—the more so that it took so little account of a difference of nature. One often hears mature mothers spoken of as warnings—signposts, more or less discouraging, of the way daughters may go. But there was nothing deterrent in the idea that Charlotte, at fifty-five, should be as beautiful, even though it were conditioned on her being as pale and preoccupied, as Mrs. Marden. At twenty-two she had a kind of rosy blankness and she was admirably handsome. Her head had the charming shape of her mother's, and her features the same fine order. Then there were looks and movements and tones (moments when you could scarcely say whether it were aspect or sound), which, between the two personalities, were a reflection, a recall.

These ladies had a small fortune and a cheerful little house at Brighton, full of portraits and tokens and trophies (stuffed animals on the top of bookcases, and sallow, varnished fish under glass), to which Mrs. Marden professed herself attached by pious memories. Her husband had been 'ordered' there in ill-health, to spend the last years of his life, and she had already mentioned to me that it was a place in which she felt herself still under the protection of his goodness. His goodness appeared to have been great, and she sometimes had the air of defending it against mysterious imputations. Some sense of protection, of an influence invoked and cherished, was evidently necessary to her; she had a dim wistfulness, a longing for security. She wanted friends and she had a good many. She was kind to me on our first meeting, and I never suspected her of the vulgar purpose of 'making up' to me—a suspicion, of course, unduly frequent in conceited young men. It never struck me that she wanted me for her daughter, nor yet, like some unnatural mammas, for herself. It was as if they had had a common deep, shy need and had been ready to say: 'Oh, be friendly to us and be trustful! Don't be afraid, you won't be expected to marry us.' "Of course there's something about mamma; that's really what makes her such a dear!" Charlotte said to me, confidentially, at an early stage of our acquaintance. She worshipped her mother's appearance. It was the only thing she was vain of; she accepted the raised eyebrows as a charming ultimate fact. "She looks as if she were waiting for the doctor, dear mamma," she said on another occasion. "Perhaps *you're* the doctor; do you think you are?" It appeared in the event that I had some healing power. At any rate when I learned, for she once dropped the remark, that Mrs. Marden also thought there was something 'awfully strange' about Charlotte, the relation between the two ladies became extremely interesting. It was happy enough, at bottom; each had the other so much on her mind.

On the Parade the stream of strollers held its course, and Charlotte presently went by with Teddy Bostwick. She smiled and nodded and continued, but when she came back she stopped and spoke to us. Captain Bostwick positively declined to go in, he said the occasion was too jolly: might they therefore take another turn? Her mother dropped a "Do as you like", and the girl gave me an impertinent smile over her shoulder as they quitted us. Teddy looked at me with his glass in one eye; but I didn't mind that; it was only of Miss Marden I was thinking as I observed to my companion, laughing:

"She's a bit of a coquette, you know."

"Don't say that—don't say that!" Mrs. Marden murmured.

"The nicest girls always are—just a little," I was magnanimous enough to plead.

"Then why are they always punished?"

The intensity of the question startled me—it had come out in such a vivid flash. Therefore I had to think a moment before I inquired: "What do you know about it?"

"I was a bad girl myself."

"And were you punished?"

"I carry it through life," said Mrs. Marden, looking away from me. "Ah!" she suddenly panted, in the next breath, rising to her feet and staring at her daughter, who had reappeared again with Captain Bostwick. She stood a few seconds, with the queerest expression in her face; then she sank upon the seat again and I saw that she had blushed crimson. Charlotte, who had observed her movement, came straight up to her and, taking her hand with quick tenderness, seated herself on the other side of her. The girl had turned pale—she gave her mother a fixed, frightened look. Mrs. Marden, who had had some shock which escaped our detection, recovered herself; that is she sat quiet and inexpressive, gazing at the indifferent crowd, the sunny air, the slumbering sea. My eye happened to fall, however, on the interlocked hands of the two ladies, and I quickly guessed that the grasp of the elder one was violent. Bostwick stood before them, wondering what was the matter and asking me from his little vacant disk if I knew; which led Charlotte to say to him after a moment, with a certain irritation: "Don't stand there that way, Captain Bostwick; go away—*please* go away."

I got up at this, hoping that Mrs. Marden wasn't ill; but she immediately begged that we would not go away, that we would particularly stay and that we would presently come Home to lunch. She drew me down beside her and for a moment I felt her hand pressing my arm in a way that might have been an involuntary betrayal of distress and might have been a private signal. What she might have wished to point out to me I couldn't divine: perhaps she had seen somebody or something abnormal in the crowd. She explained to us in a few minutes that she was all right; that she was only liable to palpitations—they came as quickly as they went. It was time to move, and we moved. The incident was felt to be closed. Bostwick and I lunched with our sociable friends, and when I walked away with him he declared that he had never seen such dear kind creatures.

Mrs. Marden had made us promise to come back the next day to tea, and had exhorted us in general to come as often as we could. Yet the next day, when at five o'clock I knocked at the door of the pretty house, it was to learn that the ladies had gone up to town. They had left a message for us with the butler: he was to say that they had suddenly been called—were very sorry. They would be absent a few days. This was all I could extract from the dumb domestic. I went again three days later, but they were still away; and it was not till the end of a week that I got a note from Mrs. Marden, saying 'We are back; do come and forgive us.' It was on this occasion, I remember (the occasion of my going just after getting the note), that she told me she had intuitions. I don't know how many people there were in England at that time in that predicament, but there were very few who would have mentioned it; so that the announcement struck me as original, especially as her point was that some of these uncanny promptings were connected with me. There were other people present—idle Brighton folk, old women with frightened eyes and irrelevant interjections—and I had but a few minutes' talk with Charlotte; but the day after this I met them both at dinner and had the satisfaction of sitting next to Miss Marden. I recall that hour as the hour on which it first completely came over me that she was a beautiful, liberal creature. I had seen her personality in patches and gleams, like a song sung in snatches, but now it was before me in a large rosy glow, as if it had been a full volume of sound—I heard the whole of the air. It was sweet, fresh music—I was often to hum it over.

After dinner I had a few words with Mrs. Marden; it was at the moment, late in the evening, when tea was handed about. A servant passed near us with a tray, I asked her if she would have a cup, and, on her assenting, took one and handed it to her. She put out her hand for it and I gave it to her, safely as I supposed; but as she was in the act of receiving it she started and faltered, so that the cup and saucer dropped with a crash of porcelain and without, on the part of my interlocutress, the usual woman's movement to save her dress. I stooped to pick up the fragments and when I raised myself Mrs. Marden was looking across the room at her daughter, who looked back at her smiling, but with an anxious light in her eyes. 'Dear mamma, what on earth is the matter with you?' the silent question seemed to say. Mrs. Marden coloured, just as she had done after her strange movement on the Parade the other week, and I was therefore surprised when she said to me with unexpected assurance: "You should really have a steadier hand!" I had begun to stammer a defence of my hand when I became aware that she had fixed her eyes upon me with an intense appeal. It was ambiguous at first and only added to my confusion; then suddenly I understood, as plainly as if she had murmured 'Make believe it was you—

make believe it was you.' The servant came back to take the morsels of the cup and wipe up the spilt tea, and while I was in the midst of making believe Mrs. Marden abruptly brushed away from me and from her daughter's attention and went into another room. I noticed that she gave no heed to the state of her dress.

I saw nothing more of either of them that evening, but the next morning, in the King's Road, I met Miss Marden with a roll of music in her muff. She told me she had been a little way alone, to practice duets with a friend, and I asked her if she would go a little way further in company. She gave me leave to attend her to her door, and as we stood before it I inquired if I might go in. "No, not to-day—I don't want you," she said, candidly, though not roughly; while the words caused me to direct a wistful, disconcerted gaze at one of the windows of the house. It fell upon the white face of Mrs. Marden, who was looking out at us from the drawing-room. She stood there long enough for me to see that it *was* she and not an apparition, as I had thought for a second, and then she vanished before her daughter had observed her. The girl, during our walk, had said nothing about her. As I had been told they didn't want me I left them alone a little, after which circumstances supervened that kept us still longer apart. I finally went up to London, and while there I received a pressing invitation to come immediately down to Tranton, a pretty old place in Sussex belonging to a couple whose acquaintance I had lately made.

I went to Tranton from town, and on arriving found the Mardens, with a dozen other people, in the house. The first thing Mrs. Marden said was: "Will you forgive me?" and when I asked what I had to forgive she answered: "My throwing my tea over you." I replied that it had gone over herself; whereupon she said: "At any rate I was very rude; but some day I think you'll understand, and then you'll make allowances for me." The first day I was there she dropped two or three of these references (she had already indulged in more than one), to the mystic initiation that was in store for me; so that I began, as the phrase is, to chaff her about it, to say I would rather it were less wonderful and take it out at once. She answered that when it should come to me I would have to take it out—there would be little enough option. That it *would* come was privately clear to her, a deep presentiment, which was the only reason she had ever mentioned the matter. Didn't I remember she had told me she had intuitions? From the first time of her seeing me she had been sure there were things I should not escape knowing. Meanwhile there was nothing to do but wait and keep cool, not to be precipitate. She particularly wished not to be any more nervous than she was. And I was above all not to be nervous myself—one got used to everything. I declared that though I couldn't make out what she was talking about I was terribly frightened; the absence of a clue gave such a range to one's imagination. I exaggerated on purpose; for if Mrs. Marden was mystifying I can scarcely say she was alarming. I couldn't imagine what she meant, but I wondered more than I shuddered. I might have said to myself that she was a little wrong in the upper story; but that never occurred to me. She struck me as hopelessly right.

There were other girls in the house, but Charlotte Marden was the most charming; which was so generally felt to be the case that she really interfered with the slaughter of ground game. There were two or three men, and I was of the number, who actually preferred her to the society of the beaters. In short she was recognised as a form of sport superior and exquisite. She was kind to all of us—she made us go out late and come in early. I don't know whether she flirted, but several other members of the party thought *they* did. Indeed, as regards himself, Teddy Bostwick, who had come over from Brighton, was visibly sure.

The third day I was at Tranton was a Sunday, and there was a very pretty walk to morning service over the fields. It was grey, windless weather, and the bell of the little old church that nestled in the hollow of the Sussex down sounded near and domestic. We were a straggling procession, in the mild damp air (which, as always at that season, gave one the feeling that after the trees were bare there was more of it—a larger sky), and I managed to fall a good way behind with Miss Marden. I remember entertaining, as we moved together over the turf, a strong impulse to say something intensely personal, something violent and important, important for *me*—such as that I had never seen her so lovely, or that that particular moment was the sweetest of my life. But always, in youth, such words have been on the lips many times before they are spoken; and I had the sense, not that I didn't know her well enough (I cared little for that), but that she didn't know *me*. In the church, where there were old Tranton tombs and brasses, the big Tranton pew was full. Several of us were scattered, and I found a seat for Miss Marden, and another for myself beside it, at a distance from her mother and from most of our friends. There were two or three decent rustics on the bench, who moved in further to make room for us, and I took my place first, to cut off my companion from our neighbours. After she was seated there was still a space left, which remained empty till service was about half over.

This at least was the moment at which I became aware that another person had entered and had taken the seat. When I noticed him he had apparently been for some minutes in the pew, for he had settled himself and put down his hat beside him, and, with his hands crossed on the knob of his cane, was gazing before him at the altar. He was a pale young man in black, with the air of a gentleman. I was slightly startled on perceiving him, for Miss Marden had not attracted my attention to his entrance by moving to make room for him. After a few minutes, observing that he had no prayer-book, I reached across my neighbour and placed mine before him, on the ledge of the pew; a manœuvre the motive of which was not unconnected with the possibility that, in my own destitution, Miss Marden would give me one side of *her* velvet volume to hold. The pretext, however, was destined to fail for at the moment I offered him the book the intruder—whose intrusion I had so condoned—rose from his place without thanking me, stepped noiselessly out of the pew (it had no door), and, so discreetly as to attract no attention, passed down the centre of the church. A few minutes had sufficed for his devotions. His behaviour was unbecoming, his early departure even more than his late arrival; but he managed so quietly that we were not incommoded, and I perceived, on turning a little to glance after him, that nobody was disturbed by his withdrawal. I only noticed, and with surprise, that Mrs. Marden had been so affected by it as to rise, involuntarily, an instant, in her place. She stared at him as he passed, but he passed very quickly, and she as quickly dropped down again, though not too soon to catch my eye across the church. Five minutes later I asked Miss Marden, in a low voice, if she would kindly pass me back my prayer-book—I had waited to see if she would spontaneously perform the act. She restored this aid to devotion, but had been so far from troubling herself about it that she could say to me as she did so: "Why on earth did you put it there?" I was on the point of answering her when she dropped on her knees, and I held my tongue. I had only been going to say: 'To be decently civil.'

After the benediction, as we were leaving our places, I was slightly surprised, again, to see that Mrs. Marden, instead of going out with her companions, had come up the aisle to join us, having apparently something to say to her daughter. She said it, but in an instant I observed that it was only a pretext—her real Business was with me. She pushed Charlotte forward and suddenly murmured to me: "Did you see him?"

"The gentleman who sat down here? How could I help seeing him?"

"Hush!" she said, with the intensest excitement; "don't *speak* to her—don't tell her!" She slipped her hand into my arm, to keep me near her, to keep me, it seemed, away from her daughter. The precaution was unnecessary, for Teddy Bostwick had already taken possession of Miss Marden, and as they passed out of church in front of me I saw one of the other men close up on her other hand. It appeared to be considered that I had had my turn. Mrs. Marden withdrew her hand from my arm as soon as we got out, but not before I felt that she had really needed the support. "Don't speak to any one—don't tell any one!" she went on.

"I don't understand. Tell them what?"

"Why, that you saw him."

"Surely they saw him for themselves."

"Not one of them, not one of them." She spoke in a tone of such passionate decision that I glanced at her—she was staring straight before her. But she felt the challenge of my eyes and she stopped short, in the old brown timber porch of the church, with the others well in advance of us, and said, looking at me now and in a quite extraordinary manner: "You're the only person, the only person in the world."

"But *you*, dear madam?"

"Oh me—of course. That's my curse!" And with this she moved rapidly away from me to join the body of the party. I hovered on its outskirts on the way home, for I had food for rumination. Whom had I seen and why was the apparition—it rose before my mind's eye very vividly again—invisible to the others? If an exception had been made for Mrs. Marden, why did it constitute a curse, and why was I to share so questionable an advantage? This inquiry, carried on in my own locked breast, kept me doubtless silent enough during luncheon. After luncheon I went out on the old terrace to smoke a cigarette, but I had only taken a couple of turns when I perceived Mrs. Marden's moulded mask at the window of one of the rooms which opened on the crooked flags. It reminded me of the same flitting presence at the window at Brighton the day I met Charlotte and walked Home with her. But this time my ambiguous friend didn't vanish; she tapped on the pane and motioned me to come in. She was in a queer little apartment, one of the many reception-rooms of which the ground-floor at Tranton consisted; it was known as the Indian room and had a decoration vaguely Oriental—bamboo lounges, lacquered screens, lanterns with long fringes and strange idols in cabinets, objects not held to conduce to sociability. The place was little used, and when I went round to her we had it to ourselves. As soon as I entered she said to me: "Please tell me this; are you in love with my daughter?"

I hesitated a moment. "Before I answer your question will you kindly tell me what gives you the idea? I don't consider that I have been very forward."

Mrs. Marden, contradicting me with her beautiful anxious eyes, gave me no satisfaction on the point I mentioned; she only went on strenuously:

"Did you say nothing to her on the way to church?"

"What makes you think I said anything?"

"The fact that you saw him."

"Saw whom, dear Mrs. Marden?"

"Oh, you know," she answered, gravely, even a little reproachfully, as if I were trying to humiliate her by making her name the unnamable.

"Do you mean the gentleman who formed the subject of your strange statement in church—the one who came into the pew?"

"You saw him, you saw him!" Mrs. Marden panted, with a strange mixture of dismay and relief.

"Of course I saw him; and so did you."

"It didn't follow. Did you feel it to be inevitable?"

I was puzzled again. "Inevitable?"

"That you *should* see him?"

"Certainly, since I'm not blind."

"You might have been; every one else is." I was wonderfully at sea, and I frankly confessed it to my interlocutress; but the case was not made clearer by her presently exclaiming: "I knew you would, from the moment you should be really in love with her! I knew it would be the test—what do I mean?—the proof."

"Are there such strange bewilderments attached to that high state?" I asked, smiling.

"You perceive there are. You see him, you see him!" Mrs. Marden announced, with tremendous exaltation. "You'll see him again."

"I've no objection; but I shall take more interest in him if you'll kindly tell me who he is."

She hesitated, looking down a moment; then she said, raising her eyes: "I'll tell you if you'll tell me first what you said to her on the way to church."

"Has she told you I said anything?"

"Do I need that?" smiled Mrs. Marden.

"Oh yes, I remember—your intuitions! But I'm sorry to see they're at fault this time; because I really said nothing to your daughter that was the least out of the way."

"Are you very sure?"

"On my honour, Mrs. Marden."

"Then you consider that you're not in love with her?"

"That's another affair!" I laughed.

"You are—you *are*! You wouldn't have seen him if you hadn't been."

"Who the deuce is he, then, madam?" I inquired with some irritation.

She would still only answer me with another question. "Didn't you at least *want* to say something to her—didn't you come very near it?"

The question was much to the point; it justified the famous intuitions. "Very near it—it was the turn of a hair. I don't know what kept me quiet."

"That was quite enough," said Mrs. Marden. "It isn't what you say that determines it; it's what you feel. *That's* what he goes by."

I was annoyed, at last, by her reiterated reference to an identity yet to be established, and I clasped my hands with an air of supplication which covered much real impatience, a sharper curiosity and even the first short throbs of a certain sacred dread. "I entreat you to tell me whom you're talking about."

She threw up her arms, looking away from me, as if to shake off both reserve and responsibility. "Sir Edmund Orme."

"And who is Sir Edmund Orme?"

At the moment I spoke she gave a start. "Hush, here they come." Then as, following the direction of her eyes, I saw Charlotte Marden on the terrace, at the window, she added, with an intensity of warning: "Don't notice him—never!"

Charlotte, who had had her hands beside her eyes, peering into the room and smiling, made a sign that she was to be admitted, on which I went and opened the long window. Her mother turned away, and the girl came in with a laughing challenge: "What plot, in the world are you two hatching here?" Some plan—I forget what—was in prospect for the afternoon, as to which Mrs. Marden's participation or consent was solicited—my adhesion was taken for granted—and she had been half over the place in her quest. I was flurried, because I saw that Mrs. Marden was flurried (when she turned round to meet her daughter she covered it by a kind of extravagance, throwing herself on the girl's neck and embracing her), and to pass it off I said, fancifully, to Charlotte:

"I've been asking your mother for your hand."

"Oh, indeed, and has she given it?" Miss Marden answered, gaily.

"She was just going to when you appeared there."

"Well, it's only for a moment—I'll leave you free."

"Do you like him, Charlotte?" Mrs. Marden asked, with a candour I scarcely expected.

"It's difficult to say it *before* him isn't it?" the girl replied, entering into the humour of the thing, but looking at me as if she didn't like me.

She would have had to say it before another person as well, for at that moment there stepped into the room from the terrace (the window had been left open), a gentleman who had come into sight, at least into mine, only within the instant. Mrs. Marden had said "Here *they* come," but he appeared to have followed her daughter at a certain distance. I immediately recognised him as the personage who had sat beside us in church. This time I saw him better, saw that his face and his whole air were strange. I speak of him as a personage, because one felt, indescribably, as if a reigning prince had come into the room. He held himself with a kind of habitual majesty, as if he were different from us. Yet he looked fixedly and gravely at me, till I wondered what he expected of me. Did he consider that I should bend my knee or kiss his hand? He turned his eyes in the same way on Mrs. Marden, but she knew what to do. After the first agitation produced by his approach she took no notice of him whatever; it made me remember her passionate adjuration to me. I had to achieve a great effort to imitate her, for though I knew nothing about him but that he was Sir Edmund Orme I felt his presence as a strong appeal, almost as an oppression. He stood there without speaking—young, pale, handsome, clean-shaven, decorous, with extraordinary light blue eyes and something old-fashioned, like a portrait of years ago, in his head, his manner of wearing his hair. He was in complete mourning (one immediately felt that he was very well dressed), and he carried his hat in his hand. He looked again strangely hard at me, harder than any one in the world had ever looked before; and I remember feeling rather cold and wishing he would say something. No silence had ever seemed to me so soundless. All this was of course an impression intensely rapid; but that it had consumed some instants was proved to me suddenly by the aspect of Charlotte Marden, who stared from her mother to me and back again (he never looked at her, and she had no appearance of looking at him), and then broke out with: "What on earth is the matter with you? You've such odd faces!" I felt the colour come back to mine, and when she went on in the same tone: "One would think you had seen a ghost!" I was conscious that I had turned very red. Sir Edmund Orme never blushed, and I could see that he had no capacity for embarrassment. One had met people of that sort, but never any one with such a grand indifference.

"Don't be impertinent; and go and tell them all that I'll join them," said Mrs. Marden with much dignity, but with a quaver in her voice.

"And will you come—*you*?" the girl asked, turning away. I made no answer, taking the question, somehow, as meant for her companion. But he was more silent than I, and when she reached the door (she was going out that way), she stopped, with her hand on the knob, and looked at me, repeating it. I assented, springing forward to open the door for her, and as she passed out she exclaimed to me mockingly: "You haven't got your wits about you—you sha'n't have my hand!"

I closed the door and turned round to find that Sir Edmund Orme had during the moment my back was presented to him retired by the window. Mrs. Marden stood there and we looked at each other long. It had only then—as the girl flitted away—come Home to me that her daughter was unconscious of what had happened. It was *that*, oddly enough, that gave me a sudden, sharp shake, and not my own perception of our visitor, which appeared perfectly natural. It made the fact vivid to me that she had been equally unaware of him in church, and the two facts together—now that they were over—set my heart more sensibly beating. I wiped my forehead, and Mrs. Marden broke out with a low distressful wail: "Now you know my life—now you know my life!"

"In God's name who is he—*what* is he?"

"He's a man I wronged."

"How did you wrong him?"

"Oh, awfully—years ago."

"Years ago? Why, he's very young."

"Young—young?" cried Mrs. Marden. "He was born before *I* was!"

"Then why does he look so?"

She came nearer to me, she laid her hand on my arm, and there was something in her face that made me shrink a little. "Don't you understand—don't you *feel*?" she murmured, reproachfully.

"I feel very queer!" I laughed; and I was conscious that my laugh betrayed it.

"He's dead!" said Mrs. Marden, from her white face.

"Dead?" I panted. "Then that gentleman was-?" I couldn't even say the word.

"Call him what you like—there are twenty vulgar names. He's a perfect presence."

"He's a splendid presence!" I cried. "The place is haunted—*haunted*!" I exulted in the word as if it represented the fulfilment of my dearest dream.

"It isn't the place—more's the pity! That has nothing to do with it!"

"Then it's you, dear lady?" I said, as if this were still better.

"No, nor me either—I wish it were!"

"Perhaps it's me," I suggested with a sickly smile.

"It's nobody but my child—my innocent, innocent child!" And with this Mrs. Marden broke down—she dropped into a chair and burst into tears. I stammered some question—I pressed on her some bewildered appeal, but she waved me off, unexpectedly and passionately. I persisted—couldn't I help her, couldn't I intervene? "You *have* intervened," she sobbed; "you're *in* it, you're in it."

"I'm very glad to be in anything so curious," I boldly declared.

"Glad or not, you can't get out of it."

"I don't want to get out of it—it's too interesting."

"I'm glad you like it. Go away."

"But I want to know more about it."

"You'll see all you want—go away!"

"But I want to understand what I see."

"How can you—when I don't understand myself?"

"We'll do so together—we'll make it out."

At this she got up, doing what she could to obliterate her tears. "Yes, it will be better together—that's why I've liked you."

"Oh, we'll see it through!" I declared.

"Then you must control yourself better."

"I will, I will—with practice."

"You'll get used to it," said Mrs. Marden, in a tone I never forgot. "But go and join them—I'll come in a moment."

I passed out to the terrace and I felt that I had a part to play. So far from dreading another encounter with the 'perfect presence', as Mrs. Marden called it, I was filled with an excitement that was positively joyous. I desired a renewal of the sensation—I opened myself wide to the impression; I went round the house as quickly as if I expected to overtake Sir Edmund Orme. I didn't overtake him just then, but the day was not to close without my recognising that, as Mrs. Marden had said, I should see all I wanted of him.

We took, or most of us took, the collective sociable walk which, in the English country-house, is the consecrated pastime on Sunday afternoons. We were restricted to such a regulated ramble as the ladies were good for; the afternoons, moreover, were short, and by five o'clock we were restored to the fireside in the hall, with a sense, on my part at least, that we might have done a little more for our tea. Mrs. Marden had said she would join us, but she had not appeared; her daughter, who had seen her again before we went out, only explained that she was tired. She remained invisible all the afternoon, but this was a detail to which I gave as little heed as I had given to the circumstance of my not having Miss Marden to myself during all our walk. I was too much taken up with another emotion to care; I felt beneath my feet the threshold of the strange door, in my life, which had suddenly been thrown open and out of which unspeakable vibrations played up through me like a fountain. I had heard all my days of apparitions, but it was a different thing to have seen one and to know that I should in all probability see it familiarly, as it were, again. I was on the look-out for it, as a pilot for the flash of a revolving light, and I was ready to generalise on the sinister subject, to declare that ghosts were much less alarming and much more amusing than was commonly supposed. There is no doubt that I was extremely nervous. I couldn't get over the distinction conferred upon me—the exception (in the way of mystic enlargement of vision), made in my favour. At the same time I think I did justice to Mrs. Marden's absence; it was a commentary on what she had said to me—"Now you know my life." She had probably been seeing Sir Edmund Orme for years, and, not having my firm fibre, she had broken down under him. Her nerve was gone, though she had also been able to attest that, in a degree, one got used to him. She had got used to breaking down.

Afternoon tea, when the dusk fell early, was a friendly hour at Tranton; the firelight played into the wide, white last-century hall; sympathies almost confessed themselves, lingering together, before dressing, on deep sofas, in muddy boots, for last words, after walks; and even solitary absorption in the third volume of a novel that was wanted by some one else seemed a form of geniality. I watched my moment and went over to Charlotte Marden when I saw she was about to withdraw. The ladies had left the place one by one, and after I had addressed myself particularly to Miss Marden the three men who were near her gradually dispersed. We had a little vague talk—she appeared preoccupied, and heaven knows *I* was—after which she said she must go: she should be late for dinner. I proved to her by book that she had plenty of time, and she objected that she must at any rate go up to see her mother: she was afraid she was unwell.

"On the contrary, she's better than she has been for a long time—I'll guarantee that," I said. "She has found out that she can have confidence in me, and that has done her good." Miss Marden had dropped into her chair again. I was standing before her, and she looked up at me without a smile—with a dim distress in her beautiful eyes; not exactly as if I were hurting her, but as if she were no longer disposed to treat as a joke what had passed (whatever it was, it was at the same time difficult to be serious about it), between her mother and myself. But I could answer her inquiry in all kindness and candour, for I was really conscious that the poor lady had put off a part of her burden on me and was proportionately relieved and eased. "I'm sure she has slept all the afternoon as she hasn't slept for years," I went on. "You have only to ask her."

Charlotte got up again. "You make yourself out very useful."

"You've a good quarter of an hour," I said. "Haven't I a right to talk to you a little this way, alone, when your mother has given me your hand?"

"And is it *your* mother who has given me yours? I'm much obliged to her, but I don't want it. I think our hands are not our mothers'—they happen to be our own!" laughed the girl.

"Sit down, sit down and let me tell you!" I pleaded.

I still stood before her, urgently, to see if she wouldn't oblige me. She hesitated a moment, looking vaguely this way and that, as if under a compulsion that was slightly painful. The empty hall was quiet—we heard the loud ticking of the great clock. Then she slowly sank down and I drew a chair close to her. This made me face round to the fire again, and with the movement I perceived, disconcertedly, that we were not alone. The next instant, more strangely than I can say, my discomposure, instead of increasing, dropped, for the person before the fire was Sir Edmund Orme. He stood there as I had seen him in the Indian room, looking at me with the expressionless attention which borrowed its sternness from his sombre distinction. I knew so much more about him now that I had to check a movement of recognition, an acknowledgment of his presence. When once I was aware of it, and that it lasted, the sense that we had company, Charlotte and I, quitted me; it was impressed on me on the contrary that I was more intensely alone with Miss Marden. She evidently saw nothing to look at, and I made a tremendous and very nearly successful effort to conceal from her that my own situation was different. I say 'very nearly', because she watched me an instant—while my words were arrested—in a way that made me fear she was going to say again, as she had said in the Indian room: 'What on earth is the matter with you?'

What the matter with me was I quickly told her, for the full knowledge of it rolled over me with the touching spectacle of her unconsciousness. It was touching that she became, in the presence of this extraordinary portent. What was portended, danger or sorrow, bliss or bane, was a minor question; all I saw, as she sat there, was that, innocent and charming, she was close to a horror, as she might have thought it, that happened to be veiled from her but that might at any moment be disclosed. I didn't mind it now, as I found, but nothing was more possible than she should, and if it wasn't curious and interesting it might easily be very dreadful. If I didn't mind it for myself, as I afterwards saw, this was largely because I was so taken up with the idea of protecting her. My heart beat high with this idea, on the spot; I determined to do everything I could to keep her sense sealed. What I could do might have been very obscure to me if I had not, in all this, become more aware than of anything else that I loved her. The way to save her was to love her, and the way to love her was to tell her, now and here, that I did so. Sir Edmund Orme didn't prevent me, especially as after a moment he turned his back to us and stood looking discreetly at the fire. At the end of another moment he leaned his head on his arm, against the chimneypiece, with an air of gradual dejection, like a spirit still more weary than discreet. Charlotte Marden was startled by what I said to her, and she jumped up to escape it; but she took no offence—my tenderness was too real. She only moved about the room with a deprecating murmur, and I was so busy following up any little advantage that I might have obtained that I didn't notice in what manner Sir Edmund Orme disappeared. I only observed presently that he had gone. This made no difference—he had been so small a hindrance; I only remember being struck, suddenly, with something inexorable in the slow, sweet, sad headshake that Miss Marden gave me.

"I don't ask for an answer now," I said; "I only want you to be sure—to know how much depends on it."

"Oh, I don't want to give it to you, now or ever!" she replied. "I hate the subject, please—I wish one could be let alone." And then, as if I might have found something harsh in this irrepressible, artless cry of beauty beset, she added quickly, vaguely, kindly, as she left the room: "Thank you, thank you—thank you so much!"

At dinner I could be generous enough to be glad, for her, that I was placed on the same side of the table with her, where she couldn't see me. Her mother was nearly opposite to me, and just after we had sat down Mrs. Marden gave me one long, deep look, in which all our strange communion was expressed. It meant of course 'She has told me,' but it meant other things beside. At any rate I know what my answering look to her conveyed: 'I've seen him again—I've seen him again!' This didn't prevent Mrs. Marden from treating her neighbours with her usual scrupulous blandness. After dinner, when, in the drawing-room, the men joined the ladies and I went straight up to her to tell her how I wished we could have some private conversation, she said immediately, in a low tone, looking down at her fan while she opened and shut it:

"He's here—he's here."

"Here?" I looked round the room, but I was disappointed.

"Look where *she* is," said Mrs. Marden, with just the faintest asperity. Charlotte was in fact not in the main saloon, but in an apartment into which it opened and which was known as the morning-room. I took a few steps and saw her, through a doorway, upright in the middle of the room, talking with three gentlemen whose backs were practically turned to me. For a moment my quest seemed vain; then I recognised that one of the gentlemen—the middle one—was Sir Edmund Orme. This time it *was* surprising that the others didn't see him. Charlotte seemed to be looking straight at him, addressing her conversation to him. She saw me after an instant, however, and immediately turned her eyes away. I went back to her mother with an annoyed sense that the girl would think I was watching *her*, which would be unjust. Mrs. Marden had found a small sofa—a little apart—and I sat down beside her. There were some questions I had so wanted to go into that I wished we were once more in the Indian room. I presently gathered, however, that our privacy was all-sufficient. We communicated so closely and completely now, and with such silent reciprocities, that it would in every circumstance be adequate.

"Oh, yes, he's there," I said; "and at about a quarter-past seven he was in the hall."

"I knew it at the time, and I was so glad!"

"So glad?"

"That it was your affair, this time, and not mine. It's a rest for me."

"Did you sleep all the afternoon?" I asked.

"As I haven't done for months. But how did you know that?"

"As you knew, I take it, that Sir Edmund was in the hall. We shall evidently each of us know things now—where the other is concerned."

"Where *he's* concerned," Mrs. Marden amended. "It's a blessing, the way you take it," she added, with a long, mild sigh.

"I take it as a man who's in love with your daughter."

"Of course—of course." Intense as I now felt my desire for the girl to be, I couldn't help laughing a little at the tone of these words; and it led my companion immediately to say: "Otherwise you wouldn't have seen him."

"But every one doesn't see him who's in love with her, or there would be dozens."

"They're not in love with her as you are."

"I can, of course, only speak for myself; and I found a moment, before dinner, to do so."

"She told me immediately."

"And have I any hope—any chance?"

"That's what I long for, what I pray for."

"Ah, how can I thank you enough?" I murmured.

"I believe it will all pass—if she loves you," Mrs. Marden continued.

"It will all pass?"

"We shall never see him again."

"Oh, if she loves me I don't care how often I see him!"

"Ah, you take it better than *I* could," said my companion. "You have the Happiness not to know—not to understand."

"I don't indeed. What on earth does he want?"

"He wants to make me suffer." She turned her wan face upon me with this, and I saw now for the first time, fully, how perfectly, if this had been Sir Edmund Orme's purpose, he had succeeded. "For what I did to him," Mrs. Marden explained.

"And what did you do to him?"

She looked at me a moment. "I killed him." As I had seen him fifty yards away only five minutes before the words gave me a start. "Yes, I make you jump; be careful. He's there still, but he killed himself. I broke his heart—he thought me awfully bad. We were to have been married, but I broke it off—just at the last. I saw some one I liked better; I had no reason but that. It wasn't for interest, or money, or position, or anything of that sort. All those things were his. It was simply that I fell in love with Captain Marden. When I saw *him* I felt that I couldn't marry any one else. I wasn't in love with Edmund Orme—my mother, my elder sister had brought it about. But he did love me. I told him I didn't care—that I couldn't, that I wouldn't. I threw him over, and he took something, some abominable drug or draught that proved fatal. It was dreadful, it was horrible, he was found that way—he died in agony. I married Captain Marden, but not for five years. I was happy, perfectly happy; time obliterates. But when my husband died I began to see him."

I had listened intently, but I wondered. "To see your husband?"

"Never, never—*that* way, thank God! To see *him*, with Chartie—always with Chartie. The first time it nearly killed me—about seven years ago, when she first came out. Never when I'm by myself—only with her. Sometimes not for months, then every day for a week. I've tried everything to break the spell—doctors and *régimes* and climates; I've prayed to God on my knees. That day at Brighton, on the Parade with you, when you thought I was ill, that was the first for an age. And then, in the evening, when I knocked my tea over you, and the day you were at the door with Charlotte and I saw you from the window—each time he was there."

"I see, I see." I was more thrilled than I could say. "It's an apparition like another."

"Like another? Have you ever seen another?"

"No, I mean the sort of thing one has heard of. It's tremendously interesting to encounter a case."

"Do you call me a 'case'?" Mrs. Marden asked, with exquisite resentment.

"I mean myself."

"Oh, you're the right one!" she exclaimed. "I was right when I trusted you."

"I'm devoutly grateful you did; but what made you do it?"

"I had thought the whole thing out—I had had time to in those dreadful years, while he was punishing me in my daughter."

"Hardly that," I objected, "if she never knew."

"That has been my terror, that she *will*, from one occasion to another. I've an unspeakable dread of the effect on her."

"She sha'n't, she sha'n't!" I declared, so loud that several people looked round. Mrs. Marden made me get up, and I had no more talk with her that evening. The next day I told her I must take my departure from Tranton—it was neither comfortable nor considerate to remain as a rejected suitor. She was disconcerted, but she accepted my reasons, only saying to me out of her mournful eyes: 'You'll leave me alone then with my burden?' It was of course understood between us that for many weeks to come there would be no discretion in 'worrying poor Charlotte': such were the terms in which, with odd feminine and maternal inconsistency, she alluded to an attitude on my part that she favoured. I was prepared to be heroically considerate, but it seemed to me that even this delicacy permitted me to say a word to Miss Marden before I went. I begged her, after breakfast, to take a turn with me on the terrace, and as she hesitated, looking at me distantly, I informed her that it was only to ask her a question and to say good-bye—I was leaving Tranton for *her*.

She came out with me, and we passed slowly round the house three or four times. Nothing is finer than this great airy platform, from which every look is a sweep of the country, with the sea on the furthest edge. It might have been that as we passed the windows we were conspicuous to our friends in the house, who would divine, sarcastically, why I was so significantly bolting. But I didn't care; I only wondered whether they wouldn't really this time make out Sir Edmund Orme, who joined us on one of our turns and strolled slowly on the other side of my companion. Of what transcendent essence he was composed I knew not; I have no theory about him (leaving that to others), any more than I have one about such or such another of my fellow-mortals whom I have elbowed in life. He was as positive, as individual, as ultimate a fact as any of these. Above all he was as respectable, as sensitive a fact; so that I should no more have thought of taking a liberty, of practicing an experiment with him, of touching him, for instance, or speaking to him, since he set the example of silence, than I should have thought of committing any other social grossness. He had always, as I saw more fully later, the perfect propriety of his position—had always the appearance of being dressed and, in attitude and aspect, of comporting himself, as the occasion demanded. He looked strange, incontestably, but somehow he always looked right. I very soon came to attach an idea of beauty to his unmentionable presence, the beauty of an old story of love and pain. What I ended by feeling was that he was on my side, that he was watching over my interest, that he was looking to it that my heart shouldn't be broken. Oh, he had taken it seriously, his own catastrophe—he had certainly proved that in his day. If poor Mrs. Marden, as she told me, had thought it out, I also subjected the case to the finest analysis of which my intellect was capable. It was a case of retributive justice. The mother was to pay, in suffering, for the suffering she had inflicted, and as the disposition to jilt a lover might have been transmitted to the daughter, the daughter was to be watched, so that *she* might be made to suffer should she do an equal wrong. She might reproduce her mother in character as vividly as she did in face. On the day she should transgress, in other words, her eyes would be opened suddenly and unpitiedly to the 'perfect presence', which she would have to work as she could into her conception of a young lady's universe. I had no great fear for her, because I didn't believe she was, in any cruel degree, a coquette. We should have a good deal of ground to get over before I, at least, should be in a position to be sacrificed by her. She couldn't throw me over before she had made a little more of me. The question I asked her on the terrace that morning was whether I might continue, during the winter, to come to Mrs. Marden's house. I promised not to come too often and not to speak to her for three months of the question I had raised the day before. She replied that I might do as I liked, and on this we parted.

I carried out the vow I had made her; I held my tongue for my three months. Unexpectedly to myself there were moments of this time when she struck me as capable of playing with a man. I wanted so to make her like me that I became subtle and ingenious, wonderfully alert, patiently diplomatic. Sometimes I thought I had earned my reward, brought her to the point of saying: 'Well, well, you're the best of them all—you may speak to me now.' Then there was a greater blankness than ever in her beauty, and on certain days a mocking light in her eyes, of which the meaning seemed to be: 'If you don't take care, I *will* accept you, to have done with you the more effectually.' Mrs. Marden was a great help to me simply by believing in me, and I valued her faith all the more that it continued even though there was a sudden intermission of the miracle that had been wrought for me. After our visit to Tranton Sir Edmund Orme gave us a holiday, and I confess it was at first a disappointment to me. I felt less designated, less connected with Charlotte. "Oh, don't cry till you're out of the wood," her mother said; "he has let me off sometimes for six months. He'll break out again when you least expect it—he knows what he's about." For her these weeks were happy, and she was wise enough not to talk about me to the girl. She was so good as to assure me that I was taking the right way, that I looked as if I felt secure and that in the long run women give way to that. She had known them do it even when the man was a fool for looking so—or was a fool on any terms. For herself she felt it to be a good time, a sort of St Martin's summer of the soul. She was better than she had been for years, and she had me to thank for it. The sense of visitation was light upon her—she wasn't in anguish every time she looked round. Charlotte contradicted me very often, but she contradicted herself still more. That winter was a wonder of mildness, and we often sat out in the sun. I walked up and down with Charlotte, and Mrs. Marden, sometimes on a bench, sometimes in a bath-chair, waited for us and smiled at us as we passed. I always looked out for a sign in her face—'He's with you, he's with you' (she would see him before I should), but nothing came; the season had brought us also a sort of spiritual softness. Toward the end of April the air was so like June that, meeting my two friends one night at some Brighton sociability—an evening party with amateur music—I drew Miss Marden unresistingly out upon a balcony to which a window in one of the rooms stood open. The night was close and thick, the stars were dim, and below us, under the cliff, we heard the regular rumble of the sea. We listened to it a little and we heard mixed with it, from within the house, the sound of a violin accompanied by a piano—a performance which had been our pretext for passing out.

"Do you like me a little better?" I asked, abruptly, after a minute. "Could you listen to me again?"

I had no sooner spoken than she laid her hand quickly, with a certain force, on my arm. "Hush!—isn't there some one there?" She was looking into the gloom of the far end of the balcony. This balcony ran the whole width of the house, a width very great in the best of the old houses at Brighton. We were lighted a little by the open window behind us, but the other windows, curtained within, left the darkness undiminished, so that I made out but dimly the figure of a gentleman standing there and looking at us. He was in evening dress, like a guest—I saw the vague shine of his white shirt and the pale oval of his face—and he might perfectly have been a guest who had stepped out in advance of us to take the air. Miss Marden took him for one at first—then evidently, even in a few seconds, she saw that the intensity of his gaze was unconventional. What else she saw I couldn't determine; I was too taken up with my own impression to do more than feel the quick contact of her uneasiness. My own impression was in fact the strongest of sensations, a sensation of horror; for what could the thing mean but that the girl at last saw? I heard her give a sudden, gasping "Ah!" and move quickly into the house. It was only afterwards that I knew that I myself had had a totally new emotion—my horror passing into anger, and my anger into a stride along the balcony with a gesture of reprobation. The case was simplified to the vision of a frightened girl whom I loved. I advanced to vindicate her security, but I found nothing there to meet me. It was either all a mistake or Sir Edmund Orme had vanished.

I followed Miss Marden immediately, but there were symptoms of confusion in the drawing-room when I passed in. A lady had fainted, the music had stopped; there was a shuffling of chairs and a pressing forward. The lady was not Charlotte, as I feared, but Mrs. Marden, who had suddenly been taken ill. I remember the relief with which I learned this, for to see Charlotte stricken would have been anguish, and her mother's condition gave a channel to her agitation. It was of course all a matter for the people of the house and for the ladies, and I could have no share in attending to my friends or in conducting them to their carriage. Mrs. Marden revived and insisted on going Home, after which I uneasily withdrew.

I called the next morning to ask about her and was informed that she was better, but when I asked if Miss Marden would see me the message sent down was that it was impossible. There was nothing for me to do all day but to roam about with a beating heart. But toward evening I received a line in pencil, brought by hand—'Please come; mother wishes you.' Five minutes afterward I was at the door again and ushered into the drawing-room. Mrs. Marden lay upon the sofa, and as soon as I looked at her I saw the shadow of death in her face. But the first thing she said was that she was better, ever so much better; her poor old heart had been behaving queerly again, but now it was quiet. She gave me her hand and I bent over her with my eyes in hers, and in this way I was able to read what she didn't speak—'I'm really very ill, but appear to take what I say exactly as I say it.' Charlotte stood there beside her, looking not frightened now, but intensely grave, and not meeting my eyes. "She has told me—she has told me!" her mother went on.

"She has told you?" I stared from one of them to the other, wondering if Mrs. Marden meant that the girl had spoken to her of the circumstances on the balcony.

"That you spoke to her again—that you're admirably faithful."

I felt a thrill of joy at this; it showed me that that memory had been uppermost, and also that Charlotte had wished to say the thing that would soothe her mother most, not the thing that would alarm her. Yet I now knew, myself, as well as if Mrs. Marden had told me, that she knew and had known at the moment what her daughter had seen. "I spoke—I spoke, but she gave me no answer," I said.

"She will now, won't you, Chartie? I want it so, I want it!" the poor lady murmured, with ineffable wistfulness.

"You're very good to me," Charlotte said to me, seriously and sweetly, looking fixedly on the carpet. There was something different in her, different from all the past. She had recognised something, she felt a coercion. I could see that she was trembling.

"Ah, if you would let me show you *how* good I can be!" I exclaimed, holding out my hands to her. As I uttered the words I was touched with the knowledge that something had happened. A form had constituted itself on the other side of the bed, and the form leaned over Mrs. Marden. My whole being went forth into a mute prayer that Charlotte shouldn't see it and that I should be able to betray nothing. The impulse to glance toward Mrs. Marden was even stronger than the involuntary movement of taking in Sir Edmund Orme; but I could resist even that, and Mrs. Marden was perfectly still. Charlotte got up to give me her hand, and with the definite act she saw. She gave, with a shriek, one stare of dismay, and another sound, like a wail of one of the lost, fell at the same instant on my ear. But I had already sprung toward the girl to cover her, to veil her face. She had already thrown herself into my arms. I held her there a moment—bending over her, given up to her, feeling each of her throbs with my own and not knowing which was which; then, all of a sudden, coldly, I gathered that we were alone. She released herself. The figure beside the sofa had vanished; but Mrs. Marden lay in her place with closed eyes, with something in her stillness that gave us both another terror. Charlotte expressed it in the cry of "Mother, mother!" with which she flung herself down. I fell on my knees beside her. Mrs. Marden had passed away.

Was the sound I heard when Chartie shrieked—the other and still more tragic sound I mean—the despairing cry of the poor lady's death-shock or the articulate sob (it was like a waft from a great tempest), of the exorcised and pacified spirit? Possibly the latter, for that was, mercifully, the last of Sir Edmund Orme.

THE ALTAR OF THE DEAD

CHAPTER I

He had a mortal dislike, poor Stransom, to lean anniversaries, and loved them still less when they made a pretence of a figure. Celebrations and suppressions were equally painful to him, and but one of the former found a place in his life. He had kept each year in his own fashion the date of Mary Antrim's death. It would be more to the point perhaps to say that this occasion kept him: it kept him at least effectually from doing anything else. It took hold of him again and again with a hand of which time had softened but never loosened the touch. He waked to his feast of memory as consciously as he would have waked to his marriage-morn. Marriage had had of old but too little to say to the matter: for the girl who was to have been his bride there had been no bridal embrace. She had died of a malignant fever after the wedding-day had been fixed, and he had lost before fairly tasting it an affection that promised to fill his life to the brim.

Of that benediction, however, it would have been false to say this life could really be emptied: it was still ruled by a pale ghost, still ordered by a sovereign presence. He had not been a man of numerous passions, and even in all these years no sense had grown stronger with him than the sense of being bereft. He had needed no priest and no altar to make him for ever widowed. He had done many things in the world—he had done almost all but one: he had never, never forgotten. He had tried to put into his existence whatever else might take up room in it, but had failed to make it more than a house of which the mistress was eternally absent. She was most absent of all on the recurrent December day that his tenacity set apart. He had no arranged observance of it, but his nerves made it all their own. They drove him forth without mercy, and the goal of his pilgrimage was far. She had been buried in a London suburb, a part then of Nature's breast, but which he had seen lose one after another every feature of freshness. It was in truth during the moments he stood there that his eyes beheld the place least. They looked at another image, they opened to another light. Was it a credible future? Was it an incredible past? Whatever the answer it was an immense escape from the actual.

It's true that if there weren't other dates than this there were other memories; and by the time George Stransom was fifty-five such memories had greatly multiplied. There were other ghosts in his life than the ghost of Mary Antrim. He had perhaps not had more losses than most men, but he had counted his losses more; he hadn't seen death more closely, but had in a manner felt it more deeply. He had formed little by little the habit of numbering his Dead: it had come to him early in life that there was something one had to do for them. They were there in their simplified intensified essence, their conscious absence and expressive patience, as personally there as if they had only been stricken dumb. When all sense of them failed, all sound of them ceased, it was as if their purgatory were really still on earth: they asked so little that they got, poor things, even less, and died again, died every day, of the hard usage of life. They had no organised service, no reserved place, no honour, no shelter, no safety. Even ungenerous people provided for the living, but even those who were called most generous did nothing for the others. So on George Stransom's part had grown up with the years a resolve that he at least would do something, do it, that is, for his own—would perform the great charity without reproach. Every man had his own, and every man had, to meet this charity, the ample resources of the soul.

It was doubtless the voice of Mary Antrim that spoke for them best; as the years at any rate went by he found himself in regular communion with these postponed pensioners, those whom indeed he always called in his thoughts the Others. He spared them the moments, he organised the charity. Quite how it had risen he probably never could have told you, but what came to pass was that an altar, such as was after all within everybody's compass, lighted with perpetual candles and dedicated to these secret rites, reared itself in his spiritual spaces. He had wondered of old, in some embarrassment, whether he had a religion; being very sure, and not a little content, that he hadn't at all events the religion some of the people he had known wanted him to have. Gradually this question was straightened out for him: it became clear to him that the religion instilled by his earliest consciousness had been simply the religion of the Dead. It suited his inclination, it satisfied his spirit, it gave employment to his piety. It answered his love of great offices, of a solemn and splendid ritual; for no shrine could be more bedecked and no ceremonial more stately than those to which his worship was attached. He had no imagination about these things but that they were accessible to any one who should feel the need of them. The poorest could build such temples of the spirit—could make them blaze with candles and smoke with incense, make them flush with pictures and flowers. The cost, in the common phrase, of keeping them up fell wholly on the generous heart.

CHAPTER II

He had this year, on the eve of his anniversary, as happened, an emotion not unconnected with that range of feeling. Walking home at the close of a busy day he was arrested in the London street by the particular effect of a shop-front that lighted the dull brown air with its mercenary grin and before which several persons were gathered. It was the window of a jeweller whose diamonds and sapphires seemed to laugh, in flashes like high notes of sound, with the mere joy of knowing how much more they were 'worth' than most of the dingy pedestrians staring at them from the other side of the pane. Stransom lingered long enough to suspend, in a vision, a string of pearls about the white neck of Mary Antrim, and then was kept an instant longer by the sound of a voice he knew. Next him was a mumbling old woman, and beyond the old woman a gentleman with a lady on his arm. It was from him, from Paul Creston, the voice had proceeded: he was talking with the lady of some precious object in the window. Stransom had no sooner recognised him than the old woman turned away; but just with this growth of opportunity came a felt strangeness that stayed him in the very act of laying his hand on his friend's arm. It lasted but the instant, only that space sufficed for the flash of a wild question. Was not Mrs. Creston dead?—the ambiguity met him there in the short drop of her husband's voice, the drop conjugal, if it ever was, and in the way the two figures leaned to each other. Creston, making a step to look at something else, came nearer, glanced at him, started and exclaimed—behaviour the effect of which was at first only to leave Stransom staring, staring back across the months at the different face, the wholly other face, the poor man had shown him last, the blurred ravaged mask bent over the open grave by which they had stood together. That son of affliction wasn't in mourning now; he detached his arm from his companion's to grasp the hand of the older friend. He coloured as well as smiled in the strong light of the shop when Stransom raised a tentative hat to the lady. Stransom had just time to see she was pretty before he found himself gaping at a fact more portentous. 'My dear fellow, let me make you acquainted with my wife.'

Creston had blushed and stammered over it, but in half a minute, at the rate we live in polite society, it had practically become, for our friend, the mere memory of a shock. They stood there and laughed and talked; Stransom had instantly whisked the shock out of the way, to keep it for private consumption. He felt himself grimace, he heard himself exaggerate the proper, but was conscious of turning not a little faint. That new woman, that hired performer, Mrs. Creston? Mrs. Creston had been more living for him than any woman but one. This lady had a face that shone as publicly as the jeweler's window, and in the happy candour with which she wore her monstrous character was an effect of gross immodesty. The character of Paul Creston's wife thus attributed to her was monstrous for reasons Stransom could judge his friend to know perfectly that he knew. The happy pair had just arrived from America, and Stransom hadn't needed to be told this to guess the nationality of the lady. Somehow it deepened the foolish air that her husband's confused cordiality was unable to conceal. Stransom recalled that he had heard of poor Creston's having, while his bereavement was still fresh, crossed the sea for what people in such predicaments call a little change. He had found the little change indeed, he had brought the little change back; it was the little change that stood there and that, do what he would, he couldn't, while he showed those high front teeth of his, look other than a conscious ass about. They were going into the shop, Mrs. Creston said, and she begged Mr. Stransom to come with them and help to decide. He thanked her, opening his watch and pleading an engagement for which he was already late, and they parted while she shrieked into the fog, 'Mind now you come to see me right away!' Creston had had the delicacy not to suggest that, and Stransom hoped it hurt him somewhere to hear her scream it to all the echoes.

He felt quite determined, as he walked away, never in his life to go near her. She was perhaps a human being, but Creston oughtn't to have shown her without precautions, oughtn't indeed to have shown her at all. His precautions should have been those of a forger or a murderer, and the people at home would never have mentioned extradition. This was a wife for foreign service or purely external use; a decent consideration would have spared her the injury of comparisons. Such was the first flush of George Stransom's reaction; but as he sat alone that night—there were particular hours he always passed alone—the harshness dropped from it and left only the pity. He could spend an evening with Kate Creston, if the man to whom she had given everything couldn't. He had known her twenty years, and she was the only woman for whom he might perhaps have been unfaithful. She was all cleverness and sympathy and charm; her house had been the very easiest in all the world and her friendship the very firmest. Without accidents he had loved her, without accidents every one had loved her: she had made the passions about her as regular as the moon makes the tides. She had been also of course far too good for her husband, but he never suspected it, and in nothing had she been more admirable than in the exquisite art with which she tried to keep every one else (keeping Creston was no trouble) from finding it out. Here was a man to whom she had devoted her life and for whom she had given it up—dying to bring into the world a child of his bed; and she had had only to submit to her fate to have, ere the grass was green on her grave, no more existence for him than a domestic servant he had replaced. The frivolity, the indecency of it made Stransom's eyes fill; and he had that evening a sturdy sense that he alone, in a world without delicacy, had a right to hold up his head. While he smoked, after dinner, he had a book in his lap, but he had no eyes for his page: his eyes, in the swarming void of things, seemed to have caught Kate Creston's, and it was into their sad silences he looked. It was to him her sentient spirit had turned, knowing it to be of her he would think. He thought for a long time of how the closed eyes of dead women could still live—how they could open again, in a quiet lamplit room, long after they had looked their last. They had looks that survived—had them as great poets had quoted lines.

The newspaper lay by his chair—the thing that came in the afternoon and the servants thought one wanted; without sense for what was in it he had mechanically unfolded and then dropped it. Before he went to bed he took it up, and this time, at the top of a paragraph, he was caught by five words that made him start. He stood staring, before the fire, at the 'Death of Sir Acton Hague, K.C.B.,' the man who ten years earlier had been the nearest of his friends and whose deposition from this eminence had practically left it without an occupant. He had seen him after their rupture, but hadn't now seen him for years. Standing there before the fire he turned cold as he read what had befallen him. Promoted a short time previous to the governorship of the Westward Islands, Acton Hague had died, in the bleak honour of this exile, of an illness consequent on the bite of a poisonous snake. His career was compressed by the newspaper into a dozen lines, the perusal of which excited on George Stransom's part no warmer feeling than one of relief at the absence of any mention of their quarrel, an incident accidentally tainted at the time, thanks to their joint immersion in large affairs, with a horrible publicity. Public indeed was the wrong Stransom had, to his own sense, suffered, the insult he had blankly taken from the only man with whom he had ever been intimate; the friend, almost adored, of his University years, the subject, later, of his passionate loyalty: so public that he had never spoken of it to a human creature, so public that he had completely overlooked it. It had made the difference for him that friendship too was all over, but it had only made just that one. The shock of interests had been private, intensely so; but the action taken by Hague had been in the face of men. To-day it all seemed to have occurred merely to the end that George Stransom should think of him as 'Hague' and measure exactly how much he himself could resemble a stone. He went cold, suddenly and horribly cold, to bed.

CHAPTER III

The next day, in the afternoon, in the great grey suburb, he knew his long walk had tired him. In the dreadful cemetery alone he had been on his feet an hour. Instinctively, coming back, they had taken him a devious course, and it was a desert in which no circling cabman hovered over possible prey. He paused on a corner and measured the dreariness; then he made out through the gathered dusk that he was in one of those tracts of London which are less gloomy by night than by day, because, in the former case of the civil gift of light. By day there was nothing, but by night there were lamps, and George Stransom was in a mood that made lamps good in themselves. It wasn't that they could show him anything, it was only that they could burn clear. To his surprise, however, after a while, they did show him something: the arch of a high doorway approached by a low terrace of steps, in the depth of which—it formed a dim vestibule—the raising of a curtain at the moment he passed gave him a glimpse of an avenue of gloom with a glow of tapers at the end. He stopped and looked up, recognising the place as a church. The thought quickly came to him that since he was tired he might rest there; so that after a moment he had in turn pushed up the leathern curtain and gone in. It was a temple of the old persuasion, and there had evidently been a function—perhaps a service for the dead; the high altar was still a blaze of candles. This was an exhibition he always liked, and he dropped into a seat with relief. More than it had ever yet come home to him it struck him as good there should be churches.

This one was almost empty and the other altars were dim; a verger shuffled about, an old woman coughed, but it seemed to Stransom there was hospitality in the thick sweet air. Was it only the savour of the incense or was it something of larger intention? He had at any rate quitted the great grey suburb and come nearer to the warm centre. He presently ceased to feel intrusive, gaining at last even a sense of community with the only worshipper in his neighbourhood, the sombre presence of a woman, in mourning unrelieved, whose back was all he could see of her and who had sunk deep into prayer at no great distance from him. He wished he could sink, like her, to the very bottom, be as motionless, as rapt in prostration. After a few moments he shifted his seat; it was almost indelicate to be so aware of her. But Stransom subsequently quite lost himself, floating away on the sea of light. If occasions like this had been more frequent in his life he would have had more present the great original type, set up in a myriad temples, of the unapproachable shrine he had erected in his mind. That shrine had begun in vague likeness to church pomps, but the echo had ended by growing more distinct than the sound. The sound now rang out, the type blazed at him with all its fires and with a mystery of radiance in which endless meanings could glow. The thing became as he sat there his appropriate altar and each starry candle an appropriate vow. He numbered them, named them, grouped them—it was the silent roll-call of his Dead. They made together a brightness vast and intense, a brightness in which the mere chapel of his thoughts grew so dim that as it faded away he asked himself if he shouldn't find his real comfort in some material act, some outward worship.

This idea took possession of him while, at a distance, the black-robed lady continued prostrate; he was quietly thrilled with his conception, which at last brought him to his feet in the sudden excitement of a plan. He wandered softly through the aisles, pausing in the different chapels, all save one applied to a special devotion. It was in this clear recess, lampless and unapplied, that he stood longest—the length of time it took him fully to grasp the conception of gilding it with his bounty. He should snatch it from no other rites and associate it with nothing profane; he would simply take it as it should be given up to him and make it a masterpiece of splendour and a mountain of fire. Tended sacredly all the year, with the sanctifying church round it, it would always be ready for his offices. There would be difficulties, but from the first they presented themselves only as difficulties surmounted. Even for a person so little affiliated the thing would be a matter of arrangement. He saw it all in advance, and how bright in especial the place would become to him in the intermissions of toil and the dusk of afternoons; how rich in assurance at all times, but especially in the indifferent world. Before withdrawing he drew nearer again to the spot where he had first sat down, and in the movement he met the lady whom he had seen praying and who was now on her way to the door. She passed him quickly, and he had only a glimpse of her pale face and her unconscious, almost sightless eyes. For that instant she looked faded and handsome.

This was the origin of the rites more public, yet certainly esoteric, that he at last found himself able to establish. It took a long time, it took a year, and both the process and the result would have been—for any who knew—a vivid picture of his good faith. No one did know, in fact—no one but the bland ecclesiastics whose acquaintance he had promptly sought, whose objections he had softly overridden, whose curiosity and sympathy he had artfully charmed, whose assent to his eccentric munificence he had eventually won, and who had asked for concessions in exchange for indulgences. Stransom had of course at an early stage of his enquiry been referred to the Bishop, and the Bishop had been delightfully human, the Bishop had been almost amused. Success was within sight, at any rate from the moment the attitude of those whom it concerned became liberal in response to liberality. The altar and the sacred shell that half encircled it, consecrated to an ostensible and customary worship, were to be splendidly maintained; all that Stransom reserved to himself was the number of his lights and the free enjoyment of his intention. When the intention had taken complete effect the enjoyment became even greater than he had ventured to hope. He liked to think of this effect when far from it, liked to convince himself of it yet again when near. He was not often indeed so near as that a visit to it hadn't perforce something of the patience of a pilgrimage; but the time he gave to his devotion came to seem to him more a contribution to his other interests than a betrayal of them. Even a loaded life might be easier when one had added a new necessity to it.

How much easier was probably never guessed by those who simply knew there were hours when he disappeared and for many of whom there was a vulgar reading of what they used to call his plunges. These plunges were into depths quieter than the deep sea-caves, and the habit had at the end of a year or two become the one it would have cost him most to relinquish. Now they had really, his Dead, something that was indefensibly theirs; and he liked to think that they might in cases be the Dead of others, as well as that the Dead of others might be invoked there under the protection of what he had done.

Whoever bent a knee on the carpet he had laid down appeared to him to act in the spirit of his intention. Each of his lights had a name for him, and from time to time a new light was kindled. This was what he had fundamentally agreed for, that there should always be room for them all. What those who passed or lingered saw was simply the most resplendent of the altars called suddenly into vivid usefulness, with a quiet elderly man, for whom it evidently had a fascination, often seated there in a maze or a doze; but half the satisfaction of the spot for this mysterious and fitful worshipper was that he found the years of his life there, and the ties, the affections, the struggles, the submissions, the conquests, if there had been such, a record of that adventurous journey in which the beginnings and the endings of human relations are the lettered mile-stones. He had in general little taste for the past as a part of his own history; at other times and in other places it mostly seemed to him pitiful to consider and impossible to repair; but on these occasions he accepted it with something of that positive gladness with which one adjusts one's self to an ache that begins to succumb to treatment. To the treatment of time the malady of life begins at a given moment to succumb; and these were doubtless the hours at which that truth most came home to him. The day was written for him there on which he had first become acquainted with death, and the successive phases of the acquaintance were marked each with a flame.

The flames were gathering thick at present, for Stransom had entered that dark defile of our earthly descent in which some one dies every day. It was only yesterday that Kate Creston had flashed out her white fire; yet already there were younger stars ablaze on the tips of the tapers. Various persons in whom his interest had not been intense drew closer to him by entering this company. He went over it, head by head, till he felt like the shepherd of a huddled flock, with all a shepherd's vision of differences imperceptible. He knew his candles apart, up to the colour of the flame, and would still have known them had their positions all been changed. To other imaginations they might stand for other things—that they should stand for something to be hushed before was all he desired; but he was intensely conscious of the personal note of each and of the distinguishable way it contributed to the concert. There were hours at which he almost caught himself wishing that certain of his friends would now die, that he might establish with them in this manner a connexion more charming than, as it happened, it was possible to enjoy with them in life. In regard to those from whom one was separated by the long curves of the globe such a connexion could only be an improvement: it brought them instantly within reach. Of course there were gaps in the constellation, for Stransom knew he could only pretend to act for his own, and it wasn't every figure passing before his eyes into the great obscure that was entitled to a memorial. There was a strange sanctification in death, but some characters were more sanctified by being forgotten than by being remembered. The greatest blank in the shining page was the memory of Acton Hague, of which he inveterately tried to rid himself. For Acton Hague no flame could ever rise on any altar of his.

CHAPTER IV

Every year, the day he walked back from the great graveyard, he went to church as he had done the day his idea was born. It was on this occasion, as it happened, after a year had passed, that he began to observe his altar to be haunted by a worshipper at least as frequent as himself. Others of the faithful, and in the rest of the church, came and went, appealing sometimes, when they disappeared, to a vague or to a particular recognition; but this unfailing presence was always to be observed when he arrived and still in possession when he departed. He was surprised, the first time, at the promptitude with which it assumed an identity for him—the identity of the lady whom two years before, on his anniversary, he had seen so intensely bowed, and of whose tragic face he had had so flitting a vision. Given the time that had passed, his recollection of her was fresh enough to make him wonder. Of himself she had of course no impression, or rather had had none at first: the time came when her manner of transacting her business suggested her having gradually guessed his call to be of the same order. She used his altar for her own purpose—he could only hope that sad and solitary as she always struck him, she used it for her own Dead. There were interruptions, infidelities, all on his part, calls to other associations and duties; but as the months went on he found her whenever he returned, and he ended by taking pleasure in the thought that he had given her almost the contentment he had given himself. They worshipped side by side so often that there were moments when he wished he might be sure, so straight did their prospect stretch away of growing old together in their rites. She was younger than he, but she looked as if her Dead were at least as numerous as his candles. She had no colour, no sound, no fault, and another of the things about which he had made up his mind was that she had no fortune. Always black-robed, she must have had a succession of sorrows. People weren't poor, after all, whom so many losses could overtake; they were positively rich when they had had so much to give up. But the air of this devoted and indifferent woman, who always made, in any attitude, a beautiful accidental line, conveyed somehow to Stransom that she had known more kinds of trouble than one.

He had a great love of music and little time for the joy of it; but occasionally, when workaday noises were muffled by Saturday afternoons, it used to come back to him that there were glories. There were moreover friends who reminded him of this and side by side with whom he found himself sitting out concerts. On one of these winter afternoons, in St. James's Hall, he became aware after he had seated himself that the lady he had so often seen at church was in the place next him and was evidently alone, as he also this time happened to be. She was at first too absorbed in the consideration of the programme to heed him, but when she at last glanced at him he took advantage of the movement to speak to her, greeting her with the remark that he felt as if he already knew her. She smiled as she said 'Oh yes, I recognise you'; yet in spite of this admission of long acquaintance it was the first he had seen of her smile. The effect of it was suddenly to contribute more to that acquaintance than all the previous meetings had done. He hadn't 'taken in,' he said to himself, that she was so pretty. Later, that evening—it was while he rolled along in a hansom on his way to dine out—he added that he hadn't taken in that she was so interesting. The next morning in the midst of his work he quite suddenly and irrelevantly reflected that his impression of her, beginning so far back, was like a winding river that had at last reached the sea.

His work in fact was blurred a little all that day by the sense of what had now passed between them. It wasn't much, but it had just made the difference. They had listened together to Beethoven and Schumann; they had talked in the pauses, and at the end, when at the door, to which they moved together, he had asked her if he could help her in the matter of getting away. She had thanked him and put up her umbrella, slipping into the crowd without an allusion to their meeting yet again and leaving him to remember at leisure that not a word had been exchanged about the usual scene of that coincidence. This omission struck him now as natural and then again as perverse. She mightn't in the least have allowed his warrant for speaking to her, and yet if she hadn't he would have judged her an underbred woman. It was odd that when nothing had really ever brought them together he should have been able successfully to assume they were in a manner old friends—that this negative quantity was somehow more than they could express. His success, it was true, had been qualified by her quick escape, so that there grew up in him an absurd desire to put it to some better test. Save in so far as some other poor chance might help him, such a test could be only to meet her afresh at church. Left to himself he would have gone to church the very next afternoon, just for the curiosity of seeing if he should find her there. But he wasn't left to himself, a fact he discovered quite at the last, after he had virtually made up his mind to go. The influence that kept him away really revealed to him how little to himself his Dead ever left him. He went only for them—for nothing else in the world.

The force of this revulsion kept him away ten days: he hated to connect the place with anything but his offices or to give a glimpse of the curiosity that had been on the point of moving him. It was absurd to weave a tangle about a matter so simple as a custom of devotion that might with ease have been daily or hourly; yet the tangle got itself woven. He was sorry, he was disappointed: it was as if a long happy spell had been broken and he had lost a familiar security. At the last, however, he asked himself if he was to stay away for ever from the fear of this muddle about motives. After an interval neither longer nor shorter than usual he re-entered the church with a clear conviction that he should scarcely heed the presence or the absence of the lady of the concert. This indifference didn't prevent his at once noting that for the only time since he had first seen her she wasn't on the spot. He had now no scruple about giving her time to arrive, but she didn't arrive, and when he went away still missing her he was profanely and consentingly sorry. If her absence made the tangle more intricate, that was all her own doing. By the end of another year it was very intricate indeed; but by that time he didn't in the least care, and it was only his cultivated consciousness that had given him scruples. Three times in three months he had gone to church without finding her, and he felt he hadn't needed these occasions to show him his suspense had dropped. Yet it was, incongruously, not indifference, but a refinement of delicacy that had kept him from asking the sacristan, who would of course immediately have recognised his description of her, whether she had been seen at other hours. His delicacy had kept him from asking any question about her at any time, and it was exactly the same virtue that had left him so free to be decently civil to her at the concert.

This happy advantage now served him anew, enabling him when she finally met his eyes—it was after a fourth trial—to predetermine quite fixedly his awaiting her retreat. He joined her in the street as soon as she had moved, asking her if he might accompany her a certain distance. With her placid permission he went as far as a house in the neighbourhood at which she had business: she let him know it was not where she lived. She lived, as she said, in a mere slum, with an old aunt, a person in connexion with whom she spoke of the engrossment of humdrum duties and regular occupations. She wasn't, the mourning niece, in her first youth, and her vanished freshness had left something behind that, for Stransom, represented the proof it had been tragically sacrificed. Whatever she gave him the assurance of she gave without references. She might have been a divorced duchess—she might have been an old maid who taught the harp.

CHAPTER V

They fell at last into the way of walking together almost every time they met, though for a long time still they never met but at church. He couldn't ask her to come and see him, and as if she hadn't a proper place to receive him she never invited her friend. As much as himself she knew the world of London, but from an undiscussed instinct of privacy they haunted the region not mapped on the social chart. On the return she always made him leave her at the same corner. She looked with him, as a pretext for a pause, at the depressed things in suburban shop-fronts; and there was never a word he had said to her that she hadn't beautifully understood. For long ages he never knew her name, any more than she had ever pronounced his own; but it was not their names that mattered, it was only their perfect practice and their common need.

These things made their whole relation so impersonal that they hadn't the rules or reasons people found in ordinary friendships. They didn't care for the things it was supposed necessary to care for in the intercourse of the world. They ended one day—they never knew which of them expressed it first—by throwing out the idea that they didn't care for each other. Over this idea they grew quite intimate; they rallied to it in a way that marked a fresh start in their confidence. If to feel deeply together about certain things wholly distinct from themselves didn't constitute a safety, where was safety to be looked for? Not lightly nor often, not without occasion nor without emotion, any more than in any other reference by serious people to a mystery of their faith; but when something had happened to warm, as it were, the air for it, they came as near as they could come to calling their Dead by name. They felt it was coming very near to utter their thought at all. The word 'they' expressed enough; it limited the mention, it had a dignity of its own, and if, in their talk, you had heard our friends use it, you might have taken them for a pair of pagans of old alluding decently to the domesticated gods. They never knew—at least Stransom never knew—how they had learned to be sure about each other. If it had been with each a question of what the other was there for, the certitude had come in some fine way of its own. Any faith, after all, has the instinct of propagation, and it was as natural as it was beautiful that they should have taken pleasure on the spot in the imagination of a following. If the following was for each but a following of one it had proved in the event sufficient. Her debt, however, of course was much greater than his, because while she had only given him a worshipper he had given her a splendid temple. Once she said she pitied him for the length of his list—she had counted his candles almost as often as himself—and this made him wonder what could have been the length of hers. He had wondered before at the coincidence of their losses, especially as from time to time a new candle was set up. On some occasion some accident led him to express this curiosity, and she answered as if in surprise that he hadn't already understood. 'Oh for me, you know, the more there are the better—there could never be too many. I should like hundreds and hundreds—I should like thousands; I should like a great mountain of light.'

Then of course in a flash he understood. 'Your Dead are only One?'

She hung back at this as never yet. 'Only One,' she answered, colouring as if now he knew her guarded secret. It really made him feel he knew less than before, so difficult was it for him to reconstitute a life in which a single experience had so belittled all others. His own life, round its central hollow, had been packed close enough. After this she appeared to have regretted her confession, though at the moment she spoke there had been pride in her very embarrassment. She declared to him that his own was the larger, the dearer possession—the portion one would have chosen if one had been able to choose; she assured him she could perfectly imagine some of the echoes with which his silences were peopled. He knew she couldn't: one's relation to what one had loved and hated had been a relation too distinct from the relations of others. But this didn't affect the fact that they were growing old together in their piety. She was a feature of that piety, but even at the ripe stage of acquaintance in which they occasionally arranged to meet at a concert or to go together to an exhibition she was not a feature of anything else. The most that happened was that his worship became paramount. Friend by friend dropped away till at last there were more emblems on his altar than houses left him to enter. She was more than any other the friend who remained, but she was unknown to all the rest. Once when she had discovered, as they called it, a new star, she used the expression that the chapel at last was full.

'Oh no,' Stransom replied, 'there is a great thing wanting for that! The chapel will never be full till a candle is set up before which all the others will pale. It will be the tallest candle of all.'

Her mild wonder rested on him. 'What candle do you mean?'

'I mean, dear lady, my own.'

He had learned after a long time that she earned money by her pen, writing under a pseudonym she never disclosed in magazines he never saw. She knew too well what he couldn't read and what she couldn't write, and she taught him to cultivate indifference with a success that did much for their good relations. Her invisible industry was a convenience to him; it helped his contented thought of her, the thought that rested in the dignity of her proud obscure life, her little remunerated art and her little impenetrable home. Lost, with her decayed relative, in her dim suburban world, she came to the surface for him in distant places. She was really the priestess of his altar, and whenever he quitted England he committed it to her keeping. She proved to him afresh that women have more of the spirit of religion than men; he felt his fidelity pale and faint in comparison with hers. He often said to her that since he had so little time to live he rejoiced in her having so much; so glad was he to think she would guard the temple when he should have been called. He had a great plan for that, which of course he told her too, a bequest of money to keep it up in undiminished state. Of the administration of this fund he would appoint her superintendent, and if the spirit should move her she might kindle a taper even for him.

'And who will kindle one even for me?' she then seriously asked.

CHAPTER VI

She was always in mourning, yet the day he came back from the longest absence he had yet made her appearance immediately told him she had lately had a bereavement. They met on this occasion as she was leaving the church, so that postponing his own entrance he instantly offered to turn round and walk away with her. She considered, then she said: 'Go in now, but come and see me in an hour.' He knew the small vista of her street, closed at the end and as dreary as an empty pocket, where the pairs of shabby little houses, semi-detached but indissolubly united, were like married couples on bad terms. Often, however, as he had gone to the beginning he had never gone beyond. Her aunt was dead—that he immediately guessed, as well as that it made a difference; but when she had for the first time mentioned her number he found himself, on her leaving him, not a little agitated by this sudden liberality. She wasn't a person with whom, after all, one got on so very fast: it had taken him months and months to learn her name, years and years to learn her address. If she had looked, on this reunion, so much older to him, how in the world did he look to her? She had reached the period of life he had long since reached, when, after separations, the marked clock-face of the friend we meet announces the hour we have tried to forget. He couldn't have said what he expected as, at the end of his waiting, he turned the corner where for years he had always paused; simply not to pause was a efficient cause for emotion. It was an event, somehow; and in all their long acquaintance there had never been an event. This one grew larger when, five minutes later, in the faint elegance of her little drawing-room, she quavered out a greeting that showed the measure she took of it. He had a strange sense of having come for something in particular; strange because literally there was nothing particular between them, nothing save that they were at one on their great point, which had long ago become a magnificent matter of course. It was true that after she had said 'You can always come now, you know,' the thing he was there for seemed already to have happened. He asked her if it was the death of her aunt that made the difference; to which she replied: 'She never knew I knew you. I wished her not to.' The beautiful clearness of her candour—her faded beauty was like a summer twilight—disconnected the words from any image of deceit. They might have struck him as the record of a deep dissimulation; but she had always given him a sense of noble reasons. The vanished aunt was present, as he looked about him, in the small complacencies of the room, the beaded velvet and the fluted moreen; and though, as we know, he had the worship of the Dead, he found himself not definitely regretting this lady. If she wasn't in his long list, however, she was in her niece's short one, and Stransom presently observed to the latter that now at least, in the place they haunted together, she would have another object of devotion.

'Yes, I shall have another. She was very kind to me. It's that that's the difference.'

He judged, wondering a good deal before he made any motion to leave her, that the difference would somehow be very great and would consist of still other things than her having let him come in. It rather chilled him, for they had been happy together as they were. He extracted from her at any rate an intimation that she should now have means less limited, that her aunt's tiny fortune had come to her, so that there was henceforth only one to consume what had formerly been made to suffice for two. This was a joy to Stransom, because it had hitherto been equally impossible for him either to offer her presents or contentedly to stay his hand. It was too ugly to be at her side that way, abounding himself and yet not able to overflow—a demonstration that would have been signally a false note. Even her better situation too seemed only to draw out in a sense the loneliness of her future. It would merely help her to live more and more for their small ceremonial, and this at a time when he himself had begun wearily to feel that, having set it in motion, he might depart. When they had sat a while in the pale parlour she got up—'This isn't my room: let us go into mine.' They had only to cross the narrow hall, as he found, to pass quite into another air. When she had closed the door of the second room, as she called it, he felt at last in real possession of her. The place had the flush of life—it was expressive; its dark red walls were articulate with memories and relics. These were simple things—photographs and water-colours, scraps of writing framed and ghosts of flowers embalmed; but a moment sufficed to show him they had a common meaning. It was here she had lived and worked, and she had already told him she would make no change of scene. He read the reference in the objects about her—the general one to places and times; but after a minute he distinguished among them a small portrait of a gentleman. At a distance and without their glasses his eyes were only so caught by it as to feel a vague curiosity. Presently this impulse carried him nearer, and in another moment he was staring at the picture in stupefaction and with the sense that some sound had broken from him. He was further conscious that he showed his companion a white face when he turned round on her gasping: 'Acton Hague!'

She matched his great wonder. 'Did you know him?'

'He was the friend of all my youth—of my early manhood. And you knew him?'

She coloured at this and for a moment her answer failed; her eyes embraced everything in the place, and a strange irony reached her lips as she echoed: 'Knew him?'

Then Stransom understood, while the room heaved like the cabin of a ship, that its whole contents cried out with him, that it was a museum in his honour, that all her later years had been addressed to him and that the shrine he himself had reared had been passionately converted to this use. It was all for Acton Hague that she had kneeled every day at his altar. What need had there been for a consecrated candle when he was present in the whole array? The revelation so smote our friend in the face that he dropped into a seat and sat silent. He had quickly felt her shaken by the force of his shock, but as she sank on the sofa beside him and laid her hand on his arm he knew almost as soon that she mightn't resent it as much as she'd have liked.

CHAPTER VII

He learned in that instant two things: one being that even in so long a time she had gathered no knowledge of his great intimacy and his great quarrel; the other that in spite of this ignorance, strangely enough, she supplied on the spot a reason for his stupor. 'How extraordinary,' he presently exclaimed, 'that we should never have known!'

She gave a wan smile which seemed to Stransom stranger even than the fact itself. 'I never, never spoke of him.'

He looked again about the room. 'Why then, if your life had been so full of him?'

'Mayn't I put you that question as well? Hadn't your life also been full of him?'

'Anyone's, every one's life who had the wonderful experience of knowing him. I never spoke of him,' Stransom added in a moment, 'because he did me—years ago—an unforgettable wrong.' She was silent, and with the full effect of his presence all about them it almost startled her guest to hear no protest escape her. She accepted his words, he turned his eyes to her again to see in what manner she accepted them. It was with rising tears and a rare sweetness in the movement of putting out her hand to take his own. Nothing more wonderful had ever appeared to him than, in that little chamber of remembrance and homage, to see her convey with such exquisite mildness that as from Acton Hague any injury was credible. The clock ticked in the stillness—Hague had probably given it to her—and while he let her hold his hand with a tenderness that was almost an assumption of responsibility for his old pain as well as his new, Stransom after a minute broke out: 'Good God, how he must have used you!'

She dropped his hand at this, got up and, moving across the room, made straight a small picture to which, on examining it, he had given a slight push. Then turning round on him with her pale gaiety recovered, 'I've forgiven him!' she declared.

'I know what you've done,' said Stransom 'I know what you've done for years.' For a moment they looked at each other through it all with their long community of service in their eyes. This short passage made, to his sense, for the woman before him, an immense, an absolutely naked confession; which was presently, suddenly blushing red and changing her place again, what she appeared to learn he perceived in it. He got up and 'How you must have loved him!' he cried.

'Women aren't like men. They can love even where they've suffered.'

'Women are wonderful,' said Stransom. 'But I assure you I've forgiven him too.'

'If I had known of anything so strange I wouldn't have brought you here.'

'So that we might have gone on in our ignorance to the last?'

'What do you call the last?' she asked, smiling still.

At this he could smile back at her. 'You'll see—when it comes.'

She thought of that. 'This is better perhaps; but as we were—it was good.'

He put her the question. 'Did it never happen that he spoke of me?'

Considering more intently she made no answer, and he then knew he should have been adequately answered by her asking how often he himself had spoken of their terrible friend. Suddenly a brighter light broke in her face and an excited idea sprang to her lips in the appeal: 'You have forgiven him?'

'How, if I hadn't, could I linger here?'

She visibly winced at the deep but unintended irony of this; but even while she did so she panted quickly: 'Then in the lights on your altar—?'

'There's never a light for Acton Hague!'

She stared with a dreadful fall, 'But if he's one of your Dead?'

'He's one of the world's, if you like—he's one of yours. But he's not one of mine. Mine are only the Dead who died possessed of me. They're mine in death because they were mine in life.'

'He was yours in life then, even if for a while he ceased to be. If you forgave him you went back to him. Those whom we've once loved—'

'Are those who can hurt us most,' Stransom broke in.

'Ah it's not true—you've not forgiven him!' she wailed with a passion that startled him.

He looked at her as never yet. 'What was it he did to you?'

'Everything!' Then abruptly she put out her hand in farewell. 'Good-bye.'

He turned as cold as he had turned that night he read the man's death. 'You mean that we meet no more?'

'Not as we've met—not there!'

He stood aghast at this snap of their great bond, at the renouncement that rang out in the word she so expressively sounded. 'But what's changed—for you?'

She waited in all the sharpness of a trouble that for the first time since he had known her made her splendidly stern. 'How can you understand now when you didn't understand before?'

'I didn't understand before only because I didn't know. Now that I know, I see what I've been living with for years,' Stransom went on very gently.

She looked at him with a larger allowance, doing this gentleness justice. 'How can I then, on this new knowledge of my own, ask you to continue to live with it?'

'I set up my altar, with its multiplied meanings,' Stransom began; but she quietly interrupted him.

'You set up your altar, and when I wanted one most I found it magnificently ready. I used it with the gratitude I've always shown you, for I knew it from of old to be dedicated to Death. I told you long ago that my Dead weren't many. Yours were, but all you had done for them was none too much for my worship! You had placed a great light for Each—I gathered them together for One!'

'We had simply different intentions,' he returned. 'That, as you say, I perfectly knew, and I don't see why your intention shouldn't still sustain you.'

'That's because you're generous—you can imagine and think. But the spell is broken.'

It seemed to poor Stransom, in spite of his resistance, that it really was, and the prospect stretched grey and void before him. All he could say, however, was: 'I hope you'll try before you give up.'

'If I had known you had ever known him I should have taken for granted he had his candle,' she presently answered. 'What's changed, as you say, is that on making the discovery I find he never has had it. That makes my attitude'—she paused as thinking how to express it, then said simply—'all wrong.'

'Come once again,' he pleaded.

'Will you give him his candle?' she asked.

He waited, but only because it would sound ungracious; not because of a doubt of his feeling. 'I can't do that!' he declared at last.

'Then good-bye.' And she gave him her hand again.

He had got his dismissal; besides which, in the agitation of everything that had opened out to him, he felt the need to recover himself as he could only do in solitude. Yet he lingered—lingered to see if she had no compromise to express, no attenuation to propose. But he only met her great lamenting eyes, in which indeed he read that she was as sorry for him as for any one else. This made him say: 'At least, in any case, I may see you here.'

'Oh yes, come if you like. But I don't think it will do.'

He looked round the room once more, knowing how little he was sure it would do. He felt also stricken and more and more cold, and his chill was like an ague in which he had to make an effort not to shake. Then he made doleful reply: 'I must try on my side—if you can't try on yours.' She came out with him to the hall and into the doorway, and here he put her the question he held he could least answer from his own wit. 'Why have you never let me come before?'

'Because my aunt would have seen you, and I should have had to tell her how I came to know you.'

'And what would have been the objection to that?'

'It would have entailed other explanations; there would at any rate have been that danger.'

'Surely she knew you went every day to church,' Stransom objected.

'She didn't know what I went for.'

'Of me then she never even heard?'

'You'll think I was deceitful. But I didn't need to be!'

He was now on the lower door-step, and his hostess held the door half-closed behind him. Through what remained of the opening he saw her framed face. He made a supreme appeal. 'What did he do to you?'

'It would have come out—she would have told you. That fear at my heart—that was my reason!' And she closed the door, shutting him out.

CHAPTER VIII

He had ruthlessly abandoned her—that of course was what he had done. Stransom made it all out in solitude, at leisure, fitting the unmatched pieces gradually together and dealing one by one with a hundred obscure points. She had known Hague only after her present friend's relations with him had wholly terminated; obviously indeed a good while after; and it was natural enough that of his previous life she should have ascertained only what he had judged good to communicate. There were passages it was quite conceivable that even in moments of the tenderest expansion he should have withheld. Of many facts in the career of a man so in the eye of the world there was of course a common knowledge; but this lady lived apart from public affairs, and the only time perfectly clear to her would have been the time following the dawn of her own drama. A man in her place would have 'looked up' the past—would even have consulted old newspapers. It remained remarkable indeed that in her long contact with the partner of her retrospect no accident had lighted a train; but there was no arguing about that; the accident had in fact come: it had simply been that security had prevailed. She had taken what Hague had given her, and her blankness in respect of his other connexions was only a touch in the picture of that plasticity Stransom had supreme reason to know so great a master could have been trusted to produce.

This picture was for a while all our friend saw: he caught his breath again and again as it came over him that the woman with whom he had had for years so fine a point of contact was a woman whom Acton Hague, of all men in the world, had more or less fashioned. Such as she sat there to-day she was ineffaceably stamped with him. Beneficent, blameless as Stransom held her, he couldn't rid himself of the sense that he had been, as who should say, swindled. She had imposed upon him hugely, though she had known it as little as he. All this later past came back to him as a time grotesquely misspent. Such at least were his first reflexions; after a while he found himself more divided and only, as the end of it, more troubled. He imagined, recalled, reconstituted, figured out for himself the truth she had refused to give him; the effect of which was to make her seem to him only more saturated with her fate. He felt her spirit, through the whole strangeness, finer than his own to the very degree in which she might have been, in which she certainly had been, more wronged. A women, when wronged, was always more wronged than a man, and there were conditions when the least she could have got off with was more than the most he could have to bear. He was sure this rare creature wouldn't have got off with the least. He was awestruck at the thought of such a surrender—such a prostration. Moulded indeed she had been by powerful hands, to have converted her injury into an exaltation so sublime. The fellow had only had to die for everything that was ugly in him to be washed out in a torrent. It was vain to try to guess what had taken place, but nothing could be clearer than that she had ended by accusing herself. She absolved him at every point, she adored her very wounds. The passion by which he had profited had rushed back after its ebb, and now the tide of tenderness, arrested for ever at flood, was too deep even to fathom. Stransom sincerely considered that he had forgiven him; but how little he had achieved the miracle that she had achieved! His forgiveness was silence, but hers was mere unuttered sound. The light she had demanded for his altar would have broken his silence with a blare; whereas all the lights in the church were for her too great a hush.

She had been right about the difference—she had spoken the truth about the change: Stransom was soon to know himself as perversely but sharply jealous. His tide had ebbed, not flowed; if he had 'forgiven' Acton Hague, that forgiveness was a motive with a broken spring. The very fact of her appeal for a material sign, a sign that should make her dead lover equal there with the others, presented the concession to her friend as too handsome for the case. He had never thought of himself as hard, but an exorbitant article might easily render him so. He moved round and round this one, but only in widening circles—the more he looked at it the less acceptable it seemed. At the same time he had no illusion about the effect of his refusal; he perfectly saw how it would make for a rupture. He left her alone a week, but when at last he again called this conviction was cruelly confirmed. In the interval he had kept away from the church, and he needed no fresh assurance from her to know she hadn't entered it. The change was complete enough: it had broken up her life. Indeed it had broken up his, for all the fires of his shrine seemed to him suddenly to have been quenched. A great indifference fell upon him, the weight of which was in itself a pain; and he never knew what his devotion had been for him till in that shock it ceased like a dropped watch. Neither did he know with how large a confidence he had counted on the final service that had now failed: the mortal deception was that in this abandonment the whole future gave way.

These days of her absence proved to him of what she was capable; all the more that he never dreamed she was vindictive or even resentful. It was not in anger she had forsaken him; it was in simple submission to hard reality, to the stern logic of life. This came home to him when he sat with her again in the room in which her late aunt's conversation lingered like the tone of a cracked piano. She tried to make him forget how much they were estranged, but in the very presence of what they had given up it was impossible not to be sorry for her. He had taken from her so much more than she had taken from him. He argued with her again, told her she could now have the altar to herself; but she only shook her head with pleading sadness, begging him not to waste his breath on the impossible, the extinct. Couldn't he see that in relation to her private need the rites he had established were practically an elaborate exclusion? She regretted nothing that had happened; it had all been right so long as she didn't know, and it was only that now she knew too much and that from the moment their eyes were open they would simply have to conform. It had doubtless been happiness enough for them to go on together so long. She was gentle, grateful, resigned; but this was only the form of a deep immutability. He saw he should never more cross the threshold of the second room, and he felt how much this alone would make a stranger of him and give a conscious stiffness to his visits. He would have hated to plunge again into that well of reminders, but he enjoyed quite as little the vacant alternative.

After he had been with her three or four times it struck him that to have come at last into her house had had the horrid effect of diminishing their intimacy. He had known her better, had liked her in greater freedom, when they merely walked together or kneeled together. Now they only pretended; before they had been nobly sincere. They began to try their walks again, but it proved a lame imitation, for these things, from the first, beginning or ending, had been connected with their visits to the church. They had either strolled away as they came out or gone in to rest on the return. Stransom, besides, now faltered; he couldn't walk as of old. The omission made everything false; it was a dire mutilation of their lives. Our friend was frank and monotonous, making no mystery of his remonstrance and no secret of his predicament. Her response, whatever it was, always came to the same thing—an implied invitation to him to judge, if he spoke of predicaments, of how much comfort she had in hers. For him indeed was no comfort even in complaint, since every allusion to what had befallen them but made the author of their trouble more present. Acton Hague was between them—that was the essence of the matter, and never so much between them as when they were face to face. Then Stransom, while still wanting to banish him, had the strangest sense of striving for an ease that would involve having accepted him. Deeply disconcerted by what he knew, he was still worse tormented by really not knowing. Perfectly aware that it would have been horribly vulgar to abuse his old friend or to tell his companion the story of their quarrel, it yet vexed him that her depth of reserve should give him no opening and should have the effect of a magnanimity greater even than his own.

He challenged himself, denounced himself, asked himself if he were in love with her that he should care so much what adventures she had had. He had never for a moment allowed he was in love with her; therefore nothing could have surprised him more than to discover he was jealous. What but jealousy could give a man that sore contentious wish for the detail of what would make him suffer? Well enough he knew indeed that he should never have it from the only person who to-day could give it to him. She let him press her with his sombre eyes, only smiling at him with an exquisite mercy and breathing equally little the word that would expose her secret and the word that would appear to deny his literal right to bitterness. She told nothing, she judged nothing; she accepted everything but the possibility of her return to the old symbols. Stransom divined that for her too they had been vividly individual, had stood for particular hours or particular attributes—particular links in her chain. He made it clear to himself, as he believed, that his difficulty lay in the fact that the very nature of the plea for his faithless friend constituted a prohibition; that it happened to have come from her was precisely the vice that attached to it. To the voice of impersonal generosity he felt sure he would have listened; he would have deferred to an advocate who, speaking from abstract justice, knowing of his denial without having known Hague, should have had the imagination to say: 'Ah, remember only the best of him; pity him; provide for him.' To provide for him on the very ground of having discovered another of his turpitudes was not to pity but to glorify him. The more Stransom thought the more he made out that whatever this relation of Hague's it could only have been a deception more or less finely practised. Where had it come into the life that all men saw? Why had one never heard of it if it had had the frankness of honourable things? Stransom knew enough of his other ties, of his obligations and appearances, not to say enough of his general character, to be sure there had been some infamy. In one way or another this creature had been coldly sacrificed. That was why at the last as well as the first he must still leave him out and out.

CHAPTER IX

And yet this was no solution, especially after he had talked again to his friend of all it had been his plan she should finally do for him. He had talked in the other days, and she had responded with a frankness qualified only by a courteous reluctance, a reluctance that touched him, to linger on the question of his death. She had then practically accepted the charge, suffered him to feel he could depend upon her to be the eventual guardian of his shrine; and it was in the name of what had so passed between them that he appealed to her not to forsake him in his age. She listened at present with shining coldness and all her habitual forbearance to insist on her terms; her deprecation was even still tenderer, for it expressed the compassion of her own sense that he was abandoned. Her terms, however, remained the same, and scarcely the less audible for not being uttered; though he was sure that secretly even more than he she felt bereft of the satisfaction his solemn trust was to have provided her. They both missed the rich future, but she missed it most, because after all it was to have been entirely hers; and it was her acceptance of the loss that gave him the full measure of her preference for the thought of Acton Hague over any other thought whatever. He had humour enough to laugh rather grimly when he said to himself: 'Why the deuce does she like him so much more than she likes me?'—the reasons being really so conceivable. But even his faculty of analysis left the irritation standing, and this irritation proved perhaps the greatest misfortune that had ever overtaken him. There had been nothing yet that made him so much want to give up. He had of course by this time well reached the age of renouncement; but it had not hitherto been vivid to him that it was time to give up everything.

Practically, at the end of six months, he had renounced the friendship once so charming and comforting. His privation had two faces, and the face it had turned to him on the occasion of his last attempt to cultivate that friendship was the one he could look at least. This was the privation he inflicted; the other was the privation he bore. The conditions she never phrased he used to murmur to himself in solitude: 'One more, one more—only just one.' Certainly he was going down; he often felt it when he caught himself, over his work, staring at vacancy and giving voice to that inanity. There was proof enough besides in his being so weak and so ill. His irritation took the form of melancholy, and his melancholy that of the conviction that his health had quite failed. His altar moreover had ceased to exist; his chapel, in his dreams, was a great dark cavern. All the lights had gone out—all his Dead had died again. He couldn't exactly see at first how it had been in the power of his late companion to extinguish them, since it was neither for her nor by her that they had been called into being. Then he understood that it was essentially in his own soul the revival had taken place, and that in the air of this soul they were now unable to breathe. The candles might mechanically burn, but each of them had lost its lustre. The church had become a void; it was his presence, her presence, their common presence, that had made the indispensable medium. If anything was wrong everything was—her silence spoiled the tune.

Then when three months were gone he felt so lonely that he went back; reflecting that as they had been his best society for years his Dead perhaps wouldn't let him forsake them without doing something more for him. They stood there, as he had left them, in their tall radiance, the bright cluster that had already made him, on occasions when he was willing to compare small things with great, liken them to a group of sea-lights on the edge of the ocean of life. It was a relief to him, after a while, as he sat there, to feel they had still a virtue. He was more and more easily tired, and he always drove now; the action of his heart was weak and gave him none of the reassurance conferred by the action of his fancy. None the less he returned yet again, returned several times, and finally, during six months, haunted the place with a renewal of frequency and a strain of impatience. In winter the church was unwarmed and exposure to cold forbidden him, but the glow of his shrine was an influence in which he could almost bask. He sat and wondered to what he had reduced his absent associate and what she now did with the hours of her absence. There were other churches, there were other altars, there were other candles; in one way or another her piety would still operate; he couldn't absolutely have deprived her of her rites. So he argued, but without contentment; for he well enough knew there was no other such rare semblance of the mountain of light she had once mentioned to him as the satisfaction of her need. As this semblance again gradually grew great to him and his pious practice more regular, he found a sharper and sharper pang in the imagination of her darkness; for never so much as in these weeks had his rites been real, never had his gathered company seemed so to respond and even to invite. He lost himself in the large lustre, which was more and more what he had from the first wished it to be—as dazzling as the vision of heaven in the mind of a child. He wandered in the fields of light; he passed, among the tall tapers, from tier to tier, from fire to fire, from name to name, from the white intensity of one clear emblem, of one saved soul, to another. It was in the quiet sense of having saved his souls that his deep strange instinct rejoiced. This was no dim theological rescue, no boon of a contingent world; they were saved better than faith or works could save them, saved for the warm world they had shrunk from dying to, for actuality, for continuity, for the certainty of human remembrance.

By this time he had survived all his friends; the last straight flame was three years old, there was no one to add to the list. Over and over he called his roll, and it appeared to him compact and complete. Where should he put in another, where, if there were no other objection, would it stand in its place in the rank? He reflected, with a want of sincerity of which he was quite conscious, that it would be difficult to determine that place. More and more, besides, face to face with his little legion, over endless histories, handling the empty shells and playing with the silence—more and more he could see that he had never introduced an alien. He had had his great companions, his indulgences—there were cases in which they had been immense; but what had his devotion after all been if it hadn't been at bottom a respect? He was, however, himself surprised at his stiffness; by the end of the winter the responsibility of it was what was uppermost in his thoughts. The refrain had grown old to them, that plea for just one more. There came a day when, for simple exhaustion, if symmetry should demand just one he was ready so far to meet symmetry. Symmetry was harmony, and the idea of harmony began to haunt him; he said to himself that harmony was of course everything. He took, in fancy, his composition to pieces, redistributing it into other lines, making other juxtapositions and contrasts. He shifted this and that candle, he made the spaces different, he effaced the disfigurement of a possible gap. There were subtle and complex relations, a scheme of cross-reference, and moments in which he seemed to catch a glimpse of the void so sensible to the woman who wandered in exile or sat where he had seen her with the portrait of Acton Hague. Finally, in this way, he arrived at a conception of the total, the ideal, which left a clear opportunity for just another figure. 'Just one more—to round it off; just one more, just one,' continued to hum in his head. There was a strange confusion in the thought, for he felt the day to be near when he too should be one of the Others. What in this event would the Others matter to him, since they only mattered to the living? Even as one of the Dead what would his altar matter to him, since his particular dream of keeping it up had melted away? What had harmony to do with the case if his lights were all to be quenched? What he had hoped for was an instituted thing. He might perpetuate it on some other pretext, but his special meaning would have dropped. This meaning was to have lasted with the life of the one other person who understood it.

In March he had an illness during which he spent a fortnight in bed, and when he revived a little he was told of two things that had happened. One was that a lady whose name was not known to the servants (she left none) had been three times to ask about him; the other was that in his sleep and on an occasion when his mind evidently wandered he was heard to murmur again and again: 'Just one more—just one.' As soon as he found himself able to go out, and before the doctor in attendance had pronounced him so, he drove to see the lady who had come to ask about him. She was not at home; but this gave him the opportunity, before his strength should fall again, to take his way to the church. He entered it alone; he had declined, in a happy manner he possessed of being able to decline effectively, the company of his servant or of a nurse. He knew now perfectly what these good people thought; they had discovered his clandestine connexion, the magnet that had drawn him for so many years, and doubtless attached a significance of their own to the odd words they had repeated to him. The nameless lady was the clandestine connexion—a fact nothing could have made clearer than his indecent haste to rejoin her. He sank on his knees before his altar while his head fell over on his hands. His weakness, his life's weariness overtook him. It seemed to him he had come for the great surrender. At first he asked himself how he should get away; then, with the failing belief in the power, the very desire to move gradually left him. He had come, as he always came, to lose himself; the fields of light were still there to stray in; only this time, in straying, he would never come back. He had given himself to his Dead, and it was good: this time his Dead would keep him. He couldn't rise from his knees; he believed he should never rise again; all he could do was to lift his face and fix his eyes on his lights. They looked unusually, strangely splendid, but the one that always drew him most had an unprecedented lustre. It was the central voice of the choir, the glowing heart of the brightness, and on this occasion it seemed to expand, to spread great wings of flame. The whole altar flared—dazzling and blinding; but the source of the vast radiance burned clearer than the rest, gathering itself into form, and the form was human beauty and human charity, was the far-off face of Mary Antrim. She smiled at him from the glory of heaven—she brought the glory down with her to take him. He bowed his head in submission and at the same moment another wave rolled over him. Was it the quickening of joy to pain? In the midst of his joy at any rate he felt his buried face grow hot as with some communicated knowledge that had the force of a reproach. It suddenly made him contrast that very rapture with the bliss he had refused to another. This breath of the passion immortal was all that other had asked; the descent of Mary Antrim opened his spirit with a great compunctious throb for the descent of Acton Hague. It was as if Stransom had read what her eyes said to him.

After a moment he looked round in a despair that made him feel as if the source of life were ebbing. The church had been empty—he was alone; but he wanted to have something done, to make a last appeal. This idea gave him strength for an effort; he rose to his feet with a movement that made him turn, supporting himself by the back of a bench. Behind him was a prostrate figure, a figure he had seen before; a woman in deep mourning, bowed in grief or in prayer. He had seen her in other days—the first time of his entrance there, and he now slightly wavered, looking at her again till she seemed aware he had noticed her. She raised her head and met his eyes: the partner of his long worship had come back. She looked across at him an instant with a face wondering and scared; he saw he had made her afraid. Then quickly rising she came straight to him with both hands out.

'Then you could come? God sent you!' he murmured with a happy smile.

'You're very ill—you shouldn't be here,' she urged in anxious reply.

'God sent me too, I think. I was ill when I came, but the sight of you does wonders.' He held her hands, which steadied and quickened him. 'I've something to tell you.'

'Don't tell me!' she tenderly pleaded; 'let me tell you. This afternoon, by a miracle, the sweetest of miracles, the sense of our difference left me. I was out—I was near, thinking, wandering alone, when, on the spot, something changed in my heart. It's my confession—there it is. To come back, to come back on the instant—the idea gave me wings. It was as if I suddenly saw something—as if it all became possible. I could come for what you yourself came for: that was enough. So here I am. It's not for my own—that's over. But I'm here for them.' And breathless, infinitely relieved by her low precipitate explanation, she looked with eyes that reflected all its splendour at the magnificence of their altar.

'They're here for you,' Stransom said, 'they're present to-night as they've never been. They speak for you—don't you see?—in a passion of light; they sing out like a choir of angels. Don't you hear what they say?—they offer the very thing you asked of me.'

'Don't talk of it—don't think of it; forget it!' She spoke in hushed supplication, and while the alarm deepened in her eyes she disengaged one of her hands and passed an arm round him to support him better, to help him to sink into a seat.

He let himself go, resting on her; he dropped upon the bench and she fell on her knees beside him, his own arm round her shoulder. So he remained an instant, staring up at his shrine. 'They say there's a gap in the array—they say it's not full, complete. Just one more,' he went on, softly—'isn't that what you wanted? Yes, one more, one more.'

'Ah no more—no more!' she wailed, as with a quick new horror of it, under her breath.

'Yes, one more,' he repeated, simply; 'just one!' And with this his head dropped on her shoulder; she felt that in his weakness he had fainted. But alone with him in the dusky church a great dread was on her of what might still happen, for his face had the whiteness of death.

THE ASPERN PAPERS

I

I had taken Mrs. Prest into my confidence; in truth without her I should have made but little advance, for the fruitful idea in the whole business dropped from her friendly lips. It was she who invented the short cut, who severed the Gordian knot. It is not supposed to be the nature of women to rise as a general thing to the largest and most liberal view—I mean of a practical scheme; but it has struck me that they sometimes throw off a bold conception—such as a man would not have risen to—with singular serenity. "Simply ask them to take you in on the footing of a lodger"—I don't think that unaided I should have risen to that. I was beating about the bush, trying to be ingenious, wondering by what combination of arts I might become an acquaintance, when she offered this happy suggestion that the way to become an acquaintance was first to become an inmate. Her actual knowledge of the Misses Bordereau was scarcely larger than mine, and indeed I had brought with me from England some definite facts which were new to her. Their name had been mixed up ages before with one of the greatest names of the century, and they lived now in Venice in obscurity, on very small means, unvisited, unapproachable, in a dilapidated old palace on an out-of-the-way canal: this was the substance of my friend's impression of them. She herself had been established in Venice for fifteen years and had done a great deal of good there; but the circle of her benevolence did not include the two shy, mysterious and, as it was somehow supposed, scarcely respectable Americans (they were believed to have lost in their long exile all national quality, besides having had, as their name implied, some French strain in their origin), who asked no favors and desired no attention. In the early years of her residence she had made an attempt to see them, but this had been successful only as regards the little one, as Mrs. Prest called the niece; though in reality as I afterward learned she was considerably the bigger of the two. She had heard Miss Bordereau was ill and had a suspicion that she was in want; and she had gone to the house to offer assistance, so that if there were suffering (and American suffering), she should at least not have it on her conscience. The "little one" received her in the great cold, tarnished Venetian sala, the central hall of the house, paved with marble and roofed with dim crossbeams, and did not even ask her to sit down. This was not encouraging for me, who wished to sit so fast, and I remarked as much to Mrs. Prest. She however replied with profundity, "Ah, but there's all the difference: I went to confer a favor and you will go to ask one. If they are proud you will be on the right side." And she offered to show me their house to begin with—to row me thither in her gondola. I let her know that I had already been to look at it half a dozen times; but I accepted her invitation, for it charmed me to hover about the place. I had made my way to it the day after my arrival in Venice (it had been described to me in advance by the friend in England to whom I owed definite information as to their possession of the papers), and I had besieged it with my eyes while I considered my plan of campaign. Jeffrey Aspern had never been in it that I knew of; but some note of his voice seemed to abide there by a roundabout implication, a faint reverberation.

Mrs. Prest knew nothing about the papers, but she was interested in my curiosity, as she was always interested in the joys and sorrows of her friends. As we went, however, in her gondola, gliding there under the sociable hood with the bright Venetian picture framed on either side by the movable window, I could see that she was amused by my infatuation, the way my interest in the papers had become a fixed idea. "One would think you expected to find in them the answer to the riddle of the universe," she said; and I denied the impeachment only by replying that if I had to choose between that precious solution and a bundle of Jeffrey Aspern's letters I knew indeed which would appear to me the greater boon. She pretended to make light of his genius, and I took no pains to defend him. One doesn't defend one's god: one's god is in himself a defense. Besides, today, after his long comparative obscuration, he hangs high in the heaven of our literature, for all the world to see; he is a part of the light by which we walk. The most I said was that he was no doubt not a woman's poet: to which she rejoined aptly enough that he had been at least Miss Bordereau's. The strange thing had been for me to discover in England that she was still alive: it was as if I had been told Mrs. Siddons was, or Queen Caroline, or the famous Lady Hamilton, for it seemed to me that she belonged to a generation as extinct. "Why, she must be tremendously old—at least a hundred," I had said; but on coming to consider dates I saw that it was not strictly necessary that she should have exceeded by very much the common span. Nonetheless she was very far advanced in life, and her relations with Jeffrey Aspern had occurred in her early womanhood. "That is her excuse," said Mrs. Prest, half-sententiously and yet also somewhat as if she were ashamed of making a speech so little in the real tone of Venice. As if a woman needed an excuse for having loved the divine poet! He had been not only one of the most brilliant minds of his day (and in those years, when the century was young, there were, as everyone knows, many), but one of the most genial men and one of the handsomest.

The niece, according to Mrs. Prest, was not so old, and she risked the conjecture that she was only a grandniece. This was possible; I had nothing but my share in the very limited knowledge of my English fellow worshipper John Cumnor, who had never seen the couple. The world, as I say, had recognized Jeffrey Aspern, but Cumnor and I had recognized him most. The multitude, today, flocked to his temple, but of that temple he and I regarded ourselves as the ministers. We held, justly, as I think, that we had done more for his memory than anyone else, and we had done it by opening lights into his life. He had nothing to fear from us because he had nothing to fear from the truth, which alone at such a distance of time we could be interested in establishing. His early death had been the only dark spot in his life, unless the papers in Miss Bordereau's hands should perversely bring out others. There had been an impression about 1825 that he had "treated her badly," just as there had been an impression that he had "served," as the London populace says, several other ladies in the same way. Each of these cases Cumnor and I had been able to investigate, and we had never failed to acquit him conscientiously of shabby behavior. I judged him perhaps more indulgently than my friend; certainly, at any rate, it appeared to me that no man could have walked straighter in the given circumstances. These were almost always awkward. Half the women of his time, to speak liberally, had flung themselves at his head, and out of this pernicious fashion many complications, some of them grave, had not failed to arise. He was not a woman's poet, as I had said to Mrs. Prest, in the modern phase of his reputation; but the situation had been different when the man's own voice was mingled with his song. That voice, by every testimony, was one of the sweetest ever heard. "Orpheus and the Maenads!" was the exclamation that rose to my lips when I first turned over his correspondence. Almost all the Maenads were unreasonable, and many of them insupportable; it struck me in short that he was kinder, more considerate than, in his place (if I could imagine myself in such a place!) I should have been.

It was certainly strange beyond all strangeness, and I shall not take up space with attempting to explain it, that whereas in all these other lines of research we had to deal with phantoms and dust, the mere echoes of echoes, the one living source of information that had lingered on into our time had been unheeded by us. Every one of Aspern's contemporaries had, according to our belief, passed away; we had not been able to look into a single pair of eyes into which his had looked or to feel a transmitted contact in any aged hand that his had touched. Most dead of all did poor Miss Bordereau appear, and yet she alone had survived. We exhausted in the course of months our wonder that we had not found her out sooner, and the substance of our explanation was that she had kept so quiet. The poor lady on the whole had had reason for doing so. But it was a revelation to us that it was possible to keep so quiet as that in the latter half of the nineteenth century—the age of newspapers and telegrams and photographs and interviewers. And she had taken no great trouble about it either: she had not hidden herself away in an undiscoverable hole; she had boldly settled down in a city of exhibition. The only secret of her safety that we could perceive was that Venice contained so many curiosities that were greater than she. And then accident had somehow favored her, as was shown for example in the fact that Mrs. Prest had never happened to mention her to me, though I had spent three weeks in Venice—under her nose, as it were—five years before. Mrs. Prest had not mentioned this much to anyone; she appeared almost to have forgotten she was there. Of course she had not the responsibilities of an editor. It was no explanation of the old woman's having eluded us to say that she lived abroad, for our researches had again and again taken us (not only by correspondence but by personal inquiry) to France, to Germany, to Italy, in which countries, not counting his important stay in England, so many of the too few years of Aspern's career were spent. We were glad to think at least that in all our publishings (some people consider I believe that we have overdone them), we had only touched in passing and in the most discreet manner on Miss Bordereau's connection. Oddly enough, even if we had had the material (and we often wondered what had become of it), it would have been the most difficult episode to handle.

The gondola stopped, the old palace was there; it was a house of the class which in Venice carries even in extreme dilapidation the dignified name. "How charming! It's gray and pink!" my companion exclaimed; and that is the most comprehensive description of it. It was not particularly old, only two or three centuries; and it had an air not so much of decay as of quiet discouragement, as if it had rather missed its career. But its wide front, with a stone balcony from end to end of the piano nobile or most important floor, was architectural enough, with the aid of various pilasters and arches; and the stucco with which in the intervals it had long ago been endued was rosy in the April afternoon. It overlooked a clean, melancholy, unfrequented canal, which had a narrow riva or convenient footway on either side. "I don't know why—there are no brick gables," said Mrs. Prest, "but this corner has seemed to me before more Dutch than Italian, more like Amsterdam than like Venice. It's perversely clean, for reasons of its own; and though you can pass on foot scarcely anyone ever thinks of doing so. It has the air of a Protestant Sunday. Perhaps the people are afraid of the Misses Bordereau. I daresay they have the reputation of witches."

I forget what answer I made to this—I was given up to two other reflections. The first of these was that if the old lady lived in such a big, imposing house she could not be in any sort of misery and therefore would not be tempted by a chance to let a couple of rooms. I expressed this idea to Mrs. Prest, who gave me a very logical reply. "If she didn't live in a big house how could it be a question of her having rooms to spare? If she were not amply lodged herself you would lack ground to approach her. Besides, a big house here, and especially in this quartier perdu, proves nothing at all: it is perfectly compatible with a state of penury. Dilapidated old palazzi, if you will go out of the way for them, are to be had for five shillings a year. And as for the people who live in them—no, until you have explored Venice socially as much as I have you can form no idea of their domestic desolation. They live on nothing, for they have nothing to live on." The other idea that had come into my head was connected with a high blank wall which appeared to confine an expanse of ground on one side of the house. Blank I call it, but it was figured over with the patches that please a painter, repaired breaches, crumblings of plaster, extrusions of brick that had turned pink with time; and a few thin trees, with the poles of certain rickety trellises, were visible over the top. The place was a garden, and apparently it belonged to the house. It suddenly occurred to me that if it did belong to the house I had my pretext.

I sat looking out on all this with Mrs. Prest (it was covered with the golden glow of Venice) from the shade of our felze, and she asked me if I would go in then, while she waited for me, or come back another time. At first I could not decide—it was doubtless very weak of me. I wanted still to think I *might* get a footing, and I was afraid to meet failure, for it would leave me, as I remarked to my companion, without another arrow for my bow. "Why not another?" she inquired as I sat there hesitating and thinking it over; and she wished to know why even now and before taking the trouble of becoming an inmate (which might be wretchedly uncomfortable after all, even if it succeeded), I had not the resource of simply offering them a sum of money down. In that way I might obtain the documents without bad nights.

"Dearest lady," I exclaimed, "excuse the impatience of my tone when I suggest that you must have forgotten the very fact (surely I communicated it to you) which pushed me to throw myself upon your ingenuity. The old woman won't have the documents spoken of; they are personal, delicate, intimate, and she hasn't modern notions, God bless her! If I should sound that note first I should certainly spoil the game. I can arrive at the papers only by putting her off her guard, and I can put her off her guard only by ingratiating diplomatic practices. Hypocrisy, duplicity are my only chance. I am sorry for it, but for Jeffrey Aspern's sake I would do worse still. First I must take tea with her; then tackle the main job." And I told over what had happened to John Cumnor when he wrote to her. No notice whatever had been taken of his first letter, and the second had been answered very sharply, in six lines, by the niece. "Miss Bordereau requested her to say that she could not imagine what he meant by troubling them. They had none of Mr. Aspern's papers, and if they had should never think of showing them to anyone on any account whatever. She didn't know what he was talking about and begged he would let her alone." I certainly did not want to be met that way.

"Well," said Mrs. Prest after a moment, provokingly, "perhaps after all they haven't any of his things. If they deny it flat how are you sure?"

"John Cumnor is sure, and it would take me long to tell you how his conviction, or his very strong presumption—strong enough to stand against the old lady's not unnatural fib—has built itself up. Besides, he makes much of the internal evidence of the niece's letter."

"The internal evidence?"

"Her calling him 'Mr. Aspern.'"

"I don't see what that proves."

"It proves familiarity, and familiarity implies the possession of mementoes, or relics. I can't tell you how that 'Mr.' touches me—how it bridges over the gulf of time and brings our hero near to me—nor what an edge it gives to my desire to see Juliana. You don't say, 'Mr.' Shakespeare."

"Would I, any more, if I had a box full of his letters?"

"Yes, if he had been your lover and someone wanted them!" And I added that John Cumnor was so convinced, and so all the more convinced by Miss Bordereau's tone, that he would have come himself to Venice on the business were it not that for him there was the obstacle that it would be difficult to disprove his identity with the person who had written to them, which the old ladies would be sure to suspect in spite of dissimulation and a change of name. If they were to ask him point-blank if he were not their correspondent it would be too awkward for him to lie; whereas I was fortunately not tied in that way. I was a fresh hand and could say no without lying.

"But you will have to change your name," said Mrs. Prest. "Juliana lives out of the world as much as it is possible to live, but none the less she has probably heard of Mr. Aspern's editors; she perhaps possesses what you have published."

"I have thought of that," I returned; and I drew out of my pocketbook a visiting card, neatly engraved with a name that was not my own.

"You are very extravagant; you might have written it," said my companion.

"This looks more genuine."

"Certainly, you are prepared to go far! But it will be awkward about your letters; they won't come to you in that mask."

"My banker will take them in, and I will go every day to fetch them. It will give me a little walk."

"Shall you only depend upon that?" asked Mrs. Prest. "Aren't you coming to see me?"

"Oh, you will have left Venice, for the hot months, long before there are any results. I am prepared to roast all summer—as well as hereafter, perhaps you'll say! Meanwhile, John Cumnor will bombard me with letters addressed, in my feigned name, to the care of the padrona."

"She will recognize his hand," my companion suggested.

"On the envelope he can disguise it."

"Well, you're a precious pair! Doesn't it occur to you that even if you are able to say you are not Mr. Cumnor in person they may still suspect you of being his emissary?"

"Certainly, and I see only one way to parry that."

"And what may that be?"

I hesitated a moment. "To make love to the niece."

"Ah," cried Mrs. Prest, "wait till you see her!"

II

"I must work the garden—I must work the garden," I said to myself, five minutes later, as I waited, upstairs, in the long, dusky sala, where the bare scagliola floor gleamed vaguely in a chink of the closed shutters. The place was impressive but it looked cold and cautious. Mrs. Prest had floated away, giving me a rendezvous at the end of half an hour by some neighboring water steps; and I had been let into the house, after pulling the rusty bell wire, by a little red-headed, white-faced maidservant, who was very young and not ugly and wore clicking pattens and a shawl in the fashion of a hood. She had not contented herself with opening the door from above by the usual arrangement of a creaking pulley, though she had looked down at me first from an upper window, dropping the inevitable challenge which in Italy precedes the hospitable act. As a general thing I was irritated by this survival of medieval manners, though as I liked the old I suppose I ought to have liked it; but I was so determined to be genial that I took my false card out of my pocket and held it up to her, smiling as if it were a magic token. It had the effect of one indeed, for it brought her, as I say, all the way down. I begged her to hand it to her mistress, having first written on it in Italian the words, "Could you very kindly see a gentleman, an American, for a moment?" The little maid was not hostile, and I reflected that even that was perhaps something gained. She colored, she smiled and looked both frightened and pleased. I could see that my arrival was a great affair, that visits were rare in that house, and that she was a person who would have liked a sociable place. When she pushed forward the heavy door behind me I felt that I had a foot in the citadel. She pattered across the damp, stony lower hall and I followed her up the high staircase—stonier still, as it seemed—without an invitation. I think she had meant I should wait for her below, but such was not my idea, and I took up my station in the sala. She flitted, at the far end of it, into impenetrable regions, and I looked at the place with my heart beating as I had known it to do in the dentist's parlor. It was gloomy and stately, but it owed its character almost entirely to its noble shape and to the fine architectural doors—as high as the doors of houses—which, leading into the various rooms, repeated themselves on either side at intervals. They were surmounted with old faded painted escutcheons, and here and there, in the spaces between them, brown pictures, which I perceived to be bad, in battered frames, were suspended. With the exception of several straw-bottomed chairs with their backs to the wall, the grand obscure vista contained nothing else to minister to effect. It was evidently never used save as a passage, and little even as that. I may add that by the time the door opened again through which the maidservant had escaped, my eyes had grown used to the want of light.

I had not meant by my private ejaculation that I must myself cultivate the soil of the tangled enclosure which lay beneath the windows, but the lady who came toward me from the distance over the hard, shining floor might have supposed as much from the way in which, as I went rapidly to meet her, I exclaimed, taking care to speak Italian: "The garden, the garden—do me the pleasure to tell me if it's yours!"

She stopped short, looking at me with wonder; and then, "Nothing here is mine," she answered in English, coldly and sadly.

"Oh, you are English; how delightful!" I remarked, ingenuously. "But surely the garden belongs to the house?"

"Yes, but the house doesn't belong to me." She was a long, lean, pale person, habited apparently in a dull-colored dressing gown, and she spoke with a kind of mild literalness. She did not ask me to sit down, any more than years before (if she were the niece) she had asked Mrs. Prest, and we stood face to face in the empty pompous hall.

"Well then, would you kindly tell me to whom I must address myself? I'm afraid you'll think me odiously intrusive, but you know I *must* have a garden—upon my honor I must!"

Her face was not young, but it was simple; it was not fresh, but it was mild. She had large eyes which were not bright, and a great deal of hair which was not "dressed," and long fine hands which were—possibly—not clean. She clasped these members almost convulsively as, with a confused, alarmed look, she broke out, "Oh, don't take it away from us; we like it ourselves!"

"You have the use of it then?"

"Oh, yes. If it wasn't for that!" And she gave a shy, melancholy smile.

"Isn't it a luxury, precisely? That's why, intending to be in Venice some weeks, possibly all summer, and having some literary work, some reading and writing to do, so that I must be quiet, and yet if possible a great deal in the open air—that's why I have felt that a garden is really indispensable. I appeal to your own experience," I went on, smiling. "Now can't I look at yours?"

"I don't know, I don't understand," the poor woman murmured, planted there and letting her embarrassed eyes wander all over my strangeness.

"I mean only from one of those windows—such grand ones as you have here—if you will let me open the shutters." And I walked toward the back of the house. When I had advanced halfway I stopped and waited, as if I took it for granted she would accompany me. I had been of necessity very abrupt, but I strove at the same time to give her the impression of extreme courtesy. "I have been looking at furnished rooms all over the place, and it seems impossible to find any with a garden attached. Naturally in a place like Venice gardens are rare. It's absurd if you like, for a man, but I can't live without flowers."

"There are none to speak of down there." She came nearer to me, as if, though she mistrusted me, I had drawn her by an invisible thread. I went on again, and she continued as she followed me: "We have a few, but they are very common. It costs too much to cultivate them; one has to have a man."

"Why shouldn't I be the man?" I asked. "I'll work without wages; or rather I'll put in a gardener. You shall have the sweetest flowers in Venice."

She protested at this, with a queer little sigh which might also have been a gush of rapture at the picture I presented. Then she observed, "We don't know you—we don't know you."

"You know me as much as I know you: that is much more, because you know my name. And if you are English I am almost a countryman."

"We are not English," said my companion, watching me helplessly while I threw open the shutters of one of the divisions of the wide high window.

"You speak the language so beautifully: might I ask what you are?" Seen from above the garden was certainly shabby; but I perceived at a glance that it had great capabilities. She made no rejoinder, she was so lost in staring at me, and I exclaimed, "You don't mean to say you are also by chance American?"

"I don't know; we used to be."

"Used to be? Surely you haven't changed?"

"It's so many years ago—we are nothing."

"So many years that you have been living here? Well, I don't wonder at that; it's a grand old house. I suppose you all use the garden," I went on, "but I assure you I shouldn't be in your way. I would be very quiet and stay in one corner."

"We all use it?" she repeated after me, vaguely, not coming close to the window but looking at my shoes. She appeared to think me capable of throwing her out.

"I mean all your family, as many as you are."

"There is only one other; she is very old—she never goes down."

"Only one other, in all this great house!" I feigned to be not only amazed but almost scandalized. "Dear lady, you must have space then to spare!"

"To spare?" she repeated, in the same dazed way.

"Why, you surely don't live (two quiet women—I see *you* are quiet, at any rate) in fifty rooms!" Then with a burst of hope and cheer I demanded: "Couldn't you let me two or three? That would set me up!"

I had not struck the note that translated my purpose, and I need not reproduce the whole of the tune I played. I ended by making my interlocutress believe that I was an honorable person, though of course I did not even attempt to persuade her that I was not an eccentric one. I repeated that I had studies to pursue; that I wanted quiet; that I delighted in a garden and had vainly sought one up and down the city; that I would undertake that before another month was over the dear old house should be smothered in flowers. I think it was the flowers that won my suit, for I afterward found that Miss Tita (for such the name of this high tremulous spinster proved somewhat incongruously to be) had an insatiable appetite for them. When I speak of my suit as won I mean that before I left her she had promised that she would refer the question to her aunt. I inquired who her aunt might be and she answered, "Why, Miss Bordereau!" with an air of surprise, as if I might have been expected to know. There were contradictions like this in Tita Bordereau which, as I observed later, contributed to make her an odd and affecting person. It was the study of the two ladies to live so that the world should not touch them, and yet they had never altogether accepted the idea that it never heard of them. In Tita at any rate a grateful susceptibility to human contact had not died out, and contact of a limited order there would be if I should come to live in the house.

"We have never done anything of the sort; we have never had a lodger or any kind of inmate." So much as this she made a point of saying to me. "We are very poor, we live very badly. The rooms are very bare—that you might take; they have nothing in them. I don't know how you would sleep, how you would eat."

"With your permission, I could easily put in a bed and a few tables and chairs. *C'est la moindre des choses* and the affair of an hour or two. I know a little man from whom I can hire what I should want for a few months, for a trifle, and my gondolier can bring the things round in his boat. Of course in this great house you must have a second kitchen, and my servant, who is a wonderfully handy fellow" (this personage was an evocation of the moment), "can easily cook me a chop there. My tastes and habits are of the simplest; I live on flowers!" And then I ventured to add that if they were very poor it was all the more reason they should let their rooms. They were bad economists—I had never heard of such a waste of material.

I saw in a moment that the good lady had never before been spoken to in that way, with a kind of humorous firmness which did not exclude sympathy but was on the contrary founded on it. She might easily have told me that my sympathy was impertinent, but this by good fortune did not occur to her. I left her with the understanding that she would consider the matter with her aunt and that I might come back the next day for their decision.

"The aunt will refuse; she will think the whole proceeding very louche!" Mrs. Prest declared shortly after this, when I had resumed my place in her gondola. She had put the idea into my head and now (so little are women to be counted on) she appeared to take a despondent view of it. Her pessimism provoked me and I pretended to have the best hopes; I went so far as to say that I had a distinct presentiment that I should succeed. Upon this Mrs. Prest broke out, "Oh, I see what's in your head! You fancy you have made such an impression in a quarter of an hour that she is dying for you to come and can be depended upon to bring the old one round. If you do get in you'll count it as a triumph."

I did count it as a triumph, but only for the editor (in the last analysis), not for the man, who had not the tradition of personal conquest. When I went back on the morrow the little maidservant conducted me straight through the long sala (it opened there as before in perfect perspective and was lighter now, which I thought a good omen) into the apartment from which the recipient of my former visit had emerged on that occasion. It was a large shabby parlor, with a fine old painted ceiling and a strange figure sitting alone at one of the windows. They come back to me now almost with the palpitation they caused, the successive feelings that accompanied my consciousness that as the door of the room closed behind me I was really face to face with the Juliana of some of Aspern's most exquisite and most renowned lyrics. I grew used to her afterward, though never completely; but as she sat there before me my heart beat as fast as if the miracle of resurrection had taken place for my benefit. Her presence seemed somehow to contain his, and I felt nearer to him at that first moment of seeing her than I ever had been before or ever have been since. Yes, I remember my emotions in their order, even including a curious little tremor that took me when I saw that the niece was not there. With her, the day before, I had become sufficiently familiar, but it almost exceeded my courage (much as I had longed for the event) to be left alone with such a terrible relic as the aunt. She was too strange, too literally resurgent. Then came a check, with the perception that we were not really face to face, inasmuch as she had over her eyes a horrible green shade which, for her, served almost as a mask. I believed for the instant that she had put it on expressly, so that from underneath it she might scrutinize me without being scrutinized herself. At the same time it increased the presumption that there was a ghastly death's-head lurking behind it. The divine Juliana as a grinning skull—the vision hung there until it passed. Then it came to me that she *was* tremendously old—so old that death might take her at any moment, before I had time to get what I wanted from her. The next thought was a correction to that; it lighted up the situation. She would die next week, she would die tomorrow—then I could seize her papers. Meanwhile she sat there neither moving nor speaking. She was very small and shrunken, bent forward, with her hands in her lap. She was dressed in black, and her head was wrapped in a piece of old black lace which showed no hair.

My emotion keeping me silent she spoke first, and the remark she made was exactly the most unexpected.

III

"Our house is very far from the center, but the little canal is very *comme il faut*."

"It's the sweetest corner of Venice and I can imagine nothing more charming," I hastened to reply. The old lady's voice was very thin and weak, but it had an agreeable, cultivated murmur, and there was wonder in the thought that that individual note had been in Jeffrey Aspern's ear.

"Please to sit down there. I hear very well," she said quietly, as if perhaps I had been shouting at her; and the chair she pointed to was at a certain distance. I took possession of it, telling her that I was perfectly aware that I had intruded, that I had not been properly introduced and could only throw myself upon her indulgence. Perhaps the other lady, the one I had had the honor of seeing the day before, would have explained to her about the garden. That was literally what had given me courage to take a step so unconventional. I had fallen in love at sight with the whole place (she herself probably was so used to it that she did not know the impression it was capable of making on a stranger), and I had felt it was really a case to risk something. Was her own kindness in receiving me a sign that I was not wholly out in my calculation? It would render me extremely happy to think so. I could give her my word of honor that I was a most respectable, inoffensive person and that as an inmate they would be barely conscious of my existence. I would conform to any regulations, any restrictions if they would only let me enjoy the garden. Moreover I should be delighted to give her references, guarantees; they would be of the very best, both in Venice and in England as well as in America.

She listened to me in perfect stillness and I felt that she was looking at me with great attention, though I could see only the lower part of her bleached and shriveled face. Independently of the refining process of old age it had a delicacy which once must have been great. She had been very fair, she had had a wonderful complexion. She was silent a little after I had ceased speaking; then she inquired, "If you are so fond of a garden why don't you go to terra firma, where there are so many far better than this?"

"Oh, it's the combination!" I answered, smiling; and then, with rather a flight of fancy, "It's the idea of a garden in the middle of the sea."

"It's not in the middle of the sea; you can't see the water."

I stared a moment, wondering whether she wished to convict me of fraud. "Can't see the water? Why, dear madam, I can come up to the very gate in my boat."

She appeared inconsequent, for she said vaguely in reply to this, "Yes, if you have got a boat. I haven't any; it's many years since I have been in one of the gondolas." She uttered these words as if the gondolas were a curious faraway craft which she knew only by hearsay.

"Let me assure you of the pleasure with which I would put mine at your service!" I exclaimed. I had scarcely said this, however, before I became aware that the speech was in questionable taste and might also do me the injury of making me appear too eager, too possessed of a hidden motive. But the old woman remained impenetrable and her attitude bothered me by suggesting that she had a fuller vision of me than I had of her. She gave me no thanks for my somewhat extravagant offer but remarked that the lady I had seen the day before was her niece; she would presently come in. She had asked her to stay away a little on purpose, because she herself wished to see me at first alone. She relapsed into silence, and I asked myself why she had judged this necessary and what was coming yet; also whether I might venture on some judicious remark in praise of her companion. I went so far as to say that I should be delighted to see her again: she had been so very courteous to me, considering how odd she must have thought me—a declaration which drew from Miss Bordereau another of her whimsical speeches.

"She has very good manners; I bred her up myself!" I was on the point of saying that that accounted for the easy grace of the niece, but I arrested myself in time, and the next moment the old woman went on: "I don't care who you may be—I don't want to know; it signifies very little today." This had all the air of being a formula of dismissal, as if her next words would be that I might take myself off now that she had had the amusement of looking on the face of such a monster of indiscretion. Therefore I was all the more surprised when she added, with her soft, venerable quaver, "You may have as many rooms as you like—if you will pay a good deal of money."

I hesitated but for a single instant, long enough to ask myself what she meant in particular by this condition. First it struck me that she must have really a large sum in her mind; then I reasoned quickly that her idea of a large sum would probably not correspond to my own. My deliberation, I think, was not so visible as to diminish the promptitude with which I replied, "I will pay with pleasure and of course in advance whatever you may think is proper to ask me."

"Well then, a thousand francs a month," she rejoined instantly, while her baffling green shade continued to cover her attitude.

The figure, as they say, was startling and my logic had been at fault. The sum she had mentioned was, by the Venetian measure of such matters, exceedingly large; there was many an old palace in an out-of-the-way corner that I might on such terms have enjoyed by the year. But so far as my small means allowed I was prepared to spend money, and my decision was quickly taken. I would pay her with a smiling face what she asked, but in that case I would give myself the compensation of extracting the papers from her for nothing. Moreover if she had asked five times as much I should have risen to the occasion; so odious would it have appeared to me to stand chaffering with Aspern's Juliana. It was queer enough to have a question of money with her at all. I assured her that her views perfectly met my own and that on the morrow I should have the pleasure of putting three months' rent into her hand. She received this announcement with serenity and with no apparent sense that after all it would be becoming of her to say that I ought to see the rooms first. This did not occur to her and indeed her serenity was mainly what I wanted. Our little bargain was just concluded when the door opened and the younger lady appeared on the threshold. As soon as Miss Bordereau saw her niece she cried out almost gaily, "He will give three thousand—three thousand tomorrow!"

Miss Tita stood still, with her patient eyes turning from one of us to the other; then she inquired, scarcely above her breath, "Do you mean francs?"

"Did you mean francs or dollars?" the old woman asked of me at this.

"I think francs were what you said," I answered, smiling.

"That is very good," said Miss Tita, as if she had become conscious that her own question might have looked overreaching.

"What do *you* know? You are ignorant," Miss Bordereau remarked; not with acerbity but with a strange, soft coldness.

"Yes, of money—certainly of money!" Miss Tita hastened to exclaim.

"I am sure you have your own branches of knowledge," I took the liberty of saying, genially. There was something painful to me, somehow, in the turn the conversation had taken, in the discussion of the rent.

"She had a very good education when she was young. I looked into that myself," said Miss Bordereau. Then she added, "But she has learned nothing since."

"I have always been with you," Miss Tita rejoined very mildly, and evidently with no intention of making an epigram.

"Yes, but for that!" her aunt declared with more satirical force. She evidently meant that but for this her niece would never have got on at all; the point of the observation however being lost on Miss Tita, though she blushed at hearing her history revealed to a stranger. Miss Bordereau went on, addressing herself to me: "And what time will you come tomorrow with the money?"

"The sooner the better. If it suits you I will come at noon."

"I am always here but I have my hours," said the old woman, as if her convenience were not to be taken for granted.

"You mean the times when you receive?"

"I never receive. But I will see you at noon, when you come with the money."

"Very good, I shall be punctual;" and I added, "May I shake hands with you, on our contract?" I thought there ought to be some little form, it would make me really feel easier, for I foresaw that there would be no other. Besides, though Miss Bordereau could not today be called personally attractive and there was something even in her wasted antiquity that bade one stand at one's distance, I felt an irresistible desire to hold in my own for a moment the hand that Jeffrey Aspern had pressed.

For a minute she made no answer, and I saw that my proposal failed to meet with her approbation. She indulged in no movement of withdrawal, which I half-expected; she only said coldly, "I belong to a time when that was not the custom."

I felt rather snubbed but I exclaimed good humoredly to Miss Tita, "Oh, you will do as well!" I shook hands with her while she replied, with a small flutter, "Yes, yes, to show it's all arranged!"

"Shall you bring the money in gold?" Miss Bordereau demanded, as I was turning to the door.

I looked at her for a moment. "Aren't you a little afraid, after all, of keeping such a sum as that in the house?" It was not that I was annoyed at her avidity but I was really struck with the disparity between such a treasure and such scanty means of guarding it.

"Whom should I be afraid of if I am not afraid of you?" she asked with her shrunken grimness.

"Ah well," said I, laughing, "I shall be in point of fact a protector and I will bring gold if you prefer."

"Thank you," the old woman returned with dignity and with an inclination of her head which evidently signified that I might depart. I passed out of the room, reflecting that it would not be easy to circumvent her. As I stood in the sala again I saw that Miss Tita had followed me, and I supposed that as her aunt had neglected to suggest that I should take a look at my quarters it was her purpose to repair the omission. But she made no such suggestion; she only stood there with a dim, though not a languid smile, and with an effect of irresponsible, incompetent youth which was almost comically at variance with the faded facts of her person. She was not infirm, like her aunt, but she struck me as still more helpless, because her inefficiency was spiritual, which was not the case with Miss Bordereau's. I waited to see if she would offer to show me the rest of the house, but I did not precipitate the question, inasmuch as my plan was from this moment to spend as much of my time as possible in her society. I only observed at the end of a minute:

"I have had better fortune than I hoped. It was very kind of her to see me. Perhaps you said a good word for me."

"It was the idea of the money," said Miss Tita.

"And did you suggest that?"

"I told her that you would perhaps give a good deal."

"What made you think that?"

"I told her I thought you were rich."

"And what put that idea into your head?"

"I don't know; the way you talked."

"Dear me, I must talk differently now," I declared. "I'm sorry to say it's not the case."

"Well," said Miss Tita, "I think that in Venice the forestieri, in general, often give a great deal for something that after all isn't much." She appeared to make this remark with a comforting intention, to wish to remind me that if I had been extravagant I was not really foolishly singular. We walked together along the sala, and as I took its magnificent measure I said to her that I was afraid it would not form a part of my quartiere. Were my rooms by chance to be among those that opened into it? "Not if you go above, on the second floor," she answered with a little startled air, as if she had rather taken for granted I would know my proper place.

"And I infer that that's where your aunt would like me to be."

"She said your apartments ought to be very distinct."

"That certainly would be best." And I listened with respect while she told me that up above I was free to take whatever I liked; that there was another staircase, but only from the floor on which we stood, and that to pass from it to the garden-story or to come up to my lodging I should have in effect to cross the great hall. This was an immense point gained; I foresaw that it would constitute my whole leverage in my relations with the two ladies. When I asked Miss Tita how I was to manage at present to find my way up she replied with an access of that sociable shyness which constantly marked her manner.

"Perhaps you can't. I don't see—unless I should go with you." She evidently had not thought of this before.

We ascended to the upper floor and visited a long succession of empty rooms. The best of them looked over the garden; some of the others had a view of the blue lagoon, above the opposite rough-tiled housetops. They were all dusty and even a little disfigured with long neglect, but I saw that by spending a few hundred francs I should be able to convert three or four of them into a convenient habitation. My experiment was turning out costly, yet now that I had all but taken possession I ceased to allow this to trouble me. I mentioned to my companion a few of the things that I should put in, but she replied rather more precipitately than usual that I might do exactly what I liked; she seemed to wish to notify me that the Misses Bordereau would take no overt interest in my proceedings. I guessed that her aunt had instructed her to adopt this tone, and I may as well say now that I came afterward to distinguish perfectly (as I believed) between the speeches she made on her own responsibility and those the old lady imposed upon her. She took no notice of the unswept condition of the rooms and indulged in no explanations nor apologies. I said to myself that this was a sign that Juliana and her niece (disenchanting idea!) were untidy persons, with a low Italian standard; but I afterward recognized that a lodger who had forced an entrance had no locus standi as a critic. We looked out of a good many windows, for there was nothing within the rooms to look at, and still I wanted to linger. I asked her what several different objects in the prospect might be, but in no case did she appear to know. She was evidently not familiar with the view—it was as if she had not looked at it for years—and I presently saw that she was too preoccupied with something else to pretend to care for it. Suddenly she said—the remark was not suggested:

"I don't know whether it will make any difference to you, but the money is for me."

"The money?"

"The money you are going to bring."

"Why, you'll make me wish to stay here two or three years." I spoke as benevolently as possible, though it had begun to act on my nerves that with these women so associated with Aspern the pecuniary question should constantly come back.

"That would be very good for me," she replied, smiling.

"You put me on my honor!"

She looked as if she failed to understand this, but went on: "She wants me to have more. She thinks she is going to die."

"Ah, not soon, I hope!" I exclaimed with genuine feeling. I had perfectly considered the possibility that she would destroy her papers on the day she should feel her end really approach. I believed that she would cling to them till then, and I think I had an idea that she read Aspern's letters over every night or at least pressed them to her withered lips. I would have given a good deal to have a glimpse of the latter spectacle. I asked Miss Tita if the old lady were seriously ill, and she replied that she was only very tired—she had lived so very, very long. That was what she said herself—she wanted to die for a change. Besides, all her friends were dead long ago; either they ought to have remained or she ought to have gone. That was another thing her aunt often said—she was not at all content.

"But people don't die when they like, do they?" Miss Tita inquired. I took the liberty of asking why, if there was actually enough money to maintain both of them, there would not be more than enough in case of her being left alone. She considered this difficult problem a moment and then she said, "Oh, well, you know, she takes care of me. She thinks that when I'm alone I shall be a great fool, I shall not know how to manage."

"I should have supposed that you took care of her. I'm afraid she is very proud."

"Why, have you discovered that already?" Miss Tita cried with the glimmer of an illumination in her face.

"I was shut up with her there for a considerable time, and she struck me, she interested me extremely. It didn't take me long to make my discovery. She won't have much to say to me while I'm here."

"No, I don't think she will," my companion averred.

"Do you suppose she has some suspicion of me?"

Miss Tita's honest eyes gave me no sign that I had touched a mark. "I shouldn't think so—letting you in after all so easily."

"Oh, so easily! she has covered her risk. But where is it that one could take an advantage of her?"

"I oughtn't to tell you if I knew, ought I?" And Miss Tita added, before I had time to reply to this, smiling dolefully, "Do you think we have any weak points?"

"That's exactly what I'm asking. You would only have to mention them for me to respect them religiously."

She looked at me, at this, with that air of timid but candid and even gratified curiosity with which she had confronted me from the first; and then she said, "There is nothing to tell. We are terribly quiet. I don't know how the days pass. We have no life."

"I wish I might think that I should bring you a little."

"Oh, we know what we want," she went on. "It's all right."

There were various things I desired to ask her: how in the world they did live; whether they had any friends or visitors, any relations in America or in other countries. But I judged such an inquiry would be premature; I must leave it to a later chance. "Well, don't *you* be proud," I contented myself with saying. "Don't hide from me altogether."

"Oh, I must stay with my aunt," she returned, without looking at me. And at the same moment, abruptly, without any ceremony of parting, she quitted me and disappeared, leaving me to make my own way downstairs. I remained a while longer, wandering about the bright desert (the sun was pouring in) of the old house, thinking the situation over on the spot. Not even the pattering little serva came to look after me, and I reflected that after all this treatment showed confidence.

IV

Perhaps it did, but all the same, six weeks later, toward the middle of June, the moment when Mrs. Prest undertook her annual migration, I had made no measurable advance. I was obliged to confess to her that I had no results to speak of. My first step had been unexpectedly rapid, but there was no appearance that it would be followed by a second. I was a thousand miles from taking tea with my hostesses—that privilege of which, as I reminded Mrs. Prest, we both had had a vision. She reproached me with wanting boldness, and I answered that even to be bold you must have an opportunity: you may push on through a breach but you can't batter down a dead wall. She answered that the breach I had already made was big enough to admit an army and accused me of wasting precious hours in whimpering in her salon when I ought to have been carrying on the struggle in the field. It is true that I went to see her very often, on the theory that it would console me (I freely expressed my discouragement) for my want of success on my own premises. But I began to perceive that it did not console me to be perpetually chaffed for my scruples, especially when I was really so vigilant; and I was rather glad when my derisive friend closed her house for the summer. She had expected to gather amusement from the drama of my intercourse with the Misses Bordereau, and she was disappointed that the intercourse, and consequently the drama, had not come off. "They'll lead you on to your ruin," she said before she left Venice. "They'll get all your money without showing you a scrap." I think I settled down to my business with more concentration after she had gone away.

It was a fact that up to that time I had not, save on a single brief occasion, had even a moment's contact with my queer hostesses. The exception had occurred when I carried them according to my promise the terrible three thousand francs. Then I found Miss Tita waiting for me in the hall, and she took the money from my hand so that I did not see her aunt. The old lady had promised to receive me, but she apparently thought nothing of breaking that vow. The money was contained in a bag of chamois leather, of respectable dimensions, which my banker had given me, and Miss Tita had to make a big fist to receive it. This she did with extreme solemnity, though I tried to treat the affair a little as a joke. It was in no jocular strain, yet it was with simplicity, that she inquired, weighing the money in her two palms: "Don't you think it's too much?" To which I replied that that would depend upon the amount of pleasure I should get for it. Hereupon she turned away from me quickly, as she had done the day before, murmuring in a tone different from any she had used hitherto: "Oh, pleasure, pleasure—there's no pleasure in this house!"

After this, for a long time, I never saw her, and I wondered that the common chances of the day should not have helped us to meet. It could only be evident that she was immensely on her guard against them; and in addition to this the house was so big that for each other we were lost in it. I used to look out for her hopefully as I crossed the sala in my comings and goings, but I was not rewarded with a glimpse of the tail of her dress. It was as if she never peeped out of her aunt's apartment. I used to wonder what she did there week after week and year after year. I had never encountered such a violent parti pris of seclusion; it was more than keeping quiet—it was like hunted creatures feigning death. The two ladies appeared to have no visitors whatever and no sort of contact with the world. I judged at least that people could not have come to the house and that Miss Tita could not have gone out without my having some observation of it. I did what I disliked myself for doing (reflecting that it was only once in a way): I questioned my servant about their habits and let him divine that I should be interested in any information he could pick up. But he picked up amazingly little for a knowing Venetian: it must be added that where there is a perpetual fast there are very few crumbs on the floor. His cleverness in other ways was sufficient, if it was not quite all that I had attributed to him on the occasion of my first interview with Miss Tita. He had helped my gondolier to bring me round a boatload of furniture; and when these articles had been carried to the top of the palace and distributed according to our associated wisdom he organized my household with such promptitude as was consistent with the fact that it was composed exclusively of himself. He made me in short as comfortable as I could be with my indifferent prospects. I should have been glad if he had fallen in love with Miss Bordereau's maid or, failing this, had taken her in aversion; either event might have brought about some kind of catastrophe, and a catastrophe might have led to some parley. It was my idea that she would have been sociable, and I myself on various occasions saw her flit to and fro on domestic errands, so that I was sure she was accessible. But I tasted of no gossip from that fountain, and I afterward learned that Pasquale's affections were fixed upon an object that made him heedless of other women. This was a young lady with a powdered face, a yellow cotton gown, and much leisure, who used often to come to see him. She practiced, at her convenience, the art of a stringer of beads (these ornaments are made in Venice, in profusion; she had her pocket full of them, and I used to find them on the floor of my apartment), and kept an eye on the maiden in the house. It was not for me of course to make the domestics tattle, and I never said a word to Miss Bordereau's cook.

It seemed to me a proof of the old lady's determination to have nothing to do with me that she should never have sent me a receipt for my three months' rent. For some days I looked out for it and then, when I had given it up, I wasted a good deal of time in wondering what her reason had been for neglecting so indispensable and familiar a form. At first I was tempted to send her a reminder, after which I relinquished the idea (against my judgment as to what was right in the particular case), on the general ground of wishing to keep quiet. If Miss Bordereau suspected me of ulterior aims she would suspect me less if I should be businesslike, and yet I consented not to be so. It was possible she intended her omission as an impertinence, a visible irony, to show how she could overreach people who attempted to overreach her. On that hypothesis it was well to let her see that one did not notice her little tricks. The real reading of the matter, I afterward perceived, was simply the poor old woman's desire to emphasize the fact that I was in the enjoyment of a favor as rigidly limited as it had been liberally bestowed. She had given me part of her house, and now she would not give me even a morsel of paper with her name on it. Let me say that even at first this did not make me too miserable, for the whole episode was essentially delightful to me. I foresaw that I should have a summer after my own literary heart, and the sense of holding my opportunity was much greater than the sense of losing it. There could be no Venetian business without patience, and since I adored the place I was much more in the spirit of it for having laid in a large provision. That spirit kept me perpetual company and seemed to look out at me from the revived immortal face—in which all his genius shone—of the great poet who was my prompter. I had invoked him and he had come; he hovered before me half the time; it was as if his bright ghost had returned to earth to tell me that he regarded the affair as his own no less than mine and that we should see it fraternally, cheerfully to a conclusion. It was as if he had said, "Poor dear, be easy with her; she has some natural prejudices; only give her time. Strange as it may appear to you she was very attractive in 1820. Meanwhile are we not in Venice together, and what better place is there for the meeting of dear friends? See how it glows with the advancing summer; how the sky and the sea and the rosy air and the marble of the palaces all shimmer and melt together." My eccentric private errand became a part of the general romance and the general glory—I felt even a mystic companionship, a moral fraternity with all those who in the past had been in the service of art. They had worked for beauty, for a devotion; and what else was I doing? That element was in everything that Jeffrey Aspern had written, and I was only bringing it to the light.

I lingered in the sala when I went to and fro; I used to watch—as long as I thought decent—the door that led to Miss Bordereau's part of the house. A person observing me might have supposed I was trying to cast a spell upon it or attempting some odd experiment in hypnotism. But I was only praying it would open or thinking what treasure probably lurked behind it. I hold it singular, as I look back, that I should never have doubted for a moment that the sacred relics were there; never have failed to feel a certain joy at being under the same roof with them. After all they were under my hand—they had not escaped me yet; and they made my life continuous, in a fashion, with the illustrious life they had touched at the other end. I lost myself in this satisfaction to the point of assuming—in my quiet extravagance—that poor Miss Tita also went back, went back, as I used to phrase it. She did indeed, the gentle spinster, but not quite so far as Jeffrey Aspern, who was simply hearsay to her, quite as he was to me. Only she had lived for years with Juliana, she had seen and handled the papers and (even though she was stupid) some esoteric knowledge had rubbed off on her. That was what the old woman represented—esoteric knowledge; and this was the idea with which my editorial heart used to thrill. It literally beat faster often, of an evening, when I had been out, as I stopped with my candle in the re-echoing hall on my way up to bed. It was as if at such a moment as that, in the stillness, after the long contradiction of the day, Miss Bordereau's secrets were in the air, the wonder of her survival more palpable. These were the acute impressions. I had them in another form, with more of a certain sort of reciprocity, during the hours that I sat in the garden looking up over the top of my book at the closed windows of my hostess. In these windows no sign of life ever appeared; it was as if, for fear of my catching a glimpse of them, the two ladies passed their days in the dark. But this only proved to me that they had something to conceal; which was what I had wished to demonstrate. Their motionless shutters became as expressive as eyes consciously closed, and I took comfort in thinking that at all events through invisible themselves they saw me between the lashes.

I made a point of spending as much time as possible in the garden, to justify the picture I had originally given of my horticultural passion. And I not only spent time, but (hang it! as I said) I spent money. As soon as I had got my rooms arranged and could give the proper thought to the matter I surveyed the place with a clever expert and made terms for having it put in order. I was sorry to do this, for personally I liked it better as it was, with its weeds and its wild, rough tangle, its sweet, characteristic Venetian shabbiness. I had to be consistent, to keep my promise that I would smother the house in flowers. Moreover I formed this graceful project that by flowers I would make my way—I would succeed by big nosegays. I would batter the old women with lilies—I would bombard their citadel with roses. Their door would have to yield to the pressure when a mountain of carnations should be piled up against it. The place in truth had been brutally neglected. The Venetian capacity for dawdling is of the largest, and for a good many days unlimited litter was all my gardener had to show for his ministrations. There was a great digging of holes and carting about of earth, and after a while I grew so impatient that I had thoughts of sending for my bouquets to the nearest stand. But I reflected that the ladies would see through the chinks of their shutters that they must have been bought and might make up their minds from this that I was a humbug. So I composed myself and finally, though the delay was long, perceived some appearances of bloom. This encouraged me, and I waited serenely enough till they multiplied. Meanwhile the real summer days arrived and began to pass, and as I look back upon them they seem to me almost the happiest of my life. I took more and more care to be in the garden whenever it was not too hot. I had an arbor arranged and a low table and an armchair put into it; and I carried out books and portfolios (I had always some business of writing in hand), and worked and waited and mused and hoped, while the golden hours elapsed and the plants drank in the light and the inscrutable old palace turned pale and then, as the day waned, began to flush in it and my papers rustled in the wandering breeze of the Adriatic.

Considering how little satisfaction I got from it at first it is remarkable that I should not have grown more tired of wondering what mystic rites of ennui the Misses Bordereau celebrated in their darkened rooms; whether this had always been the tenor of their life and how in previous years they had escaped elbowing their neighbors. It was clear that they must have had other habits and other circumstances; that they must once have been young or at least middle-aged. There was no end to the questions it was possible to ask about them and no end to the answers it was not possible to frame. I had known many of my country-people in Europe and was familiar with the strange ways they were liable to take up there; but the Misses Bordereau formed altogether a new type of the American absentee. Indeed it was plain that the American name had ceased to have any application to them—I had seen this in the ten minutes I spent in the old woman's room. You could never have said whence they came, from the appearance of either of them; wherever it was they had long ago dropped the local accent and fashion. There was nothing in them that one recognized, and putting the question of speech aside they might have been Norwegians or Spaniards. Miss Bordereau, after all, had been in Europe nearly three-quarters of a century; it appeared by some verses addressed to her by Aspern on the occasion of his own second absence from America—verses of which Cumnor and I had after infinite conjecture established solidly enough the date—that she was even then, as a girl of twenty, on the foreign side of the sea. There was an implication in the poem (I hope not just for the phrase) that he had come back for her sake. We had no real light upon her circumstances at that moment, any more than we had upon her origin, which we believed to be of the sort usually spoken of as modest. Cumnor had a theory that she had been a governess in some family in which the poet visited and that, in consequence of her position, there was from the first something unavowed, or rather something positively clandestine, in their relations. I on the other hand had hatched a little romance according to which she was the daughter of an artist, a painter or a sculptor, who had left the western world when the century was fresh, to study in the ancient schools. It was essential to my hypothesis that this amiable man should have lost his wife, should have been poor and unsuccessful and should have had a second daughter, of a disposition quite different from Juliana's. It was also indispensable that he should have been accompanied to Europe by these young ladies and should have established himself there for the remainder of a struggling, saddened life. There was a further implication that Miss Bordereau had had in her youth a perverse and adventurous, albeit a generous and fascinating character, and that she had passed through some singular vicissitudes. By what passions had she been ravaged, by what sufferings had she been blanched, what store of memories had she laid away for the monotonous future?

I asked myself these things as I sat spinning theories about her in my arbor and the bees droned in the flowers. It was incontestable that, whether for right or for wrong, most readers of certain of Aspern's poems (poems not as ambiguous as the sonnets—scarcely more divine, I think—of Shakespeare) had taken for granted that Juliana had not always adhered to the steep footway of renunciation. There hovered about her name a perfume of reckless passion, an intimation that she had not been exactly as the respectable young person in general. Was this a sign that her singer had betrayed her, had given her away, as we say nowadays, to posterity? Certain it is that it would have been difficult to put one's finger on the passage in which her fair fame suffered an imputation. Moreover was not any fame fair enough that was so sure of duration and was associated with works immortal through their beauty? It was a part of my idea that the young lady had had a foreign lover (and an unedifying tragical rupture) before her meeting with Jeffrey Aspern. She had lived with her father and sister in a queer old-fashioned, expatriated, artistic Bohemia, in the days when the aesthetic was only the academic and the painters who knew the best models for a contadina and pifferaro wore peaked hats and long hair. It was a society less furnished than the coteries of today (in its ignorance of the wonderful chances, the opportunities of the early bird, with which its path was strewn), with tatters of old stuff and fragments of old crockery; so that Miss Bordereau appeared not to have picked up or have inherited many objects of importance. There was no enviable bric-a-brac, with its provoking legend of cheapness, in the room in which I had seen her. Such a fact as that suggested bareness, but nonetheless it worked happily into the sentimental interest I had always taken in the early movements of my countrymen as visitors to Europe. When Americans went abroad in 1820 there was something romantic, almost heroic in it, as compared with the perpetual ferryings of the present hour, when photography and other conveniences have annihilated surprise. Miss Bordereau sailed with her family on a tossing brig, in the days of long voyages and sharp differences; she had her emotions on the top of yellow diligences, passed the night at inns where she dreamed of travelers' tales, and was struck, on reaching the Eternal City, with the elegance of Roman pearls and scarfs. There was something touching to me in all that, and my imagination frequently went back to the period. If Miss Bordereau carried it there of course Jeffrey Aspern at other times had done so a great deal more. It was a much more important fact, if one were looking at his genius critically, that he had lived in the days before the general transfusion. It had happened to me to regret that he had known Europe at all; I should have liked to see what he would have written without that experience, by which he had incontestably been enriched. But as his fate had ordered otherwise I went with him—I tried to judge how the Old World would have struck him. It was not only there, however, that I watched him; the relations he had entertained with the new had even a livelier interest. His own country after all had had most of his life, and his muse, as they said at that time, was essentially American. That was originally what I had loved him for: that at a period when our native land was nude and crude and provincial, when the famous "atmosphere" it is supposed to lack was not even missed, when literature was lonely there and art and form almost impossible, he had found means to live and write like one of the first; to be free and general and not at all afraid; to feel, understand, and express everything.

V

I was seldom at home in the evening, for when I attempted to occupy myself in my apartments the lamplight brought in a swarm of noxious insects, and it was too hot for closed windows. Accordingly I spent the late hours either on the water (the moonlight of Venice is famous), or in the splendid square which serves as a vast forecourt to the strange old basilica of Saint Mark. I sat in front of Florian's cafe, eating ices, listening to music, talking with acquaintances: the traveler will remember how the immense cluster of tables and little chairs stretches like a promontory into the smooth lake of the Piazza. The whole place, of a summer's evening, under the stars and with all the lamps, all the voices and light footsteps on marble (the only sounds of the arcades that enclose it), is like an open-air saloon dedicated to cooling drinks and to a still finer degustation—that of the exquisite impressions received during the day. When I did not prefer to keep mine to myself there was always a stray tourist, disencumbered of his Baedeker, to discuss them with, or some domesticated painter rejoicing in the return of the season of strong effects. The wonderful church, with its low domes and bristling embroideries, the mystery of its mosaic and sculpture, looking ghostly in the tempered gloom, and the sea breeze passed between the twin columns of the Piazzetta, the lintels of a door no longer guarded, as gently as if a rich curtain were swaying there. I used sometimes on these occasions to think of the Misses Bordereau and of the pity of their being shut up in apartments which in the Venetian July even Venetian vastness did not prevent from being stuffy. Their life seemed miles away from the life of the Piazza, and no doubt it was really too late to make the austere Juliana change her habits. But poor Miss Tita would have enjoyed one of Florian's ices, I was sure; sometimes I even had thoughts of carrying one home to her. Fortunately my patience bore fruit, and I was not obliged to do anything so ridiculous.

One evening about the middle of July I came in earlier than usual—I forget what chance had led to this—and instead of going up to my quarters made my way into the garden. The temperature was very high; it was such a night as one would gladly have spent in the open air, and I was in no hurry to go to bed. I had floated home in my gondola, listening to the slow splash of the oar in the narrow dark canals, and now the only thought that solicited me was the vague reflection that it would be pleasant to recline at one's length in the fragrant darkness on a garden bench. The odor of the canal was doubtless at the bottom of that aspiration and the breath of the garden, as I entered it, gave consistency to my purpose. It was delicious—just such an air as must have trembled with Romeo's vows when he stood among the flowers and raised his arms to his mistress's balcony. I looked at the windows of the palace to see if by chance the example of Verona (Verona being not far off) had been followed; but everything was dim, as usual, and everything was still. Juliana, on summer nights in her youth, might have murmured down from open windows at Jeffrey Aspern, but Miss Tita was not a poet's mistress any more than I was a poet. This however did not prevent my gratification from being great as I became aware on reaching the end of the garden that Miss Tita was seated in my little bower. At first I only made out an indistinct figure, not in the least counting on such an overture from one of my hostesses; it even occurred to me that some sentimental maidservant had stolen in to keep a tryst with her sweetheart. I was going to turn away, not to frighten her, when the figure rose to its height and I recognized Miss Bordereau's niece. I must do myself the justice to say that I did not wish to frighten her either, and much as I had longed for some such accident I should have been capable of retreating. It was as if I had laid a trap for her by coming home earlier than usual and adding to that eccentricity by creeping into the garden. As she rose she spoke to me, and then I reflected that perhaps, secure in my almost inveterate absence, it was her nightly practice to take a lonely airing. There was no trap, in truth, because I had had no suspicion. At first I took for granted that the words she uttered expressed discomfiture at my arrival; but as she repeated them—I had not caught them clearly—I had the surprise of hearing her say, "Oh, dear, I'm so very glad you've come!" She and her aunt had in common the property of unexpected speeches. She came out of the arbor almost as if she were going to throw herself into my arms.

I hasten to add that she did nothing of the kind; she did not even shake hands with me. It was a gratification to her to see me and presently she told me why—because she was nervous when she was out-of-doors at night alone. The plants and bushes looked so strange in the dark, and there were all sorts of queer sounds—she could not tell what they were—like the noises of animals. She stood close to me, looking about her with an air of greater security but without any demonstration of interest in me as an individual. Then I guessed that nocturnal prowlings were not in the least her habit, and I was also reminded (I had been struck with the circumstance in talking with her before I took possession) that it was impossible to overestimate her simplicity.

"You speak as if you were lost in the backwoods," I said, laughing. "How you manage to keep out of this charming place when you have only three steps to take to get into it is more than I have yet been able to discover. You hide away mighty well so long as I am on the premises, I know; but I had a hope that you peeped out a little at other times. You and your poor aunt are worse off than Carmelite nuns in their cells. Should you mind telling me how you exist without air, without exercise, without any sort of human contact? I don't see how you carry on the common business of life."

She looked at me as if I were talking some strange tongue, and her answer was so little of an answer that I was considerably irritated. "We go to bed very early—earlier than you would believe." I was on the point of saying that this only deepened the mystery when she gave me some relief by adding, "Before you came we were not so private. But I never have been out at night."

"Never in these fragrant alleys, blooming here under your nose?"

"Ah," said Miss Tita, "they were never nice till now!" There was an unmistakable reference in this and a flattering comparison, so that it seemed to me I had gained a small advantage. As it would help me to follow it up to establish a sort of grievance I asked her why, since she thought my garden nice, she had never thanked me in any way for the flowers I had been sending up in such quantities for the previous three weeks. I had not been discouraged—there had been, as she would have observed, a daily armful; but I had been brought up in the common forms and a word of recognition now and then would have touched me in the right place.

"Why I didn't know they were for me!"

"They were for both of you. Why should I make a difference?"

Miss Tita reflected as if she might by thinking of a reason for that, but she failed to produce one. Instead of this she asked abruptly, "Why in the world do you want to know us?"

"I ought after all to make a difference," I replied. "That question is your aunt's; it isn't yours. You wouldn't ask it if you hadn't been put up to it."

"She didn't tell me to ask you," Miss Tita replied without confusion; she was the oddest mixture of the shrinking and the direct.

"Well, she has often wondered about it herself and expressed her wonder to you. She has insisted on it, so that she has put the idea into your head that I am insufferably pushing. Upon my word I think I have been very discreet. And how completely your aunt must have lost every tradition of sociability, to see anything out of the way in the idea that respectable intelligent people, living as we do under the same roof, should occasionally exchange a remark! What could be more natural? We are of the same country, and we have at least some of the same tastes, since, like you, I am intensely fond of Venice."

My interlocutress appeared incapable of grasping more than one clause in any proposition, and she declared quickly, eagerly, as if she were answering my whole speech: "I am not in the least fond of Venice. I should like to go far away!"

"Has she always kept you back so?" I went on, to show her that I could be as irrelevant as herself.

"She told me to come out tonight; she has told me very often," said Miss Tita. "It is I who wouldn't come. I don't like to leave her."

"Is she too weak, is she failing?" I demanded, with more emotion, I think, than I intended to show. I judged this by the way her eyes rested upon me in the darkness. It embarrassed me a little, and to turn the matter off I continued genially: "Do let us sit down together comfortably somewhere, and you will tell me all about her."

Miss Tita made no resistance to this. We found a bench less secluded, less confidential, as it were, than the one in the arbor; and we were still sitting there when I heard midnight ring out from those clear bells of Venice which vibrate with a solemnity of their own over the lagoon and hold the air so much more than the chimes of other places. We were together more than an hour, and our interview gave, as it struck me, a great lift to my undertaking. Miss Tita accepted the situation without a protest; she had avoided me for three months, yet now she treated me almost as if these three months had made me an old friend. If I had chosen I might have inferred from this that though she had avoided me she had given a good deal of consideration to doing so. She paid no attention to the flight of time—never worried at my keeping her so long away from her aunt. She talked freely, answering questions and asking them and not even taking advantage of certain longish pauses with which they inevitably alternated to say she thought she had better go in. It was almost as if she were waiting for something—something I might say to her—and intended to give me my opportunity. I was the more struck by this as she told me that her aunt had been less well for a good many days and in a way that was rather new. She was weaker; at moments it seemed as if she had no strength at all; yet more than ever before she wished to be left alone. That was why she had told her to come out—not even to remain in her own room, which was alongside; she said her niece irritated her, made her nervous. She sat still for hours together, as if she were asleep; she had always done that, musing and dozing; but at such times formerly she gave at intervals some small sign of life, of interest, liking her companion to be near her with her work. Miss Tita confided to me that at present her aunt was so motionless that she sometimes feared she was dead; moreover she took hardly any food—one couldn't see what she lived on. The great thing was that she still on most days got up; the serious job was to dress her, to wheel her out of her bedroom. She clung to as many of her old habits as possible and she had always, little company as they had received for years, made a point of sitting in the parlor.

I scarcely knew what to think of all this—of Miss Tita's sudden conversion to sociability and of the strange circumstance that the more the old lady appeared to decline toward her end the less she should desire to be looked after. The story did not hang together, and I even asked myself whether it were not a trap laid for me, the result of a design to make me show my hand. I could not have told why my companions (as they could only by courtesy be called) should have this purpose—why they should try to trip up so lucrative a lodger. At any rate I kept on my guard, so that Miss Tita should not have occasion again to ask me if I had an *arrière-pensée*. Poor woman, before we parted for the night my mind was at rest as to *her* capacity for entertaining one.

She told me more about their affairs than I had hoped; there was no need to be prying, for it evidently drew her out simply to feel that I listened, that I cared. She ceased wondering why I cared, and at last, as she spoke of the brilliant life they had led years before, she almost chattered. It was Miss Tita who judged it brilliant; she said that when they first came to live in Venice, years and years before (I saw that her mind was essentially vague about dates and the order in which events had occurred), there was scarcely a week that they had not some visitor or did not make some delightful passeggio in the city. They had seen all the curiosities; they had even been to the Lido in a boat (she spoke as if I might think there was a way on foot); they had had a collation there, brought in three baskets and spread out on the grass. I asked her what people they had known and she said, Oh! very nice ones—the Cavaliere Bombicci and the Contessa Altemura, with whom they had had a great friendship. Also English people—the Churtons and the Goldies and Mrs. Stock-Stock, whom they had loved dearly; she was dead and gone, poor dear. That was the case with most of their pleasant circle (this expression was Miss Tita's own), though a few were left, which was a wonder considering how they had neglected them. She mentioned the names of two or three Venetian old women; of a certain doctor, very clever, who was so kind—he came as a friend, he had really given up practice; of the avvocato Pochintesta, who wrote beautiful poems and had addressed one to her aunt. These people came to see them without fail every year, usually at the capo d'anno, and of old her aunt used to make them some little present—her aunt and she together: small things that she, Miss Tita, made herself, like paper lampshades or mats for the decanters of wine at dinner or those woolen things that in cold weather were worn on the wrists. The last few years there had not been many presents; she could not think what to make, and her aunt had lost her interest and never suggested. But the people came all the same; if the Venetians liked you once they liked you forever.

There was something affecting in the good faith of this sketch of former social glories; the picnic at the Lido had remained vivid through the ages, and poor Miss Tita evidently was of the impression that she had had a brilliant youth. She had in fact had a glimpse of the Venetian world in its gossiping, home-keeping, parsimonious, professional walks; for I observed for the first time that she had acquired by contact something of the trick of the familiar, soft-sounding, almost infantile speech of the place. I judged that she had imbibed this invertebrate dialect from the natural way the names of things and people—mostly purely local—rose to her lips. If she knew little of what they represented she knew still less of anything else. Her aunt had drawn in—her failing interest in the table mats and lampshades was a sign of that—and she had not been able to mingle in society or to entertain it alone; so that the matter of her reminiscences struck one as an old world altogether. If she had not been so decent her references would have seemed to carry one back to the queer rococo Venice of Casanova. I found myself falling into the error of thinking of her too as one of Jeffrey Aspern's contemporaries; this came from her having so little in common with my own. It was possible, I said to myself, that she had not even heard of him; it might very well be that Juliana had not cared to lift even for her the veil that covered the temple of her youth. In this case she perhaps would not know of the existence of the papers, and I welcomed that presumption—it made me feel more safe with her—until I remembered that we had believed the letter of disavowal received by Cumnor to be in the handwriting of the niece. If it had been dictated to her she had of course to know what it was about; yet after all the effect of it was to repudiate the idea of any connection with the poet. I held it probable at all events that Miss Tita had not read a word of his poetry. Moreover if, with her companion, she had always escaped the interviewer there was little occasion for her having got it into her head that people were "after" the letters. People had not been after them, inasmuch as they had not heard of them; and Cumnor's fruitless feeler would have been a solitary accident.

When midnight sounded Miss Tita got up; but she stopped at the door of the house only after she had wandered two or three times with me round the garden. "When shall I see you again?" I asked before she went in; to which she replied with promptness that she should like to come out the next night. She added however that she should not come—she was so far from doing everything she liked.

"You might do a few things that *I* like," I said with a sigh.

"Oh, you—I don't believe you!" she murmured at this, looking at me with her simple solemnity.

"Why don't you believe me?"

"Because I don't understand you."

"That is just the sort of occasion to have faith." I could not say more, though I should have liked to, as I saw that I only mystified her; for I had no wish to have it on my conscience that I might pass for having made love to her. Nothing less should I have seemed to do had I continued to beg a lady to "believe in me" in an Italian garden on a midsummer night. There was some merit in my scruples, for Miss Tita lingered and lingered: I perceived that she felt that she should not really soon come down again and wished therefore to protract the present. She insisted too on making the talk between us personal to ourselves; and altogether her behavior was such as would have been possible only to a completely innocent woman.

"I shall like the flowers better now that I know they are also meant for me."

"How could you have doubted it? If you will tell me the kind you like best I will send a double lot of them."

"Oh, I like them all best!" Then she went on, familiarly: "Shall you study—shall you read and write—when you go up to your rooms?"

"I don't do that at night, at this season. The lamplight brings in the animals."

"You might have known that when you came."

"I did know it!"

"And in winter do you work at night?"

"I read a good deal, but I don't often write." She listened as if these details had a rare interest, and suddenly a temptation quite at variance with the prudence I had been teaching myself associated itself with her plain, mild face. Ah yes, she was safe and I could make her safer! It seemed to me from one moment to another that I could not wait longer—that I really must take a sounding. So I went on: "In general before I go to sleep—very often in bed (it's a bad habit, but I confess to it), I read some great poet. In nine cases out of ten it's a volume of Jeffrey Aspern."

I watched her well as I pronounced that name but I saw nothing wonderful. Why should I indeed—was not Jeffrey Aspern the property of the human race?

"Oh, we read him—we *have* read him," she quietly replied.

"He is my poet of poets—I know him almost by heart."

For an instant Miss Tita hesitated; then her sociability was too much for her.

"Oh, by heart—that's nothing!" she murmured, smiling. "My aunt used to know him—to know him"—she paused an instant and I wondered what she was going to say—"to know him as a visitor."

"As a visitor?" I repeated, staring.

"He used to call on her and take her out."

I continued to stare. "My dear lady, he died a hundred years ago!"

"Well," she said mirthfully, "my aunt is a hundred and fifty."

"Mercy on us!" I exclaimed; "why didn't you tell me before? I should like so to ask her about him."

"She wouldn't care for that—she wouldn't tell you," Miss Tita replied.

"I don't care what she cares for! She *must* tell me—it's not a chance to be lost."

"Oh, you should have come twenty years ago: then she still talked about him."

"And what did she say?" I asked eagerly.

"I don't know—that he liked her immensely."

"And she—didn't she like him?"

"She said he was a god." Miss Tita gave me this information flatly, without expression; her tone might have made it a piece of trivial gossip. But it stirred me deeply as she dropped the words into the summer night; it seemed such a direct testimony.

"Fancy, fancy!" I murmured. And then, "Tell me this, please—has she got a portrait of him? They are distressingly rare."

"A portrait? I don't know," said Miss Tita; and now there was discomfiture in her face. "Well, good night!" she added; and she turned into the house.

I accompanied her into the wide, dusky, stone-paved passage which on the ground floor corresponded with our grand sala. It opened at one end into the garden, at the other upon the canal, and was lighted now only by the small lamp that was always left for me to take up as I went to bed. An extinguished candle which Miss Tita apparently had brought down with her stood on the same table with it. "Good night, good night!" I replied, keeping beside her as she went to get her light. "Surely you would know, shouldn't you, if she had one?"

"If she had what?" the poor lady asked, looking at me queerly over the flame of her candle.

"A portrait of the god. I don't know what I wouldn't give to see it."

"I don't know what she has got. She keeps her things locked up." And Miss Tita went away, toward the staircase, with the sense evidently that she had said too much.

I let her go—I wished not to frighten her—and I contented myself with remarking that Miss Bordereau would not have locked up such a glorious possession as that—a thing a person would be proud of and hang up in a prominent place on the parlor wall. Therefore of course she had not any portrait. Miss Tita made no direct answer to this and, candle in hand, with her back to me, ascended two or three stairs. Then she stopped short and turned round, looking at me across the dusky space.

"Do you write—do you write?" There was a shake in her voice—she could scarcely bring out what she wanted to ask.

"Do I write? Oh, don't speak of my writing on the same day with Aspern's!"

"Do you write about *him*—do you pry into his life?"

"Ah, that's your aunt's question; it can't be yours!" I said, in a tone of slightly wounded sensibility.

"All the more reason then that you should answer it. Do you, please?"

I thought I had allowed for the falsehoods I should have to tell; but I found that in fact when it came to the point I had not. Besides, now that I had an opening there was a kind of relief in being frank. Lastly (it was perhaps fanciful, even fatuous), I guessed that Miss Tita personally would not in the last resort be less my friend. So after a moment's hesitation I answered, "Yes, I have written about him and I am looking for more material. In heaven's name have you got any?"

"Santo Dio!" she exclaimed, without heeding my question; and she hurried upstairs and out of sight. I might count upon her in the last resort, but for the present she was visibly alarmed. The proof of it was that she began to hide again, so that for a fortnight I never beheld her. I found my patience ebbing and after four or five days of this I told the gardener to stop the flowers.

VI

One afternoon, as I came down from my quarters to go out, I found Miss Tita in the sala: it was our first encounter on that ground since I had come to the house. She put on no air of being there by accident; there was an ignorance of such arts in her angular, diffident directness. That I might be quite sure she was waiting for me she informed me of the fact and told me that Miss Bordereau wished to see me: she would take me into the room at that moment if I had time. If I had been late for a love tryst I would have stayed for this, and I quickly signified that I should be delighted to wait upon the old lady. "She wants to talk with you—to know you," Miss Tita said, smiling as if she herself appreciated that idea; and she led me to the door of her aunt's apartment. I stopped her a moment before she had opened it, looking at her with some curiosity. I told her that this was a great satisfaction to me and a great honor; but all the same I should like to ask what had made Miss Bordereau change so suddenly. It was only the other day that she wouldn't suffer me near her. Miss Tita was not embarrassed by my question; she had as many little unexpected serenities as if she told fibs, but the odd part of them was that they had on the contrary their source in her truthfulness. "Oh, my aunt changes," she answered; "it's so terribly dull—I suppose she's tired."

"But you told me that she wanted more and more to be alone."

Poor Miss Tita colored, as if she found me over-insistent. "Well, if you don't believe she wants to see you—I haven't invented it! I think people often are capricious when they are very old."

"That's perfectly true. I only wanted to be clear as to whether you have repeated to her what I told you the other night."

"What you told me?"

"About Jeffrey Aspern—that I am looking for materials."

"If I had told her do you think she would have sent for you?"

"That's exactly what I want to know. If she wants to keep him to herself she might have sent for me to tell me so."

"She won't speak of him," said Miss Tita. Then as she opened the door she added in a lower tone, "I have told her nothing."

The old woman was sitting in the same place in which I had seen her last, in the same position, with the same mystifying bandage over her eyes. her welcome was to turn her almost invisible face to me and show me that while she sat silent she saw me clearly. I made no motion to shake hands with her; I felt too well on this occasion that that was out of place forever. It had been sufficiently enjoined upon me that she was too sacred for that sort of reciprocity—too venerable to touch. There was something so grim in her aspect (it was partly the accident of her green shade), as I stood there to be measured, that I ceased on the spot to feel any doubt as to her knowing my secret, though I did not in the least suspect that Miss Tita had not just spoken the truth. She had not betrayed me, but the old woman's brooding instinct had served her; she had turned me over and over in the long, still hours, and she had guessed. The worst of it was that she looked terribly like an old woman who at a pinch would burn her papers. Miss Tita pushed a chair forward, saying to me, "This will be a good place for you to sit." As I took possession of it I asked after Miss Bordereau's health; expressed the hope that in spite of the very hot weather it was satisfactory. She replied that it was good enough—good enough; that it was a great thing to be alive.

"Oh, as to that, it depends upon what you compare it with!" I exclaimed, laughing.

"I don't compare—I don't compare. If I did that I should have given everything up long ago."

I liked to think that this was a subtle allusion to the rapture she had known in the society of Jeffrey Aspern—though it was true that such an allusion would have accorded ill with the wish I imputed to her to keep him buried in her soul. What it accorded with was my constant conviction that no human being had ever had a more delightful social gift than his, and what it seemed to convey was that nothing in the world was worth speaking of if one pretended to speak of that. But one did not! Miss Tita sat down beside her aunt, looking as if she had reason to believe some very remarkable conversation would come off between us.

"It's about the beautiful flowers," said the old lady; "you sent us so many—I ought to have thanked you for them before. But I don't write letters and I receive only at long intervals."

She had not thanked me while the flowers continued to come, but she departed from her custom so far as to send for me as soon as she began to fear that they would not come any more. I noted this; I remembered what an acquisitive propensity she had shown when it was a question of extracting gold from me, and I privately rejoiced at the happy thought I had had in suspending my tribute. She had missed it and she was willing to make a concession to bring it back. At the first sign of this concession I could only go to meet her. "I am afraid you have not had many, of late, but they shall begin again immediately—tomorrow, tonight."

"Oh, do send us some tonight!" Miss Tita cried, as if it were an immense circumstance.

"What else should you do with them? It isn't a manly taste to make a bower of your room," the old woman remarked.

"I don't make a bower of my room, but I am exceedingly fond of growing flowers, of watching their ways. There is nothing unmanly in that: it has been the amusement of philosophers, of statesmen in retirement; even I think of great captains."

"I suppose you know you can sell them—those you don't use," Miss Bordereau went on. "I daresay they wouldn't give you much for them; still, you could make a bargain."

"Oh, I have never made a bargain, as you ought to know. My gardener disposes of them and I ask no questions."

"I would ask a few, I can promise you!" said Miss Bordereau; and it was the first time I had heard her laugh. I could not get used to the idea that this vision of pecuniary profit was what drew out the divine Juliana most.

"Come into the garden yourself and pick them; come as often as you like; come every day. They are all for you," I pursued, addressing Miss Tita and carrying off this veracious statement by treating it as an innocent joke. "I can't imagine why she doesn't come down," I added, for Miss Bordereau's benefit.

"You must make her come; you must come up and fetch her," said the old woman, to my stupefaction. "That odd thing you have made in the corner would be a capital place for her to sit."

The allusion to my arbor was irreverent; it confirmed the impression I had already received that there was a flicker of impertinence in Miss Bordereau's talk, a strange mocking lambency which must have been a part of her adventurous youth and which had outlived passions and faculties. Nonetheless I asked, "Wouldn't it be possible for you to come down there yourself? Wouldn't it do you good to sit there in the shade, in the sweet air?"

"Oh, sir, when I move out of this it won't be to sit in the air, and I'm afraid that any that may be stirring around me won't be particularly sweet! It will be a very dark shade indeed. But that won't be just yet," Miss Bordereau continued cannily, as if to correct any hopes that this courageous allusion to the last receptacle of her mortality might lead me to entertain. "I have sat here many a day and I have had enough of arbors in my time. But I'm not afraid to wait till I'm called."

Miss Tita had expected some interesting talk, but perhaps she found it less genial on her aunt's side (considering that I had been sent for with a civil intention) than she had hoped. As if to give the conversation a turn that would put our companion in a light more favorable she said to me, "Didn't I tell you the other night that she had sent me out? You see that I can do what I like!"

"Do you pity her—do you teach her to pity herself?" Miss Bordereau demanded before I had time to answer this appeal. "She has a much easier life than I had when I was her age."

"You must remember that it has been quite open to me to think you rather inhuman."

"Inhuman? That's what the poets used to call the women a hundred years ago. Don't try that; you won't do as well as they!" Juliana declared. "There is no more poetry in the world—that I know of at least. But I won't bandy words with you," she pursued, and I well remember the old-fashioned, artificial sound she gave to the speech. "You have made me talk, talk! It isn't good for me at all." I got up at this and told her I would take no more of her time; but she detained me to ask, "Do you remember, the day I saw you about the rooms, that you offered us the use of your gondola?" And when I assented, promptly, struck again with her disposition to make a "good thing" of being there and wondering what she now had in her eye, she broke out, "Why don't you take that girl out in it and show her the place?"

"Oh, dear Aunt, what do you want to do with me?" cried the "girl" with a piteous quaver. "I know all about the place!"

"Well then, go with him as a cicerone!" said Miss Bordereau with an effort of something like cruelty in her implacable power of retort—an incongruous suggestion that she was a sarcastic, profane, cynical old woman. "Haven't we heard that there have been all sorts of changes in all these years? You ought to see them and at your age (I don't mean because you're so young) you ought to take the chances that come. You're old enough, my dear, and this gentleman won't hurt you. He will show you the famous sunsets, if they still go on—*do* they go on? The sun set for me so long ago. But that's not a reason. Besides, I shall never miss you; you think you are too important. Take her to the Piazza; it used to be very pretty," Miss Bordereau continued, addressing herself to me. "What have they done with the funny old church? I hope it hasn't tumbled down. Let her look at the shops; she may take some money, she may buy what she likes."

Poor Miss Tita had got up, discountenanced and helpless, and as we stood there before her aunt it would certainly have seemed to a spectator of the scene that the old woman was amusing herself at our expense. Miss Tita protested, in a confusion of exclamations and murmurs; but I lost no time in saying that if she would do me the honor to accept the hospitality of my boat I would engage that she should not be bored. Or if she did not want so much of my company the boat itself, with the gondolier, was at her service; he was a capital oar and she might have every confidence. Miss Tita, without definitely answering this speech, looked away from me, out of the window, as if she were going to cry; and I remarked that once we had Miss Bordereau's approval we could easily come to an understanding. We would take an hour, whichever she liked, one of the very next days. As I made my obeisance to the old lady I asked her if she would kindly permit me to see her again.

For a moment she said nothing; then she inquired, "Is it very necessary to your happiness?"

"It diverts me more than I can say."

"You are wonderfully civil. Don't you know it almost kills *me*?"

"How can I believe that when I see you more animated, more brilliant than when I came in?"

"That is very true, Aunt," said Miss Tita. "I think it does you good."

"Isn't it touching, the solicitude we each have that the other shall enjoy herself?" sneered Miss Bordereau. "If you think me brilliant today you don't know what you are talking about; you have never seen an agreeable woman. Don't try to pay me a compliment; I have been spoiled," she went on. "My door is shut, but you may sometimes knock."

With this she dismissed me, and I left the room. The latch closed behind me, but Miss Tita, contrary to my hope, had remained within. I passed slowly across the hall and before taking my way downstairs I waited a little. My hope was answered; after a minute Miss Tita followed me. "That's a delightful idea about the Piazza," I said. "When will you go—tonight, tomorrow?"

She had been disconcerted, as I have mentioned, but I had already perceived and I was to observe again that when Miss Tita was embarrassed she did not (as most women would have done) turn away from you and try to escape, but came closer, as it were, with a deprecating, clinging appeal to be spared, to be protected. Her attitude was perpetually a sort of prayer for assistance, for explanation; and yet no woman in the world could have been less of a comedian. From the moment you were kind to her she depended on you absolutely; her self-consciousness dropped from her and she took the greatest intimacy, the innocent intimacy which was the only thing she could conceive, for granted. She told me she did not know what had got into her aunt; she had changed so quickly, she had got some idea. I replied that she must find out what the idea was and then let me know; we would go and have an ice together at Florian's, and she should tell me while we listened to the band.

"Oh, it will take me a long time to find out!" she said, rather ruefully; and she could promise me this satisfaction neither for that night nor for the next. I was patient now, however, for I felt that I had only to wait; and in fact at the end of the week, one lovely evening after dinner, she stepped into my gondola, to which in honor of the occasion I had attached a second oar.

We swept in the course of five minutes into the Grand Canal; whereupon she uttered a murmur of ecstasy as fresh as if she had been a tourist just arrived. She had forgotten how splendid the great waterway looked on a clear, hot summer evening, and how the sense of floating between marble palaces and reflected lights disposed the mind to sympathetic talk. We floated long and far, and though Miss Tita gave no high-pitched voice to her satisfaction I felt that she surrendered herself. She was more than pleased, she was transported; the whole thing was an immense liberation. The gondola moved with slow strokes, to give her time to enjoy it, and she listened to the plash of the oars, which grew louder and more musically liquid as we passed into narrow canals, as if it were a revelation of Venice. When I asked her how long it was since she had been in a boat she answered, "Oh, I don't know; a long time—not since my aunt began to be ill." This was not the only example she gave me of her extreme vagueness about the previous years and the line which marked off the period when Miss Bordereau flourished. I was not at liberty to keep her out too long, but we took a considerable *girl* before going to the Piazza. I asked her no questions, keeping the conversation on purpose away from her domestic situation and the things I wanted to know; I poured treasures of information about Venice into her ears, described Florence and Rome, discoursed to her on the charms and advantages of travel. She reclined, receptive, on the deep leather cushions, turned her eyes conscientiously to everything I pointed out to her, and never mentioned to me till sometime afterward that she might be supposed to know Florence better than I, as she had lived there for years with Miss Bordereau. At last she asked, with the shy impatience of a child, "Are we not really going to the Piazza? That's what I want to see!" I immediately gave the order that we should go straight; and then we sat silent with the expectation of arrival. As some time still passed, however, she said suddenly, of her own movement, "I have found out what is the matter with my aunt: she is afraid you will go!"

"What has put that into her head?"

"She has had an idea you have not been happy. That is why she is different now."

"You mean she wants to make me happier?"

"Well, she wants you not to go; she wants you to stay."

"I suppose you mean on account of the rent," I remarked candidly.

Miss Tita's candor showed itself a match for my own. "Yes, you know; so that I shall have more."

"How much does she want you to have?" I asked, laughing. "She ought to fix the sum, so that I may stay till it's made up."

"Oh, that wouldn't please me," said Miss Tita. "It would be unheard of, your taking that trouble."

"But suppose I should have my own reasons for staying in Venice?"

"Then it would be better for you to stay in some other house."

"And what would your aunt say to that?"

"She wouldn't like it at all. But I should think you would do well to give up your reasons and go away altogether."

"Dear Miss Tita," I said, "it's not so easy to give them up!"

She made no immediate answer to this, but after a moment she broke out: "I think I know what your reasons are!"

"I daresay, because the other night I almost told you how I wish you would help me to make them good."

"I can't do that without being false to my aunt."

"What do you mean, being false to her?"

"Why, she would never consent to what you want. She has been asked, she has been written to. It made her fearfully angry."

"Then she *has* got papers of value?" I demanded quickly.

"Oh, she has got everything!" sighed Miss Tita with a curious weariness, a sudden lapse into gloom.

These words caused all my pulses to throb, for I regarded them as precious evidence. For some minutes I was too agitated to speak, and in the interval the gondola approached the Piazzetta. After we had disembarked I asked my companion whether she would rather walk round the square or go and sit at the door of the cafe; to which she replied that she would do whichever I liked best—I must only remember again how little time she had. I assured her there was plenty to do both, and we made the circuit of the long arcades. Her spirits revived at the sight of the bright shop windows, and she lingered and stopped, admiring or disapproving of their contents, asking me what I thought of things, theorizing about prices. My attention wandered from her; her words of a while before, "Oh, she has got everything!" echoed so in my consciousness. We sat down at last in the crowded circle at Florian's, finding an unoccupied table among those that were ranged in the square. It was a splendid night and all the world was out-of-doors; Miss Tita could not have wished the elements more auspicious for her return to society. I saw that she enjoyed it even more than she told; she was agitated with the multitude of her impressions. She had forgotten what an attractive thing the world is, and it was coming over her that somehow she had for the best years of her life been cheated of it. This did not make her angry; but as she looked all over the charming scene her face had, in spite of its smile of appreciation, the flush of a sort of wounded surprise. She became silent, as if she were thinking with a secret sadness of opportunities, forever lost, which ought to have been easy; and this gave me a chance to say to her, "Did you mean a while ago that your aunt has a plan of keeping me on by admitting me occasionally to her presence?"

"She thinks it will make a difference with you if you sometimes see her. She wants you so much to stay that she is willing to make that concession."

"And what good does she consider that I think it will do me to see her?"

"I don't know; she thinks it's interesting," said Miss Tita simply. "You told her you found it so."

"So I did; but everyone doesn't think so."

"No, of course not, or more people would try."

"Well, if she is capable of making that reflection she is capable of making this further one," I went on: "that I must have a particular reason for not doing as others do, in spite of the interest she offers—for not leaving her alone." Miss Tita looked as if she failed to grasp this rather complicated proposition; so I continued, "If you have not told her what I said to you the other night may she not at least have guessed it?"

"I don't know; she is very suspicious."

"But she has not been made so by indiscreet curiosity, by persecution?"

"No, no; it isn't that," said Miss Tita, turning on me a somewhat troubled face. "I don't know how to say it: it's on account of something—ages ago, before I was born—in her life."

"Something? What sort of thing?" I asked as if I myself could have no idea.

"Oh, she has never told me," Miss Tita answered; and I was sure she was speaking the truth.

Her extreme limpidity was almost provoking, and I felt for the moment that she would have been more satisfactory if she had been less ingenuous. "Do you suppose it's something to which Jeffrey Aspern's letters and papers—I mean the things in her possession—have reference?"

"I daresay it is!" my companion exclaimed as if this were a very happy suggestion. "I have never looked at any of those things."

"None of them? Then how do you know what they are?"

"I don't," said Miss Tita placidly. "I have never had them in my hands. But I have seen them when she has had them out."

"Does she have them out often?"

"Not now, but she used to. She is very fond of them."

"In spite of their being compromising?"

"Compromising?" Miss Tita repeated as if she was ignorant of the meaning of the word. I felt almost as one who corrupts the innocence of youth.

"I mean their containing painful memories."

"Oh, I don't think they are painful."

"You mean you don't think they affect her reputation?"

At this a singular look came into the face of Miss Bordereau's niece—a kind of confession of helplessness, an appeal to me to deal fairly, generously with her. I had brought her to the Piazza, placed her among charming influences, paid her an attention she appreciated, and now I seemed to let her perceive that all this had been a bribe—a bribe to make her turn in some way against her aunt. She was of a yielding nature and capable of doing almost anything to please a person who was kind to her; but the greatest kindness of all would be not to presume too much on this. It was strange enough, as I afterward thought, that she had not the least air of resenting my want of consideration for her aunt's character, which would have been in the worst possible taste if anything less vital (from my point of view) had been at stake. I don't think she really measured it. "Do you mean that she did something bad?" she asked in a moment.

"Heaven forbid I should say so, and it's none of my business. Besides, if she did," I added, laughing, "it was in other ages, in another world. But why should she not destroy her papers?"

"Oh, she loves them too much."

"Even now, when she may be near her end?"

"Perhaps when she's sure of that she will."

"Well, Miss Tita," I said, "it's just what I should like you to prevent."

"How can I prevent it?"

"Couldn't you get them away from her?"

"And give them to you?"

This put the case very crudely, though I am sure there was no irony in her intention. "Oh, I mean that you might let me see them and look them over. It isn't for myself; there is no personal avidity in my desire. It is simply that they would be of such immense interest to the public, such immeasurable importance as a contribution to Jeffrey Aspern's history."

She listened to me in her usual manner, as if my speech were full of reference to things she had never heard of, and I felt particularly like the reporter of a newspaper who forces his way into a house of mourning. This was especially the case when after a moment she said. "There was a gentleman who some time ago wrote to her in very much those words. He also wanted her papers."

"And did she answer him?" I asked, rather ashamed of myself for not having her rectitude.

"Only when he had written two or three times. He made her very angry."

"And what did she say?"

"She said he was a devil," Miss Tita replied simply.

"She used that expression in her letter?"

"Oh, no; she said it to me. She made me write to him."

"And what did you say?"

"I told him there were no papers at all."

"Ah, poor gentleman!" I exclaimed.

"I knew there were, but I wrote what she bade me."

"Of course you had to do that. But I hope I shall not pass for a devil."

"It will depend upon what you ask me to do for you," said Miss Tita, smiling.

"Oh, if there is a chance of *your* thinking so my affair is in a bad way! I shan't ask you to steal for me, nor even to fib—for you can't fib, unless on paper. But the principal thing is this—to prevent her from destroying the papers."

"Why, I have no control of her," said Miss Tita. "It's she who controls me."

"But she doesn't control her own arms and legs, does she? The way she would naturally destroy her letters would be to burn them. Now she can't burn them without fire, and she can't get fire unless you give it to her."

"I have always done everything she has asked," my companion rejoined. "Besides, there's Olimpia."

I was on the point of saying that Olimpia was probably corruptible, but I thought it best not to sound that note. So I simply inquired if that faithful domestic could not be managed.

"Everyone can be managed by my aunt," said Miss Tita. And then she observed that her holiday was over; she must go home.

I laid my hand on her arm, across the table, to stay her a moment. "What I want of you is a general promise to help me."

"Oh, how can I—how can I?" she asked, wondering and troubled. She was half-surprised, half-frightened at my wishing to make her play an active part.

"This is the main thing: to watch her carefully and warn me in time, before she commits that horrible sacrilege."

"I can't watch her when she makes me go out."

"That's very true."

"And when you do, too."

"Mercy on us; do you think she will have done anything tonight?"

"I don't know; she is very cunning."

"Are you trying to frighten me?" I asked.

I felt this inquiry sufficiently answered when my companion murmured in a musing, almost envious way, "Oh, but she loves them—she loves them!"

This reflection, repeated with such emphasis, gave me great comfort; but to obtain more of that balm I said, "If she shouldn't intend to destroy the objects we speak of before her death she will probably have made some disposition by will."

"By will?"

"Hasn't she made a will for your benefit?"

"Why, she has so little to leave. That's why she likes money," said Miss Tita.

"Might I ask, since we are really talking things over, what you and she live on?"

"On some money that comes from America, from a lawyer. He sends it every quarter. It isn't much!"

"And won't she have disposed of that?"

My companion hesitated—I saw she was blushing. "I believe it's mine," she said; and the look and tone which accompanied these words betrayed so the absence of the habit of thinking of herself that I almost thought her charming. The next instant she added, "But she had a lawyer once, ever so long ago. And some people came and signed something."

"They were probably witnesses. And you were not asked to sign? Well then," I argued rapidly and hopefully, "it is because you are the legatee; she has left all her documents to you!"

"If she has it's with very strict conditions," Miss Tita responded, rising quickly, while the movement gave the words a little character of decision. They seemed to imply that the bequest would be accompanied with a command that the articles bequeathed should remain concealed from every inquisitive eye and that I was very much mistaken if I thought she was the person to depart from an injunction so solemn.

"Oh, of course you will have to abide by the terms," I said; and she uttered nothing to mitigate the severity of this conclusion. Nonetheless, later, just before we disembarked at her own door, on our return, which had taken place almost in silence, she said to me abruptly, "I will do what I can to help you." I was grateful for this—it was very well so far as it went; but it did not keep me from remembering that night in a worried waking hour that I now had her word for it to reinforce my own impression that the old woman was very cunning.

VII

The fear of what this side of her character might have led her to do made me nervous for days afterward. I waited for an intimation from Miss Tita; I almost figured to myself that it was her duty to keep me informed, to let me know definitely whether or no Miss Bordereau had sacrificed her treasures. But as she gave no sign I lost patience and determined to judge so far as was possible with my own senses. I sent late one afternoon to ask if I might pay the ladies a visit, and my servant came back with surprising news. Miss Bordereau could be approached without the least difficulty; she had been moved out into the sala and was sitting by the window that overlooked the garden. I descended and found this picture correct; the old lady had been wheeled forth into the world and had a certain air, which came mainly perhaps from some brighter element in her dress, of being prepared again to have converse with it. It had not yet, however, begun to flock about her; she was perfectly alone and, though the door leading to her own quarters stood open, I had at first no glimpse of Miss Tita. The window at which she sat had the afternoon shade and, one of the shutters having been pushed back, she could see the pleasant garden, where the summer sun had by this time dried up too many of the plants—she could see the yellow light and the long shadows.

"Have you come to tell me that you will take the rooms for six months more?" she asked as I approached her, startling me by something coarse in her cupidity almost as much as if she had not already given me a specimen of it. Juliana's desire to make our acquaintance lucrative had been, as I have sufficiently indicated, a false note in my image of the woman who had inspired a great poet with immortal lines; but I may say here definitely that I recognized after all that it behooved me to make a large allowance for her. It was I who had kindled the unholy flame; it was I who had put into her head that she had the means of making money. She appeared never to have thought of that; she had been living wastefully for years, in a house five times too big for her, on a footing that I could explain only by the presumption that, excessive as it was, the space she enjoyed cost her next to nothing and that small as were her revenues they left her, for Venice, an appreciable margin. I had descended on her one day and taught her to calculate, and my almost extravagant comedy on the subject of the garden had presented me irresistibly in the light of a victim. Like all persons who achieve the miracle of changing their point of view when they are old she had been intensely converted; she had seized my hint with a desperate, tremulous clutch.

I invited myself to go and get one of the chairs that stood, at a distance, against the wall (she had given herself no concern as to whether I should sit or stand); and while I placed it near her I began, gaily, "Oh, dear madam, what an imagination you have, what an intellectual sweep! I am a poor devil of a man of letters who lives from day to day. How can I take palaces by the year? My existence is precarious. I don't know whether six months hence I shall have bread to put in my mouth. I have treated myself for once; it has been an immense luxury. But when it comes to going on—!"

"Are your rooms too dear? If they are you can have more for the same money," Juliana responded. "We can arrange, we can combinare, as they say here."

"Well yes, since you ask me, they are too dear," I said. "Evidently you suppose me richer than I am."

She looked at me in her barricaded way. "If you write books don't you sell them?"

"Do you mean don't people buy them? A little—not so much as I could wish. Writing books, unless one be a great genius—and even then!—is the last road to fortune. I think there is no more money to be made by literature."

"Perhaps you don't choose good subjects. What do you write about?" Miss Bordereau inquired.

"About the books of other people. I'm a critic, an historian, in a small way." I wondered what she was coming to.

"And what other people, now?"

"Oh, better ones than myself: the great writers mainly—the great philosophers and poets of the past; those who are dead and gone and can't speak for themselves."

"And what do you say about them?"

"I say they sometimes attached themselves to very clever women!" I answered, laughing. I spoke with great deliberation, but as my words fell upon the air they struck me as imprudent. However, I risked them and I was not sorry, for perhaps after all the old woman would be willing to treat. It seemed to be tolerably obvious that she knew my secret: why therefore drag the matter out? But she did not take what I had said as a confession; she only asked:

"Do you think it's right to rake up the past?"

"I don't know that I know what you mean by raking it up; but how can we get at it unless we dig a little? The present has such a rough way of treading it down."

"Oh, I like the past, but I don't like critics," the old woman declared with her fine tranquility.

"Neither do I, but I like their discoveries."

"Aren't they mostly lies?"

"The lies are what they sometimes discover," I said, smiling at the quiet impertinence of this. "They often lay bare the truth."

"The truth is God's, it isn't man's; we had better leave it alone. Who can judge of it—who can say?"

"We are terribly in the dark, I know," I admitted; "but if we give up trying what becomes of all the fine things? What becomes of the work I just mentioned, that of the great philosophers and poets? It is all vain words if there is nothing to measure it by."

"You talk as if you were a tailor," said Miss Bordereau whimsically; and then she added quickly, in a different manner, "This house is very fine; the proportions are magnificent. Today I wanted to look at this place again. I made them bring me out here. When your man came, just now, to learn if I would see you, I was on the point of sending for you, to ask if you didn't mean to go on. I wanted to judge what I'm letting you have. This sala is very grand," she pursued, like an auctioneer, moving a little, as I guessed, her invisible eyes. "I don't believe you often have lived in such a house, eh?"

"I can't often afford to!" I said.

"Well then, how much will you give for six months?"

I was on the point of exclaiming—and the air of excruciation in my face would have denoted a moral face—"Don't, Juliana; for *his* sake, don't!" But I controlled myself and asked less passionately: "Why should I remain so long as that?"

"I thought you liked it," said Miss Bordereau with her shriveled dignity.

"So I thought I should."

For a moment she said nothing more, and I left my own words to suggest to her what they might. I half-expected her to say, coldly enough, that if I had been disappointed we need not continue the discussion, and this in spite of the fact that I believed her now to have in her mind (however it had come there) what would have told her that my disappointment was natural. But to my extreme surprise she ended by observing: "If you don't think we have treated you well enough perhaps we can discover some way of treating you better." This speech was somehow so incongruous that it made me laugh again, and I excused myself by saying that she talked as if I were a sulky boy, pouting in the corner, to be "brought round." I had not a grain of complaint to make; and could anything have exceeded Miss Tita's graciousness in accompanying me a few nights before to the Piazza? At this the old woman went on: "Well, you brought it on yourself!" And then in a different tone, "She is a very nice girl." I assented cordially to this proposition, and she expressed the hope that I did so not merely to be obliging, but that I really liked her. Meanwhile I wondered still more what Miss Bordereau was coming to. "Except for me, today," she said, "she has not a relation in the world." Did she by describing her niece as amiable and unencumbered wish to represent her as a parti?

It was perfectly true that I could not afford to go on with my rooms at a fancy price and that I had already devoted to my undertaking almost all the hard cash I had set apart for it. My patience and my time were by no means exhausted, but I should be able to draw upon them only on a more usual Venetian basis. I was willing to pay the venerable woman with whom my pecuniary dealings were such a discord twice as much as any other padrona di casa would have asked, but I was not willing to pay her twenty times as much. I told her so plainly, and my plainness appeared to have some success, for she exclaimed, "Very good; you have done what I asked—you have made an offer!"

"Yes, but not for half a year. Only by the month."

"Oh, I must think of that then." She seemed disappointed that I would not tie myself to a period, and I guessed that she wished both to secure me and to discourage me; to say severely, "Do you dream that you can get off with less than six months? Do you dream that even by the end of that time you will be appreciably nearer your victory?" What was more in my mind was that she had a fancy to play me the trick of making me engage myself when in fact she had annihilated the papers. There was a moment when my suspense on this point was so acute that I all but broke out with the question, and what kept it back was but a kind of instinctive recoil (lest it should be a mistake), from the last violence of self-exposure. She was such a subtle old witch that one could never tell where one stood with her. You may imagine whether it cleared up the puzzle when, just after she had said she would think of my proposal and without any formal transition, she drew out of her pocket with an embarrassed hand a small object wrapped in crumpled white paper. She held it there a moment and then she asked, "Do you know much about curiosities?"

"About curiosities?"

"About antiquities, the old gimcracks that people pay so much for today. Do you know the kind of price they bring?"

I thought I saw what was coming, but I said ingenuously, "Do you want to buy something?"

"No, I want to sell. What would an amateur give me for that?" She unfolded the white paper and made a motion for me to take from her a small oval portrait. I possessed myself of it with a hand of which I could only hope that she did not perceive the tremor, and she added, "I would part with it only for a good price."

At the first glance I recognized Jeffrey Aspern, and I was well aware that I flushed with the act. As she was watching me however I had the consistency to exclaim, "What a striking face! Do tell me who it is."

"It's an old friend of mine, a very distinguished man in his day. He gave it to me himself, but I'm afraid to mention his name, lest you never should have heard of him, critic and historian as you are. I know the world goes fast and one generation forgets another. He was all the fashion when I was young."

She was perhaps amazed at my assurance, but I was surprised at hers; at her having the energy, in her state of health and at her time of life, to wish to sport with me that way simply for her private entertainment—the humor to test me and practice on me. This, at least, was the interpretation that I put upon her production of the portrait, for I could not believe that she really desired to sell it or cared for any information I might give her. What she wished was to dangle it before my eyes and put a prohibitive price on it. "The face comes back to me, it torments me," I said, turning the object this way and that and looking at it very critically. It was a careful but not a supreme work of art, larger than the ordinary miniature and representing a young man with a remarkably handsome face, in a high-collared green coat and a buff waistcoat. I judged the picture to have a valuable quality of resemblance and to have been painted when the model was about twenty-five years old. There are, as all the world knows, three other portraits of the poet in existence, but none of them is of so early a date as this elegant production. "I have never seen the original but I have seen other likenesses," I went on. "You expressed doubt of this generation having heard of the gentleman, but he strikes me for all the world as a celebrity. Now who is he? I can't put my finger on him—I can't give him a label. Wasn't he a writer? Surely he's a poet." I was determined that it should be she, not I, who should first pronounce Jeffrey Aspern's name.

My resolution was taken in ignorance of Miss Bordereau's extremely resolute character, and her lips never formed in my hearing the syllables that meant so much for her. She neglected to answer my question but raised her hand to take back the picture, with a gesture which though ineffectual was in a high degree peremptory. "It's only a person who should know for himself that would give me my price," she said with a certain dryness.

"Oh, then, you have a price?" I did not restore the precious thing; not from any vindictive purpose but because I instinctively clung to it. We looked at each other hard while I retained it.

"I know the least I would take. What it occurred to me to ask you about is the most I shall be able to get."

She made a movement, drawing herself together as if, in a spasm of dread at having lost her treasure, she were going to attempt the immense effort of rising to snatch it from me. I instantly placed it in her hand again, saying as I did so, "I should like to have it myself, but with your ideas I could never afford it."

She turned the small oval plate over in her lap, with its face down, and I thought I saw her catch her breath a little, as if she had had a strain or an escape. This however did not prevent her saying in a moment, "You would buy a likeness of a person you don't know, by an artist who has no reputation?"

"The artist may have no reputation, but that thing is wonderfully well painted," I replied, to give myself a reason.

"It's lucky you thought of saying that, because the painter was my father."

"That makes the picture indeed precious!" I exclaimed, laughing; and I may add that a part of my laughter came from my satisfaction in finding that I had been right in my theory of Miss Bordereau's origin. Aspern had of course met the young lady when he went to her father's studio as a sitter. I observed to Miss Bordereau that if she would entrust me with her property for twenty-four hours I should be happy to take advice upon it; but she made no answer to this save to slip it in silence into her pocket. This convinced me still more that she had no sincere intention of selling it during her lifetime, though she may have desired to satisfy herself as to the sum her niece, should she leave it to her, might expect eventually to obtain for it. "Well, at any rate I hope you will not offer it without giving me notice," I said as she remained irresponsive. "Remember that I am a possible purchaser."

"I should want your money first!" she returned with unexpected rudeness; and then, as if she bethought herself that I had just cause to complain of such an insinuation and wished to turn the matter off, asked abruptly what I talked about with her niece when I went out with her that way in the evening.

"You speak as if we had set up the habit," I replied. "Certainly I should be very glad if it were to become a habit. But in that case I should feel a still greater scruple at betraying a lady's confidence."

"Her confidence? Has she got confidence?"

"Here she is—she can tell you herself," I said; for Miss Tita now appeared on the threshold of the old woman's parlor. "Have you got confidence, Miss Tita? Your aunt wants very much to know."

"Not in her, not in her!" the younger lady declared, shaking her head with a dolefulness that was neither jocular not affected. "I don't know what to do with her; she has fits of horrid imprudence. She is so easily tired—and yet she has begun to roam—to drag herself about the house." And she stood looking down at her immemorial companion with a sort of helpless wonder, as if all their years of familiarity had not made her perversities, on occasion, any more easy to follow.

"I know what I'm about. I'm not losing my mind. I daresay you would like to think so," said Miss Bordereau with a cynical little sigh.

"I don't suppose you came out here yourself. Miss Tita must have had to lend you a hand," I interposed with a pacifying intention.

"Oh, she insisted that we should push her; and when she insists!" said Miss Tita in the same tone of apprehension; as if there were no knowing what service that she disapproved of her aunt might force her next to render.

"I have always got most things done I wanted, thank God! The people I have lived with have humored me," the old woman continued, speaking out of the gray ashes of her vanity.

"I suppose you mean that they have obeyed you."

"Well, whatever it is, when they like you."

"It's just because I like you that I want to resist," said Miss Tita with a nervous laugh.

"Oh, I suspect you'll bring Miss Bordereau upstairs next to pay me a visit," I went on; to which the old lady replied:

"Oh, no; I can keep an eye on you from here!"

"You are very tired; you will certainly be ill tonight!" cried Miss Tita.

"Nonsense, my dear; I feel better at this moment than I have done for a month. Tomorrow I shall come out again. I want to be where I can see this clever gentleman."

"Shouldn't you perhaps see me better in your sitting room?" I inquired.

"Don't you mean shouldn't you have a better chance at me?" she returned, fixing me a moment with her green shade.

"Ah, I haven't that anywhere! I look at you but I don't see you."

"You excite her dreadfully—and that is not good," said Miss Tita, giving me a reproachful, appealing look.

"I want to watch you—I want to watch you!" the old lady went on.

"Well then, let us spend as much of our time together as possible—I don't care where—and that will give you every facility."

"Oh, I've seen you enough for today. I'm satisfied. Now I'll go home." Miss Tita laid her hands on the back of her aunt's chair and began to push, but I begged her to let me take her place. "Oh, yes, you may move me this way—you shan't in any other!" Miss Bordereau exclaimed as she felt herself propelled firmly and easily over the smooth, hard floor. Before we reached the door of her own apartment she commanded me to stop, and she took a long, last look up and down the noble sala. "Oh, it's a magnificent house!" she murmured; after which I pushed her forward. When we had entered the parlor Miss Tita told me that she should now be able to manage, and at the same moment the little red-haired donna came to meet her mistress. Miss Tita's idea was evidently to get her aunt immediately back to bed. I confess that in spite of this urgency I was guilty of the indiscretion of lingering; it held me there to think that I was nearer the documents I coveted—that they were probably put away somewhere in the faded, unsociable room. The place had indeed a bareness which did not suggest hidden treasures; there were no dusky nooks nor curtained corners, no massive cabinets nor chests with iron bands. Moreover it was possible, it was perhaps even probable that the old lady had consigned her relics to her bedroom, to some battered box that was shoved under the bed, to the drawer of some lame dressing table, where they would be in the range of vision by the dim night lamp. Nonetheless I scrutinized every article of furniture, every conceivable cover for a hoard, and noticed that there were half a dozen things with drawers, and in particular a tall old secretary, with brass ornaments of the style of the Empire—a receptacle somewhat rickety but still capable of keeping a great many secrets. I don't know why this article fascinated me so, inasmuch as I certainly had no definite purpose of breaking into it; but I stared at it so hard that Miss Tita noticed me and changed color. Her doing this made me think I was right and that wherever they might have been before the Aspern papers at that moment languished behind the peevish little lock of the secretary. it was hard to remove my eyes from the dull mahogany front when I reflected that a simple panel divided me from the goal of my hopes; but I remembered my prudence and with an effort took leave of Miss Bordereau. To make the effort graceful I said to her that I should certainly bring her an opinion about the little picture.

"The little picture?" Miss Tita asked, surprised.

"What do YOU know about it, my dear?" the old woman demanded. "You needn't mind. I have fixed my price."

"And what may that be?"

"A thousand pounds."

"Oh Lord!" cried poor Miss Tita irrepressibly.

"Is that what she talks to you about?" said Miss Bordereau.

"Imagine your aunt's wanting to know!" I had to separate from Miss Tita with only those words, though I should have liked immensely to add, "For heaven's sake meet me tonight in the garden!"

VIII

As it turned out the precaution had not been needed, for three hours later, just as I had finished my dinner, Miss Bordereau's niece appeared, unannounced, in the open doorway of the room in which my simple repasts were served. I remember well that I felt no surprise at seeing her; which is not a proof that I did not believe in her timidity. It was immense, but in a case in which there was a particular reason for boldness it never would have prevented her from running up to my rooms. I saw that she was now quite full of a particular reason; it threw her forward—made her seize me, as I rose to meet her, by the arm.

"My aunt is very ill; I think she is dying!"

"Never in the world," I answered bitterly. "Don't you be afraid!"

"Do go for a doctor—do, do! Olimpia is gone for the one we always have, but she doesn't come back; I don't know what has happened to her. I told her that if he was not at home she was to follow him where he had gone; but apparently she is following him all over Venice. I don't know what to do—she looks so as if she were sinking."

"May I see her, may I judge?" I asked. "Of course I shall be delighted to bring someone; but hadn't we better send my man instead, so that I may stay with you?"

Miss Tita assented to this and I dispatched my servant for the best doctor in the neighborhood. I hurried downstairs with her, and on the way she told me that an hour after I quitted them in the afternoon Miss Bordereau had had an attack of "oppression," a terrible difficulty in breathing. This had subsided but had left her so exhausted that she did not come up: she seemed all gone. I repeated that she was not gone, that she would not go yet; whereupon Miss Tita gave me a sharper sidelong glance than she had ever directed at me and said, "Really, what do you mean? I suppose you don't accuse her of making believe!" I forget what reply I made to this, but I grant that in my heart I thought the old woman capable of any weird maneuver. Miss Tita wanted to know what I had done to her; her aunt had told her that I had made her so angry. I declared I had done nothing—I had been exceedingly careful; to which my companion rejoined that Miss Bordereau had assured her she had had a scene with me—a scene that had upset her. I answered with some resentment that it was a scene of her own making—that I couldn't think what she was angry with me for unless for not seeing my way to give a thousand pounds for the portrait of Jeffrey Aspern. "And did she show you that? Oh, gracious—oh, deary me!" groaned Miss Tita, who appeared to feel that the situation was passing out of her control and that the elements of her fate were thickening around her. I said that I would give anything to possess it, yet that I had not a thousand pounds; but I stopped when we came to the door of Miss Bordereau's room. I had an immense curiosity to pass it, but I thought it my duty to represent to Miss Tita that if I made the invalid angry she ought perhaps to be spared the sight of me. "The sight of you? Do you think she can *see*?" my companion demanded almost with indignation. I did think so but forebore to say it, and I softly followed my conductress.

I remember that what I said to her as I stood for a moment beside the old woman's bed was, "Does she never show you her eyes then? Have you never seen them?" Miss Bordereau had been divested of her green shade, but (it was not my fortune to behold Juliana in her nightcap) the upper half of her face was covered by the fall of a piece of dingy lacelike muslin, a sort of extemporized hood which, wound round her head, descended to the end of her nose, leaving nothing visible but her white withered cheeks and puckered mouth, closed tightly and, as it were consciously. Miss Tita gave me a glance of surprise, evidently not seeing a reason for my impatience. "You mean that she always wears something? She does it to preserve them."

"Because they are so fine?"

"Oh, today, today!" And Miss Tita shook her head, speaking very low. "But they used to be magnificent!"

"Yes indeed, we have Aspern's word for that." And as I looked again at the old woman's wrappings I could imagine that she had not wished to allow people a reason to say that the great poet had overdone it. But I did not waste my time in considering Miss Bordereau, in whom the appearance of respiration was so slight as to suggest that no human attention could ever help her more. I turned my eyes all over the room, rummaging with them the closets, the chests of drawers, the tables. Miss Tita met them quickly and read, I think, what was in them; but she did not answer it, turning away restlessly, anxiously, so that I felt rebuked, with reason, for a preoccupation that was almost profane in the presence of our dying companion. All the same I took another look, endeavoring to pick out mentally the place to try first, for a person who should wish to put his hand on Miss Bordereau's papers directly after her death. The room was a dire confusion; it looked like the room of an old actress. There were clothes hanging over chairs, odd-looking shabby bundles here and there, and various pasteboard boxes piled together, battered, bulging, and discolored, which might have been fifty years old. Miss Tita after a moment noticed the direction of my eyes again and, as if she guessed how I judged the air of the place (forgetting I had no business to judge it at all), said, perhaps to defend herself from the imputation of complicity in such untidiness:

"She likes it this way; we can't move things. There are old bandboxes she has had most of her life." Then she added, half taking pity on my real thought, "Those things were *there*." And she pointed to a small, low trunk which stood under a sofa where there was just room for it. It appeared to be a queer, superannuated coffer, of painted wood, with elaborate handles and shriveled straps and with the color (it had last been endued with a coat of light green) much rubbed off. It evidently had traveled with Juliana in the olden time—in the days of her adventures, which it had shared. It would have made a strange figure arriving at a modern hotel.

"*Were* there—they aren't now?" I asked, startled by Miss Tita's implication.

She was going to answer, but at that moment the doctor came in—the doctor whom the little maid had been sent to fetch and whom she had at last overtaken. My servant, going on his own errand, had met her with her companion in tow, and in the sociable Venetian spirit, retracing his steps with them, had also come up to the threshold of Miss Bordereau's room, where I saw him peeping over the doctor's shoulder. I motioned him away the more instantly that the sight of his prying face reminded me that I myself had almost as little to do there—an admonition confirmed by the sharp way the little doctor looked at me, appearing to take me for a rival who had the field before him. He was a short, fat, brisk gentleman who wore the tall hat of his profession and seemed to look at everything but his patient. He looked particularly at me, as if it struck him that I should be better for a dose, so that I bowed to him and left him with the women, going down to smoke a cigar in the garden. I was nervous; I could not go further; I could not leave the place. I don't know exactly what I thought might happen, but it seemed to me important to be there. I wandered about in the alleys—the warm night had come on—smoking cigar after cigar and looking at the light in Miss Bordereau's windows. They were open now, I could see; the situation was different. Sometimes the light moved, but not quickly; it did not suggest the hurry of a crisis. Was the old woman dying, or was she already dead? Had the doctor said that there was nothing to be done at her tremendous age but to let her quietly pass away; or had he simply announced with a look a little more conventional that the end of the end had come? Were the other two women moving about to perform the offices that follow in such a case? It made me uneasy not to be nearer, as if I thought the doctor himself might carry away the papers with him. I bit my cigar hard as it came over me again that perhaps there were now no papers to carry!

I wandered about for an hour—for an hour and a half. I looked out for Miss Tita at one of the windows, having a vague idea that she might come there to give me some sign. Would she not see the red tip of my cigar moving about in the dark and feel that I wanted eminently to know what the doctor had said? I am afraid it is a proof my anxieties had made me gross that I should have taken in some degree for granted that at such an hour, in the midst of the greatest change that could take place in her life, they were uppermost also in Miss Tita's mind. My servant came down and spoke to me; he knew nothing save that the doctor had gone after a visit of half an hour. If he had stayed half an hour then Miss Bordereau was still alive: it could not have taken so much time as that to enunciate the contrary. I sent the man out of the house; there were moments when the sense of his curiosity annoyed me, and this was one of them. *he* had been watching my cigar tip from an upper window, if Miss Tita had not; he could not know what I was after and I could not tell him, though I was conscious he had fantastic private theories about me which he thought fine and which I, had I known them, should have thought offensive.

I went upstairs at last but I ascended no higher than the sala. The door of Miss Bordereau's apartment was open, showing from the parlor the dimness of a poor candle. I went toward it with a light tread, and at the same moment Miss Tita appeared and stood looking at me as I approached. "She's better—she's better," she said, even before I had asked. "The doctor has given her something; she woke up, came back to life while he was there. He says there is no immediate danger."

"No immediate danger? Surely he thinks her condition strange!"

"Yes, because she had been excited. That affects her dreadfully."

"It will do so again then, because she excites herself. She did so this afternoon."

"Yes; she mustn't come out any more," said Miss Tita, with one of her lapses into a deeper placidity.

"What is the use of making such a remark as that if you begin to rattle her about again the first time she bids you?"

"I won't—I won't do it any more."

"You must learn to resist her," I went on.

"Oh, yes, I shall; I shall do so better if you tell me it's right."

"You mustn't do it for me; you must do it for yourself. It all comes back to you, if you are frightened."

"Well, I am not frightened now," said Miss Tita cheerfully. "She is very quiet."

"Is she conscious again—does she speak?"

"No, she doesn't speak, but she takes my hand. She holds it fast."

"Yes," I rejoined, "I can see what force she still has by the way she grabbed that picture this afternoon. But if she holds you fast how comes it that you are here?"

Miss Tita hesitated a moment; though her face was in deep shadow (she had her back to the light in the parlor and I had put down my own candle far off, near the door of the sala), I thought I saw her smile ingenuously. "I came on purpose—I heard your step."

"Why, I came on tiptoe, as inaudibly as possible."

"Well, I heard you," said Miss Tita.

"And is your aunt alone now?"

"Oh, no; Olimpia is sitting there."

On my side I hesitated. "Shall we then step in there?" And I nodded at the parlor; I wanted more and more to be on the spot.

"We can't talk there—she will hear us."

I was on the point of replying that in that case we would sit silent, but I was too conscious that this would not do, as there was something I desired immensely to ask her. So I proposed that we should walk a little in the sala, keeping more at the other end, where we should not disturb the old lady. Miss Tita assented unconditionally; the doctor was coming again, she said, and she would be there to meet him at the door. We strolled through the fine superfluous hall, where on the marble floor—particularly as at first we said nothing—our footsteps were more audible than I had expected. When we reached the other end—the wide window, inveterately closed, connecting with the balcony that overhung the canal—I suggested that we should remain there, as she would see the doctor arrive still better. I opened the window and we passed out on the balcony. The air of the canal seemed even heavier, hotter than that of the sala. The place was hushed and void; the quiet neighborhood had gone to sleep. A lamp, here and there, over the narrow black water, glimmered in double; the voice of a man going homeward singing, with his jacket on his shoulder and his hat on his ear, came to us from a distance. This did not prevent the scene from being very comme il faut, as Miss Bordereau had called it the first time I saw her. Presently a gondola passed along the canal with its slow rhythmical plash, and as we listened we watched it in silence. It did not stop, it did not carry the doctor; and after it had gone on I said to Miss Tita:

"And where are they now—the things that were in the trunk?"

"In the trunk?"

"That green box you pointed out to me in her room. You said her papers had been there; you seemed to imply that she had transferred them."

"Oh, yes; they are not in the trunk," said Miss Tita.

"May I ask if you have looked?"

"Yes, I have looked—for you."

"How for me, dear Miss Tita? Do you mean you would have given them to me if you had found them?" I asked, almost trembling.

She delayed to reply and I waited. Suddenly she broke out, "I don't know what I would do—what I wouldn't!"

"Would you look again—somewhere else?"

She had spoken with a strange unexpected emotion, and she went on in the same tone: "I can't—I can't—while she lies there. It isn't decent."

"No, it isn't decent," I replied gravely. "Let the poor lady rest in peace." And the words, on my lips, were not hypocritical, for I felt reprimanded and shamed.

Miss Tita added in a moment, as if she had guessed this and were sorry for me, but at the same time wished to explain that I did drive her on or at least did insist too much: "I can't deceive her that way. I can't deceive her—perhaps on her deathbed."

"Heaven forbid I should ask you, though I have been guilty myself!"

"You have been guilty?"

"I have sailed under false colors." I felt now as if I must tell her that I had given her an invented name, on account of my fear that her aunt would have heard of me and would refuse to take me in. I explained this and also that I had really been a party to the letter written to them by John Cumnor months before.

She listened with great attention, looking at me with parted lips, and when I had made my confession she said, "Then your real name—what is it?" She repeated it over twice when I had told her, accompanying it with the exclamation "Gracious, gracious!" Then she added, "I like your own best."

"So do I," I said, laughing. "Ouf! it's a relief to get rid of the other."

"So it was a regular plot—a kind of conspiracy?"

"Oh, a conspiracy—we were only two," I replied, leaving out Mrs. Prest of course.

She hesitated; I thought she was perhaps going to say that we had been very base. But she remarked after a moment, in a candid, wondering way, "How much you must want them!"

"Oh, I do, passionately!" I conceded, smiling. And this chance made me go on, forgetting my compunction of a moment before. "How can she possibly have changed their place herself? How can she walk? How can she arrive at that sort of muscular exertion? How can she lift and carry things?"

"Oh, when one wants and when one has so much will!" said Miss Tita, as if she had thought over my question already herself and had simply had no choice but that answer—the idea that in the dead of night, or at some moment when the coast was clear, the old woman had been capable of a miraculous effort.

"Have you questioned Olimpia? Hasn't she helped her—hasn't she done it for her?" I asked; to which Miss Tita replied promptly and positively that their servant had had nothing to do with the matter, though without admitting definitely that she had spoken to her. It was as if she were a little shy, a little ashamed now of letting me see how much she had entered into my uneasiness and had me on her mind. Suddenly she said to me, without any immediate relevance:

"I feel as if you were a new person, now that you have got a new name."

"It isn't a new one; it is a very good old one, thank heaven!"

She looked at me a moment. "I do like it better."

"Oh, if you didn't I would almost go on with the other!"

"Would you really?"

I laughed again, but for all answer to this inquiry I said, "Of course if she can rummage about that way she can perfectly have burnt them."

"You must wait—you must wait," Miss Tita moralized mournfully; and her tone ministered little to my patience, for it seemed after all to accept that wretched possibility. I would teach myself to wait, I declared nevertheless; because in the first place I could not do otherwise and in the second I had her promise, given me the other night, that she would help me.

"Of course if the papers are gone that's no use," she said; not as if she wished to recede, but only to be conscientious.

"Naturally. But if you could only find out!" I groaned, quivering again.

"I thought you said you would wait."

"Oh, you mean wait even for that?"

"For what then?"

"Oh, nothing," I replied, rather foolishly, being ashamed to tell her what had been implied in my submission to delay—the idea that she would do more than merely find out. I know not whether she guessed this; at all events she appeared to become aware of the necessity for being a little more rigid.

"I didn't promise to deceive, did I? I don't think I did."

"It doesn't much matter whether you did or not, for you couldn't!"

I don't think Miss Tita would have contested this event had she not been diverted by our seeing the doctor's gondola shoot into the little canal and approach the house. I noted that he came as fast as if he believed that Miss Bordereau was still in danger. We looked down at him while he disembarked and then went back into the sala to meet him. When he came up however I naturally left Miss Tita to go off with him alone, only asking her leave to come back later for news.

I went out of the house and took a long walk, as far as the Piazza, where my restlessness declined to quit me. I was unable to sit down (it was very late now but there were people still at the little tables in front of the cafes); I could only walk round and round, and I did so half a dozen times. I was uncomfortable, but it gave me a certain pleasure to have told Miss Tita who I really was. At last I took my way home again, slowly getting all but inextricably lost, as I did whenever I went out in Venice: so that it was considerably past midnight when I reached my door. The sala, upstairs, was as dark as usual and my lamp as I crossed it found nothing satisfactory to show me. I was disappointed, for I had notified Miss Tita that I would come back for a report, and I thought she might have left a light there as a sign. The door of the ladies' apartment was closed; which seemed an intimation that my faltering friend had gone to bed, tired of waiting for me. I stood in the middle of the place, considering, hoping she would hear me and perhaps peep out, saying to myself too that she would never go to bed with her aunt in a state so critical; she would sit up and watch—she would be in a chair, in her dressing gown. I went nearer the door; I stopped there and listened. I heard nothing at all and at last I tapped gently. No answer came and after another minute I turned the handle. There was no light in the room; this ought to have prevented me from going in, but it had no such effect. If I have candidly narrated the importunities, the indelicacies, of which my desire to possess myself of Jeffrey Aspern's papers had rendered me capable I need not shrink from confessing this last indiscretion. I think it was the worst thing I did; yet there were extenuating circumstances. I was deeply though doubtless not disinterestedly anxious for more news of the old lady, and Miss Tita had accepted from me, as it were, a rendezvous which it might have been a point of honor with me to keep. It may be said that her leaving the place dark was a positive sign that she released me, and to this I can only reply that I desired not to be released.

The door of Miss Bordereau's room was open and I could see beyond it the faintness of a taper. There was no sound—my footstep caused no one to stir. I came further into the room; I lingered there with my lamp in my hand. I wanted to give Miss Tita a chance to come to me if she were with her aunt, as she must be. I made no noise to call her; I only waited to see if she would not notice my light. She did not, and I explained this (I found afterward I was right) by the idea that she had fallen asleep. If she had fallen asleep her aunt was not on her mind, and my explanation ought to have led me to go out as I had come. I must repeat again that it did not, for I found myself at the same moment thinking of something else. I had no definite purpose, no bad intention, but I felt myself held to the spot by an acute, though absurd, sense of opportunity. For what I could not have said, inasmuch as it was not in my mind that I might commit a theft. Even if it had been I was confronted with the evident fact that Miss Bordereau did not leave her secretary, her cupboard, and the drawers of her tables gaping. I had no keys, no tools, and no ambition to smash her furniture. Nonetheless it came to me that I was now, perhaps alone, unmolested, at the hour of temptation and secrecy, nearer to the tormenting treasure than I had ever been. I held up my lamp, let the light play on the different objects as if it could tell me something. Still there came no movement from the other room. If Miss Tita was sleeping she was sleeping sound. Was she doing so—generous creature—on purpose to leave me the field? Did she know I was there and was she just keeping quiet to see what I would do—what I *could* do? But what could I do, when it came to that? She herself knew even better than I how little.

I stopped in front of the secretary, looking at it very idiotically; for what had it to say to me after all? In the first place it was locked, and in the second it almost surely contained nothing in which I was interested. Ten to one the papers had been destroyed; and even if they had not been destroyed the old woman would not have put them in such a place as that after removing them from the green trunk—would not have transferred them, if she had the idea of their safety on her brain, from the better hiding place to the worse. The secretary was more conspicuous, more accessible in a room in which she could no longer mount guard. It opened with a key, but there was a little brass handle, like a button, as well; I saw this as I played my lamp over it. I did something more than this at that moment: I caught a glimpse of the possibility that Miss Tita wished me really to understand. If she did not wish me to understand, if she wished me to keep away, why had she not locked the door of communication between the sitting room and the sala? That would have been a definite sign that I was to leave them alone. If I did not leave them alone she meant me to come for a purpose—a purpose now indicated by the quick, fantastic idea that to oblige me she had unlocked the secretary. She had not left the key, but the lid would probably move if I touched the button. This theory fascinated me, and I bent over very close to judge. I did not propose to do anything, not even—not in the least—to let down the lid; I only wanted to test my theory, to see if the cover *would* move. I touched the button with my hand—a mere touch would tell me; and as I did so (it is embarrassing for me to relate it), I looked over my shoulder. It was a chance, an instinct, for I had not heard anything. I almost let my luminary drop and certainly I stepped back, straightening myself up at what I saw. Miss Bordereau stood there in her nightdress, in the doorway of her room, watching me; her hands were raised, she had lifted the everlasting curtain that covered half her face, and for the first, the last, the only time I beheld her extraordinary eyes. They glared at me, they made me horribly ashamed. I never shall forget her strange little bent white tottering figure, with its lifted head, her attitude, her expression; neither shall I forget the tone in which as I turned, looking at her, she hissed out passionately, furiously:

"Ah, you publishing scoundrel!"

I know not what I stammered, to excuse myself, to explain; but I went toward her, to tell her I meant no harm. She waved me off with her old hands, retreating before me in horror; and the next thing I knew she had fallen back with a quick spasm, as if death had descended on her, into Miss Tita's arms.

IX

I left Venice the next morning, as soon as I learned that the old lady had not succumbed, as I feared at the moment, to the shock I had given her—the shock I may also say she had given me. How in the world could I have supposed her capable of getting out of bed by herself? I failed to see Miss Tita before going; I only saw the donna, whom I entrusted with a note for her younger mistress. In this note I mentioned that I should be absent but for a few days. I went to Treviso, to Bassano, to Castelfranco; I took walks and drives and looked at musty old churches with ill-lighted pictures and spent hours seated smoking at the doors of cafes, where there were flies and yellow curtains, on the shady side of sleepy little squares. In spite of these pastimes, which were mechanical and perfunctory, I scantily enjoyed my journey: there was too strong a taste of the disagreeable in my life. I had been devilish awkward, as the young men say, to be found by Miss Bordereau in the dead of night examining the attachment of her bureau; and it had not been less so to have to believe for a good many hours afterward that it was highly probable I had killed her. In writing to Miss Tita I attempted to minimize these irregularities; but as she gave me no word of answer I could not know what impression I made upon her. It rankled in my mind that I had been called a publishing scoundrel, for certainly I did publish and certainly I had not been very delicate. There was a moment when I stood convinced that the only way to make up for this latter fault was to take myself away altogether on the instant; to sacrifice my hopes and relieve the two poor women forever of the oppression of my intercourse. Then I reflected that I had better try a short absence first, for I must already have had a sense (unexpressed and dim) that in disappearing completely it would not be merely my own hopes that I should condemn to extinction. It would perhaps be sufficient if I stayed away long enough to give the elder lady time to think she was rid of me. That she would wish to be rid of me after this (if I was not rid of her) was now not to be doubted: that nocturnal scene would have cured her of the disposition to put up with my company for the sake of my dollars. I said to myself that after all I could not abandon Miss Tita, and I continued to say this even while I observed that she quite failed to comply with my earnest request (I had given her two or three addresses, at little towns, post restante) that she would let me know how she was getting on. I would have made my servant write to me but that he was unable to manage a pen. It struck me there was a kind of scorn in Miss Tita's silence (little disdainful as she had ever been), so that I was uncomfortable and sore. I had scruples about going back and yet I had others about not doing so, for I wanted to put myself on a better footing. The end of it was that I did return to Venice on the twelfth day; and as my gondola gently bumped against Miss Bordereau's steps a certain palpitation of suspense told me that I had done myself a violence in holding off so long.

I had faced about so abruptly that I had not telegraphed to my servant. He was therefore not at the station to meet me, but he poked out his head from an upper window when I reached the house. "They have put her into the earth, la vecchia," he said to me in the lower hall, while he shouldered my valise; and he grinned and almost winked, as if he knew I should be pleased at the news.

"She's dead!" I exclaimed, giving him a very different look.

"So it appears, since they have buried her."

"It's all over? When was the funeral?"

"The other yesterday. But a funeral you could scarcely call it, signore; it was a dull little passeggio of two gondolas. Poveretta!" the man continued, referring apparently to Miss Tita. His conception of funerals was apparently that they were mainly to amuse the living.

I wanted to know about Miss Tita—how she was and where she was—but I asked him no more questions till we had got upstairs. Now that the fact had met me I took a bad view of it, especially of the idea that poor Miss Tita had had to manage by herself after the end. What did she know about arrangements, about the steps to take in such a case? Poveretta indeed! I could only hope that the doctor had given her assistance and that she had not been neglected by the old friends of whom she had told me, the little band of the faithful whose fidelity consisted in coming to the house once a year. I elicited from my servant that two old ladies and an old gentleman had in fact rallied round Miss Tita and had supported her (they had come for her in a gondola of their own) during the journey to the cemetery, the little red-walled island of tombs which lies to the north of the town, on the way to Murano. It appeared from these circumstances that the Misses Bordereau were Catholics, a discovery I had never made, as the old woman could not go to church and her niece, so far as I perceived, either did not or went only to early mass in the parish, before I was stirring. Certainly even the priests respected their seclusion; I had never caught the whisk of the curato's skirt. That evening, an hour later, I sent my servant down with five words written on a card, to ask Miss Tita if she would see me for a few moments. She was not in the house, where he had sought her, he told me when he came back, but in the garden walking about to refresh herself and gathering flowers. He had found her there and she would be very happy to see me.

I went down and passed half an hour with poor Miss Tita. She had always had a look of musty mourning (as if she were wearing out old robes of sorrow that would not come to an end), and in this respect there was no appreciable change in her appearance. But she evidently had been crying, crying a great deal—simply, satisfyingly, refreshingly, with a sort of primitive, retarded sense of loneliness and violence. But she had none of the formalism or the self-consciousness of grief, and I was almost surprised to see her standing there in the first dusk with her hands full of flowers, smiling at me with her reddened eyes. Her white face, in the frame of her mantilla, looked longer, leaner than usual. I had had an idea that she would be a good deal disgusted with me—would consider that I ought to have been on the spot to advise her, to help her; and, though I was sure there was no rancor in her composition and no great conviction of the importance of her affairs, I had prepared myself for a difference in her manner, for some little injured look, half-familiar, half-estranged, which should say to my conscience, "Well, you are a nice person to have professed things!" But historic truth compels me to declare that Tita Bordereau's countenance expressed unqualified pleasure in seeing her late aunt's lodger. That touched him extremely, and he thought it simplified his situation until he found it did not. I was as kind to her that evening as I knew how to be, and I walked about the garden with her for half an hour. There was no explanation of any sort between us; I did not ask her why she had not answered my letter. Still less did I repeat what I had said to her in that communication; if she chose to let me suppose that she had forgotten the position in which Miss Bordereau surprised me that night and the effect of the discovery on the old woman I was quite willing to take it that way: I was grateful to her for not treating me as if I had killed her aunt.

We strolled and strolled and really not much passed between us save the recognition of her bereavement, conveyed in my manner and in a visible air that she had of depending on me now, since I let her see that I took an interest in her. Miss Tita had none of the pride that makes a person wish to preserve the look of independence; she did not in the least pretend that she knew at present what would become of her. I forebore to touch particularly on that, however, for I certainly was not prepared to say that I would take charge of her. I was cautious; not ignobly, I think, for I felt that her knowledge of life was so small that in her unsophisticated vision there would be no reason why—since I seemed to pity her—I should not look after her. She told me how her aunt had died, very peacefully at the last, and how everything had been done afterward by the care of her good friends (fortunately, thanks to me, she said, smiling, there was money in the house; and she repeated that when once the Italians like you they are your friends for life); and when we had gone into this she asked me about my giro, my impressions, the places I had seen. I told her what I could, making it up partly, I am afraid, as in my depression I had not seen much; and after she had heard me she exclaimed, quite as if she had forgotten her aunt and her sorrow, "Dear, dear, how much I should like to do such things—to take a little journey!" It came over me for the moment that I ought to propose some tour, say I would take her anywhere she liked; and I remarked at any rate that some excursion—to give her a change—might be managed: we would think of it, talk it over. I said never a word to her about the Aspern documents; asked no questions as to what she had ascertained or what had otherwise happened with regard to them before Miss Bordereau's death. It was not that I was not on pins and needles to know, but that I thought it more decent not to betray my anxiety so soon after the catastrophe. I hoped she herself would say something, but she never glanced that way, and I thought this natural at the time. Later however, that night, it occurred to me that her silence was somewhat strange; for if she had talked of my movements, of anything so detached as the Giorgione at Castelfranco, she might have alluded to what she could easily remember was in my mind. It was not to be supposed that the emotion produced by her aunt's death had blotted out the recollection that I was interested in that lady's relics, and I fidgeted afterward as it came to me that her reticence might very possibly mean simply that nothing had been found. We separated in the garden (it was she who said she must go in); now that she was alone in the rooms I felt that (judged, at any rate, by Venetian ideas) I was on rather a different footing in regard to visiting her there. As I shook hands with her for goodnight I asked her if she had any general plan—had thought over what she had better do. "Oh, yes, oh, yes, but I haven't settled anything yet," she replied quite cheerfully. Was her cheerfulness explained by the impression that I would settle for her?

I was glad the next morning that we had neglected practical questions, for this gave me a pretext for seeing her again immediately. There was a very practical question to be touched upon. I owed it to her to let her know formally that of course I did not expect her to keep me on as a lodger, and also to show some interest in her own tenure, what she might have on her hands in the way of a lease. But I was not destined, as it happened, to converse with her for more than an instant on either of these points. I sent her no message; I simply went down to the sala and walked to and fro there. I knew she would come out; she would very soon discover I was there. Somehow I preferred not to be shut up with her; gardens and big halls seemed better places to talk. It was a splendid morning, with something in the air that told of the waning of the long Venetian summer; a freshness from the sea which stirred the flowers in the garden and made a pleasant draught in the house, less shuttered and darkened now than when the old woman was alive. It was the beginning of autumn, of the end of the golden months. With this it was the end of my experiment—or would be in the course of half an hour, when I should really have learned that the papers had been reduced to ashes. After that there would be nothing left for me but to go to the station; for seriously (and as it struck me in the morning light) I could not linger there to act as guardian to a piece of middle-aged female helplessness. If she had not saved the papers wherein should I be indebted to her? I think I winced a little as I asked myself how much, if she *had* saved them, I should have to recognize and, as it were, to reward such a courtesy. Might not that circumstance after all saddle me with a guardianship? If this idea did not make me more uncomfortable as I walked up and down it was because I was convinced I had nothing to look to. If the old woman had not destroyed everything before she pounced upon me in the parlor she had done so afterward.

It took Miss Tita rather longer than I had expected to guess that I was there; but when at last she came out she looked at me without surprise. I said to her that I had been waiting for her, and she asked why I had not let her know. I was glad the next day that I had checked myself before remarking that I had wished to see if a friendly intuition would not tell her: it became a satisfaction to me that I had not indulged in that rather tender joke. What I did say was virtually the truth—that I was too nervous, since I expected her now to settle my fate.

"Your fate?" said Miss Tita, giving me a queer look; and as she spoke I noticed a rare change in her. She was different from what she had been the evening before—less natural, less quiet. She had been crying the day before and she was not crying now, and yet she struck me as less confident. It was as if something had happened to her during the night, or at least as if she had thought of something that troubled her—something in particular that affected her relations with me, made them more embarrassing and complicated. Had she simply perceived that her aunt's not being there now altered my position?

"I mean about our papers. *Are* there any? You must know now."

"Yes, there are a great many; more than I supposed." I was struck with the way her voice trembled as she told me this.

"Do you mean that you have got them in there—and that I may see them?"

"I don't think you can see them," said Miss Tita with an extraordinary expression of entreaty in her eyes, as if the dearest hope she had in the world now was that I would not take them from her. But how could she expect me to make such a sacrifice as that after all that had passed between us? What had I come back to Venice for but to see them, to take them? My delight in learning they were still in existence was such that if the poor woman had gone down on her knees to beseech me never to mention them again I would have treated the proceeding as a bad joke. "I have got them but I can't show them," she added.

"Not even to me? Ah, Miss Tita!" I groaned, with a voice of infinite remonstrance and reproach.

She colored, and the tears came back to her eyes; I saw that it cost her a kind of anguish to take such a stand but that a dreadful sense of duty had descended upon her. It made me quite sick to find myself confronted with that particular obstacle; all the more that it appeared to me I had been extremely encouraged to leave it out of account. I almost considered that Miss Tita had assured me that if she had no greater hindrance than that—! "You don't mean to say you made her a deathbed promise? It was precisely against your doing anything of that sort that I thought I was safe. Oh, I would rather she had burned the papers outright than that!"

"No, it isn't a promise," said Miss Tita.

"Pray what is it then?"

She hesitated and then she said, "She tried to burn them, but I prevented it. She had hid them in her bed."

"In her bed?"

"Between the mattresses. That's where she put them when she took them out of the trunk. I can't understand how she did it, because Olimpia didn't help her. She tells me so, and I believe her. My aunt only told her afterward, so that she shouldn't touch the bed—anything but the sheets. So it was badly made," added Miss Tita simply.

"I should think so! And how did she try to burn them?"

"She didn't try much; she was too weak, those last days. But she told me—she charged me. Oh, it was terrible! She couldn't speak after that night; she could only make signs."

"And what did you do?"

"I took them away. I locked them up."

"In the secretary?"

"Yes, in the secretary," said Miss Tita, reddening again.

"Did you tell her you would burn them?"

"No, I didn't—on purpose."

"On purpose to gratify me?"

"Yes, only for that."

"And what good will you have done me if after all you won't show them?"

"Oh, none; I know that—I know that."

"And did she believe you had destroyed them?"

"I don't know what she believed at the last. I couldn't tell—she was too far gone."

"Then if there was no promise and no assurance I can't see what ties you."

"Oh, she hated it so—she hated it so! She was so jealous. But here's the portrait—you may have that," Miss Tita announced, taking the little picture, wrapped up in the same manner in which her aunt had wrapped it, out of her pocket.

"I may have it—do you mean you give it to me?" I questioned, staring, as it passed into my hand.

"Oh, yes."

"But it's worth money—a large sum."

"Well!" said Miss Tita, still with her strange look.

I did not know what to make of it, for it could scarcely mean that she wanted to bargain like her aunt. She spoke as if she wished to make me a present. "I can't take it from you as a gift," I said, "and yet I can't afford to pay you for it according to the ideas Miss Bordereau had of its value. She rated it at a thousand pounds."

"Couldn't we sell it?" asked Miss Tita.

"God forbid! I prefer the picture to the money."

"Well then keep it."

"You are very generous."

"So are you."

"I don't know why you should think so," I replied; and this was a truthful speech, for the singular creature appeared to have some very fine reference in her mind, which I did not in the least seize.

"Well, you have made a great difference for me," said Miss Tita.

I looked at Jeffrey Aspern's face in the little picture, partly in order not to look at that of my interlocutress, which had begun to trouble me, even to frighten me a little—it was so self-conscious, so unnatural. I made no answer to this last declaration; I only privately consulted Jeffrey Aspern's delightful eyes with my own (they were so young and brilliant, and yet so wise, so full of vision); I asked him what on earth was the matter with Miss Tita. He seemed to smile at me with friendly mockery, as if he were amused at my case. I had got into a pickle for him—as if he needed it! He was unsatisfactory, for the only moment since I had known him. Nevertheless, now that I held the little picture in my hand I felt that it would be a precious possession. "Is this a bribe to make me give up the papers?" I demanded in a moment, perversely. "Much as I value it, if I were to be obliged to choose, the papers are what I should prefer. Ah, but ever so much!"

"How can you choose—how can you choose?" Miss Tita asked, slowly, lamentably.

"I see! Of course there is nothing to be said, if you regard the interdiction that rests upon you as quite insurmountable. In this case it must seem to you that to part with them would be an impiety of the worst kind, a simple sacrilege!"

Miss Tita shook her head, full of her dolefulness. "You would understand if you had known her. I'm afraid," she quavered suddenly—"I'm afraid! She was terrible when she was angry."

"Yes, I saw something of that, that night. She was terrible. Then I saw her eyes. Lord, they were fine!"

"I see them—they stare at me in the dark!" said Miss Tita.

"You are nervous, with all you have been through."

"Oh, yes, very—very!"

"You mustn't mind; that will pass away," I said, kindly. Then I added, resignedly, for it really seemed to me that I must accept the situation, "Well, so it is, and it can't be helped. I must renounce." Miss Tita, at this, looking at me, gave a low, soft moan, and I went on: "I only wish to heaven she had destroyed them; then there would be nothing more to say. And I can't understand why, with her ideas, she didn't."

"Oh, she lived on them!" said Miss Tita.

"You can imagine whether that makes me want less to see them," I answered, smiling. "But don't let me stand here as if I had it in my soul to tempt you to do anything base. Naturally you will understand if I give up my rooms. I leave Venice immediately."

And I took up my hat, which I had placed on a chair. We were still there rather awkwardly, on our feet, in the middle of the sala. She had left the door of the apartments open behind her but she had not led me that way.

A kind of spasm came into her face as she saw me take my hat. "Immediately—do you mean today?" The tone of the words was tragical—they were a cry of desolation.

"Oh, no; not so long as I can be of the least service to you."

"Well, just a day or two more—just two or three days," she panted. Then controlling herself, she added in another manner, "She wanted to say something to me—the last day—something very particular, but she couldn't."

"Something very particular?"

"Something more about the papers."

"And did you guess—have you any idea?"

"No, I have thought—but I don't know. I have thought all kinds of things."

"And for instance?"

"Well, that if you were a relation it would be different."

"If I were a relation?"

"If you were not a stranger. Then it would be the same for you as for me. Anything that is mine—would be yours, and you could do what you like. I couldn't prevent you—and you would have no responsibility."

She brought out this droll explanation with a little nervous rush, as if she were speaking words she had got by heart. They gave me an impression of subtlety and at first I failed to follow. But after a moment her face helped me to see further, and then a light came into my mind. It was embarrassing, and I bent my head over Jeffrey Aspern's portrait. What an odd expression was in his face! "Get out of it as you can, my dear fellow!" I put the picture into the pocket of my coat and said to Miss Tita, "Yes, I'll sell it for you. I shan't get a thousand pounds by any means, but I shall get something good."

She looked at me with tears in her eyes, but she seemed to try to smile as she remarked, "We can divide the money."

"No, no, it shall be all yours." Then I went on, "I think I know what your poor aunt wanted to say. She wanted to give directions that her papers should be buried with her."

Miss Tita appeared to consider this suggestion for a moment; after which she declared, with striking decision, "Oh no, she wouldn't have thought that safe!"

"It seems to me nothing could be safer."

"She had an idea that when people want to publish they are capable—" And she paused, blushing.

"Of violating a tomb? Mercy on us, what must she have thought of me!"

"She was not just, she was not generous!" Miss Tita cried with sudden passion.

The light that had come into my mind a moment before increased. "Ah, don't say that, for we *are* a dreadful race." Then I pursued, "If she left a will, that may give you some idea."

"I have found nothing of the sort—she destroyed it. She was very fond of me," Miss Tita added incongruously. "She wanted me to be happy. And if any person should be kind to me—she wanted to speak of that."

I was almost awestricken at the astuteness with which the good lady found herself inspired, transparent astuteness as it was and sewn, as the phrase is, with white thread. "Depend upon it she didn't want to make any provision that would be agreeable to me."

"No, not to you but to me. She knew I should like it if you could carry out your idea. Not because she cared for you but because she did think of me," Miss Tita went on with her unexpected, persuasive volubility. "You could see them—you could use them." She stopped, seeing that I perceived the sense of that conditional—stopped long enough for me to give some sign which I did not give. She must have been conscious, however, that though my face showed the greatest embarrassment that was ever painted on a human countenance it was not set as a stone, it was also full of compassion. It was a comfort to me a long time afterward to consider that she could not have seen in me the smallest symptom of disrespect. "I don't know what to do; I'm too tormented, I'm too ashamed!" she continued with vehemence. Then turning away from me and burying her face in her hands she burst into a flood of tears. If she did not know what to do it may be imagined whether I did any better. I stood there dumb, watching her while her sobs resounded in the great empty hall. In a moment she was facing me again, with her streaming eyes. "I would give you everything—and she would understand, where she is—she would forgive me!"

"Ah, Miss Tita—ah, Miss Tita," I stammered, for all reply. I did not know what to do, as I say, but at a venture I made a wild, vague movement in consequence of which I found myself at the door. I remember standing there and saying, "It wouldn't do—it wouldn't do!" pensively, awkwardly, grotesquely, while I looked away to the opposite end of the sala as if there were a beautiful view there. The next thing I remember is that I was downstairs and out of the house. My gondola was there and my gondolier, reclining on the cushions, sprang up as soon as he saw me. I jumped in and to his usual "Dove commanda?" I replied, in a tone that made him stare, "Anywhere, anywhere; out into the lagoon!"

He rowed me away and I sat there prostrate, groaning softly to myself, with my hat pulled over my face. What in the name of the preposterous did she mean if she did not mean to offer me her hand? That was the price—that was the price! And did she think I wanted it, poor deluded, infatuated, extravagant lady? My gondolier, behind me, must have seen my ears red as I wondered, sitting there under the fluttering tenda, with my hidden face, noticing nothing as we passed—wondered whether her delusion, her infatuation had been my own reckless work. Did she think I had made love to her, even to get the papers? I had not, I had not; I repeated that over to myself for an hour, for two hours, till I was wearied if not convinced. I don't know where my gondolier took me; we floated aimlessly about in the lagoon, with slow, rare strokes. At last I became conscious that we were near the Lido, far up, on the right hand, as you turn your back to Venice, and I made him put me ashore. I wanted to walk, to move, to shed some of my bewilderment. I crossed the narrow strip and got to the sea beach—I took my way toward Malamocco. But presently I flung myself down again on the warm sand, in the breeze, on the coarse dry grass. It took it out of me to think I had been so much at fault, that I had unwittingly but nonetheless deplorably trifled. But I had not given her cause—distinctly I had not. I had said to Mrs. Prest that I would make love to her; but it had been a joke without consequences and I had never said it to Tita Bordereau. I had been as kind as possible, because I really liked her; but since when had that become a crime where a woman of such an age and such an appearance was concerned? I am far from remembering clearly the succession of events and feelings during this long day of confusion, which I spent entirely in wandering about, without going home, until late at night; it only comes back to me that there were moments when I pacified my conscience and others when I lashed it into pain. I did not laugh all day—that I do recollect; the case, however it might have struck others, seemed to me so little amusing. It would have been better perhaps for me to feel the comic side of it. At any rate, whether I had given cause or not it went without saying that I could not pay the price. I could not accept. I could not, for a bundle of tattered papers, marry a ridiculous, pathetic, provincial old woman. it was a proof that she did not think the idea would come to me, her having determined to suggest it herself in that practical, argumentative, heroic way, in which the timidity however had been so much more striking than the boldness that her reasons appeared to come first and her feelings afterward.

As the day went on I grew to wish that I had never heard of Aspern's relics, and I cursed the extravagant curiosity that had put John Cumnor on the scent of them. We had more than enough material without them, and my predicament was the just punishment of that most fatal of human follies, our not having known when to stop. It was very well to say it was no predicament, that the way out was simple, that I had only to leave Venice by the first train in the morning, after writing a note to Miss Tita, to be placed in her hand as soon as I got clear of the house; for it was a strong sign that I was embarrassed that when I tried to make up the note in my mind in advance (I would put it on paper as soon as I got home, before going to bed), I could not think of anything but "How can I thank you for the rare confidence you have placed in me?" That would never do; it sounded exactly as if an acceptance were to follow. Of course I might go away without writing a word, but that would be brutal and my idea was still to exclude brutal solutions. As my confusion cooled I was lost in wonder at the importance I had attached to Miss Bordereau's crumpled scraps; the thought of them became odious to me, and I was as vexed with the old witch for the superstition that had prevented her from destroying them as I was with myself for having already spent more money than I could afford in attempting to control their fate. I forget what I did, where I went after leaving the Lido and at what hour or with what recovery of composure I made my way back to my boat. I only know that in the afternoon, when the air was aglow with the sunset, I was standing before the church of Saints John and Paul and looking up at the small square-jawed face of Bartolommeo Colleoni, the terrible condottiere who sits so sturdily astride of his huge bronze horse, on the high pedestal on which Venetian gratitude maintains him. The statue is incomparable, the finest of all mounted figures, unless that of Marcus Aurelius, who rides benignant before the Roman Capitol, be finer: but I was not thinking of that; I only found myself staring at the triumphant captain as if he had an oracle on his lips. The western light shines into all his grimness at that hour and makes it wonderfully personal. But he continued to look far over my head, at the red immersion of another day—he had seen so many go down into the lagoon through the centuries—and if he were thinking of battles and stratagems they were of a different quality from any I had to tell him of. He could not direct me what to do, gaze up at him as I might. Was it before this or after that I wandered about for an hour in the small canals, to the continued stupefaction of my gondolier, who had never seen me so restless and yet so void of a purpose and could extract from me no order but "Go anywhere—everywhere—all over the place"? He reminded me that I had not lunched and expressed therefore respectfully the hope that I would dine earlier. He had had long periods of leisure during the day, when I had left the boat and rambled, so that I was not obliged to consider him, and I told him that that day, for a change, I would touch no meat. It was an effect of poor Miss Tita's proposal, not altogether auspicious, that I had quite lost my appetite. I don't know why it happened that on this occasion I was more than ever struck with that queer air of sociability, of cousinship and family life, which makes up half the expression of Venice. Without streets and vehicles, the uproar of wheels, the brutality of horses, and with its little winding ways where people crowd together, where voices sound as in the corridors of a house, where the human step circulates as if it skirted the angles of furniture and shoes never wear out, the place has the character of an immense collective apartment, in which Piazza San Marco is the most ornamented corner and palaces and churches, for the rest, play the part of great divans of repose, tables of entertainment, expanses of decoration. And somehow the splendid common domicile, familiar, domestic, and resonant, also resembles a theater, with actors clicking over bridges and, in straggling processions, tripping along fondamentas. As you sit in your gondola the footways that in certain parts edge the canals assume to the eye the importance of a stage, meeting it at the same angle, and the Venetian figures, moving to and fro against the battered scenery of their little houses of comedy, strike you as members of an endless dramatic troupe.

I went to bed that night very tired, without being able to compose a letter to Miss Tita. Was this failure the reason why I became conscious the next morning as soon as I awoke of a determination to see the poor lady again the first moment she would receive me? That had something to do with it, but what had still more was the fact that during my sleep a very odd revulsion had taken place in my spirit. I found myself aware of this almost as soon as I opened my eyes; it made me jump out of my bed with the movement of a man who remembers that he has left the house door ajar or a candle burning under a shelf. Was I still in time to save my goods? That question was in my heart; for what had now come to pass was that in the unconscious cerebration of sleep I had swung back to a passionate appreciation of Miss Bordereau's papers. They were now more precious than ever, and a kind of ferocity had come into my desire to possess them. The condition Miss Tita had attached to the possession of them no longer appeared an obstacle worth thinking of, and for an hour, that morning, my repentant imagination brushed it aside. It was absurd that I should be able to invent nothing; absurd to renounce so easily and turn away helpless from the idea that the only way to get hold of the papers was to unite myself to her for life. I would not unite myself and yet I would have them. I must add that by the time I sent down to ask if she would see me I had invented no alternative, though to do so I had had all the time that I was dressing. This failure was humiliating, yet what could the alternative be? Miss Tita sent back word that I might come; and as I descended the stairs and crossed the sala to her door—this time she received me in her aunt's forlorn parlor—I hoped she would not think my errand was to tell her I accepted her hand. She certainly would have made the day before the reflection that I declined it.

As soon as I came into the room I saw that she had drawn this inference, but I also saw something which had not been in my forecast. Poor Miss Tita's sense of her failure had produced an extraordinary alteration in her, but I had been too full of my literary concupiscence to think of that. Now I perceived it; I can scarcely tell how it startled me. She stood in the middle of the room with a face of mildness bent upon me, and her look of forgiveness, of absolution, made her angelic. It beautified her; she was younger; she was not a ridiculous old woman. This optical trick gave her a sort of phantasmagoric brightness, and while I was still the victim of it I heard a whisper somewhere in the depths of my conscience: "Why not, after all—why not?" It seemed to me I was ready to pay the price. Still more distinctly however than the whisper I heard Miss Tita's own voice. I was so struck with the different effect she made upon me that at first I was not clearly aware of what she was saying; then I perceived she had bade me goodbye—she said something about hoping I should be very happy.

"Goodbye—goodbye?" I repeated with an inflection interrogative and probably foolish.

I saw she did not feel the interrogation, she only heard the words; she had strung herself up to accepting our separation and they fell upon her ear as a proof. "Are you going today?" she asked. "But it doesn't matter, for whenever you go I shall not see you again. I don't want to." And she smiled strangely, with an infinite gentleness. She had never doubted that I had left her the day before in horror. How could she, since I had not come back before night to contradict, even as a simple form, such an idea? And now she had the force of soul—Miss Tita with force of soul was a new conception—to smile at me in her humiliation.

"What shall you do—where shall you go?" I asked.

"Oh, I don't know. I have done the great thing. I have destroyed the papers."

"Destroyed them?" I faltered.

"Yes; what was I to keep them for? I burned them last night, one by one, in the kitchen."

"One by one?" I repeated, mechanically.

"It took a long time—there were so many." The room seemed to go round me as she said this, and a real darkness for a moment descended upon my eyes. When it passed Miss Tita was there still, but the transfiguration was over and she had changed back to a plain, dingy, elderly person. It was in this character she spoke as she said, "I can't stay with you longer, I can't;" and it was in this character that she turned her back upon me, as I had turned mine upon her twenty-four hours before, and moved to the door of her room. Here she did what I had not done when I quitted her—she paused long enough to give me one look. I have never forgotten it and I sometimes still suffer from it, though it was not resentful. No, there was no resentment, nothing hard or vindictive in poor Miss Tita; for when, later, I sent her in exchange for the portrait of Jeffrey Aspern a larger sum of money than I had hoped to be able to gather for her, writing to her that I had sold the picture, she kept it with thanks; she never sent it back. I wrote to her that I had sold the picture, but I admitted to Mrs. Prest, at the time (I met her in London, in the autumn), that it hangs above my writing table. When I look at it my chagrin at the loss of the letters becomes almost intolerable.

THE BEAST IN THE JUNGLE

CHAPTER I

What determined the speech that startled him in the course of their encounter scarcely matters, being probably but some words spoken by himself quite without intention—spoken as they lingered and slowly moved together after their renewal of acquaintance. He had been conveyed by friends an hour or two before to the house at which she was staying; the party of visitors at the other house, of whom he was one, and thanks to whom it was his theory, as always, that he was lost in the crowd, had been invited over to luncheon. There had been after luncheon much dispersal, all in the interest of the original motive, a view of Weatherend itself and the fine things, intrinsic features, pictures, heirlooms, treasures of all the arts, that made the place almost famous; and the great rooms were so numerous that guests could wander at their will, hang back from the principal group and in cases where they took such matters with the last seriousness give themselves up to mysterious appreciations and measurements. There were persons to be observed, singly or in couples, bending toward objects in out-of-the-way corners with their hands on their knees and their heads nodding quite as with the emphasis of an excited sense of smell. When they were two they either mingled their sounds of ecstasy or melted into silences of even deeper import, so that there were aspects of the occasion that gave it for Marcher much the air of the "look round," previous to a sale highly advertised, that excites or quenches, as may be, the dream of acquisition. The dream of acquisition at Weatherend would have had to be wild indeed, and John Marcher found himself, among such suggestions, disconcerted almost equally by the presence of those who knew too much and by that of those who knew nothing. The great rooms caused so much poetry and history to press upon him that he needed some straying apart to feel in a proper relation with them, though this impulse was not, as happened, like the gloating of some of his companions, to be compared to the movements of a dog sniffing a cupboard. It had an issue promptly enough in a direction that was not to have been calculated.

It led, briefly, in the course of the October afternoon, to his closer meeting with May Bartram, whose face, a reminder, yet not quite a remembrance, as they sat much separated at a very long table, had begun merely by troubling him rather pleasantly. It affected him as the sequel of something of which he had lost the beginning. He knew it, and for the time quite welcomed it, as a continuation, but didn't know what it continued, which was an interest or an amusement the greater as he was also somehow aware—yet without a direct sign from her—that the young woman herself hadn't lost the thread. She hadn't lost it, but she wouldn't give it back to him, he saw, without some putting forth of his hand for it; and he not only saw that, but saw several things more, things odd enough in the light of the fact that at the moment some accident of grouping brought them face to face he was still merely fumbling with the idea that any contact between them in the past would have had no importance. If it had had no importance he scarcely knew why his actual impression of her should so seem to have so much; the answer to which, however, was that in such a life as they all appeared to be leading for the moment one could but take things as they came. He was satisfied, without in the least being able to say why, that this young lady might roughly have ranked in the house as a poor relation; satisfied also that she was not there on a brief visit, but was more or less a part of the establishment—almost a working, a remunerated part. Didn't she enjoy at periods a protection that she paid for by helping, among other services, to show the place and explain it, deal with the tiresome people, answer questions about the dates of the building, the styles of the furniture, the authorship of the pictures, the favourite haunts of the ghost? It wasn't that she looked as if you could have given her shillings—it was impossible to look less so. Yet when she finally drifted toward him, distinctly handsome, though ever so much older—older than when he had seen her before—it might have been as an effect of her guessing that he had, within the couple of hours, devoted more imagination to her than to all the others put together, and had thereby penetrated to a kind of truth that the others were too stupid for. She was there on harder terms than any one; she was there as a consequence of things suffered, one way and another, in the interval of years; and she remembered him very much as she was remembered—only a good deal better.

By the time they at last thus came to speech they were alone in one of the rooms—remarkable for a fine portrait over the chimney-place—out of which their friends had passed, and the charm of it was that even before they had spoken they had practically arranged with each other to stay behind for talk. The charm, happily, was in other things too—partly in there being scarce a spot at Weatherend without something to stay behind for. It was in the way the autumn day looked into the high windows as it waned; the way the red light, breaking at the close from under a low sombre sky, reached out in a long shaft and played over old wainscots, old tapestry, old gold, old colour. It was most of all perhaps in the way she came to him as if, since she had been turned on to deal with the simpler sort, he might, should he choose to keep the whole thing down, just take her mild attention for a part of her general business. As soon as he heard her voice, however, the gap was filled up and the missing link supplied; the slight irony he divined in her attitude lost its advantage. He almost jumped at it to get there before her. "I met you years and years ago in Rome. I remember all about it." She confessed to disappointment—she had been so sure he didn't; and to prove how well he did he began to pour forth the particular recollections that popped up as he called for them. Her face and her voice, all at his service now, worked the miracle—the impression operating like the torch of a lamplighter who touches into flame, one by one, a long row of gas-jets. Marcher flattered himself the illumination was brilliant, yet he was really still more pleased on her showing him, with amusement, that in his haste to make everything right he had got most things rather wrong. It hadn't been at Rome—it had been at Naples; and it hadn't been eight years before—it had been more nearly ten. She hadn't been, either, with her uncle and aunt, but with her mother and brother; in addition to which it was not with the Pembles he had been, but with the Boyers, coming down in their company from Rome—a point on which she insisted, a little to his confusion, and as to which she had her evidence in hand. The Boyers she had known, but didn't know the Pembles, though she had heard of them, and it was the people he was with who had made them acquainted. The incident of the thunderstorm that had raged round them with such violence as to drive them for refuge into an excavation—this incident had not occurred at the Palace of the Caesars, but at Pompeii, on an occasion when they had been present there at an important find.

He accepted her amendments, he enjoyed her corrections, though the moral of them was, she pointed out, that he really didn't remember the least thing about her; and he only felt it as a drawback that when all was made strictly historic there didn't appear much of anything left. They lingered together still, she neglecting her office—for from the moment he was so clever she had no proper right to him—and both neglecting the house, just waiting as to see if a memory or two more wouldn't again breathe on them. It hadn't taken them many minutes, after all, to put down on the table, like the cards of a pack, those that constituted their respective hands; only what came out was that the pack was unfortunately not perfect—that the past, invoked, invited, encouraged, could give them, naturally, no more than it had. It had made them anciently meet—her at twenty, him at twenty-five; but nothing was so strange, they seemed to say to each other, as that, while so occupied, it hadn't done a little more for them. They looked at each other as with the feeling of an occasion missed; the present would have been so much better if the other, in the far distance, in the foreign land, hadn't been so stupidly meagre. There weren't, apparently, all counted, more than a dozen little old things that had succeeded in coming to pass between them; trivialities of youth, simplicities of freshness, stupidities of ignorance, small possible germs, but too deeply buried—too deeply (didn't it seem?) to sprout after so many years. Marcher could only feel he ought to have rendered her some service—saved her from a capsized boat in the bay or at least recovered her dressing-bag, filched from her cab in the streets of Naples by a lazzarone with a stiletto. Or it would have been nice if he could have been taken with fever all alone at his hotel, and she could have come to look after him, to write to his people, to drive him out in convalescence. Then they would be in possession of the something or other that their actual show seemed to lack. It yet somehow presented itself, this show, as too good to be spoiled; so that they were reduced for a few minutes more to wondering a little helplessly why—since they seemed to know a certain number of the same people—their reunion had been so long averted. They didn't use that name for it, but their delay from minute to minute to join the others was a kind of confession that they didn't quite want it to be a failure. Their attempted supposition of reasons for their not having met but showed how little they knew of each other. There came in fact a moment when Marcher felt a positive pang. It was vain to pretend she was an old friend, for all the communities were wanting, in spite of which it was as an old friend that he saw she would have suited him. He had new ones enough—was surrounded with them for instance on the stage of the other house; as a new one he probably wouldn't have so much as noticed her. He would have liked to invent something, get her to make-believe with him that some passage of a romantic or critical kind had originally occurred. He was really almost reaching out in imagination—as against time—for something that would do, and saying to himself that if it didn't come this sketch of a fresh start would show for quite awkwardly bungled. They would separate, and now for no second or no third chance. They would have tried and not succeeded. Then it was, just at the turn, as he afterwards made it out to himself, that, everything else failing, she herself decided to take up the case and, as it were, save the situation. He felt as soon as she spoke that she had been consciously keeping back what she said and hoping to get on without it; a scruple in her that immensely touched him when, by the end of three or four minutes more, he was able to measure it. What she brought out, at any rate, quite cleared the air and supplied the link—the link it was so odd he should frivolously have managed to lose.

"You know you told me something I've never forgotten and that again and again has made me think of you since; it was that tremendously hot day when we went to Sorrento, across the bay, for the breeze. What I allude to was what you said to me, on the way back, as we sat under the awning of the boat enjoying the cool. Have you forgotten?"

He had forgotten, and was even more surprised than ashamed. But the great thing was that he saw in this no vulgar reminder of any "sweet" speech. The vanity of women had long memories, but she was making no claim on him of a compliment or a mistake. With another woman, a totally different one, he might have feared the recall possibly even some imbecile "offer." So, in having to say that he had indeed forgotten, he was conscious rather of a loss than of a gain; he already saw an interest in the matter of her mention. "I try to think—but I give it up. Yet I remember the Sorrento day."

"I'm not very sure you do," May Bartram after a moment said; "and I'm not very sure I ought to want you to. It's dreadful to bring a person back at any time to what he was ten years before. If you've lived away from it," she smiled, "so much the better."

"Ah if you haven't why should I?" he asked.

"Lived away, you mean, from what I myself was?"

"From what I was. I was of course an ass," Marcher went on; "but I would rather know from you just the sort of ass I was than—from the moment you have something in your mind—not know anything."

Still, however, she hesitated. "But if you've completely ceased to be that sort—?"

"Why I can then all the more bear to know. Besides, perhaps I haven't."

"Perhaps. Yet if you haven't," she added, "I should suppose you'd remember. Not indeed that I in the least connect with my impression the invidious name you use. If I had only thought you foolish," she explained, "the thing I speak of wouldn't so have remained with me. It was about yourself." She waited as if it might come to him; but as, only meeting her eyes in wonder, he gave no sign, she burnt her ships. "Has it ever happened?"

Then it was that, while he continued to stare, a light broke for him and the blood slowly came to his face, which began to burn with recognition.

"Do you mean I told you—?" But he faltered, lest what came to him shouldn't be right, lest he should only give himself away.

"It was something about yourself that it was natural one shouldn't forget—that is if one remembered you at all. That's why I ask you," she smiled, "if the thing you then spoke of has ever come to pass?"

Oh then he saw, but he was lost in wonder and found himself embarrassed. This, he also saw, made her sorry for him, as if her allusion had been a mistake. It took him but a moment, however, to feel it hadn't been, much as it had been a surprise. After the first little shock of it her knowledge on the contrary began, even if rather strangely, to taste sweet to him. She was the only other person in the world then who would have it, and she had had it all these years, while the fact of his having so breathed his secret had unaccountably faded from him. No wonder they couldn't have met as if nothing had happened. "I judge," he finally said, "that I know what you mean. Only I had strangely enough lost any sense of having taken you so far into my confidence."

"Is it because you've taken so many others as well?"

"I've taken nobody. Not a creature since then."

"So that I'm the only person who knows?"

"The only person in the world."

"Well," she quickly replied, "I myself have never spoken. I've never, never repeated of you what you told me." She looked at him so that he perfectly believed her. Their eyes met over it in such a way that he was without a doubt. "And I never will."

She spoke with an earnestness that, as if almost excessive, put him at ease about her possible derision. Somehow the whole question was a new luxury to him—that is from the moment she was in possession. If she didn't take the sarcastic view she clearly took the sympathetic, and that was what he had had, in all the long time, from no one whomsoever. What he felt was that he couldn't at present have begun to tell her, and yet could profit perhaps exquisitely by the accident of having done so of old. "Please don't then. We're just right as it is."

"Oh I am," she laughed, "if you are!" To which she added: "Then you do still feel in the same way?"

It was impossible he shouldn't take to himself that she was really interested, though it all kept coming as a perfect surprise. He had thought of himself so long as abominably alone, and lo he wasn't alone a bit. He hadn't been, it appeared, for an hour—since those moments on the Sorrento boat. It was she who had been, he seemed to see as he looked at her—she who had been made so by the graceless fact of his lapse of fidelity. To tell her what he had told her—what had it been but to ask something of her? something that she had given, in her charity, without his having, by a remembrance, by a return of the spirit, failing another encounter, so much as thanked her. What he had asked of her had been simply at first not to laugh at him. She had beautifully not done so for ten years, and she was not doing so now. So he had endless gratitude to make up. Only for that he must see just how he had figured to her. "What, exactly, was the account I gave—?"

"Of the way you did feel? Well, it was very simple. You said you had had from your earliest time, as the deepest thing within you, the sense of being kept for something rare and strange, possibly prodigious and terrible, that was sooner or later to happen to you, that you had in your bones the foreboding and the conviction of, and that would perhaps overwhelm you."

"Do you call that very simple?" John Marcher asked.

She thought a moment. "It was perhaps because I seemed, as you spoke, to understand it."

"You do understand it?" he eagerly asked.

Again she kept her kind eyes on him. "You still have the belief?"

"Oh!" he exclaimed helplessly. There was too much to say.

"Whatever it's to be," she clearly made out, "it hasn't yet come."

He shook his head in complete surrender now. "It hasn't yet come. Only, you know, it isn't anything I'm to do, to achieve in the world, to be distinguished or admired for. I'm not such an ass as that. It would be much better, no doubt, if I were."

"It's to be something you're merely to suffer?"

"Well, say to wait for—to have to meet, to face, to see suddenly break out in my life; possibly destroying all further consciousness, possibly annihilating me; possibly, on the other hand, only altering everything, striking at the root of all my world and leaving me to the consequences, however they shape themselves."

She took this in, but the light in her eyes continued for him not to be that of mockery. "Isn't what you describe perhaps but the expectation—or at any rate the sense of danger, familiar to so many people—of falling in love?"

John Marcher thought. "Did you ask me that before?"

"No—I wasn't so free-and-easy then. But it's what strikes me now."

"Of course," he said after a moment, "it strikes you. Of course it strikes me. Of course what's in store for me may be no more than that. The only thing is," he went on, "that I think if it had been that I should by this time know."

"Do you mean because you've been in love?" And then as he but looked at her in silence: "You've been in love, and it hasn't meant such a cataclysm, hasn't proved the great affair?"

"Here I am, you see. It hasn't been overwhelming."

"Then it hasn't been love," said May Bartram.

"Well, I at least thought it was. I took it for that—I've taken it till now. It was agreeable, it was delightful, it was miserable," he explained. "But it wasn't strange. It wasn't what my affair's to be."

"You want something all to yourself—something that nobody else knows or has known?"

"It isn't a question of what I 'want'—God knows I don't want anything. It's only a question of the apprehension that haunts me—that I live with day by day."

He said this so lucidly and consistently that he could see it further impose itself. If she hadn't been interested before she'd have been interested now.

"Is it a sense of coming violence?"

Evidently now too again he liked to talk of it. "I don't think of it as—when it does come—necessarily violent. I only think of it as natural and as of course above all unmistakeable. I think of it simply as the thing. The thing will of itself appear natural."

"Then how will it appear strange?"

Marcher bethought himself. "It won't—to me."

"To whom then?"

"Well," he replied, smiling at last, "say to you."

"Oh then I'm to be present?"

"Why you are present—since you know."

"I see." She turned it over. "But I mean at the catastrophe."

At this, for a minute, their lightness gave way to their gravity; it was as if the long look they exchanged held them together. "It will only depend on yourself—if you'll watch with me."

"Are you afraid?" she asked.

"Don't leave me now," he went on.

"Are you afraid?" she repeated.

"Do you think me simply out of my mind?" he pursued instead of answering. "Do I merely strike you as a harmless lunatic?"

"No," said May Bartram. "I understand you. I believe you."

"You mean you feel how my obsession—poor old thing—may correspond to some possible reality?"

"To some possible reality."

"Then you will watch with me?"

She hesitated, then for the third time put her question. "Are you afraid?"

"Did I tell you I was—at Naples?"

"No, you said nothing about it."

"Then I don't know. And I should like to know," said John Marcher. "You'll tell me yourself whether you think so. If you'll watch with me you'll see."

"Very good then." They had been moving by this time across the room, and at the door, before passing out, they paused as for the full wind-up of their understanding. "I'll watch with you," said May Bartram.

CHAPTER II

The fact that she "knew"—knew and yet neither chaffed him nor betrayed him—had in a short time begun to constitute between them a goodly bond, which became more marked when, within the year that followed their afternoon at Weatherend, the opportunities for meeting multiplied. The event that thus promoted these occasions was the death of the ancient lady her great-aunt, under whose wing, since losing her mother, she had to such an extent found shelter, and who, though but the widowed mother of the new successor to the property, had succeeded—thanks to a high tone and a high temper—in not forfeiting the supreme position at the great house. The deposition of this personage arrived but with her death, which, followed by many changes, made in particular a difference for the young woman in whom Marcher's expert attention had recognised from the first a dependent with a pride that might ache though it didn't bristle. Nothing for a long time had made him easier than the thought that the aching must have been much soothed by Miss Bartram's now finding herself able to set up a small home in London. She had acquired property, to an amount that made that luxury just possible, under her aunt's extremely complicated will, and when the whole matter began to be straightened out, which indeed took time, she let him know that the happy issue was at last in view. He had seen her again before that day, both because she had more than once accompanied the ancient lady to town and because he had paid another visit to the friends who so conveniently made of Weatherend one of the charms of their own hospitality. These friends had taken him back there; he had achieved there again with Miss Bartram some quiet detachment; and he had in London succeeded in persuading her to more than one brief absence from her aunt. They went together, on these latter occasions, to the National Gallery and the South Kensington Museum, where, among vivid reminders, they talked of Italy at large—not now attempting to recover, as at first, the taste of their youth and their ignorance. That recovery, the first day at Weatherend, had served its purpose well, had given them quite enough; so that they were, to Marcher's sense, no longer hovering about the head-waters of their stream, but had felt their boat pushed sharply off and down the current.

They were literally afloat together; for our gentleman this was marked, quite as marked as that the fortunate cause of it was just the buried treasure of her knowledge. He had with his own hands dug up this little hoard, brought to light—that is to within reach of the dim day constituted by their discretions and privacies—the object of value the hiding-place of which he had, after putting it into the ground himself, so strangely, so long forgotten. The rare luck of his having again just stumbled on the spot made him indifferent to any other question; he would doubtless have devoted more time to the odd accident of his lapse of memory if he hadn't been moved to devote so much to the sweetness, the comfort, as he felt, for the future, that this accident itself had helped to keep fresh. It had never entered into his plan that any one should "know", and mainly for the reason that it wasn't in him to tell any one. That would have been impossible, for nothing but the amusement of a cold world would have waited on it. Since, however, a mysterious fate had opened his mouth betimes, in spite of him, he would count that a compensation and profit by it to the utmost. That the right person should know tempered the asperity of his secret more even than his shyness had permitted him to imagine; and May Bartram was clearly right, because—well, because there she was. Her knowledge simply settled it; he would have been sure enough by this time had she been wrong. There was that in his situation, no doubt, that disposed him too much to see her as a mere confidant, taking all her light for him from the fact—the fact only—of her interest in his predicament; from her mercy, sympathy, seriousness, her consent not to regard him as the funniest of the funny. Aware, in fine, that her price for him was just in her giving him this constant sense of his being admirably spared, he was careful to remember that she had also a life of her own, with things that might happen to her, things that in friendship one should likewise take account of. Something fairly remarkable came to pass with him, for that matter, in this connexion—something represented by a certain passage of his consciousness, in the suddenest way, from one extreme to the other.

He had thought himself, so long as nobody knew, the most disinterested person in the world, carrying his concentrated burden, his perpetual suspense, ever so quietly, holding his tongue about it, giving others no glimpse of it nor of its effect upon his life, asking of them no allowance and only making on his side all those that were asked. He hadn't disturbed people with the queerness of their having to know a haunted man, though he had had moments of rather special temptation on hearing them say they were forsooth "unsettled." If they were as unsettled as he was—he who had never been settled for an hour in his life—they would know what it meant. Yet it wasn't, all the same, for him to make them, and he listened to them civilly enough. This was why he had such good—though possibly such rather colourless—manners; this was why, above all, he could regard himself, in a greedy world, as decently—as in fact perhaps even a little sublimely—unselfish. Our point is accordingly that he valued this character quite sufficiently to measure his present danger of letting it lapse, against which he promised himself to be much on his guard. He was quite ready, none the less, to be selfish just a little, since surely no more charming occasion for it had come to him. "Just a little," in a word, was just as much as Miss Bartram, taking one day with another, would let him. He never would be in the least coercive, and would keep well before him the lines on which consideration for her—the very highest—ought to proceed. He would thoroughly establish the heads under which her affairs, her requirements, her peculiarities—he went so far as to give them the latitude of that name—would come into their intercourse. All this naturally was a sign of how much he took the intercourse itself for granted. There was nothing more to be done about that. It simply existed; had sprung into being with her first penetrating question to him in the autumn light there at Weatherend. The real form it should have taken on the basis that stood out large was the form of their marrying. But the devil in this was that the very basis itself put marrying out of the question. His conviction, his apprehension, his obsession, in short, wasn't a privilege he could invite a woman to share; and that consequence of it was precisely what was the matter with him. Something or other lay in wait for him, amid the twists and the turns of the months and the years, like a crouching Beast in the Jungle. It signified little whether the crouching Beast were destined to slay him or to be slain. The definite point was the inevitable spring of the creature; and the definite lesson from that was that a man of feeling didn't cause himself to be accompanied by a lady on a tiger-hunt. Such was the image under which he had ended by figuring his life.

They had at first, none the less, in the scattered hours spent together, made no allusion to that view of it; which was a sign he was handsomely alert to give that he didn't expect, that he in fact didn't care, always to be talking about it. Such a feature in one's outlook was really like a hump on one's back. The difference it made every minute of the day existed quite independently of discussion. One discussed of course like a hunchback, for there was always, if nothing else, the hunchback face. That remained, and she was watching him; but people watched best, as a general thing, in silence, so that such would be predominantly the manner of their vigil. Yet he didn't want, at the same time, to be tense and solemn; tense and solemn was what he imagined he too much showed for with other people. The thing to be, with the one person who knew, was easy and natural—to make the reference rather than be seeming to avoid it, to avoid it rather than be seeming to make it, and to keep it, in any case, familiar, facetious even, rather than pedantic and portentous. Some such consideration as the latter was doubtless in his mind for instance when he wrote pleasantly to Miss Bartram that perhaps the great thing he had so long felt as in the lap of the gods was no more than this circumstance, which touched him so nearly, of her acquiring a house in London. It was the first allusion they had yet again made, needing any other hitherto so little; but when she replied, after having given him the news, that she was by no means satisfied with such a trifle as the climax to so special a suspense, she almost set him wondering if she hadn't even a larger conception of singularity for him than he had for himself. He was at all events destined to become aware little by little, as time went by, that she was all the while looking at his life, judging it, measuring it, in the light of the thing she knew, which grew to be at last, with the consecration of the years, never mentioned between them save as "the real truth" about him. That had always been his own form of reference to it, but she adopted the form so quietly that, looking back at the end of a period, he knew there was no moment at which it was traceable that she had, as he might say, got inside his idea, or exchanged the attitude of beautifully indulging for that of still more beautifully believing him.

It was always open to him to accuse her of seeing him but as the most harmless of maniacs, and this, in the long run—since it covered so much ground—was his easiest description of their friendship. He had a screw loose for her but she liked him in spite of it and was practically, against the rest of the world, his kind wise keeper, unremunerated but fairly amused and, in the absence of other near ties, not disreputably occupied. The rest of the world of course thought him queer, but she, she only, knew how, and above all why, queer; which was precisely what enabled her to dispose the concealing veil in the right folds. She took his gaiety from him—since it had to pass with them for gaiety—as she took everything else; but she certainly so far justified by her unerring touch his finer sense of the degree to which he had ended by convincing her. She at least never spoke of the secret of his life except as "the real truth about you," and she had in fact a wonderful way of making it seem, as such, the secret of her own life too. That was in fine how he so constantly felt her as allowing for him; he couldn't on the whole call it anything else. He allowed for himself, but she, exactly, allowed still more; partly because, better placed for a sight of the matter, she traced his unhappy perversion through reaches of its course into which he could scarce follow it. He knew how he felt, but, besides knowing that, she knew how he looked as well; he knew each of the things of importance he was insidiously kept from doing, but she could add up the amount they made, understand how much, with a lighter weight on his spirit, he might have done, and thereby establish how, clever as he was, he fell short. Above all she was in the secret of the difference between the forms he went through—those of his little office under Government, those of caring for his modest patrimony, for his library, for his garden in the country, for the people in London whose invitations he accepted and repaid—and the detachment that reigned beneath them and that made of all behaviour, all that could in the least be called behaviour, a long act of dissimulation. What it had come to was that he wore a mask painted with the social simper, out of the eye-holes of which there looked eyes of an expression not in the least matching the other features. This the stupid world, even after years, had never more than half discovered. It was only May Bartram who had, and she achieved, by an art indescribable, the feat of at once—or perhaps it was only alternately—meeting the eyes from in front and mingling her own vision, as from over his shoulder, with their peep through the apertures.

So while they grew older together she did watch with him, and so she let this association give shape and colour to her own existence. Beneath her forms as well detachment had learned to sit, and behaviour had become for her, in the social sense, a false account of herself. There was but one account of her that would have been true all the while and that she could give straight to nobody, least of all to John Marcher. Her whole attitude was a virtual statement, but the perception of that only seemed called to take its place for him as one of the many things necessarily crowded out of his consciousness. If she had moreover, like himself, to make sacrifices to their real truth, it was to be granted that her compensation might have affected her as more prompt and more natural. They had long periods, in this London time, during which, when they were together, a stranger might have listened to them without in the least pricking up his ears; on the other hand the real truth was equally liable at any moment to rise to the surface, and the auditor would then have wondered indeed what they were talking about. They had from an early hour made up their mind that society was, luckily, unintelligent, and the margin allowed them by this had fairly become one of their commonplaces. Yet there were still moments when the situation turned almost fresh—usually under the effect of some expression drawn from herself. Her expressions doubtless repeated themselves, but her intervals were generous. "What saves us, you know, is that we answer so completely to so usual an appearance: that of the man and woman whose friendship has become such a daily habit—or almost—as to be at last indispensable." That for instance was a remark she had frequently enough had occasion to make, though she had given it at different times different developments. What we are especially concerned with is the turn it happened to take from her one afternoon when he had come to see her in honour of her birthday. This anniversary had fallen on a Sunday, at a season of thick fog and general outward gloom; but he had brought her his customary offering, having known her now long enough to have established a hundred small traditions. It was one of his proofs to himself, the present he made her on her birthday, that he hadn't sunk into real selfishness. It was mostly nothing more than a small trinket, but it was always fine of its kind, and he was regularly careful to pay for it more than he thought he could afford. "Our habit saves you, at least, don't you see? because it makes you, after all, for the vulgar, indistinguishable from other men. What's the most inveterate mark of men in general? Why the capacity to spend endless time with dull women—to spend it I won't say without being bored, but without minding that they are, without being driven off at a tangent by it; which comes to the same thing. I'm your dull woman, a part of the daily bread for which you pray at church. That covers your tracks more than anything."

"And what covers yours?" asked Marcher, whom his dull woman could mostly to this extent amuse. "I see of course what you mean by your saving me, in this way and that, so far as other people are concerned—I've seen it all along. Only what is it that saves you? I often think, you know, of that."

She looked as if she sometimes thought of that too, but rather in a different way. "Where other people, you mean, are concerned?"

"Well, you're really so in with me, you know—as a sort of result of my being so in with yourself. I mean of my having such an immense regard for you, being so tremendously mindful of all you've done for me. I sometimes ask myself if it's quite fair. Fair I mean to have so involved and—since one may say it—interested you. I almost feel as if you hadn't really had time to do anything else."

"Anything else but be interested?" she asked. "Ah what else does one ever want to be? If I've been 'watching' with you, as we long ago agreed I was to do, watching's always in itself an absorption."

"Oh certainly," John Marcher said, "if you hadn't had your curiosity—! Only doesn't it sometimes come to you as time goes on that your curiosity isn't being particularly repaid?"

May Bartram had a pause. "Do you ask that, by any chance, because you feel at all that yours isn't? I mean because you have to wait so long."

Oh he understood what she meant! "For the thing to happen that never does happen? For the Beast to jump out? No, I'm just where I was about it. It isn't a matter as to which I can choose, I can decide for a change. It isn't one as to which there can be a change. It's in the lap of the gods. One's in the hands of one's law—there one is. As to the form the law will take, the way it will operate, that's its own affair."

"Yes," Miss Bartram replied; "of course one's fate's coming, of course it has come in its own form and its own way, all the while. Only, you know, the form and the way in your case were to have been—well, something so exceptional and, as one may say, so particularly your own."

Something in this made him look at her with suspicion. "You say 'were to have been,' as if in your heart you had begun to doubt."

"Oh!" she vaguely protested.

"As if you believed," he went on, "that nothing will now take place."

She shook her head slowly but rather inscrutably. "You're far from my thought."

He continued to look at her. "What then is the matter with you?"

"Well," she said after another wait, "the matter with me is simply that I'm more sure than ever my curiosity, as you call it, will be but too well repaid."

They were frankly grave now; he had got up from his seat, had turned once more about the little drawing-room to which, year after year, he brought his inevitable topic; in which he had, as he might have said, tasted their intimate community with every sauce, where every object was as familiar to him as the things of his own house and the very carpets were worn with his fitful walk very much as the desks in old counting-houses are worn by the elbows of generations of clerks. The generations of his nervous moods had been at work there, and the place was the written history of his whole middle life. Under the impression of what his friend had just said he knew himself, for some reason, more aware of these things; which made him, after a moment, stop again before her. "Is it possibly that you've grown afraid?"

"Afraid?" He thought, as she repeated the word, that his question had made her, a little, change colour; so that, lest he should have touched on a truth, he explained very kindly: "You remember that that was what you asked me long ago—that first day at Weatherend."

"Oh yes, and you told me you didn't know—that I was to see for myself. We've said little about it since, even in so long a time."

"Precisely," Marcher interposed—"quite as if it were too delicate a matter for us to make free with. Quite as if we might find, on pressure, that I am afraid. For then," he said, "we shouldn't, should we? quite know what to do."

She had for the time no answer to this question. "There have been days when I thought you were. Only, of course," she added, "there have been days when we have thought almost anything."

"Everything. Oh!" Marcher softly groaned, as with a gasp, half spent, at the face, more uncovered just then than it had been for a long while, of the imagination always with them. It had always had it's incalculable moments of glaring out, quite as with the very eyes of the very Beast, and, used as he was to them, they could still draw from him the tribute of a sigh that rose from the depths of his being. All they had thought, first and last, rolled over him; the past seemed to have been reduced to mere barren speculation. This in fact was what the place had just struck him as so full of—the simplification of everything but the state of suspense. That remained only by seeming to hang in the void surrounding it. Even his original fear, if fear it as had been, had lost itself in the desert. "I judge, however," he continued, "that you see I'm not afraid now."

"What I see, as I make it out, is that you've achieved something almost unprecedented in the way of getting used to danger. Living with it so long and so closely you've lost your sense of it; you know it's there, but you're indifferent, and you cease even, as of old, to have to whistle in the dark. Considering what the danger is," May Bartram wound up, "I'm bound to say I don't think your attitude could well be surpassed."

John Marcher faintly smiled. "It's heroic?"

"Certainly—call it that."

It was what he would have liked indeed to call it. "I am then a man of courage?"

"That's what you were to show me."

He still, however, wondered. "But doesn't the man of courage know what he's afraid of—or not afraid of? I don't know that, you see. I don't focus it. I can't name it. I only know I'm exposed."

"Yes, but exposed—how shall I say?—so directly. So intimately. That's surely enough."

"Enough to make you feel then—as what we may call the end and the upshot of our watch—that I'm not afraid?"

"You're not afraid. But it isn't," she said, "the end of our watch. That is it isn't the end of yours. You've everything still to see."

"Then why haven't you?" he asked. He had had, all along, to-day, the sense of her keeping something back, and he still had it. As this was his first impression of that it quite made a date. The case was the more marked as she didn't at first answer; which in turn made him go on. "You know something I don't." Then his voice, for that of a man of courage, trembled a little. "You know what's to happen." Her silence, with the face she showed, was almost a confession—it made him sure. "You know, and you're afraid to tell me. It's so bad that you're afraid I'll find out."

All this might be true, for she did look as if, unexpectedly to her, he had crossed some mystic line that she had secretly drawn round her. Yet she might, after all, not have worried; and the real climax was that he himself, at all events, needn't. "You'll never find out."

CHAPTER III

It was all to have made, none the less, as I have said, a date; which came out in the fact that again and again, even after long intervals, other things that passed between them were in relation to this hour but the character of recalls and results. Its immediate effect had been indeed rather to lighten insistence—almost to provoke a reaction; as if their topic had dropped by its own weight and as if moreover, for that matter, Marcher had been visited by one of his occasional warnings against egotism. He had kept up, he felt, and very decently on the whole, his consciousness of the importance of not being selfish, and it was true that he had never sinned in that direction without promptly enough trying to press the scales the other way. He often repaired his fault, the season permitting, by inviting his friend to accompany him to the opera; and it not infrequently thus happened that, to show he didn't wish her to have but one sort of food for her mind, he was the cause of her appearing there with him a dozen nights in the month. It even happened that, seeing her home at such times, he occasionally went in with her to finish, as he called it, the evening, and, the better to make his point, sat down to the frugal but always careful little supper that awaited his pleasure. His point was made, he thought, by his not eternally insisting with her on himself; made for instance, at such hours, when it befell that, her piano at hand and each of them familiar with it, they went over passages of the opera together. It chanced to be on one of these occasions, however, that he reminded her of her not having answered a certain question he had put to her during the talk that had taken place between them on her last birthday. "What is it that saves you?"—saved her, he meant, from that appearance of variation from the usual human type. If he had practically escaped remark, as she pretended, by doing, in the most important particular, what most men do—find the answer to life in patching up an alliance of a sort with a woman no better than himself—how had she escaped it, and how could the alliance, such as it was, since they must suppose it had been more or less noticed, have failed to make her rather positively talked about?

"I never said," May Bartram replied, "that it hadn't made me a good deal talked about."

"Ah well then you're not 'saved.'"

"It hasn't been a question for me. If you've had your woman I've had," she said, "my man."

"And you mean that makes you all right?"

Oh it was always as if there were so much to say!

"I don't know why it shouldn't make me—humanly, which is what we're speaking of—as right as it makes you."

"I see," Marcher returned. "'Humanly,' no doubt, as showing that you're living for something. Not, that is, just for me and my secret."

May Bartram smiled. "I don't pretend it exactly shows that I'm not living for you. It's my intimacy with you that's in question."

He laughed as he saw what she meant. "Yes, but since, as you say, I'm only, so far as people make out, ordinary, you're—aren't you? no more than ordinary either. You help me to pass for a man like another. So if I am, as I understand you, you're not compromised. Is that it?"

She had another of her waits, but she spoke clearly enough. "That's it. It's all that concerns me—to help you to pass for a man like another."

He was careful to acknowledge the remark handsomely. "How kind, how beautiful, you are to me! How shall I ever repay you?"

She had her last grave pause, as if there might be a choice of ways. But she chose. "By going on as you are."

It was into this going on as he was that they relapsed, and really for so long a time that the day inevitably came for a further sounding of their depths. These depths, constantly bridged over by a structure firm enough in spite of its lightness and of its occasional oscillation in the somewhat vertiginous air, invited on occasion, in the interest of their nerves, a dropping of the plummet and a measurement of the abyss. A difference had been made moreover, once for all, by the fact that she had all the while not appeared to feel the need of rebutting his charge of an idea within her that she didn't dare to express—a charge uttered just before one of the fullest of their later discussions ended. It had come up for him then that she "knew" something and that what she knew was bad—too bad to tell him. When he had spoken of it as visibly so bad that she was afraid he might find it out, her reply had left the matter too equivocal to be let alone and yet, for Marcher's special sensibility, almost too formidable again to touch. He circled about it at a distance that alternately narrowed and widened and that still wasn't much affected by the consciousness in him that there was nothing she could "know," after all, any better than he did. She had no source of knowledge he hadn't equally—except of course that she might have finer nerves. That was what women had where they were interested; they made out things, where people were concerned, that the people often couldn't have made out for themselves. Their nerves, their sensibility, their imagination, were conductors and revealers, and the beauty of May Bartram was in particular that she had given herself so to his case. He felt in these days what, oddly enough, he had never felt before, the growth of a dread of losing her by some catastrophe—some catastrophe that yet wouldn't at all be the catastrophe: partly because she had almost of a sudden begun to strike him as more useful to him than ever yet, and partly by reason of an appearance of uncertainty in her health, co-incident and equally new. It was characteristic of the inner detachment he had hitherto so successfully cultivated and to which our whole account of him is a reference, it was characteristic that his complications, such as they were, had never yet seemed so as at this crisis to thicken about him, even to the point of making him ask himself if he were, by any chance, of a truth, within sight or sound, within touch or reach, within the immediate jurisdiction, of the thing that waited.

When the day came, as come it had to, that his friend confessed to him her fear of a deep disorder in her blood, he felt somehow the shadow of a change and the chill of a shock. He immediately began to imagine aggravations and disasters, and above all to think of her peril as the direct menace for himself of personal privation. This indeed gave him one of those partial recoveries of equanimity that were agreeable to him—it showed him that what was still first in his mind was the loss she herself might suffer. "What if she should have to die before knowing, before seeing—?" It would have been brutal, in the early stages of her trouble, to put that question to her; but it had immediately sounded for him to his own concern, and the possibility was what most made him sorry for her. If she did "know," moreover, in the sense of her having had some—what should he think?—mystical irresistible light, this would make the matter not better, but worse, inasmuch as her original adoption of his own curiosity had quite become the basis of her life. She had been living to see what would be to be seen, and it would quite lacerate her to have to give up before the accomplishment of the vision. These reflexions, as I say, quickened his generosity; yet, make them as he might, he saw himself, with the lapse of the period, more and more disconcerted. It lapsed for him with a strange steady sweep, and the oddest oddity was that it gave him, independently of the threat of much inconvenience, almost the only positive surprise his career, if career it could be called, had yet offered him. She kept the house as she had never done; he had to go to her to see her—she could meet him nowhere now, though there was scarce a corner of their loved old London in which she hadn't in the past, at one time or another, done so; and he found her always seated by her fire in the deep old-fashioned chair she was less and less able to leave. He had been struck one day, after an absence exceeding his usual measure, with her suddenly looking much older to him than he had ever thought of her being; then he recognised that the suddenness was all on his side—he had just simply and suddenly noticed. She looked older because inevitably, after so many years, she was old, or almost; which was of course true in still greater measure of her companion. If she was old, or almost, John Marcher assuredly was, and yet it was her showing of the lesson, not his own, that brought the truth home to him. His surprises began here; when once they had begun they multiplied; they came rather with a rush: it was as if, in the oddest way in the world, they had all been kept back, sown in a thick cluster, for the late afternoon of life, the time at which for people in general the unexpected has died out.

One of them was that he should have caught himself—for he had so done—really wondering if the great accident would take form now as nothing more than his being condemned to see this charming woman, this admirable friend, pass away from him. He had never so unreservedly qualified her as while confronted in thought with such a possibility; in spite of which there was small doubt for him that as an answer to his long riddle the mere effacement of even so fine a feature of his situation would be an abject anticlimax. It would represent, as connected with his past attitude, a drop of dignity under the shadow of which his existence could only become the most grotesques of failures. He had been far from holding it a failure—long as he had waited for the appearance that was to make it a success. He had waited for quite another thing, not for such a thing as that. The breath of his good faith came short, however, as he recognised how long he had waited, or how long at least his companion had. That she, at all events, might be recorded as having waited in vain—this affected him sharply, and all the more because of his it first having done little more than amuse himself with the idea. It grew more grave as the gravity of her condition grew, and the state of mind it produced in him, which he himself ended by watching as if it had been some definite disfigurement of his outer person, may pass for another of his surprises. This conjoined itself still with another, the really stupefying consciousness of a question that he would have allowed to shape itself had he dared. What did everything mean—what, that is, did she mean, she and her vain waiting and her probable death and the soundless admonition of it all—unless that, at this time of day, it was simply, it was overwhelmingly too late? He had never at any stage of his queer consciousness admitted the whisper of such a correction; he had never till within these last few months been so false to his conviction as not to hold that what was to come to him had time, whether he struck himself as having it or not. That at last, at last, he certainly hadn't it, to speak of, or had it but in the scantiest measure—such, soon enough, as things went with him, became the inference with which his old obsession had to reckon: and this it was not helped to do by the more and more confirmed appearance that the great vagueness casting the long shadow in which he had lived had, to attest itself, almost no margin left. Since it was in Time that he was to have met his fate, so it was in Time that his fate was to have acted; and as he waked up to the sense of no longer being young, which was exactly the sense of being stale, just as that, in turn, was the sense of being weak, he waked up to another matter beside. It all hung together; they were subject, he and the great vagueness, to an equal and indivisible law. When the possibilities themselves had accordingly turned stale, when the secret of the gods had grown faint, had perhaps even quite evaporated, that, and that only, was failure. It wouldn't have been failure to be bankrupt, dishonoured, pilloried, hanged; it was failure not to be anything. And so, in the dark valley into which his path had taken its unlooked-for twist, he wondered not a little as he groped. He didn't care what awful crash might overtake him, with what ignominy or what monstrosity he might yet he associated—since he wasn't after all too utterly old to suffer—if it would only be decently proportionate to the posture he had kept, all his life, in the threatened presence of it. He had but one desire left—that he shouldn't have been "sold."

CHAPTER IV

Then it was that, one afternoon, while the spring of the year was young and new she met all in her own way his frankest betrayal of these alarms. He had gone in late to see her, but evening hadn't settled and she was presented to him in that long fresh light of waning April days which affects us often with a sadness sharper than the greyest hours of autumn. The week had been warm, the spring was supposed to have begun early, and May Bartram sat, for the first time in the year, without a fire; a fact that, to Marcher's sense, gave the scene of which she formed part a smooth and ultimate look, an air of knowing, in its immaculate order and cold meaningless cheer, that it would never see a fire again. Her own aspect—he could scarce have said why—intensified this note. Almost as white as wax, with the marks and signs in her face as numerous and as fine as if they had been etched by a needle, with soft white draperies relieved by a faded green scarf on the delicate tone of which the years had further refined, she was the picture of a serene and exquisite but impenetrable sphinx, whose head, or indeed all whose person, might have been powdered with silver. She was a sphinx, yet with her white petals and green fronds she might have been a lily too—only an artificial lily, wonderfully imitated and constantly kept, without dust or stain, though not exempt from a slight droop and a complexity of faint creases, under some clear glass bell. The perfection of household care, of high polish and finish, always reigned in her rooms, but they now looked most as if everything had been wound up, tucked in, put away, so that she might sit with folded hands and with nothing more to do. She was "out of it," to Marcher's vision; her work was over; she communicated with him as across some gulf or from some island of rest that she had already reached, and it made him feel strangely abandoned. Was it—or rather wasn't it—that if for so long she had been watching with him the answer to their question must have swum into her ken and taken on its name, so that her occupation was verily gone? He had as much as charged her with this in saying to her, many months before, that she even then knew something she was keeping from him. It was a point he had never since ventured to press, vaguely fearing as he did that it might become a difference, perhaps a disagreement, between them. He had in this later time turned nervous, which was what he in all the other years had never been; and the oddity was that his nervousness should have waited till he had begun to doubt, should have held off so long as he was sure. There was something, it seemed to him, that the wrong word would bring down on his head, something that would so at least ease off his tension. But he wanted not to speak the wrong word; that would make everything ugly. He wanted the knowledge he lacked to drop on him, if drop it could, by its own august weight. If she was to forsake him it was surely for her to take leave. This was why he didn't directly ask her again what she knew; but it was also why, approaching the matter from another side, he said to her in the course of his visit: "What do you regard as the very worst that at this time of day can happen to me?"

He had asked her that in the past often enough; they had, with the odd irregular rhythm of their intensities and avoidances, exchanged ideas about it and then had seen the ideas washed away by cool intervals, washed like figures traced in sea-sand. It had ever been the mark of their talk that the oldest allusions in it required but a little dismissal and reaction to come out again, sounding for the hour as new. She could thus at present meet his enquiry quite freshly and patiently. "Oh yes, I've repeatedly thought, only it always seemed to me of old that I couldn't quite make up my mind. I thought of dreadful things, between which it was difficult to choose; and so must you have done."

"Rather! I feel now as if I had scarce done anything else. I appear to myself to have spent my life in thinking of nothing but dreadful things. A great many of them I've at different times named to you, but there were others I couldn't name."

"They were too, too dreadful?"

"Too, too dreadful—some of them."

She looked at him a minute, and there came to him as he met it, an inconsequent sense that her eyes, when one got their full clearness, were still as beautiful as they had been in youth, only beautiful with a strange cold light—a light that somehow was a part of the effect, if it wasn't rather a part of the cause, of the pale hard sweetness of the season and the hour. "And yet," she said at last, "there are horrors we've mentioned."

It deepened the strangeness to see her, as such a figure in such a picture, talk of "horrors," but she was to do in a few minutes something stranger yet—though even of this he was to take the full measure but afterwards—and the note of it already trembled. It was, for the matter of that, one of the signs that her eyes were having again the high flicker of their prime. He had to admit, however, what she said. "Oh yes, there were times when we did go far." He caught himself in the act of speaking as if it all were over. Well, he wished it were; and the consummation depended for him clearly more and more on his friend.

But she had now a soft smile. "Oh far—!"

It was oddly ironic. "Do you mean you're prepared to go further?"

She was frail and ancient and charming as she continued to look at him, yet it was rather as if she had lost the thread. "Do you consider that we went far?"

"Why I thought it the point you were just making—that we had looked most things in the face."

"Including each other?" She still smiled. "But you're quite right. We've had together great imaginations, often great fears; but some of them have been unspoken."

"Then the worst—we haven't faced that. I could face it, I believe, if I knew what you think it. I feel," he explained, "as if I had lost my power to conceive such things." And he wondered if he looked as blank as he sounded. "It's spent."

"Then why do you assume," she asked, "that mine isn't?"

"Because you've given me signs to the contrary. It isn't a question for you of conceiving, imagining, comparing. It isn't a question now of choosing." At last he came out with it. "You know something I don't. You've shown me that before."

These last words had affected her, he made out in a moment, exceedingly, and she spoke with firmness. "I've shown you, my dear, nothing."

He shook his head. "You can't hide it."

"Oh, oh!" May Bartram sounded over what she couldn't hide. It was almost a smothered groan.

"You admitted it months ago, when I spoke of it to you as of something you were afraid I should find out. Your answer was that I couldn't, that I wouldn't, and I don't pretend I have. But you had something therefore in mind, and I see now how it must have been, how it still is, the possibility that, of all possibilities, has settled itself for you as the worst. This," he went on, "is why I appeal to you. I'm only afraid of ignorance to-day—I'm not afraid of knowledge." And then as for a while she said nothing: "What makes me sure is that I see in your face and feel here, in this air and amid these appearances, that you're out of it. You've done. You've had your experience. You leave me to my fate."

Well, she listened, motionless and white in her chair, as on a decision to be made, so that her manner was fairly an avowal, though still, with a small fine inner stiffness, an imperfect surrender. "It would be the worst," she finally let herself say. "I mean the thing I've never said."

It hushed him a moment. "More monstrous than all the monstrosities we've named?"

"More monstrous. Isn't that what you sufficiently express," she asked, "in calling it the worst?"

Marcher thought. "Assuredly—if you mean, as I do, something that includes all the loss and all the shame that are thinkable."

"It would if it should happen," said May Bartram. "What we're speaking of, remember, is only my idea."

"It's your belief," Marcher returned. "That's enough for me. I feel your beliefs are right. Therefore if, having this one, you give me no more light on it, you abandon me."

"No, no!" she repeated. "I'm with you—don't you see?—still." And as to make it more vivid to him she rose from her chair—a movement she seldom risked in these days—and showed herself, all draped and all soft, in her fairness and slimness. "I haven't forsaken you."

It was really, in its effort against weakness, a generous assurance, and had the success of the impulse not, happily, been great, it would have touched him to pain more than to pleasure. But the cold charm in her eyes had spread, as she hovered before him, to all the rest of her person, so that it was for the minute almost a recovery of youth. He couldn't pity her for that; he could only take her as she showed—as capable even yet of helping him. It was as if, at the same time, her light might at any instant go out; wherefore he must make the most of it. There passed before him with intensity the three or four things he wanted most to know; but the question that came of itself to his lips really covered the others. "Then tell me if I shall consciously suffer."

She promptly shook her head. "Never!"

It confirmed the authority he imputed to her, and it produced on him an extraordinary effect. "Well, what's better than that? Do you call that the worst?"

"You think nothing is better?" she asked.

She seemed to mean something so special that he again sharply wondered, though still with the dawn of a prospect of relief. "Why not, if one doesn't know?" After which, as their eyes, over his question, met in a silence, the dawn deepened, and something to his purpose came prodigiously out of her very face. His own, as he took it in, suddenly flushed to the forehead, and he gasped with the force of a perception to which, on the instant, everything fitted. The sound of his gasp filled the air; then he became articulate. "I see—if I don't suffer!"

In her own look, however, was doubt. "You see what?"

"Why what you mean—what you've always meant."

She again shook her head. "What I mean isn't what I've always meant. It's different."

"It's something new?"

She hung back from it a little. "Something new. It's not what you think. I see what you think."

His divination drew breath then; only her correction might be wrong. "It isn't that I am a blockhead?" he asked between faintness and grimness. "It isn't that it's all a mistake?"

"A mistake?" she pityingly echoed. That possibility, for her, he saw, would be monstrous; and if she guaranteed him the immunity from pain it would accordingly not be what she had in mind. "Oh no," she declared; "it's nothing of that sort. You've been right."

Yet he couldn't help asking himself if she weren't, thus pressed, speaking but to save him. It seemed to him he should be most in a hole if his history should prove all a platitude. "Are you telling me the truth, so that I shan't have been a bigger idiot than I can bear to know? I haven't lived with a vain imagination, in the most besotted illusion? I haven't waited but to see the door shut in my face?"

She shook her head again. "However the case stands that isn't the truth. Whatever the reality, it is a reality. The door isn't shut. The door's open," said May Bartram.

"Then something's to come?"

She waited once again, always with her cold sweet eyes on him. "It's never too late." She had, with her gliding step, diminished the distance between them, and she stood nearer to him, close to him, a minute, as if still charged with the unspoken. Her movement might have been for some finer emphasis of what she was at once hesitating and deciding to say. He had been standing by the chimney-piece, fireless and sparely adorned, a small perfect old French clock and two morsels of rosy Dresden constituting all its furniture; and her hand grasped the shelf while she kept him waiting, grasped it a little as for support and encouragement. She only kept him waiting, however; that is he only waited. It had become suddenly, from her movement and attitude, beautiful and vivid to him that she had something more to give him; her wasted face delicately shone with it—it glittered almost as with the white lustre of silver in her expression. She was right, incontestably, for what he saw in her face was the truth, and strangely, without consequence, while their talk of it as dreadful was still in the air, she appeared to present it as inordinately soft. This, prompting bewilderment, made him but gape the more gratefully for her revelation, so that they continued for some minutes silent, her face shining at him, her contact imponderably pressing, and his stare all kind but all expectant. The end, none the less, was that what he had expected failed to come to him. Something else took place instead, which seemed to consist at first in the mere closing of her eyes. She gave way at the same instant to a slow fine shudder, and though he remained staring—though he stared in fact but the harder—turned off and regained her chair. It was the end of what she had been intending, but it left him thinking only of that.

"Well, you don't say—?"

She had touched in her passage a bell near the chimney and had sunk back strangely pale. "I'm afraid I'm too ill."

"Too ill to tell me?" it sprang up sharp to him, and almost to his lips, the fear she might die without giving him light. He checked himself in time from so expressing his question, but she answered as if she had heard the words.

"Don't you know—now?"

"'Now'—?" She had spoken as if some difference had been made within the moment. But her maid, quickly obedient to her bell, was already with them. "I know nothing." And he was afterwards to say to himself that he must have spoken with odious impatience, such an impatience as to show that, supremely disconcerted, he washed his hands of the whole question.

"Oh!" said May Bartram.

"Are you in pain?" he asked as the woman went to her.

"No," said May Bartram.

Her maid, who had put an arm round her as if to take her to her room, fixed on him eyes that appealingly contradicted her; in spite of which, however, he showed once more his mystification.

"What then has happened?"

She was once more, with her companion's help, on her feet, and, feeling withdrawal imposed on him, he had blankly found his hat and gloves and had reached the door. Yet he waited for her answer. "What was to," she said.

CHAPTER V

He came back the next day, but she was then unable to see him, and as it was literally the first time this had occurred in the long stretch of their acquaintance he turned away, defeated and sore, almost angry—or feeling at least that such a break in their custom was really the beginning of the end—and wandered alone with his thoughts, especially with the one he was least able to keep down. She was dying and he would lose her; she was dying and his life would end. He stopped in the Park, into which he had passed, and stared before him at his recurrent doubt. Away from her the doubt pressed again; in her presence he had believed her, but as he felt his forlornness he threw himself into the explanation that, nearest at hand, had most of a miserable warmth for him and least of a cold torment. She had deceived him to save him—to put him off with something in which he should be able to rest. What could the thing that was to happen to him be, after all, but just this thing that had began to happen? Her dying, her death, his consequent solitude—that was what he had figured as the Beast in the Jungle, that was what had been in the lap of the gods. He had had her word for it as he left her—what else on earth could she have meant? It wasn't a thing of a monstrous order; not a fate rare and distinguished; not a stroke of fortune that overwhelmed and immortalized; it had only the stamp of the common doom. But poor Marcher at this hour judged the common doom sufficient. It would serve his turn, and even as the consummation of infinite waiting he would bend his pride to accept it. He sat down on a bench in the twilight. He hadn't been a fool. Something had been, as she had said, to come. Before he rose indeed it had quite struck him that the final fact really matched with the long avenue through which he had had to reach it. As sharing his suspense and as giving herself all, giving her life, to bring it to an end, she had come with him every step of the way. He had lived by her aid, and to leave her behind would be cruelly, damnably to miss her. What could be more overwhelming than that?

Well, he was to know within the week, for though she kept him a while at bay, left him restless and wretched during a series of days on each of which he asked about her only again to have to turn away, she ended his trial by receiving him where she had always received him. Yet she had been brought out at some hazard into the presence of so many of the things that were, consciously, vainly, half their past, and there was scant service left in the gentleness of her mere desire, all too visible, to check his obsession and wind up his long trouble. That was clearly what she wanted; the one thing more for her own peace while she could still put out her hand. He was so affected by her state that, once seated by her chair, he was moved to let everything go; it was she herself therefore who brought him back, took up again, before she dismissed him, her last word of the other time. She showed how she wished to leave their business in order. "I'm not sure you understood. You've nothing to wait for more. It has come."

Oh how he looked at her! "Really?"

"Really."

"The thing that, as you said, was to?"

"The thing that we began in our youth to watch for."

Face to face with her once more he believed her; it was a claim to which he had so abjectly little to oppose. "You mean that it has come as a positive definite occurrence, with a name and a date?"

"Positive. Definite. I don't know about the 'name,' but, oh with a date!"

He found himself again too helplessly at sea. "But come in the night—come and passed me by?"

May Bartram had her strange faint smile. "Oh no, it hasn't passed you by!"

"But if I haven't been aware of it and it hasn't touched me—?"

"Ah your not being aware of it"—and she seemed to hesitate an instant to deal with this—"your not being aware of it is the strangeness in the strangeness. It's the wonder of the wonder." She spoke as with the softness almost of a sick child, yet now at last, at the end of all, with the perfect straightness of a sibyl. She visibly knew that she knew, and the effect on him was of something co-ordinate, in its high character, with the law that had ruled him. It was the true voice of the law; so on her lips would the law itself have sounded. "It has touched you," she went on. "It has done its office. It has made you all its own."

"So utterly without my knowing it?"

"So utterly without your knowing it." His hand, as he leaned to her, was on the arm of her chair, and, dimly smiling always now, she placed her own on it. "It's enough if I know it."

"Oh!" he confusedly breathed, as she herself of late so often had done.

"What I long ago said is true. You'll never know now, and I think you ought to be content. You've had it," said May Bartram.

"But had what?"

"Why what was to have marked you out. The proof of your law. It has acted. I'm too glad," she then bravely added, "to have been able to see what it's not."

He continued to attach his eyes to her, and with the sense that it was all beyond him, and that she was too, he would still have sharply challenged her hadn't he so felt it an abuse of her weakness to do more than take devoutly what she gave him, take it hushed as to a revelation. If he did speak, it was out of the foreknowledge of his loneliness to come. "If you're glad of what it's 'not' it might then have been worse?"

She turned her eyes away, she looked straight before her; with which after a moment: "Well, you know our fears."

He wondered. "It's something then we never feared?"

On this slowly she turned to him. "Did we ever dream, with all our dreams, that we should sit and talk of it thus?"

He tried for a little to make out that they had; but it was as if their dreams, numberless enough, were in solution in some thick cold mist through which thought lost itself. "It might have been that we couldn't talk."

"Well"—she did her best for him—"not from this side. This, you see," she said, "is the other side."

"I think," poor Marcher returned, "that all sides are the same to me." Then, however, as she gently shook her head in correction: "We mightn't, as it were, have got across—?"

"To where we are—no. We're here"—she made her weak emphasis.

"And much good does it do us!" was her friend's frank comment.

"It does us the good it can. It does us the good that it isn't here. It's past. It's behind," said May Bartram. "Before—" but her voice dropped.

He had got up, not to tire her, but it was hard to combat his yearning. She after all told him nothing but that his light had failed—which he knew well enough without her. "Before—?" he blankly echoed.

"Before you see, it was always to come. That kept it present."

"Oh I don't care what comes now! Besides," Marcher added, "it seems to me I liked it better present, as you say, than I can like it absent with your absence."

"Oh mine!"—and her pale hands made light of it.

"With the absence of everything." He had a dreadful sense of standing there before her for—so far as anything but this proved, this bottomless drop was concerned—the last time of their life. It rested on him with a weight he felt he could scarce bear, and this weight it apparently was that still pressed out what remained in him of speakable protest. "I believe you; but I can't begin to pretend I understand. Nothing, for me, is past; nothing will pass till I pass myself, which I pray my stars may be as soon as possible. Say, however," he added, "that I've eaten my cake, as you contend, to the last crumb—how can the thing I've never felt at all be the thing I was marked out to feel?"

She met him perhaps less directly, but she met him unperturbed. "You take your 'feelings' for granted. You were to suffer your fate. That was not necessarily to know it."

"How in the world—when what is such knowledge but suffering?"

She looked up at him a while in silence. "No—you don't understand."

"I suffer," said John Marcher.

"Don't, don't!"

"How can I help at least that?"

"Don't!" May Bartram repeated.

She spoke it in a tone so special, in spite of her weakness, that he stared an instant—stared as if some light, hitherto hidden, had shimmered across his vision. Darkness again closed over it, but the gleam had already become for him an idea. "Because I haven't the right—?"

"Don't know—when you needn't," she mercifully urged. "You needn't—for we shouldn't."

"Shouldn't?" If he could but know what she meant!

"No— it's too much."

"Too much?" he still asked but with a mystification that was the next moment of a sudden to give way. Her words, if they meant something, affected him in this light—the light also of her wasted face—as meaning all, and the sense of what knowledge had been for herself came over him with a rush which broke through into a question. "Is it of that then you're dying?"

She but watched him, gravely at first, as to see, with this, where he was, and she might have seen something or feared something that moved her sympathy. "I would live for you still—if I could." Her eyes closed for a little, as if, withdrawn into herself, she were for a last time trying. "But I can't!" she said as she raised them again to take leave of him.

She couldn't indeed, as but too promptly and sharply appeared, and he had no vision of her after this that was anything but darkness and doom. They had parted for ever in that strange talk; access to her chamber of pain, rigidly guarded, was almost wholly forbidden him; he was feeling now moreover, in the face of doctors, nurses, the two or three relatives attracted doubtless by the presumption of what she had to "leave," how few were the rights, as they were called in such cases, that he had to put forward, and how odd it might even seem that their intimacy shouldn't have given him more of them. The stupidest fourth cousin had more, even though she had been nothing in such a person's life. She had been a feature of features in his, for what else was it to have been so indispensable? Strange beyond saying were the ways of existence, baffling for him the anomaly of his lack, as he felt it to be, of producible claim. A woman might have been, as it were, everything to him, and it might yet present him, in no connexion that any one seemed held to recognise. If this was the case in these closing weeks it was the case more sharply on the occasion of the last offices rendered, in the great grey London cemetery, to what had been mortal, to what had been precious, in his friend. The concourse at her grave was not numerous, but he saw himself treated as scarce more nearly concerned with it than if there had been a thousand others. He was in short from this moment face to face with the fact that he was to profit extraordinarily little by the interest May Bartram had taken in him. He couldn't quite have said what he expected, but he hadn't surely expected this approach to a double privation. Not only had her interest failed him, but he seemed to feel himself unattended—and for a reason he couldn't seize—by the distinction, the dignity, the propriety, if nothing else, of the man markedly bereaved. It was as if, in the view of society he had not been markedly bereaved, as if there still failed some sign or proof of it, and as if none the less his character could never be affirmed nor the deficiency ever made up. There were moments as the weeks went by when he would have liked, by some almost aggressive act, to take his stand on the intimacy of his loss, in order that it might be questioned and his retort, to the relief of his spirit, so recorded; but the moments of an irritation more helpless followed fast on these, the moments during which, turning things over with a good conscience but with a bare horizon, he found himself wondering if he oughtn't to have begun, so to speak, further back.

He found himself wondering indeed at many things, and this last speculation had others to keep it company. What could he have done, after all, in her lifetime, without giving them both, as it were, away? He couldn't have made known she was watching him, for that would have published the superstition of the Beast. This was what closed his mouth now—now that the Jungle had been thrashed to vacancy and that the Beast had stolen away. It sounded too foolish and too flat; the difference for him in this particular, the extinction in his life of the element of suspense, was such as in fact to surprise him. He could scarce have said what the effect resembled; the abrupt cessation, the positive prohibition, of music perhaps, more than anything else, in some place all adjusted and all accustomed to sonority and to attention. If he could at any rate have conceived lifting the veil from his image at some moment of the past (what had he done, after all, if not lift it to her?) so to do this to-day, to talk to people at large of the Jungle cleared and confide to them that he now felt it as safe, would have been not only to see them listen as to a goodwife's tale, but really to hear himself tell one. What it presently came to in truth was that poor Marcher waded through his beaten grass, where no life stirred, where no breath sounded, where no evil eye seemed to gleam from a possible lair, very much as if vaguely looking for the Beast, and still more as if acutely missing it. He walked about in an existence that had grown strangely more spacious, and, stopping fitfully in places where the undergrowth of life struck him as closer, asked himself yearningly, wondered secretly and sorely, if it would have lurked here or there. It would have at all events sprung; what was at least complete was his belief in the truth itself of the assurance given him. The change from his old sense to his new was absolute and final: what was to happen had so absolutely and finally happened that he was as little able to know a fear for his future as to know a hope; so absent in short was any question of anything still to come. He was to live entirely with the other question, that of his unidentified past, that of his having to see his fortune impenetrably muffled and masked.

The torment of this vision became then his occupation; he couldn't perhaps have consented to live but for the possibility of guessing. She had told him, his friend, not to guess; she had forbidden him, so far as he might, to know, and she had even in a sort denied the power in him to learn: which were so many things, precisely, to deprive him of rest. It wasn't that he wanted, he argued for fairness, that anything past and done should repeat itself; it was only that he shouldn't, as an anticlimax, have been taken sleeping so sound as not to be able to win back by an effort of thought the lost stuff of consciousness. He declared to himself at moments that he would either win it back or have done with consciousness for ever; he made this idea his one motive in fine, made it so much his passion that none other, to compare with it, seemed ever to have touched him. The lost stuff of consciousness became thus for him as a strayed or stolen child to an unappeasable father; he hunted it up and down very much as if he were knocking at doors and enquiring of the police. This was the spirit in which, inevitably, he set himself to travel; he started on a journey that was to be as long as he could make it; it danced before him that, as the other side of the globe couldn't possibly have less to say to him, it might, by a possibility of suggestion, have more. Before he quitted London, however, he made a pilgrimage to May Bartram's grave, took his way to it through the endless avenues of the grim suburban necropolis, sought it out in the wilderness of tombs, and, though he had come but for the renewal of the act of farewell, found himself, when he had at last stood by it, beguiled into long intensities. He stood for an hour, powerless to turn away and yet powerless to penetrate the darkness of death; fixing with his eyes her inscribed name and date, beating his forehead against the fact of the secret they kept, drawing his breath, while he waited, as if some sense would in pity of him rise from the stones. He kneeled on the stones, however, in vain; they kept what they concealed; and if the face of the tomb did become a face for him it was because her two names became a pair of eyes that didn't know him. He gave them a last long look, but no palest light broke.

CHAPTER VI

He stayed away, after this, for a year; he visited the depths of Asia, spending himself on scenes of romantic interest, of superlative sanctity; but what was present to him everywhere was that for a man who had known what he had known the world was vulgar and vain. The state of mind in which he had lived for so many years shone out to him, in reflexion, as a light that coloured and refined, a light beside which the glow of the East was garish cheap and thin. The terrible truth was that he had lost—with everything else—a distinction as well the things he saw couldn't help being common when he had become common to look at them. He was simply now one of them himself—he was in the dust, without a peg for the sense of difference; and there were hours when, before the temples of gods and the sepulchers of kings, his spirit turned for nobleness of association to the barely discriminated slab in the London suburb. That had become for him, and more intensely with time and distance, his one witness of a past glory. It was all that was left to him for proof or pride, yet the past glories of Pharaohs were nothing to him as he thought of it. Small wonder then that he came back to it on the morrow of his return. He was drawn there this time as irresistibly as the other, yet with a confidence, almost, that was doubtless the effect of the many months that had elapsed. He had lived, in spite of himself, into his change of feeling, and in wandering over the earth had wandered, as might be said, from the circumference to the centre of his desert. He had settled to his safety and accepted perforce his extinction; figuring to himself, with some colour, in the likeness of certain little old men he remembered to have seen, of whom, all meagre and wizened as they might look, it was related that they had in their time fought twenty duels or been loved by ten princesses. They indeed had been wondrous for others while he was but wondrous for himself; which, however, was exactly the cause of his haste to renew the wonder by getting back, as he might put it, into his own presence. That had quickened his steps and checked his delay. If his visit was prompt it was because he had been separated so long from the part of himself that alone he now valued.

It's accordingly not false to say that he reached his goal with a certain elation and stood there again with a certain assurance. The creature beneath the sod knew of his rare experience, so that, strangely now, the place had lost for him its mere blankness of expression. It met him in mildness—not, as before, in mockery; it wore for him the air of conscious greeting that we find, after absence, in things that have closely belonged to us and which seem to confess of themselves to the connexion. The plot of ground, the graven tablet, the tended flowers affected him so as belonging to him that he resembled for the hour a contented landlord reviewing a piece of property. Whatever had happened—well, had happened. He had not come back this time with the vanity of that question, his former worrying "What, what?" now practically so spent. Yet he would none the less never again so cut himself off from the spot; he would come back to it every month, for if he did nothing else by its aid he at least held up his head. It thus grew for him, in the oddest way, a positive resource; he carried out his idea of periodical returns, which took their place at last among the most inveterate of his habits. What it all amounted to, oddly enough, was that in his finally so simplified world this garden of death gave him the few square feet of earth on which he could still most live. It was as if, being nothing anywhere else for any one, nothing even for himself, he were just everything here, and if not for a crowd of witnesses or indeed for any witness but John Marcher, then by clear right of the register that he could scan like an open page. The open page was the tomb of his friend, and there were the facts of the past, there the truth of his life, there the backward reaches in which he could lose himself. He did this from time to time with such effect that he seemed to wander through the old years with his hand in the arm of a companion who was, in the most extraordinary manner, his other, his younger self; and to wander, which was more extraordinary yet, round and round a third presence—not wandering she, but stationary, still, whose eyes, turning with his revolution, never ceased to follow him, and whose seat was his point, so to speak, of orientation. Thus in short he settled to live—feeding all on the sense that he once had lived, and dependent on it not alone for a support but for an identity.

It sufficed him in its way for months and the year elapsed; it would doubtless even have carried him further but for an accident, superficially slight, which moved him, quite in another direction, with a force beyond any of his impressions of Egypt or of India. It was a thing of the merest chance—the turn, as he afterwards felt, of a hair, though he was indeed to live to believe that if light hadn't come to him in this particular fashion it would still have come in another. He was to live to believe this, I say, though he was not to live, I may not less definitely mention, to do much else. We allow him at any rate the benefit of the conviction, struggling up for him at the end, that, whatever might have happened or not happened, he would have come round of himself to the light. The incident of an autumn day had put the match to the train laid from of old by his misery. With the light before him he knew that even of late his ache had only been smothered. It was strangely drugged, but it throbbed; at the touch it began to bleed. And the touch, in the event, was the face of a fellow-mortal. This face, one grey afternoon when the leaves were thick in the alleys, looked into Marcher's own, at the cemetery, with an expression like the cut of a blade. He felt it, that is, so deep down that he winced at the steady thrust. The person who so mutely assaulted him was a figure he had noticed, on reaching his own goal, absorbed by a grave a short distance away, a grave apparently fresh, so that the emotion of the visitor would probably match it for frankness. This fact alone forbade further attention, though during the time he stayed he remained vaguely conscious of his neighbour, a middle-aged man apparently, in mourning, whose bowed back, among the clustered monuments and mortuary yews, was constantly presented. Marcher's theory that these were elements in contact with which he himself revived, had suffered, on this occasion, it may be granted, a marked, an excessive check. The autumn day was dire for him as none had recently been, and he rested with a heaviness he had not yet known on the low stone table that bore May Bartram's name. He rested without power to move, as if some spring in him, some spell vouchsafed, had suddenly been broken for ever. If he could have done that moment as he wanted he would simply have stretched himself on the slab that was ready to take him, treating it as a place prepared to receive his last sleep. What in all the wide world had he now to keep awake for? He stared before him with the question, and it was then that, as one of the cemetery walks passed near him, he caught the shock of the face.

His neighbour at the other grave had withdrawn, as he himself, with force enough in him, would have done by now, and was advancing along the path on his way to one of the gates. This brought him close, and his pace, was slow, so that—and all the more as there was a kind of hunger in his look—the two men were for a minute directly confronted.

Marcher knew him at once for one of the deeply stricken—a perception so sharp that nothing else in the picture comparatively lived, neither his dress, his age, nor his presumable character and class; nothing lived but the deep ravage of the features that he showed. He showed them—that was the point; he was moved, as he passed, by some impulse that was either a signal for sympathy or, more possibly, a challenge to an opposed sorrow. He might already have been aware of our friend, might at some previous hour have noticed in him the smooth habit of the scene, with which the state of his own senses so scantly consorted, and might thereby have been stirred as by an overt discord. What Marcher was at all events conscious of was in the first place that the image of scarred passion presented to him was conscious too—of something that profaned the air; and in the second that, roused, startled, shocked, he was yet the next moment looking after it, as it went, with envy. The most extraordinary thing that had happened to him—though he had given that name to other matters as well—took place, after his immediate vague stare, as a consequence of this impression. The stranger passed, but the raw glare of his grief remained, making our friend wonder in pity what wrong, what wound it expressed, what injury not to be healed. What had the man had, to make him by the loss of it so bleed and yet live?

Something—and this reached him with a pang—that he, John Marcher, hadn't; the proof of which was precisely John Marcher's arid end. No passion had ever touched him, for this was what passion meant; he had survived and maundered and pined, but where had been his deep ravage? The extraordinary thing we speak of was the sudden rush of the result of this question. The sight that had just met his eyes named to him, as in letters of quick flame, something he had utterly, insanely missed, and what he had missed made these things a train of fire, made them mark themselves in an anguish of inward throbs. He had seen outside of his life, not learned it within, the way a woman was mourned when she had been loved for herself: such was the force of his conviction of the meaning of the stranger's face, which still flared for him as a smoky torch. It hadn't come to him, the knowledge, on the wings of experience; it had brushed him, jostled him, upset him, with the disrespect of chance, the insolence of accident. Now that the illumination had begun, however, it blazed to the zenith, and what he presently stood there gazing at was the sounded void of his life. He gazed, he drew breath, in pain; he turned in his dismay, and, turning, he had before him in sharper incision than ever the open page of his story. The name on the table smote him as the passage of his neighbour had done, and what it said to him, full in the face, was that she was what he had missed. This was the awful thought, the answer to all the past, the vision at the dread clearness of which he turned as cold as the stone beneath him. Everything fell together, confessed, explained, overwhelmed; leaving him most of all stupefied at the blindness he had cherished. The fate he had been marked for he had met with a vengeance—he had emptied the cup to the lees; he had been the man of his time, the man, to whom nothing on earth was to have happened. That was the rare stroke—that was his visitation. So he saw it, as we say, in pale horror, while the pieces fitted and fitted. So she had seen it while he didn't, and so she served at this hour to drive the truth home. It was the truth, vivid and monstrous, that all the while he had waited the wait was itself his portion. This the companion of his vigil had at a given moment made out, and she had then offered him the chance to baffle his doom. One's doom, however, was never baffled, and on the day she told him his own had come down she had seen him but stupidly stare at the escape she offered him.

The escape would have been to love her; then, then he would have lived. She had lived—who could say now with what passion?—since she had loved him for himself;

whereas he had never thought of her (ah how it hugely glared at him!) but in the chill of his egotism and the light of her use. Her spoken words came back to him—the chain stretched and stretched. The Beast had lurked indeed, and the Beast, at its hour, had sprung; it had sprung in that twilight of the cold April when, pale, ill, wasted, but all beautiful, and perhaps even then recoverable, she had risen from her chair to stand before him and let him imaginably guess. It had sprung as he didn't guess; it had sprung as she hopelessly turned from him, and the mark, by the time he left her, had fallen where it was to fall. He had justified his fear and achieved his fate; he had failed, with the last exactitude, of all he was to fail of; and a moan now rose to his lips as he remembered she had prayed he mightn't know. This horror of waking—this was knowledge, knowledge under the breath of which the very tears in his eyes seemed to freeze. Through them, none the less, he tried to fix it and hold it; he kept it there before him so that he might feel the pain. That at least, belated and bitter, had something of the taste of life. But the bitterness suddenly sickened him, and it was as if, horribly, he saw, in the truth, in the cruelty of his image, what had been appointed and done. He saw the Jungle of his life and saw the lurking Beast; then, while he looked, perceived it, as by a stir of the air, rise, huge and hideous, for the leap that was to settle him. His eyes darkened—it was close; and, instinctively turning, in his hallucination, to avoid it, he flung himself, face down, on the tomb.

THE DEATH OF THE LION

CHAPTER I

I had simply, I suppose, a change of heart, and it must have begun when I received my manuscript back from Mr. Pinhorn. Mr. Pinhorn was my "chief," as he was called in the office: he had the high mission of bringing the paper up. This was a weekly periodical, which had been supposed to be almost past redemption when he took hold of it. It was Mr. Deedy who had let the thing down so dreadfully: he was never mentioned in the office now save in connexion with that misdemeanour. Young as I was I had been in a manner taken over from Mr. Deedy, who had been owner as well as editor; forming part of a promiscuous lot, mainly plant and office-furniture, which poor Mrs. Deedy, in her bereavement and depression, parted with at a rough valuation. I could account for my continuity but on the supposition that I had been cheap. I rather resented the practice of fathering all flatness on my late protector, who was in his unhonoured grave; but as I had my way to make I found matter enough for complacency in being on a "staff." At the same time I was aware of my exposure to suspicion as a product of the old lowering system. This made me feel I was doubly bound to have ideas, and had doubtless been at the bottom of my proposing to Mr. Pinhorn that I should lay my lean hands on Neil Paraday. I remember how he looked at me—quite, to begin with, as if he had never heard of this celebrity, who indeed at that moment was by no means in the centre of the heavens; and even when I had knowingly explained he expressed but little confidence in the demand for any such stuff. When I had reminded him that the great principle on which we were supposed to work was just to create the demand we required, he considered a moment and then returned: "I see—you want to write him up."

"Call it that if you like."

"And what's your inducement?"

"Bless my soul—my admiration!"

Mr. Pinhorn pursed up his mouth. "Is there much to be done with him?"

"Whatever there is we should have it all to ourselves, for he hasn't been touched."

This argument was effective and Mr. Pinhorn responded. "Very well, touch him." Then he added: "But where can you do it?"

"Under the fifth rib!"

Mr. Pinhorn stared. "Where's that?"

"You want me to go down and see him?" I asked when I had enjoyed his visible search for the obscure suburb I seemed to have named.

"I don't 'want' anything—the proposal's your own. But you must remember that that's the way we do things now," said Mr. Pinhorn with another dig Mr. Deedy.

Unregenerate as I was I could read the queer implications of this speech. The present owner's superior virtue as well as his deeper craft spoke in his reference to the late editor as one of that baser sort who deal in false representations. Mr. Deedy would as soon have sent me to call on Neil Paraday as he would have published a "holiday-number"; but such scruples presented themselves as mere ignoble thrift to his successor, whose own sincerity took the form of ringing door-bells and whose definition of genius was the art of finding people at home. It was as if Mr. Deedy had published reports without his young men's having, as Pinhorn would have said, really been there. I was unregenerate, as I have hinted, and couldn't be concerned to straighten out the journalistic morals of my chief, feeling them indeed to be an abyss over the edge of which it was better not to peer. Really to be there this time moreover was a vision that made the idea of writing something subtle about Neil Paraday only the more inspiring. I would be as considerate as even Mr. Deedy could have wished, and yet I should be as present as only Mr. Pinhorn could conceive. My allusion to the sequestered manner in which Mr. Paraday lived—it had formed part of my explanation, though I knew of it only by hearsay—was, I could divine, very much what had made Mr. Pinhorn nibble. It struck him as inconsistent with the success of his paper that any one should be so sequestered as that. And then wasn't an immediate exposure of everything just what the public wanted? Mr. Pinhorn effectually called me to order by reminding me of the promptness with which I had met Miss Braby at Liverpool on her return from her fiasco in the States. Hadn't we published, while its freshness and flavour were unimpaired, Miss Braby's own version of that great international episode? I felt somewhat uneasy at this lumping of the actress and the author, and I confess that after having enlisted Mr. Pinhorn's sympathies I procrastinated a little. I had succeeded better than I wished, and I had, as it happened, work nearer at hand. A few days later I called on Lord Crouchley and carried off in triumph the most unintelligible statement that had yet appeared of his lordship's reasons for his change of front. I thus set in motion in the daily papers columns of virtuous verbiage. The following week I ran down to Brighton for a chat, as Mr. Pinhorn called it, with Mrs. Bounder, who gave me, on the subject of her divorce, many curious particulars that had not been articulated in court. If ever an article flowed from the primal fount it was that article on Mrs. Bounder. By this time, however, I became aware that Neil Paraday's new book was on the point of appearing and that its approach had been the ground of my original appeal to Mr. Pinhorn, who was now annoyed with me for having lost so many days. He bundled me off—we would at least not lose another. I've always thought his sudden alertness a remarkable example of the journalistic instinct. Nothing had occurred, since I first spoke to him, to create a visible urgency, and no enlightenment could possibly have reached him. It was a pure case of profession flair—he had smelt the coming glory as an animal smells its distant prey.

CHAPTER II

I may as well say at once that this little record pretends in no degree to be a picture either of my introduction to Mr. Paraday or of certain proximate steps and stages. The scheme of my narrative allows no space for these things, and in any case a prohibitory sentiment would hang about my recollection of so rare an hour. These meagre notes are essentially private, so that if they see the light the insidious forces that, as my story itself shows, make at present for publicity will simply have overmastered my precautions. The curtain fell lately enough on the lamentable drama. My memory of the day I alighted at Mr. Paraday's door is a fresh memory of kindness, hospitality, compassion, and of the wonderful illuminating talk in which the welcome was conveyed. Some voice of the air had taught me the right moment, the moment of his life at which an act of unexpected young allegiance might most come home to him. He had recently recovered from a long, grave illness. I had gone to the neighbouring inn for the night, but I spent the evening in his company, and he insisted the next day on my sleeping under his roof. I hadn't an indefinite leave: Mr. Pinhorn supposed us to put our victims through on the gallop. It was later, in the office, that the rude motions of the jig were set to music. I fortified myself, however, as my training had taught me to do, by the conviction that nothing could be more advantageous for my article than to be written in the very atmosphere. I said nothing to Mr. Paraday about it, but in the morning, after my remove from the inn, while he was occupied in his study, as he had notified me he should need to be, I committed to paper the main heads of my impression. Then thinking to commend myself to Mr. Pinhorn by my celerity, I walked out and posted my little packet before luncheon. Once my paper was written I was free to stay on, and if it was calculated to divert attention from my levity in so doing I could reflect with satisfaction that I had never been so clever. I don't mean to deny of course that I was aware it was much too good for Mr. Pinhorn; but I was equally conscious that Mr. Pinhorn had the supreme shrewdness of recognising from time to time the cases in which an article was not too bad only because it was too good. There was nothing he loved so much as to print on the right occasion a thing he hated. I had begun my visit to the great man on a Monday, and on the Wednesday his book came out. A copy of it arrived by the first post, and he let me go out into the garden with it immediately after breakfast, I read it from beginning to end that day, and in the evening he asked me to remain with him the rest of the week and over the Sunday.

That night my manuscript came back from Mr. Pinhorn, accompanied with a letter the gist of which was the desire to know what I meant by trying to fob off on him such stuff. That was the meaning of the question, if not exactly its form, and it made my mistake immense to me. Such as this mistake was I could now only look it in the face and accept it. I knew where I had failed, but it was exactly where I couldn't have succeeded. I had been sent down to be personal and then in point of fact hadn't been personal at all: what I had dispatched to London was just a little finicking feverish study of my author's talent. Anything less relevant to Mr. Pinhorn's purpose couldn't well be imagined, and he was visibly angry at my having (at his expense, with a second-class ticket) approached the subject of our enterprise only to stand off so helplessly. For myself, I knew but too well what had happened, and how a miracle—as pretty as some old miracle of legend—had been wrought on the spot to save me. There had been a big brush of wings, the flash of an opaline robe, and then, with a great cool stir of the air, the sense of an angel's having swooped down and caught me to his bosom. He held me only till the danger was over, and it all took place in a minute. With my manuscript back on my hands I understood the phenomenon better, and the reflexions I made on it are what I meant, at the beginning of this anecdote, by my change of heart. Mr. Pinhorn's note was not only a rebuke decidedly stern, but an invitation immediately to send him—it was the case to say so—the genuine article, the revealing and reverberating sketch to the promise of which, and of which alone, I owed my squandered privilege. A week or two later I recast my peccant paper and, giving it a particular application to Mr. Paraday's new book, obtained for it the hospitality of another journal, where, I must admit, Mr. Pinhorn was so far vindicated as that it attracted not the least attention.

CHAPTER III

I was frankly, at the end of three days, a very prejudiced critic, so that one morning when, in the garden, my great man had offered to read me something I quite held my breath as I listened. It was the written scheme of another book—something put aside long ago, before his illness, but that he had lately taken out again to reconsider. He had been turning it round when I came down on him, and it had grown magnificently under this second hand. Loose liberal confident, it might have passed for a great gossiping eloquent letter—the overflow into talk of an artist's amorous plan. The theme I thought singularly rich, quite the strongest he had yet treated; and this familiar statement of it, full too of fine maturities, was really, in summarised splendour, a mine of gold, a precious independent work. I remember rather profanely wondering whether the ultimate production could possibly keep at the pitch. His reading of the fond epistle, at any rate, made me feel as if I were, for the advantage of posterity, in close correspondence with him—were the distinguished person to whom it had been affectionately addressed. It was a high distinction simply to be told such things. The idea he now communicated had all the freshness, the flushed fairness, of the conception untouched and untried: it was Venus rising from the sea and before the airs had blown upon her. I had never been so throbbingly present at such an unveiling. But when he had tossed the last bright word after the others, as I had seen cashiers in banks, weighing mounds of coin, drop a final sovereign into the tray, I knew a sudden prudent alarm.

"My dear master, how, after all, are you going to do it? It's infinitely noble, but what time it will take, what patience and independence, what assured, what perfect conditions! Oh for a lone isle in a tepid sea!"

"Isn't this practically a lone isle, and aren't you, as an encircling medium, tepid enough?" he asked, alluding with a laugh to the wonder of my young admiration and the narrow limits of his little provincial home. "Time isn't what I've lacked hitherto: the question hasn't been to find it, but to use it. Of course my illness made, while it lasted, a great hole—but I dare say there would have been a hole at any rate. The earth we tread has more pockets than a billiard-table. The great thing is now to keep on my feet."

"That's exactly what I mean."

Neil Paraday looked at me with eyes—such pleasant eyes as he had—in which, as I now recall their expression, I seem to have seen a dim imagination of his fate. He was fifty years old, and his illness had been cruel, his convalescence slow. "It isn't as if I weren't all right."

"Oh if you weren't all right I wouldn't look at you!" I tenderly said.

We had both got up, quickened as by this clearer air, and he had lighted a cigarette. I had taken a fresh one, which with an intenser smile, by way of answer to my exclamation, he applied to the flame of his match. "If I weren't better I shouldn't have thought of that!" He flourished his script in his hand.

"I don't want to be discouraging, but that's not true," I returned. "I'm sure that during the months you lay here in pain you had visitations sublime. You thought of a thousand things. You think of more and more all the while. That's what makes you, if you'll pardon my familiarity, so respectable. At a time when so many people are spent you come into your second wind. But, thank God, all the same, you're better! Thank God, too, you're not, as you were telling me yesterday, 'successful.' If you weren't a failure what would be the use of trying? That's my one reserve on the subject of your recovery—that it makes you 'score,' as the newspapers say. It looks well in the newspapers, and almost anything that does that's horrible. 'We are happy to announce that Mr. Paraday, the celebrated author, is again in the enjoyment of excellent health.' Somehow I shouldn't like to see it."

"You won't see it; I'm not in the least celebrated—my obscurity protects me. But couldn't you bear even to see I was dying or dead?" my host enquired.

"Dead—*passe encore*; there's nothing so safe. One never knows what a living artist may do—one has mourned so many. However, one must make the worst of it. You must be as dead as you can."

"Don't I meet that condition in having just published a book?"

"Adequately, let us hope; for the book's verily a masterpiece."

At this moment the parlour-maid appeared in the door that opened from the garden: Paraday lived at no great cost, and the frisk of petticoats, with a timorous "Sherry, sir?" was about his modest mahogany. He allowed half his income to his wife, from whom he had succeeded in separating without redundancy of legend. I had a general faith in his having behaved well, and I had once, in London, taken Mrs. Paraday down to dinner. He now turned to speak to the maid, who offered him, on a tray, some card or note, while, agitated, excited, I wandered to the end of the precinct. The idea of his security became supremely dear to me, and I asked myself if I were the same young man who had come down a few days before to scatter him to the four winds. When I retraced my steps he had gone into the house, and the woman—the second London post had come in—had placed my letters and a newspaper on a bench. I sat down there to the letters, which were a brief business, and then, without heeding the address, took the paper from its envelope. It was the journal of highest renown, *The Empire* of that morning. It regularly came to Paraday, but I remembered that neither of us had yet looked at the copy already delivered. This one had a great mark on the "editorial" page, and, uncrumpling the wrapper, I saw it to be directed to my host and stamped with the name of his publishers. I instantly divined that *The Empire* had spoken of him, and I've not forgotten the odd little shock of the circumstance. It checked all eagerness and made me drop the paper a moment. As I sat there conscious of a palpitation I think I had a vision of what was to be. I had also a vision of the letter I would presently address to Mr. Pinhorn, breaking, as it were, with Mr. Pinhorn. Of course, however, the next minute the voice of *The Empire* was in my ears.

The article wasn't, I thanked heaven, a review; it was a "leader," the last of three, presenting Neil Paraday to the human race. His new book, the fifth from his hand, had been but a day or two out, and *The Empire*, already aware of it, fired, as if on the birth of a prince, a salute of a whole column. The guns had been booming these three hours in the house without our suspecting them. The big blundering newspaper had discovered him, and now he was proclaimed and anointed and crowned. His place was assigned him as publicly as if a fat usher with a wand had pointed to the topmost chair; he was to pass up and still up, higher and higher, between the watching faces and the envious sounds—away up to the dais and the throne. The article was "epoch-making," a landmark in his life; he had taken rank at a bound, waked up a national glory. A national glory was needed, and it was an immense convenience he was there. What all this meant rolled over me, and I fear I grew a little faint—it meant so much more than I could say "yea" to on the spot. In a flash, somehow, all was different; the tremendous wave I speak of had swept something away. It had knocked down, I suppose, my little customary altar, my twinkling tapers and my flowers, and had reared itself into the likeness of a temple vast and bare. When Neil Paraday should come out of the house he would come out a contemporary. That was what had happened: the poor man was to be squeezed into his horrible age. I felt as if he had been overtaken on the crest of the hill and brought back to the city. A little more and he would have dipped down the short cut to posterity and escaped.

CHAPTER IV

When he came out it was exactly as if he had been in custody, for beside him walked a stout man with a big black beard, who, save that he wore spectacles, might have been a policeman, and in whom at a second glance I recognised the highest contemporary enterprise.

"This is Mr. Morrow," said Paraday, looking, I thought, rather white: "he wants to publish heaven knows what about me."

I winced as I remembered that this was exactly what I myself had wanted. "Already?" I cried with a sort of sense that my friend had fled to me for protection.

Mr. Morrow glared, agreeably, through his glasses: they suggested the electric headlights of some monstrous modem ship, and I felt as if Paraday and I were tossing terrified under his bows. I saw his momentum was irresistible. "I was confident that I should be the first in the field. A great interest is naturally felt in Mr. Paraday's surroundings," he heavily observed.

"I hadn't the least idea of it," said Paraday, as if he had been told he had been snoring.

"I find he hasn't read the article in *The Empire*," Mr. Morrow remarked to me. "That's so very interesting—it's something to start with," he smiled. He had begun to pull off his gloves, which were violently new, and to look encouragingly round the little garden. As a "surrounding" I felt how I myself had already been taken in; I was a little fish in the stomach of a bigger one. "I represent," our visitor continued, "a syndicate of influential journals, no less than thirty-seven, whose public—whose publics, I may say—are in peculiar sympathy with Mr. Paraday's line of thought. They would greatly appreciate any expression of his views on the subject of the art he so nobly exemplifies. In addition to my connexion with the syndicate just mentioned I hold a particular commission from *The Tatler*, whose most prominent department, 'Smatter and Chatter'—I dare say you've often enjoyed it—attracts such attention. I was honoured only last week, as a representative of *The Tatler*, with the confidence of Guy Walsingham, the brilliant author of 'Obsessions.' She pronounced herself thoroughly pleased with my sketch of her method; she went so far as to say that I had made her genius more comprehensible even to herself."

Neil Paraday had dropped on the garden-bench and sat there at once detached and confounded; he looked hard at a bare spot in the lawn, as if with an anxiety that had suddenly made him grave. His movement had been interpreted by his visitor as an invitation to sink sympathetically into a wicker chair that stood hard by, and while Mr. Morrow so settled himself I felt he had taken official possession and that there was no undoing it. One had heard of unfortunate people's having "a man in the house," and this was just what we had. There was a silence of a moment, during which we seemed to acknowledge in the only way that was possible the presence of universal fate; the sunny stillness took no pity, and my thought, as I was sure Paraday's was doing, performed within the minute a great distant revolution. I saw just how emphatic I should make my rejoinder to Mr. Pinhorn, and that having come, like Mr. Morrow, to betray, I must remain as long as possible to save. Not because I had brought my mind back, but because our visitors last words were in my ear, I presently enquired with gloomy irrelevance if Guy Walsingham were a woman.

"Oh yes, a mere pseudonym—rather pretty, isn't it?—and convenient, you know, for a lady who goes in for the larger latitude. 'Obsessions, by Miss So-and-so,' would look a little odd, but men are more naturally indelicate. Have you peeped into 'Obsessions'?" Mr. Morrow continued sociably to our companion.

Paraday, still absent, remote, made no answer, as if he hadn't heard the question: a form of intercourse that appeared to suit the cheerful Mr. Morrow as well as any other. Imperturbably bland, he was a man of resources—he only needed to be on the spot. He had pocketed the whole poor place while Paraday and I were wool-gathering, and I could imagine that he had already got his "heads." His system, at any rate, was justified by the inevitability with which I replied, to save my friend the trouble: "Dear no—he hasn't read it. He doesn't read such things!" I unwarily added.

"Things that are *too* far over the fence, eh?" I was indeed a godsend to Mr. Morrow. It was the psychological moment; it determined the appearance of his note-book, which, however, he at first kept slightly behind him, even as the dentist approaching his victim keeps the horrible forceps. "Mr. Paraday holds with the good old proprieties—I see!" And thinking of the thirty-seven influential journals, I found myself, as I found poor Paraday, helplessly assisting at the promulgation of this ineptitude. "There's no point on which distinguished views are so acceptable as on this question—raised perhaps more strikingly than ever by Guy Walsingham—of the permissibility of the larger latitude. I've an appointment, precisely in connexion with it, next week, with Dora Forbes, author of 'The Other Way Round,' which everybody's talking about. Has Mr. Paraday glanced at 'The Other Way Round'?" Mr. Morrow now frankly appealed to me. I took on myself to repudiate the supposition, while our companion, still silent, got up nervously and walked away. His visitor paid no heed to his withdrawal; but opened out the note-book with a more fatherly pat. "Dora Forbes, I gather, takes the ground, the same as Guy Walsingham's, that the larger latitude has simply got to come. He holds that it has got to be squarely faced. Of course *his* sex makes him a less prejudiced witness. But an authoritative word from Mr. Paraday—from the point of view of his sex, you know—would go right round the globe. He takes the line that we *haven't* got to face it?"

I was bewildered: it sounded somehow as if there were three sexes. My interlocutor's pencil was poised, my private responsibility great. I simply sat staring, none the less, and only found presence of mind to say: "Is this Miss Forbes a gentleman?"

Mr. Morrow had a subtle smile. "It wouldn't be 'Miss'—there's a wife!"

"I mean is she a man?"

"The wife?"—Mr. Morrow was for a moment as confused as myself. But when I explained that I alluded to Dora Forbes in person he informed me, with visible amusement at my being so out of it, that this was the "pen-name" of an indubitable male—he had a big red moustache. "He goes in for the slight mystification because the ladies are such popular favourites. A great deal of interest is felt in his acting on that idea—which is clever, isn't it?—and there's every prospect of its being widely imitated." Our host at this moment joined us again, and Mr. Morrow remarked invitingly that he should be happy to make a note of any observation the movement in question, the bid for success under a lady's name, might suggest to Mr. Paraday. But the poor man, without catching the allusion, excused himself, pleading that, though greatly honoured by his visitor's interest, he suddenly felt unwell and should have to take leave of him—have to go and lie down and keep quiet. His young friend might be trusted to answer for him, but he hoped Mr. Morrow didn't expect great things even of his young friend. His young friend, at this moment, looked at Neil Paraday with an anxious eye, greatly wondering if he were doomed to be ill again; but Paraday's own kind face met his question reassuringly, seemed to say in a glance intelligible enough: "Oh I'm not ill, but I'm scared: get him out of the house as quietly as possible." Getting newspaper-men out of the house was odd business for an emissary of Mr. Pinhorn, and I was so exhilarated by the idea of it that I called after him as he left us: "Read the article in *The Empire* and you'll soon be all right!"

CHAPTER V

"Delicious my having come down to tell him of it!" Mr. Morrow ejaculated. "My cab was at the door twenty minutes after *The Empire* had been laid on my breakfast-table. Now what have you got for me?" he continued, dropping again into his chair, from which, however, he the next moment eagerly rose. "I was shown into the drawing-room, but there must be more to see—his study, his literary sanctum, the little things he has about, or other domestic objects and features. He wouldn't be lying down on his study-table? There's a great interest always felt in the scene of an author's labours. Sometimes we're favoured with very delightful peeps. Dora Forbes showed me all his table-drawers, and almost jammed my hand into one into which I made a dash! I don't ask that of you, but if we could talk things over right there where he sits I feel as if I should get the keynote."

I had no wish whatever to be rude to Mr. Morrow, I was much too initiated not to tend to more diplomacy; but I had a quick inspiration, and I entertained an insurmountable, an almost superstitious objection to his crossing the threshold of my friend's little lonely shabby consecrated workshop. "No, no—we shan't get at his life that way," I said. "The way to get at his life is to—But wait a moment!" I broke off and went quickly into the house, whence I in three minutes reappeared before Mr. Morrow with the two volumes of Paraday's new book. "His life's here," I went on, "and I'm so full of this admirable thing that I can't talk of anything else. The artist's life's his work, and this is the place to observe him. What he has to tell us he tells us with *this* perfection. My dear sir, the best interviewer is the best reader."

Mr. Morrow good-humouredly protested. "Do you mean to say that no other source of information should be open to us?"

"None other till this particular one—by far the most copious—has been quite exhausted. Have you exhausted it, my dear sir? Had you exhausted it when you came down here? It seems to me in our time almost wholly neglected, and something should surely be done to restore its ruined credit. It's the course to which the artist himself at every step, and with such pathetic confidence, refers us. This last book of Mr. Paraday's is full of revelations."

"Revelations?" panted Mr. Morrow, whom I had forced again into his chair.

"The only kind that count. It tells you with a perfection that seems to me quite final all the author thinks, for instance, about the advent of the 'larger latitude.'"

"Where does it do that?" asked Mr. Morrow, who had picked up the second volume and was insincerely thumbing it.

"Everywhere—in the whole treatment of his case. Extract the opinion, disengage the answer—those are the real acts of homage."

Mr. Morrow, after a minute, tossed the book away. "Ah but you mustn't take me for a reviewer."

"Heaven forbid I should take you for anything so dreadful! You came down to perform a little act of sympathy, and so, I may confide to you, did I. Let us perform our little act together. These pages overflow with the testimony we want: let us read them and taste them and interpret them. You'll of course have perceived for yourself that one scarcely does read Neil Paraday till one reads him aloud; he gives out to the ear an extraordinary full tone, and it's only when you expose it confidently to that test that you really get near his style. Take up your book again and let me listen, while you pay it out, to that wonderful fifteenth chapter. If you feel you can't do it justice, compose yourself to attention while I produce for you—I think I can!—this scarcely less admirable ninth."

Mr. Morrow gave me a straight look which was as hard as a blow between the eyes; he had turned rather red, and a question had formed itself in his mind which reached my sense as distinctly as if he had uttered it: "What sort of a damned fool are *you*?" Then he got up, gathering together his hat and gloves, buttoning his coat, projecting hungrily all over the place the big transparency of his mask. It seemed to flare over Fleet Street and somehow made the actual spot distressingly humble: there was so little for it to feed on unless he counted the blisters of our stucco or saw his way to do something with the roses. Even the poor roses were common kinds. Presently his eyes fell on the manuscript from which Paraday had been reading to me and which still lay on the bench. As my own followed them I saw it looked promising, looked pregnant, as if it gently throbbed with the life the reader had given it. Mr. Morrow indulged in a nod at it and a vague thrust of his umbrella. "What's that?"

"Oh, it's a plan—a secret."

"A secret!" There was an instant's silence, and then Mr. Morrow made another movement. I may have been mistaken, but it affected me as the translated impulse of the desire to lay hands on the manuscript, and this led me to indulge in a quick anticipatory grab which may very well have seemed ungraceful, or even impertinent, and which at any rate left Mr. Paraday's two admirers very erect, glaring at each other while one of them held a bundle of papers well behind him. An instant later Mr. Morrow quitted me abruptly, as if he had really carried something off with him. To reassure myself, watching his broad back recede, I only grasped my manuscript the tighter. He went to the back door of the house, the one he had come out from, but on trying the handle he appeared to find it fastened. So he passed round into the front garden, and by listening intently enough I could presently hear the outer gate close behind him with a bang. I thought again of the thirty-seven influential journals and wondered what would be his revenge. I hasten to add that he was magnanimous: which was just the most dreadful thing he could have been. *The Tatler* published a charming chatty familiar account of Mr. Paraday's "Home-life," and on the wings of the thirty-seven influential journals it went, to use Mr. Morrow's own expression, right round the globe.

CHAPTER VI

A week later, early in May, my glorified friend came up to town, where, it may be veraciously recorded he was the king of the beasts of the year. No advancement was ever more rapid, no exaltation more complete, no bewilderment more teachable. His book sold but moderately, though the article in *The Empire* had done unwonted wonders for it; but he circulated in person to a measure that the libraries might well have envied. His formula had been found—he was a "revelation." His momentary terror had been real, just as mine had been—the overclouding of his passionate desire to be left to finish his work. He was far from unsociable, but he had the finest conception of being let alone that I've ever met. For the time, none the less, he took his profit where it seemed most to crowd on him, having in his pocket the portable sophistries about the nature of the artist's task. Observation too was a kind of work and experience a kind of success; London dinners were all material and London ladies were fruitful toil. "No one has the faintest conception of what I'm trying for," he said to me, "and not many have read three pages that I've written; but I must dine with them first—they'll find out why when they've time." It was rather rude justice perhaps; but the fatigue had the merit of being a new sort, while the phantasmagoric town was probably after all less of a battlefield than the haunted study. He once told me that he had had no personal life to speak of since his fortieth year, but had had more than was good for him before. London closed the parenthesis and exhibited him in relations; one of the most inevitable of these being that in which he found himself to Mrs. Weeks Wimbush, wife of the boundless brewer and proprietress of the universal menagerie. In this establishment, as everybody knows, on occasions when the crush is great, the animals rub shoulders freely with the spectators and the lions sit down for whole evenings with the lambs.

It had been ominously clear to me from the first that in Neil Paraday this lady, who, as all the world agreed, was tremendous fun, considered that she had secured a prime attraction, a creature of almost heraldic oddity. Nothing could exceed her enthusiasm over her capture, and nothing could exceed the confused apprehensions it excited in me. I had an instinctive fear of her which I tried without effect to conceal from her victim, but which I let her notice with perfect impunity. Paraday heeded it, but she never did, for her conscience was that of a romping child. She was a blind violent force to which I could attach no more idea of responsibility than to the creaking of a sign in the wind. It was difficult to say what she conduced to but circulation. She was constructed of steel and leather, and all I asked of her for our tractable friend was not to do him to death. He had consented for a time to be of india-rubber, but my thoughts were fixed on the day he should resume his shape or at least get back into his box. It was evidently all right, but I should be glad when it was well over. I had a special fear—the impression was ineffaceable of the hour when, after Mr. Morrow's departure, I had found him on the sofa in his study. That pretext of indisposition had not in the least been meant as a snub to the envoy of *The Tatler*—he had gone to lie down in very truth. He had felt a pang of his old pain, the result of the agitation wrought in him by this forcing open of a new period. His old programme, his old ideal even had to be changed. Say what one would, success was a complication and recognition had to be reciprocal. The monastic life, the pious illumination of the missal in the convent cell were things of the gathered past. It didn't engender despair, but at least it required adjustment. Before I left him on that occasion we had passed a bargain, my part of which was that I should make it my business to take care of him. Let whoever would represent the interest in his presence (I must have had a mystical prevision of Mrs. Weeks Wimbush) I should represent the interest in his work—or otherwise expressed in his absence. These two interests were in their essence opposed; and I doubt, as youth is fleeting, if I shall ever again know the intensity of joy with which I felt that in so good a cause I was willing to make myself odious.

One day in Sloane Street I found myself questioning Paraday's landlord, who had come to the door in answer to my knock. Two vehicles, a barouche and a smart hansom, were drawn up before the house.

"In the drawing-room, sir? Mrs. Weeks Wimbush."

"And in the dining-room?"

"A young lady, sir—waiting: I think a foreigner."

It was three o'clock, and on days when Paraday didn't lunch out he attached a value to these appropriated hours. On which days, however, didn't the dear man lunch out? Mrs. Wimbush, at such a crisis, would have rushed round immediately after her own repast. I went into the dining-room first, postponing the pleasure of seeing how, upstairs, the lady of the barouche would, on my arrival, point the moral of my sweet solicitude. No one took such an interest as herself in his doing only what was good for him, and she was always on the spot to see that he did it. She made appointments with him to discuss the best means of economising his time and protecting his privacy. She further made his health her special business, and had so much sympathy with my own zeal for it that she was the author of pleasing fictions on the subject of what my devotion had led me to give up. I gave up nothing (I don't count Mr. Pinhorn) because I had nothing, and all I had as yet achieved was to find myself also in the menagerie. I had dashed in to save my friend, but I had only got domesticated and wedged; so that I could do little more for him than exchange with him over people's heads looks of intense but futile intelligence.

CHAPTER VII

The young lady in the dining-room had a brave face, black hair, blue eyes, and in her lap a big volume. "I've come for his autograph," she said when I had explained to her that I was under bonds to see people for him when he was occupied. "I've been waiting half an hour, but I'm prepared to wait all day." I don't know whether it was this that told me she was American, for the propensity to wait all day is not in general characteristic of her race. I was enlightened probably not so much by the spirit of the utterance as by some quality of its sound. At any rate I saw she had an individual patience and a lovely frock, together with an expression that played among her pretty features like a breeze among flowers. Putting her book on the table she showed me a massive album, showily bound and full of autographs of price. The collection of faded notes, of still more faded "thoughts," of quotations, platitudes, signatures, represented a formidable purpose.

I could only disclose my dread of it. "Most people apply to Mr. Paraday by letter, you know."

"Yes, but he doesn't answer. I've written three times."

"Very true," I reflected; "the sort of letter you mean goes straight into the fire."

"How do you know the sort I mean?" My interlocutress had blushed and smiled, and in a moment she added: "I don't believe he gets many like them!"

"I'm sure they're beautiful, but he burns without reading." I didn't add that I had convinced him he ought to.

"Isn't he then in danger of burning things of importance?"

"He would perhaps be so if distinguished men hadn't an infallible nose for nonsense."

She looked at me a moment—her face was sweet and gay. "Do *you* burn without reading too?"—in answer to which I assured her that if she'd trust me with her repository I'd see that Mr. Paraday should write his name in it.

She considered a little. "That's very well, but it wouldn't make me see him."

"Do you want very much to see him?" It seemed ungracious to catechise so charming a creature, but somehow I had never yet taken my duty to the great author so seriously.

"Enough to have come from America for the purpose."

I stared. "All alone?"

"I don't see that that's exactly your business, but if it will make me more seductive I'll confess that I'm quite by myself. I had to come alone or not come at all."

She was interesting; I could imagine she had lost parents, natural protectors—could conceive even she had inherited money. I was at a pass of my own fortunes when keeping hansoms at doors seemed to me pure swagger. As a trick of this bold and sensitive girl, however, it became romantic—a part of the general romance of her freedom, her errand, her innocence. The confidence of young Americans was notorious, and I speedily arrived at a conviction that no impulse could have been more generous than the impulse that had operated here. I foresaw at that moment that it would make her my peculiar charge, just as circumstances had made Neil Paraday. She would be another person to look after, so that one's honour would be concerned in guiding her straight. These things became clearer to me later on; at the instant I had scepticism enough to observe to her, as I turned the pages of her volume, that her net had all the same caught many a big fish. She appeared to have had fruitful access to the great ones of the earth; there were people moreover whose signatures she had presumably secured without a personal interview. She couldn't have worried George Washington and Friedrich Schiller and Hannah More. She met this argument, to my surprise, by throwing up the album without a pang. It wasn't even her own; she was responsible for none of its treasures. It belonged to a girl-friend in America, a young lady in a western city. This young lady had insisted on her bringing it, to pick up more autographs: she thought they might like to see, in Europe, in what company they would be. The "girl-friend," the western city, the immortal names, the curious errand, the idyllic faith, all made a story as strange to me, and as beguiling, as some tale in the Arabian Nights. Thus it was that my informant had encumbered herself with the ponderous tome; but she hastened to assure me that this was the first time she had brought it out. For her visit to Mr. Paraday it had simply been a pretext. She didn't really care a straw that he should write his name; what she did want was to look straight into his face.

I demurred a little. "And why do you require to do that?"

"Because I just love him!" Before I could recover from the agitating effect of this crystal ring my companion had continued: "Hasn't there ever been any face that you've wanted to look into?"

How could I tell her so soon how much I appreciated the opportunity of looking into hers? I could only assent in general to the proposition that there were certainly for every one such yearnings, and even such faces; and I felt the crisis demand all my lucidity, all my wisdom. "Oh yes, I'm a student of physiognomy. Do you mean," I pursued, "that you've a passion for Mr. Paraday's books?"

"They've been everything to me and a little more beside—I know them by heart. They've completely taken hold of me. There's no author about whom I'm in such a state as I'm in about Neil Paraday."

"Permit me to remark then," I presently returned, "that you're one of the right sort."

"One of the enthusiasts? Of course I am!"

"Oh there are enthusiasts who are quite of the wrong. I mean you're one of those to whom an appeal can be made."

"An appeal?" Her face lighted as if with the chance of some great sacrifice.

If she was ready for one it was only waiting for her, and in a moment I mentioned it. "Give up this crude purpose of seeing him! Go away without it. That will be far better."

She looked mystified, then turned visibly pale. "Why, hasn't he any personal charm?" The girl was terrible and laughable in her bright directness.

"Ah that dreadful word 'personally'!" I wailed; "we're dying of it, for you women bring it out with murderous effect. When you meet with a genius as fine as this idol of ours let him off the dreary duty of being a personality as well. Know him only by what's best in him and spare him for the same sweet sake."

My young lady continued to look at me in confusion and mistrust, and the result of her reflexion on what I had just said was to make her suddenly break out: "Look here, sir—what's the matter with him?"

"The matter with him is that if he doesn't look out people will eat a great hole in his life."

She turned it over. "He hasn't any disfigurement?"

"Nothing to speak of!"

"Do you mean that social engagements interfere with his occupations?"

"That but feebly expresses it."

"So that he can't give himself up to his beautiful imagination?"

"He's beset, badgered, bothered—he's pulled to pieces on the pretext of being applauded. People expect him to give them his time, his golden time, who wouldn't themselves give five shillings for one of his books."

"Five? I'd give five thousand!"

"Give your sympathy—give your forbearance. Two-thirds of those who approach him only do it to advertise themselves."

"Why it's too bad!" the girl exclaimed with the face of an angel. "It's the first time I was ever called crude!" she laughed.

I followed up my advantage. "There's a lady with him now who's a terrible complication, and who yet hasn't read, I'm sure, ten pages he ever wrote."

My visitor's wide eyes grew tenderer. "Then how does she talk—?"

"Without ceasing. I only mention her as a single case. Do you want to know how to show a superlative consideration? Simply avoid him."

"Avoid him?" she despairingly breathed.

"Don't force him to have to take account of you; admire him in silence, cultivate him at a distance and secretly appropriate his message. Do you want to know," I continued, warming to my idea, "how to perform an act of homage really sublime?" Then as she hung on my words: "Succeed in never seeing him at all!"

"Never at all?"—she suppressed a shriek for it.

"The more you get into his writings the less you'll want to, and you'll be immensely sustained by the thought of the good you're doing him."

She looked at me without resentment or spite, and at the truth I had put before her with candour, credulity, pity. I was afterwards happy to remember that she must have gathered from my face the liveliness of my interest in herself. "I think I see what you mean."

"Oh I express it badly, but I should be delighted if you'd let me come to see you—to explain it better."

She made no response to this, and her thoughtful eyes fell on the big album, on which she presently laid her hands as if to take it away. "I did use to say out West that they might write a little less for autographs—to all the great poets, you know—and study the thoughts and style a little more."

"What do they care for the thoughts and style? They didn't even understand you. I'm not sure," I added, "that I do myself, and I dare say that you by no means make me out." She had got up to go, and though I wanted her to succeed in not seeing Neil Paraday I wanted her also, inconsequently, to remain in the house. I was at any rate far from desiring to hustle her off. As Mrs. Weeks Wimbush, upstairs, was still saving our friend in her own way, I asked my young lady to let me briefly relate, in illustration of my point, the little incident of my having gone down into the country for a profane purpose and been converted on the spot to holiness. Sinking again into her chair to listen she showed a deep interest in the anecdote. Then thinking it over gravely she returned with her odd intonation:

"Yes, but you do see him!" I had to admit that this was the case; and I wasn't so prepared with an effective attenuation as I could have wished. She eased the situation off, however, by the charming quaintness with which she finally said: "Well, I wouldn't want him to be lonely!" This time she rose in earnest, but I persuaded her to let me keep the album to show Mr. Paraday. I assured her I'd bring it back to her myself. "Well, you'll find my address somewhere in it on a paper!" she sighed all resignedly at the door.

CHAPTER VIII

I blush to confess it, but I invited Mr. Paraday that very day to transcribe into the album one of his most characteristic passages. I told him how I had got rid of the strange girl who had brought it—her ominous name was Miss Hurter and she lived at an hotel; quite agreeing with him moreover as to the wisdom of getting rid with equal promptitude of the book itself. This was why I carried it to Albemarle Street no later than on the morrow. I failed to find her at home, but she wrote to me and I went again; she wanted so much to hear more about Neil Paraday. I returned repeatedly, I may briefly declare, to supply her with this information. She had been immensely taken, the more she thought of it, with that idea of mine about the act of homage: it had ended by filling her with a generous rapture. She positively desired to do something sublime for him, though indeed I could see that, as this particular flight was difficult, she appreciated the fact that my visits kept her up. I had it on my conscience to keep her up: I neglected nothing that would contribute to it, and her conception of our cherished author's independence became at last as fine as his very own. "Read him, read him—that will be an education in decency," I constantly repeated; while, seeking him in his works even as God in nature, she represented herself as convinced that, according to my assurance, this was the system that had, as she expressed it, weaned her. We read him together when I could find time, and the generous creature's sacrifice was fed by our communion. There were twenty selfish women about whom I told her and who stirred her to a beautiful rage. Immediately after my first visit her sister, Mrs. Milsom, came over from Paris, and the two ladies began to present, as they called it, their letters. I thanked our stars that none had been presented to Mr. Paraday. They received invitations and dined out, and some of these occasions enabled Fanny Hurter to perform, for consistency's sake, touching feats of submission. Nothing indeed would now have induced her even to look at the object of her admiration. Once, hearing his name announced at a party, she instantly left the room by another door and then straightway quitted the house. At another time when I was at the opera with them—Mrs. Milsom had invited me to their box—I attempted to point Mr. Paraday out to her in the stalls. On this she asked her sister to change places with her and, while that lady devoured the great man through a powerful glass, presented, all the rest of the evening, her inspired back to the house. To torment her tenderly I pressed the glass upon her, telling her how wonderfully near it brought our friend's handsome head. By way of answer she simply looked at me in charged silence, letting me see that tears had gathered in her eyes. These tears, I may remark, produced an effect on me of which the end is not yet. There was a moment when I felt it my duty to mention them to Neil Paraday, but I was deterred by the reflexion that there were questions more relevant to his happiness.

These question indeed, by the end of the season, were reduced to a single one—the question of reconstituting so far as might be possible the conditions under which he had produced his best work. Such conditions could never all come back, for there was a new one that took up too much place; but some perhaps were not beyond recall. I wanted above all things to see him sit down to the subject he had, on my making his acquaintance, read me that admirable sketch of. Something told me there was no security but in his doing so before the new factor, as we used to say at Mr. Pinhorn's, should render the problem incalculable. It only half-reassured me that the sketch itself was so copious and so eloquent that even at the worst there would be the making of a small but complete book, a tiny volume which, for the faithful, might well become an object of adoration. There would even not be wanting critics to declare, I foresaw, that the plan was a thing to be more thankful for than the structure to have been reared on it. My impatience for the structure, none the less, grew and grew with the interruptions. He had on coming up to town begun to sit for his portrait to a young painter, Mr. Rumble, whose little game, as we also used to say at Mr. Pinhorn's, was to be the first to perch on the shoulders of renown. Mr. Rumble's studio was a circus in which the man of the hour, and still more the woman, leaped through the hoops of his showy frames almost as electrically as they burst into telegrams and "specials." He pranced into the exhibitions on their back; he was the reporter on canvas, the Vandyke up to date, and there was one roaring year in which Mrs. Bounder and Miss Braby, Guy Walsingham and Dora Forbes proclaimed in chorus from the same pictured walls that no one had yet got ahead of him.

Paraday had been promptly caught and saddled, accepting with characteristic good-humour his confidential hint that to figure in his show was not so much a consequence as a cause of immortality. From Mrs. Wimbush to the last "representative" who called to ascertain his twelve favourite dishes, it was the same ingenuous assumption that he would rejoice in the repercussion. There were moments when I fancied I might have had more patience with them if they hadn't been so fatally benevolent. I hated at all events Mr. Rumble's picture, and had my bottled resentment ready when, later on, I found my distracted friend had been stuffed by Mrs. Wimbush into the mouth of another cannon. A young artist in whom she was intensely interested, and who had no connexion with Mr. Rumble, was to show how far he could make him go. Poor Paraday, in return, was naturally to write something somewhere about the young artist. She played her victims against each other with admirable ingenuity, and her establishment was a huge machine in which the tiniest and the biggest wheels went round to the same treadle. I had a scene with her in which I tried to express that the function of such a man was to exercise his genius—not to serve as a hoarding for pictorial posters. The people I was perhaps angriest with were the editors of magazines who had introduced what they called new features, so aware were they that the newest feature of all would be to make him grind their axes by contributing his views on vital topics and taking part in the periodical prattle about the future of fiction. I made sure that before I should have done with him there would scarcely be a current form of words left me to be sick of; but meanwhile I could make surer still of my animosity to bustling ladies for whom he drew the water that irrigated their social flower-beds.

I had a battle with Mrs. Wimbush over the artist she protected, and another over the question of a certain week, at the end of July, that Mr. Paraday appeared to have contracted to spend with her in the country. I protested against this visit; I intimated that he was too unwell for hospitality without a *nuance*, for caresses without imagination; I begged he might rather take the time in some restorative way. A sultry air of promises, of ponderous parties, hung over his August, and he would greatly profit by the interval of rest. He hadn't told me he was ill again that he had had a warning; but I hadn't needed this, for I found his reticence his worst symptom. The only thing he said to me was that he believed a comfortable attack of something or other would set him up: it would put out of the question everything but the exemptions he prized. I'm afraid I shall have presented him as a martyr in a very small cause if I fail to explain that he surrendered himself much more liberally than I surrendered him. He filled his lungs, for the most part; with the comedy of his queer fate: the tragedy was in the spectacles through which I chose to look. He was conscious of inconvenience, and above all of a great renouncement; but how could he have heard a mere dirge in the bells of his accession? The sagacity and the jealousy were mine, and his the impressions and the harvest. Of course, as regards Mrs. Wimbush, I was worsted in my encounters, for wasn't the state of his health the very reason for his coming to her at Prestidge? Wasn't it precisely at Prestidge that he was to be coddled, and wasn't the dear Princess coming to help her to coddle him? The dear Princess, now on a visit to England, was of a famous foreign house, and, in her gilded cage, with her retinue of keepers and feeders, was the most expensive specimen in the good lady's collection. I don't think her august presence had had to do with Paraday's consenting to go, but it's not impossible he had operated as a bait to the illustrious stranger. The party had been made up for him, Mrs. Wimbush averred, and every one was counting on it, the dear Princess most of all. If he was well enough he was to read them something absolutely fresh, and it was on that particular prospect the Princess had set her heart. She was so fond of genius in *any* walk of life, and was so used to it and understood it so well: she was the greatest of Mr. Paraday's admirers, she devoured everything he wrote. And then he read like an angel. Mrs. Wimbush reminded me that he had again and again given her, Mrs. Wimbush, the privilege of listening to him.

I looked at her a moment. "What has he read to you?" I crudely enquired.

For a moment too she met my eyes, and for the fraction of a moment she hesitated and coloured. "Oh all sorts of things!"

I wondered if this were an imperfect recollection or only a perfect fib, and she quite understood my unuttered comment on her measure of such things. But if she could forget Neil Paraday's beauties she could of course forget my rudeness, and three days later she invited me, by telegraph, to join the party at Prestidge. This time she might indeed have had a story about what I had given up to be near the master. I addressed from that fine residence several communications to a young lady in London, a young lady whom, I confess, I quitted with reluctance and whom the reminder of what she herself could give up was required to make me quit at all. It adds to the gratitude I owe her on other grounds that she kindly allows me to transcribe from my letters a few of the passages in which that hateful sojourn is candidly commemorated.

CHAPTER IX

"I suppose I ought to enjoy the joke of what's going on here," I wrote, "but somehow it doesn't amuse me. Pessimism on the contrary possesses me and cynicism deeply engages. I positively feel my own flesh sore from the brass nails in Neil Paraday's social harness. The house is full of people who like him, as they mention, awfully, and with whom his talent for talking nonsense has prodigious success. I delight in his nonsense myself; why is it therefore that I grudge these happy folk their artless satisfaction? Mystery of the human heart—abyss of the critical spirit! Mrs. Wimbush thinks she can answer that question, and as my want of gaiety has at last worn out her patience she has given me a glimpse of her shrewd guess. I'm made restless by the selfishness of the insincere friend—I want to monopolise Paraday in order that he may push me on. To be intimate with him is a feather in my cap; it gives me an importance that I couldn't naturally pretend to, and I seek to deprive him of social refreshment because I fear that meeting more disinterested people may enlighten him as to my real motive. All the disinterested people here are his particular admirers and have been carefully selected as such. There's supposed to be a copy of his last book in the house, and in the hall I come upon ladies, in attitudes, bending gracefully over the first volume. I discreetly avert my eyes, and when I next look round the precarious joy has been superseded by the book of life. There's a sociable circle or a confidential couple, and the relinquished volume lies open on its face and as dropped under extreme coercion. Somebody else presently finds it and transfers it, with its air of momentary desolation, to another piece of furniture. Every one's asking every one about it all day, and every one's telling every one where they put it last. I'm sure it's rather smudgy about the twentieth page. I've a strong impression, too, that the second volume is lost—has been packed in the bag of some departing guest; and yet everybody has the impression that somebody else has read to the end. You see therefore that the beautiful book plays a great part in our existence. Why should I take the occasion of such distinguished honours to say that I begin to see deeper into Gustave Flaubert's doleful refrain about the hatred of literature? I refer you again to the perverse constitution of man.

"The Princess is a massive lady with the organisation of an athlete and the confusion of tongues of a *valet de place*. She contrives to commit herself extraordinarily little in a great many languages, and is entertained and conversed with in detachments and relays, like an institution which goes on from generation to generation or a big building contracted for under a forfeit. She can't have a personal taste any more than, when her husband succeeds, she can have a personal crown, and her opinion on any matter is rusty and heavy and plain—made, in the night of ages, to last and be transmitted. I feel as if I ought to 'tip' some one a fee for my glimpse of it. She has been told everything in the world and has never perceived anything, and the echoes of her education respond awfully to the rash footfall—I mean the casual remark—in the cold Valhalla of her memory. Mrs. Wimbush delights in her wit and says there's nothing so charming as to hear Mr. Paraday draw it out. He's perpetually detailed for this job, and he tells me it has a peculiarly exhausting effect. Every one's beginning—at the end of two days—to sidle obsequiously away from her, and Mrs. Wimbush pushes him again and again into the breach. None of the uses I have yet seen him put to infuriate me quite so much. He looks very fagged and has at last confessed to me that his condition makes him uneasy—has even promised me he'll go straight home instead of returning to his final engagements in town. Last night I had some talk with him about going to-day, cutting his visit short; so sure am I that he'll be better as soon as he's shut up in his lighthouse. He told me that this is what he would like to do; reminding me, however, that the first lesson of his greatness has been precisely that he can't do what he likes. Mrs. Wimbush would never forgive him if he should leave her before the Princess has received the last hand. When I hint that a violent rupture with our hostess would be the best thing in the world for him he gives me to understand that if his reason assents to the proposition his courage hangs woefully back. He makes no secret of being mortally afraid of her, and when I ask what harm she can do him that she hasn't already done he simply repeats: 'I'm afraid, I'm afraid! Don't enquire too closely,' he said last night; 'only believe that I feel a sort of terror. It's strange, when she's so kind! At any rate, I'd as soon overturn that piece of priceless Sèvres as tell her I must go before my date.' It sounds dreadfully weak, but he has some reason, and he pays for his imagination, which puts him (I should hate it) in the place of others and makes him feel, even against himself, their feelings, their appetites, their motives. It's indeed inveterately against himself that he makes his imagination act. What a pity he has such a lot of it! He's too beastly intelligent. Besides, the famous reading's still to come off, and it has been postponed a day to allow Guy Walsingham to arrive. It appears this eminent lady's staying at a house a few miles off, which means of course that Mrs. Wimbush has forcibly annexed her. She's to come over in a day or two—Mrs. Wimbush wants her to hear Mr. Paraday.

"To-day's wet and cold, and several of the company, at the invitation of the Duke, have driven over to luncheon at Bigwood. I saw poor Paraday wedge himself, by command, into the little supplementary seat of a brougham in which the Princess and our hostess were already ensconced. If the front glass isn't open on his dear old back perhaps he'll survive. Bigwood, I believe, is very grand and frigid, all marble and precedence, and I wish him well out of the adventure. I can't tell you how much more and more *your* attitude to him, in the midst of all this, shines out by contrast. I never willingly talk to these people about him, but see what a comfort I find it to scribble to you! I appreciate it—it keeps me warm; there are no fires in the house. Mrs. Wimbush goes by the calendar, the temperature goes by the weather, the weather goes by God knows what, and the Princess is easily heated. I've nothing but my acrimony to warm me, and have been out under an umbrella to restore my circulation. Coming in an hour ago I found Lady Augusta Minch rummaging about the hall. When I asked her what she was looking for she said she had mislaid something that Mr. Paraday had lent her. I ascertained in a moment that the article in question is a manuscript, and I've a foreboding that it's the noble morsel he read me six weeks ago. When I expressed my surprise that he should have bandied about anything so precious (I happen to know it's his only copy—in the most beautiful hand in all the world) Lady Augusta confessed to me that she hadn't had it from himself, but from Mrs. Wimbush, who had wished to give her a glimpse of it as a salve for her not being able to stay and hear it read.

"'Is that the piece he's to read,' I asked, 'when Guy Walsingham arrives?'

"'It's not for Guy Walsingham they're waiting now, it's for Dora Forbes,' Lady Augusta said. 'She's coming, I believe, early to-morrow. Meanwhile Mrs. Wimbush has found out about *him*, and is actively wiring to him. She says he also must hear him.'

"'You bewilder me a little,' I replied; 'in the age we live in one gets lost among the genders and the pronouns. The clear thing is that Mrs. Wimbush doesn't guard such a treasure so jealously as she might.'

"'Poor dear, she has the Princess to guard! Mr. Paraday lent her the manuscript to look over.'

"'She spoke, you mean, as if it were the morning paper?'

"Lady Augusta stared—my irony was lost on her. 'She didn't have time, so she gave me a chance first; because unfortunately I go to-morrow to Bigwood.'

"'And your chance has only proved a chance to lose it?'

"'I haven't lost it. I remember now—it was very stupid of me to have forgotten. I told my maid to give it to Lord Dorimont—or at least to his man.'

"'And Lord Dorimont went away directly after luncheon.'

"'Of course he gave it back to my maid—or else his man did,' said Lady Augusta. 'I dare say it's all right.'

"The conscience of these people is like a summer sea. They haven't time to look over a priceless composition; they've only time to kick it about the house. I suggested that the 'man,' fired with a noble emulation, had perhaps kept the work for his own perusal; and her ladyship wanted to know whether, if the thing shouldn't reappear for the grand occasion appointed by our hostess, the author wouldn't have something else to read that would do just as well. Their questions are too delightful! I declared to Lady Augusta briefly that nothing in the world can ever do so well as the thing that does best; and at this she looked a little disconcerted. But I added that if the manuscript had gone astray our little circle would have the less of an effort of attention to make. The piece in question was very long—it would keep them three hours.

"'Three hours! Oh the Princess will get up!' said Lady Augusta.

"'I thought she was Mr. Paraday's greatest admirer.'

"'I dare say she is—she's so awfully clever. But what's the use of being a Princess—'

"'If you can't dissemble your love?' I asked as Lady Augusta was vague. She said at any rate she'd question her maid; and I'm hoping that when I go down to dinner I shall find the manuscript has been recovered."

CHAPTER X

"It has not been recovered," I wrote early the next day, "and I'm moreover much troubled about our friend. He came back from Bigwood with a chill and, being allowed to have a fire in his room, lay down a while before dinner. I tried to send him to bed and indeed thought I had put him in the way of it; but after I had gone to dress Mrs. Wimbush came up to see him, with the inevitable result that when I returned I found him under arms and flushed and feverish, though decorated with the rare flower she had brought him for his button-hole. He came down to dinner, but Lady Augusta Minch was very shy of him. To-day he's in great pain, and the advent of *ces dames*—I mean of Guy Walsingham and Dora Forbes—doesn't at all console me. It does Mrs. Wimbush, however, for she has consented to his remaining in bed so that he may be all right to-morrow for the listening circle. Guy Walsingham's already on the scene, and the Doctor for Paraday also arrived early. I haven't yet seen the author of 'Obsessions,' but of course I've had a moment by myself with the Doctor. I tried to get him to say that our invalid must go straight home—I mean to-morrow or next day; but he quite refuses to talk about the future. Absolute quiet and warmth and the regular administration of an important remedy are the points he mainly insists on. He returns this afternoon, and I'm to go back to see the patient at one o'clock, when he next takes his medicine. It consoles me a little that he certainly won't be able to read—an exertion he was already more than unfit for. Lady Augusta went off after breakfast, assuring me her first care would be to follow up the lost manuscript. I can see she thinks me a shocking busybody and doesn't understand my alarm, but she'll do what she can, for she's a good-natured woman. 'So are they all honourable men.' That was precisely what made her give the thing to Lord Dorimont and made Lord Dorimont bag it. What use *he* has for it God only knows. I've the worst forebodings, but somehow I'm strangely without passion—desperately calm. As I consider the unconscious, the well-meaning ravages of our appreciative circle I bow my head in submission to some great natural, some universal accident; I'm rendered almost indifferent, in fact quite gay (ha-ha!) by the sense of immitigable fate. Lady Augusta promises me to trace the precious object and let me have it through the post by the time Paraday's well enough to play his part with it. The last evidence is that her maid did give it to his lordship's valet. One would suppose it some thrilling number of *The Family Budget*. Mrs. Wimbush, who's aware of the accident, is much less agitated by it than she would doubtless be were she not for the hour inevitably engrossed with Guy Walsingham."

Later in the day I informed my correspondent, for whom indeed I kept a loose diary of the situation, that I had made the acquaintance of this celebrity and that she was a pretty little girl who wore her hair in what used to be called a crop. She looked so juvenile and so innocent that if, as Mr. Morrow had announced, she was resigned to the larger latitude, her superiority to prejudice must have come to her early. I spent most of the day hovering about Neil Paraday's room, but it was communicated to me from below that Guy Walsingham, at Prestidge, was a success. Toward evening I became conscious somehow that her superiority was contagious, and by the time the company separated for the night I was sure the larger latitude had been generally accepted. I thought of Dora Forbes and felt that he had no time to lose. Before dinner I received a telegram from Lady Augusta Minch. "Lord Dorimont thinks he must have left bundle in train—enquire." How could I enquire—if I was to take the word as a command? I was too worried and now too alarmed about Neil Paraday. The Doctor came back, and it was an immense satisfaction to me to be sure he was wise and interested. He was proud of being called to so distinguished a patient, but he admitted to me that night that my friend was gravely ill. It was really a relapse, a recrudescence of his old malady. There could be no question of moving him: we must at any rate see first, on the spot, what turn his condition would take. Meanwhile, on the morrow, he was to have a nurse. On the morrow the dear man was easier, and my spirits rose to such cheerfulness that I could almost laugh over Lady Augusta's second telegram: "Lord Dorimont's servant been to station—nothing found. Push enquiries." I did laugh, I'm sure, as I remembered this to be the mystic scroll I had scarcely allowed poor Mr. Morrow to point his umbrella at. Fool that I had been: the thirty-seven influential journals wouldn't have destroyed it, they'd only have printed it. Of course I said nothing to Paraday.

When the nurse arrived she turned me out of the room, on which I went downstairs. I should premise that at breakfast the news that our brilliant friend was doing well excited universal complacency, and the Princess graciously remarked that he was only to be commiserated for missing the society of Miss Collop. Mrs. Wimbush, whose social gift never shone brighter than in the dry decorum with which she accepted this fizzle in her fireworks, mentioned to me that Guy Walsingham had made a very favourable impression on her Imperial Highness. Indeed I think every one did so, and that, like the money-market or the national honour, her Imperial Highness was constitutionally sensitive. There was a certain gladness, a perceptible bustle in the air, however, which I thought slightly anomalous in a house where a great author lay critically ill. "*Le roy est mort—vive le roy*": I was reminded that another great author had already stepped into his shoes. When I came down again after the nurse had taken possession I found a strange gentleman hanging about the hall and pacing to and fro by the closed door of the drawing-room. This personage was florid and bald; he had a big red moustache and wore showy knickerbockers—characteristics all that fitted to my conception of the identity of Dora Forbes. In a moment I saw what had happened: the author of "The Other Way Round" had just alighted at the portals of Prestidge, but had suffered a scruple to restrain him from penetrating further. I recognised his scruple when, pausing to listen at his gesture of caution, I heard a shrill voice lifted in a sort of rhythmic uncanny chant. The famous reading had begun, only it was the author of "Obsessions" who now furnished the sacrifice. The new visitor whispered to me that he judged something was going on he oughtn't to interrupt.

"Miss Collop arrived last night," I smiled, "and the Princess has a thirst for the *inédit*."

Dora Forbes lifted his bushy brows. "Miss Collop?"

"Guy Walsingham, your distinguished *confrère*—or shall I say your formidable rival?"

"Oh!" growled Dora Forbes. Then he added: "Shall I spoil it if I go in?"

"I should think nothing could spoil it!" I ambiguously laughed.

Dora Forbes evidently felt the dilemma; he gave an irritated crook to his moustache. "*Shall* I go in?" he presently asked.

We looked at each other hard a moment; then I expressed something bitter that was in me, expressed it in an infernal "Do!" After this I got out into the air, but not so fast as not to hear, when the door of the drawing-room opened, the disconcerted drop of Miss Collop's public manner: she must have been in the midst of the larger latitude. Producing with extreme rapidity, Guy Walsingham has just published a work in which amiable people who are not initiated have been pained to see the genius of a sister-novelist held up to unmistakeable ridicule; so fresh an exhibition does it seem to them of the dreadful way men have always treated women. Dora Forbes, it's true, at the present hour, is immensely pushed by Mrs. Wimbush and has sat for his portrait to the young artists she protects, sat for it not only in oils but in monumental alabaster.

What happened at Prestidge later in the day is of course contemporary history. If the interruption I had whimsically sanctioned was almost a scandal, what is to be said of that general scatter of the company which, under the Doctor's rule, began to take place in the evening? His rule was soothing to behold, small comfort as I was to have at the end. He decreed in the interest of his patient an absolutely soundless house and a consequent break-up of the party. Little country practitioner as he was, he literally packed off the Princess. She departed as promptly as if a revolution had broken out, and Guy

Walsingham emigrated with her. I was kindly permitted to remain, and this was not denied even to Mrs. Wimbush. The privilege was withheld indeed from Dora Forbes; so Mrs. Wimbush kept her latest capture temporarily concealed. This was so little, however, her usual way of dealing with her eminent friends that a couple of days of it exhausted her patience, and she went up to town with him in great publicity. The sudden turn for the worse her afflicted guest had, after a brief improvement, taken on the third night raised an obstacle to her seeing him before her retreat; a fortunate circumstance doubtless, for she was fundamentally disappointed in him. This was not the kind of performance for which she had invited him to Prestidge, let alone invited the Princess. I must add that none of the generous acts marking her patronage of intellectual and other merit have done so much for her reputation as her lending Neil Paraday the most beautiful of her numerous homes to die in. He took advantage to the utmost of the singular favour. Day by day I saw him sink, and I roamed alone about the empty terraces and gardens. His wife never came near him, but I scarcely noticed it: as I paced there with rage in my heart I was too full of another wrong. In the event of his death it would fall to me perhaps to bring out in some charming form, with notes, with the tenderest editorial care, that precious heritage of his written project. But where *was* that precious heritage and were both the author and the book to have been snatched from us? Lady Augusta wrote me that she had done all she could and that poor Lord Dorimont, who had really been worried to death, was extremely sorry. I couldn't have the matter out with Mrs. Wimbush, for I didn't want to be taunted by her with desiring to aggrandise myself by a public connexion with Mr. Paraday's sweepings. She had signified her willingness to meet the expense of all advertising, as indeed she was always ready to do. The last night of the horrible series, the night before he died, I put my ear closer to his pillow.

"That thing I read you that morning, you know."

"In your garden that dreadful day? Yes!"

"Won't it do as it is?"

"It would have been a glorious book."

"It *is* a glorious book," Neil Paraday murmured. "Print it as it stands—beautifully."

"Beautifully!" I passionately promised.

It may be imagined whether, now that he's gone, the promise seems to me less sacred. I'm convinced that if such pages had appeared in his lifetime the Abbey would hold him to-day. I've kept the advertising in my own hands, but the manuscript has not been recovered. It's impossible, and at any rate intolerable, to suppose it can have been wantonly destroyed. Perhaps some hazard of a blind hand, some brutal fatal ignorance has lighted kitchen-fires with it. Every stupid and hideous accident haunts my meditations. My undiscourageable search for the lost treasure would make a long chapter. Fortunately I've a devoted associate in the person of a young lady who has every day a fresh indignation and a fresh idea, and who maintains with intensity that the prize will still turn up. Sometimes I believe her, but I've quite ceased to believe myself. The only thing for us at all events is to go on seeking and hoping together; and we should be closely united by this firm tie even were we not at present by another.

THE FRIENDS OF THE FRIENDS

I find, as you prophesied, much that's interesting, but little that helps the delicate question—the possibility of publication. Her diaries are less systematic than I hoped; she only had a blessed habit of noting and narrating. She summarised; she saved; she seldom appears indeed to have let a good story pass without catching it on the wing. I allude of course not so much to things she heard as to things she saw and felt. She writes sometimes of herself, sometimes of others, sometimes of the combination. It's under the last rubric that she's usually most vivid. But it's not, you'll understand, when she's most vivid that she's always most publishable. To tell the truth she's fearfully indiscreet, or has at least all the material for making me so. Take as an instance the fragment I send you after dividing it for your convenience into several small chapters. It's the contents of a thin blank-book which I've copied out and which has the merit of being nearly enough a rounded thing, an intelligible whole. These pages evidently date from years ago. I've read with liveliest wonder the statement they so circumstantially make and done my best to swallow the prodigy they leave to be inferred. These things would be striking, wouldn't they? to any reader; but can you imagine for a moment my placing such a document before the world, even though, as if she herself desired the world should have the benefit of it, she has given her friends neither names nor initials? Have you any sort of clue to their identity? I leave her the floor.

I

I know perfectly of course that I brought it on myself; but that doesn't make it any better. I was the first to speak of her to him—he had never even heard her mentioned. Even if I had happened not to speak some one else would have made up for it: I tried afterwards to find comfort in that reflexion. But the comfort of reflexions is thin: the only comfort that counts in life is not to have been a fool. That's a beatitude I shall doubtless never enjoy. "Why you ought to meet her and talk it over" is what I immediately said. "Birds of a feather flock together." I told him who she was and that they were birds of a feather because if he had had in his youth a strange adventure she had had about the same time just such another. It was well known to her friends—an incident she was constantly called on to describe. She was charming clever pretty unhappy; but it was none the less the thing to which she had originally owed her reputation.

Being at the age of eighteen somewhere abroad with an aunt she had had a vision of one of her parents at the moment of death. The parent was in England hundreds of miles away and so far as she knew neither dying nor dead. It was by day, in the museum of some great foreign town. She had passed alone, in advance of her companions, into a small room containing some famous work of art and occupied at that moment by two other persons. One of these was the old custodian; the second, before observing him, she took for a stranger, a tourist. She was merely conscious that he was bareheaded and seated on a bench. The instant her eyes rested on him however she beheld to her amazement her father, who, as if he had long waited for her, looked at her in singular distress and an impatience akin to reproach. She rushed to him with a bewildered cry, "Papa, what *is* it?" but this was followed by an exhibition of still livelier feeling when on her movement he simply vanished, leaving the custodian and her relations, who were by that time at her heels, to gather round her in distress. These persons, the official, the aunt, the cousins, were therefore in a manner witnesses of the fact—the fact at least of the impression made on her; and there was the further testimony of a doctor who was attending one of the party and to whom it was immediately afterwards communicated. He gave her a remedy for hysterics, but said to the aunt privately: "Wait and see if something doesn't happen at home." Something *had* happened—the poor father, suddenly and violently seized, had died that morning. The aunt, the mother's sister, received before the day was out a telegram announcing the event and requesting her to prepare her niece for it. Her niece was already prepared, and the girl's sense of this visitation remained of course indelible. We had all, as her friends, had it conveyed to us and had conveyed it creepily to each other. Twelve years had elapsed, and as a woman who had made an unhappy marriage and lived apart from her husband she had become interesting from other sources; but since the name she now bore was a name frequently borne, and since moreover her judicial separation, as things were going, could hardly count as a distinction, it was usual to qualify her as "the one, you know, who saw her father's ghost."

As for him, dear man, he had seen his mother's—so there you are! I had never heard of that till this occasion on which our closer, our pleasanter acquaintance led him, through some turn in the subject of our talk, to mention it and to inspire me in so doing with the impulse to let him know that he had a rival in the field—a person with whom he could compare notes. Later on his story became for him, perhaps because of my unduly repeating it, likewise a convenient worldly label; but it hadn't a year before been the ground on which he was introduced to me. He had other merits, just as she, poor thing, had others. I can honestly say that I was quite aware of them from the first—I discovered them sooner than he discovered mine. I remember how it struck me even at the time that his sense of mine was quickened by my having been able to match, though indeed not straight from my own experience, his curious anecdote. It dated, this anecdote, as hers did, from some dozen years before—a year in which, at Oxford, he had for some reason of his own been staying long into the "Long." He had been in the August afternoon on the river. Coming back into his room while it was still distinct daylight he found his mother standing there as if her eyes had been fixed on the door. He had had a letter from her that morning out of Wales, where she was staying with her father. At the sight of him she smiled with extraordinary radiance and extended her arms to him, and then as he sprang forward and joyfully opened his own she vanished from the place. He wrote to her that night, telling her what had happened; the letter had been carefully preserved. The next morning he heard of her death. He was through this chance of our talk extremely struck with the little prodigy I was able to produce for him. He had never encountered another case. Certainly they ought to meet, my friend and he; certainly they would have something in common. I would arrange this, wouldn't I?—if *she* didn't mind; for himself he didn't mind in the least. I had promised to speak to her of the matter as soon as possible, and within the week I was able to do so. She "minded" as little as he; she was perfectly willing to see him. And yet no meeting would occur—as meetings are commonly understood.

II

That's just half my tale—the extraordinary way it was hindered. This was the fault of a series of accidents; but the accidents, persisting for years, became, to me and to others, a subject of mirth with either party. They were droll enough at first, then they grew rather a bore. The odd thing was that both parties were amenable: it wasn't a case of their being indifferent, much less of their being indisposed. It was one of the caprices of chance, aided I suppose by some rather settled opposition of their interests and habits. His were centered in his office, his eternal inspectorship, which left him small leisure, constantly calling him away and making him break engagements. He liked society, but found it everywhere and took it at a run. She was on her side practically suburban: she lived at Richmond and never went "out." She was a woman of distinction, but not of fashion, and felt, as people said, her situation. Decidedly proud and rather whimsical, she lived her life as she had planned it. There were things one could do for her, but one couldn't make her come to one's parties. One went indeed a little more than seemed quite convenient to hers, which consisted of her cousin, a cup of tea and the view. The tea was good; but the view was familiar, though perhaps not, like the cousin—a disagreeable old maid who had been of the group at the museum and with whom she now lived—offensively so. This connexion with an inferior relative, which had partly an economic motive—she proclaimed her companion a marvelous manager—was one of those little perversities we had to forgive her. Another was her estimate of the proprieties created by her rupture with her husband. That was extreme—many persons called it even morbid. She made no advances; she cultivated scruples; she suspected, or I should perhaps rather say she remembered, slights: she was one of the few women I've known whom the particular predicament had rendered modest rather than bold. Dear thing, she had some delicacy! Especially marked were the limits she set to possible attentions from men: it was always her thought that her husband only waited to pounce on her. She discouraged if she didn't forbid the visits of male persons not senile: she said she could never be too careful.

When I first mentioned to her that I had a friend whom fate had distinguished in the same weird way as herself I put her quite at liberty to say "Oh bring him to see me!" I should have probably been able to bring him, and a situation perfectly innocent or at any rate comparatively simple would have been created. But she uttered no such word; she only said: "I must meet him certainly; yes, I shall look out for him!" That caused the first delay, and meanwhile various things happened. One of them was that as time went on she made, charming as she was, more and more friends, and that it regularly befell that these friends were sufficiently also friends of his to bring him up in conversation. It was odd that without belonging, as it were, to the same world or, according to the horrid term, the same set, my baffled pair should have happened in so many cases to fall in with the same people and make them join in the droll chorus. She had friends who didn't know each other but who inevitably and punctually recommended *him*. She had also a sort of originality, the intrinsic interest, that led her to be kept by each of us as a private resource, cultivated jealously, more or less in secret, as a person one didn't meet in society, whom it was not for every one—whom it was not for the vulgar—to approach, and with whom therefore acquaintance was particularly difficult and particularly precious. We saw her separately, with appointments and conditions, and found it made on the whole for harmony not to tell each other. Somebody had always a note from her still later than somebody else. There was some silly woman who for a long time, among the underprivileged, owed to three simple visits to Richmond a reputation for being intimate with "lots of awfully clever out-of-the-way people."

Every one has had friends it has seemed a happy thought to bring together, and every one remembers that his happiest thoughts have not been his greatest successes; but I doubt if there ever was a case in which the failure was in such direct proportion to the quantity of influence set in motion. It's really perhaps here the quantity of influence that was most remarkable. My lady and my gentleman pronounced it to me and others a subject for a roaring farce. The reason first given had with time dropped out of sight and fifty better ones flourished on top of it. They were so awfully alike: they had the same ideas and tricks and tastes, the same prejudices and superstitions and heresies; they said the same things and sometimes did them; the liked and disliked the same persons and places, the same books, authors and styles; there were touches of resemblance even in their looks and features. It established much of a propriety that they were in common parlance "nice" and almost equally handsome. But the great sameness, for wonder and chatter, was their rare perversity in regard to being photographed. They were the only persons ever heard of who had never been "taken" and who had a passionate objection to it. They just *wouldn't* be—no, not for anything any one could say. I loudly complained of this; him in particular I had so vainly desired to be able to show on my drawing-room chimney-piece in a Bond Street frame. It was at any rate the very liveliest of all the reasons why they ought to know each other—all the lively reasons reduced to naught by the strange law that made them bang so many doors in each other's face, made them the buckets in the well, the two ends of the see-saw, the two parties in the State, so that when one was up the other was down, when one was out the other was in; neither by any possibility entering a house till the other had left it or leaving it all unawares till the other was at hand. They only arrived when they had been given up, which was also precisely when they departed. They were in a word alternate and incompatible; they missed each other with an inveteracy that could be explained only by its being preconcerted. It was however so far from preconcerted that it had ended—literally after several years—by disappointing and annoying them. I don't think their curiosity was lively till it had been proved utterly vain. A great deal was of course done to help them, but it merely laid wires for them to trip. To give examples I should have to have taken notes; but I happen to remember that neither had ever been able to dine on the right occasion. The right occasion for each was the occasion that would be wrong for the other. On the wrong one they were most punctual, and there were never any but the wrong ones. The very elements conspired and the constitution of man re-enforced them. A cold, a headache, a bereavement, a storm, a fog, an earthquake, a cataclysm, infallibly intervened. The whole business was beyond a joke.

Yet as a joke it had still to be taken, though one couldn't help feeling that the joke had made the situation serious, had produced on the part of each a consciousness, an awkwardness, a positive dread of the last accident of all, the only one with any freshness left, the accident that would bring them together. The final effect of its predecessors had been to kindle this instinct. They were quite ashamed—perhaps even a little of each other. So much preparation, so much frustration: what indeed could be good enough for it all to lead up to? A mere meeting would be mere flatness. Did I see them at the end of years, they often asked, just stupidly confronted? If they were bored by the joke they might easily be bored by something else. They made exactly the same reflexions, and each in some manner was sure to hear of the other's. I really think it was this peculiar diffidence that finally controlled the situation. I mean that if they had failed for the first year or two because they couldn't help it, they kept up the habit because they had—what shall I call it?—grown nervous. It really took some lurking volition to account for anything both so regular and so ridiculous.

III

When to crown our long acquaintance I accepted his renewed offer of marriage it was humorously said, I know, that I had made the gift of his photograph a condition. This was so far true that I refused to give him mine without it. At any rate I had him at last, in his high distinction, on the chimney-piece, where the day she called to congratulate me she came nearer than she had ever done to seeing him. He had in being taken set her an example that I invited her to follow; he had sacrificed his perversity—wouldn't she sacrifice hers? She too must give me something on my engagement—wouldn't she give me the companion-piece? She laughed and shook her head; she had headshakes whose impulse seemed to come from as far away as the breeze that stirs a flower. The companion-piece to the portrait of my future husband was the portrait of his future wife. She had taken her stand—she could depart from it as little as she could explain it. It was a prejudice, an *entêtement*, a vow—she would live and die unphotographed. Now too she was alone in that state: this was what she liked; it made her so much more original. She rejoiced in the fall of her late associate and looked for a long time at his picture, about which she made no memorable remark, though she even turned it over to see the back. About our engagement she was charming—full of cordiality and sympathy. "You've known him even longer than I've *not*," she said, "and that seems a very long time." She understood how we had jogged over hill and dale and how inevitable it was that we should now rest together. I'm definite about all this because what followed is so strange that it's kind of a relief to me to mark the point up to which our relations were as natural as ever. It was I myself who in a sudden madness altered and destroyed them. I see now that she gave me no pretext and that I only found one in the way she looked at the fine face in the Bond Street frame. How then would I have had her look at it? What I had wanted from the first was to make her care for him. Well, that was what I still wanted—up to the moment of her having promised me she would on this occasion really aid me to break the silly spell that had kept them asunder. I had arranged with him to do his part if she would triumphantly do hers. I was on a different footing now—I was on a footing to answer for him. I would positively engage that at five on the following Saturday he should be on that spot. He was out of town on pressing business, but, pledged to keep his promise to the letter, would return on purpose and in abundant time. "Are you perfectly sure?" I remember she asked, looking grave and considering: I thought she had turned a little pale. She was tired, she was indisposed: it was a pity he was to see her after all at so poor a moment. If he only *could* have seen her five years before! However, I replied that this time I was sure and that success therefore depended simply on herself. At five o'clock on the Saturday she would find him in a particular chair I pointed out, the one in which he usually sat and in which—though this I didn't mention—he had been sitting when, the week before, he put the question of our future to me in the way that had brought me round. She looked at it in silence, just as she had looked at his photograph, while I repeated for the twentieth time that it was too preposterous one shouldn't somehow succeed in introducing one's dearest friend to one's second self. "*Am* I your dearest friend?" she asked with a smile that for a moment brought back her beauty. I replied by pressing her to my bosom; after which she said, "Well, I'll come. I'm extraordinarily afraid, but you may count on me."

When she left me I began to wonder what she was afraid of, for she had spoken as if she fully meant it. The next day, late in the afternoon, I had three lines from her: she found on getting home the announcement of her husband's death. She hadn't seen him for seven years, but she wished me to know it in this way before I should hear of it in another. It made however in her life, strange and sad to say, so little difference that she would scrupulously keep her appointment. I rejoiced for her—I supposed it would make at least the difference of her having more money; but even in this diversion, far from forgetting she had said that she was afraid, I seemed to catch sight of a reason for her being so. Her fear, as the evening went on, became contagious, and the contagion took in my breast the form of a sudden panic. It wasn't jealousy—it was just the dread of jealousy. I called myself a fool for not having been quiet till we were man and wife. After that I should somehow feel secure. It was only a question of waiting another month—a trifle surely for people who had waited so long. It had been plain enough that she was nervous, and now she was free her nervousness wouldn't be less. What was it therefore but a sharp foreboding? She had been hitherto the victim of interference, but it was quite possible she would henceforth be the source of it. The victim in that case would be my simple self. What had the interference been but the finger of Providence pointing out a danger? The danger was of course for poor *me*. It had been kept at bay by a series of accidents unexampled in their frequency; but the reign of accidents was now visibly at an end. I had an intimate conviction that both parties would keep the tryst. It was more and more impressed on me that they were approaching, converging. They were like the seekers for the hidden object in the game of blindfold; they had one and the other begun to "burn." We had talked about breaking the spell; well, it would be effectually broken—unless indeed it should merely take another form and overdo their encounters as it had overdone their escapes. This was something I couldn't sit still for thinking of; it kept me awake—at midnight I was full of unrest. At last I felt there was only one way of laying the ghost. If the reign of accident was over I must just take up the succession. I sat down and wrote a hurried note which would meet him on his return and which as the servants had gone to bed I sallied forth bareheaded into the empty gusty street to drop into the nearest pillar-box. It was to tell him that I shouldn't be able to be at home in the afternoon as I had hoped and that he must postpone his visit until dinner-time. This was an implication that he would find me alone.

IV

When accordingly at five she presented herself I naturally felt false and base. My act had been a momentary madness, but I had at least, as they say, to live up to it. She remained an hour; he of course never came; and I could only persist in my perfidy. I had thought it best to let her come; singular as this now seems to me I held it diminished my guilt. Yet as she sat there so visibly white and weary, stricken with a sense of everything her husband's death had opened up, I felt a really piercing pang of pity and remorse. If I didn't tell her on the spot what I had done it was because I was too ashamed. I feigned astonishment—I feigned it to the end; I protested that if ever I had had confidence I had had it that day. I blush as I tell my story—I take it as my penance. There was nothing indignant I didn't say about him; I invented suppositions, attenuations; I admitted in stupefaction, as the hands of the clock travelled, that their luck hadn't turned. She smiled at this vision of their "luck," but she looked anxious—she looked unusual: the only thing that kept me up was the fact that, oddly enough, she wore mourning—no great depths of crape, but simple and scrupulous black. She had in her bonnet three small black feathers. She carried a little muff of astrachan. This put me, by the aid of some acute reflexion, in the right. She had written to me that the sudden event made no difference for her, but apparently it made as much difference as that. If she was inclined to the usual forms why didn't she observe that of not going out the next day or two to tea? There was someone she wanted so much to see that she couldn't wait until her husband was buried. Such a betrayal of eagerness made me hard and cruel enough to practise my odious deceit, though at the same time, as the hour waxed and waned, I suspected in her something deeper still than disappointment and something less successfully concealed. I mean a strange underlying relief, the soft low emission of the breath that comes when a danger is past. What happened as she spent her barren hour with me was that at last she gave him up. She let him go for ever. She made the most graceful joke of it that I've ever seen made of anything; but it was for all that a great date in her life. She spoke with mild gaiety of all the other vain times, the long game of hide-and-seek, the unprecedented queerness of such a relation. For it *was*, or had been, a relation, wasn't it, hadn't it? That was just the absurd part of it. When she got up to go I said to her that it was more of a relation than ever, but I hadn't the face after what had occurred to propose to her for the present another opportunity. It was plain that the only valid opportunity would be my accomplished marriage. Of course she would be at my wedding? It was even to be hoped that *he* would.

"If *I* am, he won't be!"—I remember the high quaver and the little break of her laugh. I admitted there might be something in that. The thing therefore was to get us safely married first. "That won't help us. Nothing will help us!" she said as she kissed me farewell. "I shall never, never see him!" It was with those words she left me.

I could bear her disappointment as I've called it; but when a couple hours later I received him at dinner I discovered I couldn't bear his. The way my manœuver might have affected him hadn't been particularly present to me; but the result of it was the first word of reproach that had ever dropped from him. I say "reproach" because that expression is scarcely too strong for the terms in which he conveyed to me his surprise that under the extraordinary circumstances I shouldn't have found some means not to deprive him of such an occasion. I might really have managed either not to be obliged to go out or to let their meeting take place all the same. They would probably have got on, in my drawing-room, well enough without me. At this I quite broke down—I confessed my iniquity and the miserable reason of it. I hadn't put her off and I hadn't gone out; she had been there and, after waiting for him an hour, had departed in the belief that he had been absent by his own fault.

"She must think me a precious brute!" he exclaimed. "Did she say of me"—and I remember the just perceptible catch of breath in his pause—"what she had a right to say?"

"I assure you she said nothing that showed the least feeling. She looked at your photograph, she even turned round the back of it, on which your address happens to be inscribed. Yet it provoked her to no demonstration. She doesn't care as much as all that."

"Then why were you afraid of her?"

"It wasn't of her I was afraid. It was of you."

"Did you think that I'd be so sure to fall in love with her? You never alluded to such a possibility before," he went on as I remained silent. "Admirable person as you pronounced her, that wasn't the light in which you showed her to me."

"Do you mean that if it *had* been you'd have managed by now to catch a glimpse of her? I didn't fear things then," I added. "I hadn't the same reason."

He kissed me at this, and when I remembered that she had done so an hour or two before I felt for an instant as if he were taking from my lips the very pressure of hers. In spite of kisses the incident had shed a certain chill, and I suffered horribly from the sense that he had seen me guilty of a fraud. He had seen it only through my frank avowal, but I was as unhappy as if I had a stain to efface. I couldn't get over the manner of his looking at me when I spoke of her apparent indifference to his not having come. For the first time since I had known him he seemed to have expressed a doubt of my word. Before we parted I told him that I'd undeceive her—start the first thing in the morning for Richmond and there let her know that he had been blameless. At this he kissed me again. I'd expiate my sin, I said; I'd humble myself in the dust; I'd confess and ask to be forgiven. At this he kissed me once more.

V

In the train the next day this struck me as a good deal for him to have consented to; but my purpose was firm enough to carry me on. I mounted the long hill to where the view begins, and then I knocked at her door. I was a trifle mystified by the fact that her blinds were still drawn, reflecting that if in the stress of my compunction I had come early I had certainly yet allowed people time to get up.

"At home, mum? She has left home for ever."

I was extraordinarily startled by this announcement of the elderly parlour-maid. "She has gone away?"

"She's dead, mum, please." Then as I gasped at the horrible word: "She died last night."

The loud cry that escaped me sounded even in my own ears like some harsh violation of the hour. I felt for the moment as if I had killed her; I turned faint and saw through a vagueness that woman hold out her arms to me. Of what next happened I've no recollection, nor of anything but my friend's poor stupid cousin, in a darkened room, after an interval that I suppose very brief, sobbing at me in a smothered accusatory way. I can't say how long it took for me to understand, to believe and then to press back with an immense effort that pang of responsibility which, superstitiously, insanely, had been at first almost all I was conscious of. The doctor, after the fact, had been superlatively wise and clear: he was satisfied of a long-latent weakness of the heart, determined probably years before by the agitations and terrors to which her marriage had introduced her. She had had in those days cruel scenes with her husband, she had been in fear of her life. All emotion, everything in the nature of anxiety and suspense had been after that to be strongly deprecated, as in her marked cultivation of a quiet life she was evidently well aware; but who could say that any one, especially a "real lady," might be successfully protected from *every* little rub? She had had one a day or two before in the news of her husband's death—since there were shocks of all kinds, not only those of grief and surprise. For that matter she had never dreamed of so near a release: it had looked uncommonly as if he would live as long as herself. Then in the evening, in town, she had manifestly had some misadventure: something must have happened there that it would be imperative to clear up. She had come back very late—it was past eleven o'clock, and on being met in the hall by her cousin, who was extremely anxious, had allowed she was tired and must rest a moment before mounting the stairs. They had passed together into the dining-room, her companion proposing a glass of wine and bustling to pour it out. This took but a moment, and when my informant turned round our poor friend had not had time to seat herself. Suddenly, with a small moan that was barely audible, she dropped upon the sofa. She was dead. What unknown "little rub" had dealt her the blow? What concussion, in the name of wonder, *had* awaited her in town? I mentioned immediately the one thinkable ground of disturbance—her having failed to meet at my house, to which by invitation she had come at five o'clock, the gentleman I was to be married to, who had been accidentally kept away and with whom she had no acquaintance whatever. This obviously counted for little; but something else might easily have occurred: nothing in the London streets was more possible than an accident, especially an accident in those desperate cabs. What had she done, where had she gone on leaving my house? I had taken for granted that she had gone straight home. We both presently remembered that in her excursions to town she sometimes, for convenience, for refreshment, spent an hour or two at the "Gentlewoman," the quiet little ladies' club, and I promised that it should be my first care to make at that establishment an earnest appeal. Then we entered the dim and dreadful chamber where she lay locked up in death and where, asking after a little to be left alone with her, I remained for half an hour. Death had made her, had kept her beautiful; but I felt above all, as I kneeled at her bed, that it had made her, had kept her silent. It had turned the key on something I was concerned to know.

On my return from Richmond and after another duty had been performed I drove to his chambers. It was the first time, but I had often wanted to see them. On the staircase, which, as the house contained twenty sets of rooms, was unrestrictedly public, I met his servant, who went back with me and ushered me in. At the sound of my entrance he appeared in the doorway of a further room, and the instant we were alone I produced my news: "She's dead!"

"Dead?" He was tremendously struck, and I noticed he had no need to ask whom, in this abruptness, I meant.

"She died last evening—just after leaving me."

He stared with the strangest expression, his own eyes searching mine as for a trap. "Last evening—after leaving you?" He repeated my words in stupefaction. Then he brought out, so that it was in stupefaction I heard, "Impossible! I saw her."

"You 'saw' her?"

"On that spot—where you stand."

This called back to me after an instant, as if to help me take it in, the great warning of his youth. "In the hour of death—I understand: as you so beautifully saw your mother."

"Ah *not* as I saw my mother—not that way, not that way!" He was deeply moved by my news—far more moved, it was plain, than he would have been the day before: it gave me a vivid sense that, as I had then said to myself, there was indeed a relation between them and that he had actually been face to face with her. Such an idea, by its reassertion of his extraordinary privilege, would have suddenly presented him as painfully abnormal hadn't he vehemently insisted on the difference. "I saw her living. I saw her to speak to her. I saw her as I see you now."

It's remarkable that for a moment, though only for a moment, I found relief in the more personal, as it were, but also the more natural, of the two odd facts. The next, as I embraced this image of her having come to him on leaving me and of just what it accounted for in the disposal of her time, I demanded with a shade of harshness of which I was aware: "What on earth did she come for?"

He had now had a moment to think—to recover himself and judge of effects, so that if it was still with excited eyes he spoke he showed a conscious redness and made an inconsequent attempt to smile away the gravity of my words. "She came just to see me. She came—after what had passed at your home—so that we *should*, nevertheless at last meet. The impulse seemed to me exquisite, and that was the way I took it."

I looked round the room where she had been—where she had been and I never had till now. "And was the way you took it the way she expressed it?"

"She only expressed it by being here and by letting me look at her. That was enough!" he cried with an extraordinary laugh.

I wondered more and more. "You mean she didn't speak to you?"

"She said nothing. She only looked at me as I looked at her."

"And you didn't speak either?"

He gave me again his painful smile. "I thought of *you*. The situation was very delicate. I used the finest tact. But she saw she had pleased me." He even repeated his dissonant laugh.

"She evidently 'pleased' you!" Then I thought a moment. "How long did she stay?"

"How can I say? It seemed twenty minutes, but it was probably a good deal less."

"Twenty minutes of silence!" I began to have my definite view and now in fact quite to clutch at it. "Do you know you're telling me a thing positively monstrous?"

He had been standing with his back to the fire; at this, with a pleading look, he came to me. "I beseech you, dearest, to take it kindly."

I could take it kindly, and I signified as much; but I couldn't somehow, as he rather awkwardly opened his arms, let him draw me to him. So there fell between us for an appreciable time the discomfort of a great silence.

VI

He broke it by presently saying: "There's absolutely no doubt of her death?"

"Unfortunately no. I've just risen from my knees by the bed where they've laid her out."

He fixed his eyes hard on the floor; then he raised them to mine. "How does she look?"

"She looks—at peace."

He turned away again while I watched him; but after a moment he began: "At what hour then—?"

"It must have been near midnight. She dropped as she reached her house—from an affection of the heart which she knew herself and her physician knew her to have, but of which, patiently, bravely, she had never spoken to me."

He listened intently and for a minute was unable to speak. At last he broke out with an accent of which the almost boyish confidence, the really sublime simplicity, rings in my ears as I write: "Wasn't she *wonderful*!" Even at the time I was able to do it justice enough to answer that I had always told him so; but the next minute, as if after speaking he had caught a glimpse of what he might have made me feel, he went on quickly: "You can easily understand that if she didn't get home before midnight -"

I instantly took him up. "There was plenty of time for you to have seen her? How so," I asked, "when you didn't leave my house until late? I don't remember the very moment—I was preoccupied. But you know that though you said you had lots to do you sat for some time after dinner. She, on her side, was all the evening at the 'Gentlewoman,' I've just come from there—I've ascertained. She had tea there; she remained a long long time."

"What was she doing there all that long long time?"

I saw him eager to challenge at every step my account of the matter; and the more he showed this the more I was moved to emphasise that version, to prefer with apparent perversity an explanation which only deepened the marvel and the mystery, but which, of the two prodigies it had to choose from, my reviving jealousy found easiest to accept. He stood there pleading with a candour that now seems to me beautiful for the privilege of having in spite of supreme defeat known the living woman; while I, with a passion I wonder at today, though it still smoulders in a manner in its ashes, could only reply that, through a strange gift shared by her with his mother and on her own side equally hereditary, the miracle of his youth had been renewed for him, the miracle of hers for her. She had been to him—yes, and by an impulse as charming as he liked; but oh she hadn't been in the body! It was a simple question of evidence. I had had, I maintained, a definite statement of what she had done—most of the time—at the little club. The place was almost empty, but the servants had noticed her. She had sat motionless in a deep chair by the drawing-room fire; she had leaned back her head, she had closed her eyes, she had seemed softly to sleep.

"I see. But till what o'clock?"

"There," I was obliged to answer, "the servants fail me a little. The portress in particular is unfortunately a fool, even though she too is supposed to be a Gentlewoman. She was evidently at that period of time, without a substitute and against regulations, absent for some little time from the cage in which it's her business to watch the comings and goings. She's muddled, she palpably prevaricates; so I can't positively, from her observation, give you an hour. But it was remarked toward half-past ten that our poor friend was no longer in the club."

It suited him down to the ground. "She came straight here, and from here she went straight to the train."

"She couldn't have run it so close," I declared. "That was a thing she particularly never did."

"There was no need of running it close, my dear—she had plenty of time. Your memory's at fault about my having left you late: I left you, as it happens, unusually early. I'm sorry my stay with you seemed long, for I was back here by ten."

"To put yourself into your slippers," I retorted, "and fall asleep in your chair. You slept till morning—you saw her in a dream!" He looked at me in silence and with sombre eyes—eyes that showed me he had some irritation to repress. Presently I went on: "You had a visit, at an extraordinary hour, from a lady—*soit*; nothing in the world's more probable. But there are ladies and ladies. How in the name of goodness, if she was unannounced and dumb and you had into the bargain never seen the least portrait of her—how could you identify the person we're speaking of?"

"Haven't I to absolute satiety heard her described? I'll describe her for you in every particular."

"Don't!" I cried with a promptness that made him laugh once more. I coloured at this, but I continued: "Did your servant introduce her?"

"He wasn't there—he's always away when he's wanted. One of the features of this big house is that from the street-door the different floors are accessible practically without challenge. My servant makes love to a young person employed in the rooms above these, and he had a long bout of it last evening. When he's out on that job he leaves my outer door, on the staircase, so much ajar as to enable him to slip back without a sound. The door only requires a little push. She pushed it—that simply took a little courage."

"A little? It took tons! And it took all sorts of impossible calculations."

"Well, she had them—she made them. Mind you, I don't deny for a moment," he added, "that it was very very wonderful."

Something in his tone kept me a time from trusting myself to speak. At last I said: "How did she come to know where you live?"

"By remembering the address on the little label the shop-people happily left sticking to the frame I had had made for my photograph."

"And how was she dressed?"

"In mourning, my own dear. No great depths of crape, but simple and scrupulous black. She had in her bonnet three small black feathers. She carried a little muff of astrachan. She has near the left eye," he continued, "a tiny vertical scar—"

I stopped him short. "The mark of a caress from her husband." Then I added: "How close you must have been to her!" He made no answer to this, and I thought he blushed, observing which I broke off. "Well, good-bye."

"You won't stay a little?" He came to me again tenderly, and this time I suffered him. "Her visit had its beauty," he murmured as he held me, "but yours has a greater one."

I let him kiss me, but I remembered, as I had remembered the day before, that the last kiss she had given, as I supposed, in this world had been for the lips he touched. "I'm life, you see," I answered. "What you saw last night was death."

"It was life—it was life!"

He spoke with a soft stubbornness—I disengaged myself. We stood looking at each other hard. "You describe the scene—so far as you describe it at all—in terms that are incomprehensible. She was in the room before you knew it?"

"I looked up from my letter-writing—at that table under the lamp I had been wholly absorbed in it—and she stood before me."

"Then what did you do?"

"I sprang up with an ejaculation, and she, with a smile, laid her finger, ever so warningly, yet with a delicate dignity, to her lips. I knew it meant silence, but the strange thing was that it seemed immediately to explain and justify her. We at any rate stood for a time that, as I told you, I can't calculate, face to face. It was just as you and I stand now."

"Simply staring?"

He shook an impatient head. "Ah! we're not staring!"

"Yes, but we're talking."

Well, *we* were—after a fashion." He lost himself in the memory of it. "It was as friendly as this." I had on my tongue's end to ask if that was saying much for it, but I made the point instead that what they had evidently done was gaze in mutual admiration. Then I asked if recognition of her had been immediate. "Not quite," he replied, "for of course I didn't expect her; but it came to me long before she went who she was—who she could only be."

I thought a little. "And how did she at last go?"

"Just as she arrived. The door was open behind her and she passed out."

"Was she rapid—slow?"

"Rather quick. But looking behind her," he smiled to add, "I let her go, for I perfectly knew I was to take it as she wished."

I was conscious of exhaling a long vague sigh. "Well, you must take it now as *I* wish—you must let *me* go."

At this he drew near me again, detaining and persuading me, declaring with all due gallantry that I was a very different matter. I'd have given anything to have been able to ask him if he had touched her, but the words refused to form themselves: I knew to the last tenth of a tone how horrid and vulgar they'd sound. I said something else—I forget exactly what; it was feebly tortuous and intended, meanly enough, to make him tell me without my putting the question. But he didn't tell me; he only repeated, as from a glimpse of the propriety of soothing and consoling me, the sense of his declaration of some minutes before—the assurance that she was indeed exquisite, as I had always insisted, but that I was his "real" friend and his very own for ever. This led me to reassert, in the spirit of my previous rejoinder, that I had at least the merit of being alive; which in turn drew from him again the flash of contradiction I dreaded. "Oh *she* was alive! She was, she was!"

"She was dead, she was dead!" I asservated with an energy, a determination it should *be* so, which comes back to me now as almost grotesque. But the sound of the word as it rang out filled me suddenly with horror, and all the natural emotion the meaning of it might have evoked in other conditions gathered and broke in a flood. It rolled over me that here was a great affection quenched and how much I had loved and trusted her. I had a vision at the same time of the lonely beauty of her end. "She's gone—she's lost to us for ever!" I burst into sobs.

"That's exactly how I feel," he exclaimed, speaking with extreme kindness and pressing me to him for comfort. "She's gone; she's lost to us for ever; so what does it matter now?" He bent over me, and when his face had touched mine I scarcely knew if it were wet with my tears or his own.

VII

It was my theory, my conviction, it became, as I may say, my attitude, that they had still never "met"; and it was just on this ground I felt it generous to ask him to stand with me at her grave. He did so very modestly and tenderly, and I assumed, though he himself clearly cared nothing for the danger, that the solemnity of the occasion, largely made up of persons who had known them both and had a sense of the long joke, would sufficiently deprive his presence of all light association. On the question of what had happened the evening of her death little more passed between us. He on his side lacked producible corroboration—everything, that is, but a statement of the house-porter, on his own admission a most casual and intermittent personage, that between the hours of ten o'clock and midnight no less than three ladies in deep black had flitted in and out of the place. This proved far too much; we had neither of us any use for three. He knew I considered I had accounted for every fragment of her time, and we dropped the matter as settled; we abstained from further discussion. What *I* knew however was that he abstained to please me rather than because he yielded to my reasons. He didn't yield—he was only indulgent; he clung to his interpretation because he liked it better. He liked it better, I held, because it had more to say to his vanity. That, in a similar position, wouldn't have been its effect on me, though I had doubtless quite as much; but these are things of individual humour and as to which no person can judge for another. I should have supposed it more gratifying to be the subject of one of those inexplicable occurrences that are chronicled in thrilling books and disputed about at learned meetings; I could conceive, on the part of a being just engulfed in the infinite and still vibrating with human emotion, of nothing more fine and pure, more high and august, than such an impulse of reparation, of admonition, or even of curiosity. *That* was beautiful, if one would, and I should in his place have thought more of myself for being so distinguished and so selected. It was public that he had already, that he had long figured in that light, and what was such a fact itself but almost a proof? Each of the strange visitations contributed to establishing the other. He had a different feeling; but he had also, I hasten to add, an unmistakable desire not to make a stand or, as they say, a fuss about it. I might believe what I liked—the more so that the whole thing was in a manner a mystery of my producing. It was an event of my history, a puzzle of my consciousness, not of his; therefore he would take about it any tone that struck me as convenient. We had both at all events other business on hand; we were pressed with preparations for our marriage.

Mine were assuredly urgent, but I found as the days went on that to believe what I "liked" was to believe what I was more and more intimately convinced of. I found also that I didn't like it so much as that came to, or that the pleasure at all events was far from being the cause of my conviction. My obsession, as I may really call it and as I began to perceive, refused to be elbowed away, as I had hoped, by my sense of paramount duties. If I had a great deal to do I had still more to think of, and the moment came when my occupations were gravely menaced by my thoughts. I see it all now, I feel it, I live it over. It's terribly void of joy, it's full indeed to overflowing of bitterness; and yet I must do myself justice—I couldn't have been other than I was. The same strange impressions, had I to meet them again, would produce the same deep anguish, the same sharp doubts, the same still sharper certainties. Oh it's all easier to remember than to write, but even could I retrace the business hour by hour, could I find terms for the inexpressible, the ugliness and pain would quickly stay my hand. Let me then note very simply and briefly that a week before our wedding-day, three weeks after her death, I knew in all my fibres that I had something very serious to look in the face and that if I was to make the effort I must make it on the spot and before another hour should elapse. My unextinguished jealousy—that was the Medusa-mask. It hadn't died with her death, it had lividly survived, and it was fed by suspicions unspeakable. They *would* be unspeakable today, that is, if I hadn't felt the sharp need of uttering them at the time. This need took possession of me—to save me, as it seemed from my fate. When once it had done so I saw—in the urgency of the case, the diminishing hours and shrinking interval—only one issue, that of absolute promptness and frankness. I could at least not do him the wrong of delaying another day; I could at least treat my difficulty as too fine for any subterfuge. Therefore very quietly, but none the less abruptly and hideously, I put it before him on a certain evening that we must reconsider our situation and recognize that it had completely altered.

He stared bravely. "How in the world altered?"

"Another person has come between us."

He took but an instant to think. "I won't pretend not to know whom you mean." He smiled in pity for my aberration, but he meant to be kind. "A woman dead and buried!"

"She's buried, but she's not dead. She's dead for the world—she's dead for me. But she's not dead for you."

"You hark back to the different construction we put on her appearance that evening?"

"No," I answered, "I hark back to nothing. I've no need of it. I've more than enough with what's before me."

"And pray, darling, what may that be?"

"You're completely changed."

"By that absurdity?" he laughed.

"Not so much by that one as by other absurdities that have followed it."

"And what may *they* have been?"

We had faced each other fairly, with eyes that didn't flinch; but his had a dim strange light, and my certitude triumphed in his perceptible paleness. "Do you really pretend," I asked, "not to know what they are?"

"My dear child," he replied, "you describe them too sketchily!"

I considered a moment. "One may well be embarrassed to finish the picture! But from that point of view—and from the beginning—what was ever more embarrassing than your idiosyncrasy?"

He invoked his vagueness—a thing he always did beautifully. "My idiosyncrasy?"

"Your notorious, your peculiar power."

He gave a great shrug of impatience, a groan of overdone disdain. "Oh my peculiar power!"

"Your accessibility to forms of life," I coldly went on, "your command of impressions, appearances, contacts, closed—for our gain or our loss—to the rest of us. That was originally a part of the deep interest with which you inspired me—one of the reasons I was amused, I was indeed positively proud, to know you. It was a magnificent distinction; it's a magnificent distinction still. But of course I had no prevision then of the way it would operate now; and even had that been the case I should have had none of the extraordinary way of which its action would affect me."

"To what in the name of goodness," he pleadingly enquired, "are you fantastically alluding?" Then as I remained silent, gathering a tone for my charge, "How in the world *does* it operate?" he went on; "and how in the world are you affected?"

"She missed you for five years," I said, "but she never misses you now. You're making it up!"

"Making it up?" He had begun to turn from white to red.

"You see her—you see her: you see her every night!" He gave a loud sound of derision, but I felt it ring false. "She comes to you as she came that evening," I declared; "having tried it she found she liked it!" I was able, with God's help, to speak without blind passion or vulgar violence; but those were my words—and far from "sketchy" they then appeared to me—that I uttered. He had turned away in laughter, clapping his hands at my folly, but in an instant he faced me again with a change of expression that struck me. "Do you dare to deny," I then asked, "that you habitually see her?"

He had taken the line of indulgence, of meeting me halfway and kindly humouring me. At all events he to my astonishment suddenly said: "Well, my dear, what if I do?"

"It's your natural right: it belongs to your constitution and to your wonderful if not perhaps quite enviable fortune. But you'll easily understand that it separates us. I unconditionally release you."

"Release me?"

"You must choose between me and her."

He looked at me hard. "I see." Then he walked away a little, as if grasping what I had said and thinking how he had best treat it. At last he turned on me afresh. "How on earth do you know such an awfully private thing?"

"You mean because you've tried so hard to hide it? It is awfully private, and you may believe that I shall never betray you. You've done your best, you've acted your part, you've behaved, poor dear! loyally and admirably. Therefore I've watched you in silence, playing my part too; I've noted every drop in your voice, every absence in your eyes, every effort in your indifferent hand: I've waited till I was utterly sure and miserably unhappy. How *can* you hide it when you're abjectly in love with her, when you're sick almost to death with the joy of what she gives you?" I checked his quick protest with a quicker gesture. "You love her as you've *never* loved, and, passion for passion, she gives it straight back. She rules you, she holds you, she has you all! A woman, in such a case as mine, divines and feels and sees; she's not a dunce who has to be 'credibly informed.' You come to me mechanically, compunctiously, with the dregs of your tenderness and the remnant of your life. I can renounce you, but I can't share you: the best of you is hers, I know what it is and freely give you up to her for ever!"

He made a gallant fight, but it couldn't be patched up; he repeated his denial, he retracted his admission, he ridiculed my charge, of which I freely granted him moreover the indefensible extravagance. I didn't pretend for a moment that we were talking of common things; I didn't pretend for a moment that he and she were common people. Pray, if they *had* been, how should I ever have cared for them? They had enjoyed a rare extension of being and they had caught me up in their flight; only I couldn't breathe in such air and I promptly asked to be set down. Everything in the facts was monstrous, and most of all my lucid perception of them; the only thing allied to nature and truth was my having to act on that perception. I felt after I had spoken in this sense that my assurance was complete; nothing had been wanting to it but the sight of my effect on him. He disguised indeed the effect in a cloud of chaff, a diversion that gained him time and covered his retreat. He challenged my sincerity, my sanity, almost my humanity, and that of course widened our breach and confirmed our rupture. He did everything in short but convince me either that I was wrong or that he was unhappy: we separated and I left him to his inconceivable communion.

He never married, any more than I've done. When six years later, in solitude and silence, I heard of his death I hailed it as a direct contribution to my theory. It was sudden, it was never properly accounted for, it was surrounded by circumstances in which—for oh I took them to pieces!—I distinctly read an intention, the mark of his own hidden hand. It was the result of a long necessity, of an unquenchable desire. To say exactly what I mean, it was a response to an irresistible call.

THE JOLLY CORNER

CHAPTER I

"Every one asks me what I 'think' of everything," said Spencer Brydon; "and I make answer as I can—begging or dodging the question, putting them off with any nonsense. It wouldn't matter to any of them really," he went on, "for, even were it possible to meet in that stand-and-deliver way so silly a demand on so big a subject, my 'thoughts' would still be almost altogether about something that concerns only myself." He was talking to Miss Staverton, with whom for a couple of months now he had availed himself of every possible occasion to talk; this disposition and this resource, this comfort and support, as the situation in fact presented itself, having promptly enough taken the first place in the considerable array of rather unattenuated surprises attending his so strangely belated return to America. Everything was somehow a surprise; and that might be natural when one had so long and so consistently neglected everything, taken pains to give surprises so much margin for play. He had given them more than thirty years—thirty-three, to be exact; and they now seemed to him to have organised their performance quite on the scale of that licence. He had been twenty-three on leaving New York—he was fifty-six to-day; unless indeed he were to reckon as he had sometimes, since his repatriation, found himself feeling; in which case he would have lived longer than is often allotted to man. It would have taken a century, he repeatedly said to himself, and said also to Alice Staverton, it would have taken a longer absence and a more averted mind than those even of which he had been guilty, to pile up the differences, the newnesses, the queernesses, above all the bignesses, for the better or the worse, that at present assaulted his vision wherever he looked.

The great fact all the while, however, had been the incalculability; since he had supposed himself, from decade to decade, to be allowing, and in the most liberal and intelligent manner, for brilliancy of change. He actually saw that he had allowed for nothing; he missed what he would have been sure of finding, he found what he would never have imagined. Proportions and values were upside-down; the ugly things he had expected, the ugly things of his far-away youth, when he had too promptly waked up to a sense of the ugly—these uncanny phenomena placed him rather, as it happened, under the charm; whereas the "swagger" things, the modern, the monstrous, the famous things, those he had more particularly, like thousands of ingenuous enquirers every year, come over to see, were exactly his sources of dismay. They were as so many set traps for displeasure, above all for reaction, of which his restless tread was constantly pressing the spring. It was interesting, doubtless, the whole show, but it would have been too disconcerting hadn't a certain finer truth saved the situation. He had distinctly not, in this steadier light, come over all for the monstrosities; he had come, not only in the last analysis but quite on the face of the act, under an impulse with which they had nothing to do. He had come—putting the thing pompously—to look at his "property," which he had thus for a third of a century not been within four thousand miles of; or, expressing it less sordidly, he had yielded to the humour of seeing again his house on the jolly corner, as he usually, and quite fondly, described it—the one in which he had first seen the light, in which various members of his family had lived and had died, in which the holidays of his overschooled boyhood had been passed and the few social flowers of his chilled adolescence gathered, and which, alienated then for so long a period, had, through the successive deaths of his two brothers and the termination of old arrangements, come wholly into his hands. He was the owner of another, not quite so "good"—the jolly corner having been, from far back, superlatively extended and consecrated; and the value of the pair represented his main capital, with an income consisting, in these later years, of their respective rents which (thanks precisely to their original excellent type) had never been depressingly low. He could live in "Europe," as he had been in the habit of living, on the product of these flourishing New York leases, and all the better since, that of the second structure, the mere number in its long row, having within a twelvemonth fallen in, renovation at a high advance had proved beautifully possible.

These were items of property indeed, but he had found himself since his arrival distinguishing more than ever between them. The house within the street, two bristling blocks westward, was already in course of reconstruction as a tall mass of flats; he had acceded, some time before, to overtures for this conversion—in which, now that it was going forward, it had been not the least of his astonishments to find himself able, on the spot, and though without a previous ounce of such experience, to participate with a certain intelligence, almost with a certain authority. He had lived his life with his back so turned to such concerns and his face addressed to those of so different an order that he scarce knew what to make of this lively stir, in a compartment of his mind never yet penetrated, of a capacity for business and a sense for construction. These virtues, so common all round him now, had been dormant in his own organism—where it might be said of them perhaps that they had slept the sleep of the just. At present, in the splendid autumn weather—the autumn at least was a pure boon in the terrible place—he loafed about his "work" undeterred, secretly agitated; not in the least "minding" that the whole proposition, as they said, was vulgar and sordid, and ready to climb ladders, to walk the plank, to handle materials and look wise about them, to ask questions, in fine, and challenge explanations and really "go into" figures.

It amused, it verily quite charmed him; and, by the same stroke, it amused, and even more, Alice Staverton, though perhaps charming her perceptibly less. She wasn't, however, going to be better-off for it, as he was—and so astonishingly much: nothing was now likely, he knew, ever to make her better-off than she found herself, in the afternoon of life, as the delicately frugal possessor and tenant of the small house in Irving Place to which she had subtly managed to cling through her almost unbroken New York career. If he knew the way to it now better than to any other address among the dreadful multiplied numberings which seemed to him to reduce the whole place to some vast ledger-page, overgrown, fantastic, of ruled and criss-crossed lines and figures—if he had formed, for his consolation, that habit, it was really not a little because of the charm of his having encountered and recognised, in the vast wilderness of the wholesale, breaking through the mere gross generalisation of wealth and force and success, a small still scene where items and shades, all delicate things, kept the sharpness of the notes of a high voice perfectly trained, and where economy hung about like the scent of a garden. His old friend lived with one maid and herself dusted her relics and trimmed her lamps and polished her silver; she stood oft, in the awful modern crush, when she could, but she sallied forth and did battle when the challenge was really to "spirit," the spirit she after all confessed to, proudly and a little shyly, as to that of the better time, that of their common, their quite far-away and antediluvian social period and order. She made use of the street-cars when need be, the terrible things that people scrambled for as the panic-stricken at sea scramble for the boats; she affronted, inscrutably, under stress, all the public concussions and ordeals; and yet, with that slim mystifying grace of her appearance, which defied you to say if she were a fair young woman who looked older through trouble, or a fine smooth older one who looked young through successful indifference with her precious reference, above all, to memories and histories into which he could enter, she was as exquisite for him as some pale pressed flower (a rarity to begin with), and, failing other sweetnesses, she was a sufficient reward of his effort. They had communities of knowledge, "their" knowledge (this discriminating possessive was always on her lips) of presences of the other age, presences all overlaid, in his case, by the experience of a man and the freedom of a wanderer, overlaid by pleasure, by infidelity, by passages of life that were strange and dim to her, just by "Europe" in short, but still unobscured, still exposed and cherished, under that pious visitation of the spirit from which she had never been diverted.

She had come with him one day to see how his "apartment-house" was rising; he had helped her over gaps and explained to her plans, and while they were there had happened to have, before her, a brief but lively discussion with the man in charge, the representative of the building firm that had undertaken his work. He had found himself quite "standing up" to this personage over a failure on the latter's part to observe some detail of one of their noted conditions, and had so lucidly argued his case that, besides ever so prettily flushing, at the time, for sympathy in his triumph, she had afterwards said to him (though to a slightly greater effect of irony) that he had clearly for too many years neglected a real gift. If he had but stayed at home he would have anticipated the inventor of the sky-scraper. If he had but stayed at home he would have discovered his genius in time really to start some new variety of awful architectural hare and run it till it burrowed in a gold mine. He was to remember these words, while the weeks elapsed, for the small silver ring they had sounded over the queerest and deepest of his own lately most disguised and most muffled vibrations.

It had begun to be present to him after the first fortnight, it had broken out with the oddest abruptness, this particular wanton wonderment: it met him there—and this was the image under which he himself judged the matter, or at least, not a little, thrilled and flushed with it—very much as he might have been met by some strange figure, some unexpected occupant, at a turn of one of the dim passages of an empty house. The quaint analogy quite hauntingly remained with him, when he didn't indeed rather improve it by a still intenser form: that of his opening a door behind which he would have made sure of finding nothing, a door into a room shuttered and void, and yet so coming, with a great suppressed start, on some quite erect confronting presence, something planted in the middle of the place and facing him through the dusk. After that visit to the house in construction he walked with his companion to see the other and always so much the better one, which in the eastward direction formed one of the corners,—the "jolly" one precisely, of the street now so generally dishonoured and disfigured in its westward reaches, and of the comparatively conservative Avenue. The Avenue still had pretensions, as Miss Staverton said, to decency; the old people had mostly gone, the old names were unknown, and here and there an old association seemed to stray, all vaguely, like some very aged person, out too late, whom you might meet and feel the impulse to watch or follow, in kindness, for safe restoration to shelter.

They went in together, our friends; he admitted himself with his key, as he kept no one there, he explained, preferring, for his reasons, to leave the place empty, under a simple arrangement with a good woman living in the neighbourhood and who came for a daily hour to open windows and dust and sweep. Spencer Brydon had his reasons and was growingly aware of them; they seemed to him better each time he was there, though he didn't name them all to his companion, any more than he told her as yet how often, how quite absurdly often, he himself came. He only let her see for the present, while they walked through the great blank rooms, that absolute vacancy reigned and that, from top to bottom, there was nothing but Mrs. Muldoon's broomstick, in a corner, to tempt the burglar. Mrs. Muldoon was then on the premises, and she loquaciously attended the visitors, preceding them from room to room and pushing back shutters and throwing up sashes—all to show them, as she remarked, how little there was to see. There was little indeed to see in the great gaunt shell where the main dispositions and the general apportionment of space, the style of an age of ampler allowances, had nevertheless for its master their honest pleading message, affecting him as some good old servant's, some lifelong retainer's appeal for a character, or even for a retiring-pension; yet it was also a remark of Mrs. Muldoon's that, glad as she was to oblige him by her noonday round, there was a request she greatly hoped he would never make of her. If he should wish her for any reason to come in after dark she would just tell him, if he "plased," that he must ask it of somebody else.

The fact that there was nothing to see didn't militate for the worthy woman against what one might see, and she put it frankly to Miss Staverton that no lady could be expected to like, could she? "scraping up to thim top storeys in the ayvil hours." The gas and the electric light were off the house, and she fairly evoked a gruesome vision of her march through the great grey rooms—so many of them as there were too!—with her glimmering taper. Miss Staverton met her honest glare with a smile and the profession that she herself certainly would recoil from such an adventure. Spencer Brydon meanwhile held his peace—for the moment; the question of the "evil" hours in his old home had already become too grave for him. He had begun some time since to "crape," and he knew just why a packet of candles addressed to that pursuit had been stowed by his own hand, three weeks before, at the back of a drawer of the fine old sideboard that occupied, as a "fixture," the deep recess in the dining-room. Just now he laughed at his companions—quickly however changing the subject; for the reason that, in the first place, his laugh struck him even at that moment as starting the odd echo, the conscious human resonance (he scarce knew how to qualify it) that sounds made while he was there alone sent back to his ear or his fancy; and that, in the second, he imagined Alice Staverton for the instant on the point of asking him, with a divination, if he ever so prowled. There were divinations he was unprepared for, and he had at all events averted enquiry by the time Mrs. Muldoon had left them, passing on to other parts.

There was happily enough to say, on so consecrated a spot, that could be said freely and fairly; so that a whole train of declarations was precipitated by his friend's having herself broken out, after a yearning look round: "But I hope you don't mean they want you to pull this to pieces!" His answer came, promptly, with his re-awakened wrath: it was of course exactly what they wanted, and what they were "at" him for, daily, with the iteration of people who couldn't for their life understand a man's liability to decent feelings. He had found the place, just as it stood and beyond what he could express, an interest and a joy. There were values other than the beastly rent-values, and in short, in short—! But it was thus Miss Staverton took him up. "In short you're to make so good a thing of your sky-scraper that, living in luxury on those ill-gotten gains, you can afford for a while to be sentimental here!" Her smile had for him, with the words, the particular mild irony with which he found half her talk suffused; an irony without bitterness and that came, exactly, from her having so much imagination—not, like the cheap sarcasms with which one heard most people, about the world of "society," bid for the reputation of cleverness, from nobody's really having any. It was agreeable to him at this very moment to be sure that when he had answered, after a brief demur, "Well, yes; so, precisely, you may put it!" her imagination would still do him justice. He explained that even if never a dollar were to come to him from the other house he would nevertheless cherish this one; and he dwelt, further, while they lingered and wandered, on the fact of the stupefaction he was already exciting, the positive mystification he felt himself create.

He spoke of the value of all he read into it, into the mere sight of the walls, mere shapes of the rooms, mere sound of the floors, mere feel, in his hand, of the old silver-plated knobs of the several mahogany doors, which suggested the pressure of the palms of the dead the seventy years of the past in fine that these things represented, the annals of nearly three generations, counting his grandfather's, the one that had ended there, and the impalpable ashes of his long-extinct youth, afloat in the very air like microscopic motes. She listened to everything; she was a woman who answered intimately but who utterly didn't chatter. She scattered abroad therefore no cloud of words; she could assent, she could agree, above all she could encourage, without doing that. Only at the last she went a little further than he had done himself. "And then how do you know? You may still, after all, want to live here." It rather indeed pulled him up, for it wasn't what he had been thinking, at least in her sense of the words, "You mean I may decide to stay on for the sake of it?"

"Well, with such a home—!" But, quite beautifully, she had too much tact to dot so monstrous an *i*, and it was precisely an illustration of the way she didn't rattle. How could any one—of any wit—insist on any one else's "wanting" to live in New York?

"Oh," he said, "I might have lived here (since I had my opportunity early in life); I might have put in here all these years. Then everything would have been different enough—and, I dare say, 'funny' enough. But that's another matter. And then the beauty of it—I mean of my perversity, of my refusal to agree to a 'deal'—is just in the total absence of a reason. Don't you see that if I had a reason about the matter at all it would have to be the other way, and would then be inevitably a reason of dollars? There are no reasons here but of dollars. Let us therefore have none whatever—not the ghost of one."

They were back in the hall then for departure, but from where they stood the vista was large, through an open door, into the great square main saloon, with its almost antique felicity of brave spaces between windows. Her eyes came back from that reach and met his own a moment. "Are you very sure the 'ghost' of one doesn't, much rather, serve—?"

He had a positive sense of turning pale. But it was as near as they were then to come. For he made answer, he believed, between a glare and a grin: "Oh ghosts—of course the place must swarm with them! I should be ashamed of it if it didn't. Poor Mrs. Muldoon's right, and it's why I haven't asked her to do more than look in."

Miss Staverton's gaze again lost itself, and things she didn't utter, it was clear, came and went in her mind. She might even for the minute, off there in the fine room, have imagined some element dimly gathering. Simplified like the death-mask of a handsome face, it perhaps produced for her just then an effect akin to the stir of an expression in the "set" commemorative plaster. Yet whatever her impression may have been she produced instead a vague platitude. "Well, if it were only furnished and lived in—!"

She appeared to imply that in case of its being still furnished he might have been a little less opposed to the idea of a return. But she passed straight into the vestibule, as if to leave her words behind her, and the next moment he had opened the house-door and was standing with her on the steps. He closed the door and, while he re-pocketed his key, looking up and down, they took in the comparatively harsh actuality of the Avenue, which reminded him of the assault of the outer light of the Desert on the traveller emerging from an Egyptian tomb. But he risked before they stepped into the street his gathered answer to her speech. "For me it is lived in. For me it is furnished." At which it was easy for her to sigh "Ah yes!" all vaguely and discreetly; since his parents and his favourite sister, to say nothing of other kin, in numbers, had run their course and met their end there. That represented, within the walls, ineffaceable life.

It was a few days after this that, during an hour passed with her again, he had expressed his impatience of the too flattering curiosity—among the people he met—about his appreciation of New York. He had arrived at none at all that was socially producible, and as for that matter of his "thinking" (thinking the better or the worse of anything there) he was wholly taken up with one subject of thought. It was mere vain egoism, and it was moreover, if she liked, a morbid obsession. He found all things come back to the question of what he personally might have been, how he might have led his life and "turned out," if he had not so, at the outset, given it up. And confessing for the first time to the intensity within him of this absurd speculation—which but proved also, no doubt, the habit of too selfishly thinking—he affirmed the impotence there of any other source of interest, any other native appeal. "What would it have made of me, what would it have made of me? I keep for ever wondering, all idiotically; as if I could possibly know! I see what it has made of dozens of others, those I meet, and it positively aches within me, to the point of exasperation, that it would have made something of me as well. Only I can't make out what, and the worry of it, the small rage of curiosity never to be satisfied, brings back what I remember to have felt, once or twice, after judging best, for reasons, to burn some important letter unopened. I've been sorry, I've hated it—I've never known what was in the letter. You may, of course, say it's a trifle—!"

"I don't say it's a trifle," Miss Staverton gravely interrupted.

She was seated by her fire, and before her, on his feet and restless, he turned to and fro between this intensity of his idea and a fitful and unseeing inspection, through his single eye-glass, of the dear little old objects on her chimney-piece. Her interruption made him for an instant look at her harder. "I shouldn't care if you did!" he laughed, however; "and it's only a figure, at any rate, for the way I now feel. Not to have followed my perverse young course—and almost in the teeth of my father's curse, as I may say; not to have kept it up, so, 'over there,' from that day to this, without a doubt or a pang; not, above all, to have liked it, to have loved it, so much, loved it, no doubt, with such an abysmal conceit of my own preference; some variation from that, I say, must have produced some different effect for my life and for my 'form.' I should have stuck here—if it had been possible; and I was too young, at twenty-three, to judge, *pour deux sous*, whether it were possible. If I had waited I might have seen it was, and then I might have been, by staying here, something nearer to one of these types who have been hammered so hard and made so keen by their conditions. It isn't that I admire them so much—the question of any charm in them, or of any charm, beyond that of the rank money-passion, exerted by their conditions for them, has nothing to do with the matter: it's only a question of what fantastic, yet perfectly possible, development of my own nature I mayn't have missed. It comes over me that I had then a strange alter ego deep down somewhere within me, as the full-blown flower is in the small tight bud, and that I just took the course, I just transferred him to the climate, that blighted him for once and for ever."

"And you wonder about the flower," Miss Staverton said. "So do I, if you want to know; and so I've been wondering these several weeks. I believe in the flower," she continued, "I feel it would have been quite splendid, quite huge and monstrous."

"Monstrous above all!" her visitor echoed; "and I imagine, by the same stroke, quite hideous and offensive."

"You don't believe that," she returned; "if you did you wouldn't wonder. You'd know, and that would be enough for you. What you feel—and what I feel for you—is that you'd have had power."

"You'd have liked me that way?" he asked.

She barely hung fire. "How should I not have liked you?"

"I see. You'd have liked me, have preferred me, a billionaire!"

"How should I not have liked you?" she simply again asked.

He stood before her still—her question kept him motionless. He took it in, so much there was of it; and indeed his not otherwise meeting it testified to that. "I know at least what I am," he simply went on; "the other side of the medal's clear enough. I've not been edifying—I believe I'm thought in a hundred quarters to have been barely decent. I've followed strange paths and worshipped strange gods; it must have come to you again and again—in fact you've admitted to me as much—that I was leading, at any time these thirty years, a selfish frivolous scandalous life. And you see what it has made of me."

She just waited, smiling at him. "You see what it has made of me."

"Oh you're a person whom nothing can have altered. You were born to be what you are, anywhere, anyway: you've the perfection nothing else could have blighted. And don't you see how, without my exile, I shouldn't have been waiting till now—?" But he pulled up for the strange pang.

"The great thing to see," she presently said, "seems to me to be that it has spoiled nothing. It hasn't spoiled your being here at last. It hasn't spoiled this. It hasn't spoiled your speaking—" She also however faltered.

He wondered at everything her controlled emotion might mean. "Do you believe then—too dreadfully!—that I am as good as I might ever have been?"

"Oh no! Far from it!" With which she got up from her chair and was nearer to him. "But I don't care," she smiled.

"You mean I'm good enough?"

She considered a little. "Will you believe it if I say so? I mean will you let that settle your question for you?" And then as if making out in his face that he drew back from this, that he had some idea which, however absurd, he couldn't yet bargain away: "Oh you don't care either—but very differently: you don't care for anything but yourself."

Spencer Brydon recognised it—it was in fact what he had absolutely professed. Yet he importantly qualified. "He isn't myself. He's the just so totally other person. But I do want to see him," he added. "And I can. And I shall."

Their eyes met for a minute while he guessed from something in hers that she divined his strange sense. But neither of them otherwise expressed it, and her apparent understanding, with no protesting shock, no easy derision, touched him more deeply than anything yet, constituting for his stifled perversity, on the spot, an element that was like breatheable air. What she said however was unexpected. "Well, I've seen him."

"You—?"

"I've seen him in a dream."

"Oh a 'dream'—!" It let him down.

"But twice over," she continued. "I saw him as I see you now."

"You've dreamed the same dream—?"

"Twice over," she repeated. "The very same."

This did somehow a little speak to him, as it also gratified him. "You dream about me at that rate?"

"Ah about him!" she smiled.

His eyes again sounded her. "Then you know all about him." And as she said nothing more: "What's the wretch like?"

She hesitated, and it was as if he were pressing her so hard that, resisting for reasons of her own, she had to turn away. "I'll tell you some other time!"

CHAPTER II

It was after this that there was most of a virtue for him, most of a cultivated charm, most of a preposterous secret thrill, in the particular form of surrender to his obsession and of address to what he more and more believed to be his privilege. It was what in these weeks he was living for—since he really felt life to begin but after Mrs. Muldoon had retired from the scene and, visiting the ample house from attic to cellar, making sure he was alone, he knew himself in safe possession and, as he tacitly expressed it, let himself go. He sometimes came twice in the twenty-four hours; the moments he liked best were those of gathering dusk, of the short autumn twilight; this was the time of which, again and again, he found himself hoping most. Then he could, as seemed to him, most intimately wander and wait, linger and listen, feel his fine attention, never in his life before so fine, on the pulse of the great vague place: he preferred the lampless hour and only wished he might have prolonged each day the deep crepuscular spell. Later—rarely much before midnight, but then for a considerable vigil—he watched with his glimmering light; moving slowly, holding it high, playing it far, rejoicing above all, as much as he might, in open vistas, reaches of communication between rooms and by passages; the long straight chance or show, as he would have called it, for the revelation he pretended to invite. It was a practice he found he could perfectly "work" without exciting remark; no one was in the least the wiser for it; even Alice Staverton, who was moreover a well of discretion, didn't quite fully imagine.

He let himself in and let himself out with the assurance of calm proprietorship; and accident so far favoured him that, if a fat Avenue "officer" had happened on occasion to see him entering at eleven-thirty, he had never yet, to the best of his belief, been noticed as emerging at two. He walked there on the crisp November nights, arrived regularly at the evening's end; it was as easy to do this after dining out as to take his way to a club or to his hotel. When he left his club, if he hadn't been dining out, it was ostensibly to go to his hotel; and when he left his hotel, if he had spent a part of the evening there, it was ostensibly to go to his club. Everything was easy in fine; everything conspired and promoted: there was truly even in the strain of his experience something that glossed over, something that salved and simplified, all the rest of consciousness. He circulated, talked, renewed, loosely and pleasantly, old relations—met indeed, so far as he could, new expectations and seemed to make out on the whole that in spite of the career, of such different contacts, which he had spoken of to Miss Staverton as ministering so little, for those who might have watched it, to edification, he was positively rather liked than not. He was a dim secondary social success—and all with people who had truly not an idea of him. It was all mere surface sound, this murmur of their welcome, this popping of their corks—just as his gestures of response were the extravagant shadows, emphatic in proportion as they meant little, of some game of *ombres chinoises*. He projected himself all day, in thought, straight over the bristling line of hard unconscious heads and into the other, the real, the waiting life; the life that, as soon as he had heard behind him the click of his great house-door, began for him, on the jolly corner, as beguilingly as the slow opening bars of some rich music follows the tap of the conductor's wand.

He always caught the first effect of the steel point of his stick on the old marble of the hall pavement, large black-and-white squares that he remembered as the admiration of his childhood and that had then made in him, as he now saw, for the growth of an early conception of style. This effect was the dim reverberating tinkle as of some far-off bell hung who should say where?—in the depths of the house, of the past, of that mystical other world that might have flourished for him had he not, for weal or woe, abandoned it. On this impression he did ever the same thing; he put his stick noiselessly away in a corner—feeling the place once more in the likeness of some great glass bowl, all precious concave crystal, set delicately humming by the play of a moist finger round its edge. The concave crystal held, as it were, this mystical other world, and the indescribably fine murmur of its rim was the sigh there, the scarce audible pathetic wail to his strained ear, of all the old baffled forsworn possibilities. What he did therefore by this appeal of his hushed presence was to wake them into such measure of ghostly life as they might still enjoy. They were shy, all but unappeasably shy, but they weren't really sinister; at least they weren't as he had hitherto felt them—before they had taken the Form he so yearned to make them take, the Form he at moments saw himself in the light of fairly hunting on tiptoe, the points of his evening shoes, from room to room and from storey to storey.

That was the essence of his vision—which was all rank folly, if one would, while he was out of the house and otherwise occupied, but which took on the last verisimilitude as soon as he was placed and posted. He knew what he meant and what he wanted; it was as clear as the figure on a cheque presented in demand for cash. His alter ego "walked"—that was the note of his image of him, while his image of his motive for his own odd pastime was the desire to waylay him and meet him. He roamed, slowly, warily, but all restlessly, he himself did—Mrs. Muldoon had been right, absolutely, with her figure of their "craping"; and the presence he watched for would roam restlessly too. But it would be as cautious and as shifty; the conviction of its probable, in fact its already quite sensible, quite audible evasion of pursuit grew for him from night to night, laying on him finally a rigour to which nothing in his life had been comparable. It had been the theory of many superficially-judging persons, he knew, that he was wasting that life in a surrender to sensations, but he had tasted of no pleasure so fine as his actual tension, had been introduced to no sport that demanded at once the patience and the nerve of this stalking of a creature more subtle, yet at bay perhaps more formidable, than any beast of the forest. The terms, the comparisons, the very practices of the chase positively came again into play; there were even moments when passages of his occasional experience as a sportsman, stirred memories, from his younger time, of moor and mountain and desert, revived for him—and to the increase of his keenness—by the tremendous force of analogy. He found himself at moments—once he had placed his single light on some mantel-shelf or in some recess—stepping back into shelter or shade, effacing himself behind a door or in an embrasure, as he had sought of old the vantage of rock and tree; he found himself holding his breath and living in the joy of the instant, the supreme suspense created by big game alone.

He wasn't afraid (though putting himself the question as he believed gentlemen on Bengal tiger-shoots or in close quarters with the great bear of the Rockies had been known to confess to having put it); and this indeed—since here at least he might be frank!—because of the impression, so intimate and so strange, that he himself produced as yet a dread, produced certainly a strain, beyond the liveliest he was likely to feel. They fell for him into categories, they fairly became familiar, the signs, for his own perception, of the alarm his presence and his vigilance created; though leaving him always to remark, portentously, on his probably having formed a relation, his probably enjoying a consciousness, unique in the experience of man. People enough, first and last, had been in terror of apparitions, but who had ever before so turned the tables and become himself, in the apparitional world, an incalculable terror? He might have found this sublime had he quite dared to think of it; but he didn't too much insist, truly, on that side of his privilege. With habit and repetition he gained to an extraordinary degree the power to penetrate the dusk of distances and the darkness of corners, to resolve back into their innocence the treacheries of uncertain light, the evil-looking forms taken in the gloom by mere shadows, by accidents of the air, by shifting effects of perspective; putting down his dim luminary he could still wander on without it, pass into other rooms and, only knowing it was there behind him in case of need, see his way about, visually project for his purpose a comparative clearness. It made him feel, this acquired faculty, like some monstrous stealthy cat; he wondered if he would have glared at these moments with large shining yellow eyes, and what it mightn't verily be, for the poor hard-pressed alter ego, to be confronted with such a type.

He liked however the open shutters; he opened everywhere those Mrs. Muldoon had closed, closing them as carefully afterwards, so that she shouldn't notice: he liked—oh this he did like, and above all in the upper rooms!—the sense of the hard silver of the autumn stars through the window-panes, and scarcely less the flare of the street-lamps below, the white electric lustre which it would have taken curtains to keep out. This was human actual social; this was of the world he had lived in, and he was more at his ease certainly for the countenance, coldly general and impersonal, that all the while and in spite of his detachment it seemed to give him. He had support of course mostly in the rooms at the wide front and the prolonged side; it failed him considerably in the central shades and the parts at the back. But if he sometimes, on his rounds, was glad of his optical reach, so none the less often the rear of the house affected him as the very jungle of his prey. The place was there more subdivided; a large "extension" in particular, where small rooms for servants had been multiplied, abounded in nooks and corners, in closets and passages, in the ramifications especially of an ample back staircase over which he leaned, many a time, to look far down—not deterred from his gravity even while aware that he might, for a spectator, have figured some solemn simpleton playing at hide-and-seek. Outside in fact he might himself make that ironic *rapprochement*; but within the walls, and in spite of the clear windows, his consistency was proof against the cynical light of New York.

It had belonged to that idea of the exasperated consciousness of his victim to become a real test for him; since he had quite put it to himself from the first that, oh distinctly! he could "cultivate" his whole perception. He had felt it as above all open to cultivation—which indeed was but another name for his manner of spending his time. He was bringing it on, bringing it to perfection, by practice; in consequence of which it had grown so fine that he was now aware of impressions, attestations of his general postulate, that couldn't have broken upon him at once. This was the case more specifically with a phenomenon at last quite frequent for him in the upper rooms, the recognition—absolutely unmistakeable, and by a turn dating from a particular hour, his resumption of his campaign after a diplomatic drop, a calculated absence of three nights—of his being definitely followed, tracked at a distance carefully taken and to the express end that he should the less confidently, less arrogantly, appear to himself merely to pursue. It worried, it finally quite broke him up, for it proved, of all the conceivable impressions, the one least suited to his book. He was kept in sight while remaining himself—as regards the essence of his position—sightless, and his only recourse then was in abrupt turns, rapid recoveries of ground. He wheeled about, retracing his steps, as if he might so catch in his face at least the stirred air of some other quick revolution. It was indeed true that his fully dislocalised thought of these manoeuvres recalled to him Pantaloon, at the Christmas farce, buffeted and tricked from behind by ubiquitous Harlequin; but it left intact the influence of the conditions themselves each time he was re-exposed to them, so that in fact this association, had he suffered it to become constant, would on a certain side have but ministered to his intenser gravity. He had made, as I have said, to create on the premises the baseless sense of a reprieve, his three absences; and the result of the third was to confirm the after-effect of the second.

On his return that night—the night succeeding his last intermission—he stood in the hall and looked up the staircase with a certainty more intimate than any he had yet known. "He's there, at the top, and waiting—not, as in general, falling back for disappearance. He's holding his ground, and it's the first time—which is a proof, isn't it? that something has happened for him." So Brydon argued with his hand on the banister and his foot on the lowest stair; in which position he felt as never before the air chilled by his logic. He himself turned cold in it, for he seemed of a sudden to know what now was involved. "Harder pressed?—yes, he takes it in, with its thus making clear to him that I've come, as they say, 'to stay.' He finally doesn't like and can't bear it, in the sense, I mean, that his wrath, his menaced interest, now balances with his dread. I've hunted him till he has 'turned'; that, up there, is what has happened—he's the fanged or the antlered animal brought at last to bay." There came to him, as I say—but determined by an influence beyond my notation!—the acuteness of this certainty; under which however the next moment he had broken into a sweat that he would as little have consented to attribute to fear as he would have dared immediately to act upon it for enterprise. It marked none the less a prodigious thrill, a thrill that represented sudden dismay, no doubt, but also represented, and with the selfsame throb, the strangest, the most joyous, possibly the next minute almost the proudest, duplication of consciousness.

"He has been dodging, retreating, hiding, but now, worked up to anger, he'll fight!"—this intense impression made a single mouthful, as it were, of terror and applause. But what was wondrous was that the applause, for the felt fact, was so eager, since, if it was his other self he was running to earth, this ineffable identity was thus in the last resort not unworthy of him. It bristled there—somewhere near at hand, however unseen still—as the hunted thing, even as the trodden worm of the adage must at last bristle; and Brydon at this instant tasted probably of a sensation more complex than had ever before found itself consistent with sanity. It was as if it would have shamed him that a character so associated with his own should triumphantly succeed in just skulking, should to the end not risk the open; so that the drop of this danger was, on the spot, a great lift of the whole situation. Yet with another rare shift of the same subtlety he was already trying to measure by how much more he himself might now be in peril of fear; so rejoicing that he could, in another form, actively inspire that fear, and simultaneously quaking for the form in which he might passively know it.

The apprehension of knowing it must after a little have grown in him, and the strangest moment of his adventure perhaps, the most memorable or really most interesting, afterwards, of his crisis, was the lapse of certain instants of concentrated conscious combat, the sense of a need to hold on to something, even after the manner of a man slipping and slipping on some awful incline; the vivid impulse, above all, to move, to act, to charge, somehow and upon something—to show himself, in a word, that he wasn't afraid. The state of "holding on" was thus the state to which he was momentarily reduced; if there had been anything, in the great vacancy, to seize, he would presently have been aware of having clutched it as he might under a shock at home have clutched the nearest chair-back. He had been surprised at any rate—of this he was aware—into something unprecedented since his original appropriation of the place; he had closed his eyes, held them tight, for a long minute, as with that instinct of dismay and that terror of vision. When he opened them the room, the other contiguous rooms, extraordinarily, seemed lighter—so light, almost, that at first he took the change for day. He stood firm, however that might be, just where he had paused; his resistance had helped him—it was as if there were something he had tided over. He knew after a little what this was—it had been in the imminent danger of flight. He had stiffened his will against going; without this he would have made for the stairs, and it seemed to him that, still with his eyes closed, he would have descended them, would have known how, straight and swiftly, to the bottom.

Well, as he had held out, here he was—still at the top, among the more intricate upper rooms and with the gauntlet of the others, of all the rest of the house, still to run when it should be his time to go. He would go at his time—only at his time: didn't he go every night very much at the same hour? He took out his watch—there was light for that: it was scarcely a quarter past one, and he had never withdrawn so soon. He reached his lodgings for the most part at two—with his walk of a quarter of an hour. He would wait for the last quarter—he wouldn't stir till then; and he kept his watch there with his eyes on it, reflecting while he held it that this deliberate wait, a wait with an effort, which he recognised, would serve perfectly for the attestation he desired to make. It would prove his courage—unless indeed the latter might most be proved by his budging at last from his place. What he mainly felt now was that, since he hadn't originally scuttled, he had his dignities—which had never in his life seemed so many—all to preserve and to carry aloft. This was before him in truth as a physical image, an image almost worthy of an age of greater romance. That remark indeed glimmered for him only to glow the next instant with a finer light; since what age of romance, after all, could have matched either the state of his mind or, "objectively," as they said, the wonder of his situation? The only difference would have been that, brandishing his dignities over his head as in a parchment scroll, he might then—that is in the heroic time—have proceeded downstairs with a drawn sword in his other grasp.

At present, really, the light he had set down on the mantel of the next room would have to figure his sword; which utensil, in the course of a minute, he had taken the requisite number of steps to possess himself of. The door between the rooms was open, and from the second another door opened to a third. These rooms, as he remembered, gave all three upon a common corridor as well, but there was a fourth, beyond them, without issue save through the preceding. To have moved, to have heard his step again, was appreciably a help; though even in recognising this he lingered once more a little by the chimney-piece on which his light had rested. When he next moved, just hesitating where to turn, he found himself considering a circumstance that, after his first and comparatively vague apprehension of it, produced in him the start that often attends some pang of recollection, the violent shock of having ceased happily to forget. He had come into sight of the door in which the brief chain of communication ended and which he now surveyed from the nearer threshold, the one not directly facing it. Placed at some distance to the left of this point, it would have admitted him to the last room of the four, the room without other approach or egress, had it not, to his intimate conviction, been closed since his former visitation, the matter probably of a quarter of an hour before. He stared with all his eyes at the wonder of the fact, arrested again where he stood and again holding his breath while he sounded his sense. Surely it had been subsequently closed—that is it had been on his previous passage indubitably open!

He took it full in the face that something had happened between—that he couldn't have noticed before (by which he meant on his original tour of all the rooms that evening) that such a barrier had exceptionally presented itself. He had indeed since that moment undergone an agitation so extraordinary that it might have muddled for him any earlier view; and he tried to convince himself that he might perhaps then have gone into the room and, inadvertently, automatically, on coming out, have drawn the door after him. The difficulty was that this exactly was what he never did; it was against his whole policy, as he might have said, the essence of which was to keep vistas clear. He had them from the first, as he was well aware, quite on the brain: the strange apparition, at the far end of one of them, of his baffled "prey" (which had become by so sharp an irony so little the term now to apply!) was the form of success his imagination had most cherished, projecting into it always a refinement of beauty. He had known fifty times the start of perception that had afterwards dropped; had fifty times gasped to himself. "There!" under some fond brief hallucination. The house, as the case stood, admirably lent itself; he might wonder at the taste, the native architecture of the particular time, which could rejoice so in the multiplication of doors—the opposite extreme to the modern, the actual almost complete proscription of them; but it had fairly contributed to provoke this obsession of the presence encountered telescopically, as he might say, focused and studied in diminishing perspective and as by a rest for the elbow.

It was with these considerations that his present attention was charged—they perfectly availed to make what he saw portentous. He couldn't, by any lapse, have blocked that aperture; and if he hadn't, if it was unthinkable, why what else was clear but that there had been another agent? Another agent?—he had been catching, as he felt, a moment back, the very breath of him; but when had he been so close as in this simple, this logical, this completely personal act? It was so logical, that is, that one might have taken it for personal; yet for what did Brydon take it, he asked himself, while, softly panting, he felt his eyes almost leave their sockets. Ah this time at last they were, the two, the opposed projections of him, in presence; and this time, as much as one would, the question of danger loomed. With it rose, as not before, the question of courage—for what he knew the blank face of the door to say to him was "Show us how much you have!" It stared, it glared back at him with that challenge; it put to him the two alternatives: should he just push it open or not? Oh to have this consciousness was to think—and to think, Brydon knew, as he stood there, was, with the lapsing moments, not to have acted! Not to have acted—that was the misery and the pang—was even still not to act; was in fact all to feel the thing in another, in a new and terrible way. How long did he pause and how long did he debate? There was presently nothing to measure it; for his vibration had already changed—as just by the effect of its intensity. Shut up there, at bay, defiant, and with the prodigy of the thing palpably proveably done, thus giving notice like some stark signboard—under that accession of accent the situation itself had turned; and Brydon at last remarkably made up his mind on what it had turned to.

It had turned altogether to a different admonition; to a supreme hint, for him, of the value of Discretion! This slowly dawned, no doubt—for it could take its time; so perfectly, on his threshold, had he been stayed, so little as yet had he either advanced or retreated. It was the strangest of all things that now when, by his taking ten steps and applying his hand to a latch, or even his shoulder and his knee, if necessary, to a panel, all the hunger of his prime need might have been met, his high curiosity crowned, his unrest assuaged—it was amazing, but it was also exquisite and rare, that insistence should have, at a touch, quite dropped from him. Discretion—he jumped at that; and yet not, verily, at such a pitch, because it saved his nerves or his skin, but because, much more valuably, it saved the situation. When I say he "jumped" at it I feel the consonance of this term with the fact that—at the end indeed of I know not how long—he did move again, he crossed straight to the door. He wouldn't touch it—it seemed now that he might if he would: he would only just wait there a little, to show, to prove, that he wouldn't. He had thus another station, close to the thin partition by which revelation was denied him; but with his eyes bent and his hands held off in a mere intensity of stillness. He listened as if there had been something to hear, but this attitude, while it lasted, was his own communication. "If you won't then—good: I spare you and I give up. You affect me as by the appeal positively for pity: you convince me that for reasons rigid and sublime—what do I know?—we both of us should have suffered. I respect them then, and, though moved and privileged as, I believe, it has never been given to man, I retire, I renounce—never, on my honour, to try again. So rest for ever—and let me!"

That, for Brydon, was the deep sense of this last demonstration—solemn, measured, directed, as he felt it to be. He brought it to a close, he turned away; and now verily he knew how deeply he had been stirred. He retraced his steps, taking up his candle, burnt, he observed, well-nigh to the socket, and marking again, lighten it as he would, the distinctness of his footfall; after which, in a moment, he knew himself at the other side of the house. He did here what he had not yet done at these hours—he opened half a casement, one of those in the front, and let in the air of the night; a thing he would have taken at any time previous for a sharp rupture of his spell. His spell was broken now, and it didn't matter—broken by his concession and his surrender, which made it idle henceforth that he should ever come back. The empty street—its other life so marked even by great lamp-lit vacancy—was within call, within touch; he stayed there as to be in it again, high above it though he was still perched; he watched as for some comforting common fact, some vulgar human note, the passage of a scavenger or a thief, some night-bird however base. He would have blessed that sign of life; he would have welcomed positively the slow approach of his friend the policeman, whom he had hitherto only sought to avoid, and was not sure that if the patrol had come into sight he mightn't have felt the impulse to get into relation with it, to hail it, on some pretext, from his fourth floor.

The pretext that wouldn't have been too silly or too compromising, the explanation that would have saved his dignity and kept his name, in such a case, out of the papers, was not definite to him: he was so occupied with the thought of recording his Discretion—as an effect of the vow he had just uttered to his intimate adversary—that the importance of this loomed large and something had overtaken all ironically his sense of proportion. If there had been a ladder applied to the front of the house, even one of the vertiginous perpendiculars employed by painters and roofers and sometimes left standing overnight, he would have managed somehow, astride of the window-sill, to compass by outstretched leg and arm that mode of descent. If there had been some such uncanny thing as he had found in his room at hotels, a workable fire-escape in the form of notched cable or a canvas shoot, he would have availed himself of it as a proof—well, of his present delicacy. He nursed that sentiment, as the question stood, a little in vain, and even—at the end of he scarce knew, once more, how long—found it, as by the action on his mind of the failure of response of the outer world, sinking back to vague anguish. It seemed to him he had waited an age for some stir of the great grim hush; the life of the town was itself under a spell—so unnaturally, up and down the whole prospect of known and rather ugly objects, the blankness and the silence lasted. Had they ever, he asked himself, the hard-faced houses, which had begun to look livid in the dim dawn, had they ever spoken so little to any need of his spirit? Great builded voids, great crowded stillnesses put on, often, in the heart of cities, for the small hours, a sort of sinister mask, and it was of this large collective negation that Brydon presently became conscious—all the more that the break of day was, almost incredibly, now at hand, proving to him what a night he had made of it.

He looked again at his watch, saw what had become of his time-values (he had taken hours for minutes—not, as in other tense situations, minutes for hours) and the strange air of the streets was but the weak, the sullen flush of a dawn in which everything was still locked up. His choked appeal from his own open window had been the sole note of life, and he could but break off at last as for a worse despair. Yet while so deeply demoralised he was capable again of an impulse denoting—at least by his present measure—extraordinary resolution; of retracing his steps to the spot where he had turned cold with the extinction of his last pulse of doubt as to there being in the place another presence than his own. This required an effort strong enough to sicken him; but he had his reason, which over-mastered for the moment everything else. There was the whole of the rest of the house to traverse, and how should he screw himself to that if the door he had seen closed were at present open? He could hold to the idea that the closing had practically been for him an act of mercy, a chance offered him to descend, depart, get off the ground and never again profane it. This conception held together, it worked; but what it meant for him depended now clearly on the amount of forbearance his recent action, or rather his recent inaction, had engendered. The image of the "presence" whatever it was, waiting there for him to go—this image had not yet been so concrete for his nerves as when he stopped short of the point at which certainty would have come to him. For, with all his resolution, or more exactly with all his dread, he did stop short—he hung back from really seeing. The risk was too great and his fear too definite: it took at this moment an awful specific form.

He knew—yes, as he had never known anything—that, should he see the door open, it would all too abjectly be the end of him. It would mean that the agent of his shame—for his shame was the deep abjection—was once more at large and in general possession; and what glared him thus in the face was the act that this would determine for him. It would send him straight about to the window he had left open, and by that window, be long ladder and dangling rope as absent as they would, he saw himself uncontrollably insanely fatally take his way to the street. The hideous chance of this he at least could avert; but he could only avert it by recoiling in time from assurance. He had the whole house to deal with, this fact was still there; only he now knew that uncertainty alone could start him. He stole back from where he had checked himself—merely to do so was suddenly like safety—and, making blindly for the greater staircase, left gaping rooms and sounding passages behind. Here was the top of the stairs, with a fine large dim descent and three spacious landings to mark off. His instinct was all for mildness, but his feet were harsh on the floors, and, strangely, when he had in a couple of minutes become aware of this, it counted somehow for help. He couldn't have spoken, the tone of his voice would have scared him, and the common conceit or resource of "whistling in the dark" (whether literally or figuratively) have appeared basely vulgar; yet he liked none the less to hear himself go, and when he had reached his first landing—taking it all with no rush, but quite steadily—that stage of success drew from him a gasp of relief.

The house, withal, seemed immense, the scale of space again inordinate; the open rooms, to no one of which his eyes deflected, gloomed in their shuttered state like mouths of caverns; only the high skylight that formed the crown of the deep well created for him a medium in which he could advance, but which might have been, for queerness of colour, some watery under-world. He tried to think of something noble, as that his property was really grand, a splendid possession; but this nobleness took the form too of the clear delight with which he was finally to sacrifice it. They might come in now, the builders, the destroyers—they might come as soon as they would. At the end of two flights he had dropped to another zone, and from the middle of the third, with only one more left, he recognised the influence of the lower windows, of half-drawn blinds, of the occasional gleam of street-lamps, of the glazed spaces of the vestibule. This was the bottom of the sea, which showed an illumination of its own and which he even saw paved—when at a given moment he drew up to sink a long look over the banisters—with the marble squares of his childhood. By that time indubitably he felt, as he might have said in a commoner cause, better; it had allowed him to stop and draw breath, and the case increased with the sight of the old black-and-white slabs. But what he most felt was that now surely, with the element of impunity pulling him as by hard firm hands, the case was settled for what he might have seen above had he dared that last look. The closed door, blessedly remote now, was still closed—and he had only in short to reach that of the house.

He came down further, he crossed the passage forming the access to the last flight and if here again he stopped an instant it was almost for the sharpness of the thrill of assured escape. It made him shut his eyes—which opened again to the straight slope of the remainder of the stairs. Here was impunity still, but impunity almost excessive; inasmuch as the side-lights and the high fan-tracery of the entrance were glimmering straight into the hall; an appearance produced, he the next instant saw, by the fact that the vestibule gaped wide, that the hinged halves of the inner door had been thrown far back. Out of that again the question sprang at him, making his eyes, as he felt, half-start from his head, as they had done, at the top of the house, before the sign of the other door. If he had left that one open, hadn't he left this one closed, and wasn't he now in most immediate presence of some inconceivable occult activity? It was as sharp, the question, as a knife in his side, but the answer hung fire still and seemed to lose itself in the vague darkness to which the thin admitted dawn, glimmering archwise over the whole outer door, made a semicircular margin, a cold silvery nimbus that seemed to play a little as he looked—to shift and expand and contract.

It was as if there had been something within it, protected by indistinctness and corresponding in extent with the opaque surface behind, the painted panels of the last barrier to his escape, of which the key was in his pocket. The indistinctness mocked him even while he stared, affected him as somehow shrouding or challenging certitude, so that after faltering an instant on his step he let himself go with the sense that here was at last something to meet, to touch, to take, to know—something all unnatural and dreadful, but to advance upon which was the condition for him either of liberation or of supreme defeat. The penumbra, dense and dark, was the virtual screen of a figure which stood in it as still as some image erect in a niche or as some black-vizored sentinel guarding a treasure. Brydon was to know afterwards, was to recall and make out, the particular thing he had believed during the rest of his descent. He saw, in its great grey glimmering margin, the central vagueness diminish, and he felt it to be taking the very form toward which, for so many days, the passion of his curiosity had yearned. It gloomed, it loomed, it was something, it was somebody, the prodigy of a personal presence.

Rigid and conscious, spectral yet human, a man of his own substance and stature waited there to measure himself with his power to dismay. This only could it be—this only till he recognised, with his advance, that what made the face dim was the pair of raised hands that covered it and in which, so far from being offered in defiance, it was buried, as for dark deprecation. So Brydon, before him, took him in; with every fact of him now, in the higher light, hard and acute—his planted stillness, his vivid truth, his grizzled bent head and white masking hands, his queer actuality of evening-dress, of dangling double eye-glass, of gleaming silk lappet and white linen, of pearl button and gold watch-guard and polished shoe. No portrait by a great modern master could have presented him with more intensity, thrust him out of his frame with more art, as if there had been "treatment," of the consummate sort, in his every shade and salience. The revulsion, for our friend, had become, before he knew it, immense—this drop, in the act of apprehension, to the sense of his adversary's inscrutable manoeuvre. That meaning at least, while he gaped, it offered him; for he could but gape at his other self in this other anguish, gape as a proof that he, standing there for the achieved, the enjoyed, the triumphant life, couldn't be faced in his triumph. Wasn't the proof in the splendid covering hands, strong and completely spread?—so spread and so intentional that, in spite of a special verity that surpassed every other, the fact that one of these hands had lost two fingers, which were reduced to stumps, as if accidentally shot away, the face was effectually guarded and saved.

"Saved," though, would it be?—Brydon breathed his wonder till the very impunity of his attitude and the very insistence of his eyes produced, as he felt, a sudden stir which showed the next instant as a deeper portent, while the head raised itself, the betrayal of a braver purpose. The hands, as he looked, began to move, to open; then, as if deciding in a flash, dropped from the face and left it uncovered and presented. Horror, with the sight, had leaped into Brydon's throat, gasping there in a sound he couldn't utter; for the bared identity was too hideous as his, and his glare was the passion of his protest. The face, that face, Spencer Brydon's?—he searched it still, but looking away from it in dismay and denial, falling straight from his height of sublimity. It was unknown, inconceivable, awful, disconnected from any possibility!—He had been "sold," he inwardly moaned, stalking such game as this: the presence before him was a presence, the horror within him a horror, but the waste of his nights had been only grotesque and the success of his adventure an irony. Such an identity fitted his at no point, made its alternative monstrous. A thousand times yes, as it came upon him nearer now, the face was the face of a stranger. It came upon him nearer now, quite as one of those expanding fantastic images projected by the magic lantern of childhood; for the stranger, whoever he might be, evil, odious, blatant, vulgar, had advanced as for aggression, and he knew himself give ground. Then harder pressed still, sick with the force of his shock, and falling back as under the hot breath and the roused passion of a life larger than his own, a rage of personality before which his own collapsed, he felt the whole vision turn to darkness and his very feet give way. His head went round; he was going; he had gone.

CHAPTER III

What had next brought him back, clearly—though after how long?—was Mrs. Muldoon's voice, coming to him from quite near, from so near that he seemed presently to see her as kneeling on the ground before him while he lay looking up at her; himself not wholly on the ground, but half-raised and upheld—conscious, yes, of tenderness of support and, more particularly, of a head pillowed in extraordinary softness and faintly refreshing fragrance. He considered, he wondered, his wit but half at his service; then another face intervened, bending more directly over him, and he finally knew that Alice Staverton had made her lap an ample and perfect cushion to him, and that she had to this end seated herself on the lowest degree of the staircase, the rest of his long person remaining stretched on his old black-and-white slabs. They were cold, these marble squares of his youth; but he somehow was not, in this rich return of consciousness—the most wonderful hour, little by little, that he had ever known, leaving him, as it did, so gratefully, so abysmally passive, and yet as with a treasure of intelligence waiting all round him for quiet appropriation; dissolved, he might call it, in the air of the place and producing the golden glow of a late autumn afternoon. He had come back, yes—come back from further away than any man but himself had ever travelled; but it was strange how with this sense what he had come back to seemed really the great thing, and as if his prodigious journey had been all for the sake of it. Slowly but surely his consciousness grew, his vision of his state thus completing itself; he had been miraculously carried back—lifted and carefully borne as from where he had been picked up, the uttermost end of an interminable grey passage. Even with this he was suffered to rest, and what had now brought him to knowledge was the break in the long mild motion.

It had brought him to knowledge, to knowledge—yes, this was the beauty of his state; which came to resemble more and more that of a man who has gone to sleep on some news of a great inheritance, and then, after dreaming it away, after profaning it with matters strange to it, has waked up again to serenity of certitude and has only to lie and watch it grow. This was the drift of his patience—that he had only to let it shine on him. He must moreover, with intermissions, still have been lifted and borne; since why and how else should he have known himself, later on, with the afternoon glow intenser, no longer at the foot of his stairs—situated as these now seemed at that dark other end of his tunnel—but on a deep window-bench of his high saloon, over which had been spread, couch-fashion, a mantle of soft stuff lined with grey fur that was familiar to his eyes and that one of his hands kept fondly feeling as for its pledge of truth. Mrs. Muldoon's face had gone, but the other, the second he had recognised, hung over him in a way that showed how he was still propped and pillowed. He took it all in, and the more he took it the more it seemed to suffice: he was as much at peace as if he had had food and drink. It was the two women who had found him, on Mrs. Muldoon's having plied, at her usual hour, her latch-key—and on her having above all arrived while Miss Staverton still lingered near the house. She had been turning away, all anxiety, from worrying the vain bell-handle—her calculation having been of the hour of the good woman's visit; but the latter, blessedly, had come up while she was still there, and they had entered together. He had then lain, beyond the vestibule, very much as he was lying now—quite, that is, as he appeared to have fallen, but all so wondrously without bruise or gash; only in a depth of stupor. What he most took in, however, at present, with the steadier clearance, was that Alice Staverton had for a long unspeakable moment not doubted he was dead.

"It must have been that I was." He made it out as she held him. "Yes—I can only have died. You brought me literally to life. Only," he wondered, his eyes rising to her, "only, in the name of all the benedictions, how?"

It took her but an instant to bend her face and kiss him, and something in the manner of it, and in the way her hands clasped and locked his head while he felt the cool charity and virtue of her lips, something in all this beatitude somehow answered everything.

"And now I keep you," she said.

"Oh keep me, keep me!" he pleaded while her face still hung over him: in response to which it dropped again and stayed close, clingingly close. It was the seal of their situation—of which he tasted the impress for a long blissful moment in silence. But he came back. "Yet how did you know—?"

"I was uneasy. You were to have come, you remember—and you had sent no word."

"Yes, I remember—I was to have gone to you at one to-day." It caught on to their "old" life and relation—which were so near and so far. "I was still out there in my strange darkness—where was it, what was it? I must have stayed there so long." He could but wonder at the depth and the duration of his swoon.

"Since last night?" she asked with a shade of fear for her possible indiscretion.

"Since this morning—it must have been: the cold dim dawn of to-day. Where have I been," he vaguely wailed, "where have I been?" He felt her hold him close, and it was as if this helped him now to make in all security his mild moan. "What a long dark day!"

All in her tenderness she had waited a moment. "In the cold dim dawn?" she quavered.

But he had already gone on piecing together the parts of the whole prodigy. "As I didn't turn up you came straight—?"

She barely cast about. "I went first to your hotel—where they told me of your absence. You had dined out last evening and hadn't been back since. But they appeared to know you had been at your club."

"So you had the idea of this—?"

"Of what?" she asked in a moment.

"Well—of what has happened."

"I believed at least you'd have been here. I've known, all along," she said, "that you've been coming."

"'Known' it—?"

"Well, I've believed it. I said nothing to you after that talk we had a month ago—but I felt sure. I knew you would," she declared.

"That I'd persist, you mean?"

"That you'd see him."

"Ah but I didn't!" cried Brydon with his long wail. "There's somebody—an awful beast; whom I brought, too horribly, to bay. But it's not me."

At this she bent over him again, and her eyes were in his eyes. "No—it's not you." And it was as if, while her face hovered, he might have made out in it, hadn't it been so near, some particular meaning blurred by a smile. "No, thank heaven," she repeated, "it's not you! Of course it wasn't to have been."

"Ah but it was," he gently insisted. And he stared before him now as he had been staring for so many weeks. "I was to have known myself."

"You couldn't!" she returned consolingly. And then reverting, and as if to account further for what she had herself done, "But it wasn't only that, that you hadn't been at home," she went on. "I waited till the hour at which we had found Mrs. Muldoon that day of my going with you; and she arrived, as I've told you, while, failing to bring any one to the door, I lingered in my despair on the steps. After a little, if she hadn't come, by such a mercy, I should have found means to hunt her up. But it wasn't," said Alice Staverton, as if once more with her fine intentions—"it wasn't only that."

His eyes, as he lay, turned back to her. "What more then?"

She met it, the wonder she had stirred. "In the cold dim dawn, you say? Well, in the cold dim dawn of this morning I too saw you."

"Saw me—?"

"Saw him," said Alice Staverton. "It must have been at the same moment."

He lay an instant taking it in—as if he wished to be quite reasonable. "At the same moment?"

"Yes—in my dream again, the same one I've named to you. He came back to me. Then I knew it for a sign. He had come to you."

At this Brydon raised himself; he had to see her better. She helped him when she understood his movement, and he sat up, steadying himself beside her there on the window-bench and with his right hand grasping her left. "He didn't come to me."

"You came to yourself," she beautifully smiled.

"Ah I've come to myself now—thanks to you, dearest. But this brute, with his awful face—this brute's a black stranger. He's none of me, even as I might have been," Brydon sturdily declared.

But she kept the clearness that was like the breath of infallibility. "Isn't the whole point that you'd have been different?"

He almost scowled for it. "As different as that—?"

Her look again was more beautiful to him than the things of this world. "Haven't you exactly wanted to know how different? So this morning," she said, "you appeared to me."

"Like him?"

"A black stranger!"

"Then how did you know it was I?"

"Because, as I told you weeks ago, my mind, my imagination, has worked so over what you might, what you mightn't have been—to show you, you see, how I've thought of you. In the midst of that you came to me—that my wonder might be answered. So I knew," she went on; "and believed that, since the question held you too so fast, as you told me that day, you too would see for yourself. And when this morning I again saw I knew it would be because you had—and also then, from the first moment, because you somehow wanted me. He seemed to tell me of that. So why," she strangely smiled, "shouldn't I like him?"

It brought Spencer Brydon to his feet. "You 'like' that horror—?"

"I could have liked him. And to me," she said, "he was no horror. I had accepted him."

"'Accepted'—?" Brydon oddly sounded.

"Before, for the interest of his difference—yes. And as I didn't disown him, as I knew him—which you at last, confronted with him in his difference, so cruelly didn't, my dear,—well, he must have been, you see, less dreadful to me. And it may have pleased him that I pitied him."

She was beside him on her feet, but still holding his hand—still with her arm supporting him. But though it all brought for him thus a dim light, "You 'pitied' him?" he grudgingly, resentfully asked.

"He has been unhappy, he has been ravaged," she said.

"And haven't I been unhappy? Am not I—you've only to look at me!—ravaged?"

"Ah I don't say I like him better," she granted after a thought. "But he's grim, he's worn—and things have happened to him. He doesn't make shift, for sight, with your charming monocle."

"No"—it struck Brydon; "I couldn't have sported mine 'down-town.' They'd have guyed me there."

"His great convex pince-nez—I saw it, I recognised the kind—is for his poor ruined sight. And his poor right hand—!"

"Ah!" Brydon winced—whether for his proved identity or for his lost fingers. Then, "He has a million a year," he lucidly added. "But he hasn't you."

"And he isn't—no, he isn't—you!" she murmured, as he drew her to his breast.

THE MIDDLE YEARS

I

The April day was soft and bright, and poor Dencombe, happy in the conceit of reasserted strength, stood in the garden of the hotel, comparing, with a deliberation in which, however, there was still something of languor, the attractions of easy strolls. He liked the feeling of the south, so far as you could have it in the north, he liked the sandy cliffs and the clustered pines, he liked even the colourless sea. 'Bournemouth as a health-resort' had sounded like a mere advertisement, but now he was reconciled to the prosaic. The sociable country postman, passing through the garden, had just given him a small parcel, which he took out with him, leaving the hotel to the right and creeping to a convenient bench that he knew of, a safe recess in the cliff. It looked to the south, to the tinted walls of the Island, and was protected behind by the sloping shoulder of the down. He was tired enough when he reached it, and for a moment he was disappointed; he was better, of course, but better, after all, than what? He should never again, as at one or two great moments of the past, be better than himself. The infinite of life had gone, and what was left of the dose was a small glass engraved like a thermometer by the apothecary. He sat and stared at the sea, which appeared all surface and twinkle, far shallower than the spirit of man. It was the abyss of human illusion that was the real, the tideless deep. He held his packet, which had come by book-post, unopened on his knee, liking, in the lapse of so many joys (his illness had made him feel his age), to know that it was there, but taking for granted there could be no complete renewal of the pleasure, dear to young experience, of seeing one's self 'just out'. Dencombe, who had a reputation, had come out too often and knew too well in advance how he should look.

His postponement associated itself vaguely, after a little, with a group of three persons, two ladies and a young man, whom, beneath him, straggling and seemingly silent, he could see move slowly together along the sands. The gentleman had his head bent over a book and was occasionally brought to a stop by the charm of this volume, which, as Dencombe could perceive even at a distance, had a cover alluringly red. Then his companions, going a little further, waited for him to come up, poking their parasols into the beach, looking around them at the sea and sky and clearly sensible of the beauty of the day. To these things the young man with the book was still more clearly indifferent; lingering, credulous, absorbed, he was an object of envy to an observer from whose connexion with literature all such artlessness had faded. One of the ladies was large and mature; the other had the spareness of comparative youth and of a social situation possibly inferior. The large lady carried back Dencombe's imagination to the age of crinoline; she wore a hat of the shape of a mushroom, decorated with a blue veil, and had the air, in her aggressive amplitude, of clinging to a vanished fashion or even a lost cause. Presently her companion produced from under the folds of a mantle a limp, portable chair which she stiffened out and of which the large lady took possession. This act, and something in the movement of either party, instantly characterized the performers—they performed for Dencombe's recreation—as opulent matron and humble dependant. What, moreover, was the use of being an approved novelist if one couldn't establish a relation between such figures; the clever theory, for instance, that the young man was the son of the opulent matron, and that the humble dependant, the daughter of a clergyman or an officer, nourished a secret passion for him ? Was that not visible from the way she stole behind her protectress to look back at him ?—back to where he had let himself come to a full stop when his mother sat down to rest. His book was a novel; it had the catchpenny cover, and while the romance of life stood neglected at his side he lost himself in that of the circulating library. He moved mechanically to where the sand was softer, and ended by plumping down in it to finish his chapter at his ease. The humble dependant, discouraged by his remoteness, wandered, with a martyred droop of the head, in another direction, and the exorbitant lady, watching the waves, offered a confused resemblance to a flying-machine that had broken down.

When his drama began to fail Dencombe remembered that he had, after all, another pastime. Though such promptitude on the part of the publisher was rare, he was already able to draw from its wrapper his 'latest', perhaps his last. The cover of 'The Middle Years' was duly meretricious, the smell of the fresh pages the very odour of sanctity; but for the moment he went no further—he had become conscious of a strange alienation. He had forgotten what his book was about. Had the assault of his old ailment, which he had so fallaciously come to Bournemouth to ward off, interposed utter blankness as to what had preceded it ? He had finished the revision of proof before quitting London, but his subsequent fortnight in bed had passed the sponge over colour. He couldn't have chanted to himself a single sentence, couldn't have turned with curiosity or confidence to any particular page. His subject had already gone from him, leaving scarcely a superstition behind. He uttered a low moan as he breathed the chill of this dark void, so desperately it seemed to represent the completion of a sinister process. The tears filled his mild eyes; something precious had passed away. This was the pang that had been sharpest during the last few years—the sense of ebbing time, of shrinking opportunity; and now he felt not so much that his last chance was going as that it was gone indeed. He had done all that he should ever do, and yet he had not done what he wanted. This was the laceration—that practically his career was over: it was as violent as a rough hand at his throat. He rose from his seat nervously, like a creature hunted by a dread; then he fell back in his weakness and nervously opened his book. It was a single volume; he preferred single volumes and aimed at a rare compression. He began to read, and little by little, in this occupation, he was pacified and reassured. Everything came back to him, but came back with a wonder, came back, above all, with a high and magnificent beauty. He read his own prose, he turned his own leaves, and had, as he sat there with the spring sunshine on the page, an emotion peculiar and intense. His career was over, no doubt, but it was over, after all, with *that*.

He had forgotten during his illness the work of the previous year; but what he had chiefly forgotten was that it was extraordinary good. He lived once more into his story and was drawn down, as by a siren's hand, to where, in the dim underworld of fiction, the great glazed tank of art, strange silent subjects float. He recognized his motive and surrendered to his talent. Never, probably, had that talent, such as it was, been so fine. His difficulties were still there, but what was also there, to his perception, though probably, alas! to nobody's else, was the art that in most cases had surmounted them. In his surprised enjoyment of this ability he had a glimpse of a possible reprieve. Surely its force was not spent—there was life and service in it yet. It had not come to him easily, it had been backward and roundabout. It was the child of time, the nursling of delay; he had struggled and suffered for it, making sacrifices not to be counted, and now that it was really mature was it to cease to yield, to confess itself brutally beaten? There was an infinite charm for Dencombe in feeling as he had never felt before that diligence *vincit omnia*. The result produced in his little book was somehow a result beyond his conscious intention: it was as if he had planted his genius, had trusted his method, and they had grown up and flowered with this sweetness. If the achievement had been real, however, the process had been manful enough. What he saw so intensely to-day, what he felt as a nail driven in, was that only now, at the very last, had he come into possession. His development had been abnormally slow, almost grotesquely gradual. He had been hindered and retarded by experience, and for long periods had only groped his way. It had taken too much of his life to produce too little of his art. The art had come, but it had come after everything else. At such a rate a first existence was too short—long enough only to collect material; so that to fructify, to use the material, one must have a second age, an extension. This extension was what poor Dencombe sighed for. As he turned the last leaves of his volume he murmured: 'Ah for another go!—ah for a better chance!'

The three persons he had observed on the sands had vanished and then reappeared; they had now wandered up a path, an artificial and easy ascent, which led to the top of the cliff. Dencombe's bench was halfway down, on a sheltered ledge, and the large lady, a massive, heterogeneous person, with bold black eyes and kind red cheeks, now took a few moments to rest. She wore dirty gauntlets and immense diamond earrings; at first she looked vulgar, but she contradicted this announcement in an agreeable off-hand tone. While her companions stood waiting for her she spread her skirts on the end of Dencombe's seat. The young man had gold spectacles, through which, with his finger still in his red-covered book, he glanced at the volume, bound in the same shade of the same colour, lying on the lap of the original occupant of the bench. After an instant Dencombe understood that he was struck with a resemblance, had recognized the gilt stamp on the crimson cloth, was reading 'The Middle Years', and now perceived that somebody else had kept pace with him. The stranger was startled, possibly even a little ruffled, to find that he was not the only person who had been favoured with an early copy. The eyes of the two proprietors met for a moment, and Dencombe borrowed amusement from the expression of those of his competitor, those, it might even be inferred, of his admirer. They confessed to some resentment—they seemed to say: 'Hang it, has he got it *already*?—Of course he's a brute of a reviewer!' Dencombe shuffled his copy out of sight while the opulent matron, rising from her repose, broke out: 'I feel already the good of this air!'

'I can't say I do,' said the angular lady. 'I find myself quite let down.'

'I find myself horribly hungry. At what time did you order lunch?' her protectress pursued.

The young person put the question by. 'Doctor Hugh always orders it.'

'I ordered nothing to-day—I'm going to make you diet,' said their comrade.

'Then I shall go home and sleep. *Qui dort dine*!'

'Can I trust you to Miss Vernham?' asked Doctor Hugh of his elder companion.

'Don't I trust *you*?' she archly inquired.

'Not too much!' Miss Vernham, with her eyes on the ground, permitted herself to declare. 'You must come with us at least to the house,' she went on, while the personage on whom they appeared to be in attendance began to mount higher. She had got a little out of ear-shot; nevertheless Miss Vernham became, so far as Dencombe was concerned, less distinctly audible to murmur to the young man: 'I don't think you realize all you owe the Countess!'

Absently, a moment, Doctor Hugh caused his gold-rimmed spectacles to shine at her.

'Is that the way I strike you? I see—I see!'

'She's awfully good to us,' continued Miss Vernham, compelled by her interlocutor's immovability to stand there in spite of his discussion of private matters. Of what use would it have been that Dencombe should be sensitive to shades had he not detected in that immovability a strange influence from the quiet old convalescent in the great tweed cape? Miss Vernham appeared suddenly to become aware of some such connexion, for she added in a moment: 'If you want to sun yourself here you can come back after you've seen us home.'

Doctor Hugh, at this, hesitated, and Dencombe, in spite of a desire to pass for unconscious, risked a covert glance at him. What his eyes met this time, as it happened, was on the part of the young lady a queer stare, naturally vitreous, which made her aspect remind him of some figure (he couldn't name it) in a play or a novel, some sinister governess or tragic old maid. She seemed to scrutinize him, to challenge him, to say, from general spite: 'What have you got to do with us?' At the same instant the rich humour of the Countess reached them from above: 'Come, come, my little lambs, you should follow your old *bergère*!' Miss Vernham turned away at this, pursuing the ascent, and Doctor Hugh, after another mute appeal to Dencombe and a moment's evident demur, deposited his book on the bench, as if to keep his place or even as a sign that he would return, and bounded without difficulty up the rougher part of the cliff.

Equally innocent and infinite are the pleasures of observation and the resources engendered by the habit of analysing life. It amused poor Dencombe, as he dawdled in his tepid air-bath, to think that he was waiting for a revelation of something at the back of a fine young mind. He looked hard at the book on the end of the bench, but he wouldn't have touched it for the world. It served his purpose to have a theory which should not be exposed to refutation. He already felt better of his melancholy; he had, according to his old formula, put his head at the window. A passing Countess could draw off the fancy when, like the elder of the ladies who had just retreated, she was as obvious as the giantess of a caravan. It was indeed general views that were terrible; short ones, contrary to an opinion sometimes expressed, were the refuge, were the remedy. Doctor Hugh couldn't possibly be anything but a reviewer who had understandings for early copies with publishers or with newspapers. He reappeared in a quarter of an hour, with visible relief at finding Dencombe on the spot, and the gleam of white teeth in an embarrassed but generous smile. He was perceptibly disappointed at the eclipse of the other copy of the book; it was a pretext the less for speaking to the stranger. But he spoke notwithstanding; he held up his own copy and broke out pleadingly: 'Do say, if you have occasion to speak of it, that it's the best thing he has done yet!'

Dencombe responded with a laugh: 'Done yet' was so amusing to him, made such a grand avenue of the future. Better still, the young man took *him* for a reviewer. He pulled out 'The Middle Years' from under his cape, but instinctively concealed any tell-tale look of fatherhood. This was partly because a person was always a fool for calling attention to his work. 'Is that what you're going to say yourself?' he inquired of his visitor.

'I'm not quite sure I shall write anything. I don't, as a regular thing—I enjoy in peace. But it's awfully fine.'

Dencombe debated a moment. If his interlocutor had begun to abuse him he would have confessed on the spot to his identity, but there was no harm in drawing him on a little to praise. He drew him on with such success that in a few moments his new acquaintance, seated by his side, was confessing candidly that Dencombe's novels were the only ones he could read a second time. He had come the day before from London, where a friend of his, a journalist, had lent him his copy of the last—the copy sent to the office of the journal and already the subject of a 'notice' which, as was pretended there (but one had to allow for 'swagger') it had taken a full quarter of an hour to prepare. He intimated that he was ashamed for his friend, and in the case of a work demanding and repaying study, of such inferior manners; and, with his fresh appreciation and inexplicable wish to express it, he speedily became for poor Dencombe a remarkable, a delightful apparition. Chance had brought the weary man of letters face to face with the greatest admirer in the new generation whom it was supposable he possessed. The admirer, in truth, was mystifying, so rare a case was it to find a bristling young doctor—he looked like a German physiologist—enamoured of literary form. It was an accident, but happier than most accidents, so that Dencombe, exhilarated as well as confounded, spent half an hour in making his visitor talk while he kept himself quiet. He explained his premature possession of 'The Middle Years' by an allusion to the friendship of the publisher, who, knowing he was at Bournemouth for his health, had paid him this graceful attention. He admitted that he had been ill, for Doctor Hugh would infallibly have guessed it; he even went so far as to wonder whether he mightn't look for some hygienic 'tip' from a personage combining so bright an enthusiasm with a presumable knowledge of the remedies now in vogue. It would shake his faith a little perhaps to have to take a doctor seriously who could take *him* so seriously, but he enjoyed this gushing modern youth and he felt with an acute pang that there would still be work to do in a world in which such odd combinations were presented. It was not true, what he had tried for renunciation's sake to believe, that all the combinations were exhausted. They were not, they were not—they were infinite: the exhaustion was in the miserable artist.

Doctor Hugh was an ardent physiologist, saturated with the spirit of the age—in other words he had just taken his degree; but he was independent and various, he talked like a man who would have preferred to love literature best. He would fain have made fine phrases, but nature had denied him the trick. Some of the finest in 'The Middle Years' had struck him inordinately, and he took the liberty of reading them to Dencombe in support of his plea. He grew vivid, in the balmy air, to his companion, for whose deep refreshment he seemed to have been sent; and was particularly ingenuous in describing how recently he had become acquainted, and how instantly infatuated, with the only man who had put flesh between the ribs of an art that was starving on superstitions. He had not yet written to him—he was deterred by a sentiment of respect. Dencombe at this moment felicitated himself more than ever on having never answered the photographers. His visitor's attitude promised him a luxury of intercourse, but he surmised that a certain security in it, for Doctor Hugh, would depend not a little on the Countess. He learned without delay with what variety of Countess they were concerned, as well as the nature of the tie that united the curious trio. The large lady, an Englishwoman by birth and the daughter of a celebrated baritone, whose taste, without his talent, she had inherited, was the widow of a French nobleman and mistress of all that remained of the handsome fortune, the fruit of her father's earnings, that had constituted her dower. Miss Vernham, an odd creature but an accomplished pianist, was attached to her person at a salary. The Countess was generous, independent, eccentric; she travelled with her minstrel and her medical man. Ignorant and passionate, she had nevertheless moments in which she was almost irresistible. Dencombe saw her sit for her portrait in Doctor Hugh's free sketch, and felt the picture of his young friend's relation to her frame itself in his mind. This young friend, for a representative of the new psychology, was himself easily hypnotized, and if he became abnormally communicative it was only a sign of his real subjection.

Dencombe did accordingly what he wanted with him, even without being known as Dencombe.

Taken ill on a journey in Switzerland the Countess had picked him up at an hotel, and the accident of his happening to please her had made her offer him, with her imperious liberality, terms that couldn't fail to dazzle a practitioner without patients and whose resources had been drained dry by his studies. It was not the way he would have elected to spend his time, but it was time that would pass quickly, and meanwhile she was wonderfully kind. She exacted perpetual attention, but it was impossible not to like her. He gave details about his queer patient, a 'type' if there ever was one, who had in connexion with her flushed obesity and in addition to the morbid strain of a violent and aimless will a grave organic disorder; but he came back to his loved novelist, whom he was so good as to pronounce more essentially a poet than many of those who went in for verse, with a zeal excited, as all his indiscretion had been excited, by the happy chance of Dencombe's sympathy and the coincidence of their occupation. Dencombe had confessed to a slight personal acquaintance with the author of 'The Middle Years', but had not felt himself as ready as he could have wished when his companion, who had never yet encountered a being so privileged, began to be eager for particulars. He even thought that Doctor Hugh's eye at that moment emitted a glimmer of suspicion. But the young man was too inflamed to be shrewd and repeatedly caught up the book to exclaim: 'Did you notice this?' or 'Weren't you immensely struck with that?' 'There's a beautiful passage toward the end,' he broke out; and again he laid his hand upon the volume. As he turned the pages he came upon something else, while Dencombe saw him suddenly change colour. He had taken up, as it lay on the bench, Dencombe's copy instead of his own, and his neighbour immediately guessed the reason of his start. Doctor Hugh looked grave an instant; then he said: 'I see you've been altering the text!' Dencombe was a passionate corrector, a fingerer of style; the last thing he ever arrived at was a form final for himself. His ideal would have been to publish secretly, and then, on the published text, treat himself to the terrified revise, sacrificing always a first edition and beginning for posterity and even for the collectors, poor dears, with a second. This morning, in 'The Middle Years', his pencil had pricked a dozen lights. He was amused at the effect of the young man's reproach; for an instant it made him change colour. He stammered, at any rate, ambiguously; then, through a blur of ebbing consciousness, saw Doctor Hugh's mystified eyes. He only had time to feel he was about to be ill again—that emotion, excitement, fatigue, the heat of the sun, the solicitation of the air, had combined to play him a trick, before, stretching out a hand to his visitor with a plaintive cry, he lost his senses altogether.

Later he knew that he had fainted and that Doctor Hugh had got him home in a bath-chair, the conductor of which, prowling within hail for custom, had happened to remember seeing him in the garden of the hotel. He had recovered his perception in the transit, and had, in bed, that afternoon, a vague recollection of Doctor Hugh's young face, as they went together, bent over him in a comforting laugh and expressive of something more than a suspicion of his identity. That identity was ineffaceable now, and all the more that he was disappointed, disgusted. He had been rash, been stupid, had gone out too soon, stayed out too long. He oughtn't to have exposed himself to strangers, he ought to have taken his servant. He felt as if he had fallen into a hole too deep to descry any little patch of heaven. He was confused about the time that had elapsed—he pieced the fragments together. He had seen his doctor, the real one, the one who had treated him from the first and who had again been very kind. His servant was in and out on tiptoe, looking very wise after the fact. He said more than once something about the sharp young gentleman. The rest was vagueness, in so far as it wasn't despair. The vagueness, however, justified itself by dreams, dozing anxieties from which he finally emerged to the consciousness of a dark room and a shaded candle.

'You'll be all right again—I know all about you now,' said a voice near him that he knew to be young. Then his meeting with Doctor Hugh came back. He was too discouraged to joke about it yet, but he was able to perceive, after a little, that the interest of it was intense for his visitor. 'Of course I can't attend you professionally—you've got your own man, with whom I've talked and who's excellent,' Doctor Hugh went on. 'But you must let me come to see you as a good friend. I've just looked in before going to bed. You're doing beautifully, but it's a good job I was with you on the cliff. I shall come in early to-morrow. I want to do something for you. I want to do everything. You've done a tremendous lot for me.' The young man held his hand, hanging over him, and poor Dencombe, weakly aware of this living pressure, simply lay there and accepted his devotion. He couldn't do anything less—he needed help too much.

The idea of the help he needed was very present to him that night, which he spent in a lucid stillness, an intensity of thought that constituted a reaction from his hours of stupor. He was lost, he was lost—he was lost if he couldn't be saved. He was not afraid of suffering, of death; he was not even in love with life; but he had had a deep demonstration of desire. It came over him in the long, quiet hours that only with 'The Middle Years' had he taken his flight; only on that day, visited by soundless processions, had he recognized his kingdom. He had had a revelation of his range. What he dreaded was the idea that his reputation should stand on the unfinished. It was not with his past but with his future that it should properly be concerned. Illness and age rose before him like spectres with pitiless eyes; how was he to bribe such fates to give him the second chance? He had had the one chance that all men have—he had had the chance of life. He went to sleep again very late, and when he awoke Doctor Hugh was sitting by his head. There was already, by this time, something beautifully familiar in him.

'Don't think I've turned out your physician,' he said; 'I'm acting with his consent. He has been here and seen you. Somehow he seems to trust me. I told him how we happened to come together yesterday, and he recognizes that I've a peculiar right.'

Dencombe looked at him with a calculating earnestness. 'How have you squared the Countess?'

The young man blushed a little, but he laughed. 'Oh, never mind the Countess!'

'You told me she was very exacting.'

Doctor Hugh was silent a moment. 'So she is.'

'And Miss Vernham's an *intrigante*.'

'How do you know that?'

'I know everything. One *has* to, to write decently!'

'I think she's mad,' said limpid Doctor Hugh.

'Well, don't quarrel with the Countess—she's a present help to you.'

'I don't quarrel,' Doctor Hugh replied. 'But I don't get on with silly women.' Presently he added: 'You seem very much alone.'

'That often happens at my age. I've outlived, I've lost by the way.'

Doctor Hugh hesitated; then surmounting a soft scruple: 'Whom have you lost?'

'Every one.'

'Ah, no,' the young man murmured, laying a hand on his arm.

'I once had a wife—I once had a son. My wife died when my child was born, and my boy, at school, was carried off by typhoid.'

'I wish I'd been there!' said Doctor Hugh simply.

'Well—if you're here!' Dencombe answered, with a smile that, in spite of dimness, showed how much he liked to be sure of his companion's whereabouts.

'You talk strangely of your age. You're not old.'

'Hypocrite—so early!'

'I speak physiologically.'

'That's the way I've been speaking for the last five years, and it's exactly what I've been saying to myself. It isn't till we *are* old that we begin to tell ourselves we're not!'

'Yet I know I myself am young,' Doctor Hugh declared.

'Not so well as I!' laughed his patient, whose visitor indeed would have established the truth in question by the honesty with which he changed the point of view, remarking that it must be one of the charms of age—at any rate in the case of high distinction—to feel that one has laboured and achieved. Doctor Hugh employed the common phrase about earning one's rest, and it made poor Dencombe, for an instant, almost angry. He recovered himself, however, to explain, lucidly enough, that if he, ungraciously, knew nothing of such a balm, it was doubtless because he had wasted inestimable years. He had followed literature from the first, but he had taken a lifetime to get alongside of her. Only to-day, at last, had he begun to *see*, so that what he had hitherto done was a movement without a direction. He had ripened too late and was so clumsily constituted that he had had to teach himself by mistakes.

'I prefer your flowers, then, to other people's fruit, and your mistakes to other people's successes,' said gallant Doctor Hugh. 'It's for your mistakes I admire you.'

'You're happy—you don't know,' Dencombe answered.

Looking at his watch the young man had got up; he named the hour of the afternoon at which he would return. Dencombe warned him against committing himself too deeply, and expressed again all his dread of making him neglect the Countess—perhaps incur her displeasure.

'I want to be like you—I want to learn by mistakes!' Doctor Hugh laughed.

'Take care you don't make too grave a one! But do come back,' Dencombe added, with the glimmer of a new idea.

'You should have had more vanity!' Doctor Hugh spoke as if he knew the exact amount required to make a man of letters normal.

'No, no—I only should have had more time. I want another go.'

'Another go?'

'I want an extension.'

'An extension?' Again Doctor Hugh repeated Dencombe's words, with which he seemed to have been struck.

'Don't you know?—I want to what they call "live".'

The young man, for good-bye, had taken his hand, which closed with a certain force. They looked at each other hard a moment. 'You *will* live,' said Doctor Hugh.

'Don't be superficial. It's too serious!'

'You *shall* live!' Dencombe's visitor declared, turning pale.

'Ah, that's better!' And as he retired the invalid, with a troubled laugh, sank gratefully back.

All that day and all the following night he wondered if it mightn't be arranged. His doctor came again, his servant was attentive, but it was to his confident young friend that he found himself mentally appealing. His collapse on the cliff was plausibly explained, and his liberation, on a better basis, promised for the morrow; meanwhile, however, the intensity of his meditations kept him tranquil and made him indifferent. The idea that occupied him was none the less absorbing because it was a morbid fancy. Here was a clever son of the age, ingenious and ardent, who happened to have set him up for connoisseurs to worship. This servant of his altar had all the new learning in science and all the old reverence in faith; wouldn't he therefore put his knowledge at the disposal of his sympathy, his craft at the disposal of his love? Couldn't he be trusted to invent a remedy for a poor artist to whose art he had paid a tribute? If he couldn't, the alternative was hard: Dencombe would have to surrender to silence, unvindicated and undivined. The rest of the day and all the next he toyed in secret with this sweet futility. Who would work the miracle for him but the young man who could combine such lucidity with such passion? He thought of the fairy-tales of science and charmed himself into forgetting that he looked for a magic that was not of this world. Doctor Hugh was an apparition, and that placed him above the law. He came and went while his patient, who sat up, followed him with supplicating eyes. The interest of knowing the great author had made the young man begin 'The Middle Years' afresh, and would help him to find a deeper meaning in its pages. Dencombe had told him what he 'tried for'; with all his intelligence, on a first perusal, Doctor Hugh had failed to guess it. The baffled celebrity wondered then who in the world *would* guess it: he was amused once more at the fine, full way with which an intention could be missed. Yet he wouldn't rail at the general mind to-day—consoling as that ever had been: the revelation of his own slowness had seemed to make all stupidity sacred.

Doctor Hugh, after a little, was visibly worried, confessing, on inquiry, to a source of embarrassment at home. 'Stick to the Countess—don't mind me,' Dencombe said, repeatedly; for his companion was frank enough about the large lady's attitude. She was so jealous that she had fallen ill—she resented such a breach of allegiance. She paid so much for his fidelity that she must have it all: she refused him the right to other sympathies, charged him with scheming to make her die alone, for it was needless to point out how little Miss Vernham was a resource in trouble. When Doctor Hugh mentioned that the Countess would already have left Bournemouth if he hadn't kept her in bed, poor Dencombe held his arm tighter and said with decision: 'Take her straight away.' They had gone out together, walking back to the sheltered nook in which, the other day, they had met. The young man, who had given his companion a personal support, declared with emphasis that his conscience was clear—he could ride two horses at once. Didn't he dream, for his future, of a time when he should have to ride five hundred? Longing equally for virtue, Dencombe replied that in that golden age no patient would pretend to have contracted with him for his whole attention. On the part of the Countess was not such an avidity lawful? Doctor Hugh denied it, said there was no contract but only a free understanding, and that a sordid servitude was impossible to a generous spirit; he liked moreover to talk about art, and that was the subject on which, this time, as they sat together on the sunny bench, he tried most to engage the author of 'The Middle Years'. Dencombe, soaring again a little on the weak wings of convalescence and still haunted by that happy notion of an organized rescue, found another strain of eloquence to plead the cause of a certain splendid 'last manner', the very citadel, as it would prove, of his reputation, the stronghold into which his real treasure would be gathered. While his listener gave up the morning and the great still sea appeared to wait, he had a wonderful explanatory hour. Even for himself he was inspired as he told of what his treasure would consist—the precious metals he would dig from the mine, the jewels rare, strings of pearls, he would hang between the columns of his temple. He was wonderful for himself, so thick his convictions crowded; but he was still more wonderful for Doctor Hugh, who assured him, none the less, that the very pages he had just published were already encrusted with gems. The young man, however, panted for the combinations to come, and, before the face of the beautiful day, renewed to Dencombe his guarantee that his profession would hold itself responsible for such a life. Then he suddenly clapped his hand upon his watch-pocket and asked leave to absent himself for half an hour. Dencombe waited there for his return, but was at last recalled to the actual by the fall of a shadow across the ground. The shadow darkened into that of Miss Vernham, the young lady in attendance on the Countess; whom Dencombe, recognizing her, perceived so clearly to have come to speak to him that he rose from his bench to acknowledge the civility. Miss Vernham indeed proved not particularly civil; she looked strangely agitated, and her type was now unmistakable.

'Excuse me if I inquire,' she said, 'whether it's too much to hope that you may be induced to leave Doctor Hugh alone.' Then, before Dencombe, greatly disconcerted, could protest: 'You ought to be informed that you stand in his light; that you may do him a terrible injury.'

'Do you mean by causing the Countess to dispense with his services?'

'By causing her to disinherit him.' Dencombe stared at this, and Miss Vernham pursued, in the gratification of seeing she could produce an impression: 'It has depended on himself to come into something very handsome. He has had a magnificent prospect, but I think you've succeeded in spoiling it.'

'Not intentionally, I assure you. Is there no hope the accident may be repaired?' Dencombe asked.

'She was ready to do anything for him. She takes great fancies, she lets herself go—it's her way. She has no relations, she's free to dispose of her money, and she's very ill.'

'I'm very sorry to hear it,' Dencombe stammered.

'Wouldn't it be possible for you to leave Bournemouth? That's what I've come to ask of you.'

Poor Dencombe sank down on his bench. 'I'm very ill myself, but I'll try!'

Miss Vernham still stood there with her colourless eyes and the brutality of her good conscience. 'Before it's too late, please!' she said; and with this she turned her back, in order, quickly, as if it had been a business to which she could spare but a precious moment, to pass out of his sight.

Oh, yes, after this Dencombe was certainly very ill. Miss Vernham had upset him with her rough, fierce news; it was the sharpest shock to him to discover what was at stake for a penniless young man of fine parts. He sat trembling on his bench, staring at the waste of waters, feeling sick with the directness of the blow. He was indeed too weak, too unsteady, too alarmed; but he would make the effort to get away, for he couldn't accept the guilt of interference, and his honour was really involved. He would hobble home, at any rate, and then he would think what was to be done. He made his way back to the hotel and, as he went, had a characteristic vision of Miss Vernham's great motive. The Countess hated women, of course; Dencombe was lucid about that; so the hungry pianist had no personal hopes and could only console herself with the bold conception of helping Doctor Hugh in order either to marry him after he should get his money or to induce him to recognize her title to compensation and buy her off. If she had befriended him at a fruitful crisis he would really, as a man of delicacy, and she knew what to think of that point, have to reckon with her.

At the hotel Dencombe's servant insisted on his going back to bed. The invalid had talked about catching a train and had begun with orders to pack; after which his humming nerves had yielded to a sense of sickness. He consented to see his physician, who immediately was sent for, but he wished it to be understood that his door was irrevocably closed to Doctor Hugh. He had his plan, which was so fine that he rejoiced in it after getting back to bed. Doctor Hugh, suddenly finding himself snubbed without mercy, would, in natural disgust and to the joy of Miss Vernham, renew his allegiance to the Countess. When his physician arrived Dencombe learned that he was feverish and that this was very wrong: he was to cultivate calmness and try, if possible, not to think. For the rest of the day he wooed stupidity; but there was an ache that kept him sentient, the probable sacrifice of his 'extension', the limit of his course. His medical adviser was anything but pleased; his successive relapses were ominous. He charged this personage to put out a strong hand and take Doctor Hugh off his mind—it would contribute so much to his being quiet. The agitating name, in his room, was not mentioned again, but his security was a smothered fear, and it was not confirmed by the receipt, at ten o'clock that evening, of a telegram which his servant opened and read for him and to which, with an address in London, the signature of Miss Vernham was attached. 'Beseech you to use all influence to make our friend join us here in the morning. Countess much the worse for dreadful journey, but everything may still be saved.' The two ladies had gathered themselves up and had been capable in the afternoon of a spiteful revolution. They had started for the capital, and if the elder one, as Miss Vernham had announced, was very ill, she had wished to make it clear that she was proportionately reckless. Poor Dencombe, who was not reckless and who only desired that everything should indeed be 'saved', sent this missive straight off to the young man's lodging and had on the morrow the pleasure of knowing that he had quitted Bournemouth by an early train.

Two days later he pressed in with a copy of a literary journal in his hand. He had returned because he was anxious and for the pleasure of flourishing the great review of 'The Middle Years'. Here at least was something adequate—it rose to the occasion; it was an acclamation, a reparation, a critical attempt to place the author in the niche he had fairly won. Dencombe accepted and submitted; he made neither objection nor inquiry, for old complications had returned and he had had two atrocious days. He was convinced not only that he should never again leave his bed, so that his young friend might pardonably remain, but that the demand he should make on the patience of beholders would be very moderate indeed. Doctor Hugh had been to town, and he tried to find in his eyes some confession that the Countess was pacified and his legacy clinched; but all he could see there was the light of his juvenile joy in two or three of the phrases of the newspaper. Dencombe couldn't read them, but when his visitor had insisted on repeating them more than once he was able to shake an unintoxicated head. 'Ah, no; but they would have been true of what I *could* have done!'

'What people "could have done" is mainly what they've in fact done,' Doctor Hugh contended.

'Mainly, yes; but I've been an idiot!' said Dencombe.

Doctor Hugh did remain; the end was coming fast. Two days later Dencombe observed to him, by way of the feeblest of jokes, that there would now be no question whatever of a second chance. At this the young man stared; then he exclaimed: 'Why, it has come to pass—it has come to pass! The second chance has been the public's—the chance to find the point of view, to pick up the pearl!'

'Oh, the pearl!' poor Dencombe uneasily sighed. A smile as cold as a winter sunset flickered on his drawn lips as he added: 'The pearl is the unwritten—the pearl is the unalloyed, the *rest*, the lost!'

From that moment he was less and less present, heedless to all appearance of what went on around him. His disease was definitely mortal, of an action as relentless, after the short arrest that had enabled him to fall in with Doctor Hugh, as a leak in a great ship. Sinking steadily, though this visitor, a man of rare resources, now cordially approved by his physician, showed endless art in guarding him from pain, poor Dencombe kept no reckoning of favour or neglect, betrayed no symptom of regret or speculation. Yet towards the last he gave a sign of having noticed that for two days Doctor Hugh had not been in his room, a sign that consisted of his suddenly opening his eyes to ask of him if he had spent the interval with the Countess.

'The Countess is dead,' said Doctor Hugh. 'I knew that in a particular contingency she wouldn't resist. I went to her grave.'

Dencombe's eyes opened wider. 'She left you "something handsome"?'

The young man gave a laugh almost too light for a chamber of woe. 'Never a penny. She roundly cursed me.'

'Cursed you?' Dencombe murmured.

'For giving her up. I gave her up for *you*. I had to choose,' his companion explained.

'You chose to let a fortune go?'

'I chose to accept, whatever they might be, the consequences of my infatuation,' smiled Doctor Hugh. Then, as a larger pleasantry: 'A fortune be hanged! It's your own fault if I can't get your things out of my head.'

The immediate tribute to his humour was a long, bewildered moan; after which, for many hours, many days, Dencombe lay motionless and absent. A response so absolute, such a glimpse of a definite result and such a sense of credit worked together in his mind and, producing a strange commotion, slowly altered and transfigured his despair. The sense of cold submersion left him—he seemed to float without an effort. The incident was extraordinary as evidence, and it shed an intenser light. At the last he signed to Doctor Hugh to listen, and, when he was down on his knees by the pillow, brought him very near.

'You've made me think it all a delusion.'

'Not your glory, my dear friend,' stammered the young man.

'Not my glory—what there is of it! It *is* glory—to have been tested, to have had our little quality and cast our little spell. The thing is to have made somebody care. You happen to be crazy, of course, but that doesn't affect the law.'

'You're a great success!' said Doctor Hugh, putting into his young voice the ring of a marriage-bell.

Dencombe lay taking this in; then he gathered strength to speak once more. 'A second chance—*that's* the delusion. There never was to be but one. We work in the dark—we do what we can—we give what we have. Our doubt is our passion and our passion is our task. The rest is the madness of art.'

'If you've doubted, if you've despaired, you've always "done" it,' his visitor subtly argued.

'We've done something or other,' Dencombe conceded.

'Something or other is everything. It's the feasible. It's *you*!'

'Comforter!' poor Dencombe ironically sighed.

'But it's true,' insisted his friend.

'It's true. It's frustration that doesn't count.'

'Frustration's only life,' said Doctor Hugh.

'Yes, it's what passes.' Poor Dencombe was barely audible, but he had marked with the words the virtual end of his first and only chance.

THE PATAGONIA

CHAPTER I

The houses were dark in the August night and the perspective of Beacon Street, with its double chain of lamps, was a foreshortened desert. The club on the hill alone, from its semi-cylindrical front, projected a glow upon the dusky vagueness of the Common, and as I passed it I heard in the hot stillness the click of a pair of billiard-balls. As "every one" was out of town perhaps the servants, in the extravagance of their leisure, were profaning the tables. The heat was insufferable and I thought with joy of the morrow, of the deck of the steamer, the freshening breeze, the sense of getting out to sea. I was even glad of what I had learned in the afternoon at the office of the company—that at the eleventh hour an old ship with a lower standard of speed had been put on in place of the vessel in which I had taken my passage. America was roasting, England might very well be stuffy, and a slow passage (which at that season of the year would probably also be a fine one) was a guarantee of ten or twelve days of fresh air.

I strolled down the hill without meeting a creature, though I could see through the palings of the Common that that recreative expanse was peopled with dim forms. I remembered Mrs. Nettlepoint's house—she lived in those days (they are not so distant, but there have been changes) on the water-side, a little way beyond the spot at which the Public Garden terminates; and I reflected that like myself she would be spending the night in Boston if it were true that, as had been mentioned to me a few days before at Mount Desert, she was to embark on the morrow for Liverpool. I presently saw this appearance confirmed by a light above her door and in two or three of her windows, and I determined to ask for her, having nothing to do till bedtime. I had come out simply to pass an hour, leaving my hotel to the blaze of its gas and the perspiration of its porters; but it occurred to me that my old friend might very well not know of the substitution of the *Patagonia* for the *Scandinavia*, so that I should be doing her a service to prepare her mind. Besides, I could offer to help her, to look after her in the morning: lone women are grateful for support in taking ship for far countries.

It came to me indeed as I stood on her door-step that as she had a son she might not after all be so lone; yet I remembered at the same time that Jasper Nettlepoint was not quite a young man to lean upon, having—as I at least supposed—a life of his own and tastes and habits which had long since diverted him from the maternal side. If he did happen just now to be at home my solicitude would of course seem officious; for in his many wanderings—I believed he had roamed all over the globe—he would certainly have learned how to manage. None the less, in fine, I was very glad to show Mrs. Nettlepoint I thought of her. With my long absence I had lost sight of her; but I had liked her of old, she had been a good friend to my sisters, and I had in regard to her that sense which is pleasant to those who in general have gone astray or got detached, the sense that she at least knew all about me. I could trust her at any time to tell people I was respectable.

Perhaps I was conscious of how little I deserved this indulgence when it came over me that I hadn't been near her for ages. The measure of that neglect was given by my vagueness of mind about Jasper. However, I really belonged nowadays to a different generation; I was more the mother's contemporary than the son's.

Mrs. Nettlepoint was at home: I found her in her back drawing-room, where the wide windows opened to the water. The room was dusky—it was too hot for lamps—and she sat slowly moving her fan and looking out on the little arm of the sea which is so pretty at night, reflecting the lights of Cambridgeport and Charlestown. I supposed she was musing on the loved ones she was to leave behind, her married daughters, her grandchildren; but she struck a note more specifically Bostonian as she said to me, pointing with her fan to the Back Bay: "I shall see nothing more charming than that over there, you know!" She made me very welcome, but her son had told her about the *Patagonia*, for which she was sorry, as this would mean a longer voyage. She was a poor creature in any boat and mainly confined to her cabin even in weather extravagantly termed fine—as if any weather could be fine at sea.

"Ah then your son's going with you?" I asked.

"Here he comes, he'll tell you for himself much better than I can pretend to." Jasper Nettlepoint at that moment joined us, dressed in white flannel and carrying a large fan. "Well, my dear, have you decided?" his mother continued with no scant irony. "He hasn't yet made up his mind, and we sail at ten o'clock!"

"What does it matter when my things are put up?" the young man said. "There's no crowd at this moment; there will be cabins to spare. I'm waiting for a telegram—that will settle it. I just walked up to the club to see if it was come—they'll send it there because they suppose this house unoccupied. Not yet, but I shall go back in twenty minutes."

"Mercy, how you rush about in this temperature!" the poor lady exclaimed while I reflected that it was perhaps *his* billiard-balls I had heard ten minutes before. I was sure he was fond of billiards.

"Rush? not in the least. I take it uncommon easy."

"Ah I'm bound to say you do!" Mrs. Nettlepoint returned with inconsequence. I guessed at a certain tension between the pair and a want of consideration on the young man's part, arising perhaps from selfishness. His mother was nervous, in suspense, wanting to be at rest as to whether she should have his company on the voyage or be obliged to struggle alone. But as he stood there smiling and slowly moving his fan he struck me somehow as a person on whom this fact wouldn't sit too heavily. He was of the type of those whom other people worry about, not of those who worry about other people. Tall and strong, he had a handsome face, with a round head and close-curling hair; the whites of his eyes and the enamel of his teeth, under his brown moustache, gleamed vaguely in the lights of the Back Bay. I made out that he was sunburnt, as if he lived much in the open air, and that he looked intelligent but also slightly brutal, though not in a morose way. His brutality, if he had any, was bright and finished. I had to tell him who I was, but even then I saw how little he placed me and that my explanations gave me in his mind no great identity or at any rate no great importance. I foresaw that he would in intercourse make me feel sometimes very young and sometimes very old, caring himself but little which. He mentioned, as if to show our companion that he might safely be left to his own devices, that he had once started from London to Bombay at three quarters of an hour's notice.

"Yes, and it must have been pleasant for the people you were with!"

"Oh the people I was with—!" he returned; and his tone appeared to signify that such people would always have to come off as they could. He asked if there were no cold drinks in the house, no lemonade, no iced syrups; in such weather something of that sort ought always to be kept going. When his mother remarked that surely at the club they *were* kept going he went on: "Oh yes, I had various things there; but you know I've walked down the hill since. One should have something at either end. May I ring and see?" He rang while Mrs. Nettlepoint observed that with the people they had in the house, an establishment reduced naturally at such a moment to its simplest expression—they were burning up candle-ends and there were no luxuries—she wouldn't answer for the service. The matter ended in her leaving the room in quest of cordials with the female domestic who had arrived in response to the bell and in whom Jasper's appeal aroused no visible intelligence.

She remained away some time and I talked with her son, who was sociable but desultory and kept moving over the place, always with his fan, as if he were properly impatient. Sometimes he seated himself an instant on the window-sill, and then I made him out in fact thoroughly good-looking—a fine brown clean young athlete. He failed to tell me on what special contingency his decision depended; he only alluded familiarly to an expected telegram, and I saw he was probably fond at no time of the trouble of explanations. His mother's absence was a sign that when it might be a question of gratifying him she had grown used to spare no pains, and I fancied her rummaging in some close storeroom, among old preserve-pots, while the dull maid-servant held the candle awry. I don't know whether this same vision was in his own eyes; at all events it didn't prevent his saying suddenly, as he looked at his watch, that I must excuse him—he should have to go back to the club. He would return in half an hour—or in less. He walked away and I sat there alone, conscious, on the dark dismantled simplified scene, in the deep silence that rests on American towns during the hot season—there was now and then a far cry or a plash in the water, and at intervals the tinkle of the bells of the horse-cars on the long bridge, slow in the suffocating night—of the strange influence, half-sweet, half-sad, that abides in houses uninhabited or about to become so, in places muffled and bereaved, where the unheeded sofas and patient belittered tables seem (like the disconcerted dogs, to whom everything is alike sinister) to recognise the eve of a journey.

After a while I heard the sound of voices, of steps, the rustle of dresses, and I looked round, supposing these things to denote the return of Mrs. Nettlepoint and her handmaiden with the refection prepared for her son. What I saw however was two other female forms, visitors apparently just admitted, and now ushered into the room. They were not announced—the servant turned her back on them and rambled off to our hostess. They advanced in a wavering tentative unintroduced way—partly, I could see, because the place was dark and partly because their visit was in its nature experimental, a flight of imagination or a stretch of confidence. One of the ladies was stout and the other slim, and I made sure in a moment that one was talkative and the other reserved. It was further to be discerned that one was elderly and the other young, as well as that the fact of their unlikeness didn't prevent their being mother and daughter. Mrs. Nettlepoint reappeared in a very few minutes, but the interval had sufficed to establish a communication—really copious for the occasion—between the strangers and the unknown gentleman whom they found in possession, hat and stick in hand. This was not my doing—for what had I to go upon?—and still less was it the doing of the younger and the more indifferent, or less courageous, lady. She spoke but once—when her companion informed me that she was going out to Europe the next day to be married. Then she protested "Oh mother!" in a tone that struck me in the darkness as doubly odd, exciting my curiosity to see her face.

It had taken the elder woman but a moment to come to that, and to various other things, after I had explained that I myself was waiting for Mrs. Nettlepoint, who would doubtless soon come back.

"Well, she won't know me—I guess she hasn't ever heard much about me," the good lady said; "but I've come from Mrs. Allen and I guess that will make it all right. I presume you know Mrs. Allen?"

I was unacquainted with this influential personage, but I assented vaguely to the proposition. Mrs. Allen's emissary was good-humoured and familiar, but rather appealing than insistent (she remarked that if her friend *had* found time to come in the afternoon—she had so much to do, being just up for the day, that she couldn't be sure—it would be all right); and somehow even before she mentioned Merrimac Avenue (they had come all the way from there) my imagination had associated her with that indefinite social limbo known to the properly-constituted Boston mind as the South End—a nebulous region which condenses here and there into a pretty face, in which the daughters are an "improvement" on the mothers and are sometimes acquainted with gentlemen more gloriously domiciled, gentlemen whose wives and sisters are in turn not acquainted with them.

When at last Mrs. Nettlepoint came in, accompanied by candles and by a tray laden with glasses of coloured fluid which emitted a cool tinkling, I was in a position to officiate as master of the ceremonies, to introduce Mrs. Mavis and Miss Grace Mavis, to represent that Mrs. Allen had recommended them—nay, had urged them—just to come that way, informally and without fear; Mrs. Allen who had been prevented only by the pressure of occupations so characteristic of her (especially when up from Mattapoisett for a few hours' desperate shopping) from herself calling in the course of the day to explain who they were and what was the favour they had to ask of her benevolent friend. Good-natured women understand each other even when so divided as to sit residentially above and below the salt, as who should say; by which token our hostess had quickly mastered the main facts: Mrs. Allen's visit that morning in Merrimac Avenue to talk of Mrs. Amber's great idea, the classes at the public schools in vacation (she was interested with an equal charity to that of Mrs. Mavis—even in such weather!—in those of the South End) for games and exercises and music, to keep the poor unoccupied children out of the streets; then the revelation that it had suddenly been settled almost from one hour to the other that Grace should sail for Liverpool, Mr. Porterfield at last being ready. He was taking a little holiday; his mother was with him, they had come over from Paris to see some of the celebrated old buildings in England, and he had telegraphed to say that if Grace would start right off they would just finish it up and be married. It often happened that when things had dragged on that way for years they were all huddled up at the end. Of course in such a case she, Mrs. Mavis, had had to fly round. Her daughter's passage was taken, but it seemed too dreadful she should make her journey all alone, the first time she had ever been at sea, without any companion or escort. *She* couldn't go—Mr. Mavis was too sick: she hadn't even been able to get him off to the seaside.

"Well, Mrs. Nettlepoint's going in that ship," Mrs. Allen had said; and she had represented that nothing was simpler than to give her the girl in charge. When Mrs. Mavis had replied that this was all very well but that she didn't know the lady, Mrs. Allen had declared that that didn't make a speck of difference, for Mrs. Nettlepoint was kind enough for anything. It was easy enough to *know* her, if that was all the trouble! All Mrs. Mavis would have to do would be to go right up to her next morning, when she took her daughter to the ship (she would see her there on the deck with her party) and tell her fair and square what she wanted. Mrs. Nettlepoint had daughters herself and would easily understand. Very likely she'd even look after Grace a little on the other side, in such a queer situation, going out alone to the gentleman she was engaged to: she'd just help her, like a good Samaritan, to turn round before she was married. Mr. Porterfield seemed to think they wouldn't wait long, once she was there: they would have it right over at the American consul's. Mrs. Allen had said it would perhaps be better still to go and see Mrs. Nettlepoint beforehand, that day, to tell her what they wanted: then they wouldn't seem to spring it on her just as she was leaving. She herself (Mrs. Allen) would call and say a word for them if she could save ten minutes before catching her train. If she hadn't come it was because she hadn't saved her ten minutes but she had made them feel that they must come all the same. Mrs. Mavis liked that better, because on the ship in the morning there would be such a confusion. She didn't think her daughter would be any trouble—conscientiously she didn't. It was just to have some one to speak to her and not sally forth like a servant-girl going to a situation.

"I see, I'm to act as a sort of bridesmaid and to give her away," Mrs. Nettlepoint obligingly said. Kind enough in fact for anything, she showed on this occasion that it was easy enough to know her. There is notoriously nothing less desirable than an imposed aggravation of effort at sea, but she accepted without betrayed dismay the burden of the young lady's dependence and allowed her, as Mrs. Mavis said, to hook herself on. She evidently had the habit of patience, and her reception of her visitors' story reminded me afresh—I was reminded of it whenever I returned to my native land—that my dear compatriots are the people in the world who most freely take mutual accommodation for granted. They have always had to help themselves, and have rather magnanimously failed to learn just where helping others is distinguishable from that. In no country are there fewer forms and more reciprocities.

It was doubtless not singular that the ladies from Merrimac Avenue shouldn't feel they were importunate: what was striking was that Mrs. Nettlepoint didn't appear to suspect it. However, she would in any case have thought it inhuman to show this—though I could see that under the surface she was amused at everything the more expressive of the pilgrims from the South End took for granted. I scarce know whether the attitude of the younger visitor added or not to the merit of her good nature. Mr. Porterfield's intended took no part in the demonstration, scarcely spoke, sat looking at the Back Bay and the lights on the long bridge. She declined the lemonade and the other mixtures which, at Mrs. Nettlepoint's request, I offered her, while her mother partook freely of everything and I reflected—for I as freely drained a glass or two in which the ice tinkled—that Mr. Jasper had better hurry back if he wished to enjoy these luxuries.

Was the effect of the young woman's reserve meanwhile ungracious, or was it only natural that in her particular situation she shouldn't have a flow of compliment at her command? I noticed that Mrs. Nettlepoint looked at her often, and certainly though she was undemonstrative Miss Mavis was interesting. The candlelight enabled me to see that though not in the very first flower of her youth she was still fresh and handsome. Her eyes and hair were dark, her face was pale, and she held up her head as if, with its thick braids and everything else involved in it, it were an appurtenance she wasn't ashamed of. If her mother was excellent and common she was not common—not at least flagrantly so—and perhaps also not excellent. At all events she wouldn't be, in appearance at least, a dreary appendage; which in the case of a person "hooking on" was always something gained. Was it because something of a romantic or pathetic interest usually attaches to a good creature who has been the victim of a "long engagement" that this young lady made an impression on me from the first—favoured as I had been so quickly with this glimpse of her history? I could charge her certainly with no positive appeal; she only held her tongue and smiled, and her smile corrected whatever suggestion might have forced itself upon me that the spirit within her was dead—the spirit of that promise of which she found herself doomed to carry out the letter.

What corrected it less, I must add, was an odd recollection which gathered vividness as I listened to it—a mental association evoked by the name of Mr. Porterfield. Surely I had a personal impression, over-smeared and confused, of the gentleman who was waiting at Liverpool, or who presently would be, for Mrs. Nettlepoint's protégée. I had met him, known him, some time, somewhere, somehow, on the other side. Wasn't he studying something, very hard, somewhere—probably in Paris—ten years before, and didn't he make extraordinarily neat drawings, linear and architectural? Didn't he go to a table d'hôte, at two francs twenty-five, in the Rue Bonaparte, which I then frequented, and didn't he wear spectacles and a Scotch plaid arranged in a manner which seemed to say "I've trustworthy information that that's the way they do it in the Highlands"? Wasn't he exemplary to positive irritation, and very poor, poor to positive oppression, so that I supposed he had no overcoat and his tartan would be what he slept under at night? Wasn't he working very hard still, and wouldn't he be, in the natural course, not yet satisfied that he had found his feet or knew enough to launch out? He would be a man of long preparations—Miss Mavis's white face seemed to speak to one of that. It struck me that if I had been in love with her I shouldn't have needed to lay such a train for the closer approach. Architecture was his line and he was a pupil of the École des Beaux Arts. This reminiscence grew so much more vivid with me that at the end of ten minutes I had an odd sense of knowing—by implication—a good deal about the young lady.

Even after it was settled that Mrs. Nettlepoint would do everything possible for her the other visitor sat sipping our iced liquid and telling how "low" Mr. Mavis had been. At this period the girl's silence struck me as still more conscious, partly perhaps because she deprecated her mother's free flow—she was enough of an "improvement" to measure that—and partly because she was too distressed by the idea of leaving her infirm, her perhaps dying father. It wasn't indistinguishable that they were poor and that she would take out a very small purse for her trousseau. For Mr. Porterfield to make up the sum his own case would have had moreover greatly to change. If he had enriched himself by the successful practice of his profession I had encountered no edifice he had reared—his reputation hadn't come to my ears.

Mrs. Nettlepoint notified her new friends that she was a very inactive person at sea: she was prepared to suffer to the full with Miss Mavis, but not prepared to pace the deck with her, to struggle with her, to accompany her to meals. To this the girl replied that she would trouble her little, she was sure: she was convinced she should prove a wretched sailor and spend the voyage on her back. Her mother scoffed at this picture, prophesying perfect weather and a lovely time, and I interposed to the effect that if I might be trusted, as a tame bachelor fairly sea-seasoned, I should be delighted to give the new member of our party an arm or any other countenance whenever she should require it. Both the ladies thanked me for this—taking my professions with no sort of abatement—and the elder one declared that we were evidently going to be such a sociable group that it was too bad to have to stay at home. She asked Mrs. Nettlepoint if there were any one else in our party, and when our hostess mentioned her son—there was a chance of his embarking but (wasn't it absurd?) he hadn't decided yet—she returned with extraordinary candour: "Oh dear, I do hope he'll go: that would be so lovely for Grace."

Somehow the words made me think of poor Mr. Porterfield's tartan, especially as Jasper Nettlepoint strolled in again at that moment. His mother at once challenged him: it was ten o'clock; had he by chance made up his great mind? Apparently he failed to hear her, being in the first place surprised at the strange ladies and then struck with the fact that one of them wasn't strange. The young man, after a slight hesitation, greeted Miss Mavis with a handshake and a "Oh good-evening, how do you do?" He didn't utter her name—which I could see he must have forgotten; but she immediately pronounced his, availing herself of the American girl's discretion to "present" him to her mother.

"Well, you might have told me you knew him all this time!" that lady jovially cried. Then she had an equal confidence for Mrs. Nettlepoint. "It would have saved me a worry—an acquaintance already begun."

"Ah my son's acquaintances!" our hostess murmured.

"Yes, and my daughter's too!" Mrs. Mavis gaily echoed. "Mrs. Allen didn't tell us *you* were going," she continued to the young man.

"She'd have been clever if she had been able to!" Mrs. Nettlepoint sighed.

"Dear mother, I have my telegram," Jasper remarked, looking at Grace Mavis.

"I know you very little," the girl said, returning his observation.

"I've danced with you at some ball—for some sufferers by something or other."

"I think it was an inundation or a big fire," she a little languidly smiled. "But it was a long time ago—and I haven't seen you since."

"I've been in far countries—to my loss. I should have said it was a big fire."

"It was at the Horticultural Hall. I didn't remember your name," said Grace Mavis.

"That's very unkind of you, when I recall vividly that you had a pink dress."

"Oh I remember that dress—your strawberry tarletan: you looked lovely in it!" Mrs. Mavis broke out. "You must get another just like it—on the other side."

"Yes, your daughter looked charming in it," said Jasper Nettlepoint. Then he added to the girl: "Yet you mentioned my name to your mother."

"It came back to me—seeing you here. I had no idea this was your home."

"Well, I confess it isn't, much. Oh there are some drinks!"—he approached the tray and its glasses.

"Indeed there are and quite delicious"—Mrs. Mavis largely wiped her mouth.

"Won't you have another then?—a pink one, like your daughter's gown."

"With pleasure, sir. Oh do see them over," Mrs. Mavis continued, accepting from the young man's hand a third tumbler.

"My mother and that gentleman? Surely they can take care of themselves," he freely pleaded.

"Then my daughter—she has a claim as an old friend."

But his mother had by this time interposed. "Jasper, what does your telegram say?"

He paid her no heed: he stood there with his glass in his hand, looking from Mrs. Mavis to Miss Grace.

"Ah leave her to me, madam; I'm quite competent," I said to Mrs. Mavis.

Then the young man gave me his attention. The next minute he asked of the girl: "Do you mean you're going to Europe?"

"Yes, tomorrow. In the same ship as your mother."

"That's what we've come here for, to see all about it," said Mrs. Mavis.

"My son, take pity on me and tell me what light your telegram throws," Mrs. Nettlepoint went on.

"I will, dearest, when I've quenched my thirst." And he slowly drained his glass.

"Well, I declare you're worse than Gracie," Mrs. Mavis commented. "She was first one thing and then the other—but only about up to three o'clock yesterday."

"Excuse me—won't you take something?" Jasper inquired of Gracie; who however still declined, as if to make up for her mother's copious consommation. I found myself quite aware that the two ladies would do well to take leave, the question of Mrs. Nettlepoint's good will being so satisfactorily settled and the meeting of the morrow at the ship so near at hand and I went so far as to judge that their protracted stay, with their hostess visibly in a fidget, gave the last proof of their want of breeding. Miss Grace after all then was not such an improvement on her mother, for she easily might have taken the initiative of departure, in spite of Mrs. Mavis's evident "game" of making her own absorption of refreshment last as long as possible. I watched the girl with increasing interest; I couldn't help asking myself a question or two about her and even perceiving already (in a dim and general way) that rather marked embarrassment, or at least anxiety attended her. Wasn't it complicating that she should have needed, by remaining long enough, to assuage a certain suspense, to learn whether or no Jasper were going to sail? Hadn't something particular passed between them on the occasion or at the period to which we had caught their allusion, and didn't she really not know her mother was bringing her to *his* mother's, though she apparently had thought it well not to betray knowledge? Such things were symptomatic—though indeed one scarce knew of what—on the part of a young lady betrothed to that curious cross-barred phantom of a Mr. Porterfield. But I am bound to add that she gave me no further warrant for wonder than was conveyed in her all tacitly and covertly encouraging her mother to linger. Somehow I had a sense that *she* was conscious of the indecency of this. I got up myself to go, but Mrs. Nettlepoint detained me after seeing that my movement wouldn't be taken as a hint, and I felt she wished me not to leave my fellow visitors on her hands. Jasper complained of the closeness of the room, said that it was not a night to sit in a room—one ought to be out in the air, under the sky. He denounced the windows that overlooked the water for not opening upon a balcony or a terrace, until his mother, whom he hadn't yet satisfied about his telegram, reminded him that there was a beautiful balcony in front, with room for a dozen people. She assured him we would go and sit there if it would please him.

"It will be nice and cool tomorrow, when we steam into the great ocean," said Miss Mavis, expressing with more vivacity than she had yet thrown into any of her utterances my own thought of half an hour before. Mrs. Nettlepoint replied that it would probably be freezing cold, and her son murmured that he would go and try the drawing-room balcony and report upon it. Just as he was turning away he said, smiling, to Miss Mavis: "Won't you come with me and see if it's pleasant?"

"Oh well, we had better not stay all night!" her mother exclaimed, but still without moving. The girl moved, after a moment's hesitation;—she rose and accompanied Jasper to the other room. I saw how her slim tallness showed to advantage as she walked, and that she looked well as she passed, with her head thrown back, into the darkness of the other part of the house. There was something rather marked, rather surprising—I scarcely knew why, for the act in itself was simple enough—in her acceptance of such a plea, and perhaps it was our sense of this that held the rest of us somewhat stiffly silent as she remained away. I was waiting for Mrs. Mavis to go, so that I myself might go; and Mrs. Nettlepoint was waiting for her to go so that I mightn't. This doubtless made the young lady's absence appear to us longer than it really was—it was probably very brief. Her mother moreover, I think, had now a vague lapse from ease. Jasper Nettlepoint presently returned to the back drawing-room to serve his companion with our lucent syrup, and he took occasion to remark that it was lovely on the balcony: one really got some air, the breeze being from that quarter. I remembered, as he went away with his tinkling tumbler, that from *my* hand, a few minutes before, Miss Mavis had not been willing to accept this innocent offering. A little later Mrs. Nettlepoint said: "Well, if it's so pleasant there we had better go ourselves." So we passed to the front and in the other room met the two young people coming in from the balcony. I was to wonder, in the light of later things, exactly how long they had occupied together a couple of the set of cane chairs garnishing the place in summer. If it had been but five minutes that only made subsequent events more curious. "We must go, mother," Miss Mavis immediately said; and a moment after, with a little renewal of chatter as to our general meeting on the ship, the visitors had taken leave. Jasper went down with them to the door and as soon as they had got off Mrs. Nettlepoint quite richly exhaled her impression. "Ah but'll she be a bore—she'll be a bore of bores!"

"Not through talking too much, surely."

"An affectation of silence is as bad. I hate that particular *pose*; it's coming up very much now; an imitation of the English, like everything else. A girl who tries to be statuesque at sea—that will act on one's nerves!"

"I don't know what she tries to be, but she succeeds in being very handsome."

"So much the better for you. I'll leave her to you, for I shall be shut up. I like her being placed under my 'care'!" my friend cried.

"She'll be under Jasper's," I remarked.

"Ah he won't go," she wailed—"I want it too much!"

"But I didn't see it that way. I have an idea he'll go."

"Why didn't he tell me so then—when he came in?"

"He was diverted by that young woman—a beautiful unexpected girl sitting there."

"Diverted from his mother and her fond hope?—his mother trembling for his decision?"

"Well"—I pieced it together—"she's an old friend, older than we know. It was a meeting after a long separation."

"Yes, such a lot of them as he does know!" Mrs. Nettlepoint sighed.

"Such a lot of them?"

"He has so many female friends—in the most varied circles."

"Well, we can close round her then," I returned; "for I on my side know, or used to know, her young man."

"Her intended?"—she had a light of relief for this.

"The very one she's going out to. He can't, by the way," it occurred to me, "be very young now."

"How odd it sounds—her muddling after him!" said Mrs. Nettlepoint.

I was going to reply that it wasn't odd if you knew Mr. Porterfield, but I reflected that that perhaps only made it odder. I told my companion briefly who he was—that I had met him in the old Paris days, when I believed for a fleeting hour that I could learn to paint, when I lived with the *jeunesse des écoles*; and her comment on this was simply: "Well, he had better have come out for her!"

"Perhaps so. She looked to me as she sat there as if, she might change her mind at the last moment."

"About her marriage?

"About sailing. But she won't change now."

Jasper came back, and his mother instantly challenged him. "Well, *are* you going?"

"Yes, I shall go"—he was finally at peace about it. "I've got my telegram."

"Oh your telegram!"—I ventured a little to jeer.

"That charming girl's your telegram."

He gave me a look, but in the dusk I couldn't make out very well what it conveyed. Then he bent over his mother, kissing her. "My news isn't particularly satisfactory. I'm going for *you*."

"Oh you humbug!" she replied. But she was of course delighted.

CHAPTER II

People usually spend the first hours of a voyage in squeezing themselves into their cabins, taking their little precautions, either so excessive or so inadequate, wondering how they can pass so many days in such a hole and asking idiotic questions of the stewards, who appear in comparison rare men of the world. My own initiations were rapid, as became an old sailor, and so, it seemed, were Miss Mavis's, for when I mounted to the deck at the end of half an hour I found her there alone, in the stern of the ship, her eyes on the dwindling continent. It dwindled very fast for so big a place. I accosted her, having had no conversation with her amid the crowd of leave-takers and the muddle of farewells before we put off; we talked a little about the boat, our fellow-passengers and our prospects, and then I said: "I think you mentioned last night a name I know—that of Mr. Porterfield."

"Oh no I didn't!" she answered very straight while she smiled at me through her closely-drawn veil.

"Then it was your mother."

"Very likely it was my mother." And she continued to smile as if I ought to have known the difference.

"I venture to allude to him because I've an idea I used to know him," I went on.

"Oh I see." And beyond this remark she appeared to take no interest; she left it to me to make any connexion.

"That is if it's the same one." It struck me as feeble to say nothing more; so I added "My Mr. Porterfield was called David."

"Well, so is ours." "Ours" affected me as clever.

"I suppose I shall see him again if he's to meet you at Liverpool," I continued.

"Well, it will be bad if he doesn't."

It was too soon for me to have the idea that it would be bad if he did: that only came later. So I remarked that, not having seen him for so many years, it was very possible I shouldn't know him.

"Well, I've not seen him for a considerable time, but I expect I shall know him all the same."

"Oh with you it's different," I returned with harmlessly bright significance. "Hasn't he been back since those days?"

"I don't know," she sturdily professed, "what days you mean."

"When I knew him in Paris—ages ago. He was a pupil of the École des Beaux Arts. He was studying architecture."

"Well, he's studying it still," said Grace Mavis.

"Hasn't he learned it yet?"

"I don't know what he has learned. I shall see." Then she added for the benefit of my perhaps undue levity: "Architecture's very difficult and he's tremendously thorough."

"Oh yes, I remember that. He was an admirable worker. But he must have become quite a foreigner if it's so many years since he has been at home."

She seemed to regard this proposition at first as complicated; but she did what she could for me. "Oh he's not changeable. If he were changeable—"

Then, however, she paused. I daresay she had been going to observe that if he were changeable he would long ago have given her up. After an instant she went on: "He wouldn't have stuck so to his profession. You can't make much by it."

I sought to attenuate her rather odd maidenly grimness. "It depends on what you call much."

"It doesn't make you rich."

"Oh of course you've got to practise it—and to practise it long."

"Yes—so Mr. Porterfield says."

Something in the way she uttered these words made me laugh—they were so calm an implication that the gentleman in question didn't live up to his principles. But I checked myself, asking her if she expected to remain in Europe long—to what one might call settle.

"Well, it will be a good while if it takes me as long to come back as it has taken me to go out."

"And I think your mother said last night that it was your first visit."

Miss Mavis, in her deliberate way, met my eyes. "Didn't mother talk!"

"It was all very interesting."

She continued to look at me. "You don't think that," she then simply stated.

"What have I to gain then by saying it?"

"Oh men have always something to gain."

"You make me in that case feel a terrible failure! I hope at any rate that it gives you pleasure," I went on, "the idea of seeing foreign lands."

"Mercy—I should think so!"

This was almost genial, and it cheered me proportionately. "It's a pity our ship's not one of the fast ones, if you're impatient."

She was silent a little after which she brought out: "Oh I guess it'll be fast enough!"

That evening I went in to see Mrs. Nettlepoint and sat on her sea-trunk, which was pulled out from under the berth to accommodate me. It was nine o'clock but not quite dark, as our northward course had already taken us into the latitude of the longer days. She had made her nest admirably and now rested from her labours; she lay upon her sofa in a dressing-gown and a cap that became her. It was her regular practice to spend the voyage in her cabin, which smelt positively good—such was the refinement of her art; and she had a secret peculiar to herself for keeping her port open without shipping seas. She hated what she called the mess of the ship and the idea, if she should go above, of meeting stewards with plates of supererogatory food. She professed to be content with her situation—we promised to lend each other books and I assured her familiarly that I should be in and out of her room a dozen times a day—pitying me for having to mingle in society. She judged this a limited privilege, for on the deck before we left the wharf she had taken a view of our fellow-passengers.

"Oh I'm an inveterate, almost a professional observer," I replied, "and with that vice I'm as well occupied as an old woman in the sun with her knitting. It makes me, in any situation, just inordinately and submissively *see* things. I shall see them even here and shall come down very often and tell you about them. You're not interested today, but you will be tomorrow, for a ship's a great school of gossip. You won't believe the number of researches and problems you'll be engaged in by the middle of the voyage."

"I? Never in the world!—lying here with my nose in a book and not caring a straw."

"You'll participate at second hand. You'll see through my eyes, hang upon my lips, take sides, feel passions, all sorts of sympathies and indignations. I've an idea," I further developed, "that your young lady's the person on board who will interest me most."

"'Mine' indeed! She hasn't been near me since we left the dock."

"There you are—you do feel she owes you something. Well," I added, "she's very curious."

"You've such cold-blooded terms!" Mrs. Nettlepoint wailed. "Elle ne sait pas se conduire; she ought to have come to ask about me."

"Yes, since you're under her care," I laughed. "As for her not knowing how to behave—well, that's exactly what we shall see."

"You will, but not I! I wash my hands of her."

"Don't say that—don't say that."

Mrs. Nettlepoint looked at me a moment. "Why do you speak so solemnly?"

In return I considered her. "I'll tell you before we land. And have you seen much of your son?"

"Oh yes, he has come in several times. He seems very much pleased. He has got a cabin to himself."

"That's great luck," I said, "but I've an idea he's always in luck. I was sure I should have to offer him the second berth in my room."

"And you wouldn't have enjoyed that, because you don't like him," she took upon herself to say.

"What put that into your head?"

"It isn't in my head—it's in my heart, my *cœur de mère*. We guess those things. You think he's selfish. I could see it last night."

"Dear lady," I contrived promptly enough to reply, "I've no general ideas about him at all. He's just one of the phenomena I am going to observe. He seems to me a very fine young man. However," I added, "since you've mentioned last night I'll admit that I thought he rather tantalised you. He played with your suspense."

"Why he came at the last just to please me," said Mrs. Nettlepoint.

I was silent a little. "Are you sure it was for your sake?"

"Ah, perhaps it was for yours!"

I bore up, however, against this thrust, characteristic of perfidious woman when you presume to side with her against a fond tormentor. "When he went out on the balcony with that girl," I found assurance to suggest, "perhaps she asked him to come for *hers*."

"Perhaps she did. But why should he do everything she asks him—such as she is?"

"I don't know yet, but perhaps I shall know later. Not that he'll tell me—for he'll never tell me anything: he's not," I consistently opined, "one of those who tell."

"If she didn't ask him, what you say is a great wrong to her," said Mrs. Nettlepoint.

"Yes, if she didn't. But you say that to protect Jasper—not to protect her," I smiled.

"You *are* cold-blooded—it's uncanny!" my friend exclaimed.

"Ah this is nothing yet! Wait a while—you'll see. At sea in general I'm awful—I exceed the limits. If I've outraged her in thought I'll jump overboard. There are ways of asking—a man doesn't need to tell a woman that—without the crude words."

"I don't know what you imagine between them," said Mrs. Nettlepoint.

"Well, nothing," I allowed, "but what was visible on the surface. It transpired, as the newspapers say, that they were old friends."

"He met her at some promiscuous party—I asked him about it afterwards. She's not a person"—my hostess was confident—"whom he could ever think of seriously."

"That's exactly what I believe."

"You don't observe—you know—you imagine," Mrs. Nettlepoint continued to argue. "How do you reconcile her laying a trap for Jasper with her going out to Liverpool on an errand of love?"

Oh I wasn't to be caught that way! "I don't for an instant suppose she laid a trap; I believe she acted on the impulse of the moment. She's going out to Liverpool on an errand of marriage; that's not necessarily the same thing as an errand of love, especially for one who happens to have had a personal impression of the gentleman she's engaged to."

"Well, there are certain decencies which in such a situation the most abandoned of her sex would still observe. You apparently judge her capable—on no evidence—of violating them."

"Ah you don't understand the shades of things," I returned. "Decencies and violations, dear lady—there's no need for such heavy artillery! I can perfectly imagine that without the least immodesty she should have said to Jasper on the balcony, in fact if not in words: 'I'm in dreadful spirits, but if you come I shall feel better, and that will be pleasant for you too.'"

"And why is she in dreadful spirits?"

"She isn't!" I replied, laughing.

My poor friend wondered. "What then is she doing?"

"She's walking with your son."

Mrs. Nettlepoint for a moment said nothing; then she treated me to another inconsequence. "Ah she's horrid!"

"No, she's charming!" I protested.

"You mean she's 'curious'?"

"Well, for me it's the same thing!"

This led my friend of course to declare once more that I was cold-blooded. On the afternoon of the morrow we had another talk, and she told me that in the morning Miss Mavis had paid her a long visit. She knew nothing, poor creature, about anything, but her intentions were good and she was evidently in her own eyes conscientious and decorous. And Mrs. Nettlepoint concluded these remarks with the sigh "Unfortunate person!"

"You think she's a good deal to be pitied then?"

"Well, her story sounds dreary—she told me a good deal of it. She fell to talking little by little and went from one thing to another. She's in that situation when a girl *must* open herself—to some woman."

"Hasn't she got Jasper?" I asked.

"He isn't a woman. You strike me as jealous of him," my companion added.

"I daresay *he* thinks so—or will before the end. Ah no—ah no!" And I asked Mrs. Nettlepoint if our young lady struck her as, very grossly, a flirt. She gave me no answer, but went on to remark that she found it odd and interesting to see the way a girl like Grace Mavis resembled the girls of the kind she herself knew better, the girls of "society," at the same time that she differed from them; and the way the differences and resemblances were so mixed up that on certain questions you couldn't tell where you'd find her. You'd think she'd feel as you did because you had found her feeling so, and then suddenly, in regard to some other matter—which was yet quite the same—she'd be utterly wanting. Mrs. Nettlepoint proceeded to observe—to such idle speculations does the vacancy of sea-hours give encouragement—that she wondered whether it were better to be an ordinary girl very well brought up or an extraordinary girl not brought up at all.

"Oh I go in for the extraordinary girl under all circumstances."

"It's true that if you're *very* well brought up you're not, you can't be, ordinary," said Mrs. Nettlepoint, smelling her strong salts. "You're a lady, at any rate."

"And Miss Mavis is fifty miles out—is that what you mean?"

"Well—you've seen her mother."

"Yes, but I think your contention would be that among such people the mother doesn't count."

"Precisely, and that's bad."

"I see what you mean. But isn't it rather hard? If your mother doesn't know anything it's better you should be independent of her, and yet if you are that constitutes a bad note." I added that Mrs. Mavis had appeared to count sufficiently two nights before. She had said and done everything she wanted, while the girl sat silent and respectful. Grace's attitude, so far as her parent was concerned, had been eminently decent.

"Yes, but she 'squirmed' for her," said Mrs. Nettlepoint.

"Ah if you know it I may confess she has told me as much."

My friend stared. "Told *you*? There's one of the things they do!"

"Well, it was only a word. Won't you let me know whether you do think her a flirt?"

"Try her yourself—that's better than asking another woman; especially as you pretend to study folk."

"Oh your judgement wouldn't probably at all determine mine. It's as bearing on *you* I ask it." Which, however, demanded explanation, so that I was duly frank; confessing myself curious as to how far maternal immorality would go.

It made her at first but repeat my words. "Maternal immorality?"

"You desire your son to have every possible distraction on his voyage, and if you can make up your mind in the sense I refer to that will make it all right. He'll have no responsibility."

"Heavens, how you analyse!" she cried. "I haven't in the least your passion for making up my mind."

"Then if you chance it," I returned, "you'll be more immoral still."

"Your reasoning's strange," said Mrs. Nettlepoint; "when it was you who tried to put into my head yesterday that she had asked him to come."

"Yes, but in good faith."

"What do you mean, in such a case, by that?"

"Why, as girls of that sort do. Their allowance and measure in such matters," I expounded, "is much larger than that of young persons who have been, as you say, *very* well brought up; and yet I'm not sure that on the whole I don't think them thereby the more innocent. Miss Mavis is engaged, and she's to be married next week, but it's an old old story, and there's no more romance in it than if she were going to be photographed. So her usual life proceeds, and her usual life consists—and that of *ces demoiselles* in general—in having plenty of gentlemen's society. Having it I mean without having any harm from it."

Mrs. Nettlepoint had given me due attention. "Well, if there's no harm from it what are you talking about and why am I immoral?"

I hesitated, laughing. "I retract—you're sane and clear. I'm sure she thinks there won't be any harm," I added. "That's the great point."

"The great point?"

"To be settled, I mean."

"Mercy, we're not trying them!" cried my friend. "How can *we* settle it?"

"I mean of course in our minds. There will be nothing more interesting these next ten days for our minds to exercise themselves upon."

"Then they'll get terribly tired of it," said Mrs. Nettlepoint.

"No, no—because the interest will increase and the plot will thicken. It simply can't not," I insisted. She looked at me as if she thought me more than Mephistophelean, and I went back to something she had lately mentioned. "So she told you everything in her life was dreary?"

"Not everything, but most things. And she didn't tell me so much as I guessed it. She'll tell me more the next time. She'll behave properly now about coming in to see me; I told her she ought to."

"I'm glad of that," I said. "Keep her with you as much as possible."

"I don't follow you closely," Mrs. Nettlepoint replied, "but so far as I do I don't think your remarks in the best taste."

"Well, I'm too excited, I lose my head in these sports," I had to recognise—"cold-blooded as you think me. Doesn't she like Mr. Porterfield?"

"Yes, that's the worst of it."

I kept making her stare. "The worst of it?"

"He's so good—there's no fault to be found with him. Otherwise she'd have thrown it all up. It has dragged on since she was eighteen: she became engaged to him before he went abroad to study. It was one of those very young and perfectly needless blunders that parents in America might make so much less possible than they do. The thing is to insist on one's daughter waiting, on the engagement's being long; and then, after you've got that started, to take it on every occasion as little seriously as possible—to make it die out. You can easily tire it to death," Mrs. Nettlepoint competently stated. "However," she concluded, "Mr. Porterfield has taken this one seriously for some years. He has done his part to keep it alive. She says he adores her."

"His part? Surely his part would have been to marry her by this time."

"He has really no money." My friend was even more confidently able to report it than I had been.

"He ought to have got some, in seven years," I audibly reflected.

"So I think she thinks. There are some sorts of helplessness that are contemptible. However, a small difference has taken place. That's why he won't wait any longer. His mother has come out, she has something—a little—and she's able to assist him. She'll live with them and bear some of the expenses, and after her death the son will have what there is."

"How old is she?" I cynically asked.

"I haven't the least idea. But it doesn't, on his part, sound very heroic—or very inspiring for our friend here. He hasn't been to America since he first went out."

"That's an odd way of adoring her," I observed.

"I made that objection mentally, but I didn't express it to her. She met it indeed a little by telling me that he had had other chances to marry."

"That surprises me," I remarked. "But did she say," I asked, "that *she* had had?"

"No, and that's one of the things I thought nice in her; for she must have had. She didn't try to make out that he had spoiled her life. She has three other sisters and there's very little money at home. She has tried to make money; she has written little things and painted little things—and dreadful little things they must have been; too bad to think of. Her father has had a long illness and has lost his place—he was in receipt of a salary in connexion with some waterworks—and one of her sisters has lately become a widow, with children and without means. And so as in fact she never has married any one else, whatever opportunities she may have encountered, she appears to have just made up her mind to go out to Mr. Porterfield as the least of her evils. But it isn't very amusing."

"Well," I judged after all, "that only makes her doing it the more honourable. She'll go through with it, whatever it costs, rather than disappoint him after he has waited so long. It's true," I continued, "that when a woman acts from a sense of honour—!"

"Well, when she does?" said Mrs. Nettlepoint, for I hung back perceptibly.

"It's often so extravagant and unnatural a proceeding as to entail heavy costs on some one."

"You're very impertinent. We all have to pay for each other all the while and for each other's virtues as well as vices."

"That's precisely why I shall be sorry for Mr. Porterfield when she steps off the ship with her little bill. I mean with her teeth clenched."

"Her teeth are not in the least clenched. She's quite at her ease now"—Mrs. Nettlepoint could answer for that.

"Well, we must try and keep her so," I said.

"You must take care that Jasper neglects nothing." I scarce know what reflexions this innocent pleasantry of mine provoked on the good lady's part; the upshot of them at all events was to make her say: "Well, I never asked her to come; I'm very glad of that. It's all their own doing."

"'Their' own—you mean Jasper's and hers?"

"No indeed. I mean her mother's and Mrs. Allen's; the girl's too of course. They put themselves on us by main force."

"Oh yes, I can testify to that. Therefore I'm glad too. We should have missed it, I think."

"How seriously you take it!" Mrs. Nettlepoint amusedly cried.

"Ah wait a few days!"—and I got up to leave her.

CHAPTER III

The *Patagonia* was slow, but spacious and comfortable, and there was a motherly decency in her long nursing rock and her rustling old-fashioned gait, the multitudinous swish, in her wake, as of a thousand proper petticoats. It was as if she wished not to present herself in port with the splashed eagerness of a young creature. We weren't numerous enough quite to elbow each other and yet weren't too few to support—with that familiarity and relief which figures and objects acquire on the great bare field of the ocean and under the great bright glass of the sky. I had never liked the sea so much before, indeed I had never liked it at all; but now I had a revelation of how in a midsummer mood it could please. It was darkly and magnificently blue and imperturbably quiet—save for the great regular swell of its heartbeats, the pulse of its life; and there grew to be something so agreeable in the sense of floating there in infinite isolation and leisure that it was a positive godsend the *Patagonia* was no racer. One had never thought of the sea as the great place of safety, but now it came over one that there's no place so safe from the land. When it doesn't confer trouble it takes trouble away—takes away letters and telegrams and newspapers and visits and duties and efforts, all the complications, all the superfluities and superstitions that we have stuffed into our terrene life. The simple absence of the post, when the particular conditions enable you to enjoy the great fact by which it's produced, becomes in itself a positive bliss, and the clean boards of the deck turn to the stage of a play that amuses, the personal drama of the voyage, the movement and interaction, in the strong sea-light, of figures that end by representing something—something moreover of which the interest is never, even in its keenness, too great to suffer you to slumber. I at any rate dozed to excess, stretched on my rug with a French novel, and when I opened my eyes I generally saw Jasper Nettlepoint pass with the young woman confided to his mother's care on his arm. Somehow at these moments, between sleeping and waking, I inconsequently felt that my French novel had set them in motion. Perhaps this was because I had fallen into the trick, at the start, of regarding Grace Mavis almost as a married woman, which, as every one knows, is the necessary status of the heroine of such a work. Every revolution of our engine at any rate would contribute to the effect of making her one.

In the saloon, at meals, my neighbour on the right was a certain little Mrs. Peck, a very short and very round person whose head was enveloped in a "cloud" (a cloud of dirty white wool) and who promptly let me know that she was going to Europe for the education of her children. I had already perceived—an hour after we left the dock—that some energetic measure was required in their interest, but as we were not in Europe yet the redemption of the four little Pecks was stayed. Enjoying untrammelled leisure they swarmed about the ship as if they had been pirates boarding her, and their mother was as powerless to check their licence as if she had been gagged and stowed away in the hold. They were especially to be trusted to dive between the legs of the stewards when these attendants arrived with bowls of soup for the languid ladies. Their mother was too busy counting over to her fellow-passengers all the years Miss Mavis had been engaged. In the blank of our common detachment things that were nobody's business very soon became everybody's, and this was just one of those facts that are propagated with mysterious and ridiculous speed. The whisper that carries them is very small, in the great scale of things, of air and space and progress, but it's also very safe, for there's no compression, no sounding-board, to make speakers responsible. And then repetition at sea is somehow not repetition; monotony is in the air, the mind is flat and everything recurs—the bells, the meals, the stewards' faces, the romp of children, the walk, the clothes, the very shoes and buttons of passengers taking their exercise. These things finally grow at once so circumstantial and so arid that, in comparison, lights on the personal history of one's companions become a substitute for the friendly flicker of the lost fireside.

Jasper Nettlepoint sat on my left hand when he was not upstairs seeing that Miss Mavis had her repast comfortably on deck. His mother's place would have been next mine had she shown herself, and then that of the young lady under her care. These companions, in other words, would have been between us, Jasper marking the limit of the party in that quarter. Miss Mavis was present at luncheon the first day, but dinner passed without her coming in, and when it was half over Jasper remarked that he would go up and look after her.

"Isn't that young lady coming—the one who was here to lunch?" Mrs. Peck asked of me as he left the saloon.

"Apparently not. My friend tells me she doesn't like the saloon."

"You don't mean to say she's sick, do you?"

"Oh no, not in this weather. But she likes to be above."

"And is that gentleman gone up to her?"

"Yes, she's under his mother's care."

"And is his mother up there, too?" asked Mrs. Peck, whose processes were homely and direct.

"No, she remains in her cabin. People have different tastes. Perhaps that's one reason why Miss Mavis doesn't come to table," I added—"her chaperon not being able to accompany her."

"Her chaperon?" my fellow passenger echoed.

"Mrs. Nettlepoint—the lady under whose protection she happens to be."

"Protection?" Mrs. Peck stared at me a moment, moving some valued morsel in her mouth; then she exclaimed familiarly "Pshaw!" I was struck with this and was on the point of asking her what she meant by it when she continued: "Ain't we going to see Mrs. Nettlepoint?"

"I'm afraid not. She vows she won't stir from her sofa."

"Pshaw!" said Mrs. Peck again. "That's quite a disappointment."

"Do you know her then?"

"No, but I know all about her." Then my companion added: "You don't mean to say she's any real relation?"

"Do you mean to me?"

"No, to Grace Mavis."

"None at all. They're very new friends, as I happen to know. Then you're acquainted with our young lady?" I hadn't noticed the passage of any recognition between them at luncheon.

"Is she your young lady too?" asked Mrs. Peck with high significance.

"Ah when people are in the same boat—literally—they belong a little to each other."

"That's so," said Mrs. Peck. "I don't know Miss Mavis, but I know all about her—I live opposite to her on Merrimac Avenue. I don't know whether you know that part."

"Oh yes—it's very beautiful."

The consequence of this remark was another "Pshaw!" But Mrs. Peck went on: "When you've lived opposite to people like that for a long time you feel as if you had some rights in them—tit for tat! But she didn't take it up today; she didn't speak to me. She knows who I am as well as she knows her own mother."

"You had better speak to her first—she's constitutionally shy," I remarked.

"Shy? She's constitutionally tough! Why she's thirty years old," cried my neighbour. "I suppose you know where she's going."

"Oh yes—we all take an interest in that."

"That young man, I suppose, particularly." And then as I feigned a vagueness: "The handsome one who sits *there*. Didn't you tell me he's Mrs. Nettlepoint's son?"

"Oh yes—he acts as her deputy. No doubt he does all he can to carry out her function."

Mrs. Peck briefly brooded. I had spoken jocosely, but she took it with a serious face. "Well, she might let him eat his dinner in peace!" she presently put forth.

"Oh he'll come back!" I said, glancing at his place. The repast continued and when it was finished I screwed my chair round to leave the table. Mrs. Peck performed the same movement and we quitted the saloon together. Outside of it was the usual vestibule, with several seats, from which you could descend to the lower cabins or mount to the promenade-deck. Mrs. Peck appeared to hesitate as to her course and then solved the problem by going neither way. She dropped on one of the benches and looked up at me.

"I thought you said he'd come back."

"Young Nettlepoint? Yes, I see he didn't. Miss Mavis then has given him half her dinner."

"It's very kind of her! She has been engaged half her life."

"Yes, but that will soon be over."

"So I suppose—as quick as ever we land. Every one knows it on Merrimac Avenue," Mrs. Peck pursued. "Every one there takes a great interest in it."

"Ah of course—a girl like that has many friends."

But my informant discriminated. "I mean even people who don't know her."

"I see," I went on: "she's so handsome that she attracts attention—people enter into her affairs."

Mrs. Peck spoke as from the commanding centre of these. "She *used* to be pretty, but I can't say I think she's anything remarkable today. Anyhow, if she attracts attention she ought to be all the more careful what she does. You had better tell her that."

"Oh it's none of my business!" I easily made out, leaving the terrible little woman and going above. This profession, I grant, was not perfectly attuned to my real idea, or rather my real idea was not quite in harmony with my profession. The very first thing I did on reaching the deck was to notice that Miss Mavis was pacing it on Jasper Nettlepoint's arm and that whatever beauty she might have lost, according to Mrs. Peck's insinuation, she still kept enough to make one's eyes follow her. She had put on a crimson hood, which was very becoming to her and which she wore for the rest of the voyage. She walked very well, with long steps, and I remember that at this moment the sea had a gentle evening swell which made the great ship dip slowly, rhythmically, giving a movement that was graceful to graceful pedestrians and a more awkward one to the awkward. It was the loveliest hour of a fine day, the clear early evening, with the glow of the sunset in the air and a purple colour on the deep. It was always present to me that so the waters ploughed by the Homeric heroes must have looked. I became conscious on this particular occasion moreover that Grace Mavis would for the rest of the voyage be the most visible thing in one's range, the figure that would count most in the composition of groups. She couldn't help it, poor girl; nature had made her conspicuous—important, as the painters say. She paid for it by the corresponding exposure, the danger that people would, as I had said to Mrs. Peck, enter into her affairs.

Jasper Nettlepoint went down at certain times to see his mother, and I watched for one of these occasions—on the third day out—and took advantage of it to go and sit by Miss Mavis. She wore a light blue veil drawn tightly over her face, so that if the smile with which she greeted me rather lacked intensity I could account for it partly by that.

"Well, we're getting on—we're getting on," I said cheerfully, looking at the friendly twinkling sea.

"Are we going very fast?"

"Not fast, but steadily. *Ohne Hast, ohne Rast*—do you know German?"

"Well, I've studied it—some."

"It will be useful to you over there when you travel."

"Well yes, if we do. But I don't suppose we shall much. Mr. Nettlepoint says we ought," my young woman added in a moment.

"Ah of course *he* thinks so. He has been all over the world."

"Yes, he has described some of the places. They must be wonderful. I didn't know I should like it so much."

"But it isn't 'Europe' yet!" I laughed.

Well, she didn't care if it wasn't. "I mean going on this way. I could go on for ever—for ever and ever."

"Ah you know it's not always like this," I hastened to mention.

"Well, it's better than Boston."

"It isn't so good as Paris," I still more portentously noted.

"Oh I know all about Paris. There's no freshness in that. I feel as if I had been there all the time."

"You mean you've heard so much of it?"

"Oh yes, nothing else for ten years."

I had come to talk with Miss Mavis because she was attractive, but I had been rather conscious of the absence of a good topic, not feeling at liberty to revert to Mr. Porterfield. She hadn't encouraged me, when I spoke to her as we were leaving Boston, to go on with the history of my acquaintance with this gentleman; and yet now, unexpectedly, she appeared to imply—it was doubtless one of the disparities mentioned by Mrs. Nettlepoint—that he might be glanced at without indelicacy.

"I see—you mean by letters," I remarked.

"We won't live in a good part. I know enough to know that," she went on.

"Well, it isn't as if there were any very bad ones," I answered reassuringly.

"Why Mr. Nettlepoint says it's regular mean."

"And to what does he apply that expression?"

She eyed me a moment as if I were elegant at her expense, but she answered my question. "Up there in the Batignolles. I seem to make out it's worse than Merrimac Avenue."

"Worse—in what way?"

"Why, even less where the nice people live."

"He oughtn't to say that," I returned. And I ventured to back it up. "Don't you call Mr. Porterfield a nice person?"

"Oh it doesn't make any difference." She watched me again a moment through her veil, the texture of which gave her look a suffused prettiness. "Do you know him very little?" she asked.

"Mr. Porterfield?"

"No, Mr. Nettlepoint."

"Ah very little. He's very considerably my junior, you see."

She had a fresh pause, as if almost again for my elegance; but she went on: "He's younger than me too." I don't know what effect of the comic there could have been in it, but the turn was unexpected and it made me laugh. Neither do I know whether Miss Mavis took offence at my sensibility on this head, though I remember thinking at the moment with compunction that it had brought a flush to her cheek. At all events she got up, gathering her shawl and her books into her arm. "I'm going down—I'm tired."

"Tired of me, I'm afraid."

"No, not yet."

"I'm like you," I confessed. "I should like it to go on and on."

She had begun to walk along the deck to the companionway and I went with her. "Well, I guess *I* wouldn't, after all!"

I had taken her shawl from her to carry it, but at the top of the steps that led down to the cabins I had to give it back. "Your mother would be glad if she could know," I observed as we parted.

But she was proof against my graces. "If she could know what?"

"How well you're getting on." I refused to be discouraged. "And that good Mrs. Allen."

"Oh mother, mother! She made me come, she pushed me off." And almost as if not to say more she went quickly below.

I paid Mrs. Nettlepoint a morning visit after luncheon and another in the evening, before she "turned in." That same day, in the evening, she said to me suddenly: "Do you know what I've done? I've asked Jasper."

"Asked him what?"

"Why, if *she* asked him, you understand."

I wondered. "Do I understand?"

"If you don't it's because you 'regular' won't, as she says. If that girl really asked him—on the balcony—to sail with us."

"My dear lady, do you suppose that if she did he'd tell you?"

She had to recognise my acuteness. "That's just what he says. But he says she didn't."

"And do you consider the statement valuable?" I asked, laughing out. "You had better ask your young friend herself."

Mrs. Nettlepoint stared. "I couldn't do that."

On which I was the more amused that I had to explain I was only amused. "What does it signify now?"

"I thought you thought everything signified. You were so full," she cried, "of signification!"

"Yes, but we're further out now, and somehow in mid-ocean everything becomes absolute."

"What else *can* he do with decency?" Mrs. Nettlepoint went on. "If, as my son, he were never to speak to her it would be very rude and you'd think that stranger still. Then *you* would do what he does, and where would be the difference?"

"How do you know what he does? I haven't mentioned him for twenty-four hours."

"Why, she told me herself. She came in this afternoon."

"What an odd thing to tell you!" I commented.

"Not as she says it. She says he's full of attention, perfectly devoted—looks after her all the time. She seems to want me to know it, so that I may approve him for it."

"That's charming; it shows her good conscience."

"Yes, or her great cleverness."

Something in the tone in which Mrs. Nettlepoint said this caused me to return in real surprise: "Why what do you suppose she has in her mind?"

"To get hold of him, to make him go so far he can't retreat. To marry him perhaps."

"To marry him? And what will she do with Mr. Porterfield?"

"She'll ask me just to make it all right to him—or perhaps you."

"Yes, as an old friend"—and for a moment I felt it awkwardly possible. But I put to her seriously: "*Do* you see Jasper caught like that?"

"Well, he's only a boy—he's younger at least than she."

"Precisely; she regards him as a child. She remarked to me herself today, that is, that he's so much younger."

Mrs. Nettlepoint took this in. "Does she talk of it with you? That shows she has a plan, that she has thought it over!"

I've sufficiently expressed—for the interest of my anecdote—that I found an oddity in one of our young companions, but I was far from judging her capable of laying a trap for the other. Moreover my reading of Jasper wasn't in the least that he was catchable—could be made to do a thing if he didn't want to do it. Of course it wasn't impossible that he might be inclined, that he might take it—or already have taken it—into his head to go further with his mother's charge; but to believe this I should require still more proof than his always being with her. He wanted at most to "take up with her" for the voyage. "If you've questioned him perhaps you've tried to make him feel responsible," I said to my fellow critic.

"A little, but it's very difficult. Interference makes him perverse. One has to go gently. Besides, it's too absurd—think of her age. If she can't take care of herself!" cried Mrs. Nettlepoint.

"Yes, let us keep thinking of her age, though it's not so prodigious. And if things get very bad you've one resource left," I added.

She wondered. "To lock her up in her cabin?"

"No—to come out of yours."

"Ah never, never! If it takes that to save her she must be lost. Besides, what good would it do? If I were to go above she could come below."

"Yes, but you could keep Jasper with you."

"*Could* I?" Mrs. Nettlepoint demanded in the manner of a woman who knew her son.

In the saloon the next day, after dinner, over the red cloth of the tables, beneath the swinging lamps and the racks of tumblers, decanters and wine-glasses, we sat down to whist, Mrs. Peck, to oblige, taking a hand in the game. She played very badly and talked too much, and when the rubber was over assuaged her discomfiture (though not mine—we had been partners) with a Welsh rabbit and a tumbler of something hot. We had done with the cards, but while she waited for this refreshment she sat with her elbows on the table shuffling a pack.

"She hasn't spoken to me yet—she won't do it," she remarked in a moment.

"Is it possible there's any one on the ship who hasn't spoken to you?"

"Not that girl—she knows too well!" Mrs. Peck looked round our little circle with a smile of intelligence—she had familiar communicative eyes. Several of our company had assembled, according to the wont, the last thing in the evening, of those who are cheerful at sea, for the consumption of grilled sardines and devilled bones.

"What then does she know?"

"Oh she knows *I* know."

"Well, we know what Mrs. Peck knows," one of the ladies of the group observed to me with an air of privilege.

"Well, you wouldn't know if I hadn't told you—from the way she acts," said our friend with a laugh of small charm.

"She's going out to a gentleman who lives over there—he's waiting there to marry her," the other lady went on, in the tone of authentic information. I remember that her name was Mrs. Gotch and that her mouth looked always as if she were whistling.

"Oh he knows—I've told him," said Mrs. Peck.

"Well, I presume every one knows," Mrs. Gotch contributed.

"Dear madam, is it every one's business?" I asked.

"Why, don't you think it's a peculiar way to act?"—and Mrs. Gotch was evidently surprised at my little protest.

"Why it's right there—straight in front of you, like a play at the theatre—as if you had paid to see it," said Mrs. Peck. "If you don't call it public!"

"Aren't you mixing things up? What do you call public?"

"Why the way they go on. They're up there now."

"They cuddle up there half the night," said Mrs. Gotch. "I don't know when they come down. Any hour they like. When all the lights are out they're up there still."

"Oh you can't tire them out. They don't want relief—like the ship's watch!" laughed one of the gentlemen.

"Well, if they enjoy each other's society what's the harm?" another asked. "They'd do just the same on land."

"They wouldn't do it on the public streets, I presume," said Mrs. Peck. "And they wouldn't do it if Mr. Porterfield was round!"

"Isn't that just where your confusion comes in?" I made answer. "It's public enough that Miss Mavis and Mr. Nettlepoint are always together, but it isn't in the least public that she's going to be married."

"Why how can you say—when the very sailors know it! The Captain knows it and all the officers know it. They see them there, especially at night, when they're sailing the ship."

"I thought there was some rule—!" submitted Mrs. Gotch.

"Well, there is—that you've got to behave yourself," Mrs. Peck explained. "So the Captain told me—he said they have some rule. He said they have to have, when people are too undignified."

"Is that the term he used?" I inquired.

"Well, he may have said when they attract too much attention."

I ventured to discriminate. "It's we who attract the attention—by talking about what doesn't concern us and about what we really don't know."

"She said the Captain said he'd tell on her as soon as ever we arrive," Mrs. Gotch none the less serenely pursued.

"*She* said—?" I repeated, bewildered.

"Well, he did say so, that he'd think it his duty to inform Mr. Porterfield when he comes on to meet her—if they keep it up in the same way," said Mrs. Peck.

"Oh they'll keep it up, don't you fear!" one of the gentlemen exclaimed.

"Dear madam, the Captain's having his joke on you," was, however, my own congruous reply.

"No, he ain't—he's right down scandalised. He says he regards us all as a real family and wants the family not to be downright coarse." I felt Mrs. Peck irritated by my controversial tone: she challenged me with considerable spirit. "How can you say I don't know it when all the street knows it and has known it for years—for years and years?" She spoke as if the girl had been engaged at least for twenty. "What's she going out for if not to marry him?"

"Perhaps she's going to see how he looks," suggested one of the gentlemen.

"He'd look queer—if he knew."

"Well, I guess he'll know," said Mrs. Gotch.

"She'd tell him herself—she wouldn't be afraid," the gentleman went on.

"Well she might as well kill him. He'll jump overboard," Mrs. Peck could foretell.

"Jump overboard?" cried Mrs. Gotch as if she hoped then that Mr. Porterfield would be told.

"He has just been waiting for this—for long, long years," said Mrs. Peck.

"Do you happen to know him?" I asked.

She replied at her convenience. "No, but I know a lady who does. Are you going up?"

I had risen from my place—I had not ordered supper. "I'm going to take a turn before going to bed."

"Well then you'll see!"

Outside the saloon I hesitated, for Mrs. Peck's admonition made me feel for a moment that if I went up I should have entered in a manner into her little conspiracy. But the night was so warm and splendid that I had been intending to smoke a cigar in the air before going below, and I didn't see why I should deprive myself of this pleasure in order to seem not to mind Mrs. Peck. I mounted accordingly and saw a few figures sitting or moving about in the darkness. The ocean looked black and small, as it is apt to do at night, and the long mass of the ship, with its vague dim wings, seemed to take up a great part of it. There were more stars than one saw on land and the heavens struck one more than ever as larger than the earth. Grace Mavis and her companion were not, so far as I perceived at first, among the few passengers who lingered late, and I was glad, because I hated to hear her talked about in the manner of the gossips I had left at supper. I wished there had been some way to prevent it, but I could think of none but to recommend her privately to reconsider her rule of discretion. That would be a very delicate business, and perhaps it would be better to begin with Jasper, though that would be delicate too. At any rate one might let him know, in a friendly spirit, to how much remark he exposed the young lady—leaving this revelation to work its way upon him. Unfortunately I couldn't altogether believe that the pair were unconscious of the observation and the opinion of the passengers. They weren't boy and girl; they had a certain social perspective in their eye. I was meanwhile at any rate in no possession of the details of that behaviour which had made them—according to the version of my good friends in the saloon—a scandal to the ship; for though I had taken due note of them, as will already have been gathered, I had taken really no such ferocious, or at least such competent, note as Mrs. Peck. Nevertheless the probability was that they knew what was thought of them—what naturally would be—and simply didn't care. That made our heroine out rather perverse and even rather shameless; and yet somehow if these were her leanings I didn't dislike her for them. I don't know what strange secret excuses I found for her. I presently indeed encountered, on the spot, a need for any I might have at call, since, just as I was on the point of going below again, after several restless turns and—within the limit where smoking was allowed—as many puffs at a cigar as I cared for, I became aware of a couple of figures settled together behind one of the lifeboats that rested on the deck. They were so placed as to be visible only to a person going close to the rail and peering a little sidewise. I don't think I peered, but as I stood a moment beside the rail my eye was attracted by a dusky object that protruded beyond the boat and that I saw at a second glance to be the tail of a lady's dress. I bent forward an instant, but even then I saw very little more; that scarcely mattered however, as I easily concluded that the persons tucked away in so snug a corner were Jasper Nettlepoint and Mr. Porterfield's intended. Tucked away was the odious right expression, and I deplored the fact so betrayed for the pitiful bad taste in it. I immediately turned away, and the next moment found myself face to face with our vessel's skipper. I had already had some conversation with him—he had been so good as to invite me, as he had invited Mrs. Nettlepoint and her son and the young lady travelling with them, and also Mrs. Peck, to sit at his table—and had observed with pleasure that his seamanship had the grace, not universal on the Atlantic liners, of a fine-weather manner.

"They don't waste much time—your friends in there," he said, nodding in the direction in which he had seen me looking.

"Ah well, they haven't much to lose."

"That's what I mean. I'm told *she* hasn't."

I wanted to say something exculpatory, but scarcely knew what note to strike. I could only look vaguely about me at the starry darkness and the sea that seemed to sleep. "Well, with these splendid nights and this perfect air people are beguiled into late hours."

"Yes, we want a bit of a blow," the Captain said.

I demurred. "How much of one?"

"Enough to clear the decks!"

He was after all rather dry and he went about his business. He had made me uneasy, and instead of going below I took a few turns more. The other walkers dropped off pair by pair—they were all men—till at last I was alone. Then after a little I quitted the field. Jasper and his companion were still behind their lifeboat. Personally I greatly preferred our actual conditions, but as I went down I found myself vaguely wishing, in the interest of I scarcely knew what, unless it had been a mere superstitious delicacy, that we might have half a gale.

Miss Mavis turned out, in sea-phrase, early; for the next morning I saw her come up only a short time after I had finished my breakfast, a ceremony over which I contrived not to dawdle. She was alone and Jasper Nettlepoint, by a rare accident, was not on deck to help her. I went to meet her—she was encumbered as usual with her shawl, her sun-umbrella and a book—and laid my hands on her chair, placing it near the stern of the ship, where she liked best to be. But I proposed to her to walk a little before she sat down, and she took my arm after I had put her accessories into the chair. The deck was clear at that hour and the morning light gay; one had an extravagant sense of good omens and propitious airs. I forget what we spoke of first, but it was because I felt these things pleasantly; and not to torment my companion nor to test her, that I couldn't help exclaiming cheerfully after a moment, as I have mentioned having done the first day: "Well, we're getting on, we're getting on!"

"Oh yes, I count every hour."

"The last days always go quicker," I said, "and the last hours—!"

"Well, the last hours?" she asked; for I had instinctively checked myself.

"Oh one's so glad then that it's almost the same as if one had arrived. Yet we ought to be grateful when the elements have been so kind to us," I added. "I hope you'll have enjoyed the voyage."

She hesitated ever so little. "Yes, much more than I expected."

"Did you think it would be very bad?"

"Horrible, horrible!"

The tone of these words was strange, but I hadn't much time to reflect upon it, for turning round at that moment I saw Jasper Nettlepoint come toward us. He was still distant by the expanse of the white deck, and I couldn't help taking him in from head to foot as he drew nearer. I don't know what rendered me on this occasion particularly sensitive to the impression, but it struck me that I saw him as I had never seen him before, saw him, thanks to the intense sea-light, inside and out, in his personal, his moral totality. It was a quick, a vivid revelation; if it only lasted a moment it had a simplifying certifying effect. He was intrinsically a pleasing apparition, with his handsome young face and that marked absence of any drop in his personal arrangements which, more than any one I've ever seen, he managed to exhibit on shipboard. He had none of the appearance of wearing out old clothes that usually prevails there, but dressed quite straight, as I heard some one say. This gave him an assured, almost a triumphant air, as of a young man who would come best out of any awkwardness. I expected to feel my companion's hand loosen itself on my arm, as an indication that now she must go to him, and I was almost surprised she didn't drop me. We stopped as we met and Jasper bade us a friendly good-morning. Of course the remark that we had another lovely day was already indicated, and it led him to exclaim, in the manner of one to whom criticism came easily, "Yes, but with this sort of thing consider what one of the others would do!"

"One of the other ships?"

"We should be there now, or at any rate tomorrow."

"Well then I'm glad it isn't one of the others"—and I smiled at the young lady on my arm. My words offered her a chance to say something appreciative, and gave him one even more; but neither Jasper nor Grace Mavis took advantage of the occasion. What they did do, I noticed, was to look at each other rather fixedly an instant; after which she turned her eyes silently to the sea. She made no movement and uttered no sound, contriving to give me the sense that she had all at once become perfectly passive, that she somehow declined responsibility. We remained standing there with Jasper in front of us, and if the contact of her arm didn't suggest I should give her up, neither did it intimate that we had better pass on. I had no idea of giving her up, albeit one of the things I seemed to read just then into Jasper's countenance was a fine implication that she was his property. His eyes met mine for a moment, and it was exactly as if he had said to me "I know what you think, but I don't care a rap." What I really thought was that he was selfish beyond the limits: that was the substance of my little revelation. Youth is almost always selfish, just as it is almost always conceited, and, after all, when it's combined with health and good parts, good looks and good spirits, it has a right to be, and I easily forgive it if it be really youth. Still it's a question of degree, and what stuck out of Jasper Nettlepoint—if, of course, one had the intelligence for it—was that his egotism had a hardness, his love of his own way an avidity. These elements were jaunty and prosperous, they were accustomed to prevail. He was fond, very fond, of women; they were necessary to him—that was in his type; but he wasn't in the least in love with Grace Mavis. Among the reflexions I quickly made this was the one that was most to the point. There was a degree of awkwardness, after a minute, in the way we were planted there, though the apprehension of it was doubtless not in the least with himself. To dissimulate my own share in it, at any rate, I asked him how his mother might be.

His answer was unexpected. "You had better go down and see."

"Not till Miss Mavis is tired of me."

She said nothing to this and I made her walk again. For some minutes she failed to speak; then, rather abruptly, she began: "I've seen you talking to that lady who sits at our table—the one who has so many children."

"Mrs. Peck? Oh yes, one has inevitably talked with Mrs. Peck."

"Do you know her very well?"

"Only as one knows people at sea. An acquaintance makes itself. It doesn't mean very much."

"She doesn't speak to me—she might if she wanted."

"That's just what she says of you—that you might speak to her."

"Oh if she's waiting for that!" said my companion with a laugh. Then she added: "She lives in our street, nearly opposite."

"Precisely. That's the reason why she thinks you coy or haughty. She has seen you so often and seems to know so much about you."

"What does she know about me?"

"Ah you must ask her—I can't tell you!"

"I don't care what she knows," said my young lady. After a moment she went on: "She must have seen I ain't very sociable." And then, "What are you laughing at?" she asked.

"Well"—my amusement was difficult to explain—"you're not very sociable, and yet somehow you are. Mrs. Peck is, at any rate, and thought that ought to make it easy for you to enter into conversation with her."

"Oh I don't care for her conversation—I know what it amounts to." I made no reply—I scarcely knew what reply to make—and the girl went on: "I know what she thinks and I know what she says." Still I was silent, but the next moment I saw my discretion had been wasted, for Miss Mavis put to me straight: "Does she make out that she knows Mr. Porterfield?"

"No, she only claims she knows a lady who knows him."

"Yes, that's it—Mrs. Jeremie. Mrs. Jeremie's an idiot!" I wasn't in a position to controvert this, and presently my young lady said she would sit down. I left her in her chair—I saw that she preferred it—and wandered to a distance. A few minutes later I met Jasper again, and he stopped of his own accord to say: "We shall be in about six in the evening of our eleventh day—they promise it."

"If nothing happens, of course."

"Well, what's going to happen?"

"That's just what I'm wondering!" And I turned away and went below with the foolish but innocent satisfaction of thinking I had mystified him.

CHAPTER IV

"I don't know what to do, and you must help me," Mrs. Nettlepoint said to me, that evening, as soon as I looked in.

"I'll do what I can—but what's the matter?"

"She has been crying here and going on—she has quite upset me."

"Crying? She doesn't look like that."

"Exactly, and that's what startled me. She came in to see me this afternoon, as she has done before, and we talked of the weather and the run of the ship and the manners of the stewardess and other such trifles, and then suddenly, in the midst of it, as she sat there, on no visible pretext, she burst into tears. I asked her what ailed her and tried to comfort her, but she didn't explain; she said it was nothing, the effect of the sea, of the monotony, of the excitement, of leaving home. I asked her if it had anything to do with her prospects, with her marriage; whether she finds as this draws near that her heart isn't in it. I told her she mustn't be nervous, that I could enter into that—in short I said what I could. All she replied was that she is nervous, very nervous, but that it was already over; and then she jumped up and kissed me and went away. Does she look as if she has been crying?" Mrs. Nettlepoint wound up.

"How can I tell, when she never quits that horrid veil? It's as if she were ashamed to show her face."

"She's keeping it for Liverpool. But I don't like such incidents," said Mrs. Nettlepoint. "I think I ought to go above."

"And is that where you want me to help you?"

"Oh with your arm and that sort of thing, yes. But I may have to look to you for something more. I feel as if something were going to happen."

"That's exactly what I said to Jasper this morning."

"And what did he say?"

"He only looked innocent—as if he thought I meant a fog or a storm."

"Heaven forbid—it isn't that! I shall never be good-natured again," Mrs. Nettlepoint went on; "never have a girl put on me that way. You always pay for it—there are always tiresome complications. What I'm afraid of is after we get there. She'll throw up her engagement; there will be dreadful scenes; I shall be mixed up with them and have to look after her and keep her with me. I shall have to stay there with her till she can be sent back, or even take her up to London. Do you see all that?"

I listened respectfully; after which I observed: "You're afraid of your son."

She also had a pause. "It depends on how you mean it."

"There are things you might say to him—and with your manner; because you have one, you know, when you choose."

"Very likely, but what's my manner to his? Besides, I *have* said everything to him. That is I've said the great thing—that he's making her immensely talked about."

"And of course in answer to that he has asked you how you know, and you've told him you have it from me."

"I've had to tell him; and he says it's none of your business."

"I wish he'd say that," I remarked, "to my face."

"He'll do so perfectly if you give him a chance. That's where you can help me. Quarrel with him—he's rather good at a quarrel; and that will divert him and draw him off."

"Then I'm ready," I returned, "to discuss the matter with him for the rest of the voyage."

"Very well; I count on you. But he'll ask you, as he asks me, what the deuce you want him to do."

"To go to bed!"—and I'm afraid I laughed.

"Oh it isn't a joke."

I didn't want to be irritating, but I made my point. "That's exactly what I told you at first."

"Yes, but don't exult; I hate people who exult. Jasper asks of me," she went on, "why he should mind her being talked about if she doesn't mind it herself."

"I'll tell him why," I replied; and Mrs. Nettlepoint said she should be exceedingly obliged to me and repeated that she would indeed take the field.

I looked for Jasper above that same evening, but circumstances didn't favour my quest. I found him—that is I gathered he was again ensconced behind the lifeboat with Miss Mavis; but there was a needless violence in breaking into their communion, and I put off our interview till the next day. Then I took the first opportunity, at breakfast, to make sure of it. He was in the saloon when I went in and was preparing to leave the table; but I stopped him and asked if he would give me a quarter of an hour on deck a little later—there was something particular I wanted to say to him. He said "Oh yes, if you like"—with just a visible surprise, but I thought with plenty of assurance. When I had finished my breakfast I found him smoking on the forward-deck and I immediately began: "I'm going to say something you won't at all like; to ask you a question you'll probably denounce for impertinent."

"I certainly shall if I find it so," said Jasper Nettlepoint.

"Well, of course my warning has meant that I don't care if you do. I'm a good deal older than you and I'm a friend—of many years—of your mother. There's nothing I like less than to be meddlesome, but I think these things give me a certain right—a sort of privilege. Besides which my inquiry will speak for itself."

"Why so many damned preliminaries?" my young man asked through his smoke.

We looked into each other's eyes a moment. What indeed was his mother's manner—her best manner—compared with his? "Are you prepared to be responsible?"

"To you?"

"Dear no—to the young lady herself. I'm speaking of course of Miss Mavis."

"Ah yes, my mother tells me you have her greatly on your mind."

"So has your mother herself—now."

"She's so good as to say so—to oblige you."

"She'd oblige me a great deal more by reassuring me. I know perfectly of your knowing I've told her that Miss Mavis is greatly talked about."

"Yes, but what on earth does it matter?"

"It matters as a sign."

"A sign of what?"

"That she's in a false position."

Jasper puffed his cigar with his eyes on the horizon, and I had, a little unexpectedly, the sense of producing a certain effect on him. "I don't know whether it's *your* business, what you're attempting to discuss but it really strikes me it's none of mine. What have I to do with the tattle with which a pack of old women console themselves for not being sea-sick?"

"Do you call it tattle that Miss Mavis is in love with you?"

"Drivelling."

"Then," I retorted, "you're very ungrateful. The tattle of a pack of old women has this importance, that she suspects, or she knows, it exists, and that decent girls are for the most part very sensitive to that sort of thing. To be prepared not to heed it in this case she must have a reason, and the reason must be the one I've taken the liberty to call your attention to."

"In love with me in six days, just like that?"—and he still looked away through narrowed eyelids.

"There's no accounting for tastes, and six days at sea are equivalent to sixty on land. I don't want to make you too proud. Of course if you recognise your responsibility it's all right and I've nothing to say."

"I don't see what you mean," he presently returned.

"Surely you ought to have thought of that by this time. She's engaged to be married, and the gentleman she's engaged to is to meet her at Liverpool. The whole ship knows it—though I didn't tell them!—and the whole ship's watching her. It's impertinent if you like, just as I am myself, but we make a little world here together and we can't blink its conditions. What I ask you is whether you're prepared to allow her to give up the gentleman I've just mentioned for your sake."

Jasper spoke in a moment as if he didn't understand. "For my sake?"

"To marry her if she breaks with him."

He turned his eyes from the horizon to my own, and I found a strange expression in them. "Has Miss Mavis commissioned you to go into that?"

"Not in the least."

"Well then, I don't quite see—!"

"It isn't as from another I make it. Let it come from yourself—*to* yourself."

"Lord, you must think I lead myself a life!" he cried as in compassion for my simplicity. "That's a question the young lady may put to me any moment it pleases her."

"Let me then express the hope that she will. But what will you answer?"

"My dear sir, it seems to me that in spite of all the titles you've enumerated you've no reason to expect I'll tell you." He turned away, and I dedicated in perfect sincerity a deep sore sigh to the thought of our young woman. At this, under the impression of it, he faced me again and, looking at me from head to foot, demanded: "What is it you want me to do?"

"I put it to your mother that you ought to go to bed."

"You had better do that yourself!" he replied.

This time he walked off, and I reflected rather dolefully that the only clear result of my undertaking would probably have been to make it vivid to him that she was in love with him. Mrs. Nettlepoint came up as she had announced, but the day was half over: it was nearly three o'clock. She was accompanied by her son, who established her on deck, arranged her chair and her shawls, saw she was protected from sun and wind, and for an hour was very properly attentive. While this went on Grace Mavis was not visible, nor did she reappear during the whole afternoon. I hadn't observed that she had as yet been absent from the deck for so long a period. Jasper left his mother, but came back at intervals to see how she got on, and when she asked where Miss Mavis might be answered that he hadn't the least idea. I sat with my friend at her particular request: she told me she knew that if I didn't Mrs. Peck and Mrs. Gotch would make their approach, so that I must act as a watch-dog. She was flurried and fatigued with her migration, and I think that Grace Mavis's choosing this occasion for retirement suggested to her a little that she had been made a fool of. She remarked that the girl's not being there showed her for the barbarian she only could be, and that she herself was really very good so to have put herself out; her charge was a mere bore: that was the end of it. I could see that my companion's advent quickened the speculative activity of the other ladies they watched her from the opposite side of the deck, keeping their eyes fixed on her very much as the man at the wheel kept his on the course of the ship. Mrs. Peck plainly had designs, and it was from this danger that Mrs. Nettlepoint averted her face.

"It's just as we said," she remarked to me as we sat there. "It's like the buckets in the well. When I come up everything else goes down."

"No, not at all everything else—since Jasper remains here."

"Remains? I don't see him."

"He comes and goes—it's the same thing."

"He goes more than he comes. But *n'en parlons plus*; I haven't gained anything. I don't admire the sea at all—what is it but a magnified water-tank? I shan't come up again."

"I've an idea she'll stay in her cabin now," I said. "She tells me she has one to herself." Mrs. Nettlepoint replied that she might do as she liked, and I repeated to her the little conversation I had had with Jasper.

She listened with interest, but "Marry her? Mercy!" she exclaimed. "I like the fine freedom with which you give my son away."

"You wouldn't accept that?"

"Why in the world should I?"

"Then I don't understand your position."

"Good heavens, I *have* none! It isn't a position to be tired of the whole thing."

"You wouldn't accept it even in the case I put to him—that of her believing she had been encouraged to throw over poor Porterfield?"

"Not even—not even. Who can know what she believes?"

It brought me back to where we had started from. "Then you do exactly what I said you would—you show me a fine example of maternal immorality."

"Maternal fiddlesticks! It was she who began it."

"Then why did you come up today?" I asked.

"To keep you quiet."

Mrs. Nettlepoint's dinner was served on deck, but I went into the saloon. Jasper was there, but not Grace Mavis, as I had half-expected. I sought to learn from him what had become of her, if she were ill—he must have thought I had an odious pertinacity—and he replied that he knew nothing whatever about her. Mrs. Peck talked to me—or tried to—of Mrs. Nettlepoint, expatiating on the great interest it had been to see her; only it was a pity she didn't seem more sociable. To this I made answer that she was to be excused on the score of health.

"You don't mean to say she's sick on this pond?"

"No, she's unwell in another way."

"I guess I know the way!" Mrs. Peck laughed. And then she added: "I suppose she came up to look after her pet."

"Her pet?" I set my face.

"Why Miss Mavis. We've talked enough about that."

"Quite enough. I don't know what that has had to do with it. Miss Mavis, so far as I've noticed, hasn't been above today."

"Oh it goes on all the same."

"It goes on?"

"Well, it's too late."

"Too late?"

"Well, you'll see. There'll be a row."

This wasn't comforting, but I didn't repeat it on deck. Mrs. Nettlepoint returned early to her cabin, professing herself infinitely spent. I didn't know what "went on," but Grace Mavis continued not to show. I looked in late, for a good-night to my friend, and learned from her that the girl hadn't been to her. She had sent the stewardess to her room for news, to see if she were ill and needed assistance, and the stewardess had come back with mere mention of her not being there. I went above after this; the night was not quite so fair and the deck almost empty. In a moment Jasper Nettlepoint and our young lady moved past me together. "I hope you're better!" I called after her; and she tossed me over her shoulder—"Oh yes, I had a headache; but the air now does me good!"

I went down again—I was the only person there but they, and I wanted not to seem to dog their steps—and, returning to Mrs. Nettlepoint's room, found (her door was open to the little passage) that she was still sitting up.

"She's all right!" I said. "She's on the deck with Jasper."

The good lady looked up at me from her book. "I didn't know you called that all right."

"Well, it's better than something else."

"Than what else?"

"Something I was a little afraid of." Mrs. Nettlepoint continued to look at me; she asked again what that might be. "I'll tell you when we're ashore," I said.

The next day I waited on her at the usual hour of my morning visit, and found her not a little distraught. "The scenes have begun," she said; "you know I told you I shouldn't get through without them! You made me nervous last night—I haven't the least idea what you meant; but you made me horribly nervous. She came in to see me an hour ago, and I had the courage to say to her: 'I don't know why I shouldn't tell you frankly that I've been scolding my son about you.' Of course she asked what I meant by that, and I let her know. 'It seems to me he drags you about the ship too much for a girl in your position. He has the air of not remembering that you belong to some one else. There's a want of taste and even a want of respect in it.' That brought on an outbreak: she became very violent."

"Do you mean indignant?"

"Yes, indignant, and above all flustered and excited—at my presuming to suppose her relations with my son not the very simplest in the world. I might scold him as much as I liked—that was between ourselves; but she didn't see why I should mention such matters to herself. Did I think she allowed him to treat her with disrespect? That idea wasn't much of a compliment to either of them! He had treated her better and been kinder to her than most other people—there were very few on the ship who hadn't been insulting. She should be glad enough when she got off it, to her own people, to some one whom nobody would have a right to speak of. What was there in her position that wasn't perfectly natural? what was the idea of making a fuss about her position? Did I mean that she took it too easily—that she didn't think as much as she ought about Mr. Porterfield? Didn't I believe she was attached to him—didn't I believe she was just counting the hours till she saw him? That would be the happiest moment of her life. It showed how little I knew her if I thought anything else."

"All that must have been rather fine—I should have liked to hear it," I said after quite hanging on my friend's lips. "And what did you reply?"

"Oh I grovelled; I assured her that I accused her—as regards my son—of nothing worse than an excess of good nature. She helped him to pass his time—he ought to be immensely obliged. Also that it would be a very happy moment for me too when I should hand her over to Mr. Porterfield."

"And will you come up today?"

"No indeed—I think she'll do beautifully now."

I heaved this time a sigh of relief. "All's well that ends well!"

Jasper spent that day a great deal of time with his mother. She had told me how much she had lacked hitherto proper opportunity to talk over with him their movements after disembarking. Everything changes a little the last two or three days of a voyage; the spell is broken and new combinations take place. Grace Mavis was neither on deck nor at dinner, and I drew Mrs. Peck's attention to the extreme propriety with which she now conducted herself. She had spent the day in meditation and judged it best to continue to meditate.

"Ah she's afraid," said my implacable neighbour.

"Afraid of what?"

"Well, that we'll tell tales when we get there."

"Whom do you mean by 'we'?"

"Well, there are plenty—on a ship like this."

"Then I think," I returned, "we won't."

"Maybe we won't have the chance," said the dreadful little woman.

"Oh at that moment"—I spoke from a full experience—"universal geniality reigns."

Mrs. Peck however knew little of any such law. "I guess she's afraid all the same."

"So much the better!"

"Yes—so much the better!"

All the next day too the girl remained invisible, and Mrs. Nettlepoint told me she hadn't looked in. She herself had accordingly inquired by the stewardess if she might be received in Miss Mavis's own quarters, and the young lady had replied that they were littered up with things and unfit for visitors: she was packing a trunk over. Jasper made up for his devotion to his mother the day before by now spending a great deal of his time in the smoking-room. I wanted to say to him "This is much better," but I thought it wiser to hold my tongue. Indeed I had begun to feel the emotion of prospective arrival—the sense of the return to Europe always kept its intensity—and had thereby the less attention for other matters. It will doubtless appear to the critical reader that my expenditure of interest had been out of proportion to the vulgar appearances of which my story gives an account, but to this I can only reply that the event was to justify me. We sighted land, the dim yet rich coast of Ireland, about sunset, and I leaned on the bulwark and took it in. "It doesn't look like much, does it?" I heard a voice say, beside me; whereupon, turning, I found Grace Mavis at hand. Almost for the first time she had her veil up, and I thought her very pale.

"It will be more tomorrow," I said.

"Oh yes, a great deal more."

"The first sight of land, at sea, changes everything," I went on. "It always affects me as waking up from a dream. It's a return to reality."

For a moment she made me no response; then she said "It doesn't look very real yet."

"No, and meanwhile, this lovely evening, one can put it that the dream's still present."

She looked up at the sky, which had a brightness, though the light of the sun had left it and that of the stars hadn't begun. "It *is* a lovely evening."

"Oh yes, with this we shall do."

She stood some moments more, while the growing dusk effaced the line of the land more rapidly than our progress made it distinct. She said nothing more, she only looked in front of her; but her very quietness prompted me to something suggestive of sympathy and service. It was difficult indeed to strike the right note—some things seemed too wide of the mark and others too importunate. At last, unexpectedly, she appeared to give me my chance. Irrelevantly, abruptly she broke out: "Didn't you tell me you knew Mr. Porterfield?"

"Dear me, yes—I used to see him. I've often wanted to speak to you of him."

She turned her face on me and in the deepened evening I imagined her more pale. "What good would that do?"

"Why it would be a pleasure," I replied rather foolishly.

"Do you mean for you?"

"Well, yes—call it that," I smiled.

"Did you know him so well?"

My smile became a laugh and I lost a little my confidence. "You're not easy to make speeches to."

"I hate speeches!" The words came from her lips with a force that surprised me; they were loud and hard. But before I had time to wonder she went on a little differently. "Shall you know him when you see him?"

"Perfectly, I think." Her manner was so strange that I had to notice it in some way, and I judged the best way was jocularly; so I added: "Shan't you?"

"Oh perhaps you'll point him out!" And she walked quickly away. As I looked after her there came to me a perverse, rather a provoking consciousness of having during the previous days, and especially in speaking to Jasper Nettlepoint, interfered with her situation in some degree to her loss. There was an odd pang for me in seeing her move about alone; I felt somehow responsible for it and asked myself why I couldn't have kept my hands off. I had seen Jasper in the smoking-room more than once that day, as I passed it, and half an hour before this had observed, through the open door, that he was there. He had been with her so much that without him she now struck one as bereaved and forsaken. This was really better, no doubt, but superficially it moved—and I admit with the last inconsequence—one's pity. Mrs. Peck would doubtless have assured me that their separation was gammon: they didn't show together on deck and in the saloon, but they made it up elsewhere. The secret places on shipboard are not numerous; Mrs. Peck's "elsewhere" would have been vague, and I know not what licence her imagination took. It was distinct that Jasper had fallen off, but of course what had passed between them on this score wasn't so and could never be. Later on, through his mother, I had *his* version of that, but I may remark that I gave it no credit. Poor Mrs. Nettlepoint, on the other hand, was of course to give it all. I was almost capable, after the girl had left me, of going to my young man and saying: "After all, do return to her a little, just till we get in! It won't make any difference after we land." And I don't think it was the fear he would tell me I was an idiot that prevented me. At any rate the next time I passed the door of the smoking-room I saw he had left it. I paid my usual visit to Mrs. Nettlepoint that night, but I troubled her no further about Miss Mavis. She had made up her mind that everything was smooth and settled now, and it seemed to me I had worried her, and that she had worried herself, in sufficiency. I left her to enjoy the deepening foretaste of arrival, which had taken possession of her mind. Before turning in I went above and found more passengers on deck than I had ever seen so late. Jasper moved about among them alone, but I forbore to join him. The coast of Ireland had disappeared, but the night and the sea were perfect. On the way to my cabin, when I came down, I met the stewardess in one of the passages, and the idea entered my head to say to her: "Do you happen to know where Miss Mavis is?"

"Why she's in her room, sir, at this hour."

"Do you suppose I could speak to her?" It had come into my mind to ask her why she had wanted to know of me if I should recognise Mr. Porterfield.

"No sir," said the stewardess; "she has gone to bed."

"That's all right." And I followed the young lady's excellent example.

The next morning, while I dressed, the steward of my side of the ship came to me as usual to see what I wanted. But the first thing he said to, me was: "Rather a bad job, sir—a passenger missing." And while I took I scarce know what instant chill from it, "A lady, sir," he went on—"whom I think you knew. Poor Miss Mavis, sir."

"*Missing*?" I cried—staring at him and horror-stricken.

"She's not on the ship. They can't find her."

"Then where to God is she?"

I recall his queer face. "Well sir, I suppose you know that as well as I."

"Do you mean she has jumped overboard?"

"Some time in the night, sir—on the quiet. But it's beyond every one, the way she escaped notice. They usually sees 'em, sir. It must have been about half-past two. Lord, but she was sharp, sir. She didn't so much as make a splash. They say she *'ad* come against her will, sir."

I had dropped upon my sofa—I felt faint. The man went on, liking to talk as persons of his class do when they have something horrible to tell. She usually rang for the stewardess early, but this morning of course there had been no ring. The stewardess had gone in all the same about eight o'clock and found the cabin empty. That was about an hour previous. Her things were there in confusion—the things she usually wore when she went above. The stewardess thought she had been a bit odd the night before, but had waited a little and then gone back. Miss Mavis hadn't turned up—and she didn't turn up. The stewardess began to look for her—she hadn't been seen on deck or in the saloon. Besides, she wasn't dressed—not to show herself; all her clothes were in her room. There was another lady, an old lady, Mrs. Nettlepoint—I would know her—that she was sometimes with, but the stewardess had been with *her* and knew Miss Mavis hadn't come near her that morning. She had spoken to *him* and they had taken a quiet look—they had hunted everywhere. A ship's a big place, but you did come to the end of it, and if a person wasn't there why there it was. In short an hour had passed and the young lady was not accounted for: from which I might judge if she ever would be. The watch couldn't account for her, but no doubt the fishes in the sea could—poor miserable pitiful lady! The stewardess and he had of course thought it their duty to speak at once to the Doctor, and the Doctor had spoken immediately to the Captain. The Captain didn't like it—they never did, but he'd try to keep it quiet—they always did.

By the time I succeeded in pulling myself together and getting on, after a fashion, the rest of my clothes I had learned that Mrs. Nettlepoint wouldn't yet have been told, unless the stewardess had broken it to her within the previous few minutes. Her son knew, the young gentleman on the other side of the ship—he had the other steward; my man had seen him come out of his cabin and rush above, just before he came in to me. He *had* gone above, my man was sure; he hadn't gone to the old lady's cabin. I catch again the sense of my dreadfully seeing something at that moment, catch the wild flash, under the steward's words, of Jasper Nettlepoint leaping, with a mad compunction in his young agility, over the side of the ship. I hasten to add, however, that no such incident was destined to contribute its horror to poor Grace Mavis's unwitnessed and unlighted tragic act. What followed was miserable enough, but I can only glance at it. When I got to Mrs. Nettlepoint's door she was there with a shawl about her; the stewardess had just told her and she was dashing out to come to me. I made her go back—I said I would go for Jasper. I went for him but I missed him, partly no doubt because it was really at first the Captain I was after. I found this personage and found him highly scandalised, but he gave me no hope that we were in error, and his displeasure, expressed with seamanlike strength, was a definite settlement of the question. From the deck, where I merely turned round and looked, I saw the light of another summer day, the coast of Ireland green and near and the sea of a more charming colour than it had shown at all. When I came below again Jasper had passed back; he had gone to his cabin and his mother had joined him there. He remained there till we reached Liverpool—I never saw him. His mother, after a little, at his request, left him alone. All the world went above to look at the land and chatter about our tragedy, but the poor lady spent the day, dismally enough, in her room. It seemed to me, the dreadful day, intolerably long; I was thinking so of vague, of inconceivable yet inevitable Porterfield, and of my having to face him somehow on the morrow. Now of course I knew why she had asked me if I should recognise him; she had delegated to me mentally a certain pleasant office. I gave Mrs. Peck and Mrs. Gotch a wide berth—I couldn't talk to them. I could, or at least I did a little, to Mrs. Nettlepoint, but with too many reserves for comfort on either side, since I quite felt how little it would now make for ease to mention Jasper to her. I was obliged to assume by my silence that he had had nothing to do with what had happened; and of course I never really ascertained what he *had* had to do. The secret of what passed between him and the strange girl who would have sacrificed her marriage to him on so short an acquaintance remains shut up in his breast. His mother, I know, went to his door from time to time, but he refused her admission. That evening, to be human at a venture, I requested the steward to go in and ask him if he should care to see me, and the good man returned with an answer which he candidly transmitted. "Not in the least!"—Jasper apparently was almost as scandalised as the Captain.

At Liverpool, at the dock, when we had touched, twenty people came on board and I had already made out Mr. Porterfield at a distance. He was looking up at the side of the great vessel with disappointment written—for my strained eyes—in his face; disappointment at not seeing the woman he had so long awaited lean over it and wave her handkerchief to him. Every one was looking at him, every one but she—his identity flew about in a moment—and I wondered if it didn't strike him. He used to be gaunt and angular, but had grown almost fat and stooped a little. The interval between us diminished—he was on the plank and then on the deck with the jostling agents of the Customs; too soon for my equanimity. I met him instantly, however, to save him from exposure—laid my hand on him and drew him away, though I was sure he had no impression of having seen me before. It was not till afterwards that I thought this rather characteristically dull of him. I drew him far away—I was conscious of Mrs. Peck and Mrs. Gotch, looking at us as we passed—into the empty stale smoking-room: he remained speechless, and that struck me as like him. I had to speak first, he couldn't even relieve me by saying "Is anything the matter?" I broke ground by putting it, feebly, that she was ill. It was a dire moment.

THE PRIVATE LIFE

We talked of London, face to face with a great bristling, primeval glacier. The hour and the scene were one of those impressions which make up a little, in Switzerland, for the modern indignity of travel—the promiscuities and vulgarities, the station and the hotel, the gregarious patience, the struggle for a scrappy attention, the reduction to a numbered state. The high valley was pink with the mountain rose, the cool air as fresh as if the world were young. There was a faint flush of afternoon on undiminished snows, and the fraternizing tinkle of the unseen cattle came to us with a cropped and sun-warmed odour. The balconied inn stood on the very neck of the sweetest pass in the Oberland, and for a week we had had company and weather. This was felt to be great luck, for one would have made up for the other had either been bad.

The weather certainly would have made up for the company; but it was not subjected to this tax, for we had by a happy chance the *fleur des pois*: Lord and Lady Mellifont, Clare Vawdrey, the greatest (in the opinion of many) of our literary glories, and Blanche

Adney, the greatest (in the opinion of all) of our theatrical. I mention these first, because they were just the people whom in London, at that time, people tried to 'get'. People endeavoured to 'book' them six weeks ahead, yet on this occasion we had come in for them, we had all come in for each other, without the least wire-pulling. A turn of the game had pitched us together, the last of August, and we recognized our luck by remaining so, under protection of the barometer. When the golden days were over—that would come soon enough—we should wind down opposite sides of the pass and disappear over the crest of surrounding heights. We were of the same general communion, we participated in the same miscellaneous publicity. We met, in London, with irregular frequency; we were more or less governed by the laws and the language, the traditions and the shibboleths of the same dense social state. I think all of us, even the ladies, 'did' something, though we pretended we didn't when it was mentioned. Such things are not mentioned indeed in London, but it was our innocent pleasure to be different here. There had to be some way to show the difference, inasmuch as we were under the impression that this was our annual holiday. We felt at any rate that the conditions were more human than in London, or that at least we ourselves were. We were frank about this, we talked about it: it was what we were talking about as we looked at the flushing glacier, just as some one called attention to the prolonged absence of Lord Mellifont and Mrs. Adney. We were seated on the terrace of the inn, where there were benches and little tables, and those of us who were most bent on proving that we had returned to nature were, in the queer Germanic fashion, having coffee before meat.

The remark about the absence of our two companions was not taken up, not even by Lady Mellifont, not even by little Adney, the fond composer; for it had been dropped only in the briefest intermission of Clare Vawdrey's talk. (This celebrity was 'Clarence' only on the title-page.) It was just that revelation of our being after all human that was his theme. He asked the company whether, candidly, every one hadn't been tempted to say to every one else: 'I had no idea you were really so nice.' I had had, for my part, an idea that he was, and even a good deal nicer, but that was too complicated to go into then; besides it is exactly my story. There was a general understanding among us that when Vawdrey talked we should be silent, and not, oddly enough, because he at all expected it. He didn't, for of all abundant talkers he was the most unconscious, the least greedy and professional. It was rather the religion of the host, of the hostess, that prevailed among us: it was their own idea, but they always looked for a listening circle when the great novelist dined with them. On the occasion I allude to there was probably no one present with whom, in London, he had not dined, and we felt the force of this habit. He had dined even with me; and on the evening of that dinner, as on this Alpine afternoon, I had been at no pains to hold my tongue, absorbed as I inveterately was in a study of the question which always rose before me, to such a height, in his fair, square, strong stature.

This question was all the more tormenting that he never suspected himself (I am sure) of imposing it, any more than he had ever observed that every day of his life every one listened to him at dinner. He used to be called 'subjective' in the weekly papers, but in society no distinguished man could have been less so. He never talked about himself; and this was a topic on which, though it would have been tremendously worthy of him, he apparently never even reflected. He had his hours and his habits, his tailor and his hatter, his hygiene and his particular wine, but all these things together never made up an attitude. Yet they constituted the only attitude he ever adopted, and it was easy for him to refer to our being 'nicer' abroad than at home. *He* was exempt from variations, and not a shade either less or more nice in one place than in another. He differed from other people, but never from himself (save in the extraordinary sense which I will presently explain), and struck me as having neither moods nor sensibilities nor preferences. He might have been always in the same company, so far as he recognized any influence from age or condition or sex: he addressed himself to women exactly as he addressed himself to men, and gossiped with all men alike, talking no better to clever folk than to dull. I used to feel a despair at his way of liking one subject—so far as I could tell—precisely as much as another: there were some I hated so myself. I never found him anything but loud and cheerful and copious, and I never heard him utter a paradox or express a shade or play with an idea. That fancy about our being 'human' was, in his conversation, quite an exceptional flight. His opinions were sound and second-rate, and of his perceptions it was too mystifying to think. I envied him his magnificent health.

Vawdrey had marched, with his even pace and his perfectly good conscience, into the flat country of anecdote, where stories are visible from afar like windmills and signposts; but I observed after a little that Lady Mellifont's attention wandered. I happened to be sitting next her. I noticed that her eyes rambled a little anxiously over the lower slopes of the mountains. At last, after looking at her watch, she said to me: "Do you know where they went?"

"Do you mean Mrs. Adney and Lord Mellifont?"

"Lord Mellifont and Mrs. Adney." Her ladyship's speech seemed—unconsciously indeed—to correct me, but it didn't occur to me that this was because she was jealous. I imputed to her no such vulgar sentiment: in the first place, because I liked her, and in the second because it would always occur to one quickly that it was right, in any connection, to put Lord Mellifont first. He was first—extraordinarily first. I don't say greatest or wisest or most renowned, but essentially at the top of the list and the head of the table. That is a position by itself, and his wife was naturally accustomed to see him in it. My phrase had sounded as if Mrs. Adney had taken him; but it was not possible for him to be taken—he only took. No one, in the nature of things, could know this better than Lady Mellifont. I had originally been rather afraid of her, thinking her, with her stiff silences and the extreme blackness of almost everything that made up her person, somewhat hard, even a little saturnine. Her paleness seemed slightly grey, and her glossy black hair metallic, like the brooches and bands and combs with which it was inveterately adorned. She was in perpetual mourning, and wore numberless ornaments of jet and onyx, a thousand clicking chains and bugles and beads. I had heard Mrs. Adney call her the queen of night, and the term was descriptive if you understood that the night was cloudy. She had a secret, and if you didn't find it out as you knew her better you at least perceived that she was gentle and unaffected and limited, and also rather submissively sad. She was like a woman with a painless malady. I told her that I had merely seen her husband and his companion stroll down the glen together about an hour before, and suggested that Mr. Adney would perhaps know something of their intentions.

Vincent Adney, who, though he was fifty years old, looked like a good little boy on whom it had been impressed that children should not talk before company, acquitted himself with remarkable simplicity and taste of the position of husband of a great exponent of comedy. When all was said about her making it easy for him, one couldn't help admiring the charmed affection with which he took everything for granted. It is difficult for a husband who is not on the stage, or at least in the theatre, to be graceful about a wife who is; but Adney was more than graceful—he was exquisite, he was inspired. He set his beloved to music; and you remember how genuine his music could be—the only English compositions I ever saw a foreigner take an interest in. His wife was in them, somewhere, always; they were like a free, rich translation of the impression she produced. She seemed, as one listened, to pass laughing, with loosened hair, across the scene. He had been only a little fiddler at her theatre, always in his place during the acts; but she had made him something rare and misunderstood. Their superiority had become a kind of partnership, and their happiness was a part of the happiness of their friends. Adney's one discomfort was that he couldn't write a play for his wife, and the only way he meddled with her affairs was by asking impossible people if *they* couldn't.

Lady Mellifont, after looking across at him a moment, remarked to me that she would rather not put any question to him. She added the next minute: "I had rather people shouldn't see I'm nervous."

"*Are* you nervous?"

"I always become so if my husband is away from me for any time."

"Do you imagine something has happened to him?"

"Yes, always. Of course I'm used to it."

"Do you mean his tumbling over precipices—that sort of thing?"

"I don't know exactly what it is: it's the general sense that he'll never come back."

She said so much and kept back so much that the only way to treat the condition she referred to seemed the jocular. "Surely he'll never forsake you!" I laughed.

She looked at the ground a moment. "Oh, at bottom I'm easy."

"Nothing can ever happen to a man so accomplished, so infallible, so armed at all points," I went on, encouragingly.

"Oh, you don't know how he's armed!" she exclaimed, with such an odd quaver that I could account for it only by her being nervous. This idea was confirmed by her moving just afterwards, changing her seat rather pointlessly, not as if to cut our conversation short, but because she was in a fidget. I couldn't know what was the matter with her, but I was presently relieved to see Mrs. Adney come toward us. She had in her hand a big bunch of wild flowers, but she was not closely attended by Lord Mellifont. I quickly saw, however, that she had no disaster to announce; yet as I knew there was a question Lady Mellifont would like to hear answered, but did not wish to ask, I expressed to her immediately the hope that his lordship had not remained in a crevasse.

"Oh, no; he left me but three minutes ago. He has gone into the house." Blanche Adney rested her eyes on mine an instant—a mode of intercourse to which no man, for himself, could ever object. The interest, on this occasion, was quickened by the particular thing the eyes happened to say. What they usually said was only: 'Oh, yes, I'm charming, I know, but don't make a fuss about it. I only want a new part—I do, I do!' At present they added, dimly, surreptitiously, and of course sweetly—for that was the way they did everything: 'It's all right, but something did happen. Perhaps I'll tell you later.' She turned to Lady Mellifont, and the transition to simple gaiety suggested her mastery of her profession. "I've brought him safe. We had a charming walk."

"I'm so very glad," returned Lady Mellifont, with her faint smile; continuing vaguely, as she got up: "He must have gone to dress for dinner. Isn't it rather near?" She moved away, to the hotel, in her leave-taking, simplifying fashion, and the rest of us, at the mention of dinner, looked at each other's watches, as if to shift the responsibility of such grossness. The head-waiter, essentially, like all head-waiters, a man of the world, allowed us hours and places of our own, so that in the evening, apart under the lamp, we formed a compact, an indulged little circle. But it was only the Mellifonts who 'dressed' and as to whom it was recognized that they naturally *would* dress: she in exactly the same manner as on any other evening of her ceremonious existence (she was not a woman whose habits could take account of anything so mutable as fitness); and he, on the other hand, with remarkable adjustment and suitability. He was almost as much a man of the world as the head-waiter, and spoke almost as many languages; but he abstained from courting a comparison of dress-coats and white waistcoats, analyzing the occasion in a much finer way—into black velvet and blue velvet and brown velvet, for instance, into delicate harmonies of necktie and subtle informalities of shirt. He had a costume for every function and a moral for every costume; and his functions and costumes and morals were ever a part of the amusement of life—a part at any rate of its beauty and romance—for an immense circle of spectators. For his particular friends indeed these things were more than an amusement; they were a topic, a social support and of course, in addition, a subject of perpetual suspense. If his wife had not been present before dinner they were what the rest of us probably would have been putting our heads together about.

Clare Vawdrey had a fund of anecdote on the whole question: he had known Lord Mellifont almost from the beginning. It was a peculiarity of this nobleman that there could be no conversation about him that didn't instantly take the form of anecdote, and a still further distinction that there could apparently be no anecdote that was not on the whole to his honour. If he had come into a room at any moment, people might have said frankly: 'Of course we were telling stories about you!' As consciences go, in London, the general conscience would have been good. Moreover it would have been impossible to imagine his taking such a tribute otherwise than amiably, for he was always as unperturbed as an actor with the right cue. He had never in his life needed the prompter—his very embarrassments had been rehearsed. For myself, when he was talked about I always had an odd impression that we were speaking of the dead—it was with that peculiar accumulation of relish. His reputation was a kind of gilded obelisk, as if he had been buried beneath it; the body of legend and reminiscence of which he was to be the subject had crystallized in advance.

This ambiguity sprang, I suppose, from the fact that the mere sound of his name and air of his person, the general expectation he created, were, somehow, too exalted to be verified. The experience of his urbanity always came later; the prefigurement, the legend paled before the reality. I remember that on the evening I refer to the reality was particularly operative. The handsomest man of his period could never have looked better, and he sat among us like a bland conductor controlling by an harmonious play of arm an orchestra still a little rough. He directed the conversation by gestures as irresistible as they were vague; one felt as if without him it wouldn't have had anything to call a tone. This was essentially what he contributed to any occasion—what he contributed above all to English public life. He pervaded it, he coloured it, he embellished it, and without him it would scarcely have had a vocabulary. Certainly it would not have had a style; for a style was what it had in having Lord Mellifont. He *was* a style. I was freshly struck with it as, in the *salle à manger* of the little Swiss inn, we resigned ourselves to inevitable veal. Confronted with his form (I must parenthesize that it was not confronted much), Clare Vawdrey's talk suggested the reporter contrasted with the bard. It was interesting to watch the shock of characters from which, of an evening, so much would be expected. There was however no concussion—it was all muffled and minimized in Lord Mellifont's tact. It was rudimentary with him to find the solution of such a problem in playing the host, assuming responsibilities which carried with them their sacrifice. He had indeed never been a guest in his life; he was the host, the patron, the moderator at every board. If there was a defect in his manner (and I suggest it under my breath), it was that he had a little more art than any conjunction—even the most complicated—could possibly require.

At any rate one made one's reflections in noticing how the accomplished peer handled the situation and how the sturdy man of letters was unconscious that the situation (and least of all he himself as part of it), was handled. Lord Mellifont poured forth treasures of tact, and Clare Vawdrey never dreamed he was doing it.

Vawdrey had no suspicion of any such precaution even when Blanche Adney asked him if he saw yet their third act—an inquiry into which she introduced a subtlety of her own. She had a theory that he was to write her a play and that the heroine, if he would only do his duty, would be the part for which she had immemorially longed. She was forty years old (this could be no secret to those who had admired her from the first), and she could now reach out her hand and touch her uttermost goal. This gave a kind of tragic passion—perfect actress of comedy as she was—to her desire not to miss the great thing. The years had passed, and still she had missed it; none of the things she had done was the thing she had dreamed of, so that at present there was no more time to lose. This was the canker in the rose, the ache beneath the smile. It made her touching—made her sadness even sweeter than her laughter. She had done the old English and the new French, and had charmed her generation; but she was haunted by the vision of a bigger chance, of something truer to the conditions that lay near her. She was tired of Sheridan and she hated Bowdler; she called for a canvas of a finer grain. The worst of it, to my sense, was that she would never extract her modern comedy from the great mature novelist, who was as incapable of producing it as he was of threading a needle. She coddled him, she talked to him, she made love to him, as she frankly proclaimed; but she dwelt in illusions—she would have to live and die with Bowdler.

It is difficult to be cursory over this charming woman, who was beautiful without beauty and complete with a dozen deficiencies. The perspective of the stage made her over, and in society she was like the model off the pedestal. She was the picture walking about, which to the artless social mind was a perpetual surprise—a miracle. People thought she told them the secrets of the pictorial nature, in return for which they gave her relaxation and tea. She told them nothing and she drank the tea; but they had, all the same, the best of the bargain. Vawdrey was really at work on a play; but if he had begun it because he liked her I think he let it drag for the same reason. He secretly felt the atrocious difficulty—knew that from his hand the finished piece would have received no active life. At the same time nothing could be more agreeable than to have such a question open with Blanche Adney, and from time to time he put something very good into the play. If he deceived Mrs. Adney it was only because in her despair she was determined to be deceived. To her question about their third act he replied that, before dinner, he had written a magnificent passage.

"Before dinner?" I said. "Why, *cher maître*, before dinner you were holding us all spellbound on the terrace."

My words were a joke, because I thought his had been; but for the first time that I could remember I perceived a certain confusion in his face. He looked at me hard, throwing back his head quickly, the least bit like a horse who has been pulled up short. "Oh, it was before that," he replied, naturally enough.

"Before that you were playing billiards with *me*," Lord Mellifont intimated.

"Then it must have been yesterday," said Vawdrey.

But he was in a tight place. "You told me this morning you did nothing yesterday," the actress objected.

"I don't think I really know when I do things." Vawdrey looked vaguely, without helping himself, at a dish that was offered him.

"It's enough if *we* know," smiled Lord Mellifont.

"I don't believe you've written a line," said Blanche Adney.

"I think I could repeat you the scene." Vawdrey helped himself to *haricots verts*.

"Oh, do—oh, do!" two or three of us cried.

"After dinner, in the salon; it will be an immense *régal*," Lord Mellifont declared.

"I'm not sure, but I'll try," Vawdrey went on.

"Oh, you lovely man!" exclaimed the actress, who was practising Americanisms, being resigned even to an American comedy.

"But there must be this condition," said Vawdrey: "you must make your husband play."

"Play while you're reading? Never!"

"I've too much vanity," said Adney.

Lord Mellifont distinguished him. "You must give us the overture, before the curtain rises. That's a peculiarly delightful moment."

"I sha'n't read—I shall just speak," said Vawdrey.

"Better still, let me go and get your manuscript," the actress suggested.

Vawdrey replied that the manuscript didn't matter; but an hour later, in the salon, we wished he might have had it. We sat expectant, still under the spell of Adney's violin. His wife, in the foreground, on an ottoman, was all impatience and profile, and Lord Mellifont, in the chair—it was always *the* chair, Lord Mellifont's—made our grateful little group feel like a social science congress or a distribution of prizes. Suddenly, instead of beginning, our tame lion began to roar out of tune—he had clean forgotten every word. He was very sorry, but the lines absolutely wouldn't come to him; he was utterly ashamed, but his memory was a blank. He didn't look in the least ashamed—Vawdrey had never looked ashamed in his life; he was only imperturbably and merrily natural. He protested that he had never expected to make such a fool of himself, but we felt that this wouldn't prevent the incident from taking its place among his jolliest reminiscences. It was only we who were humiliated, as if he had played us a premeditated trick. This was an occasion, if ever, for Lord Mellifont's tact, which descended on us all like balm: he told us, in his charming artistic way, his way of bridging over arid intervals (he had a *débit*—there was nothing to approach it in England—like the actors of the Comédie Française), of his own collapse on a momentous occasion, the delivery of an address to a mighty multitude, when, finding he had forgotten his memoranda, he fumbled, on the terrible platform, the cynosure of every eye, fumbled vainly in irreproachable pockets for indispensable notes. But the point of his story was finer than that of Vawdrey's pleasantry; for he sketched with a few light gestures the brilliancy of a performance which had risen superior to embarrassment, had resolved itself, we were left to divine, into an effort recognised at the moment as not absolutely a blot on what the public was so good as to call his reputation.

"Play up—play up!" cried Blanche Adney, tapping her husband and remembering how, on the stage, a *contretemps* is always drowned in music. Adney threw himself upon his fiddle, and I said to Clare Vawdrey that his mistake could easily be corrected by his sending for the manuscript. If he would tell me where it was I would immediately fetch it from his room. To this he replied: "My dear fellow, I'm afraid there *is* no manuscript."

"Then you've not written anything?"

"I'll write it to-morrow."

"Ah, you trifle with us," I said, in much mystification.

Vawdrey hesitated an instant. "If there *is* anything, you'll find it on my table."

At this moment one of the others spoke to him, and Lady Mellifont remarked audibly, as if to correct gently our want of consideration, that Mr. Adney was playing something very beautiful. I had noticed before that she appeared extremely fond of music; she always listened to it in a hushed transport. Vawdrey's attention was drawn away, but it didn't seem to me that the words he had just dropped constituted a definite permission to go to his room. Moreover I wanted to speak to Blanche Adney; I had something to ask her. I had to await my chance, however, as we remained silent awhile for her husband, after which the conversation became general. It was our habit to go to bed early, but there was still a little of the evening left. Before it quite waned I found an opportunity to tell the actress that Vawdrey had given me leave to put my hand on his manuscript. She adjured me, by all I held sacred, to bring it immediately, to give it to her; and her insistence was proof against my suggestion that it would now be too late for him to begin to read: besides which the charm was broken—the others wouldn't care. It was not too late for *her* to begin; therefore I was to possess myself, without more delay, of the precious pages. I told her she should be obeyed in a moment, but I wanted her first to satisfy my just curiosity. What had happened before dinner, while she was on the hills with Lord Mellifont?

"How do you know anything happened?"

"I saw it in your face when you came back."

"And they call me an actress!" cried Mrs. Adney.

"What do they call *me*?" I inquired.

"You're a searcher of hearts—that frivolous thing an observer."

"I wish you'd let an observer write you a play!" I broke out.

"People don't care for what you write: you'd break any run of luck."

"Well, I see plays all round me," I declared; "the air is full of them to-night."

"The air? Thank you for nothing! I only wish my table-drawers were."

"Did he make love to you on the glacier?" I went on.

She stared; then broke into the graduated ecstasy of her laugh. "Lord Mellifont, poor dear? What a funny place! It would indeed be the place for *our* love!"

"Did he fall into a crevasse?" I continued.

Blanche Adney looked at me again as she had done for an instant when she came up, before dinner, with her hands full of flowers. "I don't know into what he fell. I'll tell you to-morrow."

"He did come down, then?"

"Perhaps he went up," she laughed. "It's really strange."

"All the more reason you should tell me to-night."

"I must think it over; I must puzzle it out."

"Oh, if you want conundrums I'll throw in another," I said. "What's the matter with the master?"

"The master of what?"

"Of every form of dissimulation. Vawdrey hasn't written a line."

"Go and get his papers and we'll see."

"I don't like to expose him," I said.

"Why not, if I expose Lord Mellifont?"

"Oh, I'd do anything for that," I conceded. "But why should Vawdrey have made a false statement? It's very curious."

"It's very curious," Blanche Adney repeated, with a musing air and her eyes on Lord Mellifont. Then, rousing herself, she added: "Go and look in his room."

"In Lord Mellifont's?"

She turned to me quickly. "*That* would be a way!"

"A way to what?"

"To find out—to find out!" She spoke gaily and excitedly, but suddenly checked herself. "We're talking nonsense," she said.

"We're mixing things up, but I'm struck with your idea. Get Lady Mellifont to let you."

"Oh, *she* has looked!" Mrs. Adney murmured, with the oddest dramatic expression. Then, after a movement of her beautiful uplifted hand, as if to brush away a fantastic vision, she exclaimed imperiously: "Bring me the scene—bring me the scene!"

"I go for it," I answered; "but don't tell me I can't write a play."

She left me, but my errand was arrested by the approach of a lady who had produced a birthday-book—we had been threatened with it for several evenings—and who did me the honour to solicit my autograph. She had been asking the others, and she couldn't decently leave me out. I could usually remember my name, but it always took me some time to recall my date, and even when I had done so I was never very sure. I hesitated between two days and I remarked to my petitioner that I would sign on both if it would give her any satisfaction. She said that surely I had been born only once; and I replied of course that on the day I made her acquaintance I had been born again. I mention the feeble joke only to show that, with the obligatory inspection of the other autographs, we gave some minutes to this transaction. The lady departed with her book, and then I became aware that the company had dispersed. I was alone in the little salon that had been appropriated to our use. My first impression was one of disappointment: if Vawdrey had gone to bed I didn't wish to disturb him. While I hesitated, however, I recognised that Vawdrey had not gone to bed. A window was open, and the sound of voices outside came in to me: Blanche was on the terrace with her dramatist, and they were talking about the stars. I went to the window for a glimpse—the Alpine night was splendid. My friends had stepped out together; the actress had picked up a cloak; she looked as I had seen her look in the wing of the theatre. They were silent awhile, and I heard the roar of a neighbouring torrent. I turned back into the room, and its quiet lamplight gave me an idea. Our companions had dispersed—it was late for a pastoral country—and we three should have the place to ourselves. Clare Vawdrey had written his scene—it was magnificent; and his reading it to us there, at such an hour, would be an episode intensely memorable. I would bring down his manuscript and meet the two with it as they came in.

I quitted the salon for this purpose; I had been in Vawdrey's room and knew it was on the second floor, the last in a long corridor. A minute later my hand was on the knob of his door, which I naturally pushed open without knocking. It was equally natural that in the absence of its occupant the room should be dark; the more so as, the end of the corridor being at that hour unlighted, the obscurity was not immediately diminished by the opening of the door. I was only aware at first that I had made no mistake and that, the window-curtains not being drawn, I was confronted with a couple of vague starlighted apertures. Their aid, however, was not sufficient to enable me to find what I had come for, and my hand, in my pocket, was already on the little box of matches that I always carried for cigarettes. Suddenly I withdrew it with a start, uttering an ejaculation, an apology. I had entered the wrong room; a glance prolonged for three seconds showed me a figure seated at a table near one of the windows—a figure I had at first taken for a travelling-rug thrown over a chair. I retreated, with a sense of intrusion; but as I did so I became aware, more rapidly than it takes me to express it, in the first place that this was

Vawdrey's room and in the second that, most singularly, Vawdrey himself sat before me. Checking myself on the threshold I had a momentary feeling of bewilderment, but before I knew it I had exclaimed: "Hullo! is that you, Vawdrey?"

He neither turned nor answered me, but my question received an immediate and practical reply in the opening of a door on the other side of the passage. A servant, with a candle, had come out of the opposite room, and in this flitting illumination I definitely recognised the man whom, an instant before, I had to the best of my belief left below in conversation with Mrs. Adney. His back was half turned to me, and he bent over the table in the attitude of writing, but I was conscious that I was in no sort of error about his identity. "I beg your pardon—I thought you were downstairs," I said; and as the personage gave no sign of hearing me I added: "If you're busy I won't disturb you." I backed out, closing the door—I had been in the place, I suppose, less than a minute. I had a sense of mystification, which however deepened infinitely the next instant. I stood there with my hand still on the knob of the door, overtaken by the oddest impression of my life. Vawdrey was at his table, writing, and it was a very natural place for him to be; but why was he writing in the dark and why hadn't he answered me? I waited a few seconds for the sound of some movement, to see if he wouldn't rouse himself from his abstraction—a fit conceivable in a great writer—and call out: 'Oh, my dear fellow, is it you?' But I heard only the stillness, I felt only the starlighted dusk of the room, with the unexpected presence it enclosed. I turned away, slowly retracing my steps, and came confusedly downstairs. The lamp was still burning in the salon, but the room was empty. I passed round to the door of the hotel and stepped out. Empty too was the terrace. Blanche Adney and the gentleman with her had apparently come in. I hung about five minutes; then I went to bed.

I slept badly, for I was agitated. On looking back at these queer occurrences (you will see presently that they were queer), I perhaps suppose myself more agitated than I was; for great anomalies are never so great at first as after we have reflected upon them. It takes us some time to exhaust explanations. I was vaguely nervous—I had been sharply startled; but there was nothing I could not clear up by asking Blanche Adney, the first thing in the morning, who had been with her on the terrace. Oddly enough, however, when the morning dawned—it dawned admirably—I felt less desire to satisfy myself on this point than to escape, to brush away the shadow of my stupefaction. I saw the day would be splendid, and the fancy took me to spend it, as I had spent happy days of youth, in a lonely mountain ramble. I dressed early, partook of conventional coffee, put a big roll into one pocket and a small flask into the other, and, with a stout stick in my hand, went forth into the high places. My story is not closely concerned with the charming hours I passed there—hours of the kind that make intense memories. If I roamed away half of them on the shoulders of the hills, I lay on the sloping grass for the other half and, with my cap pulled over my eyes (save a peep for immensities of view), listened, in the bright stillness, to the mountain bee and felt most things sink and dwindle. Clare Vawdrey grew small, Blanche Adney grew dim, Lord Mellifont grew old, and before the day was over I forgot that I had ever been puzzled. When in the late afternoon I made my way down to the inn there was nothing I wanted so much to find out as whether dinner would not soon be ready. To-night I dressed, in a manner, and by the time I was presentable they were all at table.

In their company again my little problem came back to me, so that I was curious to see if Vawdrey wouldn't look at me the least bit queerly. But he didn't look at me at all; which gave me a chance both to be patient and to wonder why I should hesitate to ask him my question across the table. I did hesitate, and with the consciousness of doing so came back a little of the agitation I had left behind me, or below me, during the day. I wasn't ashamed of my scruple, however: it was only a fine discretion. What I vaguely felt was that a public inquiry wouldn't have been fair. Lord Mellifont was there, of course, to mitigate with his perfect manner all consequences; but I think it was present to me that with these particular elements his lordship would not be at home. The moment we got up, therefore, I approached Mrs. Adney, asking her whether, as the evening was lovely, she wouldn't take a turn with me outside.

"You've walked a hundred miles; had you not better be quiet?" she replied.

"I'd walk a hundred miles more to get you to tell me something."

She looked at me an instant, with a little of the queerness that I had sought, but had not found, in Clare Vawdrey's eyes. "Do you mean what became of Lord Mellifont?"

"Of Lord Mellifont?" With my new speculation I had lost that thread.

"Where's your memory, foolish man? We talked of it last evening."

"Ah, yes!" I cried, recalling; "we shall have lots to discuss." I drew her out to the terrace, and before we had gone three steps I said to her: "Who was with you here last night?"

"Last night?" she repeated, as wide of the mark as I had been.

"At ten o'clock—just after our company broke up. You came out here with a gentleman; you talked about the stars."

She stared a moment; then she gave her laugh. "Are you jealous of dear Vawdrey?"

"Then it was he?"

"Certainly it was."

"And how long did he stay?"

"You have it badly. He stayed about a quarter of an hour—perhaps rather more. We walked some distance; he talked about his play. There you have it all; that is the only witchcraft I have used."

"And what did Vawdrey do afterwards?"

"I haven't the least idea. I left him and went to bed."

"At what time did you go to bed?"

"At what time did you? I happen to remember that I parted from Mr. Vawdrey at ten twenty-five," said Mrs. Adney. "I came back into the salon to pick up a book, and I noticed the clock."

"In other words you and Vawdrey distinctly lingered here from about five minutes past ten till the hour you mention?"

"I don't know how distinct we were, but we were very jolly. *Où voulez-vous en venir*?" Blanche Adney asked.

"Simply to this, dear lady: that at the time your companion was occupied in the manner you describe, he was also engaged in literary composition in his own room."

She stopped short at this, and her eyes had an expression in the darkness. She wanted to know if I challenged her veracity; and I replied that, on the contrary, I backed it up—it made the case so interesting. She returned that this would only be if she should back up mine; which, however, I had no difficulty in persuading her to do, after I had related to her circumstantially the incident of my quest of the manuscript—the manuscript which, at the time, for a reason I could now understand, appeared to have passed so completely out of her own head.

"His talk made me forget it—I forgot I sent you for it. He made up for his fiasco in the salon: he declaimed me the scene," said my companion. She had dropped on a bench to listen to me and, as we sat there, had briefly cross-examined me. Then she broke out into fresh laughter "Oh, the eccentricities of genius!"

"They seem greater even than I supposed."

"Oh, the mysteries of greatness!"

"You ought to know all about them, but they take me by surprise."

"Are you absolutely certain it was Mr. Vawdrey?" my companion asked.

"If it wasn't he, who in the world was it? That a strange gentleman, looking exactly like him, should be sitting in his room at that hour of the night and writing at his table *in the dark*," I insisted, "would be practically as wonderful as my own contention."

"Yes, why in the dark?" mused Mrs. Adney.

"Cats can see in the dark," I said.

She smiled at me dimly. "Did it look like a cat?"

"No, dear lady, but I'll tell you what it did look like—it looked like the author of Vawdrey's admirable works. It looked infinitely more like him than our friend does himself," I declared.

"Do you mean it was somebody he gets to do them?"

"Yes, while he dines out and disappoints you."

"Disappoints me?" murmured Mrs. Adney artlessly.

"Disappoints *me*—disappoints every one who looks in him for the genius that created the pages they adore. Where is it in his talk?"

"Ah, last night he was splendid," said the actress.

"He's always splendid, as your morning bath is splendid, or a sirloin of beef, or the railway service to Brighton. But he's never rare."

"I see what you mean."

"That's what makes you such a comfort to talk to. I've often wondered—now I know. There are two of them."

"What a delightful idea!"

"One goes out, the other stays at home. One is the genius, the other's the bourgeois, and it's only the bourgeois whom we personally know. He talks, he circulates, he's awfully popular, he flirts with you—"

"Whereas it's the genius *you* are privileged to see!" Mrs. Adney broke in. "I'm much obliged to you for the distinction."

I laid my hand on her arm. "See him yourself. Try it, test it, go to his room."

"Go to his room? It wouldn't be proper!" she exclaimed, in the tone of her best comedy.

"Anything is proper in such an inquiry. If you see him, it settles it."

"How charming—to settle it!" She thought a moment, then she sprang up. "Do you mean *now*?"

"Whenever you like."

"But suppose I should find the wrong one?" said Blanche Adney, with an exquisite effect.

"The wrong one? Which one do you call the right?"

"The wrong one for a lady to go and see. Suppose I shouldn't find—the genius?"

"Oh, I'll look after the other," I replied. Then, as I had happened to glance about me, I added: "Take care—here comes Lord Mellifont."

"I wish you'd look after *him*," my interlocutress murmured.

"What's the matter with him?"

"That's just what I was going to tell you."

"Tell me now; he's not coming."

Blanche Adney looked a moment. Lord Mellifont, who appeared to have emerged from the hotel to smoke a meditative cigar, had paused, at a distance from us, and stood admiring the wonders of the prospect, discernible even in the dusk. We strolled slowly in another direction, and she presently said: "My idea is almost as droll as yours."

"I don't call mine droll: it's beautiful."

"There's nothing so beautiful as the droll," Mrs. Adney declared.

"You take a professional view. But I'm all ears." My curiosity was indeed alive again.

"Well then, my dear friend, if Clare Vawdrey is double (and I'm bound to say I think that the more of him the better), his lordship there has the opposite complaint: he isn't even whole."

We stopped once more, simultaneously. "I don't understand."

"No more do I. But I have a fancy that if there are two of Mr. Vawdrey, there isn't so much as one, all told, of Lord Mellifont."

I considered a moment, then I laughed out. "I think I see what you mean!"

"That's what makes *you* a comfort. Did you ever see him alone?"

I tried to remember. "Oh, yes; he has been to see me."

"Ah, then he wasn't alone."

"And I've been to see him, in his study."

"Did he know you were there?"

"Naturally—I was announced."

Blanche Adney glanced at me like a lovely conspirator. "You mustn't be announced!" With this she walked on.

I rejoined her, breathless. "Do you mean one must come upon him when he doesn't know it?"

"You must take him unawares. You must go to his room—that's what you must do."

If I was elated by the way our mystery opened out, I was also, pardonably, a little confused. "When I know he's not there?"

"When you know he *is*."

"And what shall I see?"

"You won't see anything!" Mrs. Adney cried as we turned round.

We had reached the end of the terrace, and our movement brought us face to face with Lord Mellifont, who, resuming his walk, had now, without indiscretion, overtaken us. The sight of him at that moment was illuminating, and it kindled a great backward train, connecting itself with one's general impression of the personage. As he stood there smiling at us and waving a practised hand into the transparent night (he introduced the view as if it had been a candidate and 'supported' the very Alps), as he rose before us in the delicate fragrance of his cigar and all his other delicacies and fragrances, with more perfections, somehow, heaped upon his handsome head than one had ever seen accumulated before, he struck me as so essentially, so conspicuously and uniformly the public character that I read in a flash the answer to Blanche Adney's riddle. He was all public and had no corresponding private life, just as Clare Vawdrey was all private and had no corresponding public one. I had heard only half my companion's story, yet as we joined Lord Mellifont (he had followed us—he liked Mrs. Adney; but it was always to be conceived of him that he accepted society rather than sought it), as we participated for half an hour in the distributed wealth of his conversation, I felt with unabashed duplicity that we had, as it were, found him out. I was even more deeply diverted by that whisk of the curtain to which the actress had just treated me than I had been by my own discovery; and if I was not ashamed of my share of her secret any more than of having divided my own with her (though my own was, of the two mysteries, the more glorious for the personage involved), this was because there was no cruelty in my advantage, but on the contrary an extreme tenderness and a positive compassion. Oh, he was safe with me, and I felt moreover rich and enlightened, as if I had suddenly put the universe into my pocket. I had learned what an affair of the spot and the moment a great appearance may be. It would doubtless be too much to say that I had always suspected the possibility, in the background of his lordship's being, of some such beautiful instance; but it is at least a fact that, patronising as it sounds, I had been conscious of a certain reserve of indulgence for him. I had secretly pitied him for the perfection of his performance, had wondered what blank face such a mask had to cover, what was left to him for the immitigable hours in which a man sits down with himself, or, more serious still, with that intenser self, his lawful wife. How was he at home and what did he do when he was alone? There was something in Lady Mellifont that gave a point to these researches—something that suggested that even to her he was still the public character and that she was haunted by similar questionings. She had never cleared them up: that was her eternal trouble. We therefore knew more than she did, Blanche Adney and I; but we wouldn't tell her for the world, nor would she probably thank us for doing so. She preferred the relative grandeur of uncertainty. She was not at home with him, so she couldn't say; and with her he was not alone, so he couldn't show her. He represented to his wife and he was a hero to his servants, and what one wanted to arrive at was what really became of him when no eye could see. He rested, presumably; but what form of rest could repair such a plenitude of presence? Lady Mellifont was too proud to pry, and as she had never looked through a keyhole she remained dignified and unassuaged.

It may have been a fancy of mine that Blanche Adney drew out our companion, or it may be that the practical irony of our relation to him at such a moment made me see him more vividly: at any rate he never had struck me as so dissimilar from what he would have been if we had not offered him a reflection of his image. We were only a concourse of two, but he had never been more public. His perfect manner had never been more perfect, his remarkable tact had never been more remarkable. I had a tacit sense that it would all be in the morning papers, with a leader, and also a secretly exhilarating one that I knew something that wouldn't be, that never could be, though any enterprising journal would give one a fortune for it. I must add, however, that in spite of my enjoyment—it was almost sensual, like that of a consummate dish—I was eager to be alone again with Mrs. Adney, who owed me an anecdote. It proved impossible, that evening, for some of the others came out to see what we found so absorbing; and then Lord Mellifont bespoke a little music from the fiddler, who produced his violin and played to us divinely, on our platform of echoes, face to face with the ghosts of the mountains. Before the concert was over I missed our actress and, glancing into the window of the salon, saw that she was established with Vawdrey, who was reading to her from a manuscript. The great scene had apparently been achieved and was doubtless the more interesting to Blanche from the new lights she had gathered about its author. I judged it discreet not to disturb them, and I went to bed without seeing her again. I looked out for her betimes the next morning and, as the promise of the day was fair, proposed to her that we should take to the hills, reminding her of the high obligation she had incurred. She recognised the obligation and gratified me with her company; but before we had strolled ten yards up the pass she broke out with intensity: "My dear friend, you've no idea how it works in me! I can think of nothing else."

"Than your theory about Lord Mellifont?"

"Oh, bother Lord Mellifont! I allude to yours about Mr. Vawdrey, who is much the more interesting person of the two. I'm fascinated by that vision of his—what-do-you-call-it?"

"His alternative identity?"

"His other self: that's easier to say."

"You accept it, then, you adopt it?"

"Adopt it? I rejoice in it! It became tremendously vivid to me last evening."

"While he read to you there?"

"Yes, as I listened to him, watched him. It simplified everything, explained everything."

"That's indeed the blessing of it. Is the scene very fine?"

"Magnificent, and he reads beautifully."

"Almost as well as the other one writes!" I laughed.

This made my companion stop a moment, laying her hand on my arm. "You utter my very impression. I felt that he was reading me the work of another man."

"What a service to the other man!"

"Such a totally different person," said Mrs. Adney. We talked of this difference as we went on, and of what a wealth it constituted, what a resource for life, such a duplication of character.

"It ought to make him live twice as long as other people," I observed.

"Ought to make which of them?"

"Well, both; for after all they're members of a firm, and one of them couldn't carry on the business without the other. Moreover mere survival would be dreadful for either."

Blanche Adney was silent a little; then she exclaimed: "I don't know—I wish he *would* survive!"

"May I, on my side, inquire which?"

"If you can't guess I won't tell you."

"I know the heart of woman. You always prefer the other."

She halted again, looking round her. "Off here, away from my husband, I *can* tell you. I'm in love with him!"

"Unhappy woman, he has no passions," I answered.

"That's exactly why I adore him. Doesn't a woman with my history know that the passions of others are insupportable? An actress, poor thing, can't care for any love that's not all on *her* side; she can't afford to be repaid. My marriage proves that: marriage is ruinous. Do you know what was in my mind last night, all the while Mr. Vawdrey was reading me those beautiful speeches? An insane desire to see the author." And dramatically, as if to hide her shame, Blanche Adney passed on.

"We'll manage that," I returned. "I want another glimpse of him myself. But meanwhile please remember that I've been waiting more than forty-eight hours for the evidence that supports your sketch, intensely suggestive and plausible, of Lord Mellifont's private life."

"Oh, Lord Mellifont doesn't interest me."

"He did yesterday," I said.

"Yes, but that was before I fell in love. You blotted him out with your story."

"You'll make me sorry I told it. Come," I pleaded, "if you don't let me know how your idea came into your head I shall imagine you simply made it up."

"Let me recollect then, while we wander in this grassy valley."

We stood at the entrance of a charming crooked gorge, a portion of whose level floor formed the bed of a stream that was smooth with swiftness. We turned into it, and the soft walk beside the clear torrent drew us on and on; till suddenly, as we continued and I waited for my companion to remember, a bend of the valley showed us Lady Mellifont coming toward us. She was alone, under the canopy of her parasol, drawing her sable train over the turf; and in this form, on the devious ways, she was a sufficiently rare apparition. She usually took a footman, who marched behind her on the highroads and whose livery was strange to the mountaineers. She blushed on seeing us, as if she ought somehow to justify herself; she laughed vaguely and said she had come out for a little early stroll. We stood together a moment, exchanging platitudes, and then she remarked that she had thought she might find her husband.

"Is he in this quarter?" I inquired.

"I supposed he would be. He came out an hour ago to sketch."

"Have you been looking for him?" Mrs. Adney asked.

"A little; not very much," said Lady Mellifont.

Each of the women rested her eyes with some intensity, as it seemed to me, on the eyes of the other.

"We'll look for him *for* you, if you like," said Mrs. Adney.

"Oh, it doesn't matter. I thought I'd join him."

"He won't make his sketch if you don't," my companion hinted.

"Perhaps he will if *you* do," said Lady Mellifont.

"Oh, I dare say he'll turn up," I interposed.

"He certainly will if he knows we're here!" Blanche Adney retorted.

"Will you wait while we search?" I asked of Lady Mellifont.

She repeated that it was of no consequence; upon which Mrs. Adney went on: "We'll go into the matter for our own pleasure."

"I wish you a pleasant expedition," said her ladyship, and was turning away when I sought to know if we should inform her husband that she had followed him. She hesitated a moment; then she jerked out oddly: "I think you had better not." With this she took leave of us, floating a little stiffly down the gorge.

My companion and I watched her retreat, then we exchanged a stare, while a light ghost of a laugh rippled from the actress's lips. "She might be walking in the shrubberies at Mellifont!"

"She suspects it, you know," I replied.

"And she doesn't want him to know it. There won't be any sketch."

"Unless we overtake him," I subjoined. "In that case we shall find him producing one, in the most graceful attitude, and the queer thing is that it will be brilliant."

"Let us leave him alone—he'll have to come home without it."

"He'd rather never come home. Oh, he'll find a public!"

"Perhaps he'll do it for the cows," Blanche Adney suggested; and as I was on the point of rebuking her profanity she went on: "That's simply what I happened to discover."

"What are you speaking of?"

"The incident of day before yesterday."

"Ah, let's have it at last!"

"That's all it was—that I was like Lady Mellifont: I couldn't find him."

"Did you lose him?"

"He lost *me*—that appears to be the way of it. He thought I was gone."

"But you did find him, since you came home with him."

"It was he who found *me*. That again is what must happen. He's there from the moment he knows somebody else is."

"I understand his intermissions," I said after a short reflection, "but I don't quite seize the law that governs them."

"Oh, it's a fine shade, but I caught it at that moment. I had started to come home. I was tired, and I had insisted on his not coming back with me. We had found some rare flowers—those I brought home—and it was he who had discovered almost all of them. It amused him very much, and I knew he wanted to get more; but I was weary and I quitted him. He let me go—where else would have been his tact?—and I was too stupid then to have guessed that from the moment I was not there no flower would be gathered. I started homeward, but at the end of three minutes I found I had brought away his penknife—he had lent it to me to trim a branch—and I knew he would need it. I turned back a few steps, to call him, but before I spoke I looked about for him. You can't understand what happened then without having the place before you."

"You must take me there," I said.

"We may see the wonder here. The place was simply one that offered no chance for concealment—a great gradual hillside, without obstructions or trees. There were some rocks below me, behind which I myself had disappeared, but from which on coming back I immediately emerged again."

"Then he must have seen you."

"He was too utterly gone, for some reason best known to himself. It was probably some moment of fatigue—he's getting on, you know, so that, with the sense of returning solitude, the reaction had been proportionately great, the extinction proportionately complete. At any rate the stage was as bare as your hand."

"Could he have been somewhere else?"

"He couldn't have been, in the time, anywhere but where I had left him. Yet the place was utterly empty—as empty as this stretch of valley before us. He had vanished—he had ceased to be. But as soon as my voice rang out (I uttered his name), he rose before me like the rising sun."

"And where did the sun rise?"

"Just where it ought to—just where he would have been and where I should have seen him had he been like other people."

I had listened with the deepest interest, but it was my duty to think of objections. "How long a time elapsed between the moment you perceived his absence and the moment you called?"

"Oh, only an instant. I don't pretend it was long."

"Long enough for you to be sure?" I said.

"Sure he wasn't there?"

"Yes, and that you were not mistaken, not the victim of some hocus-pocus of your eyesight."

"I may have been mistaken, but I don't believe it. At any rate, that's just why I want you to look in his room."

I thought a moment. "How *can* I, when even his wife doesn't dare to?"

"She *wants* to; propose it to her. It wouldn't take much to make her. She does suspect."

I thought another moment. "Did he seem to know?"

"That I had missed him? So it struck me, but he thought he had been quick enough."

"Did you speak of his disappearance?"

"Heaven forbid! It seemed to me too strange."

"Quite right. And how did he look?"

Trying to think it out again and reconstitute her miracle, Blanche Adney gazed abstractedly up the valley. Suddenly she exclaimed: "Just as he looks now!" and I saw Lord Mellifont stand before us with his sketch-block. I perceived, as we met him, that he looked neither suspicious nor blank: he looked simply, as he did always, everywhere, the principal feature of the scene. Naturally he had no sketch to show us, but nothing could better have rounded off our actual conception of him than the way he fell into position as we approached. He had been selecting his point of view; he took possession of it with a flourish of the pencil. He leaned against a rock; his beautiful little box of water-colours reposed on a natural table beside him, a ledge of the bank which showed how inveterately nature ministered to his convenience. He painted while he talked and he talked while he painted; and if the painting was as miscellaneous as the talk, the talk would equally have graced an album. We waited while the exhibition went on, and it seemed indeed as if the conscious profiles of the peaks were interested in his success. They grew as black as silhouettes in paper, sharp against a livid sky from which, however, there would be nothing to fear till Lord Mellifont's sketch should be finished. Blanche Adney communed with me dumbly, and I could read the language of her eyes: 'Oh, if we could only do it as well as that! He fills the stage in a way that beats us.' We could no more have left him than we could have quitted the theatre till the play was over; but in due time we turned round with him and strolled back to the inn, before the door of which his lordship, glancing again at his picture, tore the fresh leaf from the block and presented it with a few happy words to Mrs. Adney. Then he went into the house; and a moment later, looking up from where we stood, we saw him, above, at the window of his sitting-room (he had the best apartments), watching the signs of the weather.

"He'll have to rest after this," Blanche said, dropping her eyes on her water-colour.

"Indeed he will!" I raised mine to the window: Lord Mellifont had vanished. "He's already reabsorbed."

"Reabsorbed?" I could see the actress was now thinking of something else.

"Into the immensity of things. He has lapsed again; there's an *entr'acte*."

"It ought to be long." Mrs. Adney looked up and down the terrace, and at that moment the head-waiter appeared in the doorway. Suddenly she turned to this functionary with the question: "Have you seen Mr. Vawdrey lately?"

The man immediately approached. "He left the house five minutes ago—for a walk, I think. He went down the pass; he had a book."

I was watching the ominous clouds. "He had better have had an umbrella."

The waiter smiled. "I recommended him to take one."

"Thank you," said Mrs. Adney; and the Oberkellner withdrew. Then she went on, abruptly: "Will you do me a favour?"

"Yes, if you'll do me one. Let me see if your picture is signed."

She glanced at the sketch before giving it to me. "For a wonder it isn't."

"It ought to be, for full value. May I keep it awhile?"

"Yes, if you'll do what I ask. Take an umbrella and go after Mr. Vawdrey."

"To bring him to Mrs. Adney?"

"To keep him out—as long as you can."

"I'll keep him as long as the rain holds off."

"Oh, never mind the rain!" my companion exclaimed.

"Would you have us drenched?"

"Without remorse." Then with a strange light in her eyes she added: "I'm going to try."

"To try?"

"To see the real one. Oh, if I can get at him!" she broke out with passion.

"Try, try!" I replied. "I'll keep our friend all day."

"If I can get at the one who does it"—and she paused, with shining eyes—"if I can have it out with him I shall get my part!"

"I'll keep Vawdrey for ever!" I called after her as she passed quickly into the house.

Her audacity was communicative, and I stood there in a glow of excitement. I looked at Lord Mellifont's water-colour and I looked at the gathering storm; I turned my eyes again to his lordship's windows and then I bent them on my watch. Vawdrey had so little the start of me that I should have time to overtake him—time even if I should take five minutes to go up to Lord Mellifont's sitting-room (where we had all been hospitably received), and say to him, as a messenger, that Mrs. Adney begged he would bestow upon his sketch the high consecration of his signature. As I again considered this work of art I perceived there was something it certainly did lack: what else then but so noble an autograph? It was my duty to supply the deficiency without delay, and in accordance with this conviction I instantly re-entered the hotel. I went up to Lord Mellifont's apartments; I reached the door of his salon. Here, however, I was met by a difficulty of which my extravagance had not taken account. If I were to knock I should spoil everything; yet was I prepared to dispense with this ceremony? I asked myself the question, and it embarrassed me; I turned my little picture round and round, but it didn't give me the answer I wanted. I wanted it to say: 'Open the door gently, gently, without a sound, yet very quickly: then you will see what you will see.' I had gone so far as to lay my hand upon the knob when I became aware (having my wits so about me), that exactly in the manner I was thinking of—gently, gently, without a sound—another door had moved, on the opposite side of the hall. At the same instant I found myself smiling rather constrainedly upon Lady Mellifont, who, on seeing me, had checked herself on the threshold of her room. For a moment, as she stood there, we exchanged two or three ideas that were the more singular for being unspoken. We had caught each other hovering, and we understood each other; but as I stepped over to her (so that we were separated from the sitting-room by the width of the hall), her lips formed the almost soundless entreaty: "Don't!" I could see in her conscious eyes everything that the word expressed—the confession of her own curiosity and the dread of the consequences of mine. "*Don't!*" she repeated, as I stood before her. From the moment my experiment could strike her as an act of violence I was ready to renounce it; yet I thought I detected in her frightened face a still deeper betrayal—a possibility of disappointment if I should give way. It was as if she had said: "I'll let you do it if you'll take the responsibility. Yes, with some one else I'd surprise him. But it would never do for him to think it was I."

"We soon found Lord Mellifont," I observed, in allusion to our encounter with her an hour before, "and he was so good as to give this lovely sketch to Mrs. Adney, who has asked me to come up and beg him to put in the omitted signature."

Lady Mellifont took the drawing from me, and I could guess the struggle that went on in her while she looked at it. She was silent for some time; then I felt that all her delicacies and dignities, all her old timidities and pieties were fighting against her opportunity. She turned away from me and, with the drawing, went back to her room. She was absent for a couple of minutes, and when she reappeared I could see that she had vanquished her temptation; that even, with a kind of resurgent horror, she had shrunk from it. She had deposited the sketch in the room. "If you will kindly leave the picture with me, I will see that Mrs. Adney's request is attended to," she said, with great courtesy and sweetness, but in a manner that put an end to our colloquy.

I assented, with a somewhat artificial enthusiasm perhaps, and then, to ease off our separation, remarked that we were going to have a change of weather.

"In that case we shall go—we shall go immediately," said Lady Mellifont. I was amused at the eagerness with which she made this declaration: it appeared to represent a coveted flight into safety, an escape with her threatened secret. I was the more surprised therefore when, as I was turning away, she put out her hand to take mine. She had the pretext of bidding me farewell, but as I shook hands with her on this supposition I felt that what the movement really conveyed was: 'I thank you for the help you would have given me, but it's better as it is. If I should know, who would help me then?' As I went to my room to get my umbrella I said to myself: "She's sure, but she won't put it to the proof."

A quarter of an hour later I had overtaken Clare Vawdrey in the pass, and shortly after this we found ourselves looking for refuge. The storm had not only completely gathered, but it had broken at the last with extraordinary rapidity. We scrambled up a hillside to an empty cabin, a rough structure that was hardly more than a shed for the protection of cattle. It was a tolerable shelter however, and it had fissures through which we could watch the splendid spectacle of the tempest. This entertainment lasted an hour—an hour that has remained with me as full of odd disparities. While the lightning played with the thunder and the rain gushed in on our umbrellas, I said to myself that Clare Vawdrey was disappointing. I don't know exactly what I should have predicated of a great author exposed to the fury of the elements, I can't say what particular Manfred attitude I should have expected my companion to assume, but it seemed to me somehow that I shouldn't have looked to him to regale me in such a situation with stories (which I had already heard), about the celebrated Lady Ringrose. Her ladyship formed the subject of Vawdrey's conversation during this prodigious scene, though before it was quite over he had launched out on Mr. Chafer, the scarcely less notorious reviewer. It broke my heart to hear a man like Vawdrey talk of reviewers. The lightning projected a hard clearness upon the truth, familiar to me for years, to which the last day or two had added transcendent support—the irritating certitude that for personal relations this admirable genius thought his second-best good enough. It was, no doubt, as society was made, but there was a contempt in the distinction which could not fail to be galling to an admirer. The world was vulgar and stupid, and the real man would have been a fool to come out for it when he could gossip and dine by deputy. None the less my heart sank as I felt my companion practice this economy. I don't know exactly what I wanted; I suppose I wanted him to make an exception for *me*. I almost believed he would, if he had known how I worshipped his talent. But I had never been able to translate this to him, and his application of his principle was relentless. At any rate I was more than ever sure that at such an hour his chair at home was not empty: *there* was the Manfred attitude, *there* were the responsive flashes. I could only envy Mrs. Adney her presumable enjoyment of them.

The weather drew off at last, and the rain abated sufficiently to allow us to emerge from our asylum and make our way back to the inn, where we found on our arrival that our prolonged absence had produced some agitation. It was judged apparently that the fury of the elements might have placed us in a predicament. Several of our friends were at the door, and they seemed a little disconcerted when it was perceived that we were only drenched. Clare Vawdrey, for some reason, was wetter than I, and he took his course to his room. Blanche Adney was among the persons collected to look out for us, but as Vawdrey came toward her she shrank from him, without a greeting; with a movement that I observed as almost one of estrangement she turned her back on him and went quickly into the salon. Wet as I was I went in after her; on which she immediately flung round and faced me. The first thing I saw was that she had never been so beautiful. There was a light of inspiration in her face, and she broke out to me in the quickest whisper, which was at the same time the loudest cry, I have ever heard: "I've got my *part!*"

"You went to his room—I was right?"

"Right?" Blanche Adney repeated. "Ah, my dear fellow!" she murmured.

"He was there—you saw him?"

"He saw me. It was the hour of my life!"

"It must have been the hour of his, if you were half as lovely as you are at this moment."

"He's splendid," she pursued, as if she didn't hear me. "He *is* the one who does it!" I listened, immensely impressed, and she added: "We understood each other."

"By flashes of lightning?"

"Oh, I didn't see the lightning then!"

"How long were you there?" I asked with admiration.

"Long enough to tell him I adore him."

"Ah, that's what I've never been able to tell him!" I exclaimed ruefully.

"I shall have my part—I shall have my part!" she continued, with triumphant indifference; and she flung round the room with the joy of a girl, only checking herself to say: "Go and change your clothes."

"You shall have Lord Mellifont's signature," I said.

"Oh, bother Lord Mellifont's signature! He's far nicer than Mr. Vawdrey," she went on irrelevantly.

"Lord Mellifont?" I pretended to inquire.

"Confound Lord Mellifont!" And Blanche Adney, in her elation, brushed by me, whisking again through the open door. Just outside of it she came upon her husband; whereupon, with a charming cry of "We're talking of you, my love!" she threw herself upon him and kissed him.

I went to my room and changed my clothes, but I remained there till the evening. The violence of the storm had passed over us, but the rain had settled down to a drizzle. On descending to dinner I found that the change in the weather had already broken up our party. The Mellifonts had departed in a carriage and four, they had been followed by others, and several vehicles had been bespoken for the morning. Blanche Adney's was one of them, and on the pretext that she had preparations to make she quitted us directly after dinner. Clare Vawdrey asked me what was the matter with her—she suddenly appeared to dislike him. I forget what answer I gave, but I did my best to comfort him by driving away with him the next day. Mrs. Adney had vanished when we came down; but they made up their quarrel in London, for he finished his play, which she produced. I must add that she is still, nevertheless, in want of the great part. I have a beautiful one in my head, but she doesn't come to see me to stir me up about it. Lady Mellifont always drops me a kind word when we meet, but that doesn't console me.

THE TURN OF THE SCREW

The story had held us, round the fire, sufficiently breathless, but except the obvious remark that it was gruesome, as, on Christmas Eve in an old house, a strange tale should essentially be, I remember no comment uttered till somebody happened to say that it was the only case he had met in which such a visitation had fallen on a child. The case, I may mention, was that of an apparition in just such an old house as had gathered us for the occasion—an appearance, of a dreadful kind, to a little boy sleeping in the room with his mother and waking her up in the terror of it; waking her not to dissipate his dread and soothe him to sleep again, but to encounter also, herself, before she had succeeded in doing so, the same sight that had shaken him. It was this observation that drew from Douglas—not immediately, but later in the evening—a reply that had the interesting consequence to which I call attention. Someone else told a story not particularly effective, which I saw he was not following. This I took for a sign that he had himself something to produce and that we should only have to wait. We waited in fact till two nights later; but that same evening, before we scattered, he brought out what was in his mind.

"I quite agree—in regard to Griffin's ghost, or whatever it was—that its appearing first to the little boy, at so tender an age, adds a particular touch. But it's not the first occurrence of its charming kind that I know to have involved a child. If the child gives the effect another turn of the screw, what do you say to *two* children—?"

"We say, of course," somebody exclaimed, "that they give two turns! Also that we want to hear about them."

I can see Douglas there before the fire, to which he had got up to present his back, looking down at his interlocutor with his hands in his pockets. "Nobody but me, till now, has ever heard. It's quite too horrible." This, naturally, was declared by several voices to give the thing the utmost price, and our friend, with quiet art, prepared his triumph by turning his eyes over the rest of us and going on: "It's beyond everything. Nothing at all that I know touches it."

"For sheer terror?" I remember asking.

He seemed to say it was not so simple as that; to be really at a loss how to qualify it. He passed his hand over his eyes, made a little wincing grimace. "For dreadful—dreadfulness!"

"Oh, how delicious!" cried one of the women.

He took no notice of her; he looked at me, but as if, instead of me, he saw what he spoke of. "For general uncanny ugliness and horror and pain."

"Well then," I said, "just sit right down and begin."

He turned round to the fire, gave a kick to a log, watched it an instant. Then as he faced us again: "I can't begin. I shall have to send to town." There was a unanimous groan at this, and much reproach; after which, in his preoccupied way, he explained. "The story's written. It's in a locked drawer—it has not been out for years. I could write to my man and enclose the key; he could send down the packet as he finds it." It was to me in particular that he appeared to propound this—appeared almost to appeal for aid not to hesitate. He had broken a thickness of ice, the formation of many a winter; had had his reasons for a long silence. The others resented postponement, but it was just his scruples that charmed me. I adjured him to write by the first post and to agree with us for an early hearing; then I asked him if the experience in question had been his own. To this his answer was prompt. "Oh, thank God, no!"

"And is the record yours? You took the thing down?"

"Nothing but the impression. I took that *here*"—he tapped his heart. "I've never lost it."

"Then your manuscript—?"

"Is in old, faded ink, and in the most beautiful hand." He hung fire again. "A woman's. She has been dead these twenty years. She sent me the pages in question before she died." They were all listening now, and of course there was somebody to be arch, or at any rate to draw the inference. But if he put the inference by without a smile it was also without irritation. "She was a most charming person, but she was ten years older than I. She was my sister's governess," he quietly said. "She was the most agreeable woman I've ever known in her position; she would have been worthy of any whatever. It was long ago, and this episode was long before. I was at Trinity, and I found her at home on my coming down the second summer. I was much there that year—it was a beautiful one; and we had, in her off-hours, some strolls and talks in the garden—talks in which she struck me as awfully clever and nice. Oh yes; don't grin: I liked her extremely and am glad to this day to think she liked me, too. If she hadn't she wouldn't have told me. She had never told anyone. It wasn't simply that she said so, but that I knew she hadn't. I was sure; I could see. You'll easily judge why when you hear."

"Because the thing had been such a scare?"

He continued to fix me. "You'll easily judge," he repeated: "*you* will."

I fixed him, too. "I see. She was in love."

He laughed for the first time. "You *are* acute. Yes, she was in love. That is, she had been. That came out—she couldn't tell her story without its coming out. I saw it, and she saw I saw it; but neither of us spoke of it. I remember the time and the place—the corner of the lawn, the shade of the great beeches and the long, hot summer afternoon. It wasn't a scene for a shudder; but oh—!" He quitted the fire and dropped back into his chair.

"You'll receive the packet Thursday morning?" I inquired.

"Probably not till the second post."

"Well then; after dinner—"

"You'll all meet me here?" He looked us round again. "Isn't anybody going?" It was almost the tone of hope.

"Everybody will stay!"

"I will"—and "I will!" cried the ladies whose departure had been fixed. Mrs. Griffin, however, expressed the need for a little more light. "Who was it she was in love with?"

"The story will tell," I took upon myself to reply.

"Oh, I can't wait for the story!"

"The story *won't* tell," said Douglas; "not in any literal, vulgar way."

"More's the pity, then. That's the only way I ever understand."

"Won't *you* tell, Douglas?" somebody else inquired.

He sprang to his feet again. "Yes—tomorrow. Now I must go to bed. Good night." And quickly catching up a candlestick, he left us slightly bewildered. From our end of the great brown hall we heard his step on the stair; whereupon Mrs. Griffin spoke. "Well, if I don't know who she was in love with, I know who *he* was."

"She was ten years older," said her husband.

"*Raison de plus*—at that age! But it's rather nice, his long reticence."

"Forty years!" Griffin put in.

"With this outbreak at last."

"The outbreak," I returned, "will make a tremendous occasion of Thursday night;" and everyone so agreed with me that, in the light of it, we lost all attention for everything else. The last story, however incomplete and like the mere opening of a serial, had been told; we handshook and "candlestuck," as somebody said, and went to bed.

I knew the next day that a letter containing the key had, by the first post, gone off to his London apartments; but in spite of—or perhaps just on account of—the eventual diffusion of this knowledge we quite let him alone till after dinner, till such an hour of the evening, in fact, as might best accord with the kind of emotion on which our hopes were fixed. Then he became as communicative as we could desire and indeed gave us his best reason for being so. We had it from him again before the fire in the hall, as we had had our mild wonders of the previous night. It appeared that the narrative he had promised to read us really required for a proper intelligence a few words of prologue. Let me say here distinctly, to have done with it, that this narrative, from an exact transcript of my own made much later, is what I shall presently give. Poor Douglas, before his death—when it was in sight—committed to me the manuscript that reached him on the third of these days and that, on the same spot, with immense effect, he began to read to our hushed little circle on the night of the fourth. The departing ladies who had said they would stay didn't, of course, thank heaven, stay: they departed, in consequence of arrangements made, in a rage of curiosity, as they professed, produced by the touches with which he had already worked us up. But that only made his little final auditory more compact and select, kept it, round the hearth, subject to a common thrill.

The first of these touches conveyed that the written statement took up the tale at a point after it had, in a manner, begun. The fact to be in possession of was therefore that his old friend, the youngest of several daughters of a poor country parson, had, at the age of twenty, on taking service for the first time in the schoolroom, come up to London, in trepidation, to answer in person an advertisement that had already placed her in brief correspondence with the advertiser. This person proved, on her presenting herself, for judgment, at a house in Harley Street, that impressed her as vast and imposing—this prospective patron proved a gentleman, a bachelor in the prime of life, such a figure as had never risen, save in a dream or an old novel, before a fluttered, anxious girl out of a Hampshire vicarage. One could easily fix his type; it never, happily, dies out. He was handsome and bold and pleasant, offhand and gay and kind. He struck her, inevitably, as gallant and splendid, but what took her most of all and gave her the courage she afterward showed was that he put the whole thing to her as a kind of favor, an obligation he should gratefully incur. She conceived him as rich, but as fearfully extravagant—saw him all in a glow of high fashion, of good looks, of expensive habits, of charming ways with women. He had for his own town residence a big house filled with the spoils of travel and the trophies of the chase; but it was to his country home, an old family place in Essex, that he wished her immediately to proceed.

He had been left, by the death of their parents in India, guardian to a small nephew and a small niece, children of a younger, a military brother, whom he had lost two years before. These children were, by the strangest of chances for a man in his position—a lone man without the right sort of experience or a grain of patience—very heavily on his hands. It had all been a great worry and, on his own part doubtless, a series of blunders, but he immensely pitied the poor chicks and had done all he could; had in particular sent them down to his other house, the proper place for them being of course the country, and kept them there, from the first, with the best people he could find to look after them, parting even with his own servants to wait on them and going down himself, whenever he might, to see how they were doing. The awkward thing was that they had practically no other relations and that his own affairs took up all his time. He had put them in possession of Bly, which was healthy and secure, and had placed at the head of their little establishment—but below stairs only—an excellent woman, Mrs. Grose, whom he was sure his visitor would like and who had formerly been maid to his mother. She was now housekeeper and was also acting for the time as superintendent to the little girl, of whom, without children of her own, she was, by good luck, extremely fond. There were plenty of people to help, but of course the young lady who should go down as governess would be in supreme authority. She would also have, in holidays, to look after the small boy, who had been for a term at school—young as he was to be sent, but what else could be done?—and who, as the holidays were about to begin, would be back from one day to the other. There had been for the two children at first a young lady whom they had had the misfortune to lose. She had done for them quite beautifully—she was a most respectable person—till her death, the great awkwardness of which had, precisely, left no alternative but the school for little Miles. Mrs. Grose, since then, in the way of manners and things, had done as she could for Flora; and there were, further, a cook, a housemaid, a dairywoman, an old pony, an old groom, and an old gardener, all likewise thoroughly respectable.

So far had Douglas presented his picture when someone put a question. "And what did the former governess die of?—of so much respectability?"

Our friend's answer was prompt. "That will come out. I don't anticipate."

"Excuse me—I thought that was just what you *are* doing."

"In her successor's place," I suggested, "I should have wished to learn if the office brought with it—"

"Necessary danger to life?" Douglas completed my thought. "She did wish to learn, and she did learn. You shall hear tomorrow what she learned. Meanwhile, of course, the prospect struck her as slightly grim. She was young, untried, nervous: it was a vision of serious duties and little company, of really great loneliness. She hesitated—took a couple of days to consult and consider. But the salary offered much exceeded her modest measure, and on a second interview she faced the music, she engaged." And Douglas, with this, made a pause that, for the benefit of the company, moved me to throw in—

"The moral of which was of course the seduction exercised by the splendid young man. She succumbed to it."

He got up and, as he had done the night before, went to the fire, gave a stir to a log with his foot, then stood a moment with his back to us. "She saw him only twice."

"Yes, but that's just the beauty of her passion."

A little to my surprise, on this, Douglas turned round to me. "It *was* the beauty of it. There were others," he went on, "who hadn't succumbed. He told her frankly all his difficulty—that for several applicants the conditions had been prohibitive. They were, somehow, simply afraid. It sounded dull—it sounded strange; and all the more so because of his main condition."

"Which was—?"

"That she should never trouble him—but never, never: neither appeal nor complain nor write about anything; only meet all questions herself, receive all moneys from his solicitor, take the whole thing over and let him alone. She promised to do this, and she mentioned to me that when, for a moment, disburdened, delighted, he held her hand, thanking her for the sacrifice, she already felt rewarded."

"But was that all her reward?" one of the ladies asked.

"She never saw him again."

"Oh!" said the lady; which, as our friend immediately left us again, was the only other word of importance contributed to the subject till, the next night, by the corner of the hearth, in the best chair, he opened the faded red cover of a thin old-fashioned gilt-edged album. The whole thing took indeed more nights than one, but on the first occasion the same lady put another question. "What is your title?"

"I haven't one."

"Oh, *I* have!" I said. But Douglas, without heeding me, had begun to read with a fine clearness that was like a rendering to the ear of the beauty of his author's hand.

I

I remember the whole beginning as a succession of flights and drops, a little seesaw of the right throbs and the wrong. After rising, in town, to meet his appeal, I had at all events a couple of very bad days—found myself doubtful again, felt indeed sure I had made a mistake. In this state of mind I spent the long hours of bumping, swinging coach that carried me to the stopping place at which I was to be met by a vehicle from the house. This convenience, I was told, had been ordered, and I found, toward the close of the June afternoon, a commodious fly in waiting for me. Driving at that hour, on a lovely day, through a country to which the summer sweetness seemed to offer me a friendly welcome, my fortitude mounted afresh and, as we turned into the avenue, encountered a reprieve that was probably but a proof of the point to which it had sunk. I suppose I had expected, or had dreaded, something so melancholy that what greeted me was a good surprise. I remember as a most pleasant impression the broad, clear front, its open windows and fresh curtains and the pair of maids looking out; I remember the lawn and the bright flowers and the crunch of my wheels on the gravel and the clustered treetops over which the rooks circled and cawed in the golden sky. The scene had a greatness that made it a different affair from my own scant home, and there immediately appeared at the door, with a little girl in her hand, a civil person who dropped me as decent a curtsy as if I had been the mistress or a distinguished visitor. I had received in Harley Street a narrower notion of the place, and that, as I recalled it, made me think the proprietor still more of a gentleman, suggested that what I was to enjoy might be something beyond his promise.

I had no drop again till the next day, for I was carried triumphantly through the following hours by my introduction to the younger of my pupils. The little girl who accompanied Mrs. Grose appeared to me on the spot a creature so charming as to make it a great fortune to have to do with her. She was the most beautiful child I had ever seen, and I afterward wondered that my employer had not told me more of her. I slept little that night—I was too much excited; and this astonished me, too, I recollect, remained with me, adding to my sense of the liberality with which I was treated. The large, impressive room, one of the best in the house, the great state bed, as I almost felt it, the full, figured draperies, the long glasses in which, for the first time, I could see myself from head to foot, all struck me—like the extraordinary charm of my small charge—as so many things thrown in. It was thrown in as well, from the first moment, that I should get on with Mrs. Grose in a relation over which, on my way, in the coach, I fear I had rather brooded. The only thing indeed that in this early outlook might have made me shrink again was the clear circumstance of her being so glad to see me. I perceived within half an hour that she was so glad—stout, simple, plain, clean, wholesome woman—as to be positively on her guard against showing it too much. I wondered even then a little why she should wish not to show it, and that, with reflection, with suspicion, might of course have made me uneasy.

But it was a comfort that there could be no uneasiness in a connection with anything so beatific as the radiant image of my little girl, the vision of whose angelic beauty had probably more than anything else to do with the restlessness that, before morning, made me several times rise and wander about my room to take in the whole picture and prospect; to watch, from my open window, the faint summer dawn, to look at such portions of the rest of the house as I could catch, and to listen, while, in the fading dusk, the first birds began to twitter, for the possible recurrence of a sound or two, less natural and not without, but within, that I had fancied I heard. There had been a moment when I believed I recognized, faint and far, the cry of a child; there had been another when I found myself just consciously starting as at the passage, before my door, of a light footstep. But these fancies were not marked enough not to be thrown off, and it is only in the light, or the gloom, I should rather say, of other and subsequent matters that they now come back to me. To watch, teach, "form" little Flora would too evidently be the making of a happy and useful life. It had been agreed between us downstairs that after this first occasion I should have her as a matter of course at night, her small white bed being already arranged, to that end, in my room. What I had undertaken was the whole care of her, and she had remained, just this last time, with Mrs. Grose only as an effect of our consideration for my inevitable strangeness and her natural timidity. In spite of this timidity—which the child herself, in the oddest way in the world, had been perfectly frank and brave about, allowing it, without a sign of uncomfortable consciousness, with the deep, sweet serenity indeed of one of Raphael's holy infants, to be discussed, to be imputed to her, and to determine us—I feel quite sure she would presently like me. It was part of what I already liked Mrs. Grose herself for, the pleasure I could see her feel in my admiration and wonder as I sat at supper with four tall candles and with my pupil, in a high chair and a bib, brightly facing me, between them, over bread and milk. There were naturally things that in Flora's presence could pass between us only as prodigious and gratified looks, obscure and roundabout allusions.

"And the little boy—does he look like her? Is he too so very remarkable?"

One wouldn't flatter a child. "Oh, miss, *most* remarkable. If you think well of this one!"—and she stood there with a plate in her hand, beaming at our companion, who looked from one of us to the other with placid heavenly eyes that contained nothing to check us.

"Yes; if I do—?"

"You *will* be carried away by the little gentleman!"

"Well, that, I think, is what I came for—to be carried away. I'm afraid, however," I remember feeling the impulse to add, "I'm rather easily carried away. I was carried away in London!"

I can still see Mrs. Grose's broad face as she took this in. "In Harley Street?"

"In Harley Street."

"Well, miss, you're not the first—and you won't be the last."

"Oh, I've no pretension," I could laugh, "to being the only one. My other pupil, at any rate, as I understand, comes back tomorrow?"

"Not tomorrow—Friday, miss. He arrives, as you did, by the coach, under care of the guard, and is to be met by the same carriage."

I forthwith expressed that the proper as well as the pleasant and friendly thing would be therefore that on the arrival of the public conveyance I should be in waiting for him with his little sister; an idea in which Mrs. Grose concurred so heartily that I somehow took her manner as a kind of comforting pledge—never falsified, thank heaven!—that we should on every question be quite at one. Oh, she was glad I was there!

What I felt the next day was, I suppose, nothing that could be fairly called a reaction from the cheer of my arrival; it was probably at the most only a slight oppression produced by a fuller measure of the scale, as I walked round them, gazed up at them, took them in, of my new circumstances. They had, as it were, an extent and mass for which I had not been prepared and in the presence of which I found myself, freshly, a little scared as well as a little proud. Lessons, in this agitation, certainly suffered some delay; I reflected that my first duty was, by the gentlest arts I could contrive, to win the child into the sense of knowing me. I spent the day with her out-of-doors; I arranged with her, to her great satisfaction, that it should be she, she only, who might show me the place. She showed it step by step and room by room and secret by secret, with droll, delightful, childish talk about it and with the result, in half an hour, of our becoming immense friends. Young as she was, I was struck, throughout our little tour, with her confidence and courage with the way, in empty chambers and dull corridors, on crooked staircases that made me pause and even on the summit of an old machicolated square tower that made me dizzy, her morning music, her disposition to tell me so many more things than she asked, rang out and led me on. I have not seen Bly since the day I left it, and I daresay that to my older and more informed eyes it would now appear sufficiently contracted. But as my little conductress, with her hair of gold and her frock of blue, danced before me round corners and pattered down passages, I had the view of a castle of romance inhabited by a rosy sprite, such a place as would somehow, for diversion of the young idea, take all color out of storybooks and fairytales. Wasn't it just a storybook over which I had fallen adoze and adream? No; it was a big, ugly, antique, but convenient house, embodying a few features of a building still older, half-replaced and half-utilized, in which I had the fancy of our being almost as lost as a handful of passengers in a great drifting ship. Well, I was, strangely, at the helm!

II

This came home to me when, two days later, I drove over with Flora to meet, as Mrs. Grose said, the little gentleman; and all the more for an incident that, presenting itself the second evening, had deeply disconcerted me. The first day had been, on the whole, as I have expressed, reassuring; but I was to see it wind up in keen apprehension. The postbag, that evening—it came late—contained a letter for me, which, however, in the hand of my employer, I found to be composed but of a few words enclosing another, addressed to himself, with a seal still unbroken. "This, I recognize, is from the headmaster, and the headmaster's an awful bore. Read him, please; deal with him; but mind you don't report. Not a word. I'm off!" I broke the seal with a great effort—so great a one that I was a long time coming to it; took the unopened missive at last up to my room and only attacked it just before going to bed. I had better have let it wait till morning, for it gave me a second sleepless night. With no counsel to take, the next day, I was full of distress; and it finally got so the better of me that I determined to open myself at least to Mrs. Grose.

"What does it mean? The child's dismissed his school."

She gave me a look that I remarked at the moment; then, visibly, with a quick blankness, seemed to try to take it back. "But aren't they all—?"

"Sent home—yes. But only for the holidays. Miles may never go back at all."

Consciously, under my attention, she reddened. "They won't take him?"

"They absolutely decline."

At this she raised her eyes, which she had turned from me; I saw them fill with good tears. "What has he done?"

I hesitated; then I judged best simply to hand her my letter—which, however, had the effect of making her, without taking it, simply put her hands behind her. She shook her head sadly. "Such things are not for me, miss."

My counselor couldn't read! I winced at my mistake, which I attenuated as I could, and opened my letter again to repeat it to her; then, faltering in the act and folding it up once more, I put it back in my pocket. "Is he really *bad*?"

The tears were still in her eyes. "Do the gentlemen say so?"

"They go into no particulars. They simply express their regret that it should be impossible to keep him. That can have only one meaning." Mrs. Grose listened with dumb emotion; she forbore to ask me what this meaning might be; so that, presently, to put the thing with some coherence and with the mere aid of her presence to my own mind, I went on: "That he's an injury to the others."

At this, with one of the quick turns of simple folk, she suddenly flamed up. "Master Miles! *Him* an injury?"

There was such a flood of good faith in it that, though I had not yet seen the child, my very fears made me jump to the absurdity of the idea. I found myself, to meet my friend the better, offering it, on the spot, sarcastically. "To his poor little innocent mates!"

"It's too dreadful," cried Mrs. Grose, "to say such cruel things! Why, he's scarce ten years old."

"Yes, yes; it would be incredible."

She was evidently grateful for such a profession. "See him, miss, first. *Then* believe it!" I felt forthwith a new impatience to see him; it was the beginning of a curiosity that, for all the next hours, was to deepen almost to pain. Mrs. Grose was aware, I could judge, of what she had produced in me, and she followed it up with assurance. "You might as well believe it of the little lady. Bless her," she added the next moment—"*look* at her!"

I turned and saw that Flora, whom, ten minutes before, I had established in the schoolroom with a sheet of white paper, a pencil, and a copy of nice "round o's," now presented herself to view at the open door. She expressed in her little way an extraordinary detachment from disagreeable duties, looking to me, however, with a great childish light that seemed to offer it as a mere result of the affection she had conceived for my person, which had rendered necessary that she should follow me. I needed nothing more than this to feel the full force of Mrs. Grose's comparison, and, catching my pupil in my arms, covered her with kisses in which there was a sob of atonement.

Nonetheless, the rest of the day I watched for further occasion to approach my colleague, especially as, toward evening, I began to fancy she rather sought to avoid me. I overtook her, I remember, on the staircase; we went down together, and at the bottom I detained her, holding her there with a hand on her arm. "I take what you said to me at noon as a declaration that *you've* never known him to be bad."

She threw back her head; she had clearly, by this time, and very honestly, adopted an attitude. "Oh, never known him—I don't pretend *that*!"

I was upset again. "Then you *have* known him—?"

"Yes indeed, miss, thank God!"

On reflection I accepted this. "You mean that a boy who never is—?"

"Is no boy for *me*!"

I held her tighter. "You like them with the spirit to be naughty?" Then, keeping pace with her answer, "So do I!" I eagerly brought out. "But not to the degree to contaminate—"

"To contaminate?"—my big word left her at a loss. I explained it. "To corrupt."

She stared, taking my meaning in; but it produced in her an odd laugh. "Are you afraid he'll corrupt *you*?" She put the question with such a fine bold humor that, with a laugh, a little silly doubtless, to match her own, I gave way for the time to the apprehension of ridicule.

But the next day, as the hour for my drive approached, I cropped up in another place. "What was the lady who was here before?"

"The last governess? She was also young and pretty—almost as young and almost as pretty, miss, even as you."

"Ah, then, I hope her youth and her beauty helped her!" I recollect throwing off. "He seems to like us young and pretty!"

"Oh, he *did*," Mrs. Grose assented: "it was the way he liked everyone!" She had no sooner spoken indeed than she caught herself up. "I mean that's *his* way—the master's."

I was struck. "But of whom did you speak first?"

She looked blank, but she colored. "Why, of *him*."

"Of the master?"

"Of who else?"

There was so obviously no one else that the next moment I had lost my impression of her having accidentally said more than she meant; and I merely asked what I wanted to know. "Did *she* see anything in the boy—?"

"That wasn't right? She never told me."

I had a scruple, but I overcame it. "Was she careful—particular?"

Mrs. Grose appeared to try to be conscientious. "About some things—yes."

"But not about all?"

Again she considered. "Well, miss—she's gone. I won't tell tales."

"I quite understand your feeling," I hastened to reply; but I thought it, after an instant, not opposed to this concession to pursue: "Did she die here?"

"No—she went off."

I don't know what there was in this brevity of Mrs. Grose's that struck me as ambiguous. "Went off to die?" Mrs. Grose looked straight out of the window, but I felt that, hypothetically, I had a right to know what young persons engaged for Bly were expected to do. "She was taken ill, you mean, and went home?"

"She was not taken ill, so far as appeared, in this house. She left it, at the end of the year, to go home, as she said, for a short holiday, to which the time she had put in had certainly given her a right. We had then a young woman—a nursemaid who had stayed on and who was a good girl and clever; and *she* took the children altogether for the interval. But our young lady never came back, and at the very moment I was expecting her I heard from the master that she was dead."

I turned this over. "But of what?"

"He never told me! But please, miss," said Mrs. Grose, "I must get to my work."

III

Her thus turning her back on me was fortunately not, for my just preoccupations, a snub that could check the growth of our mutual esteem. We met, after I had brought home little Miles, more intimately than ever on the ground of my stupefaction, my general emotion: so monstrous was I then ready to pronounce it that such a child as had now been revealed to me should be under an interdict. I was a little late on the scene, and I felt, as he stood wistfully looking out for me before the door of the inn at which the coach had put him down, that I had seen him, on the instant, without and within, in the great glow of freshness, the same positive fragrance of purity, in which I had, from the first moment, seen his little sister. He was incredibly beautiful, and Mrs. Grose had put her finger on it: everything but a sort of passion of tenderness for him was swept away by his presence. What I then and there took him to my heart for was something divine that I have never found to the same degree in any child—his indescribable little air of knowing nothing in the world but love. It would have been impossible to carry a bad name with a greater sweetness of innocence, and by the time I had got back to Bly with him I remained merely bewildered—so far, that is, as I was not outraged—by the sense of the horrible letter locked up in my room, in a drawer. As soon as I could compass a private word with Mrs. Grose I declared to her that it was grotesque.

She promptly understood me. "You mean the cruel charge—?"

"It doesn't live an instant. My dear woman, *look* at him!"

She smiled at my pretention to have discovered his charm. "I assure you, miss, I do nothing else! What will you say, then?" she immediately added.

"In answer to the letter?" I had made up my mind. "Nothing."

"And to his uncle?"

I was incisive. "Nothing."

"And to the boy himself?"

I was wonderful. "Nothing."

She gave with her apron a great wipe to her mouth. "Then I'll stand by you. We'll see it out."

"We'll see it out!" I ardently echoed, giving her my hand to make it a vow.

She held me there a moment, then whisked up her apron again with her detached hand. "Would you mind, miss, if I used the freedom—"

"To kiss me? No!" I took the good creature in my arms and, after we had embraced like sisters, felt still more fortified and indignant.

This, at all events, was for the time: a time so full that, as I recall the way it went, it reminds me of all the art I now need to make it a little distinct. What I look back at with amazement is the situation I accepted. I had undertaken, with my companion, to see it out, and I was under a charm, apparently, that could smooth away the extent and the far and difficult connections of such an effort. I was lifted aloft on a great wave of infatuation and pity. I found it simple, in my ignorance, my confusion, and perhaps my conceit, to assume that I could deal with a boy whose education for the world was all on the point of beginning. I am unable even to remember at this day what proposal I framed for the end of his holidays and the resumption of his studies. Lessons with me, indeed, that charming summer, we all had a theory that he was to have; but I now feel that, for weeks, the lessons must have been rather my own. I learned something—at first, certainly—that had not been one of the teachings of my small, smothered life; learned to be amused, and even amusing, and not to think for the morrow. It was the first time, in a manner, that I had known space and air and freedom, all the music of summer and all the mystery of nature. And then there was consideration—and consideration was sweet. Oh, it was a trap—not designed, but deep—to my imagination, to my delicacy, perhaps to my vanity; to whatever, in me, was most excitable. The best way to picture it all is to say that I was off my guard. They gave me so little trouble—they were of a gentleness so extraordinary. I used to speculate—but even this with a dim disconnectedness—as to how the rough future (for all futures are rough!) would handle them and might bruise them. They had the bloom of health and happiness; and yet, as if I had been in charge of a pair of little grandees, of princes of the blood, for whom everything, to be right, would have to be enclosed and protected, the only form that, in my fancy, the afteryears could take for them was that of a romantic, a really royal extension of the garden and the park. It may be, of course, above all, that what suddenly broke into this gives the previous time a charm of stillness—that hush in which something gathers or crouches. The change was actually like the spring of a beast.

In the first weeks the days were long; they often, at their finest, gave me what I used to call my own hour, the hour when, for my pupils, teatime and bedtime having come and gone, I had, before my final retirement, a small interval alone. Much as I liked my companions, this hour was the thing in the day I liked most; and I liked it best of all when, as the light faded—or rather, I should say, the day lingered and the last calls of the last birds sounded, in a flushed sky, from the old trees—I could take a turn into the grounds and enjoy, almost with a sense of property that amused and flattered me, the beauty and dignity of the place. It was a pleasure at these moments to feel myself tranquil and justified; doubtless, perhaps, also to reflect that by my discretion, my quiet good sense and general high propriety, I was giving pleasure—if he ever thought of it!—to the person to whose pressure I had responded. What I was doing was what he had earnestly hoped and directly asked of me, and that I *could*, after all, do it proved even a greater joy than I had expected. I daresay I fancied myself, in short, a remarkable young woman and took comfort in the faith that this would more publicly appear. Well, I needed to be remarkable to offer a front to the remarkable things that presently gave their first sign.

It was plump, one afternoon, in the middle of my very hour: the children were tucked away, and I had come out for my stroll. One of the thoughts that, as I don't in the least shrink now from noting, used to be with me in these wanderings was that it would be as charming as a charming story suddenly to meet someone. Someone would appear there at the turn of a path and would stand before me and smile and approve. I didn't ask more than that—I only asked that he should *know*; and the only way to be sure he knew would be to see it, and the kind light of it, in his handsome face. That was exactly present to me—by which I mean the face was—when, on the first of these occasions, at the end of a long June day, I stopped short on emerging from one of the plantations and coming into view of the house. What arrested me on the spot—and with a shock much greater than any vision had allowed for—was the sense that my imagination had, in a flash, turned real. He did stand there!—but high up, beyond the lawn and at the very top of the tower to which, on that first morning, little Flora had conducted me. This tower was one of a pair—square, incongruous, crenelated structures—that were distinguished, for some reason, though I could see little difference, as the new and the old. They flanked opposite ends of the house and were probably architectural absurdities, redeemed in a measure indeed by not being wholly disengaged nor of a height too pretentious, dating, in their gingerbread antiquity, from a romantic revival that was already a respectable past. I admired them, had fancies about them, for we could all profit in a degree, especially when they loomed through the dusk, by the grandeur of their actual battlements; yet it was not at such an elevation that the figure I had so often invoked seemed most in place.

It produced in me, this figure, in the clear twilight, I remember, two distinct gasps of emotion, which were, sharply, the shock of my first and that of my second surprise. My second was a violent perception of the mistake of my first: the man who met my eyes was not the person I had precipitately supposed. There came to me thus a bewilderment of vision of which, after these years, there is no living view that I can hope to give. An unknown man in a lonely place is a permitted object of fear to a young woman privately bred; and the figure that faced me was—a few more seconds assured me—as little anyone else I knew as it was the image that had been in my mind. I had not seen it in Harley Street—I had not seen it anywhere. The place, moreover, in the strangest way in the world, had, on the instant, and by the very fact of its appearance, become a solitude. To me at least, making my statement here with a deliberation with which I have never made it, the whole feeling of the moment returns. It was as if, while I took in—what I did take in—all the rest of the scene had been stricken with death. I can hear again, as I write, the intense hush in which the sounds of evening dropped. The rooks stopped cawing in the golden sky, and the friendly hour lost, for the minute, all its voice. But there was no other change in nature, unless indeed it were a change that I saw with a stranger sharpness. The gold was still in the sky, the clearness in the air, and the man who looked at me over the battlements was as definite as a picture in a frame. That's how I thought, with extraordinary quickness, of each person that he might have been and that he was not. We were confronted across our distance quite long enough for me to ask myself with intensity who then he was and to feel, as an effect of my inability to say, a wonder that in a few instants more became intense.

The great question, or one of these, is, afterward, I know, with regard to certain matters, the question of how long they have lasted. Well, this matter of mine, think what you will of it, lasted while I caught at a dozen possibilities, none of which made a difference for the better, that I could see, in there having been in the house—and for how long, above all?—a person of whom I was in ignorance. It lasted while I just bridled a little with the sense that my office demanded that there should be no such ignorance and no such person. It lasted while this visitant, at all events—and there was a touch of the strange freedom, as I remember, in the sign of familiarity of his wearing no hat—seemed to fix me, from his position, with just the question, just the scrutiny through the fading light, that his own presence provoked. We were too far apart to call to each other, but there was a moment at which, at shorter range, some challenge between us, breaking the hush, would have been the right result of our straight mutual stare. He was in one of the angles, the one away from the house, very erect, as it struck me, and with both hands on the ledge. So I saw him as I see the letters I form on this page; then, exactly, after a minute, as if to add to the spectacle, he slowly changed his place—passed, looking at me hard all the while, to the opposite corner of the platform. Yes, I had the sharpest sense that during this transit he never took his eyes from me, and I can see at this moment the way his hand, as he went, passed from one of the crenelations to the next. He stopped at the other corner, but less long, and even as he turned away still markedly fixed me. He turned away; that was all I knew.

IV

It was not that I didn't wait, on this occasion, for more, for I was rooted as deeply as I was shaken. Was there a "secret" at Bly—a mystery of Udolpho or an insane, an unmentionable relative kept in unsuspected confinement? I can't say how long I turned it over, or how long, in a confusion of curiosity and dread, I remained where I had had my collision; I only recall that when I re-entered the house darkness had quite closed in. Agitation, in the interval, certainly had held me and driven me, for I must, in circling about the place, have walked three miles; but I was to be, later on, so much more overwhelmed that this mere dawn of alarm was a comparatively human chill. The most singular part of it, in fact—singular as the rest had been—was the part I became, in the hall, aware of in meeting Mrs. Grose. This picture comes back to me in the general train—the impression, as I received it on my return, of the wide white panelled space, bright in the lamplight and with its portraits and red carpet, and of the good surprised look of my friend, which immediately told me she had missed me. It came to me straightway, under her contact, that, with plain heartiness, mere relieved anxiety at my appearance, she knew nothing whatever that could bear upon the incident I had there ready for her. I had not suspected in advance that her comfortable face would pull me up, and I somehow measured the importance of what I had seen by my thus finding myself hesitate to mention it. Scarce anything in the whole history seems to me so odd as this fact that my real beginning of fear was one, as I may say, with the instinct of sparing my companion. On the spot, accordingly, in the pleasant hall and with her eyes on me, I, for a reason that I couldn't then have phrased, achieved an inward resolution—offered a vague pretext for my lateness and, with the plea of the beauty of the night and of the heavy dew and wet feet, went as soon as possible to my room.

Here it was another affair; here, for many days after, it was a queer affair enough. There were hours, from day to day—or at least there were moments, snatched even from clear duties—when I had to shut myself up to think. It was not so much yet that I was more nervous than I could bear to be as that I was remarkably afraid of becoming so; for the truth I had now to turn over was, simply and clearly, the truth that I could arrive at no account whatever of the visitor with whom I had been so inexplicably and yet, as it seemed to me, so intimately concerned. It took little time to see that I could sound without forms of inquiry and without exciting remark any domestic complications. The shock I had suffered must have sharpened all my senses; I felt sure, at the end of three days and as the result of mere closer attention, that I had not been practiced upon by the servants nor made the object of any "game." Of whatever it was that I knew, nothing was known around me. There was but one sane inference: someone had taken a liberty rather gross. That was what, repeatedly, I dipped into my room and locked the door to say to myself. We had been, collectively, subject to an intrusion; some unscrupulous traveler, curious in old houses, had made his way in unobserved, enjoyed the prospect from the best point of view, and then stolen out as he came. If he had given me such a bold hard stare, that was but a part of his indiscretion. The good thing, after all, was that we should surely see no more of him.

This was not so good a thing, I admit, as not to leave me to judge that what, essentially, made nothing else much signify was simply my charming work. My charming work was just my life with Miles and Flora, and through nothing could I so like it as through feeling that I could throw myself into it in trouble. The attraction of my small charges was a constant joy, leading me to wonder afresh at the vanity of my original fears, the distaste I had begun by entertaining for the probable gray prose of my office. There was to be no gray prose, it appeared, and no long grind; so how could work not be charming that presented itself as daily beauty? It was all the romance of the nursery and the poetry of the schoolroom. I don't mean by this, of course, that we studied only fiction and verse; I mean I can express no otherwise the sort of interest my companions inspired. How can I describe that except by saying that instead of growing used to them—and it's a marvel for a governess: I call the sisterhood to witness!—I made constant fresh discoveries. There was one direction, assuredly, in which these discoveries stopped: deep obscurity continued to cover the region of the boy's conduct at school. It had been promptly given me, I have noted, to face that mystery without a pang. Perhaps even it would be nearer the truth to say that—without a word—he himself had cleared it up. He had made the whole charge absurd. My conclusion bloomed there with the real rose flush of his innocence: he was only too fine and fair for the little horrid, unclean school world, and he had paid a price for it. I reflected acutely that the sense of such differences, such superiorities of quality, always, on the part of the majority—which could include even stupid, sordid headmasters—turn infallibly to the vindictive.

Both the children had a gentleness (it was their only fault, and it never made Miles a muff) that kept them—how shall I express it?—almost impersonal and certainly quite unpunishable. They were like the cherubs of the anecdote, who had—morally, at any rate—nothing to whack! I remember feeling with Miles in especial as if he had had, as it were, no history. We expect of a small child a scant one, but there was in this beautiful little boy something extraordinarily sensitive, yet extraordinarily happy, that, more than in any creature of his age I have seen, struck me as beginning anew each day. He had never for a second suffered. I took this as a direct disproof of his having really been chastised. If he had been wicked he would have "caught" it, and I should have caught it by the rebound—I should have found the trace. I found nothing at all, and he was therefore an angel. He never spoke of his school, never mentioned a comrade or a master; and I, for my part, was quite too much disgusted to allude to them. Of course I was under the spell, and the wonderful part is that, even at the time, I perfectly knew I was. But I gave myself up to it; it was an antidote to any pain, and I had more pains than one. I was in receipt in these days of disturbing letters from home, where things were not going well. But with my children, what things in the world mattered? That was the question I used to put to my scrappy retirements. I was dazzled by their loveliness.

There was a Sunday—to get on—when it rained with such force and for so many hours that there could be no procession to church; in consequence of which, as the day declined, I had arranged with Mrs. Grose that, should the evening show improvement, we would attend together the late service. The rain happily stopped, and I prepared for our walk, which, through the park and by the good road to the village, would be a matter of twenty minutes. Coming downstairs to meet my colleague in the hall, I remembered a pair of gloves that had required three stitches and that had received them—with a publicity perhaps not edifying—while I sat with the children at their tea, served on Sundays, by exception, in that cold, clean temple of mahogany and brass, the "grown-up" dining room. The gloves had been dropped there, and I turned in to recover them. The day was gray enough, but the afternoon light still lingered, and it enabled me, on crossing the threshold, not only to recognize, on a chair near the wide window, then closed, the articles I wanted, but to become aware of a person on the other side of the window and looking straight in. One step into the room had sufficed; my vision was instantaneous; it was all there. The person looking straight in was the person who had already appeared to me. He appeared thus again with I won't say greater distinctness, for that was impossible, but with a nearness that represented a forward stride in our intercourse and made me, as I met him, catch my breath and turn cold. He was the same—he was the same, and seen, this time, as he had been seen before, from the waist up, the window, though the dining room was on the ground floor, not going down to the terrace on which he stood. His face was close to the glass, yet the effect of this better view was, strangely, only to show me how intense the former had been. He remained but a few seconds—long enough to convince me he also saw and recognized; but it was as if I had been looking at him for years and had known him always. Something, however, happened this time that had not happened before; his stare into my face, through the glass and across the room, was as deep and hard as then, but it quitted me for a moment during which I could still watch it, see it fix successively several other things. On the spot there came to me the added shock of a certitude that it was not for me he had come there. He had come for someone else.

The flash of this knowledge—for it was knowledge in the midst of dread—produced in me the most extraordinary effect, started as I stood there, a sudden vibration of duty and courage. I say courage because I was beyond all doubt already far gone. I bounded straight out of the door again, reached that of the house, got, in an instant, upon the drive, and, passing along the terrace as fast as I could rush, turned a corner and came full in sight. But it was in sight of nothing now—my visitor had vanished. I stopped, I almost dropped, with the real relief of this; but I took in the whole scene—I gave him time to reappear. I call it time, but how long was it? I can't speak to the purpose today of the duration of these things. That kind of measure must have left me: they couldn't have lasted as they actually appeared to me to last. The terrace and the whole place, the lawn and the garden beyond it, all I could see of the park, were empty with a great emptiness. There were shrubberies and big trees, but I remember the clear assurance I felt that none of them concealed him. He was there or was not there: not there if I didn't see him. I got hold of this; then, instinctively, instead of returning as I had come, went to the window. It was confusedly present to me that I ought to place myself where he had stood. I did so; I applied my face to the pane and looked, as he had looked, into the room. As if, at this moment, to show me exactly what his range had been, Mrs. Grose, as I had done for himself just before, came in from the hall. With this I had the full image of a repetition of what had already occurred. She saw me as I had seen my own visitant; she pulled up short as I had done; I gave her something of the shock that I had received. She turned white, and this made me ask myself if I had blanched as much. She stared, in short, and retreated on just *my* lines, and I knew she had then passed out and come round to me and that I should presently meet her. I remained where I was, and while I waited I thought of more things than one. But there's only one I take space to mention. I wondered why *she* should be scared.

V

Oh, she let me know as soon as, round the corner of the house, she loomed again into view. "What in the name of goodness is the matter—?" She was now flushed and out of breath.

I said nothing till she came quite near. "With me?" I must have made a wonderful face. "Do I show it?"

"You're as white as a sheet. You look awful."

I considered; I could meet on this, without scruple, any innocence. My need to respect the bloom of Mrs. Grose's had dropped, without a rustle, from my shoulders, and if I wavered for the instant it was not with what I kept back. I put out my hand to her and she took it; I held her hard a little, liking to feel her close to me. There was a kind of support in the shy heave of her surprise. "You came for me for church, of course, but I can't go."

"Has anything happened?"

"Yes. You must know now. Did I look very queer?"

"Through this window? Dreadful!"

"Well," I said, "I've been frightened." Mrs. Grose's eyes expressed plainly that *she* had no wish to be, yet also that she knew too well her place not to be ready to share with me any marked inconvenience. Oh, it was quite settled that she *must* share! "Just what you saw from the dining room a minute ago was the effect of that. What *I* saw—just before—was much worse."

Her hand tightened. "What was it?"

"An extraordinary man. Looking in."

"What extraordinary man?"

"I haven't the least idea."

Mrs. Grose gazed round us in vain. "Then where is he gone?"

"I know still less."

"Have you seen him before?"

"Yes—once. On the old tower."

She could only look at me harder. "Do you mean he's a stranger?"

"Oh, very much!"

"Yet you didn't tell me?"

"No—for reasons. But now that you've guessed—"

Mrs. Grose's round eyes encountered this charge. "Ah, I haven't guessed!" she said very simply. "How can I if *you* don't imagine?"

"I don't in the very least."

"You've seen him nowhere but on the tower?"

"And on this spot just now."

Mrs. Grose looked round again. "What was he doing on the tower?"

"Only standing there and looking down at me."

She thought a minute. "Was he a gentleman?"

I found I had no need to think. "No." She gazed in deeper wonder. "No."

"Then nobody about the place? Nobody from the village?"

"Nobody—nobody. I didn't tell you, but I made sure."

She breathed a vague relief: this was, oddly, so much to the good. It only went indeed a little way. "But if he isn't a gentleman—"

"What *is* he? He's a horror."

"A horror?"

"He's—God help me if I know *what* he is!"

Mrs. Grose looked round once more; she fixed her eyes on the duskier distance, then, pulling herself together, turned to me with abrupt inconsequence. "It's time we should be at church."

"Oh, I'm not fit for church!"

"Won't it do you good?"

"It won't do *them*—! I nodded at the house.

"The children?"

"I can't leave them now."

"You're afraid—?"

I spoke boldly. "I'm afraid of *him*."

Mrs. Grose's large face showed me, at this, for the first time, the faraway faint glimmer of a consciousness more acute: I somehow made out in it the delayed dawn of an idea I myself had not given her and that was as yet quite obscure to me. It comes back to me that I thought instantly of this as something I could get from her; and I felt it to be connected with the desire she presently showed to know more. "When was it—on the tower?"

"About the middle of the month. At this same hour."

"Almost at dark," said Mrs. Grose.

"Oh, no, not nearly. I saw him as I see you."

"Then how did he get in?"

"And how did he get out?" I laughed. "I had no opportunity to ask him! This evening, you see," I pursued, "he has not been able to get in."

"He only peeps?"

"I hope it will be confined to that!" She had now let go my hand; she turned away a little. I waited an instant; then I brought out: "Go to church. Goodbye. I must watch."

Slowly she faced me again. "Do you fear for them?"

We met in another long look. "Don't *you*?" Instead of answering she came nearer to the window and, for a minute, applied her face to the glass. "You see how he could see," I meanwhile went on.

She didn't move. "How long was he here?"

"Till I came out. I came to meet him."

Mrs. Grose at last turned round, and there was still more in her face. "*I* couldn't have come out."

"Neither could I!" I laughed again. "But I did come. I have my duty."

"So have I mine," she replied; after which she added: "What is he like?"

"I've been dying to tell you. But he's like nobody."

"Nobody?" she echoed.

"He has no hat." Then seeing in her face that she already, in this, with a deeper dismay, found a touch of picture, I quickly added stroke to stroke. "He has red hair, very red, close-curling, and a pale face, long in shape, with straight, good features and little, rather queer whiskers that are as red as his hair. His eyebrows are, somehow, darker; they look particularly arched and as if they might move a good deal. His eyes are sharp, strange—awfully; but I only know clearly that they're rather small and very fixed. His mouth's wide, and his lips are thin, and except for his little whiskers he's quite clean-shaven. He gives me a sort of sense of looking like an actor."

"An actor!" It was impossible to resemble one less, at least, than Mrs. Grose at that moment.

"I've never seen one, but so I suppose them. He's tall, active, erect," I continued, "but never—no, never!—a gentleman."

My companion's face had blanched as I went on; her round eyes started and her mild mouth gaped. "A gentleman?" she gasped, confounded, stupefied: "a gentleman *he*?"

"You know him then?"

She visibly tried to hold herself. "But he *is* handsome?"

I saw the way to help her. "Remarkably!"

"And dressed—?"

"In somebody's clothes. "They're smart, but they're not his own."

She broke into a breathless affirmative groan: "They're the master's!"

I caught it up. "You *do* know him?"

She faltered but a second. "Quint!" she cried.

"Quint?"

"Peter Quint—his own man, his valet, when he was here!"

"When the master was?"

Gaping still, but meeting me, she pieced it all together. "He never wore his hat, but he did wear—well, there were waistcoats missed. They were both here—last year. Then the master went, and Quint was alone."

I followed, but halting a little. "Alone?"

"Alone with *us*." Then, as from a deeper depth, "In charge," she added.

"And what became of him?"

She hung fire so long that I was still more mystified. "He went, too," she brought out at last.

"Went where?"

Her expression, at this, became extraordinary. "God knows where! He died."

"Died?" I almost shrieked.

She seemed fairly to square herself, plant herself more firmly to utter the wonder of it. "Yes. Mr. Quint is dead."

VI

It took of course more than that particular passage to place us together in presence of what we had now to live with as we could—my dreadful liability to impressions of the order so vividly exemplified, and my companion's knowledge, henceforth—a knowledge half consternation and half compassion—of that liability. There had been, this evening, after the revelation left me, for an hour, so prostrate—there had been, for either of us, no attendance on any service but a little service of tears and vows, of prayers and promises, a climax to the series of mutual challenges and pledges that had straightway ensued on our retreating together to the schoolroom and shutting ourselves up there to have everything out. The result of our having everything out was simply to reduce our situation to the last rigor of its elements. She herself had seen nothing, not the shadow of a shadow, and nobody in the house but the governess was in the governess's plight; yet she accepted without directly impugning my sanity the truth as I gave it to her, and ended by showing me, on this ground, an awestricken tenderness, an expression of the sense of my more than questionable privilege, of which the very breath has remained with me as that of the sweetest of human charities.

What was settled between us, accordingly, that night, was that we thought we might bear things together; and I was not even sure that, in spite of her exemption, it was she who had the best of the burden. I knew at this hour, I think, as well as I knew later, what I was capable of meeting to shelter my pupils; but it took me some time to be wholly sure of what my honest ally was prepared for to keep terms with so compromising a contract. I was queer company enough—quite as queer as the company I received; but as I trace over what we went through I see how much common ground we must have found in the one idea that, by good fortune, *could* steady us. It was the idea, the second movement, that led me straight out, as I may say, of the inner chamber of my dread. I could take the air in the court, at least, and there Mrs. Grose could join me. Perfectly can I recall now the particular way strength came to me before we separated for the night. We had gone over and over every feature of what I had seen.

"He was looking for someone else, you say—someone who was not you?"

"He was looking for little Miles." A portentous clearness now possessed me. "*That's* whom he was looking for."

"But how do you know?"

"I know, I know, I know!" My exaltation grew. "And *you* know, my dear!"

She didn't deny this, but I required, I felt, not even so much telling as that. She resumed in a moment, at any rate: "What if *he* should see him?"

"Little Miles? That's what he wants!"

She looked immensely scared again. "The child?"

"Heaven forbid! The man. He wants to appear to *them*." That he might was an awful conception, and yet, somehow, I could keep it at bay; which, moreover, as we lingered there, was what I succeeded in practically proving. I had an absolute certainty that I should see again what I had already seen, but something within me said that by offering myself bravely as the sole subject of such experience, by accepting, by inviting, by surmounting it all, I should serve as an expiatory victim and guard the tranquility of my companions. The children, in especial, I should thus fence about and absolutely save. I recall one of the last things I said that night to Mrs. Grose.

"It does strike me that my pupils have never mentioned—"

She looked at me hard as I musingly pulled up. "His having been here and the time they were with him?"

"The time they were with him, and his name, his presence, his history, in any way."

"Oh, the little lady doesn't remember. She never heard or knew."

"The circumstances of his death?" I thought with some intensity. "Perhaps not. But Miles would remember—Miles would know."

"Ah, don't try him!" broke from Mrs. Grose.

I returned her the look she had given me. "Don't be afraid." I continued to think. "It *is* rather odd."

"That he has never spoken of him?"

"Never by the least allusion. And you tell me they were 'great friends'?"

"Oh, it wasn't *him*!" Mrs. Grose with emphasis declared. "It was Quint's own fancy. To play with him, I mean—to spoil him." She paused a moment; then she added: "Quint was much too free."

This gave me, straight from my vision of his face—*such* a face!—a sudden sickness of disgust. "Too free with *my* boy?"

"Too free with everyone!"

I forbore, for the moment, to analyze this description further than by the reflection that a part of it applied to several of the members of the household, of the half-dozen maids and men who were still of our small colony. But there was everything, for our apprehension, in the lucky fact that no discomfortable legend, no perturbation of scullions, had ever, within anyone's memory attached to the kind old place. It had neither bad name nor ill fame, and Mrs. Grose, most apparently, only desired to cling to me and to quake in silence. I even put her, the very last thing of all, to the test. It was when, at midnight, she had her hand on the schoolroom door to take leave. "I have it from you then—for it's of great importance—that he was definitely and admittedly bad?"

"Oh, not admittedly. *I* knew it—but the master didn't."

"And you never told him?"

"Well, he didn't like tale-bearing—he hated complaints. He was terribly short with anything of that kind, and if people were all right to *him*—"

"He wouldn't be bothered with more?" This squared well enough with my impressions of him: he was not a trouble-loving gentleman, nor so very particular perhaps about some of the company *he* kept. All the same, I pressed my interlocutress. "I promise you *I* would have told!"

She felt my discrimination. "I daresay I was wrong. But, really, I was afraid."

"Afraid of what?"

"Of things that man could do. Quint was so clever—he was so deep."

I took this in still more than, probably, I showed. "You weren't afraid of anything else? Not of his effect—?"

"His effect?" she repeated with a face of anguish and waiting while I faltered.

"On innocent little precious lives. They were in your charge."

"No, they were not in mine!" she roundly and distressfully returned. "The master believed in him and placed him here because he was supposed not to be well and the country air so good for him. So he had everything to say. Yes"—she let me have it—"even about *them*."

"Them—that creature?" I had to smother a kind of howl. "And you could bear it!"

"No. I couldn't—and I can't now!" And the poor woman burst into tears.

A rigid control, from the next day, was, as I have said, to follow them; yet how often and how passionately, for a week, we came back together to the subject! Much as we had discussed it that Sunday night, I was, in the immediate later hours in especial—for it may be imagined whether I slept—still haunted with the shadow of something she had not told me. I myself had kept back nothing, but there was a word Mrs. Grose had kept back. I was sure, moreover, by morning, that this was not from a failure of frankness, but because on every side there were fears. It seems to me indeed, in retrospect, that by the time the morrow's sun was high I had restlessly read into the fact before us almost all the meaning they were to receive from subsequent and more cruel occurrences. What they gave me above all was just the sinister figure of the living man—the dead one would keep awhile!—and of the months he had continuously passed at Bly, which, added up, made a formidable stretch. The limit of this evil time had arrived only when, on the dawn of a winter's morning, Peter Quint was found, by a laborer going to early work, stone dead on the road from the village: a catastrophe explained—superficially at least—by a visible wound to his head; such a wound as might have been produced—and as, on the final evidence, *had* been—by a fatal slip, in the dark and after leaving the public house, on the steepish icy slope, a wrong path altogether, at the bottom of which he lay. The icy slope, the turn mistaken at night and in liquor, accounted for much—practically, in the end and after the inquest and boundless chatter, for everything; but there had been matters in his life—strange passages and perils, secret disorders, vices more than suspected—that would have accounted for a good deal more.

I scarce know how to put my story into words that shall be a credible picture of my state of mind; but I was in these days literally able to find a joy in the extraordinary flight of heroism the occasion demanded of me. I now saw that I had been asked for a service admirable and difficult; and there would be a greatness in letting it be seen—oh, in the right quarter!—that I could succeed where many another girl might have failed. It was an immense help to me—I confess I rather applaud myself as I look back!—that I saw my service so strongly and so simply. I was there to protect and defend the little creatures in the world the most bereaved and the most lovable, the appeal of whose helplessness had suddenly become only too explicit, a deep, constant ache of one's own committed heart. We were cut off, really, together; we were united in our danger. They had nothing but me, and I—well, I had *them*. It was in short a magnificent chance. This chance presented itself to me in an image richly material. I was a screen—I was to stand before them. The more I saw, the less they would. I began to watch them in a stifled suspense, a disguised excitement that might well, had it continued too long, have turned to something like madness. What saved me, as I now see, was that it turned to something else altogether. It didn't last as suspense—it was superseded by horrible proofs. Proofs, I say, yes—from the moment I really took hold.

This moment dated from an afternoon hour that I happened to spend in the grounds with the younger of my pupils alone. We had left Miles indoors, on the red cushion of a deep window seat; he had wished to finish a book, and I had been glad to encourage a purpose so laudable in a young man whose only defect was an occasional excess of the restless. His sister, on the contrary, had been alert to come out, and I strolled with her half an hour, seeking the shade, for the sun was still high and the day exceptionally warm. I was aware afresh, with her, as we went, of how, like her brother, she contrived—it was the charming thing in both children—to let me alone without appearing to drop me and to accompany me without appearing to surround. They were never importunate and yet never listless. My attention to them all really went to seeing them amuse themselves immensely without me: this was a spectacle they seemed actively to prepare and that engaged me as an active admirer. I walked in a world of their invention—they had no occasion whatever to draw upon mine; so that my time was taken only with being, for them, some remarkable person or thing that the game of the moment required and that was merely, thanks to my superior, my exalted stamp, a happy and highly distinguished sinecure. I forget what I was on the present occasion; I only remember that I was something very important and very quiet and that Flora was playing very hard. We were on the edge of the lake, and, as we had lately begun geography, the lake was the Sea of Azof.

Suddenly, in these circumstances, I became aware that, on the other side of the Sea of Azof, we had an interested spectator. The way this knowledge gathered in me was the strangest thing in the world—the strangest, that is, except the very much stranger in which it quickly merged itself. I had sat down with a piece of work—for I was something or other that could sit—on the old stone bench which overlooked the pond; and in this position I began to take in with certitude, and yet without direct vision, the presence, at a distance, of a third person. The old trees, the thick shrubbery, made a great and pleasant shade, but it was all suffused with the brightness of the hot, still hour. There was no ambiguity in anything; none whatever, at least, in the conviction I from one moment to another found myself forming as to what I should see straight before me and across the lake as a consequence of raising my eyes. They were attached at this juncture to the stitching in which I was engaged, and I can feel once more the spasm of my effort not to move them till I should so have steadied myself as to be able to make up my mind what to do. There was an alien object in view—a figure whose right of presence I instantly, passionately questioned. I recollect counting over perfectly the possibilities, reminding myself that nothing was more natural, for instance, then the appearance of one of the men about the place, or even of a messenger, a postman, or a tradesman's boy, from the village. That reminder had as little effect on my practical certitude as I was conscious—still even without looking—of its having upon the character and attitude of our visitor.

Nothing was more natural than that these things should be the other things that they absolutely were not.

Of the positive identity of the apparition I would assure myself as soon as the small clock of my courage should have ticked out the right second; meanwhile, with an effort that was already sharp enough, I transferred my eyes straight to little Flora, who, at the moment, was about ten yards away. My heart had stood still for an instant with the wonder and terror of the question whether she too would see; and I held my breath while I waited for what a cry from her, what some sudden innocent sign either of interest or of alarm, would tell me. I waited, but nothing came; then, in the first place—and there is something more dire in this, I feel, than in anything I have to relate—I was determined by a sense that, within a minute, all sounds from her had previously dropped; and, in the second, by the circumstance that, also within the minute, she had, in her play, turned her back to the water. This was her attitude when I at last looked at her—looked with the confirmed conviction that we were still, together, under direct personal notice. She had picked up a small flat piece of wood, which happened to have in it a little hole that had evidently suggested to her the idea of sticking in another fragment that might figure as a mast and make the thing a boat. This second morsel, as I watched her, she was very markedly and intently attempting to tighten in its place. My apprehension of what she was doing sustained me so that after some seconds I felt I was ready for more. Then I again shifted my eyes—I faced what I had to face.

VII

I got hold of Mrs. Grose as soon after this as I could; and I can give no intelligible account of how I fought out the interval. Yet I still hear myself cry as I fairly threw myself into her arms: "They *know*—it's too monstrous: they know, they know!"

"And what on earth—?" I felt her incredulity as she held me.

"Why, all that *we* know—and heaven knows what else besides!" Then, as she released me, I made it out to her, made it out perhaps only now with full coherency even to myself. "Two hours ago, in the garden"—I could scarce articulate—"Flora *saw*!"

Mrs. Grose took it as she might have taken a blow in the stomach. "She has told you?" she panted.

"Not a word—that's the horror. She kept it to herself! The child of eight, *that* child!" Unutterable still, for me, was the stupefaction of it.

Mrs. Grose, of course, could only gape the wider. "Then how do you know?"

"I was there—I saw with my eyes: saw that she was perfectly aware."

"Do you mean aware of *him*?"

"No—of *her*." I was conscious as I spoke that I looked prodigious things, for I got the slow reflection of them in my companion's face. "Another person—this time; but a figure of quite as unmistakable horror and evil: a woman in black, pale and dreadful—with such an air also, and such a face!—on the other side of the lake. I was there with the child—quiet for the hour; and in the midst of it she came."

"Came how—from where?"

"From where they come from! She just appeared and stood there—but not so near."

"And without coming nearer?"

"Oh, for the effect and the feeling, she might have been as close as you!"

My friend, with an odd impulse, fell back a step. "Was she someone you've never seen?"

"Yes. But someone the child has. Someone *you* have." Then, to show how I had thought it all out: "My predecessor—the one who died."

"Miss Jessel?"

"Miss Jessel. You don't believe me?" I pressed.

She turned right and left in her distress. "How can you be sure?"

This drew from me, in the state of my nerves, a flash of impatience. "Then ask Flora—*she's* sure!" But I had no sooner spoken than I caught myself up. "No, for God's sake, *don't*!" She'll say she isn't—she'll lie!"

Mrs. Grose was not too bewildered instinctively to protest. "Ah, how *can* you?"

"Because I'm clear. Flora doesn't want me to know."

"It's only then to spare you."

"No, no—there are depths, depths! The more I go over it, the more I see in it, and the more I see in it, the more I fear. I don't know what I *don't* see—what I *don't* fear!"

Mrs. Grose tried to keep up with me. "You mean you're afraid of seeing her again?"

"Oh, no; that's nothing—now!" Then I explained. "It's of *not* seeing her."

But my companion only looked wan. "I don't understand you."

"Why, it's that the child may keep it up—and that the child assuredly *will*—without my knowing it."

At the image of this possibility Mrs. Grose for a moment collapsed, yet presently to pull herself together again, as if from the positive force of the sense of what, should we yield an inch, there would really be to give way to. "Dear, dear—we must keep our heads! And after all, if she doesn't mind it—!" She even tried a grim joke. "Perhaps she likes it!"

"Likes *such* things—a scrap of an infant!"

"Isn't it just a proof of her blessed innocence?" my friend bravely inquired.

She brought me, for the instant, almost round. "Oh, we must clutch at *that*—we must cling to it! If it isn't a proof of what you say, it's a proof of—God knows what! For the woman's a horror of horrors."

Mrs. Grose, at this, fixed her eyes a minute on the ground; then at last raising them, "Tell me how you know," she said.

"Then you admit it's what she was?" I cried.

"Tell me how you know," my friend simply repeated.

"Know? By seeing her! By the way she looked."

"At you, do you mean—so wickedly?"

"Dear me, no—I could have borne that. She gave me never a glance. She only fixed the child."

Mrs. Grose tried to see it. "Fixed her?"

"Ah, with such awful eyes!"

She stared at mine as if they might really have resembled them. "Do you mean of dislike?"

"God help us, no. Of something much worse."

"Worse than dislike?—this left her indeed at a loss.

"With a determination—indescribable. With a kind of fury of intention."

I made her turn pale. "Intention?"

"To get hold of her." Mrs. Grose—her eyes just lingering on mine—gave a shudder and walked to the window; and while she stood there looking out I completed my statement. "*That's* what Flora knows."

After a little she turned round. "The person was in black, you say?"

"In mourning—rather poor, almost shabby. But—yes—with extraordinary beauty." I now recognized to what I had at last, stroke by stroke, brought the victim of my confidence, for she quite visibly weighed this. "Oh, handsome—very, very," I insisted; "wonderfully handsome. But infamous."

She slowly came back to me. "Miss Jessel—*was* infamous." She once more took my hand in both her own, holding it as tight as if to fortify me against the increase of alarm I might draw from this disclosure. "They were both infamous," she finally said.

So, for a little, we faced it once more together; and I found absolutely a degree of help in seeing it now so straight. "I appreciate," I said, "the great decency of your not having hitherto spoken; but the time has certainly come to give me the whole thing." She appeared to assent to this, but still only in silence; seeing which I went on: "I must have it now. Of what did she die? Come, there was something between them."

"There was everything."

"In spite of the difference—?"

"Oh, of their rank, their condition"—she brought it woefully out. "*She* was a lady."

I turned it over; I again saw. "Yes—she was a lady."

"And he so dreadfully below," said Mrs. Grose.

I felt that I doubtless needn't press too hard, in such company, on the place of a servant in the scale; but there was nothing to prevent an acceptance of my companion's own measure of my predecessor's abasement. There was a way to deal with that, and I dealt; the more readily for my full vision—on the evidence—of our employer's late clever, good-looking "own" man; impudent, assured, spoiled, depraved. "The fellow was a hound."

Mrs. Grose considered as if it were perhaps a little a case for a sense of shades. "I've never seen one like him. He did what he wished."

"With *her*?"

"With them all."

It was as if now in my friend's own eyes Miss Jessel had again appeared. I seemed at any rate, for an instant, to see their evocation of her as distinctly as I had seen her by the pond; and I brought out with decision: "It must have been also what *she* wished!"

Mrs. Grose's face signified that it had been indeed, but she said at the same time: "Poor woman—she paid for it!"

"Then you do know what she died of?" I asked.

"No—I know nothing. I wanted not to know; I was glad enough I didn't; and I thanked heaven she was well out of this!"

"Yet you had, then, your idea—"

"Of her real reason for leaving? Oh, yes—as to that. She couldn't have stayed. Fancy it here—for a governess! And afterward I imagined—and I still imagine. And what I imagine is dreadful."

"Not so dreadful as what *I* do," I replied; on which I must have shown her—as I was indeed but too conscious—a front of miserable defeat. It brought out again all her compassion for me, and at the renewed touch of her kindness my power to resist broke down. I burst, as I had, the other time, made her burst, into tears; she took me to her motherly breast, and my lamentation overflowed. "I don't do it!" I sobbed in despair; "I don't save or shield them! It's far worse than I dreamed—they're lost!"

VIII

What I had said to Mrs. Grose was true enough: there were in the matter I had put before her depths and possibilities that I lacked resolution to sound; so that when we met once more in the wonder of it we were of a common mind about the duty of resistance to extravagant fancies. We were to keep our heads if we should keep nothing else—difficult indeed as that might be in the face of what, in our prodigious experience, was least to be questioned. Late that night, while the house slept, we had another talk in my room, when she went all the way with me as to its being beyond doubt that I had seen exactly what I had seen. To hold her perfectly in the pinch of that, I found I had only to ask her how, if I had "made it up," I came to be able to give, of each of the persons appearing to me, a picture disclosing, to the last detail, their special marks—a portrait on the exhibition of which she had instantly recognized and named them. She wished of course—small blame to her!—to sink the whole subject; and I was quick to assure her that my own interest in it had now violently taken the form of a search for the way to escape from it. I encountered her on the ground of a probability that with recurrence—for recurrence we took for granted—I should get used to my danger, distinctly professing that my personal exposure had suddenly become the least of my discomforts. It was my new suspicion that was intolerable; and yet even to this complication the later hours of the day had brought a little ease.

On leaving her, after my first outbreak, I had of course returned to my pupils, associating the right remedy for my dismay with that sense of their charm which I had already found to be a thing I could positively cultivate and which had never failed me yet. I had simply, in other words, plunged afresh into Flora's special society and there become aware—it was almost a luxury!—that she could put her little conscious hand straight upon the spot that ached. She had looked at me in sweet speculation and then had accused me to my face of having "cried." I had supposed I had brushed away the ugly signs: but I could literally—for the time, at all events—rejoice, under this fathomless charity, that they had not entirely disappeared. To gaze into the depths of blue of the child's eyes and pronounce their loveliness a trick of premature cunning was to be guilty of a cynicism in preference to which I naturally preferred to abjure my judgment and, so far as might be, my agitation. I couldn't abjure for merely wanting to, but I could repeat to Mrs. Grose—as I did there, over and over, in the small hours—that with their voices in the air, their pressure on one's heart, and their fragrant faces against one's cheek, everything fell to the ground but their incapacity and their beauty. It was a pity that, somehow, to settle this once for all, I had equally to re-enumerate the signs of subtlety that, in the afternoon, by the lake had made a miracle of my show of self-possession. It was a pity to be obliged to reinvestigate the certitude of the moment itself and repeat how it had come to me as a revelation that the inconceivable communion I then surprised was a matter, for either party, of habit. It was a pity that I should have had to quaver out again the reasons for my not having, in my delusion, so much as questioned that the little girl saw our visitant even as I actually saw Mrs. Grose herself, and that she wanted, by just so much as she did thus see, to make me suppose she didn't, and at the same time, without showing anything, arrive at a guess as to whether I myself did! It was a pity that I needed once more to describe the portentous little activity by which she sought to divert my attention—the perceptible increase of movement, the greater intensity of play, the singing, the gabbling of nonsense, and the invitation to romp.

Yet if I had not indulged, to prove there was nothing in it, in this review, I should have missed the two or three dim elements of comfort that still remained to me. I should not for instance have been able to asseverate to my friend that I was certain—which was so much to the good—that *I* at least had not betrayed myself. I should not have been prompted, by stress of need, by desperation of mind—I scarce know what to call it—to invoke such further aid to intelligence as might spring from pushing my colleague fairly to the wall. She had told me, bit by bit, under pressure, a great deal; but a small shifty spot on the wrong side of it all still sometimes brushed my brow like the wing of a bat; and I remember how on this occasion—for the sleeping house and the concentration alike of our danger and our watch seemed to help—I felt the importance of giving the last jerk to the curtain. "I don't believe anything so horrible," I recollect saying; "no, let us put it definitely, my dear, that I don't. But if I did, you know, there's a thing I should require now, just without sparing you the least bit more—oh, not a scrap, come!—to get out of you. What was it you had in mind when, in our distress, before Miles came back, over the letter from his school, you said, under my insistence, that you didn't pretend for him that he had not literally *ever* been 'bad'? He has *not* literally 'ever,' in these weeks that I myself have lived with him and so closely watched him; he has been an imperturbable little prodigy of delightful, lovable goodness. Therefore you might perfectly have made the claim for him if you had not, as it happened, seen an exception to take. What was your exception, and to what passage in your personal observation of him did you refer?"

It was a dreadfully austere inquiry, but levity was not our note, and, at any rate, before the gray dawn admonished us to separate I had got my answer. What my friend had had in mind proved to be immensely to the purpose. It was neither more nor less than the circumstance that for a period of several months Quint and the boy had been perpetually together. It was in fact the very appropriate truth that she had ventured to criticize the propriety, to hint at the incongruity, of so close an alliance, and even to go so far on the subject as a frank overture to Miss Jessel. Miss Jessel had, with a most strange manner, requested her to mind her business, and the good woman had, on this, directly approached little Miles. What she had said to him, since I pressed, was that *she* liked to see young gentlemen not forget their station.

I pressed again, of course, at this. "You reminded him that Quint was only a base menial?"

"As you might say! And it was his answer, for one thing, that was bad."

"And for another thing?" I waited. "He repeated your words to Quint?"

"No, not that. It's just what he *wouldn't*!" she could still impress upon me. "I was sure, at any rate," she added, "that he didn't. But he denied certain occasions."

"What occasions?"

"When they had been about together quite as if Quint were his tutor—and a very grand one—and Miss Jessel only for the little lady. When he had gone off with the fellow, I mean, and spent hours with him."

"He then prevaricated about it—he said he hadn't?" Her assent was clear enough to cause me to add in a moment: "I see. He lied."

"Oh!" Mrs. Grose mumbled. This was a suggestion that it didn't matter; which indeed she backed up by a further remark. "You see, after all, Miss Jessel didn't mind. She didn't forbid him."

I considered. "Did he put that to you as a justification?"

At this she dropped again. "No, he never spoke of it."

"Never mentioned her in connection with Quint?"

She saw, visibly flushing, where I was coming out. "Well, he didn't show anything. He denied," she repeated; "he denied."

Lord, how I pressed her now! "So that you could see he knew what was between the two wretches?"

"I don't know—I don't know!" the poor woman groaned.

"You do know, you dear thing," I replied; "only you haven't my dreadful boldness of mind, and you keep back, out of timidity and modesty and delicacy, even the impression that, in the past, when you had, without my aid, to flounder about in silence, most of all made you miserable. But I shall get it out of you yet! There was something in the boy that suggested to you," I continued, "that he covered and concealed their relation."

"Oh, he couldn't prevent—"

"Your learning the truth? I daresay! But, heavens," I fell, with vehemence, athinking, "what it shows that they must, to that extent, have succeeded in making of him!"

"Ah, nothing that's not nice *now*!" Mrs. Grose lugubriously pleaded.

"I don't wonder you looked queer," I persisted, "when I mentioned to you the letter from his school!"

"I doubt if I looked as queer as you!" she retorted with homely force. "And if he was so bad then as that comes to, how is he such an angel now?"

"Yes, indeed—and if he was a fiend at school! How, how, how? Well," I said in my torment, "you must put it to me again, but I shall not be able to tell you for some days. Only, put it to me again!" I cried in a way that made my friend stare. "There are directions in which I must not for the present let myself go." Meanwhile I returned to her first example—the one to which she had just previously referred—of the boy's happy capacity for an occasional slip. "If Quint—on your remonstrance at the time you speak of—was a base menial, one of the things Miles said to you, I find myself guessing, was that you were another." Again her admission was so adequate that I continued: "And you forgave him that?"

"Wouldn't *you*?"

"Oh, yes!" And we exchanged there, in the stillness, a sound of the oddest amusement. Then I went on: "At all events, while he was with the man—"

"Miss Flora was with the woman. It suited them all!"

It suited me, too, I felt, only too well; by which I mean that it suited exactly the particularly deadly view I was in the very act of forbidding myself to entertain. But I so far succeeded in checking the expression of this view that I will throw, just here, no further light on it than may be offered by the mention of my final observation to Mrs. Grose. "His having lied and been impudent are, I confess, less engaging specimens than I had hoped to have from you of the outbreak in him of the little natural man. Still," I mused, "They must do, for they make me feel more than ever that I must watch."

It made me blush, the next minute, to see in my friend's face how much more unreservedly she had forgiven him than her anecdote struck me as presenting to my own tenderness an occasion for doing. This came out when, at the schoolroom door, she quitted me. "Surely you don't accuse *him*—"

"Of carrying on an intercourse that he conceals from me? Ah, remember that, until further evidence, I now accuse nobody." Then, before shutting her out to go, by another passage, to her own place, "I must just wait," I wound up.

IX

I waited and waited, and the days, as they elapsed, took something from my consternation. A very few of them, in fact, passing, in constant sight of my pupils, without a fresh incident, sufficed to give to grievous fancies and even to odious memories a kind of brush of the sponge. I have spoken of the surrender to their extraordinary childish grace as a thing I could actively cultivate, and it may be imagined if I neglected now to address myself to this source for whatever it would yield. Stranger than I can express, certainly, was the effort to struggle against my new lights; it would doubtless have been, however, a greater tension still had it not been so frequently successful. I used to wonder how my little charges could help guessing that I thought strange things about them; and the circumstances that these things only made them more interesting was not by itself a direct aid to keeping them in the dark. I trembled lest they should see that they *were* so immensely more interesting. Putting things at the worst, at all events, as in meditation I so often did, any clouding of their innocence could only be—blameless and foredoomed as they were—a reason the more for taking risks. There were moments when, by an irresistible impulse, I found myself catching them up and pressing them to my heart. As soon as I had done so I used to say to myself: "What will they think of that? Doesn't it betray too much?" It would have been easy to get into a sad, wild tangle about how much I might betray; but the real account, I feel, of the hours of peace that I could still enjoy was that the immediate charm of my companions was a beguilement still effective even under the shadow of the possibility that it was studied. For if it occurred to me that I might occasionally excite suspicion by the little outbreaks of my sharper passion for them, so too I remember wondering if I mightn't see a queerness in the traceable increase of their own demonstrations.

They were at this period extravagantly and preternaturally fond of me; which, after all, I could reflect, was no more than a graceful response in children perpetually bowed over and hugged. The homage of which they were so lavish succeeded, in truth, for my nerves, quite as well as if I never appeared to myself, as I may say, literally to catch them at a purpose in it. They had never, I think, wanted to do so many things for their poor protectress; I mean—though they got their lessons better and better, which was naturally what would please her most—in the way of diverting, entertaining, surprising her; reading her passages, telling her stories, acting her charades, pouncing out at her, in disguises, as animals and historical characters, and above all astonishing her by the "pieces" they had secretly got by heart and could interminably recite. I should never get to the bottom—were I to let myself go even now—of the prodigious private commentary, all under still more private correction, with which, in these days, I overscored their full hours. They had shown me from the first a facility for everything, a general faculty which, taking a fresh start, achieved remarkable flights. They got their little tasks as if they loved them, and indulged, from the mere exuberance of the gift, in the most unimposed little miracles of memory. They not only popped out at me as tigers and as Romans, but as Shakespeareans, astronomers, and navigators. This was so singularly the case that it had presumably much to do with the fact as to which, at the present day, I am at a loss for a different explanation: I allude to my unnatural composure on the subject of another school for Miles. What I remember is that I was content not, for the time, to open the question, and that contentment must have sprung from the sense of his perpetually striking show of cleverness. He was too clever for a bad governess, for a parson's daughter, to spoil; and the strangest if not the brightest thread in the pensive embroidery I just spoke of was the impression I might have got, if I had dared to work it out, that he was under some influence operating in his small intellectual life as a tremendous incitement.

If it was easy to reflect, however, that such a boy could postpone school, it was at least as marked that for such a boy to have been "kicked out" by a schoolmaster was a mystification without end. Let me add that in their company now—and I was careful almost never to be out of it—I could follow no scent very far. We lived in a cloud of music and love and success and private theatricals. The musical sense in each of the children was of the quickest, but the elder in especial had a marvelous knack of catching and repeating. The schoolroom piano broke into all gruesome fancies; and when that failed there were confabulations in corners, with a sequel of one of them going out in the highest spirits in order to "come in" as something new. I had had brothers myself, and it was no revelation to me that little girls could be slavish idolaters of little boys. What surpassed everything was that there was a little boy in the world who could have for the inferior age, sex, and intelligence so fine a consideration. They were extraordinarily at one, and to say that they never either quarreled or complained is to make the note of praise coarse for their quality of sweetness. Sometimes, indeed, when I dropped into coarseness, I perhaps came across traces of little understandings between them by which one of them should keep me occupied while the other slipped away. There is a naive side, I suppose, in all diplomacy; but if my pupils practiced upon me, it was surely with the minimum of grossness. It was all in the other quarter that, after a lull, the grossness broke out.

I find that I really hang back; but I must take my plunge. In going on with the record of what was hideous at Bly, I not only challenge the most liberal faith—for which I little care; but—and this is another matter—I renew what I myself suffered, I again push my way through it to the end. There came suddenly an hour after which, as I look back, the affair seems to me to have been all pure suffering; but I have at least reached the heart of it, and the straightest road out is doubtless to advance. One evening—with nothing to lead up or to prepare it—I felt the cold touch of the impression that had breathed on me the night of my arrival and which, much lighter then, as I have mentioned, I should probably have made little of in memory had my subsequent sojourn been less agitated. I had not gone to bed; I sat reading by a couple of candles. There was a roomful of old books at Bly—last-century fiction, some of it, which, to the extent of a distinctly deprecated renown, but never to so much as that of a stray specimen, had reached the sequestered home and appealed to the unavowed curiosity of my youth. I remember that the book I had in my hand was Fielding's Amelia; also that I was wholly awake. I recall further both a general conviction that it was horribly late and a particular objection to looking at my watch. I figure, finally, that the white curtain draping, in the fashion of those days, the head of Flora's little bed, shrouded, as I had assured myself long before, the perfection of childish rest. I recollect in short that, though I was deeply interested in my author, I found myself, at the turn of a page and with his spell all scattered, looking straight up from him and hard at the door of my room. There was a moment during which I listened, reminded of the faint sense I had had, the first night, of there being something undefinably astir in the house, and noted the soft breath of the open casement just move the half-drawn blind. Then, with all the marks of a deliberation that must have seemed magnificent had there been anyone to admire it, I laid down my book, rose to my feet, and, taking a candle, went straight out of the room and, from the passage, on which my light made little impression, noiselessly closed and locked the door.

I can say now neither what determined nor what guided me, but I went straight along the lobby, holding my candle high, till I came within sight of the tall window that presided over the great turn of the staircase. At this point I precipitately found myself aware of three things. They were practically simultaneous, yet they had flashes of succession. My candle, under a bold flourish, went out, and I perceived, by the uncovered window, that the yielding dusk of earliest morning rendered it unnecessary. Without it, the next instant, I saw that there was someone on the stair. I speak of sequences, but I required no lapse of seconds to stiffen myself for a third encounter with Quint. The apparition had reached the landing halfway up and was therefore on the spot nearest the window, where at sight of me, it stopped short and fixed me exactly as it had fixed me from the tower and from the garden. He knew me as well as I knew him; and so, in the cold, faint twilight, with a glimmer in the high glass and another on the polish of the oak stair below, we faced each other in our common intensity. He was absolutely, on this occasion, a living, detestable, dangerous presence. But that was not the wonder of wonders; I reserve this distinction for quite another circumstance: the circumstance that dread had unmistakably quitted me and that there was nothing in me there that didn't meet and measure him.

I had plenty of anguish after that extraordinary moment, but I had, thank God, no terror. And he knew I had not—I found myself at the end of an instant magnificently aware of this. I felt, in a fierce rigor of confidence, that if I stood my ground a minute I should cease—for the time, at least—to have him to reckon with; and during the minute, accordingly, the thing was as human and hideous as a real interview: hideous just because it *was* human, as human as to have met alone, in the small hours, in a sleeping house, some enemy, some adventurer, some criminal. It was the dead silence of our long gaze at such close quarters that gave the whole horror, huge as it was, its only note of the unnatural. If I had met a murderer in such a place and at such an hour, we still at least would have spoken. Something would have passed, in life, between us; if nothing had passed, one of us would have moved. The moment was so prolonged that it would have taken but little more to make me doubt if even *I* were in life. I can't express what followed it save by saying that the silence itself—which was indeed in a manner an attestation of my strength—became the element into which I saw the figure disappear; in which I definitely saw it turn as I might have seen the low wretch to which it had once belonged turn on receipt of an order, and pass, with my eyes on the villainous back that no hunch could have more disfigured, straight down the staircase and into the darkness in which the next bend was lost.

X

I remained awhile at the top of the stair, but with the effect presently of understanding that when my visitor had gone, he had gone: then I returned to my room. The foremost thing I saw there by the light of the candle I had left burning was that Flora's little bed was empty; and on this I caught my breath with all the terror that, five minutes before, I had been able to resist. I dashed at the place in which I had left her lying and over which (for the small silk counterpane and the sheets were disarranged) the white curtains had been deceivingly pulled forward; then my step, to my unutterable relief, produced an answering sound: I perceived an agitation of the window blind, and the child, ducking down, emerged rosily from the other side of it. She stood there in so much of her candor and so little of her nightgown, with her pink bare feet and the golden glow of her curls. She looked intensely grave, and I had never had such a sense of losing an advantage acquired (the thrill of which had just been so prodigious) as on my consciousness that she addressed me with a reproach. "You naughty: where *have* you been?"—instead of challenging her own irregularity I found myself arraigned and explaining. She herself explained, for that matter, with the loveliest, eagerest simplicity. She had known suddenly, as she lay there, that I was out of the room, and had jumped up to see what had become of me. I had dropped, with the joy of her reappearance, back into my chair—feeling then, and then only, a little faint; and she had pattered straight over to me, thrown herself upon my knee, given herself to be held with the flame of the candle full in the wonderful little face that was still flushed with sleep. I remember closing my eyes an instant, yieldingly, consciously, as before the excess of something beautiful that shone out of the blue of her own. "You were looking for me out of the window?" I said. "You thought I might be walking in the grounds?"

"Well, you know, I thought someone was"—she never blanched as she smiled out that at me.

Oh, how I looked at her now! "And did you see anyone?"

"Ah, *no*!" she returned, almost with the full privilege of childish inconsequence, resentfully, though with a long sweetness in her little drawl of the negative.

At that moment, in the state of my nerves, I absolutely believed she lied; and if I once more closed my eyes it was before the dazzle of the three or four possible ways in which I might take this up. One of these, for a moment, tempted me with such singular intensity that, to withstand it, I must have gripped my little girl with a spasm that, wonderfully, she submitted to without a cry or a sign of fright. Why not break out at her on the spot and have it all over?—give it to her straight in her lovely little lighted face? "You see, you see, you *know* that you do and that you already quite suspect I believe it; therefore, why not frankly confess it to me, so that we may at least live with it together and learn perhaps, in the strangeness of our fate, where we are and what it means?" This solicitation dropped, alas, as it came: if I could immediately have succumbed to it I might have spared myself—well, you'll see what. Instead of succumbing I sprang again to my feet, looked at her bed, and took a helpless middle way. "Why did you pull the curtain over the place to make me think you were still there?"

Flora luminously considered; after which, with her little divine smile: "Because I don't like to frighten you!"

"But if I had, by your idea, gone out—?"

She absolutely declined to be puzzled; she turned her eyes to the flame of the candle as if the question were as irrelevant, or at any rate as impersonal, as Mrs. Marcet or nine-times-nine. "Oh, but you know," she quite adequately answered, "that you might come back, you dear, and that you *have*!" And after a little, when she had got into bed, I had, for a long time, by almost sitting on her to hold her hand, to prove that I recognized the pertinence of my return.

You may imagine the general complexion, from that moment, of my nights. I repeatedly sat up till I didn't know when; I selected moments when my roommate unmistakably slept, and, stealing out, took noiseless turns in the passage and even pushed as far as to where I had last met Quint. But I never met him there again; and I may as well say at once that I on no other occasion saw him in the house. I just missed, on the staircase, on the other hand, a different adventure. Looking down it from the top I once recognized the presence of a woman seated on one of the lower steps with her back presented to me, her body half-bowed and her head, in an attitude of woe, in her hands. I had been there but an instant, however, when she vanished without looking round at me. I knew, nonetheless, exactly what dreadful face she had to show; and I wondered whether, if instead of being above I had been below, I should have had, for going up, the same nerve I had lately shown Quint. Well, there continued to be plenty of chance for nerve. On the eleventh night after my latest encounter with that gentleman—they were all numbered now—I had an alarm that perilously skirted it and that indeed, from the particular quality of its unexpectedness, proved quite my sharpest shock. It was precisely the first night during this series that, weary with watching, I had felt that I might again without laxity lay myself down at my old hour. I slept immediately and, as I afterward knew, till about one o'clock; but when I woke it was to sit straight up, as completely roused as if a hand had shook me. I had left a light burning, but it was now out, and I felt an instant certainty that Flora had extinguished it. This brought me to my feet and straight, in the darkness, to her bed, which I found she had left. A glance at the window enlightened me further, and the striking of a match completed the picture.

The child had again got up—this time blowing out the taper, and had again, for some purpose of observation or response, squeezed in behind the blind and was peering out into the night. That she now saw—as she had not, I had satisfied myself, the previous time—was proved to me by the fact that she was disturbed neither by my reillumination nor by the haste I made to get into slippers and into a wrap. Hidden, protected, absorbed, she evidently rested on the sill—the casement opened forward—and gave herself up. There was a great still moon to help her, and this fact had counted in my quick decision. She was face to face with the apparition we had met at the lake, and could now communicate with it as she had not then been able to do. What I, on my side, had to care for was, without disturbing her, to reach, from the corridor, some other window in the same quarter. I got to the door without her hearing me; I got out of it, closed it, and listened, from the other side, for some sound from her. While I stood in the passage I had my eyes on her brother's door, which was but ten steps off and which, indescribably, produced in me a renewal of the strange impulse that I lately spoke of as my temptation. What if I should go straight in and march to *his* window?—what if, by risking to his boyish bewilderment a revelation of my motive, I should throw across the rest of the mystery the long halter of my boldness?

This thought held me sufficiently to make me cross to his threshold and pause again. I preternaturally listened; I figured to myself what might portentously be; I wondered if his bed were also empty and he too were secretly at watch. It was a deep, soundless minute, at the end of which my impulse failed. He was quiet; he might be innocent; the risk was hideous; I turned away. There was a figure in the grounds—a figure prowling for a sight, the visitor with whom Flora was engaged; but it was not the visitor most concerned with my boy. I hesitated afresh, but on other grounds and only for a few seconds; then I had made my choice. There were empty rooms at Bly, and it was only a question of choosing the right one. The right one suddenly presented itself to me as the lower one—though high above the gardens—in the solid corner of the house that I have spoken of as the old tower. This was a large, square chamber, arranged with some state as a bedroom, the extravagant size of which made it so inconvenient that it had not for years, though kept by Mrs. Grose in exemplary order, been occupied. I had often admired it and I knew my way about in it; I had only, after just faltering at the first chill gloom of its disuse, to pass across it and unbolt as quietly as I could one of the shutters. Achieving this transit, I uncovered the glass without a sound and, applying my face to the pane, was able, the darkness without being much less than within, to see that I commanded the right direction. Then I saw something more. The moon made the night extraordinarily penetrable and showed me on the lawn a person, diminished by distance, who stood there motionless and as if fascinated, looking up to where I had appeared—looking, that is, not so much straight at me as at something that was apparently above me. There was clearly another person above me—there was a person on the tower; but the presence on the lawn was not in the least what I had conceived and had confidently hurried to meet. The presence on the lawn—I felt sick as I made it out—was poor little Miles himself.

XI

It was not till late next day that I spoke to Mrs. Grose; the rigor with which I kept my pupils in sight making it often difficult to meet her privately, and the more as we each felt the importance of not provoking—on the part of the servants quite as much as on that of the children—any suspicion of a secret flurry or that of a discussion of mysteries. I drew a great security in this particular from her mere smooth aspect. There was nothing in her fresh face to pass on to others my horrible confidences. She believed me, I was sure, absolutely: if she hadn't I don't know what would have become of me, for I couldn't have borne the business alone. But she was a magnificent monument to the blessing of a want of imagination, and if she could see in our little charges nothing but their beauty and amiability, their happiness and cleverness, she had no direct communication with the sources of my trouble. If they had been at all visibly blighted or battered, she would doubtless have grown, on tracing it back, haggard enough to match them; as matters stood, however, I could feel her, when she surveyed them, with her large white arms folded and the habit of serenity in all her look, thank the Lord's mercy that if they were ruined the pieces would still serve. Flights of fancy gave place, in her mind, to a steady fireside glow, and I had already begun to perceive how, with the development of the conviction that—as time went on without a public accident—our young things could, after all, look out for themselves, she addressed her greatest solicitude to the sad case presented by their instructress. That, for myself, was a sound simplification: I could engage that, to the world, my face should tell no tales, but it would have been, in the conditions, an immense added strain to find myself anxious about hers.

At the hour I now speak of she had joined me, under pressure, on the terrace, where, with the lapse of the season, the afternoon sun was now agreeable; and we sat there together while, before us, at a distance, but within call if we wished, the children strolled to and fro in one of their most manageable moods. They moved slowly, in unison, below us, over the lawn, the boy, as they went, reading aloud from a storybook and passing his arm round his sister to keep her quite in touch. Mrs. Grose watched them with positive placidity; then I caught the suppressed intellectual creak with which she conscientiously turned to take from me a view of the back of the tapestry. I had made her a receptacle of lurid things, but there was an odd recognition of my superiority—my accomplishments and my function—in her patience under my pain. She offered her mind to my disclosures as, had I wished to mix a witch's broth and proposed it with assurance, she would have held out a large clean saucepan. This had become thoroughly her attitude by the time that, in my recital of the events of the night, I reached the point of what Miles had said to me when, after seeing him, at such a monstrous hour, almost on the very spot where he happened now to be, I had gone down to bring him in; choosing then, at the window, with a concentrated need of not alarming the house, rather that method than a signal more resonant. I had left her meanwhile in little doubt of my small hope of representing with success even to her actual sympathy my sense of the real splendor of the little inspiration with which, after I had got him into the house, the boy met my final articulate challenge. As soon as I appeared in the moonlight on the terrace, he had come to me as straight as possible; on which I had taken his hand without a word and led him, through the dark spaces, up the staircase where Quint had so hungrily hovered for him, along the lobby where I had listened and trembled, and so to his forsaken room.

Not a sound, on the way, had passed between us, and I had wondered—oh, *how* I had wondered!—if he were groping about in his little mind for something plausible and not too grotesque. It would tax his invention, certainly, and I felt, this time, over his real embarrassment, a curious thrill of triumph. It was a sharp trap for the inscrutable! He couldn't play any longer at innocence; so how the deuce would he get out of it? There beat in me indeed, with the passionate throb of this question an equal dumb appeal as to how the deuce *I* should. I was confronted at last, as never yet, with all the risk attached even now to sounding my own horrid note. I remember in fact that as we pushed into his little chamber, where the bed had not been slept in at all and the window, uncovered to the moonlight, made the place so clear that there was no need of striking a match—I remember how I suddenly dropped, sank upon the edge of the bed from the force of the idea that he must know how he really, as they say, "had" me. He could do what he liked, with all his cleverness to help him, so long as I should continue to defer to the old tradition of the criminality of those caretakers of the young who minister to superstitions and fears. He "had" me indeed, and in a cleft stick; for who would ever absolve me, who would consent that I should go unhung, if, by the faintest tremor of an overture, I were the first to introduce into our perfect intercourse an element so dire? No, no: it was useless to attempt to convey to Mrs. Grose, just as it is scarcely less so to attempt to suggest here, how, in our short, stiff brush in the dark, he fairly shook me with admiration. I was of course thoroughly kind and merciful; never, never yet had I placed on his little shoulders hands of such tenderness as those with which, while I rested against the bed, I held him there well under fire. I had no alternative but, in form at least, to put it to him.

"You must tell me now—and all the truth. What did you go out for? What were you doing there?"

I can still see his wonderful smile, the whites of his beautiful eyes, and the uncovering of his little teeth shine to me in the dusk. "If I tell you why, will you understand?" My heart, at this, leaped into my mouth. *would* he tell me why? I found no sound on my lips to press it, and I was aware of replying only with a vague, repeated, grimacing nod. He was gentleness itself, and while I wagged my head at him he stood there more than ever a little fairy prince. It was his brightness indeed that gave me a respite. Would it be so great if he were really going to tell me? "Well," he said at last, "just exactly in order that you should do this."

"Do what?"

"Think me—for a change—*bad*!" I shall never forget the sweetness and gaiety with which he brought out the word, nor how, on top of it, he bent forward and kissed me. It was practically the end of everything. I met his kiss and I had to make, while I folded him for a minute in my arms, the most stupendous effort not to cry. He had given exactly the account of himself that permitted least of my going behind it, and it was only with the effect of confirming my acceptance of it that, as I presently glanced about the room, I could say—

"Then you didn't undress at all?"

He fairly glittered in the gloom. "Not at all. I sat up and read."

"And when did you go down?"

"At midnight. When I'm bad I *am* bad!"

"I see, I see—it's charming. But how could you be sure I would know it?"

"Oh, I arranged that with Flora." His answers rang out with a readiness! "She was to get up and look out."

"Which is what she did do." It was I who fell into the trap!

"So she disturbed you, and, to see what she was looking at, you also looked—you saw."

"While you," I concurred, "caught your death in the night air!"

He literally bloomed so from this exploit that he could afford radiantly to assent. "How otherwise should I have been bad enough?" he asked. Then, after another embrace, the incident and our interview closed on my recognition of all the reserves of goodness that, for his joke, he had been able to draw upon.

XII

The particular impression I had received proved in the morning light, I repeat, not quite successfully presentable to Mrs. Grose, though I reinforced it with the mention of still another remark that he had made before we separated. "It all lies in half a dozen words," I said to her, "words that really settle the matter. 'Think, you know, what I *might* do!' He threw that off to show me how good he is. He knows down to the ground what he 'might' do. That's what he gave them a taste of at school."

"Lord, you do change!" cried my friend.

"I don't change—I simply make it out. The four, depend upon it, perpetually meet. If on either of these last nights you had been with either child, you would clearly have understood. The more I've watched and waited the more I've felt that if there were nothing else to make it sure it would be made so by the systematic silence of each. *never*, by a slip of the tongue, have they so much as alluded to either of their old friends, any more than Miles has alluded to his expulsion. Oh, yes, we may sit here and look at them, and they may show off to us there to their fill; but even while they pretend to be lost in their fairytale they're steeped in their vision of the dead restored. He's not reading to her," I declared; "they're talking of *them*—they're talking horrors! I go on, I know, as if I were crazy; and it's a wonder I'm not. What I've seen would have made *you* so; but it has only made me more lucid, made me get hold of still other things."

My lucidity must have seemed awful, but the charming creatures who were victims of it, passing and repassing in their interlocked sweetness, gave my colleague something to hold on by; and I felt how tight she held as, without stirring in the breath of my passion, she covered them still with her eyes. "Of what other things have you got hold?"

"Why, of the very things that have delighted, fascinated, and yet, at bottom, as I now so strangely see, mystified and troubled me. Their more than earthly beauty, their absolutely unnatural goodness. It's a game," I went on; "it's a policy and a fraud!"

"On the part of little darlings—?"

"As yet mere lovely babies? Yes, mad as that seems!" The very act of bringing it out really helped me to trace it—follow it all up and piece it all together. "They haven't been good—they've only been absent. It has been easy to live with them, because they're simply leading a life of their own. They're not mine—they're not ours. They're his and they're hers!"

"Quint's and that woman's?"

"Quint's and that woman's. They want to get to them."

Oh, how, at this, poor Mrs. Grose appeared to study them! "But for what?"

"For the love of all the evil that, in those dreadful days, the pair put into them. And to ply them with that evil still, to keep up the work of demons, is what brings the others back."

"Laws!" said my friend under her breath. The exclamation was homely, but it revealed a real acceptance of my further proof of what, in the bad time—for there had been a worse even than this!—must have occurred. There could have been no such justification for me as the plain assent of her experience to whatever depth of depravity I found credible in our brace of scoundrels. It was in obvious submission of memory that she brought out after a moment: "They *were* rascals! But what can they now do?" she pursued.

"Do?" I echoed so loud that Miles and Flora, as they passed at their distance, paused an instant in their walk and looked at us. "Don't they do enough?" I demanded in a lower tone, while the children, having smiled and nodded and kissed hands to us, resumed their exhibition. We were held by it a minute; then I answered: "They can destroy them!" At this my companion did turn, but the inquiry she launched was a silent one, the effect of which was to make me more explicit. "They don't know, as yet, quite how—but they're trying hard. They're seen only across, as it were, and beyond—in strange places and on high places, the top of towers, the roof of houses, the outside of windows, the further edge of pools; but there's a deep design, on either side, to shorten the distance and overcome the obstacle; and the success of the tempters is only a question of time. They've only to keep to their suggestions of danger."

"For the children to come?"

"And perish in the attempt!" Mrs. Grose slowly got up, and I scrupulously added: "Unless, of course, we can prevent!"

Standing there before me while I kept my seat, she visibly turned things over. "Their uncle must do the preventing. He must take them away."

"And who's to make him?"

She had been scanning the distance, but she now dropped on me a foolish face. "You, miss."

"By writing to him that his house is poisoned and his little nephew and niece mad?"

"But if they *are*, miss?"

"And if I am myself, you mean? That's charming news to be sent him by a governess whose prime undertaking was to give him no worry."

Mrs. Grose considered, following the children again. "Yes, he do hate worry. That was the great reason—"

"Why those fiends took him in so long? No doubt, though his indifference must have been awful. As I'm not a fiend, at any rate, I shouldn't take him in."

My companion, after an instant and for all answer, sat down again and grasped my arm. "Make him at any rate come to you."

I stared. "To *me*?" I had a sudden fear of what she might do. "'Him'?"

"He ought to *be* here—he ought to help."

I quickly rose, and I think I must have shown her a queerer face than ever yet. "You see me asking him for a visit?" No, with her eyes on my face she evidently couldn't. Instead of it even—as a woman reads another—she could see what I myself saw: his derision, his amusement, his contempt for the breakdown of my resignation at being left alone and for the fine machinery I had set in motion to attract his attention to my slighted charms. She didn't know—no one knew—how proud I had been to serve him and to stick to our terms; yet she nonetheless took the measure, I think, of the warning I now gave her. "If you should so lose your head as to appeal to him for me—"

She was really frightened. "Yes, miss?"

"I would leave, on the spot, both him and you."

XIII

It was all very well to join them, but speaking to them proved quite as much as ever an effort beyond my strength—offered, in close quarters, difficulties as insurmountable as before. This situation continued a month, and with new aggravations and particular notes, the note above all, sharper and sharper, of the small ironic consciousness on the part of my pupils. It was not, I am as sure today as I was sure then, my mere infernal imagination: it was absolutely traceable that they were aware of my predicament and that this strange relation made, in a manner, for a long time, the air in which we moved. I don't mean that they had their tongues in their cheeks or did anything vulgar, for that was not one of their dangers: I do mean, on the other hand, that the element of the unnamed and untouched became, between us, greater than any other, and that so much avoidance could not have been so successfully effected without a great deal of tacit arrangement. It was as if, at moments, we were perpetually coming into sight of subjects before which we must stop short, turning suddenly out of alleys that we perceived to be blind, closing with a little bang that made us look at each other—for, like all bangs, it was something louder than we had intended—the doors we had indiscreetly opened. All roads lead to Rome, and there were times when it might have struck us that almost every branch of study or subject of conversation skirted forbidden ground. Forbidden ground was the question of the return of the dead in general and of whatever, in especial, might survive, in memory, of the friends little children had lost. There were days when I could have sworn that one of them had, with a small invisible nudge, said to the other: "She thinks she'll do it this time—but she *won't*!" To "do it" would have been to indulge for instance—and for once in a way—in some direct reference to the lady who had prepared them for my discipline. They had a delightful endless appetite for passages in my own history, to which I had again and again treated them; they were in possession of everything that had ever happened to me, had had, with every circumstance the story of my smallest adventures and of those of my brothers and sisters and of the cat and the dog at home, as well as many particulars of the eccentric nature of my father, of the furniture and arrangement of our house, and of the conversation of the old women of our village. There were things enough, taking one with another, to chatter about, if one went very fast and knew by instinct when to go round. They pulled with an art of their own the strings of my invention and my memory; and nothing else perhaps, when I thought of such occasions afterward, gave me so the suspicion of being watched from under cover. It was in any case over *my* life, *my* past, and *my* friends alone that we could take anything like our ease—a state of affairs that led them sometimes without the least pertinence to break out into sociable reminders. I was invited—with no visible connection—to repeat afresh

Goody Gosling's celebrated mot or to confirm the details already supplied as to the cleverness of the vicarage pony.

It was partly at such junctures as these and partly at quite different ones that, with the turn my matters had now taken, my predicament, as I have called it, grew most sensible. The fact that the days passed for me without another encounter ought, it would have appeared, to have done something toward soothing my nerves. Since the light brush, that second night on the upper landing, of the presence of a woman at the foot of the stair, I had seen nothing, whether in or out of the house, that one had better not have seen. There was many a corner round which I expected to come upon Quint, and many a situation that, in a merely sinister way, would have favored the appearance of Miss Jessel. The summer had turned, the summer had gone; the autumn had dropped upon Bly and had blown out half our lights. The place, with its gray sky and withered garlands, its bared spaces and scattered dead leaves, was like a theater after the performance—all strewn with crumpled playbills. There were exactly states of the air, conditions of sound and of stillness, unspeakable impressions of the *kind* of ministering moment, that brought back to me, long enough to catch it, the feeling of the medium in which, that June evening out of doors, I had had my first sight of Quint, and in which, too, at those other instants, I had, after seeing him through the window, looked for him in vain in the circle of shrubbery. I recognized the signs, the portents—I recognized the moment, the spot. But they remained unaccompanied and empty, and I continued unmolested; if unmolested one could call a young woman whose sensibility had, in the most extraordinary fashion, not declined but deepened. I had said in my talk with Mrs. Grose on that horrid scene of Flora's by the lake—and had perplexed her by so saying—that it would from that moment distress me much more to lose my power than to keep it. I had then expressed what was vividly in my mind: the truth that, whether the children really saw or not—since, that is, it was not yet definitely proved—I greatly preferred, as a safeguard, the fullness of my own exposure. I was ready to know the very worst that was to be known. What I had then had an ugly glimpse of was that my eyes might be sealed just while theirs were most opened. Well, my eyes *were* sealed, it appeared, at present—a consummation for which it seemed blasphemous not to thank God. There was, alas, a difficulty about that: I would have thanked him with all my soul had I not had in a proportionate measure this conviction of the secret of my pupils.

How can I retrace today the strange steps of my obsession? There were times of our being together when I would have been ready to swear that, literally, in my presence, but with my direct sense of it closed, they had visitors who were known and were welcome. Then it was that, had I not been deterred by the very chance that such an injury might prove greater than the injury to be averted, my exultation would have broken out. "They're here, they're here, you little wretches," I would have cried, "and you can't deny it now!" The little wretches denied it with all the added volume of their sociability and their tenderness, in just the crystal depths of which—like the flash of a fish in a stream—the mockery of their advantage peeped up. The shock, in truth, had sunk into me still deeper than I knew on the night when, looking out to see either Quint or Miss Jessel under the stars, I had beheld the boy over whose rest I watched and who had immediately brought in with him—had straightway, there, turned it on me—the lovely upward look with which, from the battlements above me, the hideous apparition of Quint had played. If it was a question of a scare, my discovery on this occasion had scared me more than any other, and it was in the condition of nerves produced by it that I made my actual inductions. They harassed me so that sometimes, at odd moments, I shut myself up audibly to rehearse—it was at once a fantastic relief and a renewed despair—the manner in which I might come to the point. I approached it from one side and the other while, in my room, I flung myself about, but I always broke down in the monstrous utterance of names. As they died away on my lips, I said to myself that I should indeed help them to represent something infamous, if, by pronouncing them, I should violate as rare a little case of instinctive delicacy as any schoolroom, probably, had ever known. When I said to myself: "*they* have the manners to be silent, and you, trusted as you are, the baseness to speak!" I felt myself crimson and I covered my face with my hands. After these secret scenes I chattered more than ever, going on volubly enough till one of our prodigious, palpable hushes occurred—I can call them nothing else—the strange, dizzy lift or swim (I try for terms!) into a stillness, a pause of all life, that had nothing to do with the more or less noise that at the moment we might be engaged in making and that I could hear through any deepened exhilaration or quickened recitation or louder strum of the piano. Then it was that the others, the outsiders, were there. Though they were not angels, they "passed," as the French say, causing me, while they stayed, to tremble with the fear of their addressing to their younger victims some yet more infernal message or more vivid image than they had thought good enough for myself.

What it was most impossible to get rid of was the cruel idea that, whatever I had seen, Miles and Flora saw *more*—things terrible and unguessable and that sprang from dreadful passages of intercourse in the past. Such things naturally left on the surface, for the time, a chill which we vociferously denied that we felt; and we had, all three, with repetition, got into such splendid training that we went, each time, almost automatically, to mark the close of the incident, through the very same movements. It was striking of the children, at all events, to kiss me inveterately with a kind of wild irrelevance and never to fail—one or the other—of the precious question that had helped us through many a peril. "When do you think he *will* come? Don't you think we *ought* to write?"—there was nothing like that inquiry, we found by experience, for carrying off an awkwardness. "He" of course was their uncle in Harley Street; and we lived in much profusion of theory that he might at any moment arrive to mingle in our circle. It was impossible to have given less encouragement than he had done to such a doctrine, but if we had not had the doctrine to fall back upon we should have deprived each other of some of our finest exhibitions. He never wrote to them—that may have been selfish, but it was a part of the flattery of his trust of me; for the way in which a man pays his highest tribute to a woman is apt to be but by the more festal celebration of one of the sacred laws of his comfort; and I held that I carried out the spirit of the pledge given not to appeal to him when I let my charges understand that their own letters were but charming literary exercises. They were too beautiful to be posted; I kept them myself; I have them all to this hour. This was a rule indeed which only added to the satiric effect of my being plied with the supposition that he might at any moment be among us. It was exactly as if my charges knew how almost more awkward than anything else that might be for me. There appears to me, moreover, as I look back, no note in all this more extraordinary than the mere fact that, in spite of my tension and of their triumph, I never lost patience with them. Adorable they must in truth have been, I now reflect, that I didn't in these days hate them! Would exasperation, however, if relief had longer been postponed, finally have betrayed me? It little matters, for relief arrived. I call it relief, though it was only the relief that a snap brings to a strain or the burst of a thunderstorm to a day of suffocation. It was at least change, and it came with a rush.

XIV

Walking to church a certain Sunday morning, I had little Miles at my side and his sister, in advance of us and at Mrs. Grose's, well in sight. It was a crisp, clear day, the first of its order for some time; the night had brought a touch of frost, and the autumn air, bright and sharp, made the church bells almost gay. It was an odd accident of thought that I should have happened at such a moment to be particularly and very gratefully struck with the obedience of my little charges. Why did they never resent my inexorable, my perpetual society? Something or other had brought nearer home to me that I had all but pinned the boy to my shawl and that, in the way our companions were marshaled before me, I might have appeared to provide against some danger of rebellion. I was like a gaoler with an eye to possible surprises and escapes. But all this belonged—I mean their magnificent little surrender—just to the special array of the facts that were most abysmal. Turned out for Sunday by his uncle's tailor, who had had a free hand and a notion of pretty waistcoats and of his grand little air, Miles's whole title to independence, the rights of his sex and situation, were so stamped upon him that if he had suddenly struck for freedom I should have had nothing to say. I was by the strangest of chances wondering how I should meet him when the revolution unmistakably occurred. I call it a revolution because I now see how, with the word he spoke, the curtain rose on the last act of my dreadful drama, and the catastrophe was precipitated. "Look here, my dear, you know," he charmingly said, "when in the world, please, am I going back to school?"

Transcribed here the speech sounds harmless enough, particularly as uttered in the sweet, high, casual pipe with which, at all interlocutors, but above all at his eternal governess, he threw off intonations as if he were tossing roses. There was something in them that always made one "catch," and I caught, at any rate, now so effectually that I stopped as short as if one of the trees of the park had fallen across the road. There was something new, on the spot, between us, and he was perfectly aware that I recognized it, though, to enable me to do so, he had no need to look a whit less candid and charming than usual. I could feel in him how he already, from my at first finding nothing to reply, perceived the advantage he had gained. I was so slow to find anything that he had plenty of time, after a minute, to continue with his suggestive but inconclusive smile: "You know, my dear, that for a fellow to be with a lady *always*—!" His "my dear" was constantly on his lips for me, and nothing could have expressed more the exact shade of the sentiment with which I desired to inspire my pupils than its fond familiarity. It was so respectfully easy.

But, oh, how I felt that at present I must pick my own phrases! I remember that, to gain time, I tried to laugh, and I seemed to see in the beautiful face with which he watched me how ugly and queer I looked. "And always with the same lady?" I returned.

He neither blanched nor winked. The whole thing was virtually out between us. "Ah, of course, she's a jolly, 'perfect' lady; but, after all, I'm a fellow, don't you see? that's—well, getting on."

I lingered there with him an instant ever so kindly. "Yes, you're getting on." Oh, but I felt helpless!

I have kept to this day the heartbreaking little idea of how he seemed to know that and to play with it. "And you can't say I've not been awfully good, can you?"

I laid my hand on his shoulder, for, though I felt how much better it would have been to walk on, I was not yet quite able. "No, I can't say that, Miles."

"Except just that one night, you know—!"

"That one night?" I couldn't look as straight as he.

"Why, when I went down—went out of the house."

"Oh, yes. But I forget what you did it for."

"You forget?"—he spoke with the sweet extravagance of childish reproach. "Why, it was to show you I could!"

"Oh, yes, you could."

"And I can again."

I felt that I might, perhaps, after all, succeed in keeping my wits about me. "Certainly. But you won't."

"No, not *that* again. It was nothing."

"It was nothing," I said. "But we must go on."

He resumed our walk with me, passing his hand into my arm. "Then when *am* I going back?"

I wore, in turning it over, my most responsible air. "Were you very happy at school?"

He just considered. "Oh, I'm happy enough anywhere!"

"Well, then," I quavered, "if you're just as happy here—!"

"Ah, but that isn't everything! Of course *you* know a lot—"

"But you hint that you know almost as much?" I risked as he paused.

"Not half I want to!" Miles honestly professed. "But it isn't so much that."

"What is it, then?"

"Well—I want to see more life."

"I see; I see." We had arrived within sight of the church and of various persons, including several of the household of Bly, on their way to it and clustered about the door to see us go in. I quickened our step; I wanted to get there before the question between us opened up much further; I reflected hungrily that, for more than an hour, he would have to be silent; and I thought with envy of the comparative dusk of the pew and of the almost spiritual help of the hassock on which I might bend my knees. I seemed literally to be running a race with some confusion to which he was about to reduce me, but I felt that he had got in first when, before we had even entered the churchyard, he threw out—

"I want my own sort!"

It literally made me bound forward. "There are not many of your own sort, Miles!" I laughed. "Unless perhaps dear little Flora!"

"You really compare me to a baby girl?"

This found me singularly weak. "Don't you, then, *love* our sweet Flora?"

"If I didn't—and you, too; if I didn't—!" he repeated as if retreating for a jump, yet leaving his thought so unfinished that, after we had come into the gate, another stop, which he imposed on me by the pressure of his arm, had become inevitable. Mrs. Grose and Flora had passed into the church, the other worshippers had followed, and we were, for the minute, alone among the old, thick graves. We had paused, on the path from the gate, by a low, oblong, tablelike tomb.

"Yes, if you didn't—?"

He looked, while I waited, at the graves. "Well, you know what!" But he didn't move, and he presently produced something that made me drop straight down on the stone slab, as if suddenly to rest. "Does my uncle think what *you* think?"

I markedly rested. "How do you know what I think?"

"Ah, well, of course I don't; for it strikes me you never tell me. But I mean does *he* know?"

"Know what, Miles?"

"Why, the way I'm going on."

I perceived quickly enough that I could make, to this inquiry, no answer that would not involve something of a sacrifice of my employer. Yet it appeared to me that we were all, at Bly, sufficiently sacrificed to make that venial. "I don't think your uncle much cares."

Miles, on this, stood looking at me. "Then don't you think he can be made to?"

"In what way?"

"Why, by his coming down."

"But who'll get him to come down?"

"*I* will!" the boy said with extraordinary brightness and emphasis. He gave me another look charged with that expression and then marched off alone into church.

XV

The business was practically settled from the moment I never followed him. It was a pitiful surrender to agitation, but my being aware of this had somehow no power to restore me. I only sat there on my tomb and read into what my little friend had said to me the fullness of its meaning; by the time I had grasped the whole of which I had also embraced, for absence, the pretext that I was ashamed to offer my pupils and the rest of the congregation such an example of delay. What I said to myself above all was that Miles had got something out of me and that the proof of it, for him, would be just this awkward collapse. He had got out of me that there was something I was much afraid of and that he should probably be able to make use of my fear to gain, for his own purpose, more freedom. My fear was of having to deal with the intolerable question of the grounds of his dismissal from school, for that was really but the question of the horrors gathered behind. That his uncle should arrive to treat with me of these things was a solution that, strictly speaking, I ought now to have desired to bring on; but I could so little face the ugliness and the pain of it that I simply procrastinated and lived from hand to mouth. The boy, to my deep discomposure, was immensely in the right, was in a position to say to me: "Either you clear up with my guardian the mystery of this interruption of my studies, or you cease to expect me to lead with you a life that's so unnatural for a boy." What was so unnatural for the particular boy I was concerned with was this sudden revelation of a consciousness and a plan.

That was what really overcame me, what prevented my going in. I walked round the church, hesitating, hovering; I reflected that I had already, with him, hurt myself beyond repair. Therefore I could patch up nothing, and it was too extreme an effort to squeeze beside him into the pew: he would be so much more sure than ever to pass his arm into mine and make me sit there for an hour in close, silent contact with his commentary on our talk. For the first minute since his arrival I wanted to get away from him. As I paused beneath the high east window and listened to the sounds of worship, I was taken with an impulse that might master me, I felt, completely should I give it the least encouragement. I might easily put an end to my predicament by getting away altogether. Here was my chance; there was no one to stop me; I could give the whole thing up—turn my back and retreat. It was only a question of hurrying again, for a few preparations, to the house which the attendance at church of so many of the servants would practically have left unoccupied. No one, in short, could blame me if I should just drive desperately off. What was it to get away if I got away only till dinner? That would be in a couple of hours, at the end of which—I had the acute prevision—my little pupils would play at innocent wonder about my nonappearance in their train.

"What *did* you do, you naughty, bad thing? Why in the world, to worry us so—and take our thoughts off, too, don't you know?—did you desert us at the very door?" I couldn't meet such questions nor, as they asked them, their false little lovely eyes; yet it was all so exactly what I should have to meet that, as the prospect grew sharp to me, I at last let myself go.

I got, so far as the immediate moment was concerned, away; I came straight out of the churchyard and, thinking hard, retraced my steps through the park. It seemed to me that by the time I reached the house I had made up my mind I would fly. The Sunday stillness both of the approaches and of the interior, in which I met no one, fairly excited me with a sense of opportunity. Were I to get off quickly, this way, I should get off without a scene, without a word. My quickness would have to be remarkable, however, and the question of a conveyance was the great one to settle. Tormented, in the hall, with difficulties and obstacles, I remember sinking down at the foot of the staircase—suddenly collapsing there on the lowest step and then, with a revulsion, recalling that it was exactly where more than a month before, in the darkness of night and just so bowed with evil things, I had seen the specter of the most horrible of women. At this I was able to straighten myself; I went the rest of the way up; I made, in my bewilderment, for the schoolroom, where there were objects belonging to me that I should have to take. But I opened the door to find again, in a flash, my eyes unsealed. In the presence of what I saw I reeled straight back upon my resistance.

Seated at my own table in clear noonday light I saw a person whom, without my previous experience, I should have taken at the first blush for some housemaid who might have stayed at home to look after the place and who, availing herself of rare relief from observation and of the schoolroom table and my pens, ink, and paper, had applied herself to the considerable effort of a letter to her sweetheart. There was an effort in the way that, while her arms rested on the table, her hands with evident weariness supported her head; but at the moment I took this in I had already become aware that, in spite of my entrance, her attitude strangely persisted. Then it was—with the very act of its announcing itself—that her identity flared up in a change of posture. She rose, not as if she had heard me, but with an indescribable grand melancholy of indifference and detachment, and, within a dozen feet of me, stood there as my vile predecessor. Dishonored and tragic, she was all before me; but even as I fixed and, for memory, secured it, the awful image passed away. Dark as midnight in her black dress, her haggard beauty and her unutterable woe, she had looked at me long enough to appear to say that her right to sit at my table was as good as mine to sit at hers. While these instants lasted, indeed, I had the extraordinary chill of feeling that it was I who was the intruder. It was as a wild protest against it that, actually addressing her—"You terrible, miserable woman!"—I heard myself break into a sound that, by the open door, rang through the long passage and the empty house. She looked at me as if she heard me, but I had recovered myself and cleared the air. There was nothing in the room the next minute but the sunshine and a sense that I must stay.

XVI

I had so perfectly expected that the return of my pupils would be marked by a demonstration that I was freshly upset at having to take into account that they were dumb about my absence. Instead of gaily denouncing and caressing me, they made no allusion to my having failed them, and I was left, for the time, on perceiving that she too said nothing, to study Mrs. Grose's odd face. I did this to such purpose that I made sure they had in some way bribed her to silence; a silence that, however, I would engage to break down on the first private opportunity. This opportunity came before tea: I secured five minutes with her in the housekeeper's room, where, in the twilight, amid a smell of lately baked bread, but with the place all swept and garnished, I found her sitting in pained placidity before the fire. So I see her still, so I see her best: facing the flame from her straight chair in the dusky, shining room, a large clean image of the "put away"—of drawers closed and locked and rest without a remedy.

"Oh, yes, they asked me to say nothing; and to please them—so long as they were there—of course I promised. But what had happened to you?"

"I only went with you for the walk," I said. "I had then to come back to meet a friend."

She showed her surprise. "A friend—*you*?"

"Oh, yes, I have a couple!" I laughed. "But did the children give you a reason?"

"For not alluding to your leaving us? Yes; they said you would like it better. Do you like it better?"

My face had made her rueful. "No, I like it worse!" But after an instant I added: "Did they say why I should like it better?"

"No; Master Miles only said, "We must do nothing but what she likes!"

"I wish indeed he would. And what did Flora say?"

"Miss Flora was too sweet. She said, 'Oh, of course, of course!'—and I said the same."

I thought a moment. "You were too sweet, too—I can hear you all. But nonetheless, between Miles and me, it's now all out."

"All out?" My companion stared. "But what, miss?"

"Everything. It doesn't matter. I've made up my mind. I came home, my dear," I went on, "for a talk with Miss Jessel."

I had by this time formed the habit of having Mrs. Grose literally well in hand in advance of my sounding that note; so that even now, as she bravely blinked under the signal of my word, I could keep her comparatively firm. "A talk! Do you mean she spoke?"

"It came to that. I found her, on my return, in the schoolroom."

"And what did she say?" I can hear the good woman still, and the candor of her stupefaction.

"That she suffers the torments—!"

It was this, of a truth, that made her, as she filled out my picture, gape. "Do you mean," she faltered, "—of the lost?"

"Of the lost. Of the damned. And that's why, to share them-" I faltered myself with the horror of it.

But my companion, with less imagination, kept me up. "To share them—?"

"She wants Flora." Mrs. Grose might, as I gave it to her, fairly have fallen away from me had I not been prepared. I still held her there, to show I was. "As I've told you, however, it doesn't matter."

"Because you've made up your mind? But to what?"

"To everything."

"And what do you call 'everything'?"

"Why, sending for their uncle."

"Oh, miss, in pity do," my friend broke out.

"Ah, but I will, I *will*! I see it's the only way. What's 'out,' as I told you, with Miles is that if he thinks I'm afraid to—and has ideas of what he gains by that—he shall see he's mistaken. Yes, yes; his uncle shall have it here from me on the spot (and before the boy himself, if necessary) that if I'm to be reproached with having done nothing again about more school—"

"Yes, miss—" my companion pressed me.

"Well, there's that awful reason."

There were now clearly so many of these for my poor colleague that she was excusable for being vague. "But—a—which?"

"Why, the letter from his old place."

"You'll show it to the master?"

"I ought to have done so on the instant."

"Oh, no!" said Mrs. Grose with decision.

"I'll put it before him," I went on inexorably, "that I can't undertake to work the question on behalf of a child who has been expelled—"

"For we've never in the least known what!" Mrs. Grose declared.

"For wickedness. For what else—when he's so clever and beautiful and perfect? Is he stupid? Is he untidy? Is he infirm? Is he ill-natured? He's exquisite—so it can be only *that*; and that would open up the whole thing. After all," I said, "it's their uncle's fault. If he left here such people—!"

"He didn't really in the least know them. The fault's mine." She had turned quite pale.

"Well, you shan't suffer," I answered.

"The children shan't!" she emphatically returned.

I was silent awhile; we looked at each other. "Then what am I to tell him?"

"You needn't tell him anything. *I*'ll tell him."

I measured this. "Do you mean you'll write—?" Remembering she couldn't, I caught myself up. "How do you communicate?"

"I tell the bailiff. *He* writes."

"And should you like him to write our story?"

My question had a sarcastic force that I had not fully intended, and it made her, after a moment, inconsequently break down. The tears were again in her eyes. "Ah, miss, *you* write!"

"Well—tonight," I at last answered; and on this we separated.

XVII

I went so far, in the evening, as to make a beginning. The weather had changed back, a great wind was abroad, and beneath the lamp, in my room, with Flora at peace beside me, I sat for a long time before a blank sheet of paper and listened to the lash of the rain and the batter of the gusts. Finally I went out, taking a candle; I crossed the passage and listened a minute at Miles's door. What, under my endless obsession, I had been impelled to listen for was some betrayal of his not being at rest, and I presently caught one, but not in the form I had expected. His voice tinkled out. "I say, you there—come in." It was a gaiety in the gloom!

I went in with my light and found him, in bed, very wide awake, but very much at his ease. "Well, what are *you* up to?" he asked with a grace of sociability in which it occurred to me that Mrs. Grose, had she been present, might have looked in vain for proof that anything was "out."

I stood over him with my candle. "How did you know I was there?"

"Why, of course I heard you. Did you fancy you made no noise? You're like a troop of cavalry!" he beautifully laughed.

"Then you weren't asleep?"

"Not much! I lie awake and think."

I had put my candle, designedly, a short way off, and then, as he held out his friendly old hand to me, had sat down on the edge of his bed. "What is it," I asked, "that you think of?"

"What in the world, my dear, but *you*?"

"Ah, the pride I take in your appreciation doesn't insist on that! I had so far rather you slept."

"Well, I think also, you know, of this queer business of ours."

I marked the coolness of his firm little hand. "Of what queer business, Miles?"

"Why, the way you bring me up. And all the rest!"

I fairly held my breath a minute, and even from my glimmering taper there was light enough to show how he smiled up at me from his pillow. "What do you mean by all the rest?"

"Oh, you know, you know!"

I could say nothing for a minute, though I felt, as I held his hand and our eyes continued to meet, that my silence had all the air of admitting his charge and that nothing in the whole world of reality was perhaps at that moment so fabulous as our actual relation. "Certainly you shall go back to school," I said, "if it be that that troubles you. But not to the old place—we must find another, a better. How could I know it did trouble you, this question, when you never told me so, never spoke of it at all?" His clear, listening face, framed in its smooth whiteness, made him for the minute as appealing as some wistful patient in a children's hospital; and I would have given, as the resemblance came to me, all I possessed on earth really to be the nurse or the sister of charity who might have helped to cure him. Well, even as it was, I perhaps might help! "Do you know you've never said a word to me about your school—I mean the old one; never mentioned it in any way?"

He seemed to wonder; he smiled with the same loveliness. But he clearly gained time; he waited, he called for guidance. "Haven't I?" It wasn't for *me* to help him—it was for the thing I had met!

Something in his tone and the expression of his face, as I got this from him, set my heart aching with such a pang as it had never yet known; so unutterably touching was it to see his little brain puzzled and his little resources taxed to play, under the spell laid on him, a part of innocence and consistency. "No, never—from the hour you came back. You've never mentioned to me one of your masters, one of your comrades, nor the least little thing that ever happened to you at school. Never, little Miles—no, never—have you given me an inkling of anything that *may* have happened there. Therefore you can fancy how much I'm in the dark. Until you came out, that way, this morning, you had, since the first hour I saw you, scarce even made a reference to anything in your previous life. You seemed so perfectly to accept the present." It was extraordinary how my absolute conviction of his secret precocity (or whatever I might call the poison of an influence that I dared but half to phrase) made him, in spite of the faint breath of his inward trouble, appear as accessible as an older person—imposed him almost as an intellectual equal. "I thought you wanted to go on as you are."

It struck me that at this he just faintly colored. He gave, at any rate, like a convalescent slightly fatigued, a languid shake of his head. "I don't—I don't. I want to get away."

"You're tired of Bly?"

"Oh, no, I like Bly."

"Well, then—?"

"Oh, *you* know what a boy wants!"

I felt that I didn't know so well as Miles, and I took temporary refuge. "You want to go to your uncle?"

Again, at this, with his sweet ironic face, he made a movement on the pillow. "Ah, you can't get off with that!"

I was silent a little, and it was I, now, I think, who changed color. "My dear, I don't want to get off!"

"You can't, even if you do. You can't, you can't!"—he lay beautifully staring. "My uncle must come down, and you must completely settle things."

"If we do," I returned with some spirit, "you may be sure it will be to take you quite away."

"Well, don't you understand that that's exactly what I'm working for? You'll have to tell him—about the way you've let it all drop: you'll have to tell him a tremendous lot!"

The exultation with which he uttered this helped me somehow, for the instant, to meet him rather more. "And how much will *you*, Miles, have to tell him? There are things he'll ask you!"

He turned it over. "Very likely. But what things?"

"The things you've never told me. To make up his mind what to do with you. He can't send you back—"

"Oh, I don't want to go back!" he broke in. "I want a new field."

He said it with admirable serenity, with positive unimpeachable gaiety; and doubtless it was that very note that most evoked for me the poignancy, the unnatural childish tragedy, of his probable reappearance at the end of three months with all this bravado and still more dishonor. It overwhelmed me now that I should never be able to bear that, and it made me let myself go. I threw myself upon him and in the tenderness of my pity I embraced him. "Dear little Miles, dear little Miles—!"

My face was close to his, and he let me kiss him, simply taking it with indulgent good humor. "Well, old lady?"

"Is there nothing—nothing at all that you want to tell me?"

He turned off a little, facing round toward the wall and holding up his hand to look at as one had seen sick children look. "I've told you—I told you this morning."

Oh, I was sorry for him! "That you just want me not to worry you?"

He looked round at me now, as if in recognition of my understanding him; then ever so gently, "To let me alone," he replied.

There was even a singular little dignity in it, something that made me release him, yet, when I had slowly risen, linger beside him. God knows I never wished to harass him, but I felt that merely, at this, to turn my back on him was to abandon or, to put it more truly, to lose him. "I've just begun a letter to your uncle," I said.

"Well, then, finish it!"

I waited a minute. "What happened before?"

He gazed up at me again. "Before what?"

"Before you came back. And before you went away."

For some time he was silent, but he continued to meet my eyes. "What happened?"

It made me, the sound of the words, in which it seemed to me that I caught for the very first time a small faint quaver of consenting consciousness—it made me drop on my knees beside the bed and seize once more the chance of possessing him. "Dear little Miles, dear little Miles, if you *knew* how I want to help you! It's only that, it's nothing but that, and I'd rather die than give you a pain or do you a wrong—I'd rather die than hurt a hair of you. Dear little Miles"—oh, I brought it out now even if I *should* go too far—"I just want you to help me to save you!" But I knew in a moment after this that I had gone too far. The answer to my appeal was instantaneous, but it came in the form of an extraordinary blast and chill, a gust of frozen air, and a shake of the room as great as if, in the wild wind, the casement had crashed in. The boy gave a loud, high shriek, which, lost in the rest of the shock of sound, might have seemed, indistinctly, though I was so close to him, a note either of jubilation or of terror. I jumped to my feet again and was conscious of darkness. So for a moment we remained, while I stared about me and saw that the drawn curtains were unstirred and the window tight. "Why, the candle's out!" I then cried.

"It was I who blew it, dear!" said Miles.

XVIII

The next day, after lessons, Mrs. Grose found a moment to say to me quietly: "Have you written, miss?"

"Yes—I've written." But I didn't add—for the hour—that my letter, sealed and directed, was still in my pocket. There would be time enough to send it before the messenger should go to the village. Meanwhile there had been, on the part of my pupils, no more brilliant, more exemplary morning. It was exactly as if they had both had at heart to gloss over any recent little friction. They performed the dizziest feats of arithmetic, soaring quite out of *my* feeble range, and perpetrated, in higher spirits than ever, geographical and historical jokes. It was conspicuous of course in Miles in particular that he appeared to wish to show how easily he could let me down. This child, to my memory, really lives in a setting of beauty and misery that no words can translate; there was a distinction all his own in every impulse he revealed; never was a small natural creature, to the uninitiated eye all frankness and freedom, a more ingenious, a more extraordinary little gentleman. I had perpetually to guard against the wonder of contemplation into which my initiated view betrayed me; to check the irrelevant gaze and discouraged sigh in which I constantly both attacked and renounced the enigma of what such a little gentleman could have done that deserved a penalty. Say that, by the dark prodigy I knew, the imagination of all evil *had* been opened up to him: all the justice within me ached for the proof that it could ever have flowered into an act.

He had never, at any rate, been such a little gentleman as when, after our early dinner on this dreadful day, he came round to me and asked if I shouldn't like him, for half an hour, to play to me. David playing to Saul could never have shown a finer sense of the occasion. It was literally a charming exhibition of tact, of magnanimity, and quite tantamount to his saying outright: "The true knights we love to read about never push an advantage too far. I know what you mean now: you mean that—to be let alone yourself and not followed up—you'll cease to worry and spy upon me, won't keep me so close to you, will let me go and come. Well, I 'come,' you see—but I don't go! There'll be plenty of time for that. I do really delight in your society, and I only want to show you that I contended for a principle." It may be imagined whether I resisted this appeal or failed to accompany him again, hand in hand, to the schoolroom. He sat down at the old piano and played as he had never played; and if there are those who think he had better have been kicking a football I can only say that I wholly agree with them. For at the end of a time that under his influence I had quite ceased to measure, I started up with a strange sense of having literally slept at my post. It was after luncheon, and by the schoolroom fire, and yet I hadn't really, in the least, slept: I had only done something much worse—I had forgotten. Where, all this time, was Flora? When I put the question to Miles, he played on a minute before answering and then could only say: "Why, my dear, how do *I* know?"—breaking moreover into a happy laugh which, immediately after, as if it were a vocal accompaniment, he prolonged into incoherent, extravagant song.

I went straight to my room, but his sister was not there; then, before going downstairs, I looked into several others. As she was nowhere about she would surely be with Mrs. Grose, whom, in the comfort of that theory, I accordingly proceeded in quest of. I found her where I had found her the evening before, but she met my quick challenge with blank, scared ignorance. She had only supposed that, after the repast, I had carried off both the children; as to which she was quite in her right, for it was the very first time I had allowed the little girl out of my sight without some special provision. Of course now indeed she might be with the maids, so that the immediate thing was to look for her without an air of alarm. This we promptly arranged between us; but when, ten minutes later and in pursuance of our arrangement, we met in the hall, it was only to report on either side that after guarded inquiries we had altogether failed to trace her. For a minute there, apart from observation, we exchanged mute alarms, and I could feel with what high interest my friend returned me all those I had from the first given her.

"She'll be above," she presently said—"in one of the rooms you haven't searched."

"No; she's at a distance." I had made up my mind. "She has gone out."

Mrs. Grose stared. "Without a hat?"

I naturally also looked volumes. "Isn't that woman always without one?"

"She's with *her*?"

"She's with *her*!" I declared. "We must find them."

My hand was on my friend's arm, but she failed for the moment, confronted with such an account of the matter, to respond to my pressure. She communed, on the contrary, on the spot, with her uneasiness. "And where's Master Miles?"

"Oh, *he's* with Quint. They're in the schoolroom."

"Lord, miss!" My view, I was myself aware—and therefore I suppose my tone—had never yet reached so calm an assurance.

"The trick's played," I went on; "they've successfully worked their plan. He found the most divine little way to keep me quiet while she went off."

"'Divine'?" Mrs. Grose bewilderedly echoed.

"Infernal, then!" I almost cheerfully rejoined. "He has provided for himself as well. But come!"

She had helplessly gloomed at the upper regions. "You leave him—?"

"So long with Quint? Yes—I don't mind that now."

She always ended, at these moments, by getting possession of my hand, and in this manner she could at present still stay me. But after gasping an instant at my sudden resignation, "Because of your letter?" she eagerly brought out.

I quickly, by way of answer, felt for my letter, drew it forth, held it up, and then, freeing myself, went and laid it on the great hall table. "Luke will take it," I said as I came back. I reached the house door and opened it; I was already on the steps.

My companion still demurred: the storm of the night and the early morning had dropped, but the afternoon was damp and gray. I came down to the drive while she stood in the doorway. "You go with nothing on?"

"What do I care when the child has nothing? I can't wait to dress," I cried, "and if you must do so, I leave you. Try meanwhile, yourself, upstairs."

"With *them*?" Oh, on this, the poor woman promptly joined me!

XIX

We went straight to the lake, as it was called at Bly, and I daresay rightly called, though I reflect that it may in fact have been a sheet of water less remarkable than it appeared to my untraveled eyes. My acquaintance with sheets of water was small, and the pool of Bly, at all events on the few occasions of my consenting, under the protection of my pupils, to affront its surface in the old flat-bottomed boat moored there for our use, had impressed me both with its extent and its agitation. The usual place of embarkation was half a mile from the house, but I had an intimate conviction that, wherever Flora might be, she was not near home. She had not given me the slip for any small adventure, and, since the day of the very great one that I had shared with her by the pond, I had been aware, in our walks, of the quarter to which she most inclined. This was why I had now given to Mrs. Grose's steps so marked a direction—a direction that made her, when she perceived it, oppose a resistance that showed me she was freshly mystified. "You're going to the water, Miss?—you think she's *in*—?"

"She may be, though the depth is, I believe, nowhere very great. But what I judge most likely is that she's on the spot from which, the other day, we saw together what I told you."

"When she pretended not to see—?"

"With that astounding self-possession? I've always been sure she wanted to go back alone. And now her brother has managed it for her."

Mrs. Grose still stood where she had stopped. "You suppose they really *talk* of them?"

"I could meet this with a confidence! "They say things that, if we heard them, would simply appall us."

"And if she *is* there—"

"Yes?"

"Then Miss Jessel is?"

"Beyond a doubt. You shall see."

"Oh, thank you!" my friend cried, planted so firm that, taking it in, I went straight on without her. By the time I reached the pool, however, she was close behind me, and I knew that, whatever, to her apprehension, might befall me, the exposure of my society struck her as her least danger. She exhaled a moan of relief as we at last came in sight of the greater part of the water without a sight of the child. There was no trace of Flora on that nearer side of the bank where my observation of her had been most startling, and none on the opposite edge, where, save for a margin of some twenty yards, a thick copse came down to the water. The pond, oblong in shape, had a width so scant compared to its length that, with its ends out of view, it might have been taken for a scant river. We looked at the empty expanse, and then I felt the suggestion of my friend's eyes. I knew what she meant and I replied with a negative headshake.

"No, no; wait! She has taken the boat."

My companion stared at the vacant mooring place and then again across the lake. "Then where is it?"

"Our not seeing it is the strongest of proofs. She has used it to go over, and then has managed to hide it."

"All alone—that child?"

"She's not alone, and at such times she's not a child: she's an old, old woman." I scanned all the visible shore while Mrs. Grose took again, into the queer element I offered her, one of her plunges of submission; then I pointed out that the boat might perfectly be in a small refuge formed by one of the recesses of the pool, an indentation masked, for the hither side, by a projection of the bank and by a clump of trees growing close to the water.

"But if the boat's there, where on earth's *she*?" my colleague anxiously asked.

"That's exactly what we must learn." And I started to walk further.

"By going all the way round?"

"Certainly, far as it is. It will take us but ten minutes, but it's far enough to have made the child prefer not to walk. She went straight over."

"Laws!" cried my friend again; the chain of my logic was ever too much for her. It dragged her at my heels even now, and when we had got halfway round—a devious, tiresome process, on ground much broken and by a path choked with overgrowth—I paused to give her breath. I sustained her with a grateful arm, assuring her that she might hugely help me; and this started us afresh, so that in the course of but few minutes more we reached a point from which we found the boat to be where I had supposed it. It had been intentionally left as much as possible out of sight and was tied to one of the stakes of a fence that came, just there, down to the brink and that had been an assistance to disembarking. I recognized, as I looked at the pair of short, thick oars, quite safely drawn up, the prodigious character of the feat for a little girl; but I had lived, by this time, too long among wonders and had panted to too many livelier measures. There was a gate in the fence, through which we passed, and that brought us, after a trifling interval, more into the open. Then, "There she is!" we both exclaimed at once.

Flora, a short way off, stood before us on the grass and smiled as if her performance was now complete. The next thing she did, however, was to stoop straight down and pluck—quite as if it were all she was there for—a big, ugly spray of withered fern. I instantly became sure she had just come out of the copse. She waited for us, not herself taking a step, and I was conscious of the rare solemnity with which we presently approached her. She smiled and smiled, and we met; but it was all done in a silence by this time flagrantly ominous. Mrs. Grose was the first to break the spell: she threw herself on her knees and, drawing the child to her breast, clasped in a long embrace the little tender, yielding body. While this dumb convulsion lasted I could only watch it—which I did the more intently when I saw Flora's face peep at me over our companion's shoulder. It was serious now—the flicker had left it; but it strengthened the pang with which I at that moment envied Mrs. Grose the simplicity of *her* relation. Still, all this while, nothing more passed between us save that Flora had let her foolish fern again drop to the ground. What she and I had virtually said to each other was that pretexts were useless now. When Mrs. Grose finally got up she kept the child's hand, so that the two were still before me;

and the singular reticence of our communion was even more marked in the frank look she launched me. "I'll be hanged," it said, "if *I'll* speak!"

It was Flora who, gazing all over me in candid wonder, was the first. She was struck with our bareheaded aspect. "Why, where are your things?"

"Where yours are, my dear!" I promptly returned.

She had already got back her gaiety, and appeared to take this as an answer quite sufficient. "And where's Miles?" she went on.

There was something in the small valor of it that quite finished me: these three words from her were, in a flash like the glitter of a drawn blade, the jostle of the cup that my hand, for weeks and weeks, had held high and full to the brim that now, even before speaking, I felt overflow in a deluge. "I'll tell you if you'll tell *me*—" I heard myself say, then heard the tremor in which it broke.

"Well, what?"

Mrs. Grose's suspense blazed at me, but it was too late now, and I brought the thing out handsomely. "Where, my pet, is Miss Jessel?"

XX

Just as in the churchyard with Miles, the whole thing was upon us. Much as I had made of the fact that this name had never once, between us, been sounded, the quick, smitten glare with which the child's face now received it fairly likened my breach of the silence to the smash of a pane of glass. It added to the interposing cry, as if to stay the blow, that Mrs. Grose, at the same instant, uttered over my violence—the shriek of a creature scared, or rather wounded, which, in turn, within a few seconds, was completed by a gasp of my own. I seized my colleague's arm. "She's there, she's there!"

Miss Jessel stood before us on the opposite bank exactly as she had stood the other time, and I remember, strangely, as the first feeling now produced in me, my thrill of joy at having brought on a proof. She was there, and I was justified; she was there, and I was neither cruel nor mad. She was there for poor scared Mrs. Grose, but she was there most for Flora; and no moment of my monstrous time was perhaps so extraordinary as that in which I consciously threw out to her—with the sense that, pale and ravenous demon as she was, she would catch and understand it—an inarticulate message of gratitude. She rose erect on the spot my friend and I had lately quitted, and there was not, in all the long reach of her desire, an inch of her evil that fell short. This first vividness of vision and emotion were things of a few seconds, during which Mrs. Grose's dazed blink across to where I pointed struck me as a sovereign sign that she too at last saw, just as it carried my own eyes precipitately to the child. The revelation then of the manner in which Flora was affected startled me, in truth, far more than it would have done to find her also merely agitated, for direct dismay was of course not what I had expected. Prepared and on her guard as our pursuit had actually made her, she would repress every betrayal; and I was therefore shaken, on the spot, by my first glimpse of the particular one for which I had not allowed. To see her, without a convulsion of her small pink face, not even feign to glance in the direction of the prodigy I announced, but only, instead of that, turn at *me* an expression of hard, still gravity, an expression absolutely new and unprecedented and that appeared to read and accuse and judge me—this was a stroke that somehow converted the little girl herself into the very presence that could make me quail. I quailed even though my certitude that she thoroughly saw was never greater than at that instant, and in the immediate need to defend myself I called it passionately to witness. "She's there, you little unhappy thing—there, there, *there*, and you see her as well as you see me!" I had said shortly before to Mrs. Grose that she was not at these times a child, but an old, old woman, and that description of her could not have been more strikingly confirmed than in the way in which, for all answer to this, she simply showed me, without a concession, an admission, of her eyes, a countenance of deeper and deeper, of indeed suddenly quite fixed, reprobation. I was by this time—if I can put the whole thing at all together—more appalled at what I may properly call her manner than at anything else, though it was simultaneously with this that I became aware of having Mrs. Grose also, and very formidably, to reckon with. My elder companion, the next moment, at any rate, blotted out everything but her own flushed face and her loud, shocked protest, a burst of high disapproval. "What a dreadful turn, to be sure, miss! Where on earth do you see anything?"

I could only grasp her more quickly yet, for even while she spoke the hideous plain presence stood undimmed and undaunted. It had already lasted a minute, and it lasted while I continued, seizing my colleague, quite thrusting her at it and presenting her to it, to insist with my pointing hand. "You don't see her exactly as *we* see?—you mean to say you don't now—*now*? She's as big as a blazing fire! Only look, dearest woman, *look*—!" She looked, even as I did, and gave me, with her deep groan of negation, repulsion, compassion—the mixture with her pity of her relief at her exemption—a sense, touching to me even then, that she would have backed me up if she could. I might well have needed that, for with this hard blow of the proof that her eyes were hopelessly sealed I felt my own situation horribly crumble, I felt—I saw—my livid predecessor press, from her position, on my defeat, and I was conscious, more than all, of what I should have from this instant to deal with in the astounding little attitude of Flora. Into this attitude Mrs. Grose immediately and violently entered, breaking, even while there pierced through my sense of ruin a prodigious private triumph, into breathless reassurance.

"She isn't there, little lady, and nobody's there—and you never see nothing, my sweet! How can poor Miss Jessel—when poor Miss Jessel's dead and buried? *we* know, don't we, love?—and she appealed, blundering in, to the child. "It's all a mere mistake and a worry and a joke—and we'll go home as fast as we can!"

Our companion, on this, had responded with a strange, quick primness of propriety, and they were again, with Mrs. Grose on her feet, united, as it were, in pained opposition to me. Flora continued to fix me with her small mask of reprobation, and even at that minute I prayed God to forgive me for seeming to see that, as she stood there holding tight to our friend's dress, her incomparable childish beauty had suddenly failed, had quite vanished. I've said it already—she was literally, she was hideously, hard; she had turned common and almost ugly. "I don't know what you mean. I see nobody. I see nothing. I never *have*. I think you're cruel. I don't like you!" Then, after this deliverance, which might have been that of a vulgarly pert little girl in the street, she hugged Mrs. Grose more closely and buried in her skirts the dreadful little face. In this position she produced an almost furious wail. "Take me away, take me away—oh, take me away from *her*!"

"From *me*?" I panted.

"From you—from you!" she cried.

Even Mrs. Grose looked across at me dismayed, while I had nothing to do but communicate again with the figure that, on the opposite bank, without a movement, as rigidly still as if catching, beyond the interval, our voices, was as vividly there for my disaster as it was not there for my service. The wretched child had spoken exactly as if she had got from some outside source each of her stabbing little words, and I could therefore, in the full despair of all I had to accept, but sadly shake my head at her. "If I had ever doubted, all my doubt would at present have gone. I've been living with the miserable truth, and now it has only too much closed round me. Of course I've lost you: I've interfered, and you've seen—under *her* dictation"—with which I faced, over the pool again, our infernal witness—"the easy and perfect way to meet it. I've done my best, but I've lost you. Goodbye." For Mrs. Grose I had an imperative, an almost frantic "Go, go!" before which, in infinite distress, but mutely possessed of the little girl and clearly convinced, in spite of her blindness, that something awful had occurred and some collapse engulfed us, she retreated, by the way we had come, as fast as she could move.

Of what first happened when I was left alone I had no subsequent memory. I only knew that at the end of, I suppose, a quarter of an hour, an odorous dampness and roughness, chilling and piercing my trouble, had made me understand that I must have thrown myself, on my face, on the ground and given way to a wildness of grief. I must have lain there long and cried and sobbed, for when I raised my head the day was almost done. I got up and looked a moment, through the twilight, at the gray pool and its blank, haunted edge, and then I took, back to the house, my dreary and difficult course. When I reached the gate in the fence the boat, to my surprise, was gone, so that I had a fresh reflection to make on Flora's extraordinary command of the situation. She passed that night, by the most tacit, and I should add, were not the word so grotesque a false note, the happiest of arrangements, with Mrs. Grose. I saw neither of them on my return, but, on the other hand, as by an ambiguous compensation, I saw a great deal of Miles. I saw—I can use no other phrase—so much of him that it was as if it were more than it had ever been. No evening I had passed at Bly had the portentous quality of this one; in spite of which—and in spite also of the deeper depths of consternation that had opened beneath my feet—there was literally, in the ebbing actual, an extraordinarily sweet sadness. On reaching the house I had never so much as looked for the boy; I had simply gone straight to my room to change what I was wearing and to take in, at a glance, much material testimony to Flora's rupture. Her little belongings had all been removed. When later, by the schoolroom fire, I was served with tea by the usual maid, I indulged, on the article of my other pupil, in no inquiry whatever. He had his freedom now—he might have it to the end! Well, he did have it; and it consisted—in part at least—of his coming in at about eight o'clock and sitting down with me in silence. On the removal of the tea things I had blown out the candles and drawn my chair closer: I was conscious of a mortal coldness and felt as if I should never again be warm. So, when he appeared, I was sitting in the glow with my thoughts. He paused a moment by the door as if to look at me; then—as if to share them—came to the other side of the hearth and sank into a chair. We sat there in absolute stillness; yet he wanted, I felt, to be with me.

XXI

Before a new day, in my room, had fully broken, my eyes opened to Mrs. Grose, who had come to my bedside with worse news. Flora was so markedly feverish that an illness was perhaps at hand; she had passed a night of extreme unrest, a night agitated above all by fears that had for their subject not in the least her former, but wholly her present, governess. It was not against the possible re-entrance of Miss Jessel on the scene that she protested—it was conspicuously and passionately against mine. I was promptly on my feet of course, and with an immense deal to ask; the more that my friend had discernibly now girded her loins to meet me once more. This I felt as soon as I had put to her the question of her sense of the child's sincerity as against my own. "She persists in denying to you that she saw, or has ever seen, anything?"

My visitor's trouble, truly, was great. "Ah, miss, it isn't a matter on which I can push her! Yet it isn't either, I must say, as if I much needed to. It has made her, every inch of her, quite old."

"Oh, I see her perfectly from here. She resents, for all the world like some high little personage, the imputation on her truthfulness and, as it were, her respectability. 'Miss Jessel indeed—*she*!' Ah, she's 'respectable,' the chit! The impression she gave me there yesterday was, I assure you, the very strangest of all; it was quite beyond any of the others. I *did* put my foot in it! She'll never speak to me again."

Hideous and obscure as it all was, it held Mrs. Grose briefly silent; then she granted my point with a frankness which, I made sure, had more behind it. "I think indeed, miss, she never will. She do have a grand manner about it!"

"And that manner"—I summed it up—"is practically what's the matter with her now!"

Oh, that manner, I could see in my visitor's face, and not a little else besides! "She asks me every three minutes if I think you're coming in."

"I see—I see." I, too, on my side, had so much more than worked it out. "Has she said to you since yesterday—except to repudiate her familiarity with anything so dreadful—a single other word about Miss Jessel?"

"Not one, miss. And of course you know," my friend added, "I took it from her, by the lake, that, just then and there at least, there *was* nobody."

"Rather! and, naturally, you take it from her still."

"I don't contradict her. What else can I do?"

"Nothing in the world! You've the cleverest little person to deal with. They've made them—their two friends, I mean—still cleverer even than nature did; for it was wondrous material to play on! Flora has now her grievance, and she'll work it to the end."

"Yes, miss; but to *what* end?"

"Why, that of dealing with me to her uncle. She'll make me out to him the lowest creature—!"

I winced at the fair show of the scene in Mrs. Grose's face; she looked for a minute as if she sharply saw them together. "And him who thinks so well of you!"

"He has an odd way—it comes over me now," I laughed,"—of proving it! But that doesn't matter. What Flora wants, of course, is to get rid of me."

My companion bravely concurred. "Never again to so much as look at you."

"So that what you've come to me now for," I asked, "is to speed me on my way?" Before she had time to reply, however, I had her in check. "I've a better idea—the result of my reflections. My going *would* seem the right thing, and on Sunday I was terribly near it. Yet that won't do. It's *you* who must go. You must take Flora."

My visitor, at this, did speculate. "But where in the world—?"

"Away from here. Away from *them*. Away, even most of all, now, from me. Straight to her uncle."

"Only to tell on you—?"

"No, not 'only'! To leave me, in addition, with my remedy."

She was still vague. "And what *is* your remedy?"

"Your loyalty, to begin with. And then Miles's."

She looked at me hard. "Do you think he—?"

"Won't, if he has the chance, turn on me? Yes, I venture still to think it. At all events, I want to try. Get off with his sister as soon as possible and leave me with him alone." I was amazed, myself, at the spirit I had still in reserve, and therefore perhaps a trifle the more disconcerted at the way in which, in spite of this fine example of it, she hesitated. "There's one thing, of course," I went on: "they mustn't, before she goes, see each other for three seconds." Then it came over me that, in spite of Flora's presumable sequestration from the instant of her return from the pool, it might already be too late. "Do you mean," I anxiously asked, "that they *have* met?"

At this she quite flushed. "Ah, miss, I'm not such a fool as that! If I've been obliged to leave her three or four times, it has been each time with one of the maids, and at present, though she's alone, she's locked in safe. And yet—and yet!" There were too many things.

"And yet what?"

"Well, are you so sure of the little gentleman?"

"I'm not sure of anything but *you*. But I have, since last evening, a new hope. I think he wants to give me an opening. I do believe that—poor little exquisite wretch!—he wants to speak. Last evening, in the firelight and the silence, he sat with me for two hours as if it were just coming."

Mrs. Grose looked hard, through the window, at the gray, gathering day. "And did it come?"

"No, though I waited and waited, I confess it didn't, and it was without a breach of the silence or so much as a faint allusion to his sister's condition and absence that we at last kissed for good night. All the same," I continued, "I can't, if her uncle sees her, consent to his seeing her brother without my having given the boy—and most of all because things have got so bad—a little more time."

My friend appeared on this ground more reluctant than I could quite understand. "What do you mean by more time?"

"Well, a day or two—really to bring it out. He'll then be on *my* side—of which you see the importance. If nothing comes, I shall only fail, and you will, at the worst, have helped me by doing, on your arrival in town, whatever you may have found possible." So I put it before her, but she continued for a little so inscrutably embarrassed that I came again to her aid. "Unless, indeed," I wound up, "you really want *not* to go."

I could see it, in her face, at last clear itself; she put out her hand to me as a pledge. "I'll go—I'll go. I'll go this morning."

I wanted to be very just. "If you *should* wish still to wait, I would engage she shouldn't see me."

"No, no: it's the place itself. She must leave it." She held me a moment with heavy eyes, then brought out the rest. "Your idea's the right one. I myself, miss—"

"Well?"

"I can't stay."

The look she gave me with it made me jump at possibilities. "You mean that, since yesterday, you *have* seen—?"

She shook her head with dignity. "I've *heard*—!"

"Heard?"

"From that child—horrors! There!" she sighed with tragic relief. "On my honor, miss, she says things—!" But at this evocation she broke down; she dropped, with a sudden sob, upon my sofa and, as I had seen her do before, gave way to all the grief of it.

It was quite in another manner that I, for my part, let myself go. "Oh, thank God!"

She sprang up again at this, drying her eyes with a groan. "'Thank God'?"

"It so justifies me!"

"It does that, miss!"

I couldn't have desired more emphasis, but I just hesitated. "She's so horrible?"

I saw my colleague scarce knew how to put it. "Really shocking."

"And about me?"

"About you, miss—since you must have it. It's beyond everything, for a young lady; and I can't think wherever she must have picked up—"

"The appalling language she applied to me? I can, then!" I broke in with a laugh that was doubtless significant enough.

It only, in truth, left my friend still more grave. "Well, perhaps I ought to also—since I've heard some of it before! Yet I can't bear it," the poor woman went on while, with the same movement, she glanced, on my dressing table, at the face of my watch. "But I must go back."

I kept her, however. "Ah, if you can't bear it—!"

"How can I stop with her, you mean? Why, just FOR that: to get her away. Far from this," she pursued, "far from *them*-"

"She may be different? She may be free?" I seized her almost with joy. "Then, in spite of yesterday, you *believe*—"

"In such doings?" Her simple description of them required, in the light of her expression, to be carried no further, and she gave me the whole thing as she had never done. "I believe."

Yes, it was a joy, and we were still shoulder to shoulder: if I might continue sure of that I should care but little what else happened. My support in the presence of disaster would be the same as it had been in my early need of confidence, and if my friend would answer for my honesty, I would answer for all the rest. On the point of taking leave of her, nonetheless, I was to some extent embarrassed. "There's one thing, of course—it occurs to me—to remember. My letter, giving the alarm, will have reached town before you."

I now perceived still more how she had been beating about the bush and how weary at last it had made her. "Your letter won't have got there. Your letter never went."

"What then became of it?"

"Goodness knows! Master Miles—"

"Do you mean *he* took it?" I gasped.

She hung fire, but she overcame her reluctance. "I mean that I saw yesterday, when I came back with Miss Flora, that it wasn't where you had put it. Later in the evening I had the chance to question Luke, and he declared that he had neither noticed nor touched it." We could only exchange, on this, one of our deeper mutual soundings, and it was Mrs. Grose who first brought up the plumb with an almost elated "You see!"

"Yes, I see that if Miles took it instead he probably will have read it and destroyed it."

"And don't you see anything else?"

I faced her a moment with a sad smile. "It strikes me that by this time your eyes are open even wider than mine."

They proved to be so indeed, but she could still blush, almost, to show it. "I make out now what he must have done at school." And she gave, in her simple sharpness, an almost droll disillusioned nod. "He stole!"

I turned it over—I tried to be more judicial. "Well—perhaps."

She looked as if she found me unexpectedly calm. "He stole *letters*!"

She couldn't know my reasons for a calmness after all pretty shallow; so I showed them off as I might. "I hope then it was to more purpose than in this case! The note, at any rate, that I put on the table yesterday," I pursued, "will have given him so scant an advantage—for it contained only the bare demand for an interview—that he is already much ashamed of having gone so far for so little, and that what he had on his mind last evening was precisely the need of confession." I seemed to myself, for the instant, to have mastered it, to see it all. "Leave us, leave us"—I was already, at the door, hurrying her off. "I'll get it out of him. He'll meet me—he'll confess. If he confesses, he's saved. And if he's saved—"

"Then *you* are?" The dear woman kissed me on this, and I took her farewell. "I'll save you without him!" she cried as she went.

XXII

Yet it was when she had got off—and I missed her on the spot—that the great pinch really came. If I had counted on what it would give me to find myself alone with Miles, I speedily perceived, at least, that it would give me a measure. No hour of my stay in fact was so assailed with apprehensions as that of my coming down to learn that the carriage containing Mrs. Grose and my younger pupil had already rolled out of the gates. Now I *was*, I said to myself, face to face with the elements, and for much of the rest of the day, while I fought my weakness, I could consider that I had been supremely rash. It was a tighter place still than I had yet turned round in; all the more that, for the first time, I could see in the aspect of others a confused reflection of the crisis. What had happened naturally caused them all to stare; there was too little of the explained, throw out whatever we might, in the suddenness of my colleague's act. The maids and the men looked blank; the effect of which on my nerves was an aggravation until I saw the necessity of making it a positive aid. It was precisely, in short, by just clutching the helm that I avoided total wreck; and I dare say that, to bear up at all, I became, that morning, very grand and very dry. I welcomed the consciousness that I was charged with much to do, and I caused it to be known as well that, left thus to myself, I was quite remarkably firm. I wandered with that manner, for the next hour or two, all over the place and looked, I have no doubt, as if I were ready for any onset. So, for the benefit of whom it might concern, I paraded with a sick heart.

The person it appeared least to concern proved to be, till dinner, little Miles himself. My perambulations had given me, meanwhile, no glimpse of him, but they had tended to make more public the change taking place in our relation as a consequence of his having at the piano, the day before, kept me, in Flora's interest, so beguiled and befooled. The stamp of publicity had of course been fully given by her confinement and departure, and the change itself was now ushered in by our nonobservance of the regular custom of the schoolroom. He had already disappeared when, on my way down, I pushed open his door, and I learned below that he had breakfasted—in the presence of a couple of the maids—with Mrs. Grose and his sister. He had then gone out, as he said, for a stroll; than which nothing, I reflected, could better have expressed his frank view of the abrupt transformation of my office. What he would not permit this office to consist of was yet to be settled: there was a queer relief, at all events—I mean for myself in especial—in the renouncement of one pretension. If so much had sprung to the surface, I scarce put it too strongly in saying that what had perhaps sprung highest was the absurdity of our prolonging the fiction that I had anything more to teach him. It sufficiently stuck out that, by tacit little tricks in which even more than myself he carried out the care for my dignity, I had had to appeal to him to let me off straining to meet him on the ground of his true capacity. He had at any rate his freedom now; I was never to touch it again; as I had amply shown, moreover, when, on his joining me in the schoolroom the previous night, I had uttered, on the subject of the interval just concluded, neither challenge nor hint. I had too much, from this moment, my other ideas. Yet when he at last arrived, the difficulty of applying them, the accumulations of my problem, were brought straight home to me by the beautiful little presence on which what had occurred had as yet, for the eye, dropped neither stain nor shadow.

To mark, for the house, the high state I cultivated I decreed that my meals with the boy should be served, as we called it, downstairs; so that I had been awaiting him in the ponderous pomp of the room outside of the window of which I had had from Mrs. Grose, that first scared Sunday, my flash of something it would scarce have done to call light. Here at present I felt afresh—for I had felt it again and again—how my equilibrium depended on the success of my rigid will, the will to shut my eyes as tight as possible to the truth that what I had to deal with was, revoltingly, against nature. I could only get on at all by taking "nature" into my confidence and my account, by treating my monstrous ordeal as a push in a direction unusual, of course, and unpleasant, but demanding, after all, for a fair front, only another turn of the screw of ordinary human virtue. No attempt, nonetheless, could well require more tact than just this attempt to supply, one's self, *all* the nature. How could I put even a little of that article into a suppression of reference to what had occurred? How, on the other hand, could I make reference without a new plunge into the hideous obscure? Well, a sort of answer, after a time, had come to me, and it was so far confirmed as that I was met, incontestably, by the quickened vision of what was rare in my little companion. It was indeed as if he had found even now—as he had so often found at lessons—still some other delicate way to ease me off. Wasn't there light in the fact which, as we shared our solitude, broke out with a specious glitter it had never yet quite worn?—the fact that (opportunity aiding, precious opportunity which had now come) it would be preposterous, with a child so endowed, to forego the help one might wrest from absolute intelligence? What had his intelligence been given him for but to save him? Mightn't one, to reach his mind, risk the stretch of an angular arm over his character? It was as if, when we were face to face in the dining room, he had literally shown me the way. The roast mutton was on the table, and I had dispensed with attendance. Miles, before he sat down, stood a moment with his hands in his pockets and looked at the joint, on which he seemed on the point of passing some humorous judgment. But what he presently produced was: "I say, my dear, is she really very awfully ill?"

"Little Flora? Not so bad but that she'll presently be better. London will set her up. Bly had ceased to agree with her. Come here and take your mutton."

He alertly obeyed me, carried the plate carefully to his seat, and, when he was established, went on. "Did Bly disagree with her so terribly suddenly?"

"Not so suddenly as you might think. One had seen it coming on."

"Then why didn't you get her off before?"

"Before what?"

"Before she became too ill to travel."

I found myself prompt. "She's *not* too ill to travel: she only might have become so if she had stayed. This was just the moment to seize. The journey will dissipate the influence"—oh, I was grand!—"and carry it off."

"I see, I see"—Miles, for that matter, was grand, too. He settled to his repast with the charming little "table manner" that, from the day of his arrival, had relieved me of all grossness of admonition. Whatever he had been driven from school for, it was not for ugly feeding. He was irreproachable, as always, today; but he was unmistakably more conscious. He was discernibly trying to take for granted more things than he found, without assistance, quite easy; and he dropped into peaceful silence while he felt his situation. Our meal was of the briefest—mine a vain pretense, and I had the things immediately removed. While this was done Miles stood again with his hands in his little pockets and his back to me—stood and looked out of the wide window through which, that other day, I had seen what pulled me up. We continued silent while the maid was with us—as silent, it whimsically occurred to me, as some young couple who, on their wedding journey, at the inn, feel shy in the presence of the waiter. He turned round only when the waiter had left us. "Well—so we're alone!"

XXIII

"Oh, more or less." I fancy my smile was pale. "Not absolutely. We shouldn't like that!" I went on.

"No—I suppose we shouldn't. Of course we have the others."

"We have the others—we have indeed the others," I concurred.

"Yet even though we have them," he returned, still with his hands in his pockets and planted there in front of me, "they don't much count, do they?"

I made the best of it, but I felt wan. "It depends on what you call 'much'!"

"Yes"—with all accommodation—"everything depends!" On this, however, he faced to the window again and presently reached it with his vague, restless, cogitating step. He remained there awhile, with his forehead against the glass, in contemplation of the stupid shrubs I knew and the dull things of November. I had always my hypocrisy of "work," behind which, now, I gained the sofa. Steadying myself with it there as I had repeatedly done at those moments of torment that I have described as the moments of my knowing the children to be given to something from which I was barred, I sufficiently obeyed my habit of being prepared for the worst. But an extraordinary impression dropped on me as I extracted a meaning from the boy's embarrassed back—none other than the impression that I was not barred now. This inference grew in a few minutes to sharp intensity and seemed bound up with the direct perception that it was positively *he* who was. The frames and squares of the great window were a kind of image, for him, of a kind of failure. I felt that I saw him, at any rate, shut in or shut out. He was admirable, but not comfortable: I took it in with a throb of hope. Wasn't he looking, through the haunted pane, for something he couldn't see?—and wasn't it the first time in the whole business that he had known such a lapse? The first, the very first: I found it a splendid portent. It made him anxious, though he watched himself; he had been anxious all day and, even while in his usual sweet little manner he sat at table, had needed all his small strange genius to give it a gloss. When he at last turned round to meet me, it was almost as if this genius had succumbed. "Well, I think I'm glad Bly agrees with *me*!"

"You would certainly seem to have seen, these twenty-four hours, a good deal more of it than for some time before. I hope," I went on bravely, "that you've been enjoying yourself."

"Oh, yes, I've been ever so far; all round about—miles and miles away. I've never been so free."

He had really a manner of his own, and I could only try to keep up with him. "Well, do you like it?"

He stood there smiling; then at last he put into two words—"Do *you*?"—more discrimination than I had ever heard two words contain. Before I had time to deal with that, however, he continued as if with the sense that this was an impertinence to be softened. "Nothing could be more charming than the way you take it, for of course if we're alone together now it's you that are alone most. But I hope," he threw in, "you don't particularly mind!"

"Having to do with you?" I asked. "My dear child, how can I help minding? Though I've renounced all claim to your company—you're so beyond me—I at least greatly enjoy it. What else should I stay on for?"

He looked at me more directly, and the expression of his face, graver now, struck me as the most beautiful I had ever found in it. "You stay on just for *that*?"

"Certainly. I stay on as your friend and from the tremendous interest I take in you till something can be done for you that may be more worth your while. That needn't surprise you." My voice trembled so that I felt it impossible to suppress the shake. "Don't you remember how I told you, when I came and sat on your bed the night of the storm, that there was nothing in the world I wouldn't do for you?"

"Yes, yes!" He, on his side, more and more visibly nervous, had a tone to master; but he was so much more successful than I that, laughing out through his gravity, he could pretend we were pleasantly jesting. "Only that, I think, was to get me to do something for *you*!"

"It was partly to get you to do something," I conceded. "But, you know, you didn't do it."

"Oh, yes," he said with the brightest superficial eagerness, "you wanted me to tell you something."

"That's it. Out, straight out. What you have on your mind, you know."

"Ah, then, is *that* what you've stayed over for?"

He spoke with a gaiety through which I could still catch the finest little quiver of resentful passion; but I can't begin to express the effect upon me of an implication of surrender even so faint. It was as if what I had yearned for had come at last only to astonish me. "Well, yes—I may as well make a clean breast of it. it was precisely for that."

He waited so long that I supposed it for the purpose of repudiating the assumption on which my action had been founded; but what he finally said was: "Do you mean now—here?"

"There couldn't be a better place or time." He looked round him uneasily, and I had the rare—oh, the queer!—impression of the very first symptom I had seen in him of the approach of immediate fear. It was as if he were suddenly afraid of me—which struck me indeed as perhaps the best thing to make him. Yet in the very pang of the effort I felt it vain to try sternness, and I heard myself the next instant so gentle as to be almost grotesque. "You want so to go out again?"

"Awfully!" He smiled at me heroically, and the touching little bravery of it was enhanced by his actually flushing with pain. He had picked up his hat, which he had brought in, and stood twirling it in a way that gave me, even as I was just nearly reaching port, a perverse horror of what I was doing. To do it in *any* way was an act of violence, for what did it consist of but the obtrusion of the idea of grossness and guilt on a small helpless creature who had been for me a revelation of the possibilities of beautiful intercourse? Wasn't it base to create for a being so exquisite a mere alien awkwardness? I suppose I now read into our situation a clearness it couldn't have had at the time, for I seem to see our poor eyes already lighted with some spark of a prevision of the anguish that was to come. So we circled about, with terrors and scruples, like fighters not daring to close. But it was for each other we feared! That kept us a little longer suspended and unbruised. "I'll tell you everything," Miles said—"I mean I'll tell you anything you like. You'll stay on with me, and we shall both be all right, and I *will* tell you—I *will*. But not now."

"Why not now?"

My insistence turned him from me and kept him once more at his window in a silence during which, between us, you might have heard a pin drop. Then he was before me again with the air of a person for whom, outside, someone who had frankly to be reckoned with was waiting. "I have to see Luke."

I had not yet reduced him to quite so vulgar a lie, and I felt proportionately ashamed. But, horrible as it was, his lies made up my truth. I achieved thoughtfully a few loops of my knitting. "Well, then, go to Luke, and I'll wait for what you promise. Only, in return for that, satisfy, before you leave me, one very much smaller request."

He looked as if he felt he had succeeded enough to be able still a little to bargain. "Very much smaller—?"

"Yes, a mere fraction of the whole. Tell me"—oh, my work preoccupied me, and I was offhand!—"if, yesterday afternoon, from the table in the hall, you took, you know, my letter."

XXIV

My sense of how he received this suffered for a minute from something that I can describe only as a fierce split of my attention—a stroke that at first, as I sprang straight up, reduced me to the mere blind movement of getting hold of him, drawing him close, and, while I just fell for support against the nearest piece of furniture, instinctively keeping him with his back to the window. The appearance was full upon us that I had already had to deal with here: Peter Quint had come into view like a sentinel before a prison. The next thing I saw was that, from outside, he had reached the window, and then I knew that, close to the glass and glaring in through it, he offered once more to the room his white face of damnation. It represents but grossly what took place within me at the sight to say that on the second my decision was made; yet I believe that no woman so overwhelmed ever in so short a time recovered her grasp of the *act*. It came to me in the very horror of the immediate presence that the act would be, seeing and facing what I saw and faced, to keep the boy himself unaware. The inspiration—I can call it by no other name—was that I felt how voluntarily, how transcendently, I *might*. It was like fighting with a demon for a human soul, and when I had fairly so appraised it I saw how the human soul—held out, in the tremor of my hands, at arm's length—had a perfect dew of sweat on a lovely childish forehead. The face that was close to mine was as white as the face against the glass, and out of it presently came a sound, not low nor weak, but as if from much further away, that I drank like a waft of fragrance.

"Yes—I took it."

At this, with a moan of joy, I enfolded, I drew him close; and while I held him to my breast, where I could feel in the sudden fever of his little body the tremendous pulse of his little heart, I kept my eyes on the thing at the window and saw it move and shift its posture. I have likened it to a sentinel, but its slow wheel, for a moment, was rather the prowl of a baffled beast. My present quickened courage, however, was such that, not too much to let it through, I had to shade, as it were, my flame. Meanwhile the glare of the face was again at the window, the scoundrel fixed as if to watch and wait. It was the very confidence that I might now defy him, as well as the positive certitude, by this time, of the child's unconsciousness, that made me go on. "What did you take it for?"

"To see what you said about me."

"You opened the letter?"

"I opened it."

My eyes were now, as I held him off a little again, on Miles's own face, in which the collapse of mockery showed me how complete was the ravage of uneasiness. What was prodigious was that at last, by my success, his sense was sealed and his communication stopped: he knew that he was in presence, but knew not of what, and knew still less that I also was and that I did know. And what did this strain of trouble matter when my eyes went back to the window only to see that the air was clear again and—by my personal triumph—the influence quenched? There was nothing there. I felt that the cause was mine and that I should surely get *all*. "And you found nothing!"—I let my elation out.

He gave the most mournful, thoughtful little headshake. "Nothing."

"Nothing, nothing!" I almost shouted in my joy.

"Nothing, nothing," he sadly repeated.

I kissed his forehead; it was drenched. "So what have you done with it?"

"I've burned it."

"Burned it?" It was now or never. "Is that what you did at school?"

Oh, what this brought up! "At school?"

"Did you take letters?—or other things?"

"Other things?" He appeared now to be thinking of something far off and that reached him only through the pressure of his anxiety. Yet it did reach him. "Did I *steal*?"

I felt myself redden to the roots of my hair as well as wonder if it were more strange to put to a gentleman such a question or to see him take it with allowances that gave the very distance of his fall in the world. "Was it for that you mightn't go back?"

The only thing he felt was rather a dreary little surprise. "Did you know I mightn't go back?"

"I know everything."

He gave me at this the longest and strangest look. "Everything?"

"Everything. Therefore *did* you—?" But I couldn't say it again.

Miles could, very simply. "No. I didn't steal."

My face must have shown him I believed him utterly; yet my hands—but it was for pure tenderness—shook him as if to ask him why, if it was all for nothing, he had condemned me to months of torment. "What then did you do?"

He looked in vague pain all round the top of the room and drew his breath, two or three times over, as if with difficulty. He might have been standing at the bottom of the sea and raising his eyes to some faint green twilight. "Well—I said things."

"Only that?"

"They thought it was enough!"

"To turn you out for?"

Never, truly, had a person "turned out" shown so little to explain it as this little person! He appeared to weigh my question, but in a manner quite detached and almost helpless. "Well, I suppose I oughtn't."

"But to whom did you say them?"

He evidently tried to remember, but it dropped—he had lost it. "I don't know!"

He almost smiled at me in the desolation of his surrender, which was indeed practically, by this time, so complete that I ought to have left it there. But I was infatuated—I was blind with victory, though even then the very effect that was to have brought him so much nearer was already that of added separation. "Was it to everyone?" I asked.

"No; it was only to—" But he gave a sick little headshake. "I don't remember their names."

"Were they then so many?"

"No—only a few. Those I liked."

Those he liked? I seemed to float not into clearness, but into a darker obscure, and within a minute there had come to me out of my very pity the appalling alarm of his being perhaps innocent. It was for the instant confounding and bottomless, for if he *were* innocent, what then on earth was *I*? Paralyzed, while it lasted, by the mere brush of the question, I let him go a little, so that, with a deep-drawn sigh, he turned away from me again; which, as he faced toward the clear window, I suffered, feeling that I had nothing now there to keep him from. "And did they repeat what you said?" I went on after a moment.

He was soon at some distance from me, still breathing hard and again with the air, though now without anger for it, of being confined against his will. Once more, as he had done before, he looked up at the dim day as if, of what had hitherto sustained him, nothing was left but an unspeakable anxiety. "Oh, yes," he nevertheless replied—"they must have repeated them. To those *they* liked," he added.

There was, somehow, less of it than I had expected; but I turned it over. "And these things came round—?"

"To the masters? Oh, yes!" he answered very simply. "But I didn't know they'd tell."

"The masters? They didn't—they've never told. That's why I ask you."

He turned to me again his little beautiful fevered face. "Yes, it was too bad."

"Too bad?"

"What I suppose I sometimes said. To write home."

I can't name the exquisite pathos of the contradiction given to such a speech by such a speaker; I only know that the next instant I heard myself throw off with homely force: "Stuff and nonsense!" But the next after that I must have sounded stern enough. "What *were* these things?"

My sternness was all for his judge, his executioner; yet it made him avert himself again, and that movement made *me*, with a single bound and an irrepressible cry, spring straight upon him. For there again, against the glass, as if to blight his confession and stay his answer, was the hideous author of our woe—the white face of damnation. I felt a sick swim at the drop of my victory and all the return of my battle, so that the wildness of my veritable leap only served as a great betrayal. I saw him, from the midst of my act, meet it with a divination, and on the perception that even now he only guessed, and that the window was still to his own eyes free, I let the impulse flame up to convert the climax of his dismay into the very proof of his liberation. "No more, no more, no more!" I shrieked, as I tried to press him against me, to my visitant.

"Is she *here*?" Miles panted as he caught with his sealed eyes the direction of my words. Then as his strange "she" staggered me and, with a gasp, I echoed it, "Miss Jessel, Miss Jessel!" he with a sudden fury gave me back.

I seized, stupefied, his supposition—some sequel to what we had done to Flora, but this made me only want to show him that it was better still than that. "It's not Miss Jessel! But it's at the window—straight before us. It's *there*—the coward horror, there for the last time!"

At this, after a second in which his head made the movement of a baffled dog's on a scent and then gave a frantic little shake for air and light, he was at me in a white rage, bewildered, glaring vainly over the place and missing wholly, though it now, to my sense, filled the room like the taste of poison, the wide, overwhelming presence. "It's *he*?"

I was so determined to have all my proof that I flashed into ice to challenge him. "Whom do you mean by 'he'?"

"Peter Quint—you devil!" His face gave again, round the room, its convulsed supplication. "*Where*?"

They are in my ears still, his supreme surrender of the name and his tribute to my devotion. "What does he matter now, my own?—what will he *ever* matter? *I* have you," I launched at the beast, "but he has lost you forever!" Then, for the demonstration of my work, "There, *there*!" I said to Miles.

But he had already jerked straight round, stared, glared again, and seen but the quiet day. With the stroke of the loss I was so proud of he uttered the cry of a creature hurled over an abyss, and the grasp with which I recovered him might have been that of catching him in his fall. I caught him, yes, I held him—it may be imagined with what a passion; but at the end of a minute I began to feel what it truly was that I held. We were alone with the quiet day, and his little heart, dispossessed, had stopped.

THE END

LaVergne, TN USA
07 October 2010
199986LV00005B/22/P